THE
BOOKS
OF
CALEDAN
TRILOGY

THE TAINTED CROWN
THE BROODING CROWN
THE SHATTERED CROWN

MEG COWLEY

Published in 2018 by
Jolly Creative Atelier
United Kingdom

ISBN: 978-1980506744

Books by Meg Cowley

Books of Caledan
The First Crown
The Tainted Crown
The Brooding Crown
The Shattered Crown
Books of Caledan Trilogy

Coming Soon: Sagas of Caledan trilogy

Morgana Chronicles
Arthurian legend like you've never read it before.
Magic Awakened
(More titles coming soon!)

Relic Guardians
Tomb raider meets magic in this fast paced urban fantasy.
Devious Magic
Ancient Magic
Hidden Magic
Rogue Magic
Stolen Magic
Cursed Magic
Gathered Magic

For younger readers:

Diary of a Secret Witch
Wackiest Week
Worst Witch
Mischief Magic
Diary of a Secret Witch Boxset

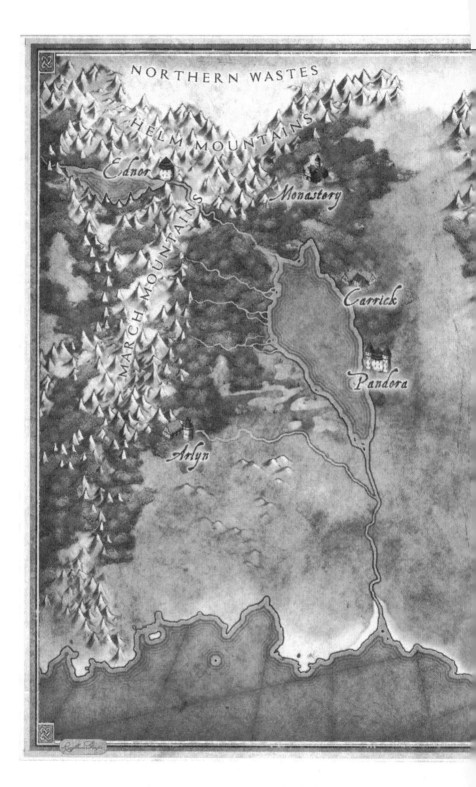

DEDICATION

For my readers

I write for me, but I publish for you.

I hope you enjoy these adventures.

I couldn't do this without you all.

Thank you for your support.

- Meg

THE
TAINTED
CROWN

ONE

Zaki struck Naisa from behind without mercy, flinching at the sickening crunch of metal upon bone. She dropped to the floor with an exclamation of surprise and pain. Breathing heavily as he raised the candelabra for another blow, Zaki stood over her, but stayed his hand. She lay stunned, her legs trapped and tangled in the folds of her dress, and bright blood oozed from her head.

"It's true," she tried to say, but her mouth would not obey her and he heard only a moan. Tears slid from the corners of her eyes, soaking into her hair and mingling with her blood. Zaki lowered the candelabra and it fell from his hand with a dull thump onto the carpet as he watched her.

"It had to be this way, sister." *This is your own fault, Naisa. You rushed me to this. I would have bought a clean death for you.*

He couldn't be sure whether he spoke to himself, to her, or to nobody. Naisa moaned again. It was fainter this time. In a few minutes, she had stilled. He leaned closer. No breath. No pulse. No life.

Zaki kicked the candelabra out of his path and strode from the room, pausing to close the door on his way out. He need not have bothered. Naisa's rooms were devoid of servants and guards, as he had arranged. Whilst the city of Pandora bustled outside, his men were silencing the rest of the castle with every pace he took.

"Long live King Zaki," he murmured to himself, savouring the sound of it.

Standing upon the dais that evening, Zaki surveyed the crowd of battle-stained men before him.

1

"Report," Zaki commanded, trying not to gag at the stench of sweat and worse things. "Sir Loren, begin." His fingers drummed upon his folded arms with impatience and nerves, hoping for good news.

"The west guard folded, Your Royal Highness. The south guard are ours and the east guard caused us great losses before we subdued them," Sir Loren recited.

"Their losses?"

"Heavy. At least half. A quarter more captured. The rest surrendered."

"Good. Imprison them all. Those who prove loyal may return to service. Our losses?"

"Not so heavy as theirs. We had the element of surprise and more men than they."

"Good. Next?" He spoke to each lord in turn, his smile growing. Pandora was his already; his enemies were dead and only pockets of resistance remained within the castle. For the most part, it seemed, the civilians in the city outside remained oblivious to the chaos there.

"What of the traitor? Where is Soren?" Zaki asked last of all. The hall fell silent. "Where is he? One of you must have found him by now," he insisted. No answer came. "Damn it! The boy has killed our queen and you have not yet seized him?" he shouted.

Few looked back with knowing faces, for few were trusted with the truth of what had happened that day. Few ever would be.

Lord Argyle spoke. "My son informs me His Roya…the traitor may be in the royal wood."

"Then, Lord Argyle, I suggest you and your son gather some men and go and search there for him," Zaki said through gritted teeth. *Do these dolts have no ingenuity?* "As for the rest of you, search harder! Hunt him down! I care not if he lives or dies; find him!"

The hall teemed with bodies scattering at his command as his retinue fell into place behind him with a snap of his fingers, Reynard first at his heels as always. "We'll search the castle again. I'm not about to pin everything on Argyle's word. Do we have the princess?"

"Aye, sir."

"Keep her out of the way."

TWO

Soft as wolves they prowled, stepping with care upon the mossy carpet of the Royal Forest as they tracked their prey. Prince Soren knew it was close; the imprints of hooves were fresh, and the blood too, for Oarwyl had caught it a glancing shot upon the thigh. Tiny splatters of the ruby liquid betrayed the stag's path, glinting in the rays of sun that pierced through to the forest floor.

Soren grinned at his friend. Oarwyl winked back. All six of the hunting party were spread in a line, pacing evenly with one another under the whispering canopy. Soren looked between them with pride, for their faces mirrored the same intent concentration. Tonight, he knew his mother, the queen, would be proud, for the royal table would dine upon one of the finest beasts of the Royal Forest.

Jaimen, his servant boy, who stood in awe of the lordlings on their hunt, sprung excitedly forward to point a quivering finger at a crushed leaf. The next part of the trail. He turned to Soren, his brown eyes bright, but he made no noise. He knew; they were close, and the hunt must not be disturbed.

Soren nodded, and Jaimen grinned; the approval he sought.

"Ungh!" Oarwyl grunted.

Soren turned to his friend just as the arrow sprouted through the front of Oarwyl's throat. Oarwyl toppled to the floor, convulsing and soon lifeless as his blood soaked into the mossy carpet beneath them.

Yet Soren had already moved, instinctively diving for cover as a hail of arrows thudded into the tree trunks around them, or sailed past. Cries to either side rang out; cries of pain.

His heart hammered against his breast as he sought the source of the attack with his senses, and his fingers scrabbled for his own bow. He suppressed a curse. His sword, one of the finest blades in all of Caledan, lay back at the camp. Useless now. His hunting knife would be no weapon against whoever assaulted them.

Sliding into a standing position using the tree trunk at his back for cover, Soren nocked an arrow to the string and prepared to draw. Now, he could hear them, even above the pounding of his heart. They crashed through the brush with no care.

This is no accident, the thought nudged him, unbidden. For what hunter would move through the woods so? They must be sure of their prey's death, or perhaps they did not care. No one else was permitted to hunt in here in any case; anyone doing so was here with less than noble intentions. Yet, who would attack the crown prince? *We are no beasts, surely they realise.*

He swallowed. Twigs snapped behind him, only feet away. Soren drew a deep breath, forcing himself into the stillness of the hunt, though his blood blazed through him, singing with tension. Ahead, he could see others amongst his friends down, but still, doubt coursed through him. Hunting accidents happened. Jaimen lay in a heap, moaning. An arrow struck him. He silenced at once. Soren's heart sank. *They do not mean to hunt beasts.*

Soren whirled around, drawing the bow with one smooth movement. A roar escaped his snarling lips as he shot the man approaching, who had been foolish enough to let his own weapon fall.

A moment of surprise; the man's eyebrows rose, and then he too crumpled to the floor.

But now, Soren was exposed, and more assailants turned his way. There were three more, he counted, stalking towards him through the trees. He was no deer, or beast, that was clear, and yet, their bows rose. Soren struck another with his next shot, and dived behind the tree again as shards of wood smashed loose from the arrow that followed him.

Green and black. They wore the marks of House Varan; a house loyal to the throne. Surely, they would know him, or recognise some of his company?

"Come out, traitor," they called to him, "or we shall drag you from your hole."

"Do you not know to whom you speak?" he shouted. "I am no traitor, or criminal, I am Crown Prince Soren. You have killed good men here today, all for naught. You shall answer for your crimes before the queen."

Jaimen's lifeless eyes gazed up, unseeing, feet before him. Soren suppressed the urge to retch, for the boy's blood mingled with the deer's upon the trail now.

"Yield," was the only reply he received, before he heard them advance once more. *Still two, maybe three, not incapacitated.* Would he have to incapacitate them, he wondered? They seemed to have no qualms against murdering innocents in cold blood; who was to say they would spare him, crown prince or not. *What on earth is the meaning of this?*

"What am I accused of?" Soren called, trying to buy more time as he nocked another arrow to his string, and loosened the knife in his belt. He would have to make a stand. He peeked around the tree, and whipped his head back at once. An arrow whistled past. *Three. One injured, but three.*

"Seize him!" The men crashed towards Soren with weapons drawn and battle cries ringing in their throats.

Soren froze, and the pounding of his blood deafened him. They were almost upon him, and his hands fumbled as he struggled to draw his knife before leaping to meet them, when a fierce cry announced the presence of another. The men turned, for a fatal moment of distraction. Soren gaped.

An armoured man sat atop a foaming horse which smashed to a halt just behind his assailants, towering over them. His sword was a slash of light as he raised it.

"Stand down!" he ordered, his voice distorted and echoing in the helm, but the Varan men turned to meet him with their blades and bows held high.

Soren moved despite his confusion. He slashed the first man's side as the horse kicked, stunning the second. Before the third could react, the stranger had dispatched him, stabbing the second who lay dazed on the floor just as Soren cut down the first. The man removed his helm to reveal the sweaty, battle-stained face of the queen's chief advisor.

"Sir Edmund!" exclaimed Soren, keeping his dripping blade ready.

The horse pranced, nostrils flaring and mouth frothing.

"These men wear the mark of House Varan—what's the meaning of this? Whoa, calm." He tried to soothe the agitated mount with shaking hands.

"Are you hurt?" Edmund dismounted, and his brows furrowed as he looked Soren up and down, his eyes darting here and there.

"I... No. I'm unharmed. But my men—"

"We must leave. Now. Your horses are still at the camp."

The prince did not move. *Too many questions. Where to begin?*

"Do you trust me?" Edmund pressed, leaning forward in his saddle.

Soren nodded.

"Then do as I say. Ride with me now!" Edmund whirled the horse about and urged it into a trot beside him.

"What's happened? What of my companions? They've been slaughtered, but some might yet live. We must help them—and seek vengeance."

"If you value your life, you will do no such thing."

"I don't understand." The man he had just killed sprang to Soren's mind, his eyes full of pain, hate, and determination as he dropped to the ground, life fading. *I just killed a man, but he was trying to kill me. They killed Jaimen and Oarwyl - and everyone else.* The woods were as silent as death now. It was incomprehensible.

Edmund turned on him. "Men loyal to the crown have just knowingly attacked you. You have had to defend your very life." His tone was harsh, and filled with anger; at odds with the usually taciturn and reserved man. "I do not have time to sit and explain, when more may yet follow them. If they found you, others may too. You are in mortal danger, and it is my duty to protect you." His voice cracked. "Fate delivered you to my hands today and I do not intend to waste the chance. I will explain, I promise, but we must leave -

7

now."

Soren considered the unwavering faith his mother placed in Edmund. He was swayed by that, yet it was with a sinking heart and growing unease that Soren followed Edmund through the forest. *What has passed?* It could not be good.

Soon, they were at the now deserted camp. The ashes of that morning's fire were long cold, and there, Soren's horse Miri waited as Edmund had promised, tethered to the tree where Soren had left her that morning. She whickered at him as he untied her. After a moment's thought, he untethered the other horses nearby. There would be no riders returning for them, and it seemed cruel to leave them to starve. It was an oddly practical thought.

Edmund led him, not west, back to the main road which would lead to Pandora, but north and east, out to the edge of the forest plateau, and the plains that surrounded the city.

It was a perilous climb down the cliffs in the fading light; impossible but for the narrow ledge that guided men and horses down. Soren was distracted from the blood that speckled the hem of his fine jacket by Miri, who had to be coaxed, pushed, and shoved almost the whole way down. The horses skittered on the narrow track, taking fright every time their passage dislodged small scatterings of stones that cascaded down the precipice to their side.

Every time the horses balked, Soren's heart leapt into his mouth with fear that he would be pushed off the path. But before the sun had set, they reached the ground. Edmund wasted no time in mounting, warning Soren to take care on the uneven ground. Soren mumbled his thanks with dull acquiescence. The descent had been excruciatingly slow and he was tiring fast as his adrenaline faded.

Several leagues to the north lay the dark bulk of woodlands which Edmund rode for. As the cooler shade of the tree canopy enveloped them, their shadowy figures melted into the forest. The thick cover was claustrophobic in contrast to the open, rolling knolls and farmland they left behind them. Soren halted, and looked back.

Framed by the trees on the fringes of the forest was the vast expanse of water; the lake was silver in the moonlight to the west.

The sweeping plains faded into the night to the east. In between lay the great hill upon which the city of Pandora stood, a huge bulk in the darkness covered with pinpricks of light. Nothing seemed amiss. The night was tranquil. Soren followed Edmund to be swallowed by the forest.

They rode until Soren was lost in the dark. The older man had been silent for hours and rode so swiftly that Soren was forced to push Miri to her limits, despite his worry she would stumble and lame herself on a stray root or rock.

Soren was too exhausted to question Edmund's urgency. Instead, when they stopped in a hollow at the base of a rocky outcrop, he dumped Miri's saddle and bags onto the floor, turned her loose, and slumped against a tree, snoring.

Midmorning sunlight streamed into the small clearing where they slept. It was late spring, the fifth month of the year, and the sound of animal and insect life buzzed around them. This place was far from any of the man-made roads that linked the hubs of civilisation together. On any other day, a tranquil haven.

Soren awoke, disorientated, and groaning at the stiffness of his body. He was surprised to find Edmund deep in concentration, attending to a small, smokeless fire. Soren took half a breath, about to question why Edmund had joined his hunting trip, when he recalled the previous day's events like he had been drenched in icy water.

Edmund turned at the sound of his movement and met his measured glare.

"Your Majesty," Edmund addressed him formally.

Soren opened his mouth to reply, pausing as he registered what Edmund had called him.

"Your Majesty?" Soren questioned, unsettled by the apprehension in Edmund's eyes. "I'm 'Your Royal Highness,' no more," he said, however he knew Edmund would not have said it mistakenly. "Explain yourself."

"It pains me to inform you thus." Edmund gestured at their surroundings. He stalled, mouth gaping as though he could not find the words. "Your mother is dead, God rest her soul."

"Impossible," Soren said. Yet, he knew the strange events of the day before would not have been without dire cause. Soren tried to frown, but his face had frozen. "I saw her the day before yesterday. She was well."

"I saw her… body… with my own eyes." Edmund rubbed his hand across his face, dragging tears away from his eyes.

Soren could not move; a thousand questions stormed through his mind, and yet his tongue held only emptiness.

"You want to know what happened," Edmund said, "but you do not know how to begin asking. Am I correct, sire?"

Soren nodded, still not believing him.

"Then I will start where I must—at the beginning," said the older man. "Forgive me, I do not wish to cause you pain, but I will not lie to you. Your uncle Zaki has been moving in shaded circles. I am sure you have noticed his repeated attempts to disrupt your grandfather's peace treaty with the southern countries. Your mother thought little of it, believing him simply to be disagreeable at times, however to my mind he is too sly.

"I set a watch upon him. Your mother disagreed with my actions, believing not a bad word against him. Only my long and trusted relationship in her council led her to accept my wishes. I am thankful that even though for her, in the end, it was all for nothing, you are saved for the kingdom."

Edmund paused for breath, whilst Soren stared at him, silent. "We watched him for many cycles of the moon: his comings and goings, his visits and visitors. All for nought, it seemed, until one day Zaki met with an esquire of Harad."

Soren scowled at that. King Harad had always been a troublesome neighbour, and ruthless in conquest. Caledan was one of few countries which had not fallen to him, but even so, he had infiltrated it by marriage; Zaki had wedded one of his daughters. Soren knew his mother intended it as a sign of allegiance, not submission; but she was no fool. Harad would be biding his time.

For this?

"Harad realises how close he is to Caledan's throne," Soren said.

"Yes. He is an ambitious man; well matched to Zaki, it would seem. The esquire left behind some correspondence, which your uncle failed to dispose. Our eyes within his household procured this for me at great personal danger. I could not believe my eyes. Harad wishes for Zaki to gain Caledan's throne and cause our royal bloodline to fall into Harad's lineage.

"Harad means to send men under his banners immediately. I took this straight to your mother, presuming as always her swift action would curtail his treacherous plan. To my surprise, her denial was total. She could not comprehend the depths of Zaki's treachery. Who would believe their own brother capable of such a thing?"

"And what then?" Soren dropped his eyes, hardly daring to ask.. "When was this? I heard nothing. I understood Uncle held the old views that women should not inherit, if only to further his own prospects, but surely he wasn't so evil as to act upon it?"

"Yesterday. I had to act with utmost haste and took the letter straight to your mother; I could not be sure Zaki would not miss it. She commanded me to leave her. I rallied the high council, warning them that we would most likely need to secure the throne now events had progressed apace. I presumed she would ask for your council, or others. I did not realise you were absent until later.

"After that, things blur. I called the Royal Guard to arms in secret, in case there was need of their help, but I believe Zaki had huge support from some of the council members and their retinues. As your mother summoned him to her chambers that afternoon, I presume to reassure herself this could not possibly be true, it was clear he had done the same with his own men. They rose too quickly for it to be otherwise. He must have decided that then was the time to act.

"I hastened to your mother's chambers, begging her to let me sit in on the meet, to protect her, but she would hear no word of it with her guards and attendants already about her. She sent me away and all I could do was urge the head of the guard to join me to protect her. I did not realise she would call him to her, alone. By the time we returned, it was too late. Her chambers were empty and Zaki was gone."

"And my mother?" Soren breathed with dread. Edmund met his gaze with a horror Soren had never before seen there. "Tell me."

Edmund's tongue darted out to moisten his lips, and he swallowed. "She was already dead." Tears rolled down his cheeks.

Soren stared at him, feeling numb. "How?" he forced himself to ask.

"A blow to the head."

Clubbed like a badger. Soren could not comprehend it. Naisa sprang into his mind's eye, smiling at him as he had seen her last before his departure on the ill-fated hunting trip.

"There was no time to care for her," Edmund said, as Soren listened with a morbid fascination, still unable to connect Edmund's words to his mother. "Caledan, perhaps now more than ever in recent years, stands on a knife-edge. I could not find either you or your sister; alas, I feared the worst."

Soren's hands tightened into fists. "Where is she?"

"Irumae was gone when I reached her chambers. It was clear there had been a struggle, however the fact there was no body or blood—" Edmund flinched, "—heartens me. We must pray she is safe. With you alive and free, Caledan has hope."

Edmund looked up, although he did not meet Soren's eye. Instead, his eyes glazed over, unseeing, seeming to speak to himself.

"So many others passed. The fighting in the great hall was violence and brutality as I have never seen the men of our Kingdom commit. What should have been friend sat with friend feasting and laughing was foe against foe cutting down man after man in a great gash of blood. This was a trap, waiting to spring into action. Every traitorous man knew his orders. I saw council member after council member loyal to the crown mobbed and cut down, whatever the cost in lives, so their voices were silenced. I can only guess what consequences this may have for Caledan. I cannot imagine how Zaki will explain this to his advantage."

"Can I go back?" Soren broke the long silence. He still could not accept Edmund's words, yet the man's emotional recount had unsettled him, adding to the feeling of unease he had awoken with. *He wouldn't lie. Not about this. Yet, he doesn't seem insane, either.*

Edmund shook his head. "I cannot guarantee your safety. As heir to the throne, Zaki will seek you out. I fear what he will do if you return."

If this is all true, there will be a funeral, Soren thought, unable to connect the idea with his mother, *but I may not go.* "What of Irumae?"

The older man paused, shifting his posture. Soren's eyes narrowed; Edmund seemed evasive, and with good cause.

"I do not know her whereabouts, or her wellbeing," Edmund admitted. "We cannot go back for her. We must journey away from here."

"To where? If I can't return to Pandora, then where can I go where I will be safe? And how can you ask me to leave Irumae if there is a chance we could help her?" Soren replied, indignant. "If things are as you say, surely there is no one keeping her safe. She's just a child!"

"*We* cannot help her, however perhaps there are others who can. We should journey to your kin in Arlyn."

"To what end? Karn is old and his forces thin, and Zaki will suspect nothing else from me. We would be walking into a trap. If we are to be safe and have some chance of a haven, we should go to a monastery – the northern monastery – and claim sanctuary. Not even Zaki would touch us there and they may help me find Irumae."

Edmund remained quiet for a moment, his mouth twisting in disapproval. "No one is to say what Zaki is or is not capable of; he is not a normal man. Besides, why would you hide away? We should fight, sire! We should wait and we should recover at Arlyn under Lord Karn's protection, and then we should fight Zaki," Edmund insisted, pounding a clenched fist on the ground beside him.

Soren scoffed. "With what army?"

"You have seen the means he has used to claim the throne, turning against his own kin and committing the vilest of sins. What hope does anyone in the Kingdom have that he will be a benevolent and great ruler like his forebears? What right-minded person will accept his rule as fair and just?"

"Edmund, my uncle has shown his cunning. What proof is there of our claim? He is bound to have created some tale to explain this all away and remove any blame from his own shoulders. I know it to be so; the Varan men called me *traitor*. Who knows what tales he has spun already. What possible evidence can we provide to stand up in any just court of law—if such a thing would be allowed—that will see him cast down? Well?"

Edmund's eyes hardened. "I have the letter." He reached into his jacket and pulled out a crumpled and bloodied parchment, complete with the broken seal of King Harad.

"How is this possible?"

"It was in your mother's rooms — a gross oversight of Zaki, I have no doubt. I recognised the seal. I knew it would be the only evidence I would be able to retrieve, so I took it. Nevertheless, the claim to the throne and for justice lies on you." He held the letter out to Soren, bowing his head.

The prince stepped forward to take it, looking at the folded piece of parchment in his hands as he traced a finger over crusted patches. The parchment was crisp and bright in contrast to the terrible crimson darkness which stained it.

"Is this...?" He dared not ask the question.

"It is hers."

They sat in silence as the life of the wood thrummed around them in the morning sun. Soren held the letter in his lap, fixated upon the patches of his mother's blood. He ignored the radiant sun imprinted on the golden wax seal and gave a cursory glance to the spiky black ink that penned the fateful message. Still unable to conceive the events, which felt altogether too bizarre to begin to accept, he cleared his throat. Edmund glanced up from his own reverie.

"So," Soren said. "We must have a plan. Are we safe enough here for the time being?"

"Yes. Zaki will realise our absence," Edmund replied. "I do not think he will know we are together. First, he will search Pandora. He will seek you with all his power and we must move swiftly if we are to survive. I do not think his intentions will be kind. I believe we should go south, to Arlyn," he insisted once more. "Your father's kin could be your best protection. I fear Zaki may send his men there, but a surer ally we may not find."

"My path lies north." Soren could not help but feel the tug. "The ceremonial crown is held at the northern monastery. If I'm to claim sanctuary, I must go there."

His lessons with the steward of Pandora, Lord Behan, replayed in his mind's eye. *The last monarch must lay in the capital for seven days of mourning and the heir to the throne must also observe this tradition, before claiming the crown with his or her own hands. The true test of kingship is whether he or she can obtain the crown.* Soren had recited it many times before.

"Zaki sees himself as heir—will he remain in Pandora for a week?"

"I believe so. He knows he must be seen to act properly. His men, however, may not," Edmund said. "Are you certain of your path? I must go to Arlyn to seek Lord Karn's advice and ask him to send an envoy to the Eldarkind on your behalf to seek their counsel. Are you sure you cannot come with me and we will journey north after? We could even journey to Ednor and seek sanctuary with the Eldarkind themselves. Zaki would not be able to reach you there."

"I'm sure," said Soren. "We must act quickly, as you say. If I have to leave Irumae, we have seven days at best if Zaki remains in Pandora. If we wait too long, we may not be safe to travel and I might not find her.

"I think you're right to seek the help of the Eldarkind, however I doubt they will act. They might shelter us but I can't go to them. If Zaki learns I'm there, he could trap me and then I'd have no way to help Irumae. I'll go to the northern monastery and ask for their help. If I can also claim the crown for myself there instead of Zaki, then perhaps I could stop him too. Will you return to me afterwards?"

"Of course. I will accompany you on the north road and swing south from there to Arlyn. You will be safe there at least; the monks will shelter you and I am sure they can help you find Irumae," said

Edmund. "I fear there will be a great struggle, but I would not leave you save where I must. As I swore fealty to your mother, I now swear it to you." He struggled to his feet with a grimace and came to kneel before Soren.

Soren regarded Edmund, who bowed before him with hands clasped over his sword, its point sunk into the soft ground. *I have a one-man army. One old man.* He touched Edmund's thinning hair with his palm and accepted his oath. He could not think of himself as a king. If he had not felt so numb, he would not have known whether to laugh or cry.

THREE

Zaki's fingers drummed upon the desk as Lord Reynard made his reports. At last, Reynard's voice trailed off, and Zaki breathed a sigh of relief. The heat was unbearable; the windows were wide open, but the air was still and close, and perspiration clogged his skin.

"Are there any more to account for?" he asked, fanning himself with a parchment.

"No, sir. All bodies have been collected and most identified." Reynard stepped forward with a list. "Here are those worthy of note."

"Excellent. Draw up orders confiscating all their lands and assets in the name of the crown. I want their houses penniless and crushed." Zaki scanned down the list, relieved by its length. His acting treasurer had already informed him that the accounts were not healthy enough to fund a potential civil war and this was a tidy way to bolster royal coffers.

Reynard hesitated.

Zaki raised an eyebrow.

"We have not yet found trace of Sir Edmund Arransson, sir," Reynard admitted.

"We must find him." Zaki fleetingly wondering if Edmund and Soren's paths had joined. "Have notices drawn for him also. An earldom for his capture, dead or alive, and a traitor's death to anyone who harbours him. Send them out with Soren's banners on the morrow, or sooner if they're done. I want these in every village and town in Caledan. Send a detachment from the local company to Edmund's estate; if he hides there, I want him found."

"As you wish, sir."

"Would that I could ride out myself." Zaki rose, frustrated. "I despise being trapped here."

"You know it to be necessary, sir. There are only six days of mourning left before you may leave in good faith."

"Six days too many." Zaki scowled. "What a blasted tradition. At least my men may come and go as they please. You must travel in my stead; lead an advance guard to the northern monastery where the crown is held. I have doubts about the allegiance of the abbot. He was far too close to my sister and I want my crown secure. It is far too important a symbol of peace and stability to the people to afford to lose it. I will ride to meet you with reinforcements the very moment I may."

Reynard bowed. "It would be my pleasure, sir." He departed. Zaki barely had time to take a refreshing gulp of his iced tea before there came a knock on the door.

"The Lord Steward," announced his manservant. Zaki swallowed a curse, forcing himself to slump in his chair and smile sadly as the Lord Steward of Pandora entered.

"How good to see you, Lord Steward Behan," he greeted the older man with a show of deference.

"Your Royal Highness." Behan bowed. "I am devastated by the loss of our fair queen and come to offer you my condolences." He sniffed and dabbed his nose with a handkerchief as Zaki observed him, trying to determine his sincerity. *I would not trust this man as far as I could throw him*, he thought.

"It is a terrible blow," Zaki was forced to reply. "My thanks for your concerns. I seek now to find Prince Soren and bring him to justice for what he has done."

"I find it so hard to believe that a prince so beloved by the people could commit such a heinous act." Behan did not skirt the issue. "How sure are you that he committed it?"

"Oh, it is beyond doubt. The queen's own guards witnessed it. One survived to tell the tale, but he died of his wounds in the night."

"How... unfortunate," murmured Behan. Zaki had no doubt that Behan was instead thinking, *how convenient*. He had never managed to win over the steward.

"Others will tell you they saw Soren running from the citadel, covered in blood," Zaki said.

Behan's attention snapped to him. "I heard the prince was on a hunt in the royal woods that day." His voice was sharp. Suspicious.

"A ruse, no doubt. My witnesses are numerous and credible." Zaki shrugged. "In the chaos, who can be sure? His allies have certainly been crushed." His voice hardened. "And all those who support him have been declared traitor for their part in this plot, to die, despairing that they have failed and that all their titles, lands and assets will be gifted to the crown in payment for their crimes."

Behan paled. "As it should be," he murmured. "I, of course, serve the crown and take no part in these matters," he added swiftly. "What of Her Royal Highness, Princess Irumae? Is she safe and well?"

"She is safe, though not well," Zaki said with feigned sadness. "My dear niece is distraught at her mother's death and brother's treason."

"She is the next in line to the throne, though."

Zaki was careful in his reaction. "She is, however she is in no fit state to assume the throne and will not hear of it. Why, she pressed me to take it."

"And did you let her, sir?"

"Of course not," Zaki hastened to add, choosing his words with care. "However, for the sake of the realm, perhaps it would be an option to consider. Perhaps it is the frailty of her sex, but the girl seems to have lost her mind. Perhaps it is worth considering a return to the old ways of male inheritance." He let the idea hang in the air.

"You would be next in line to the throne if that came to pass." Behan fiddled with the huge ring of his office that adorned his hand.

"I do not suggest this lightly. I only think of the security of Caledan, Lord Steward. Think of my father-in-law. King Harad swallows countries of weak leadership, and other sharks circle beyond our borders. Caledan must remain strong. Leaving its fate in the hands of an unstable, untrained, and untested girl could prove fatal."

"I cannot disagree with your principles, sir," Behan replied with utmost care, "but what of the succession? Legally, she is the heir to Caledan's throne if Soren is to be declared traitor and abdicated in his absence."

"I know not of the legalities," Zaki said. One *signature from Irumae countersigned by a law reader, and Caledan is as good as mine; it is too easy.* "Perhaps there is a way."

"I will consult the law readers with utmost haste to clarify this on your behalf if you wish, sir," said the steward.

For your own ends, you mean, snake, thought Zaki. Instead, he replied, "That would be most appreciated, Lord Steward. We must ensure Caledan remains strong."

Behan bowed and left with speed. Zaki could not miss the consternation upon the steward's face, well concealed as it was. He sat back in his chair, smiling at the discomfort he had caused and smug at outwitting the steward. Behan, notorious for having his finger in every pie in Pandora and many throughout Caledan, had not been expecting this, he was sure. It was satisfying to be so many steps ahead of everyone else in what felt like his own little game.

"Thank you for your promptness. Her condition has not improved in the past day, and I fear for her wellbeing," Behan said. "I thought best to call ask if you could determine the source of her malady." It was the third time he had called upon Irumae in the past hours, and each time she lay immobile and unconscious, though she breathed and there was a hint of colour upon her cheeks.

"Naturally," the royal physician answered. "My colleagues and I shall examine her. If you would be so kind?" He gestured to the door.

"Of course." Behan hurried to leave. His guard waited outside Irumae's rooms, ready to warn him should anyone call. He had distracted Zaki's men with false orders so he could conduct the medical examination in secret, fearing that the princess had come to harm after his earlier conversation with Zaki. He expected such deviousness from Harad, but his underestimation of Zaki worried him. *Who knows what he has planned.*

It seemed an age before the physicians emerged. Behan, seated upon a couch, rose eagerly. "Yes?"

The physician shook his head. "We can find no physical issues, no marks or abnormalities upon her body. We cannot examine the state of her mind, but the most likely explanation is that she is in a state of shock, understandably, and her body has shut itself down."

"Will she recover?"

"We cannot be sure," the physician answered, to the steward's dismay.

"Do not forget, I require the greatest discretion in this matter," Behan called after him as he departed.

Behan left too, hurrying to meet with the chief law reader to discuss his findings. He travelled through alleys to the back entrance of the courts, even though they were a stone's throw across the square.

"Lord Heligan." Behan rushed into the office wringing his hands, despite the secretary's protests.

"Lord Steward, such urgency?" Heligan questioned.

Behan shut the door behind him for privacy and detailed Heligan with the physician's conclusions.

Heligan sat back with a frown. "That is troubling to hear," he said.

"We must decide what is most appropriate, Heligan." Behan paced about the room. "There is the option of installing a regent in Irumae's stead, but I fear Zaki pushes for the throne. I worry Irumae has come to deliberate harm under his orders." He described the girl's condition.

"That worries me further," Heligan said. "If the law is to be kept, a regent must first be installed to rule in place of the princess, unless she herself signs over the throne willingly to him."

"He says she attempted to, though given her condition, I am unsure if that be true. Who would fill the regency?" Behan searched his knowledge of the royal family tree—only distant cousins existed. No competition for Zaki's claim.

"It would be the closest relative of age, legally," Heligan

confirmed, "or a pre-appointed regent. Alas," he continued, as Behan's face lit up with fresh hope, "there is no such arrangement. Sir Edmund signed as regent in the case of Naisa's untimely death, but just to rule until Soren came of age. There was no such safeguard in place for Irumae."

"This means Zaki is the regent, whether we will it or not," Behan said, dismayed. Heligan inclined his head in confirmation. Behan slumped in a chair. They sat silently for a few moments in the cool shade, a refreshing change after the constricting atmosphere of the castle.

"Can he take the throne from her without her cooperation?" asked Behan. Unable to sit still, he resumed his pacing.

"I had thought to look into this already. There is a loophole," Heligan admitted. "As Irumae's closest living relative, Soren could dictate her actions. However, as he has been declared traitor, this duty could be seen to fall to Zaki. He could rightfully sign her out of the succession as her guardian and representative on the grounds of her ill health."

"And sign it over to himself as next in line," Behan said, so aghast he paused. "I believe if he knows of this, he will use this to his advantage. Can this be hidden from him?" he added softly, daring to be hopeful.

"The questions is *should* it be?" Heligan's words were quiet, almost apologetic, as he stood to view the castle from his window.

"Of course! The man is selfish and self-serving, with some very troubling ideas. I cannot see how Soren could commit such a heinous act; what if Zaki has orchestrated this? His father-in-law also concerns me. I do not trust Harad would leave us alone if this were to pass. For Caledan's sake, Zaki should not rule. Soren is our rightful king and showed good promise. I pray the boy is safe—and that the princess will come to no harm."

"As do many, I am sure. Yet I am bound to tell Zaki, truthfully, what options there are if he asks it of me," said Heligan, "as are my colleagues. If this were to be concealed from him and he were to discover this, whose heads do you think would be first on the block?"

"Our roles are chosen by a ballot of our guilds." Behan frowned.

"I would not presume that makes us safe though, Behan. He has already replaced half the council with his own men and strips hereditary nobles of their rank daily. I am sure there would be a way to replace us if he wished. Our offices could be lost to a candidate of his choosing and we could find worse fates awaiting ourselves.

"Would you throw away your position so needlessly? We would be better serving if we let the cards fall where they may and ride out this storm. We need not forsake Soren or Irumae by doing so."

"So you say we ought to allow this to occur?" said Behan. "We let him stand for the regency, sign over the crown to himself and remain here, waiting and hoping that Soren returns to retake the throne?"

"I see no other choice. It will occur with or without us," Heligan said, facing him. Vexed, he rubbed his forehead. "It is not an easy choice, nor a pleasant one, and it will be dangerous for the both of us. We must speak no more of this and be seen to fully submit to the new regime. I believe only this will ensure our own survival and ensure Soren has well-placed allies, should he return."

"And if Soren returns, there is a way to undo this madness?" Behan's stomach fluttered in a frisson of nerves at Heligan's words, but he trusted his friend enough to hear him out.

"There is always a loophole," Heligan said with an uncharacteristically devious smile.

FOUR

Soren nibbled on the pathetic scraps of food they had left, whilst Edmund made all signs of their presence vanish, putting out the tiny fire and scattering the ashes wide. Soren ate the food and drank the now cold brew in silence, but Edmund suspected the young man tasted none of it. It had tasted like ash in Edmund's own mouth that morning. It was biscuits and meat strips, the crumbled and stale remnants of Soren's hunting provisions; but even if it had been the finest pastries and fruits, he doubted they would have enjoyed it.

"We must move on," Edmund prompted.

He waited for Soren to answer, but the prince stood frozen. Soren's face was a grimace, his eyes screwed as tight as his fists. Edmund's face softened. He was reminded of his own son Dane; several years older than Soren's twenty, yet he felt a strange mix of longing and worry for him. It mingled with relief, knowing Dane at least was far from harm and Pandora's chaos.

"We must move on," Edmund repeated. He sealed away his own emotions as he had been trained to do, knowing he needed to show strength in front of Soren for them to succeed. Before long, they were ready, and with last glances at the sky to mark the time and his compass to mark their position, he led them north on foot through the forest.

The greenery thinned as they passed, until the trees were so large and spaced out that both could mount their horses and ride. Their pace improved and the miles passed by to the soft drum of hooves on moss and grass, but it was slow passage compared to the open travel of the road, miles to their east.

As the sun slid once more below the horizon, they emerged onto an outcrop above the forest. A sea of green forests and rolling hills as far as the eye could see was alight with hues of gold and ruby under the descending sun—but Edmund and Soren were both too preoccupied to appreciate it. Numb with tiredness, they scrambled down the steep embankment. Almost parallel to the road, they found Carrick, the sleepy village Edmund sought, tucked away in the trees.

Avoiding both the road and the settlement, they pulled up their hoods. Both were too well known in the area to chance an encounter. Edmund knew word of the previous day's events would have passed through here first as high-speed riders flew everywhere to disperse news from the capital.

Edmund angled northwest until the village's noise faded behind them. Ahead, under the darkening canopy, a tiny, whitewashed farmhouse appeared. It was nothing much—one room downstairs and its achievement the fact it had a second floor at all—but Edmund smiled at the sight. He made straight for the barn, where he unsaddled and unpacked his horse, bidding Soren to do the same.

"Shouldn't we stay in the woods?" Soren said. "Someone could find us here!"

As if to increase his anxiety, a sudden gust of wind forced the barn door to slam shut. Moonlight flooded back in as Edmund heaved the door open, revealing an unsettled Soren gripping his sword hilt.

"We shall stay in the farmhouse. We are safe here, you have my word."

The farm door was open; unlike in the cities, doors remained unlocked in the countryside. Edmund strolled in, with Soren following behind. The familiar scent of fresh baked honey bread that met his nose made him smile. A crash sounded from upstairs as he shut the door and footsteps thundered down the stairs. Edmund could have sworn dust had shaken loose from the rafters as the occupant emerged.

Shock and surprise flitted across her face before she rushed forward to grab Edmund in a bone-crushing embrace. When she stepped back however, she scowled, standing across the bottom of the stairs, arms firmly crossed. An ancient woman of short stature, she had an imposing nature and radiated self-assurance. Grey hair was pinned up, with a few flyaway strands, and dark, quick eyes twinkled from a wrinkling face; she was a woman who took no nonsense.

"Why's it taken you so long to visit?" She was indignant, but all the same stomped to the stove in the corner to heat a kettle of water. As she turned around, she caught sight of Soren and froze.

"This house is a pigsty and I look like I've been dragged through a bush backwards!" she hissed at Edmund frantically. "Your Majesty Royal Highness." She attempted an agitated curtsy, nearly tripping over in the process.

Edmund suppressed a bemused smile as Soren looked at him, nonplussed. "My apologies, Aunt." He came forward, a few steps of his six-foot frame taking him to her, and leaned down to grab his aunt in a bear hug that overwhelmed her. "It's good to see you. It's been too long." His smile lessened as he stepped away. "You've heard the news?"

"Yes, I have, and I didn't believe a word of it for a second." Her eyes kept darting to Soren. "Now you're here, you can set the record straight." She gestured at table and chairs in the corner of the small room by a stove. A large wick burned in a table lamp, throwing bright, flickering light across them all.

"Would you like some stew?" she said, seeming worried about offending her royal guest.

Edmund laughed. "We don't bite, Aunt! Please, we're famished." This close, he could smell the tomatoes and meat and his mouth watered as he beheld the bubbling pot sat upon the hob. They set the saddlebags down in a corner, unfastening their cloaks and casting them off.

Dragging three chairs closer to the table, they sunk into them with groans as Edmund's aunt joined them, setting two wooden bowls full of stew on the table, topped with a carved spoon and a hunk of bread smeared with yellow butter. She ignored the spare chair, leaning on the mantelpiece instead.

"I suppose proper introductions are in order," said Edmund, though he could barely speak through mouthfuls of tender rabbit and vegetables. He could not remember when anything had tasted quite so good. Beside him, Soren ate in silence. "Soren, this is my Aunt Bethel, who raised me after my parents passed away when I was ten summers old."

Bethel, being of lower social standing, formally inclined her head first to the prince, who responded likewise, before raising an eyebrow to Edmund and inviting him to continue.

Edmund kept his account brief and quiet, covertly regarding Soren, but the prince focused his attention on the bowl before him, though he ate sparingly. Bethel's eyes were sympathetic as she studied the young man. "I suspect Zaki's tale of events will bear little resemblance to my own, but I can assure you that I do not lie. What have you heard?"

"Certainly not that," replied the tiny woman, looking troubled. "One of the dispatch riders passed today. It was quick; you know how they rush about. He began by announcing the passing of the queen, may she rest in peace, but he put all blame on you." Her voice reduced to a whisper.

"He claimed you had murdered your mother—please forgive me for saying this, I'm only repeating what was said—in order to steal the throne. He battled against you to save her, but was too late, and in the chaos, you escaped. Your life is proclaimed as forfeit. Yours too, Ed. There are rewards for your capture."

"What of my sister?" Soren interrupted. "Is she safe?"

Bethel shook her head. "I'm so sorry, I don't know."

Edmund and Soren tried to absorb Bethel's words. Edmund addressed the prince, both of their meals forgotten.

"Most this close to Pandora will notice something is afoot. After all, your mother, and you in turn, were popular, Soren. You will be well regarded here, far more than your uncle who has done nothing to aid Caledan's people.

"However…" Edmund paused. "I think we should tread with great care. Those further afield cannot be assumed to act in our favour and we may encounter those who would betray us at great expense to the country for their own personal gains. I think either way, for now, we have to recoup our energy. A wash, a meal, and a good nights' rest are in order." He glanced at Bethel with a question in his eyes.

She huffed at him and rolled her eyes. "Well, of course I'll keep you tonight, as if it needs to be said. You're still my little boy, Ed, no matter how far you've risen in other people's eyes. I only worry that you won't be safe here. I've got your old room under the eaves spare, you can have that."

"Soren, you take it."

Soren nodded.

The kettle whistled at last. Bethel ushered Soren up the staircase to a small room under the thatched roof and heavy beams that held it up, and Edmund followed. Bethel bustled downstairs, returning with mugs of tea just as Soren dropped his pack. She smiled and bade them goodnight—before they could thank her for her kindness, she returned downstairs as though nothing had happened.

It was a strange feeling for Edmund, stepping into his old room for the first time in several decades—almost like stepping back to his childhood. The room felt unchanged in his absence, though bare of his personal effects.

He breathed in the scent of Bethel's homemade candle burning on the small dresser, feeling wistful for the simplicity of his youth. For the first moment since before discovering the letter's existence, he felt as though he were safe, though he knew it would only be for a short time.

He too bade Soren goodnight, and retreated downstairs to sleep on the pelts before the fire, whilst Bethel retired to her pallet.

Through the walls, he heard muffled sobs. He rose to go to Soren, but checked himself and instead sat, his head bowed. He joined Soren's grief with his own silent tears. The queen he loved was dead and the country he served on the brink of disaster. It was long after the fire had died out and the tea had cooled that he wiped the crusted tears from his face and slept.

Soren struggled to stand under the low, sloping ceiling of the tiny, white-walled room. He slumped fully-clothed onto the mattress, drink forgotten as he stared at the flame, listless with exhaustion.

He bit down on his arm as sobs forced their way out, muffled by the layers of fabric in his mouth. He cried as he had never cried before—for his mother, for his father killed in battle almost ten years before, for his missing sister, and for his own misfortune. Exhausted beyond measure, he slept and the flow of tears subsided.

Hours later, the glow of early morning light and muted hubbub of the forest filtered through the shutter, waking Soren from a deep, dreamless slumber. He stared at the thatch-covered beams.

At first, he felt nothing, until anger and rebelliousness stirred—not an impulsive, heated rage, but a cold, unyielding, inexorable anger that detached him from the pain he had felt the night before. Grief had ruled him then, but now he vowed it would not escape again until he had brought Zaki to justice and found Irumae.

I must not fail.

With grim pleasure, he promised revenge on his uncle.

Edmund had already broken fast by the time Soren washed and dressed, and he helped himself to seconds whilst Soren ate. It earned him a rap on the knuckles from Bethel, who sternly ordered him to keep his hands to himself and let Soren eat first. Bethel's kind nature warmed Soren as much as the warm porridge; not even dining on the finest foods had he felt so comfortable in the palace. He relaxed, but the anger sat in his stomach as he ate.

"Off already, Ed?" Bethel asked, an eyebrow raised as Edmund retrieved their packs from upstairs. "Surely you need more rest?"

"We do," he admitted, shrugging. "I suspect Zaki's men will

come here searching for us in a while." He trailed off, looking at his aunt in concern.

"I can take care of myself," she said lightly, waving a wooden spoon at him. Soren saw that the worry in Edmund's eyes did not fade. "Well, I'm sorry it must be so. When this is over, you must promise to come and visit me. You're welcome too of course, Your Royal Highness," she added, peering around Edmund at Soren. She seemed hesitant around him when reminded of his status, but otherwise driven by habit or instinct to mother him.

"Thank you," Soren replied, wishing he could put his gratitude into better words. He had already come to feel quite at home there. The rough, home-made furniture had far more character than the castle's and Bethel's oddities—a half-knitted sock on the table, a speckled chicken pecking around the open front door, a wind chime made of woodland knickknacks—gave the cottage a far more endearing personality too.

"You're welcome any time you wish. I miss you, Ed. I don't see enough of you or Dane," Bethel said. "I didn't want to ask last night. Is he well?"

Edmund spread his hands wide. "I have had no news from him of late, nor could I send word to him. He manages my lands in the south. He will be safe there - innocence and ignorance will be his shield." He smiled, but Soren noticed how it did not reach his eyes.

Both embracing her—Soren for the unhesitant protection she had offered and danger she had placed herself in for them, and Edmund for the long time they had spent apart—they promised to return. Her eyes filled with surprise as Soren stepped back. He left with sadness, wishing he could linger in such a simple, peaceful place, but there was no choice in his mind and he would not have stayed, even if his safety had been guaranteed.

They continued to make swift progress following the road north. By nightfall, the two horses were exhausted after the ride, and nipped at the men's sleeves as they were unsaddled.

A dell some distance from the road provided shelter. The horses grazed as Edmund and Soren enjoyed a cold meal of meats and cheeses and bread, pressed on them by Bethel that morning.

They ate in silent companionship, neither feeling the need to talk, as dusk fell.

Edmund rose in the gloom to retrieve a lamp from his pack. Though its range was limited, the small clearing was soon bathed in a comforting gold light that was dappled from the lamp's rough glass panels. Soren stared into the flame, watching the dancing flicker of light and taking in the sounds of night in the woods around him.

Soren started as Edmund spoke. "Soren. I think we should discuss our plans. Do you still wish to go to the northern monastery?"

Soren's mouth tightened and his face was stern. "I do," he replied.

Edmund smiled. "Do not mistake me for chiding you. I wish to make certain in my own mind that you are resolute in yours. The monastery is not far. After tomorrow's ride, which is as far as we have come today, you will be within an hour or two's ride of the monastery. Tomorrow night, I suggest you ride for the monastery after we part. Breaking on the crossroads is far too great a risk."

"I would rather arrive at the monastery in daylight to avoid ambush." Soren frowned.

"I agree," Edmund acquiesced. "However, it is more important to reach the safety of the monastery. There should be no danger there."

"You will not come with me?"

Edmund shook his head. "I must seek help from Arlyn. The swifter I depart, the sooner I return. I may yet outrun Zaki himself and re-join you in any case. You will come to no harm at the monastery. I would trust the abbot and his brothers with my life."

Hooves drummed upon the road. Disorientated and half asleep, Edmund and Soren shrank into the earth, before rising to settle the horses. The horses stood with heads turned towards the road and ears pricked. The noise passed. The forest fell quiet again before the sounds of bird and insect life crescendoed. Soren's eyes mirrored Edmund's own apprehension.

"We had best keep moving," said Edmund.

Despite a slow pace, they reached the crossroad an hour before dusk, approaching on foot through the woods to avoid being spotted on the open road. Sure enough, when Edmund scouted ahead, sentries loitered outside the crossroad inn, laughing and idling about. The road lay in plain sight and they were well-placed to spot the comings and goings of anyone who passed whether or not they took the care to look.

"As I expected. Although Zaki may not leave the capital for another four days, he controls the army and will be sure to have his web of men spread as far and wide as possible. We must be careful," Edmund said. "We are on the north side of the road now, as is the monastery. We will bear north until it is safe for me to cross the road and bear south again."

Under the cover of dusk, they parted.

"Good fortune, Soren," Edmund said. "Follow the road north and you will find the monastery. It should be three days' ride to Arlyn and three back, so look for me in a week.

"The abbot is the wisest man I know and he shall guide and guard you; of that, I have no doubts. However, if the need arises, you must flee. This is no time for bravery and heroics; you must remain alive for the good of the realm. I know it may not be the easiest decision, but this is my advice. It will not happen, but just in case." *I leave him in safer hands than my own behind those walls.*

The prince opened his mouth to say something, then closed it and shook his head. "You're far wiser than me," Soren said. "I'll try to follow your advice, though it goes against my heart."

Edmund smiled with relief. "Well, here we are at the parting of the ways, then. We should delay no longer. Good luck and God keep you safe, Soren."

"And God keep you."

Edmund watched the prince's back fade into the gloom and silently blessed him, hoping above all else that they would meet again—that he would make it to Arlyn and back alive, unharmed and unhindered.

FIVE

Silence blanketed the room, broken by the delicate clinking of silver cutlery upon the finest porcelain tableware. Save for her lady and his manservant waiting inconspicuously outside the dining room, they were alone, yet it was no intimate dinner, for they sat at opposite ends of the large table. The gilded ceiling towered above them and weak light streamed in through tall windows. It still felt dark, cold, and unwelcoming compared to her homeland of Roher.

"How fares your business, husband?" Demara attempted to strike up a conversation. Confined to her quarters for safety, she had heard little news that week, nor seen much of her husband. Tonight was the first night he had dined with her in weeks and yet he remained as silent and closed towards her as ever.

Zaki looked up, surprised that she had spoken. "It goes well enough," he replied tersely. Meeting her glance, he laughed—a short, sharp bark—at the uncertainty in her eyes. "You are safe, fear not, and I shall be king."

Demara quieted again, although her mind buzzed with questions. *Does that mean I am to be queen? Does that mean I can never return to my home...?* "Have you found...?" She dared not name Soren in case she awakened Zaki's short temper.

"No," he replied, his attention returned to his food.

"What of the princess?" she dared to ask, laying her hands across her belly. The luxurious silk slid beneath her fingers over the bulge of her stomach. She knew what it was to be a pawn of men, bound to the fate of their choosing, and she pitied the girl. She prayed yet again that her unborn child would be a son free from the same shackles as she.

He dumped his cutlery on the plate with a crash. "Good God, still your tongue from all these questions!" She met his gaze, although she made sure not to appear too brazen. His glance softened as he saw her hands. "I forget; your condition makes you weaker. Do not concern yourself with the girl."

"I only pity that she—"

"Demara," Zaki addressed her with a warning tone, "the girl is a danger to you and our son. Feel no pity for her. Whilst she lives, I may not be secure upon the throne."

"So you will kill her?" Demara asked, her voice quiet. *Surely, he would not...*

"I have not yet decided her fate," Zaki admitted. "It is her brother who concerns me more." He wiped his mouth with his napkin and pushed back his chair. "I am done. I bid you good night. I will sleep alone tonight." With that, he called for his servant and left her alone in the gloom.

Demara lay her cutlery down on her plate with the quietest chink, her appetite lost.

Zaki's mood was buoyant - no trace of his usual irritation about him. A grin stretched his face as he stood in the company of law readers, the lord steward, and other witnesses from the royal court upon the dais. Banners bearing his sister's crest bedecked the hall.

Behan suspected they would soon be removed. He replaced the quill in the ink well; the drying ink shone brightly against the parchment before Lord Heligan blotted it with utmost care and handed the document to one of his peers in exchange for the next.

"Witness ye all, on this the nineteenth day of the fifth month of this year, the formal appointment of His Royal Highness Prince Zaki of Caledan as Regent Royale and Legal Guardian of Her Royal Highness Princess Irumae of Caledan until the day she comes of age," Heligan said as his partner held up the deed for all to see the fresh signatures of Zaki, himself, and the lord steward upon it.

The next document lay stretched out upon the ornate table. Behan kept his expression clear, though he wished he could burn every document prepared for that day.

"This document relinquishes the place of Her Royal Highness Princess Irumae in the royal succession on the grounds of her ill health," Heligan said. "I call upon her guardian to sign this document on her behalf in her absence."

"I shall sign for her," replied Zaki, stepping forward to take up the pen again.

"I call upon the Lord Steward of Pandora to bear witness to this," Heligan called.

"I shall bear witness to this," Behan said. He forced down his reluctance and stepped forward to take up the gilded quill. *Smile. Keep smiling. This can be undone. This will be undone. Please, God, let it be undone.*

"I sign myself to confirm this matter has been conducted in a legal manner." Heligan took his turn, refusing to meet Behan's eye. "Witness ye all, on this the nineteenth day of the fifth month this year, the formal renouncement of any claim to the throne of Caledan by Her Royal Highness Princess Irumae, now to be known as the Lady Irumae of Pandora."

The third and final document now lay upon the table.

"This document acknowledges His Royal Highness Prince Zaki of Caledan as the Heir Apparent to the throne of Caledan, in the absence of His Royal Highness Prince Soren of Caledan, following the death of Her Majesty Queen Naisa, first of her name, may she be at peace and with God." Heligan paused for breath. "I call upon the Regent Royale to sign this document in place of any monarch or heir."

"I shall sign as Regent Royale," said Zaki, signing swiftly.

"I call upon the nominated Heir Apparent to sign in acceptance of these terms," Heligan said, before Zaki released the quill.

"I shall sign as Heir Apparent," said Zaki, signing again.

"I call upon the Lord Steward of Pandora to bear witness to this." Heligan called Behan forward.

"I shall bear witness to this." Behan signed the document, his face impassive.

"I sign myself to confirm this matter has been conducted in a legal manner." Heligan completed the formalities. "Witness ye all, on this the nineteenth day of the fifth month this year, the formal appointment of His Royal Highness Prince Zaki of Caledan as Heir Apparent to the throne of Caledan."

Behan stepped forward. "Please make your way to the great hall for drinks to toast His Royal Highness Prince Zaki, the good health of the Lady Irumae, and the memory of Her Majesty Queen Naisa."

The murmuring crowd moved along and he made to follow, but a hand on his arm stopped him. Behan turned to find Zaki grasping his forearm, digging in his fingers like claws. Behan swallowed. "Your Royal Highness?" *Did I not sound cheerful enough about you stealing Caledan's throne?*

"Leave," Zaki commanded the few stragglers, who hurried to obey. He released Behan's arm and the steward stepped back slightly. "Why did you have a medical examination conducted upon the girl?" He glared at the older man.

Behan swallowed, trying to compose himself. "The law readers advised it a necessary precaution prior to the signing of the regency and changes in succession, sir," he improvised. *That scheming physician ran straight to Zaki.*

"Do not interfere with my niece." Zaki's eyes narrowed.

"I would not dream of it, sir," Behan stammered.

"She will be moved for her own safety and wellbeing today. If I hear you have attempted to see her again, you will be severely punished. Do I make myself clear?"

"Certainly, sir. I meant no offence."

"I am sure." Zaki scowled. "In any case, I am soon to be King of Caledan. I want the entire city to know that Soren and Irumae have been retired from the succession and that I will ascend the throne. You are to organise my coronation as swiftly as possible after mourning ends. It is your duty to ensure this runs smoothly and you I will hold personally accountable for any hitches. Go."

Behan bowed and scurried away, stumbling in his haste to escape Zaki's baleful presence.

SIX

"Come on, keep up!" Eve laughed over her shoulder. She pressed her legs into the flanks of her horse, who lengthened her stride. The mare danced around tree trunks and leapt over exposed roots with uncanny agility as the two stallions tried to keep pace.

They burst through the edge of the forest, which thinned abruptly to become open moorland bathed in bright sun. Eve reined in her horse before she lost herself in the heather, long grass, and maze of rabbit holes that could easily lame the mare. She admired the view whilst waiting for her guards to catch up.

"Eve, you must stop doing that!" the older guard scolded as they drew up beside her. His younger counterpart reined in his horse behind.

Eve grinned at him without contrition. "Sorry, Nyle. You know how I like to give Alia a free head. She's so quick!" She dismounted and gave the horse a treat and a pat.

"Who's that?" the younger man said. They turned as one to follow his pointing hand. The moor rolled away from them down into the valley, so they could see the road winding its way to Arlyn, the town nestled in the mountain foothills next to the glinting Arrow Lake. Despite the distance, the day was crisp and clear and they could see a dark-cloaked figure rushing towards the town.

"I'm not sure, Luke. Perhaps it's a dispatch rider," said Eve. "How long will it take us to return?"

"Not long," Luke replied. He shaded his eyes against the sun to see the figure better. "We should certainly reach Arlyn before him if that's your intention."

"Let's go," said Eve, unable to hide her interest. She mounted and Alia sprang into motion, wheeling around to ride home.

"Wait for us!" Nyle cried fruitlessly as he waited for Luke. "For goodness sake," he grumbled and urged his horse to follow her without waiting for his counterpart to regain his saddle.

She did not return using the wandering path up into the hills and back down to Arlyn Keep, but instead followed the fringe of the forest west for the swiftest return. Ground-nesting birds exploded out of the undergrowth, protesting as she crashed past them.

The dark rider was lost to sight now behind another rolling hill. As they both drew closer and their paths converged on Arlyn, he came into view again. Arlyn's old walls loomed before her and she turned up the hill to race alongside them, away from the main gate and the road that would take the stranger through the winding, cobbled streets of the town.

Nyle hailed her from a distance, but Eve did not slow. The two stallions did not have the same sure footing as her mare and she knew her companions were forced to turn aside. They would have to make for the main gate, which would buy her time to reach home, change her clothing, and spy on the stranger from the stables before they returned.

Alia danced up the embankment, somehow finding footing on the steep grounds, until they were on the outcropping far above the wall. For a moment, Eve paused to catch the beautiful view of Arlyn. The town sloped away towards the glittering water with the mountains soaring behind it; it was a sight that never failed to lift her heart. After a moment, she moved on. From there, she could enter the keep gardens and ride unseen to the stables.

An alarmed stable-hand dived out of her path as she rode into the stable without dismounting. She leapt from Alia and dashed upstairs to the loft. The stable-boy shook his head as he led the mare to her stall. Eve was already in the loft, batting straw hastily off the crumpled dress she had discarded there hours before. Not bothering to take off her riding pants and boots, she forced the dress over her head, shook herself into it, and gave herself a cursory glance to check it was not back to front before she climbed down.

She had changed just in time for Nyle and Luke's return. Nyle opened his mouth indignantly and paused, thrown off guard by her attire. Luke stifled a chuckle as he dismounted. He grinned at her behind Nyle's back whilst she smoothed her dress.

Before Nyle could chastise her, the dark-cloaked figure rode into the courtyard, hood down.

"Sir Edmund!" she cried with surprise as she beheld the familiar face.

Her bright voice startled Edmund. He twisted in his saddle to see Eve running towards him. Soiled boots hid beneath the folds of her skirt—ordinarily, he would have chuckled, but exhaustion and grief dulled all sense within him. He dismounted and turned to greet her as the gates thudded shut behind him.

"Lady Eve." He inclined his head as he appraised her. She had grown much since their last meeting, now slim and tall like her mother, although she still fell short of his height. Her features had sharpened from a child's to a young woman's and she had tamed her once flyaway golden hair into a long plait. She held none of the decorum and reserve he would expect from the heir of such an old house, but he appreciated her open affection.

"It's been so long! I didn't know you were coming. How are our cousins keeping? I can't wait to hear your news! Sir Edmund?" Her smile faltered at his frown.

"I would appreciate immediate audience with your father, Lady Eve. I apologise for the rudeness of my unannounced visit, but it is a matter of utmost importance, and I cannot tarry."

Eve's smile faded and she gestured for him to follow her. She hurried through the keep, down long passageways and up narrow staircases. Her long dress snatched at her ankles as she strove to stay ahead of Edmund's long strides. They approached a heavy, metal-studded, wooden door. Eve rapped on the door and heaved it open before there was any reply from within.

Warm pelts covered the wooden floor, high windows gave views of the town and lake below, and tapestries depicting the changing seasons of Arlyn covered the walls. Near the empty stone hearth was a desk covered in parchment sheets and a variety of paraphernalia. Behind it, Lord Karn of Arlyn sat, looking up at the interruption.

"Sir Edmund? I received no word of your arrival; I fear you have caught me most unprepared. Is all well?" Lord Karn asked.

"No, Lord Karn, I bring tidings which I wish were not true." Edmund paused. He glanced towards Eve. "Perhaps, Eve, you might retire. I fear my news not fit for your ears."

Eve departed with reluctance, scowling as she strode out.

Edmund drew in a deep breath and met Karn's gaze. "Naisa has been murdered," he said. A muffled cry emanated from the other side of the door. Edmund lowered his voice further before continuing.

"Zaki has usurped the throne. I do not know the full details myself, it was all I could do to escape myself and bring you tidings, but seven nights past, Zaki's murmurings of malcontent turned from nothing more than words to a full-blown overtaking of the capital. Pandora has fallen," Edmund continued. Tears pricked his eyes as Karn sagged against his desk, white-faced. "Soren escaped alongside me and I mean to follow him as soon as I may. The princess is unaccounted for." The implications hung in the air.

"I had heard murmurings of this some days hence from passing traders. I dismissed such ridiculous claims as nothing more than fear mongering." Karn shook his head in confusion. "I cannot understand that her own brother would do such a thing. If we have not heard these tidings from the dispatch riders, then perhaps he seeks to hide it from us. I am at a loss as to what to say. Come, you must rest with us a while," he insisted.

Edmund shook his head. "I cannot in good conscience do so, Karn. Soren will have already claimed sanctuary in the northern monastery. I left the prince on his way there, but I cannot disclose our business to you. I do not like to keep it from you. Suffice to say it is vital to ensure Soren's success in restoring peace, I assure you."

"Worry not, I know what you speak of." Karn bowed his head. "My brother spoke of the crown to me after he wed Naisa, though perhaps he ought not to. I believe you are correct in pursuing it, but Soren will need help. Is there any way I may be of assistance?"

"No," Edmund replied. "The risk of sheltering me is enough. I apologise for bringing this burden, but you needed to know the truth and I will confess I desired your advice. I would say to make your forces ready but do nothing. Zaki knows where your loyalties lie; at the first sign of a sword, he will crush you. All I would ask of you is to send an envoy to the Eldarkind. Mayhap they will help us again in what is to come as they helped us in our youth. Their freedoms could be at stake too. I doubt Zaki will tolerate them. What can we do?" He ran a hang through his tangled, unkempt hair.

"Indeed." Karn rubbed his forehead, and shook his head. "We cannot stand against Zaki, no matter how much I want to. We would be decimated. I can make my men ready, but we need more allies. There are many who would follow Soren after their loyalty to his mother, when faced with a choice between he or Zaki, I am certain."

"Not enough. Not enough are left, now." Edmund forced visions of their bodies stacked high around the castle from his mind.

"I wonder that we could ask the Eldarkind for their assistance."

"I wonder the same. They barely leave their valley, but I have visited them on many an occasion and I'm sorely tempted to ask for their help. They have a vested interest in the future of Caledan too. They could make the difference; their fighting skills and magic are legendary."

"Or the stuff of nightmares, depending on whether you believe the fairy tales." Karn gave a dry chuckle.

Edmund scoffed. "Nonsense, and I wish everyone knew it. We must seek them out. There is no harm in asking, but much to be lost by not." He blinked, unable to clear the gritty tiredness from his eyes, and swayed on his feet. It had been a long ride. "Thank you, though, for taking me in. And for believing me."

Karn's face clouded further.

"We will win back the throne for Soren, and defeat the usurper. Somehow." *I'm not sure how*, Edmund wondered, but he did not dare voice it.

"Time. These things take time. It would do you well to rest up a while, but at the very least you must spend the night. I insist," Karn said as Edmund protested. "You cannot gallivant around the country with no rest; we are all older than when we did such things rashly."

He smiled with fondness at Edmund, all sense of formality now gone between them, and stood up to embrace him. "It's good to see you, old friend. I wish it were under happier tidings. If you do not mind, I will need to set things in motion now, but Eve will see to it that you are comfortable and you shall join us for dinner."

Edmund bowed his head. "Certainly, friend. I am truly sorry to be the one bringing such news."

He found Eve outside, wan-faced and sat against the wall hugging her legs. Karn drew her up and held her close.

"You heard us?" he said softly. It was barely a question. She nodded into his chest. "Be brave then for our family, my little dove. We can grieve for your aunt later. There is still hope for your cousins." He stepped back to smile at her. "Come, show Edmund to the large guest room."

Eve led Edmund through corridors in silence with downcast eyes to a pleasant room overlooking the grounds, where she bade him farewell. Edmund watched her go. A new pity emerged for her as he realised her already small family had shrunk again. A servant soon appeared to prepare a bath and lay fresh clothes on an ornately carved four-poster bed draped in rich green fabrics.

After days of sleeping rough, for Edmund, this kind of forest was a far sweeter resting place for him. Following a brisk wash, he dressed himself, only to fall asleep on the comfortable bed.

Edmund woke with a start as the door opened and a maid slipped inside. He watched as she bobbed her head towards him without a word, lit the small glass lamps around the room, and left. Before long, a manservant came to guide him to where Karn and Eve awaited.

They sat in the dining room, both gazing over the town, which could be seen through the gallery of windows as pinpricks of light scattered through the gloom of dusk. Karn gave a simple grace before all three tucked into their meal.

In honour of Edmund's visit, Karn had ordered a whole piglet with roasted vegetables, potatoes and gravy. Edmund partook eagerly and the meal was so rich his tongue tingled with every mouthful. His food had run out the day before and he could barely make himself eat with decorum. Yet he could not fail to notice his companions were slow to eat and picked at their food.

"I am sure, as she is heir to the House of Arrow, that I may speak in front of Eve?" Edmund asked Karn, who sat at the opposite end of the table.

Karn nodded. His eyes flicked to his daughter, who sat unusually quietly between them. "She is of an age where I am teaching her management of the county; I suppose she must know," he said with reluctance.

"You know that Soren seeks the Crown of the Dragon Kings at the northern monastery so he may claim the throne instead of Zaki?"

Karn inclined his head.

"Zaki will also pursue it when the mourning period ends. I confess, I am unsure how well it is protected. We must ensure Zaki does not claim the crown, whilst avoiding open provocations. He now commands the army. They will follow him without question, as is their duty."

"I agree, yet how to act?" said Karn. "I must stay here, yet I have no other generals to command. This county is not a large one and we have been at peace for many years. We need the Eldarkind's council, but I have no one I could trust with a task so important and I cannot send you with your other duties; you must return to the prince's side."

"What of me, Father?" asked Eve unexpectedly. She leaned forwards. "I am your heir; I am worthy of your trust surely? Send me."

"Eve, you are my daughter and so young. How could I send you out into the world at only seventeen, knowing of its dangers?" Karn said.

"Father, you said it yourself. You're preparing me for the role. The need is great and whether you like it or not, eventually I'll have no choice but to go into the world. If you trust no one else, trust me." Eve sat back in the deepening gloom. Her face was in shadow and Edmund could not fathom her mood.

"This is too grave a matter for me to decide with a head clouded by wine," said her father indecisively. He massaged his forehead with one hand and abandoned his wine cup out of easy reach.

Edmund stirred. As he caught Eve's gaze, he saw her hopeful, wide eyes. "What of this, Karn?" he proposed. "I must needs leave tomorrow. No," he said and raised a hand as Karn began to protest. "I must. I thank you for your offer of hospitality, but I cannot avoid my duty to the prince. I will travel the north road. I could accompany Eve almost the entire way to Ednor if you would entrust her into my care." He let the suggestion hang.

"Tomorrow." Karn's tone had a darkness to it and the word sounded like a curse. Silence held until he spoke again. "Could you not ask for counsel from Ednor on our behalf?" His doubtful tone betrayed the answer he expected.

"It would delay my return to Soren by too long or I would not hesitate to do so," Edmund said.

"I have a personal guard to accompany me the rest of the way," Eve said.

"Assigning you a personal guard in the safety of Arlyn and sending them with you into the wilderness on a dangerous errand are two very different things, Eve," her father replied.

"So why did you assign them at all if they are so unnecessary?"

"You know very well why. How else are you supposed to be trained in arms and kept safe on your little wanderings into the forest, which are not so secret as you seem to think!" her father grumbled with a glare at her.

Eve flushed red and hunched in her tall chair.

"Remember, I employ them to keep you safe. Trust them and remember they report to me."

"You expect me to trust them yet you will not do so," she

muttered, her tone rebellious. "Why should I trust them when they spy on me!"

"There is more to this than trusting your guards," Karn said. Edmund thought his tone guarded.

"As always! You will not let me go to Ednor, no matter how many times I ask you. Why?"

"It is for the best," Karn replied in an even tone.

"Argh! I hate it when you say that!" Eve pushed back her chair with a mighty shove and stormed out.

Edmund regarded Karn with a raised eyebrow. His friend had once more returned his forehead to his palm, head bowed. "You will have to let her go to Ednor someday," Edmund dared to venture.

"I know!" Karn snapped. "I'm sorry. I know," he said more calmly. "I hoped this day would not come. I do not know how much longer I can stop her from travelling there. Sooner or later, she will ignore what I say and go regardless." He shrugged helplessly.

"What are you afraid of, though?"

Karn shook his head. "Many things. That she won't reach Ednor safely, that she will, what she will find there, what she will think of me as a result, what she will do when she returns, if she will return." He fell into silence and worried his forehead with his hand again.

"She will know you meant well," Edmund said.

"Eve is young and she is my daughter; her blood runs hot. She will be angry at the secrets I have kept, I know, and I fear her rashness."

"She *is* your daughter and in time, she will come to understand," Edmund insisted. "Perhaps allowing her to go will help her to reconcile sooner, rather than letting it come to her running away."

They fell into a companionable silence as the lamps burned lower around them, until Edmund's head swam. He pushed back his chair with a yawn.

"I must retire, please excuse me." Edmund's thanks for hospitality were waved away with the familiarity of old friends. He paused with his hand on the door handle. Karn looked expectantly at him.

"I leave tomorrow morning," Edmund repeated. "I know it is not ideal, but you know you can trust me to protect Eve and my offer stands to do so. For her sake and for ours, consider it. We may need the Eldarkind's help more than we can imagine." He waited for a reply, however none came. He excused himself to bed, hoping that Karn would heed his words.

SEVEN

Sentries watched and waited around the entire perimeter of the monastery. Their presence forced Soren to skulk deep in the woodlands to conceal himself, watching and cursing them. He was so close to safety, but all too far.

After three nights spent sleeping fitfully under bushes and in concealed hollows, Soren was exhausted and aching. Worse still, his remaining food had run out the previous morning. His stomach rumbled angrily as he wet his lips with water from a small beck. Without food, he was not sure how long he could continue.

His mind wandered. Today was the seventh day since his mother had been murdered. Today was the last day Zaki would have to wait before coming for the crown himself, and Soren suspected he would, given the guards surrounding the monastery. Today was the day when he, Soren, should be performing the burial and ascension rights for her amidst crowds of mourners. Instead, it would be the hands of her murderer tending to her body. He shuddered at the thought. Zaki would pay for taking that right of final farewell away from him too.

The sentries on the northern corner still huddled in their sleeping tents, or sat outside eating breakfast in the dawn mists. Soren checked his sword sat loose in its sheath—easy to draw should he need it. His bow, too difficult and slow to use in the dense vegetation, lay unstrung in his saddlebags.

Circling north, he spotted the soldier guarding the gate, who had drawn the short straw and would be lucky to break fast today. There lay no way past the man's line of sight, but Soren knew the man was alone, for now.

He suppressed the feeling of recklessness - and dizziness - and sauntered out of the trees. Soren saluted the man, who saluted back automatically, though confusion clouded his face a moment later. It was the pause Soren needed to get closer. He leapt forward and gave the sentry a blinding crack on the side of the helmed head with his sheathed sword.

The man dropped without a sound. Soren scanned around to make sure no one else had heard, and then dragged the man's prone form the ten feet or so to the tree line. Using the man's own neck-chief, he ripped it down the middle of its length to form two long thin strips; one he bound the man's hands with, the other he stuffed into the man's mouth, and pushed him out of sight beneath some bushes.

Foliage rustled behind him. Soren spun round, hand on sword, and cursed to find a second sentry just feet away. He wheeled around to face the man and charged towards him, drawing his sword. He did not cry out; to draw further attention would be fatal, but Soren knew he had to eliminate the man.

Dizzy and tired, his first blow skittered off his foe's sword with a clash that made his ears pound. Shouts converged on them from many directions but he could not look, too busy parrying a shot. He suppressed a cry as his far stronger opponent's powerful slashes jarred his arm.

As his foe drew back to land another strike, he grunted and faltered mid swing. Time slowed for Soren as he watched an arrow pierce the man's side, another his arm, and a final one his neck, each sprouting from him in quick succession as they slipped between his leather armour plates and chainmail.

Caught off-balance, the man stumbled and fell, snapping the arrow shafts clean off as he crashed upon them. Soren froze, mid-parry. His despair turned to confusion as the man gurgled and convulsed, his lifeblood slipping away. Hands grabbed Soren from behind. He shouted and twisted as he lost his balance. Hands ripped his dripping blade from him. These were no soldiers that surrounded him; they were monks.

The north gate lay open. Weapons in hand, brown-robed men poured out and drew him into the protective sanctuary of the monastery. Under the wall he went, through the gate, passed from one monk to the next; half-carried, half-dragged.

"My horse!" he managed to cry before he lost sight of the forest altogether and was rushed towards the centre of the grounds. Behind him, the gate boomed shut amidst much shouting. He barely had time to take in his surroundings as they closed in on the large building ahead.

Perimeter walls four men tall and one man wide surrounded a peaceful inner space cleared of trees to accommodate the range of buildings, gardens, and farm space. The monastery itself was several stories high, perched on the top of a small rise within the walls. Defenders could repel attackers from the ledge, which ran on the inside of the crenelated wall. In millennia gone past, they had done so against the marauders of the north, and now, they stood ready on the walls once more, as if for battle.

Monks were busy everywhere, all clad in swords and metal helmets with padded armour plates strung from their shoulders and tied around the waist. They stopped to stare as Soren was rushed through the grounds.

Soren attempted to explain who he was and the reason for his presence. The monk beside him did not break his silence or make eye contact and Soren began to doubt himself. The man showed no surprise at his news; Soren had a sudden icy flash of panic and wondered whether he had arrived at his sanctuary or delivered himself into Zaki's hands.

When he faltered, those behind him forced him to increase his pace again. Just when Soren's worry was at its peak, they reached the stone building, which towered three stories above them, and the monks turned and bowed to the prince. Before Soren could respond, they dispersed as quickly as a flock of birds taking flight, back to their duty on the walls. Soren watched them leave, bewildered.

As he turned back to the steps, he started. A huge man, coiled with tension, stood before him. The man regarded him through imperturbable eyes, muscled arms folded across his torso. Soren looked back, uncertain.

"Sire," the man said. He sunk into a bow and turned away.

"Please follow me."

That he was not in chains reassured Soren, but he still felt trepidation as the door's shadow engulfed him. Blinded by the transition from bright sunlight to gloom, he paused. As his eyes became accustomed, he was loathe to hurry after the strong man, who set a quick pace.

He marvelled as he passed through the high doorway of carved stone into a room with white, plastered, vaulted ceilings and intricate patterned windows of coloured glass, into a smaller chamber, then a corridor and a small cloister, with a covered walkway around its perimeter. It had none of the gilded grandeur of Pandora's castle or cathedral, but emanating from it was a different beauty. The stones were carved, some quite intricately; as Soren peered closer, he saw where they had weathered away, worn smooth by hundreds of years of rain and wind.

Disorientated, Soren tried to find his bearings, but the neat masonry of the colonnade rose too high to see over. It was only once he focused on the peaceful cloister that he realised his silent companion had entered the smoothly turfed space and watched him so intently he was almost glaring. Soren swallowed self-consciously as the man beckoned.

The small figure sitting bowed in its centre raised his head as they approached and rose to his feet. He was even more wizened than Soren hazily recalled from their last brief meeting in Pandora, a decade before. His beard was now so long it tucked into his belt, yet not a hair remained on his head. The old man's lively blue eyes appraised him.

"Abbot." Soren bowed deeply.

The abbot bowed in return. The monk knelt before the abbot until his head touched the ground.

"Thank you, Hador," the old man murmured. Hador rose to his feet without a word and left them.

"Your Royal Highness, it is an honour you join us and yet a sadness that you do so now." The old man spoke with a voice much stronger and richer than Soren had expected. "I am most sorry to hear of your losses. We support your cause and place ourselves and our resources at your disposal. We hope that we may aid you in your fight for justice for yourself and for Caledan."

"My thanks." Soren was lost for what else to say; where to begin.

The abbot smiled and beckoned him closer. They strolled around the cloister as Soren explained the past week's events at the abbot's bidding in as much detail as he could bear. At several points he halted, closing his eyes and breathing slow and deep to suppress the emotions that rose with recalling what had passed. At no point did the old man interrupt him. He waited each time Soren paused, a vision of calm, until the young man had finished.

"I thank you for telling me your tale. I imagine it is difficult to discuss," the abbot said.

Soren tried his best to meet the abbot's gaze, but the old man's attention was unnervingly piercing.

"We must hope that Edmund has reached Arlyn safely. You may already have noticed our visitors—" The abbot's tone remained light, although Soren caught the sarcasm. "—whom Zaki has sent to retrieve the crown. Alas though, we no longer have what you seek. The Crown of the Dragon Kings is gone." He raised a hand to quiet Soren, who exclaimed at his words. "All in good time. Come inside for a meal and I will explain what has passed here in the last week."

Soren acquiesced and followed the abbot to a large dining hall. Long, wooden trestle tables lay out across the high room, which was flooded by light filtering through the lead-paned windows. Monks wandered in and out to eat and then depart, some in silence and others talking in low voices that created an echoing murmur. All stopped to bow their head to the abbot and some paused just a little longer to stare at Soren, who stared back, intrigued.

The abbot requested a meal from the kitchen and soon a steaming plate of gravy-covered meat, vegetables, and dumplings was in front of the prince, reigniting his appetite. He ate—as politely and slowly as he could—whilst the abbot spoke.

"On the eve of your mother's passing, I dreamt a great shadow fell over the land. A monstrous blue dragon flew down from the sky. I knew what the omen of his arrival was. His name is

Brithilca and he is the guardian of Caledan."

Soren paused, his fork hovering in the air. He had not heard the name of Brithilca since his childhood, but he remembered how avidly he had followed the legend of the dragon guardian and gazed up at the throne of the dragon kings.

Legend said that Brithilca's body rested deep below the citadel, but others spoke of how the dragon throne was the petrified remains of Brithilca himself, twisted around the royal seat. Indeed, the dragon consisted of a material completely unknown to man; neither stone nor metal of any known kind, yet having properties of both, and magical ones beside.

Although Soren had not witnessed these abilities with his own eyes, he had read every existing account. For instance, it was known that when the ruler of Caledan died, the petrified dragon moved to envelop the throne in a protective shield under its wings. When the new monarch was presented to the throne, the dragon could choose whether to accept them as a worthy leader. If it deemed the human worthy, the dragon opened its wings to allow them to seat the throne and receive the Crown of the Dragon Kings upon their head.

However, if the candidate was deemed unworthy—as had happened three times in the throne's history—the throne remained out of reach under the sweeping, impenetrable cloak of the dragon's wings. This was considered to be a poor omen and in all three occurrences, the subsequent reigns were short and unhappy.

On one of these occasions, the unlucky soul had insisted upon being crowned without Brithilca's blessing. Baran the Unfortunate's reign was the shortest on record, lasting merely a few minutes, as he tried to force the wings apart with various tools and implements. The dragon did indeed move, but only to roar in his face and bathe him with dragon fire, a talent previously unknown in its repertoire of abilities.

People journeyed from far and wide to see the fabled dragon throne and hope to see it move or twitch, though they were rarely rewarded, as Soren knew from experience. He had himself spent countless hours sitting before the immobile form. "Brithilca is very good at sitting still," his amused mother had said.

"It is the greatest secret in the country that we were and remain allied with the dragons and Eldarkind," the abbot continued. "Not many people even know of their existence, but you will have learnt of them in your history studies. In the great wars a millennia ago, a pact was created between dragons, man, and Eldarkind to create a lasting peace and guardianship for the wellbeing of the world. You know of this, yes?"

Soren nodded, and the abbot proceeded.

"The spirit of Brithilca has guarded the royal family, and by extension, the wellbeing of the kingdom ever since. In times of need, he is somehow able to warn of peril, signifying that once more the three races must be united to face whatever threat is looming, or risk the undoing of the pact, which would have devastating consequences for all.

"In my dreams, Brithilca spoke to me of an impending doom on the land. He did not say what it might be, only that if not righted, terror and war would consume the world. He took the crown you seek, though I know not where, and flew away into the rising sun. When I awoke the following morning, I could not believe my eyes. The crown had truly disappeared, as if the dragon had strayed from my dreams to reality."

Soren sat in wonder, food forgotten at the thought of Brithilca being very real. As a child he wished fervently that dragons were real, had even dreamed of his own dragon. They would go adventuring together, saving townships and slaying evil villains, and he would be proclaimed the best prince that had ever lived in Caledan. Chilled, stiff, and with a numb bottom from the hard floor of the throne room, he had often daydreamed that the dragon would come to life and whisk him away on wings. He almost smiled with nostalgia at the naivety of his childish wishes.

"Will Zaki know this?" Soren said.

"Of my dream? Certainly not. I have shared this with just yourself and Hador. However, I am certain he will know of all else we have spoken of."

Soren considered the abbot's words and his own knowledge. "Then he will come here seeking the crown. What of the throne itself? Will it accept him with or without the crown?"

"I have received word that the great dragon has not yet relinquished the throne, however that news is two days old and may not reflect the results of the coronation, if it has happened yet," the abbot said. Soren raised his eyebrows, the question obvious upon his face. The abbot explained what had passed in Pandora since Soren's flight. Anger stirred again in Soren's belly as he realised the extent and detail of his uncle's scheming, but the abbot's news gave him hope that his sister, having been retired from the succession, still lived.

"I do not think the throne will accept him," the abbot continued. "Not after the sins he has committed. Instead, as the one other candidate at present, I think you are meant to seek the crown and prove your worth as the rightful ruler of Caledan."

"Where is it?" Soren asked, distracted.

To his surprise, the abbot chortled. "Well, if it were that simple to find, where would be the challenge!" His eyes twinkled with sudden merriment. Soren fell quiet and did not respond. The abbot's humorous expression faded as he saw the young man's change of mood. "Kingship; it is not meant to be an easy thing," he said gently.

Soren raised his hands wide in admission of his indecision and a sudden thought struck him. "You said that we were and remain allied with the Eldarkind... and the dragons," he said. "Dragons still exist? Truly?" The abbot nodded and Soren's mouth fell open.

The abbot filled the silence. "I think you know as well as I do that with the events of the past week, not all of the royal blood line can be trusted with such knowledge. The royals know more than most about the dragons, it is true, however only the abbot of this monastery and the ruling monarch knows everything we have to know about the dragons, the Eldarkind, the treaty, and all its implications.

"As you know, all rulers have to prove their worth before lifting the crown onto their heads. Only then can they be known to be fit for the sharing of this knowledge. Had you been crowned king in your own way, you would have found this out like your mother before you, and her father before her, and so on. Perhaps this is to be your test, even. As monks, we swear complete fealty to the crown, but as an abbot, we show responsibility and commitment above others and so we are trusted with this knowledge."

"Does Zaki know this?" Soren interrupted with sudden concern.

"There is no reason that he should," replied the abbot. "I tell you this now, because of the three direct heirs of the bloodline, you are the one worthy of carrying on the crown. Zaki has proved his great failings as a ruler, need I say more. Of Irumae, we do not know, forgive me. Thus, that leaves you—your mother's heir. I should not be telling you any of this, yet I believe it is the only option, if Zaki is not to get his hands on the crown, that you be best equipped with all the information we have. You have proved with your determination thus far that you are meant for something higher in this battle."

"What of my sister?" Soren said, dragons momentarily forgotten. "How can I help her? I'm sure she is still alive and I cannot leave her to Zaki's mercy!"

The abbot shook his head. "I can imagine how hard this is to hear from me, but Caledan must take priority before your sister. I know your heart tells you to go and save her, yet I believe for her sake, we must look to help from another direction. You need to concern yourself with the rescue of the crown and feel no guilt or shame in that decision. In seeking that, you are ensuring her safety. In the meantime, help will come to her by another means. My contacts within Pandora already search for her with all means available to them."

"I can't leave her," whispered the prince. His eyes filled with tears as he scowled at the hopelessness of the situation. "I know how important this is, but I can't leave her; she is all I have left."

"Our men arm themselves for war; as you can see, they have already begun. We may be calm in times of peace and take up the sickle and the hoe, but in times of war, hell hath no fury like our warriors. They are trained in a thousand different ways of killing and are the most skilled of their kind in the land. I can spare some more to search for your sister, but I cannot send too many for fear of arousing suspicion."

"Please," asked the prince, filling that one word with hope and desperation.

"I will see it is done," the old man replied. "Now, I am afraid we do not have much time and I must call a council of the elders. I would appreciate your attendance as there is much to discuss and decide. Zaki's forces tighten as a vice about us. They grow daily. He seeks to take the crown with no resistance or delay, to be sure. He will not be long. We have no time to dally."

The council lasted nearly all day and the sun dipped low in the sky by the time the meeting concluded. Hador's face was the only one Soren recognised. Others were introduced in quick succession, and Soren forgot most of their names. Although all present showed deference to Soren, it was clear they had no need of him to arrange their affairs. Although they consulted him politely, he knew the gestures were empty. If anything, his inexperience felt painfully obvious and he was relieved to listen.

He was used to attending councils, but never ones so filled with talk of war. It unnerved him. For all his life, Caledan had been a safe and peaceful place, and yet now there was much talk of death and the sacrifices that must be made by those who remembered less harmonious times. He shivered, worried.

It was decided the monastery would be garrisoned by the several hundred monks living there. All well trained, only their numbers concerned the council. In the confusion of the uprising, none could estimate Zaki's support; some argued a few thousand men, some argued tens of thousands. In either case, they were outnumbered and it was decided that Soren should be escorted to safety by a party trained to the highest level if an attack came.

Soren was furious as he retired with the abbot to his study. He wanted to stay and fight; more than most he had a reason to. He pictured Zaki's face across the grounds, locking eyes as his uncle became aware of him, and charging for him. The clash and squelch of his sword rending armour and flesh. Zaki's dead eyes glazed over. The sweetness of that revenge.

The abbot's room suited him; somehow grand and humble all in one. Tall bookcases surrounded three of the walls, below the high vaulted ceiling that Soren had noticed in every single room, no matter how grand or small. Volumes crammed upon every bookcase; some monstrous size, others delicate, some shiny and new, some cracked and old.

He invited Soren to sit in the chair opposite him with a wave of his hand. The abbot placed his elbows on the desk, hands together in a steeple in front of his face and cast a measured stare at the prince. After a long pause, Soren fidgeted, unsure what to say or whether to break the silence. The abbot stirred and lowered his clasped hands to the table.

"I apologise," said the abbot. "I was contemplating the best course of action. There are several options. We would do well to send envoys to the Eldarkind and the dragons each, but I suspect the dragons hold the crown and that is what you must follow. If it were not at stake, it would do you well to go to the Eldarkind. You are the highest envoy possible to send and it would be good for you to visit the home of your ancestors.

"Another time though, I think, another time. Hopefully there will be time for this 'another time'!" The abbot smiled at the prince, who smiled back uncertainly, caught off guard by the unexpected humour.

"We expect Sir Edmund two days from now at the earliest," continued the abbot. "I believe he will not tarry at Arlyn. I shall send a scout to meet him en route tonight who can, if needed, lead him to your location."

"I want to fight!" Soren said. The abbot held up a hand to silence him.

"With all due respect, you speak with the voice of the young. You cannot yet see paths that only become visible with the wisdom age and experience brings. What if you fall in the battle? Caledan would be lost to Zaki. You have been well trained, but a stray arrow may slip between your armour, and in fact, any number of mishaps could befall you. It is of the utmost importance you remain alive. Your existence may very well hold the key to the lives of Caledan's population and of others around the world.

"If you were to die, it would change the course of history. Battle will come to you, but now is not your time to fight. I do not think we can defeat Zaki, however if we can delay him and buy your freedom and success, then it is worth it. Please, trust to the wisdom of the council."

Soren's eyes dropped, ashamed of his outburst. With difficulty, he met the abbot's piercing blue eyes, which still regarded him, unwavering and unfathomable. "I apologise. If you think it best I leave, although my heart loathes this feeling of cowardice, I'll follow your advice and take to the mountains."

"I am glad. You are already learning," replied the abbot. "It relieves me to know you will be safe. I will send you with half a dozen of my best men into the hills; we have refuges there. The rest of our men will stand and fight, and that will give you the better chance of escape and success.

"I ask of you that no matter which way the battle turns, you do not return until it is over. I will post a scout to watch for Edmund and have him guided to your location. Once he arrives, if the fighting is not over, you must leave. Find the crown, prove you are the rightful king, and restore peace and justice to the land. If your heart is true, you will not fail. Now promise me that you will not return to the battle!"

Soren hesitated, then gave his agreement.

"I will hold you to your word."

Soren shivered. The old man's words had an irrevocable gravity to them. As Soren left to wash and dine before his departure, the abbot bade farewell to him.

"I fear we shall not meet again after this, Prince Soren. It gladdens my heart that the babe I blessed those long years ago has grown into such a fine young man. I wish you all the luck in your struggle ahead and hope you have many happy years ahead of you." The old man smiled.

"I will be here alongside you," insisted the prince. His confident tone masked the shiver of premonition the old man's words had sent down his spine.

"I do not fear death," replied the old man. "And I am ready to accept that may be my fate over the coming days. Please accept my blessing for your journey, in case we do not meet again."

Reluctantly, the prince agreed. The abbot placed his palm on the prince's forehead, anointed him with holy water, and intoned a simple blessing. Bowing to each other, they murmured the traditional parting and the prince departed from his company.

"God be with you, sire."

"God be with you, Abbot."

With a heavy heart, Soren shut the door of his room behind him and leaned against it. Worry for Irumae gnawed at him although he was glad to know others tried to find her. He tried to recall in the face of his mother, his father, and his sister for comfort, but his thoughts morbidly distorted into visions of his mother lying cold under stone, her spirit released to the sky without a proper goodbye. His father was a maniacally grinning skeleton beside her, the image leaping unbidden into his mind's eye.

A chasm opened in his heart and his chest ached. He slapped his face to force the memories out. It stung from the force of the blow as he busied himself washing roughly and tried not to think of anything at all.

EIGHT

It was several days before the law reader, the steward, and the heir apparent were together again, this time for the funeral of the queen, who had lain in state for seven days. Zaki's elation had not diminished since signing the last signature upon the papers.

The funeral was a grand affair, as it should have been, though muted by sadness with the entire city bedecked in black for the day. The square outside the cathedral was crowded in silent, black-clothed citizens. It was an awkward occasion; the grand Pandora cathedral held the nobility of Caledan within, yet there were significant and notable absences, Soren's and Irumae's most prominent of all.

As the next of kin, Zaki led the proceedings, dutifully playing the part of the grieving heir as he anointed Naisa's body with holy water and incense, and recited prayers over her form. Her hair had been meticulously cleaned so that not one trace of blood remained. He struggled not to smile.

Beside him in black and as quiet as ever was Demara, her eyes downcast, as they sat for the service on the cold stone pews. Zaki paid little attention and joined in to pray only when he noticed her hands clasp together beside him. Sooner than he thought, it was done and they returned to the palace for the parting feast.

The hall was full of sounds, light, and aromas as all came together to celebrate the queen's memory, but the food tasted best of all in Zaki's mouth as he savoured his success in manipulating himself on to the throne. He smiled at Demara, before excusing himself after a few courses to celebrate in private with his closest allies, leaving her isolated at the top table and ignored by all.

The sound of standing horses and men broke the silence. Filled with anticipation, Zaki sat tensely upon horseback with a detail of cavalry around him as he waited for the midnight bells to sound.

The first toll of the bell would signal midnight; the beginning of a new day and the end of the mourning period after Naisa's funeral that day. Zaki would be free to leave Pandora and he had prepared for the journey so he did not waste a single moment.

Shuttered windows and closed storefronts watched him. The city slept.

The first sonorous toll rang out and he urged his horse into action. It thundered through the open east gate and his company surged after him.

It took less than a full day to reach the northern monastery, and he outstripped most of his companions in his eagerness. It was made possible only by the constant supply of fresh mounts organised for him by Reynard and his own determination to obtain the crown of his ancestors. He did not pause to admire the sturdy build of the road, or the beauty of the forest, or the quaintness of the villages near the roadside. Inns flashed by as he rode with no desire to stop and sample their fares.

He was beyond tiredness as he came upon the encampment, filled with nervous energy as he shouted for Reynard, who ran from a tent.

"Your Royal Highness, I did not expect you so soon!" Reynard said. "I have much to tell you, sir."

"Do you have the crown?"

"No, sir, they will not release it to me." Zaki smacked a tent post. "I do have fortuitous news, sir." Reynard hastily continued. "There was an incident yesterday. We cannot be sure but it would appear that Soren has been given sanctuary within the monastery. We continue to surround it."

Zaki turned to face him. His incredulity turned to glee. "Soren is trapped here? This is excellent news!" he crowed. "They have taken in a traitor. Their lives and worldly goods are forfeit. I can crush the both of them at once and ride home with the crown. Reynard, you have done well. Send all your forces to surround the

place though the night. I want not even one rat to leave."
Tomorrow is the day I prove myself king beyond doubt.

NINE

Eve felt reckless and emboldened by the wine as she stormed along the corridor to her chamber. Above the mild tingling of tipsiness and thumping of her heart, she felt the much more charged rush of anger, partly vented by slamming her door shut behind her. For a few moments she was motionless and leaned against it, but moved into her chamber, unable to still herself.

It was a month before midsummer and the weather warm and mild. No fire burnt in the grate, so her room lay pleasantly cool, illuminated by slow-burning lamps. Dispelling some energy by pacing around the room, she turned again, unable to quell it.

It will always be like this. I will always ask and he will always refuse. I could run away. The thought arose as it had many times before. "I'm old enough to take care of myself," she contemplated aloud, distracted from her pacing.

"I know how to live off the forest and in any case, a horse could carry provisions for the journey. I can take a map from the library to show me how to find Ednor. I could even meet up with Edmund on route. No." She paused to chew on a fingernail. "He might make me return." It would have to be tonight.

Already halfway across her room to begin packing, she froze at the knock on her door. Her father opened it and peered in. His brows slanted in surprise when he beheld the bright room. She stood defensively as he entered, placing herself at the opposite side of the room as an awkward silence arose between them.

Eve kept her face impassive but the anger rose inside her once more at the unwittingly stalled attempt to break away. She waited, willing him to leave, yet her father seemed lost for words.

"I don't want you to go to Ednor," he said, with no hint of emotion. Eve narrowed her eyes at him. For the moment, she held her seething temper in check. "Will you obey me?" he asked after she did not reply. Once more, she did not answer him. He sighed.

"I could keep you here for all your life whether you liked it or not, Eve," he said as if he had taken her silence for an answer, yet there was no trace of anger or spite in his voice and he seemed half-hearted. "I could lock you in your room and never let you out." Eve tensed. Her eyes darted to the door, which he blocked, and to the now shuttered windows. There would be no escape if he willed it otherwise.

"Peace." He held up a hand. "I do not wish that. I will allow you to travel to Ednor." Eve's eyes widened, but she did not dare to speak. Her anger subsided, then surprise replaced it and distrust followed.

"Why?" she finally managed to say.

"I have need of the Eldarkind's counsel and although it pains me, you are my only heir as well as my daughter. I ask that you present yourself to Artora as befits your rank and return at once with her counsel. Will you do this for me?"

Eve acquiesced, still confused but unwilling to reject his offer.

"Well then. It's done," he said in resignation. "You will leave tomorrow with your guards and Edmund until your paths separate. I'll leave you to pack." He left without another word. Eve sat on her bed, bewildered.

Eve rose with the sun, having barely slept from the anticipation of finally being allowed to visit Ednor, the home of the legendary Eldarkind. Unable to settle, she had packed, unpacked, and repacked several times. Last of all, it was with a strange feeling that she picked up her bow and training sword.

She held the sword in her hand and stretched it out before her to tilt it this way and that, watching the colourful dawn light dance off the blade. It was a beautiful but deadly object; somehow she could not marry the two ideas.

Hollows lay dark under Edmund's eyes as he joined them for

breakfast. He seemed in better spirits than the day before, albeit quiet. Karn also seemed withdrawn. Eve itched with anticipation.

Finally, Karn broke the silence.

"I trust your preparations have been made?" he enquired.

"Yes, Father. Nyle and Luke are readying the horses and provisions now. Your pack will be brought down for you," she added to Edmund.

"Well then," Karn replied. "We should not delay. You shall both depart as soon as you are done here. I will meet you in the courtyard." He stood up and strode out, his mouth down-turned as he walked away from them.

An hour later, they assembled in the courtyard. Nyle and Luke sat mounted a short distance away whilst Karn bade farewell to his daughter and great friend. Eve observed her guards out of the corner of her eye, with her father's words from the night before clear in her memory. Luke was her senior by a couple of years and although Nyle was older by several times that gap, they still felt young enough to be of her generation; she had trusted them as her friends. Their betrayal stung.

"I wish you both well," Karn said. His face was creased with worry. "May God be with you. Ride safely, my darling, and I hope for your swift return. Edmund, I hope that you face no great perils on your travels and that we may see you soon."

Edmund strode forward and clasped Karn by the shoulders. "Goodbye, my friend. We shall meet again."

Eve threw herself at her father. He hugged her tightly in return and after a long embrace, they stepped apart. Eve struggled to conceal her excitement as she took Alia's reins from Nyle and swung herself up into the saddle. The four trotted out of the courtyard with a clatter. Eve waved at her father, who stood on the steps of the keep with a hand raised in farewell.

Far from Arlyn, forest-covered foothills of the mountain range soared to their left. The trees ended many unseen miles to their right, giving way to vast expanses of moors, grasslands, and marshland and beyond that further still, the great lake across which Pandora lay. Villages and lone inns lay here and there along the road, wherever larger streams ran down from the mountains, but they rode through the villages and past the inns without stopping.

Edmund led, with Nyle at the rear. Eve gazed at Edmund's unyielding back, proud and straight before them, her thoughts strangely lucid and impartial. She had cantered this fast many times before for great distances on hunts with her father and thus far, the day felt ordinary.

Eve tried to grasp the enormity of the coming unknown. Scenarios flashed in her mind as a small frisson gnawed at the pit of her stomach, though of fear or excitement, she could not be sure. Trying to distract herself, she gazed around. A quick glance to her left at Luke calmed her, as he caught her gaze and smiled, not having noticed her discomfort. She was glad for the familiar company before recalling that she was annoyed with him.

The road itself was busy. Being the sole clear path travelling north and south through this forest, it saw most of the wheeled and foot traffic in the area. Edmund feared his recognition or their presence being noted and pushed them on.

Just before dusk, they halted on an unremarkable stretch of road where a small beck trickled across the compacted earth on its journey down from the hills, trundling across the road and into the foliage on the other side. The road lay deserted in the deepening gloom.

The four dismounted and led the horses along the stream towards the mountains until the trees hid them well out of sight and hearing of the road. A small clearing, scarcely big enough for the four of them to lie down in, became their camp. Edmund insisted they not light a fire. Luke and Nyle, ignorant of the importance of their mission, grumbled until Edmund lightly pointed out he was a proclaimed traitor. Although disgruntled, they were forced to accept the decline in comfort.

Eve was glad Edmund had not mentioned her own task. In her brief to Luke and Nyle, she had neglected to tell them of the visit to Ednor, which would be problematic once revealed. She had not lied, having said they must travel with Edmund on his return north and omitted anything else; the relief outweighed the guilt about what she told herself was a slight deception.

After lighting a small lamp and unsaddling the horses, they set to spreading out blankets on the mossy ground, which was dry with the recent mild weather, setting one further away from the others for Eve. It was the best they could manage for decency, given the circumstances.

She preferred to bed down next to Alia in any case. The great bulk of the horse close by gave her a sense of protection. Bears seldom ventured down from the hills this far, but smaller predators lived within the woods. Eve could tell Alia remained alert and uneasy in the unfamiliar settings as she and the other horses remained standing to sleep.

Nyle picked up his blanket and moved still further away towards the road to take the first watch, and the three others settled down for the night, fully dressed, boots and all. Edmund extinguished the lamp and the camp descended into peaceful darkness, save for the occasional snorting of a horse and the rustle of a blanket.

It was an uncomfortable, but uneventful night. Luke awoke Eve the following morning by hesitantly shaking her shoulder, whilst blushing at the impropriety of his actions. He began to stammer an apology, but stopped in his tracks when she sat bolt upright.

"What time is it?" she exclaimed. Nyle and Edmund stopped packing to glance at her in surprise.

"It's around the seventh hour, my lady," replied Nyle.

"Then why am I only waking now? Why was I not woken to sit a watch?" she demanded, extricating her legs from the blanket with difficulty. She stood with her arms folded and a scowl upon her face.

"We did not wish to wake you, Lady Eve," said Nyle with a raised eyebrow.

"Am I not a member of this party?" she stormed. "Am I not fit to share in the night watch? I am my father's sole heir and raised as such. I am not some mollycoddled maiden in distress to be pandered to. Luke, Nyle, you have trained with me for some years, am I not as capable as you to defend myself?" She glared at them.

After a pause and a glance at Edmund, the two men nodded. Edmund stepped forward.

"Lady Eve," he said. "I understand their dilemma. You are the daughter of their lord. They are bound to serve and protect you and your house and also to respect and to honour you. They would not presume to dare to ask you to share in their duties, no matter how capable they may deem you to be." She relaxed and bit her lip, as Edmund looked at the two sheepish guards. A wry smile flitted across his face.

"I also doubt they are aware of the gravity of the situation." Edmund alluded to Eve's task and his own mission. "I presume these are also the self-same reasons they did not ask me to participate in the watch either.

"So, gentlemen. We are on a venture of great importance. Your courtesy is appreciated, but unnecessary. I am more than willing to participate in the watch rota, and it is evident that the Lady Eve also wishes to contribute. It would be appreciated if all four of us could wave aside status and split the night watch in future. It will not serve you well today, Masters Nyle and Luke, to be fatigued in your duties."

The two guards bowed. "Our apologies, Lady Eve, Sir Edmund," Nyle said. "We shall be careful to include you in such duties henceforth."

She agreed and saw the relief on their faces.

"It is forgiven," she said. "And you must all call me Eve." *Lady Eve*, she thought with derision. *Here am I in pants and a shirt like a man, unwashed and dirty to boot; I could not be less like a lady.*

She turned away to gather up her blanket and saddling gear. Edmund stifled a chuckle behind her back.

TEN

Edmund dreaded what state he would find the monastery in, certain that as he rode north, Zaki would also be doing the same. Knowing he could not possibly reach Soren before Zaki and that he had no power in what happened next only increased the burden. *Was I right to leave him?*

Oblivious to his troubles, Eve, Luke, and Nyle rode behind him. Although the four ran with the horses for a time to give them some form of break, they had not stopped and ate their midday meal in the saddle to avoid delay. By late afternoon, Edmund was optimistic of making the river crossing that day, where one of the great tributaries feeding the Great Lake flowed down from the mountain, just past which, those who knew where to search could find the forgotten road to Ednor.

It had once more been a solitary day in the saddle. The noise made it impractical to try to converse and there was little enough to be said. They were almost lulled into complacency and had just begun running with the horses once more to rest them, when ahead, a figure galloped into view some distance away around a bend.

There was no chance to avoid him and Edmund was sure he must have already seen them. Edmund swore, cursing their misfortune. He stopped the four of them and ordered them to mount. They obeyed instantly, and he turned in his saddle to address them.

"We are travelling north on trade purposes. Eve, you are my daughter. Luke, Nyle, you are our guards. Nyle, up front. Luke, fall behind. If we are discovered, Eve, stay back and let us capture or kill him without hesitation."

They set off at a gentle trot after composing their faces into relaxed expressions, although their hearts pounded in their chests as the rider drew closer. He approached swiftly and in a matter of minutes had met them in the road. He travelled cloaked in dark brown, though a sword sat visibly at his side and his horse was laden with light provisions. From his appearance, they could not glean much more than that regarding his identity, as they glanced surreptitiously at him in passing. He reined in his horse to one side of the road to let them pass, examining them as he did so.

"Sir Edmund!" he exclaimed as they rode by.

Edmund's reaction was swift. He forced his horse to turn on the spot and quickly had the rider surrounded by a trio of swords as Nyle and Luke followed suit. The man's horse shied and the horrified man narrowly avoided being injured as his horse tried to backtrack.

"Peace!" he cried, dismayed, and raised his hands away from his sword. "I come from the monastery! I have been sent by the abbot to warn you!"

"Warn me? Of what?" Edmund did not lower his sword.

"Sirs, Lady, I think we should step off the road to discuss it. We do not know who else may be using it," requested the man, as his horse reared again with its nostrils flaring. Edmund was cautious and still distrustful, but after some delay, he agreed, sheathed his blade, and they all dismounted to exit the road. Luke and Nyle kept their swords drawn and Eve stood to one side as Edmund faced the monk.

"You may speak freely," said Edmund.

The monk took a deep breath. "My name is Jormund. I come from the monastery by order of the abbot. He gave me a seal to show you, so you may know I am truthful in this." He fumbled as he drew forth a ring hanging from a leather thong around his neck. He presented it to Edmund, who examined it—it was indeed the seal of the abbot in miniature—and invited him to continue.

"Prince Soren reached the sanctuary of our monastery safely yesterday. However, forces loyal to Zaki have surrounded our home. He is sure to arrive today personally, but his forces already surround us." Edmund's heart sank at his words. *I sent him into danger, God forgive me.*

"Our abbot plans to smuggle the prince into the mountains with a small guard so that he is in no present danger if Zaki attacks us. I was sent to warn you."

"This is bad news, though not all unexpected, Jormund," Edmund replied, still troubled. "Thank you for seeking me. How did Soren reach the monastery yesterday? I left him nearby some days ago."

Jormund quickly explained that Zaki's forces had stopped Soren from reaching the monastery.

"I thank you for hurrying to find me." Edmund bowed his head. "It seems I have a difficult choice. Eve, I had planned to escort you to Ednor or partly there, so I had no guilt on my conscience for abandoning you in the wild. However, I must find Soren before it is too late. I hope I may trust you to the care of Luke and Nyle and I hope you will forgive me for leaving you."

"Let me accompany you!" said Eve suddenly. "I want to help my cousin!"

Edmund shook his head. "No," he said firmly. He drew her aside, away from the curious monk and her confused guards, who had plainly assumed they would be travelling together, before continuing in a low voice they could not hear.

"Your path lies towards the Eldarkind, and your father has tasked you with meeting them. You have agreed to this and your father is counting on you - as am I, as is Caledan. You are duty-bound to complete this and you may not get a chance to do so if you come with me. I do not wish to cause hostility, but I refuse to let you accompany me."

Eve scowled behind his back, but it was fear, not stubbornness that drove her. *There's still time for me to change his mind.* In the past day, she had begun to dread reaching Ednor. All the long years of anticipation and high expectations left her with a growing fear it would not measure up to the place she had imagined. Worse still, she dreaded meeting her mother's people, unsure whether they would accept her, for she was not truly one of their own.

"I'll take the first watch," Eve said in a tone that brooked no argument and stalked off with her blanket and some food. Her companions hid smiles, though Jormund's bafflement was unveiled.

Although the monk was with them on good authority, Edmund had not informed him of Eve's purpose and the monk seemed altogether at a loss about how to treat her. Behind Eve, the dim light of the solitary lamp illuminated the camp, before it fell into silence as the four men bedded down.

Throughout the night, the thunder of horses along the road and the screeching and rustling of nocturnal animals disturbed the forest. Awake and alone in the dark, Eve grew more unnerved every time sounds filtered across the landscape. The little light from the lamp behind her was small solace.

Her thoughts turned to home for comfort and repeatedly strayed to Luke. No matter how hard she tried to avoid it, she could not forget what her father had revealed. She felt unsure how to treat him. Whereas Nyle was several years her senior, she and Luke had grown up together as good friends, though distant of late; a fact not helped by her father's admission.

She considered that she and Luke had been close, being schooled together and exploring the town and surrounding land with their other friends. She remembered the happiness they had all shared, yet recalling her naivety brought forth wistfulness.

It was only when her father withdrew her from that life to become the Lady of Arlyn that responsibility soon fell on them all. Play became training and although Luke took a role with the guardsmen, frequently training alongside Eve, things had not been the same since. Status and tradition steadily dismantled their close friendship until they never idly talked or ran wild in the woods as before.

Whether she would have wanted to remain friends was beyond his or her control, but she could not forget the sadness for the fading friendship. Her life was lonely, for all its privileges. She could not decide whether to remain angry with him for breaching her privacy. Unlike Nyle, she knew Luke well enough to know he would never do so with malice.

At the end of her watch as her eyes grew heavy, Eve awoke Edmund for the second shift. Her nerves remained on edge from the creatures of the night she had heard and so she carried her bedding between Nyle and Luke, who slept a few metres apart, not wanting to feel exposed. She lay down to sleep as quietly as she could. As she did so, Nyle opened an eye and observed her guardedly.

Unseen to her in the shadows, Luke awoke and as she laid down, his breath caught to see her so near to him, her hair glowing in the lamp's illumination before she sank into the shadows beside him. His mouth dried and his heart leapt in his chest as she sighed and sunk quickly into slumber after her long watch.

That night he rested poorly, and it was with great contemplation that he took the last watch of the night. His thoughts strayed repeatedly to the sight of her reclining so near to him, so unguarded and natural, and his throat constricted. Her unexpected close proximity that night and her constant informal presence over the previous days had stirred strange feelings within him and his head was a jumble of emotions.

"We are here," Edmund said, to Eve's confusion. She had not expected the path to Ednor to be so inconspicuous. Without further explanation, he dismounted and bade them all to follow him off the road - except Jormund.

They trekked west up a slight incline until they came upon a clearing large enough for them to see the foothills. Covered in their mantle of evergreens and soaring high above them, they hid the true mountain range from view.

"It is here we part." Edmund reached into his saddlebag for the spare map he had brought. When he had opened it out on the ground, he pointed to their location on it. Nyle made to speak, but

Edmund forestalled him to explain which path they should follow.

"Ednor and the land of the Eldarkind in the mountains can be accessed solely by this pass." He focused his attention on Eve, who listened, entranced. "It is recorded that there used to be a road here, built by civilisations past and ruined before Caledonians and Eldarkind came to live here.

"The Eldarkind do not wish to mingle at large with our people anymore and so the trails were allowed to be overrun. To many, there is nothing in front of you but mountains and past that the wastes of the North, however some know better.

"I know that Eve has not described your purpose and destination to you," Edmund said to Luke and Nyle. "I know you think the Eldarkind a race extinct in the long past, but they live as they ever did, hidden away in corners of the world."

"How do you know that? Are we to chase fairy tales and dark powers?" Nyle interrupted.

"I know because I have journeyed there many times," replied Edmund. Eve saw the look he gave Nyle; one that dared the younger man to challenge him. "I ask you not to judge and to trust that this mission is of the utmost importance. You carry the safety of Caledan on your shoulders now. Heed not the petty legends of fiends and untrustworthy spell casters that they are portrayed to be in your fairy tales, for these bear no resemblance to the great and noble race that is the Eldarkind."

Luke and Nyle exchanged a shocked glance as Edmund continued.

"As you journey up into the mountains and cross over the pass, you will come into a great valley. At its longest point it is just shorter than the journey from Arlyn to here. It is there that the road is at last maintained once more and you will be able to follow the path to Ednor itself.

"From here, bear west. You will find yourself in a steep-sided valley with a stream in the bottom that runs a rusty orange with the richness of iron ore in the hills. Keep to the north side of this stream and you will soon happen upon what appear to be the remains of the old road. Admittedly, it is more of a trail now, but still discernible. If you follow that, you will reach Ednor tomorrow.

"Any questions? Peace, Eve," Edmund said at the unhappy expression upon Eve's face. Unwilling to speak in front of Luke and Nyle, she drew Edmund aside.

"I feel as if I'm going in the opposite direction to where I should be, Edmund," she said. "For so many years I've wanted to see the land where my mother was raised. My father has denied me this for reasons I still don't understand, but now, of all times, I wish I could be journeying elsewhere."

"It is a great thing, to wish for something for so long and be faced with finding out whether the reality meets your expectations," Edmund replied. "However, we all have our path through time laid out before us, and sometimes it may take us away from where we wish or towards our fears and we must face that bravely.

"Even I fear my own journey," he admitted, "but there is always a reason for everything you do. I know it is difficult but there is great value to you going to the Eldarkind, not least for your own enrichment and the fulfilment of your desire to meet your mother's people, but also to act as an envoy for our entire country. It is you that must inform them of the plight of Caledan and ask for their aid.

"You have no less a responsibility on your shoulders than I do at this moment in time. Where I go to help Soren reclaim the throne for the good of Caledan, you do the same; your path takes you one way and mine another. Yours is no less important."

"I suppose I understand," Eve acknowledged reluctantly. "I must put aside my fears in this."

"So you promise you will go as an envoy to the Eldarkind and that under no circumstances will you follow me instead?" Edmund pressed her, leaning forward. After a short pause, Eve agreed, to Edmund's relief, and they turned back to Luke and Nyle.

"Good. Let us not delay, then." Edmund picked up the map, folded it away, and offered it to Eve. "I do not need it. Do you know anything about Ednor at all?"

Eve shook her head. "Just that my mother was born there." It was said before she realised Luke and Nyle would hear. She bit her lip, mentally kicking herself.

Edmund raised an eyebrow, surprised that she knew nothing more, though he did not remark on it. Luke and Nyle froze with aghast expressions at her accidental disclosure. Edmund did not notice their reaction.

"Very well. If I am correct, for I have not heard anything of them for some time, their current ruler should still be Queen Artora. Ask for her directly and speak with the greatest courtesy when you are in her or her advisers' company. I wish I could instruct you in more length as to how to conduct yourself, as the Eldarkind have many specific ways of expressing courtesy and respect, but alas, you will have to do your best. I have faith in you."

As Eve, Luke, and Nyle led their horses west into the forest, Edmund made for the road and Jormund to continue on to the monastery.

Eve and her guards walked on, still leading the horses on foot through the woods that were too dense to allow them to ride. Because of this, they walked in single file; Nyle led Eve whilst Luke brought up the rear. Eve was glad, for it gave them no excuse or opportunity to talk and gave her time to gather her thoughts. What she could not see was the growing worry on Luke's face and Nyle's fuming countenance.

Eve puzzled over Edmund's words. Her thoughts dwelt on why her father had never before permitted her to journey to Ednor. She recalled with a sigh the faint memory of her mother's hand caressing her head, a smell of flowers and her long golden hair, which Eve had inherited, falling in a curtain as she bent to embrace Eve and tell her yet another fairy tale from the land of the Eldarkind.

After her mother's death when she was still a young girl, she had asked many times if she could journey there. It had seemed to her to be a land of magic and wonder, a place she had always yearned to visit to see the truth of the tales.

Her father—at first grief stricken and later distant—had always denied her this wish without explanation, to Eve's great frustration. They had many an argument over it, but Karn was adamant in refusing her, and in recent years, she had given up asking. She wondered why he had allowed her to go now; because he had giving up resisting, or because he had no other option.

Eve was so lost in her thoughts she did not notice the unusual hardness in Nyle's gaze as he glanced back every so often to check she and Luke were close behind, nor could she see Luke's agitation behind her. It was not until they broke for lunch did she wonder at Luke's hesitation of sitting near her and Nyle's visible bad temper.

She did not know how to break the silence. Certain her careless slip of the tongue was the reason for their bizarre behaviour towards her, she internally admonished herself for blurting out the secret of her heritage.

Though the Eldarkind had once been great, as they faded into the history of Caledan, the stories told of them grew more fanciful and false with each telling. Generations later, the noble Eldarkind had been mutated by folklore into untrustworthy, mischievous, and even sometimes malevolent beings, who haunted the night and the deeps of the world. Mere mention of them was laced with prejudice so ingrained, Eve knew any association with them as if they were real beings would sow the seeds of mistrust.

Nyle broke the silence. "What are you?" he accused, his suspicious gaze boring into her. He stood with his arms folded, looking down at where she sat on a fallen tree trunk a few feet away, whilst Luke stood to one side, not looking at either of them.

"I am who I've always been," replied Eve. She knew that here in the depth of the wilderness so far from help she would have to carefully choose her words, lest she provoke Nyle into open anger or worse. She did not know whether this could even turn Luke against her despite their many years of friendship; such were the implications.

"Nyle, you're old enough to remember my mother when you were a child. Did you ever perceive her to be evil, to be the truth of the folk stories? And have I ever given you cause to believe that I'm anything other than normal?"

He mulled over his response. "No." It was easy to see he begrudged the word.

"I know I may look different from most people. I have fair hair and light eyes, when most of our town are darker in both, and I know I take those characteristics from my mother, but you have both witnessed me grow up—Luke, you especially—and you both know me to be nothing other than my father's daughter. I hide no evil in me." She held her head high.

Nyle did not seem placated, but it was clear he had nothing else to say. They ate in awkward silence, then pressed on. To make matters more uncomfortable, a steady rain had begun to fall and although by nightfall it had ceased, they were damp and short-tempered.

They had followed the stream high into the mountain pass, where the narrow valley brought premature gloom to their travel before the sunset. Deciduous forests had given way to coniferous woods that clung to steep, rocky valley sides.

The remains of a track were visible, parting the trees to either side, and for a few hours, they had been able to saddle up the horses and ride once more. The road clung to one side of the steep valley with a stomach-churning drop to their left, and the stream was barely visible far below.

They came to a small bend high in the valley that offered some shelter and made camp under a rocky overhang. Whilst Luke and Eve unsaddled the horses and began to unpack the necessities for their evening meal, Nyle foraged further up the path for firewood so they could heat food and water and have some warmth against the altitude-induced chill in the darkening air.

Eve absentmindedly went about her tasks, until a touch on her arm made her jolt in surprise as she finished grooming Alia. She twisted to find Luke standing close behind her, her forearm now in his grasp. This close, he was taller than she was by some inches and an imposing figure in the gloom.

He saw the gleam of fear in her eyes and released her arm, half holding up his hands to show he meant no harm. She did not move, but observed him warily; tense and ready to reach for a weapon if she needed.

"I'm sorry..." he said falteringly. "I didn't mean to surprise you." He fell silent and Eve waited, still tense for a minute as he tried to compose himself. "I know it's perhaps not my place, but I wanted to ask whilst Nyle wasn't here. We used to be close; why didn't you tell me about your mother?"

"Because you would judge me like Nyle has; just like everyone else would!" she retorted. "What business is it of yours anyway? It is clear I cannot trust you, therefore it is no concern of yours at all!" she exclaimed.

She made to push past him but he grasped her arm once more. "Let go of me, Lucan!" She wrenched her hand out of his grip and stormed off down the path, feeling shaken by the experience and with her heart pounding.

Her use of his formal name felt like a physical blow and he froze, taken aback. "Eve!" he called after her. She did not respond and was soon out of sight around the bend in the track. "Damn it!" he swore, as Nyle returned with an arm full of wood.

"What's up now? Where is she?" asked Nyle.

Luke scowled.

"What did you do, Luke?"

"Nothing!" Luke exclaimed. "Look, I need to find her. Will you light the fire whilst I go search for her? She can't have gone far."

Nyle nodded, the movement barely discernible. Luke spun around and ran down the track after Eve. He found her, some minutes later, a pale figure sat on a large rock and he approached her slowly.

"Eve?"

She did not respond. He knelt in front of her. "Eve, I'm sorry for being so forward. Please, will you accept my apology?"

Her head bobbed up and down. Through her hair, she saw his relieved smile.

"Please don't take it the wrong way, I... We used to be so close. I know things are different now. You're the heir to the county and I'm nobody, but I still miss how we used to talk. I miss my friend

Evie," he trailed off into silence.

"I'm sorry too, Luke," Eve replied. She rested a hand on his head briefly before withdrawing it to her lap once more. "You startled me just now, but that was no reason for me to speak so harshly. I can see the prejudice in Nyle's eyes so clearly that I thought you might judge the worst of me too."

"You always have the benefit of the doubt in my eyes, Eve," he said. "I would never think poorly of you, or judge you, though I admit I'm surprised. I know things cannot return to the way they were, but I am always here for you. If you need someone, night or day, I'll be there. You need never feel alone."

"How can I talk to you or trust as I once did though, Luke?" Eve asked him, her eyes full of reproach. His expression changed to confusion. "You told my father of my every move. You betrayed my trust!"

"I did not mean it to be so!" he replied, distressed. "It was my job to guard you. Your father made it very clear that if I did not do my duty then I would no longer have the position."

"So you chose your job over our friendship and trust then." She spoke more bluntly than she intended. His words hurt her more than she realised. Luke crumpled at her feet and tangled his hands in his hair. Her frustrations lifted somewhat as she saw his intense discomfort.

"I did not want to leave you," he admitted, so quiet and pained that she barely heard him. "I'm sorry." He spoke louder than before. His apology was simple but she heard the urgent sincerity in his voice.

What does that mean? Eve did not know how to reply, so instead she stood, drew Luke up from where he knelt and clasped his hands in hers for the briefest moment before she dropped them. *He doesn't wish me ill, at least.*

"Shall we?" she asked, motioning towards the camp. Her anger and fear had vanished; replaced with relief and the knowledge that she had not lost her dearest friend.

As they returned to the camp together in silence, she wondered at his choice of words. *He didn't want to leave me...?*

80

ELEVEN

Armoured men parted like water before him as Zaki rode to the gates of the monastery. He had ordered his men's silent formation before dawn so that he could send a particular impression to the abbot. They stood in silent ranks, all staring forward and in full battle gear. Zaki himself felt impressed by their coordination.

The imposing wall loomed before him, broken by the closed, studded gate set into it. All seemed deserted until a voice called down from the battlements. "Who goes there?"

Reynard replied, "Here stands before you His Royal Highness, Prince Zaki of Caledan, heir to the throne. Open your gates."

"You come before us with a great host and so armed; what are your intentions?"

"We will speak with your abbot and no other," Reynard replied. "Summon him now."

"There is no need, Your Royal Highness," another voice replied. "I am here." The abbot peered over the wall, then disappeared. The gate opened before Zaki to reveal the abbot standing in his way. He was tiny in person, far smaller than Zaki remembered him. Older too, and fragile. He walked with a slight limp, Zaki noticed, and his face held years more wrinkles than Zaki recalled. The abbot was nothing more than a frail old man dressed in dowdy robes.

"I have come for the crown. Release it to me," said Zaki. He did not see the need to mince words; that only wasted his time.

"I cannot do this for you, sir," said the abbot.

Zaki paused with a frown. "Give to me one good reason why I, the legally recognised heir to the throne, may not have the crown of my forbears."

The abbot shuffled. "The crown is not here, sir."

"What a pathetic lie. This is absurd, old man. I will not ask a third time. You refuse to give me what is mine by right?"

"I cannot give what I do not possess, sir," the abbot replied.

"My men and I must search the entire monastery to find it, then," said Zaki, irked by the man's politeness and calm demeanour.

"I cannot allow you to do so, sir," the abbot protested. "These are sacred grounds."

"We will do this whether you will it or not." Zaki leered at him. "Let us in or we will enter by force."

The abbot's answer was a hand gesture to those behind him. He walked beneath the wall and through the gates. Zaki prepared to follow, but the gates shut in his face and were barred from within.

Zaki froze. It took a moment to understand what had happened and regain his composure. "You all witness this treason." Zaki stood in his saddle to address the men about him.

Not a man moved, though the eyes of those closest flicked towards him. "I hereby call upon you to defend Caledan's honour and retrieve the crown of our kings from the hands of these rebels! For Caledan!" he called.

"For Caledan!" replied his men, magnifying his words thousand-fold.

"Attack," he said to Reynard beside him. "Fire archers, battering rams, anything you like. Breach these walls, find that crown, and kill the boy."

On the other side of the wall, Soren listened to his uncle's arrogant voice with shaking fists, itching to step forward from the ranks of silent monks who stood with him. Hador moved forward infinitesimally as the abbot withdrew from the top of the walls.

"What would you have us do?"

The abbot blinked at him. "Prepare." He shook his head and sighed. "It is worse than I feared. His heart is black. I was mistaken to believe he could be reasoned wi—"

His words were drowned out in the hubbub rising from the other side of the walls, and the giant boom upon the gates.

A battering ram, Soren realised. Dust shook loose from the gates, skittering to the floor. The monks inside stepped back as one, murmuring to each other.

"Prince Soren must be evacuated as soon as darkness falls," the abbot continued grimly.

Hador nodded and saluted him, before turning away to bellow orders. Around them, monks sprang into action, scurrying in all directions to the tune of the booming battering ram. With every *boom*, Soren's heart skittered with a mix of anxiety and fear. *What's going to happen?*

"Follow me." Soren fell into step beside the abbot at his command.

TWELVE

Soren's hands fumbled with the buttons. There was no time to lose. He donned fresh traveling clothes of a dark rough cloth much simpler than those he had arrived in, as quickly as he could.

Outside, a pack of provisions and a half-dozen monks and horses awaited, Miri amongst them. He peered at their faces to try and familiarise himself, however in the dark, with scant light from the shuttered windows escaping, it was impossible to tell them apart.

The only man he could identify was Hador. "We've disabled the enemy scouts outside the northern gate, and set our own watch our there to ensure our safe passage. We have no time to waste if we are to make use of that window of opportunity." Soren did not like to think what he meant by 'disabled.'

"For now, the attack concentrates on the front gate, but we do not know how much longer it will hold." The monks shifted around him. Indeed, above his murmur, the clamor of attack was clear to here; clinking armour, the shouts of men, and the ever present boom. Before darkness had fallen, Soren had seen monks busy fortifying the gates.

"We'll proceed in complete silence and follow one of the streams north to the refuge. Muffle your swords." Hador tossed Soren a strip of fabric, which he bound around his blade.

"The abbot forbids our return until any hostile forces have departed, therefore we will remain as long as is necessary. It'll take us the night to get there without lights to guide us. We'll rope together the horses and each man should take a bridle so none of us become separated. Let's go."

Roping the horses together, they set off to the northern gate; the same portal Soren had entered just that morning, though it felt like longer. The gate opened without a sound on well-oiled hinges.

Hador led the silent line of men out. They halted so the last man in the chain could close the gate before continuing. After a few paces, soft footsteps behind them and the tiniest grate of metal on metal, Soren knew the gate had been secured once more from within.

It was a fraught walk, and they made slow progress. Under cover of darkness, not knowing where any of the army's scouts were, they dared not ride and instead led the horses through the dark, guided by the star and moonlight which fell between the clouds covering half of the sky. Reaching the tree cover a few feet from the walls, they continued downhill. Hador and the rest of the monks carried crossbow in their free hands; a brutal weapon, but an effective silencer.

Fortunately for them, or perhaps more for the enemy, they came across no scouts and soon reached the bottom of the hill on which the monastery sat. From there, they followed the stream bed up into the hills; it was wide and loud enough at this point to lead the horses up its middle and disguise any signs and sounds of their passage.

By dawn, they wandered up small wild trails in the foothills, half-hidden by grass and overcast by the tree canopy, until they reached a rock face which sheared through the treetops above them some hours later. At last, Hador halted. They untied the horses and led them individually along the bottom of the cliff for some minutes until, in the rock face, a great split opened.

Soren would not have noticed it had they not halted; by some trick of the eye, it was only visible by passing it and then looking back. A curtain of greenery that must have been purposefully grown concealed the entrance. Soren peered in. Once they had picketed the horses outside, Hador, bearing a lit candle, led him inside.

Light illuminated a narrow tunnel and then a huge space. The cavern had a rocky ceiling seven feet high sloping down towards the back to half the height of a man. A dozen straw mattresses lay piled with blankets and pillows, and chairs sat stacked next to a table. On the other wall a bookcase stood, three-quarters full of dusty books. Noting that the floor was hard-packed earth, Soren was thankful for the mattresses. His eyes burned, and his head was clouded. It had been a long night.

The men dumped their packs by the table and began to ready the room, whilst Hador dictated the watch rotas. Soren finished plumping pillows and walked outside to escape from all the dust raised in the cave; the view made him gasp. Through what seemed like a miraculous coincidence, though he supposed the location had been chosen for this very reason, a great gap in the foliage meant he could see right down onto the monastery, miles below and to the south. It was the perfect position; from below, the cave could not be identified at all.

However, his wonder turned to dismay and he let out a cry which brought the others running. A swarm of silver flashes—armoured men—had almost surrounded the monastery, most concentrated at the main gate. The size of the force, which seemed to have sprung from nowhere overnight, stunned them into silence.

The sound of their presence did not carry over such a great distance but Soren could guess their intentions; only Zaki could control and flaunt such a large force. The seven men watched. Dismay was etched in each of their faces at the size of the horde, clearly regretting that they could not add to the number of defenders to protect their home.

Looking at what faced the monastery, Soren understood the abbot's words just before they parted. *I will be lucky to see him again.* He shivered.

THIRTEEN

Eve, Luke, and Nyle drunk in the view open-mouthed. A restless night followed the previous day's turbulence and they arose with dull heads and heavy eyes. After riding further, the valley closed in around them and the trees gave way to a barren rocky landscape as the rain gave way to tentative sun. They mounted a brow, expecting rockier terrain. What they saw made them halt with incredulity.

Before them, an enormous valley sunk thousands of feet and miles into the distance. It was so long they could not see its far end in the haze. It was green and pleasant; forests and meadows as far as the eye could see and a huge lake glinting blue in the emerging sun as it faded into the distance.

To the north, Ednor lay amongst forested foothills, broken here and there by grassy meadows. In high summer the snow line lay far above the valleys and Eve saw white upon the towering peaks of the Helm Mountains; glaciers grasped the mountains and dirty snow banks stubbornly stuck in crevices and hollows.

At this distance great detail was not visible, though Ednor's buildings seemed made of the same light golden coloured stone as Arlyn, although here it appeared much paler. At Ednor's highest point, a large building dominated and Eve guessed this was where she was to go.

With a delighted laugh, she urged her horse forward to ride down into the valley as Luke and Nyle hurried to keep pace with her. Eve's excitement increased as her fear receded; forgotten as she basked in the rich, colourful beauty that contrasted the rocky, barren, and shaded path they had been following. Woods and smallholdings passed by as they rode. Trees, taller than any she had seen before, threw dappled light upon them as they rode across grassy knolls.

They reached the boundaries of Ednor just after midday and rode in without delay. Here in the secret valley, there was no need for sentries and armies, nor gates and walls. Eve was surprised to find this; even a peaceful town such as Arlyn still benefited from fortification and was under constant defence.

There was little separation between the forest and Ednor; the stone buildings complimented their surroundings, fitting within the forest inconspicuously. Eve could not decide whether it was a city or a town—or neither, for it conformed to no norms she had seen.

By comparison, Arlyn was barren and primitive and even the grandeur of Pandora could not match the muted grace of Ednor's buildings, where each building was a masterpiece. Carvings and columns adorned each one, as if they were drawn from the ground instead of constructed.

Stone ivy chased over walls, up, and around impossibly delicate stone arbours which appeared to be woven together from giant threads. Each dwelling was generously spaced from its neighbours; the buildings seemed haphazard in placement, and no boundary markings separated them.

Everywhere there was greenery, flowers, and the sound of running water. Streams trickled down from the mountains and elegant fountains burbled. Music and birdsong and laughter emanated from unseen places all around. Perhaps even more beautiful than the city were its inhabitants, the Eldarkind; golden-haired, pale-skinned and light-eyed men, women and children went about their business with a sense of unsuppressed contentment, stopping to look with surprise at the unfamiliar girl who appeared to be one of their own, riding with two dark-haired humans.

Eve rode forward unaware, engrossed by the beauty of the place and barely paying heed to Luke and Nyle, who were uncomfortable with the attention as the Eldarkind murmured in an unfamiliar tongue.

As they travelled, the ground rose and rocky outcrops thrust up from the forest floor. The valley constricted and though still wide, the tree spacing decreased, meadows opened up, and buildings now perched artfully on the valley sides. Where at last the gentle rising slops of the valley gave way to the mountains proper, they found themselves at the highest point of Ednor. A tall wall arose in front of them, with wrought gates wide open.

They passed under the archway to a courtyard and gardens where before them they beheld the great dwelling they had seen from a distance. Although the gates were open, a single guard manned it, and he approached as they made to ride through.

"Halt and dismount, please!" he called, his voice accented. "On what business are you here?"

"I am Lady Eve of Arlyn." Eve gracefully dismounted and gestured at Luke and Nyle to do the same. "I travel with my guards Luke and Nyle to seek the council of the queen as soon as possible. I apologise for our unannounced arrival and I beg for an audience."

The guard smiled and bowed. "Then it is my pleasure to welcome you to Ednor, Lady Eve. If you follow me, I shall have your horses stabled and rooms prepared for you to stay. I shall arrange for your audience as soon as possible."

"Thank you," replied Eve, surprised at the welcome. Soon the horses were stabled, and the three were led to adjacent quarters in a grand building with high ceilings and tall windows, full of light, paintings, sculptures and flowing structures. Eve's room had a view of the mountains behind Ednor. When she tore her attention away from it, she noticed a small ewer stood beside it and gratefully washed her face and hands of the stain of travel.

Before she had an opportunity to enjoy her surroundings, let alone bathe or change, another of the Eldarkind returned to invite her to meet the queen. Eve regretfully turned her back on the bath and prepared to meet Artora dressed in several days' old clothing and no doubt stinking to high heaven. She sighed and steeled herself, determined not to disappoint her father, as her guide stopped, knocked on a door, and announced her presence.

She was ushered into an airy, light room where each wall was a different fantastical mural. The far wall held wide and tall windows, with panes of glass so fine and perfect they were invisible. Eve saw gardens filled with flowers and trees, beyond which the mountains rose.

What captured Eve's gaze was the tall woman who rose at her entrance from a carved chair behind a vast desk. Golden hair streamed loosely across her shoulders and fell to her thighs, illuminated from behind by the light of the window.

She wore, to Eve's surprise, no extravagant dress or crown or jewels as Eve had seen Queen Naisa wear at Pandora, but a fine fitted shirt and pants, skilfully tailored and embroidered. Despite her face being in shadow, Eve perceived high cheekbones, symmetrical features, and keen blue eyes that fixed upon her own. Eve froze in her penetrating gaze.

"It is good to have Freya's daughter travel to our land." The woman's smile was warm, and the moment was broken. "You are most welcome, Eve of Arlyn." She stepped across the room towards Eve as her eyebrows rose in surprise that the queen knew her mother's name. "It is a pleasure to meet you. I am Artora. It is some time since I had word from Arlyn. How is your father?" The queen drew close to Eve, taller than her by a few inches, and to Eve's amazement, bent to kiss both cheeks.

"Thank you for your kind welcome, Your Majesty," replied Eve with a bow. Her cheeks burned with embarrassment for her poor state of appearance next to this impressive woman. "My father is well, thank you. However, I did not ride here for pleasure, though I have longed to for many years. I come bearing news." She presented the parchment sealed with the stamp of Arlyn to the queen, who took it and moved back to the window, to read it in the light. Her brow furrowed as she read.

"Things are indeed dark if Karn seeks my council," Artora murmured to herself. "You may call me Artora," she added, almost as an afterthought. "We do not use titles and rank so formally in Ednor, as you will see."

Thoughtfully, she folded up the letter and, balancing it on her palm, blew upon it. Eve gasped as the letter sailed lightly off the queen's hand onto the desk several feet away, as if it were no lighter than a feather with a mind of its own.

"How did you do that?" she exclaimed involuntarily, open-mouthed.

"How did I do what?" Artora turned to regard her with bafflement.

"Th-the letter. It flew!" Eve stammered.

"Magic, of course," Artora replied, as if it was obvious, but Eve's face remained blank. "Why would you not know that? Don't you know of magic?" As Eve shook her head, the queen's brows furrowed with anger, and her eyes narrowed.

"To think Freya's daughter does not know of magic. What was Karn thinking!" she said scathingly. "If magic had burst out of you unexpectedly, the consequences could have been dire!"

"Why would magic burst out of me?" Eve asked with a sense of dread.

"Your mother was one of the Eldarkind, so you will have inherited her powers." The queen frowned, as if that were obvious. "Surely you must know. Surely she told you."

"My mother didn't have any magic," said Eve with more conviction than she felt.

Dismay filled the queen's face. "You know nothing of your heritage, do you, Eve?" Eve shook her head again, feeling ashamed and confused. Her eyes dropped to the floor as her cheeks blushed once more. Artora sighed. "Your mother was one of the Eldarkind. She possessed magical abilities; we all do. She simply chose not to use her powers whilst she stayed in the mortal world and raised you, in order to keep you safe. I still thought that she must have told you of them."

"To keep me safe," Eve mouthed to herself soundlessly. She felt suddenly sad, sadder than she had felt for a long time, now realising how little she knew of a mother who had abandoned her true heritage, her own kind, and even her magical powers, and had then been rewarded with an early death from a sickness no magic could cure. She felt an awareness of the sacrifices her mother had made that she had never before perceived.

Artora studied her sympathetically. "Would you like me to tell you about your mother?" she asked gently. Eve looked up, with tears in her eyes, and nodded. The queen gestured to a chair by her desk, inviting Eve to sit, and took her own grand seat once more. A servant slipped in to leave refreshments for them both and Artora herself poured tea for them. In the silence, Eve felt as though she were a child once more; not the sophisticated ambassador she was supposed to be.

"I knew your mother better than you may think," Artora said. "Freya was my second cousin on my father's side, so in fact you would be my second cousin once removed." Eve glanced up in surprise.

"Yes, it is true!" Artora smiled at her and Eve mirrored her uncertainly, feeling a strange warmth within her at the thought of kinship. "So you may be married into royalty on your father's side, but you are royalty on your mother's." Artora let out a small, rich laugh, before her smile tempered.

"Alas, I miss her. We were close when she and I were younger, although I was several years her senior. Your mother became an envoy for us when she grew to adulthood, and I did not see much of her then; my duties kept me here.

"Oft we would send her to Pandora to confer with Queen Naisa. It was there she met your father. They fell in love and, well, that was the end of her travels. She longed for nothing more than to settle down with the man she loved and neither I nor anyone else could sway her mind.

"She returned one last time to say goodbye, many years ago now, just before you were born. She swore not to reveal our presence to anyone save Karn—he in turn doing likewise—and she swore never to use her magic outside our borders. Perhaps that is why you never knew of our magic at all, though I did not intend that."

"She told me stories," said Eve suddenly. "She told me stories about the magical kingdom of the Eldarkind, the adventures of the Eldarkind, their history, their wonderful magical powers and how they would make all right in the world, how she was of the Eldarkind. I was only a child. I never thought those tales were true. I didn't think it possible. And then she died…" She trailed off into silence.

"Yes," said the queen heavily. "And then she died. I will never understand how the illness took her of all others and so quickly too.

I wish there had been time to come to her; perhaps we could have healed her. I suppose what is past is past and we cannot change that. I am sorry though, Eve, that you never knew more of your mother, or of us."

There was a long silence as Eve contemplated Artora's words, and Artora did not press her to speak. Finally, she met the queen's eyes. "How much is there that I do not know?" she questioned.

"Eve, even I could learn of things from now until the end of time and I would not know all there is to know," replied the queen. "Of the Eldarkind and magic, there is more than I can impart to you in a short while, but I shall personally teach you what I can in the time you are here, if you would find that amenable?"

"You would do that for me?" asked Eve, surprised.

"You are my kind, and moreover my kin, Eve, and we always help those that we may, especially those of our own. Matters of politics and troubles in Caledan aside, would you like to stay for a while?" Artora invited.

"My father instructed me to return straight away," replied Eve, "although I'm unwilling to be quite so hasty." She trailed off into silence again.

"Well, regardless, you will not be departing immediately, so why not mull over it this afternoon," proposed Artora. "Tonight you and your guards may dine with the household and I, and perhaps you can give me your answer then."

Eve agreed with a shy smile, and the queen smiled back. Artora stood to dismiss her. "Excellent," she said. "Now, I understand that of course you will be tired after your journey. Please feel free to bathe in your chambers and prepare yourself for tonight. We do not dine formally, so do not trouble yourself to wear finery."

Eve smiled at the queen in thanks and, after a last glance back at the beautiful woman who stood framed in the light of the windows once more, closed the door and let herself be led away.

She spent over an hour in a hot bath mulling over everything Artora had said. Upon returning to her chambers, Eve had felt an initial flash of anger at her father for hiding so much from her, however as she thought, she realised that perhaps he had believed it was for the best, given his promise to Artora. She was determined to speak to him about it the moment she had the chance. Not for the first time she wondered why he had let her come to Ednor. Again, she found no answer.

Her reflections turned to herself; Nyle's accusing face from their confrontation the previous day swam into her mind and she dwelt upon thoughts of who and what she was. A rap at the door made her jump. Luke's voice called through it.

"Eve, are you there?" He waited for a few seconds. She did not reply. "Lady Eve?" After a pause, footsteps receded, and then there was silence.

Eve breathed a sigh of relief. She had no desire to talk to anyone; her head swam with all there was for her to consider. She resolved there was nothing more to think about that she could presently solve and closed her eyes, attempting to let the feeling of warmth wash over her.

It was no use, however. Regardless of how hard she shut her eyes or attempted to blank her thoughts, her mind whispered to her.

Who are you? It questioned insidiously, planting a growing fear within her.

FOURTEEN

The prince and the monks watched with trepidation. It was Hador who broke the silence and chivvied them away. "Come. It'll do us no good to worry over what is done. We have our orders and this is not our battle. I feel as each of you feels and I would run to defend our home, yet the abbot ordered us away for good reason."

Three of the monks nodded. The other two stared at Soren with obvious dislike and he, catching their looks, understood why. He could see the longing in their eyes to go to the aid of their comrades and their home, and their resentment at having to mind him like a baby.

He made no move to smile or frown but stared at them until they turned away and followed the others back into the cave. Hador noticed their animosity. "Take no heed of them," he murmured to the prince as soon as the others were out of earshot.

"I understand their dislike of me. If I were in their position, I would feel the same. I did ask the abbot to let me stay and fight, but his mind was made up." Soren frowned.

"The abbot is aware of your importance," replied the monk, still watching the battle below. "You are the heir to the throne, and thus the wellbeing of Caledan and its people rests in your hands. He does not wish to place you in any more danger than you are already in. It is to be our sacrifice for you that seeks to gain you the liberty to regain the crown for the good of Caledan."

"I know this," admitted the prince. "I'm still loathe to hide in the mountains when down there in plain sight is the man who murdered my mother. I'm loathe too to let anyone sacrifice themselves for me, willingly or not. I have as much cause as any of you to want to fight him, and I feel guilt staying here. What if we could make the difference? What if the addition of your six men and

I could change the fate of what lies ahead?"

"We are not to know what may or may not be," Hador said. "It was clear the abbot was not willing to take that risk. As we keep the crown, it was inevitable that Zaki would come. It would have put you in more danger for him to know of your presence there."

"What of the abbot?" asked Soren. "He said that he feared we would not meet again and it left me with the strangest shiver down my spine."

Hador looked at him keenly. "He also said those words to me. I worry they may be true. Nevertheless, try to allay your fears. The abbot has had a long and full life and has no sadness or fear at his approaching end, whenever that may be.

"Moreover, he appreciates that this is as it must be; no one may live forever. Therefore, we must be as brave as he. Do not worry about the monastery and my brethren. He entrusted it to my care as his successor and he has trained me long and well for the task, though I do not presume to be as great a man as he."

Soren reflected on this, pleasantly surprised. In the short time since they had met, Hador seemed a reasonable and just man, who was intelligent and efficient in what he did. "When are we to return?" he asked at last.

Hador did not reply for a time. "I have not decided that yet," he admitted. "The abbot forbade us to return whilst foes are at our gates. I must remain heartless in refusing my own yearning to return, so that I may help secure our future hopes." After a moment, he turned and strode away.

That day, the men busied themselves as much as they could. It was mid-afternoon when the watchman's cry brought everyone running. Moans of horror tore from their throats at the terrible sight. Murmurs broke out amongst them and frantic prayers were uttered.

The perimeter wall was intact, but the gate had fallen and a block of archers peppered outbuildings with fire arrows. Wooden and thatched buildings here and there caught alight. Although the day was still with a light breeze, the recent dry weather meant that they were aflame in minutes.

Soren could not tear his eyes away as fires spread and ranks of monks awaited the inevitable. Zaki's soldiers swarmed through the broken gate in a mass of silver. Soren knew the monks would be rushing forward too to defend their homes, but they were too few, in poor armour. *There's no chance, no chance, no chance*, the dark recesses of his mind tormented him.

The fighting was confusing from afar; no crests or banners could be seen, just a maelstrom of flashing armour accompanied by the faint sounds of battle. Fires here and there cast sickly orange glows across the grounds, as the fighting moved further into the compound. Each of the few hundred monks must have been outnumbered several to one at the very least; Soren knew even the greatest of skill would be unlikely to save them.

Soren could not imagine how twisted his uncle's mind must be to order such a horrific attack on a religious centre and he thought with revulsion of the thousands of soldiers who were now mindlessly serving Zaki, carrying out his orders with seemingly not a thought for their own morals.

He questioned right and wrong, wondering if such soldiers could be good men at heart, yet his own sense of morality was so strong, he could not see how anyone could carry out such a vile act, even if ordered to do so. It unnerved him to see such a great force intent on desecration and death.

As the red sun sank in the sky, Hador moved the men away. "We must rest," he ordered half-heartedly. He set two men on the first watch and with everyone else, retreated into the cave.

It was a long and lonely night through which no one rested, each too consumed by anxiety and fervent, muttered prayer to sleep. Just before dawn, Hador admitted there was no point trying to rest, allowing them all to rise and watch the glowing embers of the buildings they had lived in, still stubbornly alight in places.

As the sky was turning from deepest blue to bloody red at the horizon. "We are to return at once," Hador said. They all realised very little would remain when they returned, and in their heart of hearts, knew the fight was lost. Orders or no orders, there would be little to find when they returned. "Prepare the horses."

Destruction awaited. The monastery had been almost wholly razed to the ground. Debris piled higher than the haphazard half-walls that remained, and not one wall stood amongst mountains of broken and charred rock, only the central bell tower, but the bell was half caved in on the ground outside. How Zaki had achieved this in just one day, Soren had no idea.

Shattered glass and lead panes littered the ground and the smell of burning and death was on the air as they approached where the fighting had been heaviest. The dead lay twisted and still on the ground, framed by blood, their armour dulled by dust and dirt.

The seven men reached what should have been the main door, and fell still. The carnage was incomprehensible. They stood, unable to speak. It was clear there should be no survivors.

"Right, men!" Hador's hoarse voice startled them all. He ordered them to search for survivors, leaving Soren, himself, and one other, Orman, to trawl through the wreckage about them.

The others did as they were bidden and rode to the four corners of the grounds, whilst Hador applied himself with Orman and Soren to search the messy wrecks of once proud buildings. It was grim and tiring work, but not without reward, for soon Soren found a man who still had a weak pulse.

They excavated him and Hador gently lifted his head to trickle some water down his throat. The man moaned as they laid him on a square of grass—the remains of a courtyard. Hador ordered Orman to tend to the injured man.

Over the course of the afternoon, they found dozens of survivors clinging to life. The task before them was daunting; they had a few hours to recover the living and offer them medical attention, sustenance, and shelter before nightfall. Hador worked like a man possessed. He tasked four monks and Soren with bringing all survivors to the same space of grass where the first man still lay, now bandaged and asleep under Orman's watchful eyes.

One well remained unspoiled and Orman was able to draw up sufficient water from it to wash any wounds, which he then bandaged with cloth strips ripped from anything he could find. Hador worked with the horses to pull aside a particular pile of rubble, for reasons Soren did not at all understand until the monk had finished. In the middle of the cracked flagstones, he exposed a heavy slab set with a large metal ring.

He lashed ropes to the horses, tied the other end to the ring, and urged them on. Slowly but surely the slab inched up until they were able to drag it away to expose a gaping hole in the ground, where stairs could be seen fading into inky blackness. Drooping with fatigue, Hador stopped the horses with a quick word and sunk into the hole. Soon after, a warm glow emanated from within and minutes later, he came bounding up the stairs, new life in his step contrasting the deep hollows beneath his eyes.

"The cellars are intact!" he said, as a tired smile full of relief split his face. "Our brothers have saved the library and many of our greatest sacred items. They are all stored down there in the older rooms. Most importantly for now, they will shelter us during the night. There are tables and benches we can use for beds and the cold stores and larders are brimming with food and medicines."

Hador leapt down into the hole to return moments later with a makeshift stretcher. Whilst the others continued working, Hador and Soren ferried injured men into the cellar vaults. When it became clear there were no more survivors left, the other monks joined them.

Whilst one sat by the trapdoor on watch, the others created temporary beds on any surface they could find, made poultices, fetched water and provided drinks and food for any of their injured comrades who were conscious. In total, they had recovered forty-seven men from the grounds, but to their despair, the abbot could not be found.

Dusk was almost upon them when a cry from the watchman above froze them all. Hador and Soren rushed upstairs to see two silhouetted figures on horseback approaching, one oddly large and distorted. He felt mild relief it was two people and not Zaki's soldiers returning. With a sudden jolt, Soren realised it could be Edmund.

He shouted and waved to the figures, and one raised a hand in return, yet they did not speed their horses up from a slow walk. A sense of foreboding crept over him as he waited for them to approach. At his side, Hador was ashen.

The riders emerged through the low light, and the bulky figure became clearer. It was indeed Edmund, but there seemed to be something on the back of his horse—brown rags and then a flash of pale skin—Soren realised with horror it was a body. He dreaded to think who it was. He had an inkling he hoped was wrong.

Hador dropped to his knees and bowed to the ground with tears erupting from his eyes as Soren watched Edmund and an unfamiliar monk dismount and reverently lower the limp form of the abbot to the ground.

FIFTEEN

Feeling deliciously clean, Eve prepared herself with care. That evening she sat at the top table on Artora's left side. It felt good to be washed and dressed well after the previous days and she grimaced at the memory of the state of her riding clothes. She was dressed in a simple though elegant long-sleeved, green dress, embroidered in gold, that was embarassingly creased from travelling. Seated beside Artora, she felt eclipsed by the queen's effortless beauty and powerful presence.

A few others joined them, although the seat to Artora's right stood empty. Eve wondered who sat there but dared not ask. Luke and Nyle sat near the far end of the room, though Eve felt secretly glad to not have to talk to them at all let alone all evening.

"Tonight we welcome special guests." Artora stood up to announce. "To Lady Eve of Arlyn, and her escorts, welcome." Eve smiled self-consciously as Artora picked up her delicate glass, raised it into the air, and sipped from it.

Everyone rose as one to copy her; Eve, Luke, and Nyle scrambled to join them. Pale golden liquid flowed hotly down Eve's throat with an invigorating sensation.

"Oh!" she remarked in surprise.

Artora chuckled. "We make that ourselves, and rather strongly, I must admit. It is rather heady to an unfamiliar tongue!"

The meal was served and Eve tucked in with gusto to a variety of meats and vegetables, savouring the rich and varied tastes and textures, which made the best of meals after dry and tasteless travelling foods.

Artora was a skilful host and enquired about her travels and her home, yet Eve was half-hearted in her involvement; she felt out of place and still undecided about what to do.

"You're not enjoying this, are you?" Artora murmured to her.

"I'm sorry! The food is lovely, everything is lovely," stammered Eve. "But..."

"I understand, dear cousin." Artora smiled. "I gave you much to think about today, and then even more besides. It is no wonder you are distracted. However, I could teach you a great many things to help you if you wish. Will you accompany me tomorrow morning? I shall instruct you on the art of magic and the history of the Eldarkind."

Eve hesitated, so Artora persuasively continued.

"I understand some of the human perceptions of magic, Eve. It is not an evil thing, although it can be used for evil. It can also be used, as it is by us, as a great force of good. To have the skill of magic makes you neither a better nor worse person, until you choose how to use it. Do not be swayed by the perceptions of others, but choose yourself," she cautioned. "I will send someone for you tomorrow morning."

Conversation turned once more to lighter things, as those present sought the attention of the new arrivals, until the meal had run its course. Artora dismissed the guests and led Eve, Luke, and Nyle back to their quarters. Eve's head swam from the strong drinks and the whirlwind of introductions and conversations.

"Luke, Nyle, it is a pleasure to welcome you to Ednor," Artora said as they strolled down the corridors.

"Your Majesty," acknowledged Nyle.

"The pleasure is all mine, Your Majesty," murmured Luke.

The queen smiled.

"I apologise for not welcoming you both earlier. It is quite rare to have humans visit us here, so your presence is somewhat a novelty. However, I shall be unable to host you personally. I have business to tend to with the Lady Eve until she departs. Meanwhile, I grant you the freedom of Ednor. Do what you wish; we have many beautiful things to see and experience."

"Your Majesty," said Nyle, puzzled. "We have neither money nor the ability to speak in your tongue."

"I shall send an escort with you wherever you roam to act as a translator. Your expenses may be charged to my household."

Luke thanked her, his eyes wide.

Nyle bowed his head. Eve perceived his frown, though she did not remark upon it.

The queen left them near their chambers and with a quick, "good night," Eve slipped into her own and locked the door for the night, as Luke turned to speak to her. Nyle strode into his own room, leaving Luke dithering in the corridor.

He knocked on the door.

Her voice called from within. "Who is it?"

"Luke. May we talk?" he asked when she did not reply.

She paused—so long he probably thought her to be ignoring him—but the metal lock clicked open as she held the door ajar, peering out from behind it whilst she waited for him to speak. She had already unpinned her hair and it tumbled roughly over her shoulders.

"You looked beautiful tonight, my lady," he addressed her formally.

She coloured, unsure how to respond and hid behind a curtain of hair. "Thank you."

Luke cleared his throat. "How long are we to stay in Ednor?"

"I can't answer," Eve said. "There's much to be done."

Luke waited for her to expand upon her words. It was not forthcoming. "I see." He filled the silence. "Well, in that case, it's late, so I'll bid you good night." He smiled at her.

"Good night," she replied and hastily shut and bolted the door. *That was odd*, she thought, but it was late and she felt too tired to think at all. Soon, she was asleep as Ednor fell silent around her.

The following day, Eve sat in Artora's office. She had been given fresh clothes; a simple white shift with a blue kirtle, whilst Artora was once more clothed in pants and a shirt to Eve's admiration. She would have preferred similar attire, but the alternative was her stinking riding gear, which in any case had disappeared from her room the previous night.

"Thank you for joining me," said Artora, who rose to greet her. "I see no point in wasting time, as we are both unsure as to how long you will remain here. Firstly then, I shall tell you the history of the Eldarkind." She rested her forearms upon the back of her chair as she gazed over Eve's head.

"The world was created millions of years ago, although we do not know how it came to be. I know you humans have your deities; we, on the other hand, prefer to speculate," Artora began.

"Upon the earth lived the elementals; beings of pure magic. There were many. Fire and water, light and dark, air and earth, peace and war, love and hate, life and death all came together and thus the world was born. But, it was empty and barren. The elementals of fire put their warmth into the rocks so it would live and the elementals of water clothed its surface in waters so it would be nourished. The elementals of the earth put down soil so that things could grow and the elementals of air wrapped it all in sky so the planet could breathe. Light and dark came together to create a daily dance of sun and moon and spun the world around the sun to give it the changing seasons. Yet the world was still empty and barren.

"And so the elementals fashioned living beings to inhabit the world. The water was lonely, and so of the water they created all the sea life, to swim through its depths and please it. The earth was silent, and so they filled it with plants so it could resonate with their growth and life. The elementals combined all of their skills to make each of the species which inhabit the world in the air, on the earth, and in the water. However, each elemental wanted their special part to be represented best of all in the world and so they did not stop.

"Fire secretly created the dragons and gave his powers to them; they were fearsome, gigantic creatures who could breathe and control fire. Water created leviathans of the deep, so large they could consume any ship that sails the seas today and she gave them the freedom of the oceans. Air created the greatest of the giant birds who could truly explore her skies with their wings, and Earth made the insects and creatures that could burrow though his soil better than any other beings.

"No one knows who created the humans. But your kind multiplied, learned to talk, trade, coexist, and build societies. They worshipped the elementals as gods. They had the potential for great peace, but their prowess turned to war. It was clear that the planet would not survive under their dominion and the elementals despaired. And so it was agreed that Death would bestow his powers upon all life to limit man's dominion, or the rise and dominion of any other race subsequently. The elementals had given life to all the creatures across the entire world; Death gave them mortality so that their lives would be finite and in this he sacrificed himself utterly.

"The world became more balanced. Although the race of man still had the uppermost hand of all creatures, creatures coexisted after that in harmony." Artora shifted. Her gaze flicked to Eve, who listened, entranced.

"And so the elementals diminished," she continued, "to whence we know not. However, before their disappearance, for they did not want it to fail after so much of their efforts, they created a single race that could guard over all. In this race, they poured all of their honed skills.

"They made it a fair race with lives near immortal—for death could no longer take them into the void as easily as he once had done—and magic flowing through their veins so that they had the power to care for the world. In this race, the elementals instilled goodness so that they would never be tempted to ruin the world with their powers. It was thus that the Eldarkind came to be; it is said in the image of the elementals and using their language. We cared for the world and its creatures and kept the balance between all things as we still do now." At this, Eve's mouth fell open.

"Our powers have slowly declined since the pact we made with the dragons a thousand years ago. We are no longer immortal as we once were. There is a sickness in the world growing with time that even we cannot heal and our long lives wane and our powers fade as they drain to try to remedy it. Our kind has dwindled to a former shadow of what it once was.

"Nevertheless, I suppose compared to man we have lives that are far longer; several spans at least and we retain more than enough

magic. Petty human politics aside, that is the history of the world."
Artora observed Eve's face as the young woman tried to comprehend her words.

"So elementals and dragons are real?" she dared to ask, "And magic and mythical creatures?"

"Quite."

"What is the pact that you spoke of?" asked Eve. "Is that the reason your magic is fading?"

"No, it is not the reason our magic is fading. The diminishing of our powers is partly due to time. It has been so very long and magic has a tendency to spread itself about. Alas, we cannot keep it to ourselves it would seem!" The queen smiled at some inner joke, but the light upon her face faded. "There is a growing darkness in the world, so black that even we cannot fathom it with our magic and it seems to be causing our powers to wane faster than should be the case. We have noted a much quicker decline in recent generations. It is a great worry in our minds.

"Of mythical creatures, they are quite real and nearer than you may think. As humans spread throughout the land and across the seas, the leviathans of the deep that had become lonely and dumb and angry over the eons were not their friends. Many hundreds of men would die when the sea monsters rose to claim a ship—such a waste of life—and ere long we knew we had to act.

"We banished the sea monsters to the deeps. There they live now. Perhaps it was not our finest action. We were intended to be impartial to all of the species, but I fear our similarities with the humans, our weaker cousins, bred a sense of protectiveness we could not ignore.

"In a similar fashion, the dragons infringed on the human lands. As the humans grew their settlements, they took for their own livestock the animals they still farm now, sheep, cows, fowl, deer and so on. The humans also prospered financially, mining precious ores from the land and becoming skilled in fashioning works of great art and value from them.

"The dragons coveted their wealth and the tamed livestock that was effortless for them to hunt. Their coming was inevitable.

Soon, the humans found to their cost that here was an enemy they could not slay. Dragons have very few weak points in their hardened scales and they are most determined.

"Again, we aided the humans. We tried to persuade the dragons to return to their strongholds—fire mountains and hot deserts—as we had banished the sea beasts to theirs. Unlike the sea beasts however, the dragons were too clever and we were forced into a mutual agreement. They would leave the human territories if we would do the same.

"It was a difficult decision, but it seemed we had no option. The war was costly to all sides and even with our magic, we could not presume to defeat creatures also made from the very flesh of the elementals, especially those as wily as the dragons. They knew that.

"The solution, before we both tore each other's races to extinction, was to accept. We did this with one caveat; if the world was threatened, we would come together to protect it. Caledan's ruling line was created. The kings and queens were guarded with the magic of the Eldarkind and the power of the dragons, ready to awaken should the need arise. The Kingdom of Caledan was born and the Eldarkind and the dragons faded into legends and petty fairy tales, though we are both as present and real as ever."

"This is amazing," said Eve in hushed tones. "To think all these years of hearing about all those legends and stories that really live on. I wonder if I will ever see a dragon."

"Well, given the strife in the kingdom, which I will soon be forced to act upon as no doubt will they, there is every chance you will," remarked Artora, to Eve's great excitement.

Dragons!

Sixteen

The long night stretched before them as Soren and his companions cared for the injured. More slipped into the void and as dawn peered over the trees in a red haze, those tending to the sick wandered blank-eyed and increasingly quiescent. Hador beckoned to Edmund and Soren and drew them above ground. Seated amongst the wreckage of the monastery, they said little.

Hador eventually spoke, his voice weary. "You must leave," he said. "They or others may return to loot the place. You cannot be here if they do so, for we have no way to defend ourselves."

Soren and Edmund looked at each other. "Where are we to go?" mused Edmund.

"There's something I did not tell you," admitted Soren. He told Edmund of the abbot's dream, whilst Hador listened in silence.

Edmund was pensive and the pause lengthened. "So we must search for dragons then," he murmured wondrously. "What a pity he did not tell you where they are to be found."

"I believe he gave me a clue, whether he meant to or not; I think we must look to the east for the crown," Soren explained.

"I would agree with you," said Hador. His words surprised Soren. "The abbot recounted his dream to me and I inferred much the same conclusion."

Edmund pulled out his weather-worn map of Caledan and the surrounding lands, laying it upon an almost flat-topped boulder. Almost in the centre lay Pandora and to the north, their present location. He placed his finger upon that point and traced it eastwards.

"What of the Helm Mountains?" Edmund asked.

"I think not." Hador shook his head. "We would know if there were dragons hereabouts. Think of the stories at the very least;

livestock and child-stealing terrors of the night. There are no such tales."

Edmund continued his path across the map. "Then there are the open moors and wastes beneath the gap to the north and I think not much would choose to live there—too open, too bare. The Grey Mountains?"

Hador shook his head, though with less conviction. "Caledan's people live on both sides of those peaks and there are no reports of dragons there; I do not think they would remain so hidden. Think of the uproar there would be if they resided there! Perhaps once upon a time they did, but now I think not."

"Then there is just the sea," said Edmund. He traced his finger up and down the coast and squinted at the tiny writing that labelled the sparse towns and villages there.

"What about Kotyir?" Hador said.

Edmund found the point on his map. Far to the east and to the north lay an unobtrusive archipelago of islands, the Isles of Kotyir. They were unknown and unexplored; several tiny markings no bigger than a fingernail on the edge of the map as an afterthought.

"I know little of them," Edmund confessed.

"I may do," said Hador with a frown. "My hometown lays across the Grey Mountains, south of that region, though I know a little of them. Travellers from the north around those parts have a special name for those islands. They call them the Dragon Isles." Soren exclaimed, but Hador raised a hand to quiet him.

"Do not jump to that conclusion," Hador said, "for those are volcanic island that belch out fire and smoke and are dragons in themselves. Perhaps there is more to that name than ever I thought. Certainly no one dwells or travels near them."

"It is as good a lead as any we have as to where the crown may be." Soren tried to gauge Edmund's mood.

"You are not safe here, Soren," Edmund said. "If nothing else, the wilds are safe, in their own way."

Within hours they rode east through the forest. Hador sent them with blessings and provisions, and all those able to move came above ground to bid them farewell. Even those who had seemed so hostile to him in the days before seemed saddened to see him go, which puzzled Soren. He wondered whether it had been his efforts in helping their fallen that had caused their dislike to lessen.

Soren and Edmund spoke little as they rode, and the rhythmic drum of hooves lulled them into a tired stupor. Before long, the well-marked track disappeared and they rode through wide spaced trees in a light and airy part of the forest, keeping their bearing by the sun's place. The mountains to the north fell away in the distance, until had they flown above the forest, the entire world would have seemed to be an ocean of trees.

It was the following evening when the forest gave way to empty plains that stretched from the frozen tundra beyond the Helm Mountains to Pandora. The abbot's death had weighed on Soren's guilt-ridden shoulders during their ride. He was not sure how to broach the subject with Edmund.

A distance had grown between them in the silence of their ride, each man mulling over his troubled thoughts. As they sat in a small hollow at the edge of the forest, each with a back to a tree and the horses picketed nearby, dusk closed in around their still and silent forms.

"We must talk, Edmund."

Soren was almost invisible in the darkness. Edmund lit his lamp with a flint and some dry tinder. "Do not think I haven't noticed your worry. Talk with me."

"I cannot think what to say." Soren shook his head. He took a few moments to consider. Edmund did not press him to break the silence. "I watched the monastery being destroyed on Zaki's orders and it made me stop and think; how many people must die because of others?

"I suppose I began to question whether what I'm doing is right," Soren said in a low voice. "I feel guilty that the abbot and his men had to die so that I might live. What's the point of it all, Edmund? All this discord and fighting and pettiness—what's it all for? Why should others die for me?"

"You are our rightful king," replied Edmund as if the matter were that simple.

"And that justifies people dying for me? Being heir to the throne does not make me deserving of that, or even the throne."

"It is good you consider that, but do you think your uncle would be a better ruler than you?"

"That's what I can't decide." Soren looked away.

"You cannot consider that he would prove better!"

"And you would not consider it at all?" retorted Soren. They fell into silence for some minutes again. "Zaki aside, I have to consider my own fitness for the role. For all of my life I have been a prince who would someday become king, as surely as the sun rises each day. Yet I've never stopped to think about what that means.

"Being king means that I'll affect every person in this kingdom and perhaps beyond its borders; my choices will change lives perhaps or perhaps not for the better. My choices could kill people. They already have. I've stayed on this path because it's been my life and all I've known, but now it's all gone: my family, everything. Now, I only have myself left and I'm not sure who I am." The words came tumbling out as Edmund listened, barely moving.

"I cannot go back to that life. None of this can be erased. I don't know if I can live with the consequences of controlling other people's lives. Would I sacrifice another monastery full of good men for what I believe in? My conscience would not allow it. I have been frightened and grieving and confused, but this has made me realise that I cannot run from my choices and I will have to decide sooner or later whether this is worth it for the sake of those around me. If it is in the interest of the kingdom that I not pursue the throne, then I would honour that."

"What do you believe in?" Edmund questioned the prince, who took a deep breath before he replied.

"I'd like to believe peace in Caledan could be restored, so every man woman and child doesn't have to live in fear of Zaki. I'd like to believe I can make that peace," Soren added in a softer voice, "but I'm not sure if I can. I'm not sure if the cost is too high."

"They are just goals, Soren. No man is perfect," said Edmund. "But the value in him is that he always tries his best. If you were to take the throne and possess such power, would you?"

"Of course," replied Soren.

"Well, why should you not be a good ruler?" challenged his companion. "You want to do good things for the benefit of your people. Why would that make you anything less than the finest kings in your lineage?"

"What of my uncle?" asked Soren. "Surely he believes in his motives just as strongly as I do in mine?"

"Perhaps he does, but do you think they are as altruistic as yours? He covets the throne for his own gain, not for the good of the people whom he is supposed to protect. Moreover, what of your sister? Can you guarantee her safe conduct or even your own if you relinquish the throne to your uncle? Do not assume that someone other than you could and will step up to be a better ruler. The kingdom at present has two choices and no other: yourself, or Zaki.

"Besides the fact you are both of the royal bloodline and thus have the right, Zaki would not permit anyone else to rise so high; he would crush them before he saw them make a claim to the throne. So you must make the choice, not based on your merit compared to that of every other living person, but on your merit when placed beside your uncle. From his actions so far, and who you understand him to be as a person, do you think he will be the better ruler?"

"I had not considered it as such," murmured Soren, "with just he and I in contention. I can see the sense of your argument. No, I don't think he would make the better ruler. I cannot know if he would act in the best interest of others, after how he has already acted."

I really have no choice for now, Soren realised. *If I ever want to see my sister again; if I ever want to live without constant fear of my safety in exile; if I want to be sure that the kingdom is in the hands of one who will respect and protect it, then I have no choice. It has to be me.*

"So you will pursue the throne, whatever the cost?" asked Edmund.

"I will," said Soren, after a moment's hesitation. He felt

strangely calm and sure of himself for the first time. "I don't want anyone else to die for me, yet Zaki must be brought to justice for what he has done and I cannot let him claim the throne for fear of what he may do. I could not abandon my sister and flee like a coward in any case; I have to try for her sake." He frowned, but Edmund's smile was radiant.

"You have grown much more in this time than I would have thought possible, Soren. You already have the makings of a great king," Edmund said proudly, to Soren's surprise and pleasure.

"I am most happy I have your confidence and support," Soren replied. "I fear I'll need many more like you before I'm to confront Zaki with any hope of success." *I have no idea where to find such allies. I pray they materialise. I can imagine Zaki's amusement if I rode up to the gates of Pandora alone and bedraggled on my horse. He would surely laugh at me before he killed me.*

"We may find support where we least expect it," said Edmund, who must have sensed his concern, "so do not despair quite yet."

The atmosphere between them disintegrated. The niggling doubt that had occupied his mind since their flight from Pandora had vanished at last.

SEVENTEEN

It was a bitter return to Pandora. Zaki clattered through deserted late evening streets in a foul mood, driving his exhausted horse as his company straggled far behind him. He reached the citadel alone, abandoned his mount in the courtyard, and stormed into the castle, scattering surprised servants with orders to summon the council.

As he awaited them in the council chamber, dirty and travel-stained, his mood brewed further discontent until they finally assembled about the vast table.

"How do preparations for my coronation proceed?" Zaki asked Behan. He needed some good news to cool his rage.

"Very well, Your Royal Highness," Behan replied. "It will be held two days hence, if that is agreeable. We await the final arrangements."

"It will be a grand affair?"

"Naturally, sir," Master Treasurer Lord Asquith cut in. "The coffers have been replenished with the seizure of traitors' assets, so it will be magnificent."

"Good," replied Zaki, ever curt. He drummed his fingers on the table. "You will need to source me the finest crown in the vaults, Lord Steward, and organise for the archbishop to conduct the ceremony." He rose to leave but could not miss the shared look between Behan and Lord Heligan across the table from him. "Do you have an opinion to share on that?" His eyes narrowed.

Behan coloured. "No, sir. I merely wondered if the absence of the ceremonial crown will be a setback. Historically..."

"History is in the past," Zaki said through gritted teeth, "and will bear no reflection on my reign. A crown is a crown and the finest we have will be more than adequate."

114

"As you wish, sir," Behan replied. Zaki had already left without a backwards glance.

The council exchanged nervous glances.

"Are we missing something?" Asquith looked quizzically at Reynard, who exhaled in resignation.

"He did not retrieve the ceremonial crown from the monastery. The boy, Soren… We heard rumours that he sheltered there, yet we turned over every single stone and found not one trace of him or the crown. Needless to say, Zaki is not well pleased."

"Why does the abbot not come to conduct the coronation as he usually is wont to do?" Behan asked.

Reynard regarded him with a calculating look—there was no love lost between the two men—before he answered to the room at large. "The abbot is dead."

The archbishop stood with his back towards the congregation as he watched Zaki climb onto the dais with slow, measured paces. Zaki arrived before the looming stone figure of the dragon. It crouched over the throne, hiding it from view beneath the impenetrable sweep of its frozen wings.

A deep silence filled the vaulted space as the watching crowd collectively held its breath and waited. And waited. And waited. Nothing happened. The dragon did not so much as twitch.

Zaki beckoned the archbishop forward with a sharp gesture. He hurried to obey and climbed onto the dais with as much grace as he could muster. Pages scrambled after him, far less graceful under the weight of their burdens. The archbishop, beads of sweat beginning to roll down his anxious face, swept the grand purple mantle of kingship around Zaki's shoulders with a flourish and fastened it with the golden clasp.

Fur lining trailed upon the floor and stroked Zaki's neck as he began to feel uncomfortably warm. He looked into the crowd—a blinding sea of upturned faces—until Demara caught his gaze from the front row. She smiled at him, in her usual cold way, but his face seemed to have frozen and would not respond.

The archbishop knelt at Zaki's feet to offer him the royal ceremonial sword, the honour and chivalry of Caledan, which Zaki accepted. He then received the golden sceptre that denoted his right to rule, which was set with a fist-sized gleaming diamond said to represent truth and integrity.

The archbishop charged him to rule in line with the law and Zaki repeated the promises of kingship to those waiting, whilst the dragon throne stood cold and dark behind him. He knelt at the archbishop's feet as the final page approached, bearing the last plump velvet cushion upon which balanced the finest crown contained within the royal vaults.

A slight murmur arose as the silken cover concealing the crown fluttered to the ground, revealing it for the first time. Golden, set with precious metals and jewels, it was magnificent—and yet unexpected. It would be obvious to all that this was not the Crown of the Dragon Kings, the crown that had been passed from generation to generation for a thousand years. Silence fell as he rose to his feet.

"I present to you on this joyous day His Majesty King Zaki of Caledan, first of his name!" shouted the archbishop to the congregation. "Long live the king!"

"Long live the king!" the crowd obediently roared back. Cheers broke from outside, the chant taken up and repeated throughout the city, however in the cathedral silence fell once more as those gathered waited for the throne to accept the new king. Zaki met Demara's gaze again and she smiled at him encouragingly.

He turned, bowed on bended knee to the stone dragon and held himself low. His eyes opened, confused. He rose and stood. His hands shook. The dragon loomed before him. The throne was still lost to him under the protective cage of its wings. It remained unmoving.

Whispers and then murmurs began to rise from the crowd, silenced when he turned to face them. The realisation dawned. The throne had refused him. He could not begin to contemplate what this could mean, not at this moment. He stepped forward.

"I need no grand throne," he proclaimed far more bravely than he felt. "A simple chair will suffice." He called forward the archbishop. "Fetch me a damn chair," he hissed, "and have them pay allegiance to me!" The archbishop hastened to comply and he was seated within seconds, his mantle draped around him.

First of all came Demara, who knelt at his feet to kiss his hands and swear allegiance to him. A trailing line of his noble subjects followed her as Zaki locked a smile upon his face and suppressed his growing doubts.

The cheering had subsided when Demara left the cathedral and the atmosphere felt less than jubilant. The people did not clap or call to her as she passed, as she would have expected; as they would have done for her in Roher. Instead, they watched her and spoke in hushed tones.

Demara hurried into the first of the waiting open-topped carriages, helped up by her two ever present maids, who adjusted her dress and fur-lined cloak as she perched upon the cushioned seats. Trying not to shiver—the day seemed cold and the breeze brisk— Demara sat erect and poised.

She smiled to the crowd and waved gracefully to them as the carriage set off to return to the palace, puzzled when the crowd did not respond with enthusiasm. "I do not understand. What has happened?" she asked her maids through her gleaming smile.

Her maids did not reply. They sat demure and quiet opposite her.

"I see that something is not right. I command you to tell me what it is," Demara said.

"If it please you, ma'am." Joslyn leaned across to speak to her. "The coronation wasn't exactly as expected. Not very traditional," she tried to explain as Demara ceased waving to the crowd and fixed her eyes upon the maid. "The people will wonder that the abbot of the northern monastery didn't conduct the ceremony as he ought to and they will wonder why Pri— King Zaki doesn't wear the Crown of the Dragon Kings, but, ma'am, please forgive me, I only say what they'll be saying…" She trailed off.

"Tell me." Demara glared.

"The dragon throne should have accepted him." Joslyn rushed. "There's a throne hid under the wings of that stone dragon. It's magic! No one knows how it happens. The dragon's still for years and years, but when the king or queen dies, it moves and covers up the throne. When the new king or queen gets crowned, the stone dragon's supposed to move and allow them to sit the throne. But this time, it didn't."

"What does this mean?" She didn't understand the girl's garbled story but Joslyn's words at least confirmed her fear that something untoward had occurred.

"It might mean nothing, ma'am, it's just that people are superstitious and think it might be bad luck," Joslyn replied. "I'm sorry if I worried you, ma'am."

The carriage jerked to a halt outside the castle. Demara disembarked and withdrew to her quarters. "I do not require your services anymore today," she said as brightly as she could to Joslyn, who curtsied and left. She held up a hand to stay Seline as she made to leave.

"Not you, Seline. I need you." Demara slowly lowered herself onto a cushioned chair and stared out of the window.

"Are you well, my lady?" asked Seline.

"I do not know," replied Demara, downcast. "I know that you will understand me, Seline, as no one else here will. I miss our homeland. These Caledonians and their ways are so strange sometimes. I worry I will never belong here."

"Hush, my lady, do not worry yourself with these things," Seline said. She smiled at Demara as she sat at her feet. "You are the new Queen of Caledan; surely that is wonderful! No one should make you feel unworthy, for you are greater than them all."

Demara smiled faintly. "Queen. I never expected to be queen; the third daughter of a king. It does not feel quite real, I must confess, though perhaps it will when I am crowned on the morrow. I cannot see that the people will receive me well though, given the reception they have shown my husband. I worry we are not secure." Seline tried to soothe her but Demara silenced her with a wave. "I worry about everything now I am with child. I wish I were home."

"I wish that too, my lady," Seline admitted quietly. "It is cold here and unfriendly. I miss the warm sun and the long days of Roher with all my heart." They both fell silent, remembering their homeland. "Will you journey there for the birth?" Seline asked.

Demara frowned. "I know not. I suppose my child will be the heir to Caledan's throne. I am not sure if I would be allowed to leave. Perhaps I could return for a while afterwards. I have not seen my home since before I married. I know this should be my home now, but I do not belong with these people. I do not trust them." She rubbed her stomach. The growing bump was solid beneath her hands. "Will you summon Tomas for me?" she asked Seline.

"Ambassador Delgado? Of course, my lady," Seline scrambled to her feet.

Within the hour she returned, out of breath and red-faced. "He comes now, my lady."

"Thank you, Seline." Demara favoured the girl with a smile. "Send away my other ladies. I tire of them. I wish for just your company tonight."

"Of course, my lady." Seline bobbed and left as the Roherii ambassador Ser Tomas Delgado entered.

"Your Majesty." Tomas bowed low to her.

"Come, Tomas, I am ever who I was." She beckoned him forward to sit beside her, whilst she shared her worries.

"I have come from the coronation procession just now, my lady, and I see no reason why you should be concerned," Tomas said. "The crowd seemed eager to see their new king and he has made sure to guard the city well; there were many soldiers to line the route and keep the peace."

"I worry that I am not safe here, nor my child, because the coronation did not proceed as it ought to have done," she replied.

"If you seek my opinion, my lady, I would counsel you to remain positive, especially in light of your present condition. Do not overtax yourself. I will keep you informed if there is anything to be concerned by, so you can assume that if you hear nought from me that all is well."

"Thank you, Tomas." Demara smiled at him to conceal the worry which had not dissipated with his words. "I am sure you are right."

"Your Majesty, Lord Asquith seeks you."

Zaki waved the man away. The messenger scuttled out backwards, almost tripping at the door when he bowed.

"I must leave. We ride to meet your father, who is to return to oversee the smooth transition to my rule." Zaki turned back to his wife.

Demara sat in the chair opposite as usual. He could see she was weary—the pregnancy had taken its toll on her. Dark circles hung under her eyes and she slouched in the chair. *A most unladylike queen.* He did not mind, as long as she gave him a son.

"When will you return, husband? I am almost due."

"Beforehand. We will be some weeks. Do not tax yourself. My son must be healthy." He bid her a brisk farewell and left. Asquith awaited him outside.

"Your Majesty." Asquith bowed. "You summoned me?"

"We must accelerate our plans." Zaki wasted no time. "I am no fool. The coronation was a shambles. I need to reinforce my rule swiftly to ensure success. Harad already rides for Pandora, but we must ride to intercept him and impress this urgency upon him. Reynard will ride with me. You must manage affairs here in my absence. I expect all to go smoothly."

"Sire." Asquith bowed again, smooth as ever.

Zaki left with haste at the head of a great host, unannounced. It would take him weeks to reach Caledan's border and return, and he could afford no diversions.

EIGHTEEN

"What else can you tell me?" Eve asked, leaning forwards.

"Perhaps now would be the time to give you a brief insight into magic?" Artora offered, to Eve's instant agreement.

They stepped through double doors into the garden and wandered towards the mountains. Eve squinted at her surroundings as her eyes adjusted to the bright sunlight.

"Magic in Caledan is not well known and deemed not to exist by most of the population as no more than a fairytale," Artora said. "As our most powerful weapon, it is a secret of the highest order. Although there are tales of our magical abilities, they are deemed to be as fanciful as the existence of dragons due to the fact we have been hidden from the world for so very long.

"Magic itself can be described as the manipulation of pure energy that can be performed by will. It takes practice to master but can be used in complex ways and on a vast scale. Energy is not used up by magic use; it complies with the laws of matter and transforms from one form to another. Fundamentally, nothing is gained or lost and an overall equilibrium is maintained."

In her hands, a ball of water coalesced from nothing. In the blink of an eye, it turned to fire, and then to earth, and then to light, before dissipating. Eve's mouth fell open. Artora smiled.

"Magic is not straightforward to use nor accessible by anyone; only the Eldarkind were given such powers and so only those with some remnant of our blood flowing through their veins will be able to use magic. For example, the monarchy contains our blood to some degree through intermarrying in the earlier days and every now and then, a member of the bloodline will express some proficiency with magic, although for the most part it is a dormant skill. Mortals in the population with diluted forms of our bloodline can also

121

express magic to some small degree.

"It is possible, although much rarer, for any other unrelated being to use magic. It is unclear how they are able to do so. Such gifts of power appear to occur randomly and spontaneously and thankfully their powers are weak so they cannot do much harm if their skills emerge. If they have great skills, we find and train them personally," she explained.

"Most ordinary folk with such affinities to magic tend to find themselves as very proficient healers, carers, and craftspeople. You, though, should be capable of using magic—" she glanced at Eve, "—because you are a daughter of the Eldarkind. The blood should flow almost as strongly through you as it did in your mother and if your looks are anything to go by, I would think there is a very strong likelihood that you also have her powers."

Eve listened, enthralled. They wandered away from the garden and across the meadows, climbing towards the wooded slopes.

"So, I have described to you what magic is and who may use it, but I have not described how to use it. It is an odd thing to describe. Magic can be felt in the mind like a stream of raw energy, ever present, laying dormant. It can be sensed most keenly at times of high passion—anger, joy, sadness, fear and so on.

"The stream of energy is accessed, controlled, and directed simultaneously by its own language and thought, so that one may not think or speak something separately and invoke magic. Instead, most magic users must speak and have focused thought for a manipulation of energy to occur.

"In rare cases without great training, and also in childhood, magic can be used without words in situations of stress. It is possible for highly trained and skilled magic users to mentally speak, rather than physically, and still have the same desired effect; however, this is something that takes enormous levels of practice to undertake successfully.

"The language of magic is the language the elementals left the Eldarkind and so we speak with their tongue to heal the world around us. This language is one that describes the true name for each object in the world and this is how it is able to link the manipulation of anything to one's desire.

"The Eldar tongue is innately known from birth, but is awoken at a later stage, anywhere from childhood to adulthood, depending on the circumstances. It will sleep until awakened and could indeed never awaken in a person.

"Although the Eldarkind speak this language as their mother tongue, until one awakens in the magical sense and is able to reach out to the stream of energy, the language is dead on their tongue and merely a form of speech. We must also be careful, once we do awaken magically, to speak this language without directed thought unless we intend to use magic. Otherwise, this can result in unfortunate consequences if magic is used accidentally! This is something we all learn to control when we come into our skills. Perhaps this would be easier for you as your mother tongue is not the Eldar tongue.

"The Eldar tongue itself allows communication between us and all other species excepting humans, who do not understand it because they have already evolved their own complex languages. Even though the dragons are much more intelligent than other creatures in general, they are also able to understand the language and this is their primary tongue when they choose to communicate with words, which occurs in dragon to Eldarkind communication, rather than with images or sounds, which occurs in communication between dragons. They can speak in the human tongue also, although we are not sure how.

"Speakers of the Eldar tongue on a basic level are able to gauge animal emotions and on a higher level communicate in a detailed fashion, although the animals are unable to speak to us in return and instead use their usual forms of verbal and nonverbal communication, which users of the language can recognise and decode with practice.

"Magic is not a plaything, though. Although it opens up to us a great world of possibilities and allows us to reach out to any living being, magic is not something to use carelessly. Sustained magic use is limited by concentration, willpower, and mental and physical strength. No task greater than one's own strength should be attempted.

"The manipulation of energy requires your own body's life and strength to control, until you are skilled enough to successfully and subtly extract such energy from the surrounding environment to fuel your intentions. This dissuades from foolish spell casting, as you cannot use more energy than you possess to cast a spell. If you did, your very life force and physical form would be burnt up to feed the spell, which ends when it is completed, or the energy source from the magic user has completely run out.

"Magic is limited also by the knowledge of language in that particular tongue. Of course this is not an issue for Eldarkind where this is the spoken tongue and it is so innate in the strength of our blood, but it is a limitation in more diluted forms in the general population, whose innate knowledge is incomplete and warped. It is worthy to note that use of the language and directed thought by non-magical individuals produces no magical effects; they cannot access the energy stream to facilitate it."

"So you can do anything you want?" asked Eve.

"Theoretically, yes, although only the elementals possessed vast enough strength to be nearly limitless in their powers. Not even we possess either infinite knowledge or strength, even as a collective," Artora said.

Eve was silent for a while, trying to digest all she had heard, whilst Artora observed her. "You said that it is likely I am able to use magic. Are you sure?"

Artora dipped her head in silent confirmation.

"But I don't feel anything. This energy you spoke of, I don't feel it. And when I heard your people speaking in their language, it made no sense; I understood none of it. Surely that means it is not possible?"

Artora shook her head. "Eve, the signs point to your abilities and I would be astounded if your powers never awoke. It is often the case that magic does not awaken until adulthood and I believe it lays dormant within you. One moment you will be as you are and the next, it will be as if you have awoken in a new life. Perhaps you are not ready to awaken or have not met the event which is destined to awaken your powers." She saw Eve's dismayed face.

"Eve, remember what I said yesterday evening. Magic, or any other skill for that matter, does not make you evil unless you choose to use it thusly. It is a great gift, and I am confident that when the time comes, you will bear it with the appropriate sensibility."

"Perhaps I can accept that," said Eve. She bit her lip. "Does this mean I am some kind of immortal? I don't want to have to live forever if all those around me will fade."

"Alas, that I do not know and cannot guarantee," admitted Artora. "Given past precedents, one who is half-human and half-Eldarkind usually has a lifespan not quite as long as ours, but far longer than that of a human."

At that, Eve was silent.

"It is hard as an outsider to come to terms with the possibility of a life longer than those you love and it is not something you should be expected to reconcile with, especially at your young age. I would suggest you think as little of it as you can. You have many other things to consider before your lifespan becomes something to worry yourself with."

Eve still felt unease. Her excitement had been tempered by her own unknown fate. Artora had evidently decided that for the moment, Eve had enough to contemplate. It was nearing lunchtime and so she sent Eve out to dine in the gardens. Eve returned feeling calmer than before, though no less of an enigma. Basking in the sun and admiring the scenery had lulled her unsettled emotions.

"You didn't seem surprised at all when I passed you the letter from my father yesterday," Eve thought aloud. "Why is that?"

"I already knew," said Artora.

"Magic?"

"Yes."

"How?"

Artora rose from her chair to pick up a flat, round object that had been resting on one of her many shelves. She placed it gently on the table, and Eve could see it was in fact a finely crafted mirror with a border inset with white pearls. She peered at Artora in confusion. Artora gestured for her to stand.

"Look into the mirror, Eve. *Leitha Karn,*" Artora said.

Eve gasped as the silvered surface of the mirror, which had reflected the pale ceiling, plunged into the blackest colour. The dark swirled with deep greys and the mirror cleared sluggishly to reveal Eve's father writing at his desk. His face was not visible.

"Father!" Eve exclaimed. "How did you do that?"

"I used the words of power, words from our language, to seek a vision of your father as he is now in the mirror. This is how I watch the kingdoms without ever having to break the pact with the dragons by leaving my land. The word '*leitha*' is to scry, or to see far. Use of a flat, reflective surface helps fix the image one wishes to see. *Lessa,*" Artora murmured. The mirror faded back to silver, reflecting the ceiling once more.

"That's amazing. Can you use this to see anything anywhere?" asked Eve.

"Within reason," replied Artora. "You must know what you wish to seek. I could not scry a person I did not know existed in Arlyn, for example. However, if I wished to scry Arlyn itself, I would be able to see both the buildings and the people that moved through it, depending on where in the place I was looking. I might see a particular person and not knowing their name, would be able to them scry them afterwards, by picturing them very clearly in my head and directing the magic as I have just demonstrated."

"Can you scry Queen Naisa?" asked Eve, with a sudden stroke of inspiration.

"No!" Artora replied sharply. "It is impossible. It has been tried before to scry the deceased, but the veil of death masks the mirror and will not relinquish a vision. Do not ever try to interfere with the dead, should you come into magic, Eve," Artora warned, "for it is a folly that will end in your own demise. The void between this world and the next is so great that your life force would be extinguished in the fleetest of moments in the attempt to bridge it. Promise me you will never attempt it!"

"I promise," Eve said, taken aback.

The queen relaxed and picked up the mirror.

"Wait!" Eve said. "Will you scry Prince Soren?"

"Why?" Artora's eyes narrowed.

"I long to see if he is well, and Princess Irumae too. They are my cousins and had I not been bound to come here, I would have been determined to find Soren. Please, will you show me if he is alive?"

"Very well," said the queen after a pause. "*Leitha Soren!*"

The mirror's surface flooded with black, as before, and cleared. They could see Soren riding on horseback along a rutted, earthy track as leafy green trees raced past. Another horse galloped beside him, with Edmund on his back.

From what could be seen of their faces, they both had a determined air, but when Eve caught a glimpse into her cousin's eyes, she shivered. She saw a strange steely glint that had never been there before; a testament to his recent trials. Nevertheless, to all intents and purposes, he was alive and Edmund once more with him.

"*Lessa.*"

"I wonder where they journey to," Eve said.

"I have my suspicions," Artora remarked, "though I may not share them with you. He will have a great task at hand if he is to reclaim the throne. Take heart; he is alive and Edmund is with him."

"You know Edmund?" said Eve with raised eyebrows.

"Quite well. There is much that you will not know of Sir Edmund." Artora smiled. "He has visited my realm many times across the years, with news from Pandora. In any case, it is too late to follow them instead of returning home, if that was your intention."

Eve blushed. "I had thought of going to find them. I'm reluctant to return home when I feel like there's something I could be doing to help. I don't know if I'm quite ready to face my father again, either. There's so much that he hasn't told me and I want to make sense of it all before we meet again."

"As I have offered before, you are quite welcome to stay for as long as you wish."

"I appreciate your generosity," said Eve delicately. "Yet, I feel like there's still something I should be doing. I could not stay and languish in good conscience. Are you sure you cannot tell me where the prince is going? What of Irumae? Are they going to find her?"

Artora paused. "I cannot tell you the prince's destination, but no, they do not go to the aid of the princess, at least not yet." Eve opened her mouth to speak, but Artora had already guessed her intentions. "*Leitha Irumae.*"

The blackness this time seemed slower to clear. Eve realised it was because the vision showed a small, darkened room, lit by candles. It seemed to be windowless and constructed of stone, but was furnished well, with a rug on the floor and some comfortable looking furniture.

On a bed in one corner lay the princess, fully dressed. She was motionless with closed eyes. Her pale, vacant face was young and vulnerable in the sickly light.

"She has been this way in this place for many days," said Artora. "I have not seen her awaken, however we can be sure she is alive simply for the reason I can scry her at all."

"I have to help her," said Eve.

"Are you sure that is wise?" Artora raised an eyebrow.

"Probably not," Eve admitted, "but I want to help. How can I stay here or return home in good conscience? Perhaps she is hurt, or injured, and perhaps she is in danger. I would feel far too guilty knowing I might have had the chance to help her and chose not to."

Artora sighed. "I fear this may be your purpose, cousin. I would council against going alone, however. Are you to consult your father on this and request an escort?"

"No," said Eve. "He would not let me go at all, let alone lend me more men. I do not want to give him the chance to stop me. I am an adult now, free to make my own decisions and this is what I decide. He will have to realise sooner or later that he cannot always keep me safe at home."

Artora regarded her for a moment, as if measuring her up for the task. "Are you to return your two guards to him or take them with you?" asked Artora. "You are welcome to take some of my own with you should you wish."

"I'm not sure," replied Eve. "There is something about Nyle which unsettles me. Since he discovered my mother was one of the

Eldarkind, I do not feel I can trust him anymore. As for Luke...I am fairly sure I can rely on him."

"Well, perhaps Luke should accompany you," suggested Artora. "I am sure a guard of Arlyn will work in your favour. As for Nyle, he can take my news to your father. I shall send two of my own guard with you, if that is agreeable? Four will travel inconspicuously and I am sure you shall have need of my guards' skills."

"Yes, I would like that. It would give me a chance to learn much more about your people." Eve smiled. She felt content, as though the piece of a puzzle had fitted into place and revealed more of her purpose to her. It outweighed the niggling guilt that arose from becoming distracted from her original task.

"They are your people too," Artora reminded her. "In that case, the necessary arrangements shall be made and you may depart the day after tomorrow."

NINETEEN

Over the coming days, Soren and Edmund rode over vast uninhabited plains so open and wide that they felt simultaneously exposed yet insignificant. There were no hills or mountains on the horizon for days. Impressive roiling cloud structures rose overhead in nature's imitation of a cathedral and the dull, seething atmosphere made the landscape all the more imposing.

Although the plains should have been deserted, they lit no fires at night just in case. Despite it being somewhat windy, the weather remained warm enough to endure each night without proper shelter, other than small hollows in the ground, where they could find them. Before sleeping each night, they clashed in quick bouts of sword practice to warm themselves up and relieve aching muscles.

Without a fire, they had to make do with cold meals and ration the small amount of food. Along with food, Hador had given them each a crossbow with a pouch full of bolts to use both in defence and as a tool for hunting, but the plains were of any kind of animal to hunt and supplement their meals. Only birds, flying well above their range, wheeled over the plains in great swoops.

At last, after rising early on successive mornings and riding until late, they spied a smudge on the horizon which did not move with the clouds and solidified into a dark band of mountains marching down from the north. It took them a further day to ride within reach of the foothills, until at last the plains yielded to forests.

The trees seemed all the more oppressive around them after days in the endless space. However, with the forest, life also returned and Edmund soon shot a rabbit with his crossbow. As he tied the body to his saddlebag, he grinned at Soren; the forest and the rabbit meant they could have a fire and hot meal that night.

The rabbit meat stewed in their small cooking pot, bubbling away as it boiled whilst the stream they were camped beside babbled back at it. Edmund and Soren pored over their map as Edmund calculated their rough position.

"There is no road from here to the coast unfortunately, although it means there is very little chance of us meeting anyone we would rather not, which is advantageous," remarked Edmund. "We will have to cut through the mountains."

"Where are we heading?" asked Soren. He scanned the map of the coast for the various towns along its length.

"Harring." Edmund pointed out a small dot on the map where east Caledan met the sea. "It's a small town and the nearest large dwelling to the Isles of Kotyir in any case. Mostly it's fishermen who live there, though a couple of lesser noblemen have estates in this region too.

"This coast, for all its wild weather and relative remoteness from the rest of the kingdom, receives many visitors and tradesmen for the quality of its catches. There is superstition regarding dragons if we are to trust Hador's advice, which could be truer than they know. This is the nearest we will travel on land, so we could hire a small boat to take us the rest of the way."

Soren studied the map with intrigue. He had never journeyed to the other side of the coastal mountains. A thin strip of land separated mountains from the sea. On the other side, the weather was colder and the sea both freezing and fierce at this latitude. A strange quirk in geology brought together the freezing sea with a chain of volcanic islands that had risen from the depths of the sea to above its surface over many thousands of years.

Tales had been passed down from generation to generation about strange fire-breathing mountains that could form new rocky land from glowing hot molten lava, spew out black clouds high enough to be seen for many miles, and create great and treacherous mists over the sea where many a fisherman had sailed out never to return home.

Even stranger tales were told locally of the elusive and spectral flying beasts that had allegedly been sighted from a distance several times over the years flying around the islands that came inland with the mist to steal livestock and naughty children. As a rule, the islands were avoided wherever possible, but nearby inhabitants were reluctant to move too much further away because of the uncommonly good fish stocks there.

Soren had heard the tales once or twice as a child. With an amused smile, he realised that all along, those tales could be related to the dragons he had so hoped to happen upon as a child. *I wonder what they are like to meet in person. I wonder if they look like Brithilca.* He pictured the statue once more. He began to daydream as he had when he was a boy about what it would be like to meet a strange being like a dragon, but gave it up as he realised how very little he knew of them.

I only know of them what people have made up in books and pictures. In reality, they could be nothing alike. He found that exciting, yet at the same time disconcerting; he had no idea what he was getting himself into.

A sharp rap of wood on metal startled him out of his reverie, but it was Edmund, who put down the wooden spoon he had been using to stir the contents of the pot. They had a quiet meal and savoured the hot, meaty broth with special appreciation.

"A feast fit for a king." Edmund smacked his lips in satisfaction afterwards.

"Or a king-to-be, perhaps." Soren laughed and Edmund chuckled.

"That will have to do for this fine fare for the moment, I suppose."

Satisfied, they fell into slumber as the small fire died and the stream rushed past. It was not until mid-morning that they awoke.

"Damn it!" Edmund cursed. "We're late! I had hoped to be back in the saddle at dawn. That rabbit stew kept me content enough to sleep half the day away!" He kicked a stone to vent his bad temper.

"It's not that desperate, is it?" Soren half-opened his eyes and ruffled his tangled hair as he sat up.

"Not that desperate?" said Edmund. "Well, if you call being on the run from a madman and on our way to find a clan of dragons 'not that desperate,' then perhaps we ought to go back to sleep?"

"I take it back." Soren yawned. "We can still make good progress today, can't we?"

"Yes, though not as much as I had hoped."

That day, they travelled through a valley which carved the thin mountain range almost in two. High peaks towered on either side. It was barren with a rough gravelly base and a thin line of trees that separated the valley bottom from the bare grey rocks which soared up and out of sight. As they rose to the valley's end, they forded the river that had made it. Soren noted with surprise the icy coolness of the water despite it being summer.

"It's so cold!" he exclaimed to Edmund above the noise of running water and the horse hooves clattering on the loose gravel.

"It's fresh melt water from the glaciers," called Edmund. "They are so high they remain frozen all year!"

They must be high indeed, Soren realised. *I hope one day I am at leisure to explore. For all my freedoms, I have spent far too much time in the city.*

As they pressed on, mounting a small summit, the land fell away before them and gave a view all the way to the coast. Although the weather was overcast, the steely grey-blue waters in the distance stretching to the murky horizon were impressive. Edmund allowed Soren a minute's appreciation of the view before he urged him on.

"Come," he encouraged. "We need to be out of the mountains by sunset and we only have a few hours remaining of good light."

They had less time than Edmund anticipated. As they followed a rocky valley even barer than the last, the skies which had darkened since they began their descent started to drizzle and then rain until Edmund, Soren, and their horses were soaked.

When they had descended almost to sea level, the mountains fell away to either side and revealed faint lights in the distance that Edmund confirmed to be Harring. Shivering and teeth chattering, Edmund had never been as glad to see such a miserable looking place.

There was nowhere adequate to shelter overnight and so

Edmund led them into Harring. It was a muddled cluster of buildings, so dismal in the rain and dark that Edmund suspected even sunshine could not brighten it up. Harring had two inns but a small lamp caught their attention before they could decide which one to enter.

Its light shone on a damp notice pinned to a board and to their dismay, it depicted a very good likeness of both Edmund and Soren, with a huge reward for their capture. Edmund's relief at the prospect of a dry place to sleep vanished. Fear flashed through him.

"What are we to do?" asked Soren in a low voice. "We cannot stay here; we'll be recognised."

"I am not sure," replied Edmund. "I did not think Zaki would resort to this." *He is more thorough than I anticipated.* "However, we have both grown rather unkempt since we left and can pass for others against these pictures; our hair is shaggy, my beard is unkempt, and even you have some stubble. Our clothes are in a foul state and even our fine horses look less than noble."

Soren cast a glance over the horses. They were more muddy than him, but there wasn't much in it. He was glad the wilds had no mirrors. He did not want to see the state of his face. "Surely the risk is too great, but, if we do not stay here, where will we go?"

Edmund hesitated. *We could camp outside the town.* He dismissed the idea; there was little shelter to be found and no woods marked on the maps that could hide them. "I cannot tell whether this is foolish. With your consent, we shall stay the night."

The prince thought for a moment before agreeing.

"It will do us better to be warm and fed for a night, and the horses also, given what we are to attempt next. We shall risk it." Edmund suppressed his relief at Soren's response. *You're growing soft in your old age, old man,* he chastised himself, hoping he had not made a mistake.

They trotted to the nearest inn, preparing a plausible story as to who they were in muttered tones in case anyone thought to question them. After tethering the horses in the stables and untying the saddlebags to take with them, Edmund flipped a small coin at the taciturn stable-hand and requested him to unsaddle and groom the horses. He scowled at them as they walked into the inn and made no move to fulfil their requests. His eyes followed them to the door. Riding cloaks concealed their swords but were unable to hide the bows strapped to their backs.

The inside of 'The Anchor' was dingy, dull, and thoroughly unwelcoming. Nevertheless, Edmund still felt relieved to be out of the rain. A small, smoky fire burned in a damp grate and the air was unpleasant with the smell of it. Edmund and Soren shared a glance of mutual dislike and resignation at their first impression of the place as they stepped over the threshold.

It seemed that despite the early hour of the night, the locals also found it an unlikeable place, for there were only two other men sat in the yawning shadows that pooled around the inadequate lamps spotted around the room. Their gleaming eyes tracked Soren and Edmund. Soren averted his eyes and followed Edmund to the bar. The barman glanced disinterestedly at them, not offering a greeting.

"Good evening," said Edmund. After a few moments of silence from the man, he continued. "I wonder if we might seek a room for the night? My servant and I are traveling through the area and would appreciate a meal and a bed tonight."

The man sniffed loudly and replied. "Fine. Have you got horses stabled too?" As Edmund nodded, he continued. "That will cost you extra."

"How much?" asked Edmund.

The barman chewed the inside of his cheek. "Two coppers for each horse and a silver for you and the boy," he said, with a grimly gleeful smile at the inflated price.

Edmund's mouth thinned in disapproval but he counted out the coins on the bar with no word of a protest. The barkeep eagerly raised his hand. Before he could sweep the coins into his grimy apron, Edmund stopped him.

"For that extortionate price, we want meals both now and for breakfast," Edmund insisted, "and I want some meat with that too."

The barman scowled but assented and Edmund smiled, satisfied as the coins tumbled into the depths of the man's apron pockets. As they turned to sit at a table, the barman stomped off into the kitchen. The door slammed behind him. Dust fell from the beams.

"Well, we haven't been recognised," Soren mouthed.

"Ssh. May it stay that way." Edmund evaluated the two other inhabitants of the room, who regarded them with open interest.

They ate the lukewarm fare brought to them a long while later by the barman, but they were glad for it. A broth, with unnamed chunks of meat floating in it, was better than nothing. As soon as they finished, they retired to their room still under the scrutiny of the two men. Edmund latched and locked the door, then barred it with a chair as well for good measure.

The room had a double bed, if it could be called such, since it was nothing more than a wooden base with a lumpy straw mattress. A thin, patched blanket lay on top. Other than that, the room was bare. Lit by one lamp, with shuttered and locked windows, it was oppressing and dark.

Although the door and window were locked, they still took alternate watches throughout the night, not trusting the inn to be safe. Throughout the night they heard footsteps outside their door several times, but the handle was only tried once. When found locked from the inside, the perhaps opportunistic attempt to enter was abandoned. The feet and their owner padded away again.

It was a poor night's sleep and so they rose early to ride to the docks to charter a boat and forwent breakfast. The wind had fallen, but it was pervasively cold and damp in the predawn darkness. By sunrise, they were already attempting to barter passage with the sailors who were in a flurry of activity getting ready for their day's work. Man after man they asked, anyone they could see with a small craft, but to no avail.

By noon, all the boats had refused them, many having sailed before they had a chance to hail the captains. Their lack of progress left Edmund and Soren feeling frustrated and short-tempered. Chilled and tired, they retired to a dockside tavern for a hot meal and to rethink their strategy, and it was there, quite by chance, that they had the most fortunate of meetings.

The barmaid was a lively, chatty young thing, who seemed out of place in such a dull and unsociable town. Luckily for Edmund and Soren, who had attracted her interest as outsiders, her tongue was loose and without having to reveal too much of their fabricated identities and purpose, she had already furnished them with details of a fisherman who lived a few hours' ride north of the main town.

She described him as an enigma of a man, who sailed nearer to the dragon isles than he ought to; nearer than anyone else, but who somehow still managed to come to no harm and return with the reward of huge catches and strange tales. He lived an isolated life and rarely mingled with the townsfolk except to barter his fishes for other products, and this had gained him an unusual reputation.

He sounded odd enough to Edmund and Soren, however after a hopeless time on the docks that morning, they decided he might be a viable option. With a brisk thanks to the young woman, Soren and Edmund departed. In their haste, they bumped into a man entering the tavern. Edmund apologised as they brushed past him, but as he paused for the briefest moment, he could have sworn he recognised the man. The feeling passed, forgotten as he mounted his horse.

The maintained north road ended with Harring and stopped quite abruptly beyond the last house, though a discernible track lead north through the mud, rock, and grass. Urging the horses forward, they began the dismal trek along the seashore to find the sailor.

It was slow going as they picked out the pathway, and the further away from Harring they travelled the more unnerved they became. It seemed a windswept and bare place, but even more than that, utterly barren; not a creature stirred or called to break the sound of the wind. After a time, however, there seemed to be too many hoof beats upon the ground for them to be alone, yet when they looked about, they spied no one. The hairs on Edmund's neck rose and a shiver passed down his spine.

As they passed a rocky spur, they saw a horse up ahead; it stood saddled yet rider-less, and cropped the grass as it ignored them. It was only when they approached it to pass that it raised its head to wicker at them and trot away backwards.

"Ho!" a nearby voice called. The man it belonged to strolled out from behind a line of shrubs to their left, tightening his pants up. "Well now then, good sirs, how are we on this fine day?" His glance was keen and his smile did not quite reach his eyes.

"Good day, sir," Edmund responded, thrown off guard by the man's manner, so contrasting to the unfriendly folk from Harring. He made to ride on but the man passed before his mount and forced him to halt the horse again. His heart pounded out of control. *Have we been recognised?*

"Well now, what a fine horse this is," the man remarked and stroked the stallion upon his nose. "And his lady looks so fine too." He leered at Miri. Edmund tensed. The man seemed far too jovial and once more, Edmund had the feeling they had met before, but could not recall where.

"Here, Al!" called the man, startling them. Miri pranced, and Soren calmed her with a touch. "Come look at these lovely horses!" Edmund's heart sank. He lowered his hand towards his sword surreptitiously as a second figure emerged from their right. Behind him, Soren mirrored his movement.

"Oh aye, Jem, mighty fine." Al appeared.

"Mind. The horses ain't half so pretty as their riders. I'd wager no one expected to see your faces here, but they ain't half as sharp as us. A little dirt can't hide a highborn face. *Your Majesty.*" Jem cackled and bowed. The movement was mocking and exaggerated. He straightened again, and his lopsided grin widened.

Al shifted, and his cloak opened. Under it, Al held an axe. It relaxed too carefully against his hip. Instinct caused Edmund to turn back to Jem, as the quietest hiss of another blade being drawn met his ear.

Edmund yanked on his stallion's reins and the horse rose beneath him to lash out with his front legs. Jem fell back as the hoof struck him across the chest, although he managed to retain his grasp on his grimy dirk and did not fall. Upon the horse, Edmund cut an imposing figure with his drawn sword and he saw the fear reflected in Jem's eyes as he beheld the now less than helpless traveller. Edmund suddenly realised who he was; one of the two men from the inn the previous night. Contempt filled him.

TWENTY

Time in Ednor seemed to flow faster than normal and it was soon time to depart. Although Eve felt excited about the new path before her, her heart was heavy as she packed away her few possessions.

She had not seen Artora again, but her time in Ednor had exposed her to the wonders of the Eldarkind culture where she felt strangely at home. The surroundings felt familiar in a way she could not explain; almost as if she had been there in dream or another life. For her guards however, that had not been the case. She had not confided her plans in Nyle and Luke.

The three had spent their free hours exploring Ednor together, escorted by one of the Eldarkind who became a willing guide, eager to tell them of his home. Whilst Eve delighted in the sights about her in quiet awe and wonder, Nyle and Luke grew more restless. Noticing this, Eve's guilt grew, but she did not know how to tell them she would not be returning to Arlyn. Although Luke remained too shy to pry, she could see that Nyle was eager to leave and growing frustrated by their extended visit.

On the morning of their departure, they gathered in the courtyard to find their horses already assembled and tacked with saddlebags brimming with provisions. Eve had dressed once more in her now clean riding clothes.

Unbeknownst to her guards, she had also been measured over the previous days for the fitting her own personal set of light armour, a gift courtesy of the queen that now lay concealed in her saddlebags for later use. She had been given a fine and surprisingly light chainmail hauberk, with engraved metal greaves and bracers and a small helm of similar design. The night before departing, Artora also presented Eve with a long, silver dagger that had a decoratively etched handle of the blackest ebony and was accompanied by a matching black leather sheath.

From a distance it was unremarkable. Close up, the detail on the small weapon was fascinatingly intricate. Although the precious armour was stored away in the saddlebags with her bow and arrows, Eve wore the dagger around her waist with great pride, feeling overwhelmed by the queen's generosity and the kindness of her people.

As they added their few personal belongings to the bags and checked over their mounts, Artora met them with two of her kind in tow: a male and a female, both fair-haired and blue-eyed like the rest of their race. They stood behind her with neutral faces as she greeted Eve and her companions.

"It is a sad day to see you leave, dear cousin, so soon after you arrived," Artora said with affection colouring her voice, "but of course I wish you well on your travels, and the greatest of success in your endeavour."

Luke and Nyle shared a look of mutual bafflement.

Artora glanced between them, before resting her eyes on Eve. "I think it is now that your intentions must be shared, Eve."

Eve steeled herself. The moment she had been dreading had arrived. A hard knot in the pit of her stomach convulsed as she turned to face her guards. She took a deep breath to steady her nerves and wracked her brain for the best way to explain.

"I shall not be returning to Arlyn," Eve said.

"What?" Luke and Nyle exclaimed in synchronisation.

"I won't be returning to Arlyn," repeated Eve, her resolve strengthening. "There are other things I must do before I can return there. I'm going to Pandora instead, to find my cousin Irumae. My mind is made up and cannot be changed." She lifted her chin and glared at them, daring them to disagree.

Luke and Nyle gaped at her speechlessly.

"Nyle." Eve met his eyes as unflinchingly as she could. "I require you to return to my father with Queen Artora's news, and also my own."

At this, the female Eldarkind stepped forward and offered

Nyle a scroll and a small box that a simple set of clasps fastened shut. He automatically took it, though he frowned as he examined it.

Eve reached into her saddlebags to withdraw her own correspondence for him, before turning to Luke. "Luke. If you're willing, you'll accompany me."

"You cannot be serious! Have these folk addled your brain?" said Nyle.

"Who are you to question me, and how dare you slander our host and my kin!" Eve said.

Nyle glowered.

"Eve," Luke said. He chewed on his lip. "We're expected to protect you and return you safely home; your father is relying on us to do so. How could we fail in that?"

"You would be protecting me and returning me home, just not to my father's schedule," Eve said persuasively. "Nyle, you would be taking him news so that he does not fret over me."

"Yes," she said as Nyle opened his mouth, and held up her hand to stall him, "I know my continued absence would concern him. At the very least you can reassure him of my safe arrival and productive time here. He does require some news from my stay and the letter sets out everything he needs to know."

"And what do you think he will do with me when he finds out I let his beloved daughter and heir go gallivanting around the wilderness?" Nyle kicked a stone in frustration as Luke stood in silence, his brow furrowed in worry. "I'll lose my position! I'll lose everything I've worked hard for, as will Luke! Have you thought of that?"

"I have begged him in the letter to not punish you at all. I write that I left you no choice in the matter. If he disregards my words then you have my solemn promise that the moment I return, if all is not well with you, I will make it so."

"If you return," he muttered. It was clear Nyle was infuriated rather than placated. "What if we bound you and carried you to Arlyn whether you liked it or not?" He folded his arms and glared at her.

"We cannot do that!" Luke protested.

"What, so you're just going to do whatever she says and damn the consequences?" Nyle scoffed at him.

Luke hesitated, aware of Eve as she shifted her gaze to him. He met it for the fleetest of moments and cast his eyes down, also avoiding Nyle's glare.

"If she is to go regardless of our wishes, I would sooner go with her to make certain she is safe and protected, rather than return to Lord Karn without her," he murmured. "I would certainly never consider taking her anywhere by force if she felt the cause were so important, unless her life were in danger. I do not deem that to be the case now, so what other choice do I have? Yes, I too risk my position, but I would rather try to protect her as is my duty than give up and slink home like a coward."

"I am no coward!" snarled Nyle, bristling. "You have forced me into a corner." Stiff and hostile, his mouth was a thin line with the force of his displeasure. "It would seem I have no choice in the matter." He surveyed the silent group of people before him with gritted teeth.

"Thank you for your hospitality," he said. He executed a sharp, cursory bow in Artora's direction. She dipped her head to him, but he had already turned away to mount his horse. "My lady," he called back in farewell to Eve without turning as he urged his horse away.

"I feel I have made an enemy of Nyle today," said Eve, feeling troubled as he rode out of sight. "I hope this will not have repercussions."

"It will be what it will be," said Artora. She glided forward and touched Eve's shoulder reassuringly. "Come, do not let this darken your day. I have one final gift for you, dear cousin."

The male Eldarkind behind Artora handed her a small box matching the one given to Nyle. Artora passed it to Eve, who admired it for a few moments before she opened it.

It was made of an unfamiliar dark grey wood and was rectangular in shape, just over a hand-span long and wide, very thin and light. Something within gave a slight, hard rattle. As she opened the clasped lid, a gleaming silver surface caught the light and a beautiful round mirror, a smaller replica of Artora's even including the rich pearl border, was revealed lying cushioned in the box.

Eve's fingers brushed over the pearl border and she gazed at Artora in wordless thanks.

Artora beckoned her closer and bent to whisper its purpose into her ear. "As you have not yet inherited your powers, Eve, I have enchanted this mirror so that you may scry as you wish without magic of your own. Speak the words of seeing as you saw me do and you shall see what you desire. The magic shall draw off the surrounding energy of the land until you should come into your powers.

"Use it wisely though and in secrecy, for it is a great crime to needlessly breach another's privacy and this ability should never be shared carelessly. I have sent the same mirror to your father, linked to yours, so that you will be able to scry each other and share words if you need to. Keep your mirror in its case when you do not use it and keep it close."

Eve closed the box, snapped the clasps closed, and hugged it to her chest. "Thank you," she said fervently to Artora, "for everything you have done for me."

"You are welcome, dear cousin." Artora smiled. "I am glad to show the daughter of Freya kindness. Return soon."

Eve beamed.

"Luke," Artora said. Her benevolent gaze flicked to the guardsman.

Luke gawked at her, wide eyed and apprehensive.

"Walk with me."

Luke hurried to obey, though he looked terrified. Eve strained her ears and eyes as Luke followed the queen out of earshot, but could not discern anything. Exchanging some final words, Luke bowed to the queen before returning to his horse. As he passed Eve, he glanced at her with deep brown eyes that now held a troubled and thoughtful expression.

Eve looked to Artora for any clue; the queen acted as though nothing had happened and turned to the two unnamed Eldarkind, who had been murmuring away in their tongue in her absence.

"I shall introduce my escorts, as they shall be your travelling companions on the journey to Pandora. Nolwen," Artora said, as he flashed a bright smile at her, "and his sister Nelda." Nelda bowed her head.

"We should squander no more time here," Artora said, "for you have some way to travel today." She gestured at them to mount their horses. With a last few words of farewell, Nolwen and Nelda led the group out of the gates and into the city with Eve following and Luke at the rear.

Eve raised a hand to her newfound relative, who returned the gesture in kind, and wished that she might have stayed longer.

They departed in silence. The clatter of hooves meant little chance of conversation. Once they had left Ednor, the jarring noise gave way to more pleasant dull thuds as they drummed over packed earth and grass instead. Eve took her chance to approach Luke.

"What did she say to you?" she asked, as laughter floated back to them from Nolwen and Nelda, who were engaged in conversation some distance ahead. Luke regarded her for a few seconds with a strange look. She repeated her question, presuming that perhaps he had not heard.

"Nothing of importance." He averted his gaze and increased the separation between their horses as a sign of his reluctance to talk. Eve did not press him, though she was not at all convinced of his sincerity.

It took longer to climb out of the valley than it did to enter it; the journey was steeper than Eve realised. Despite this, they made it to the rim of the great valley by mid-afternoon, where they stopped for a brief respite and some food.

Eve sat near the edge of a ridge that offered an uninterrupted view of the entire vista. Looking down over the expanse before them, Eve tried to remember as much as possible about the valley, absorbing as many details as she could of the landscape.

The city they had been in mere hours before was tiny in the

distance. Although Eve had revelled in the beauty and newness of the place, she realised there was much more of the land to explore that she had not even dreamed of.

"It's beautiful, is it not?" The rich, resonant voice of Nolwen startled her out of her reverie.

"It is. There's a part of me that wishes I could stay," Eve replied with regret.

"Then you should return some day," replied Nolwen as if it were that simple. "Although it is good to travel, it is a shame to leave such a home behind. To our advantage, the sorrow of leaving makes the joy of returning all the greater. I shall leave you to your thoughts." He apologised for disturbing her.

Now her train of thought was broken however, she no longer wished to linger, for she knew she could stare at the view all day and not tire of it. Seeing Luke lunching on a rock, she decided to try to determine his strange conversation with the queen.

"So what did she say to you?" Eve asked.

"Nothing of importance," he repeated after noting her sudden presence with a raised eyebrow. "What was her gift to you?"

"A trinket, nothing of importance," she replied casually. Luke nodded and smiled as she turned away and she knew he was just as unconvinced with her response as she was with his.

She had no further success in talking to him that day and so, around a small campfire that night, she tried to become more familiar with her strange new companions. Observing them during the day, they seemed unreserved, with lively personalities, and found constant reasons to smile and laugh that she did not quite understand.

Although they conversed with each other in the tongue of the Eldarkind, they could speak the common tongue of Caledan, albeit with a strange lilting accent. They had harmonious voices that seemed to ebb and flow and Eve found that their foreign conversations were like listening to music, because of the constant shifting of pitch, timbre, and other qualities of their vocals.

They both resembled others of their race, but Nolwen wore his hair uncommonly short, cropped close to his head in a mass of short waves, rather than long as Eve had seen most other male Eldarkind styled. Nelda kept her hair longer and held back in a neat and practical braid with none of the intricacies or decoration that might adorn her brow in Ednor.

Both were outfitted in slim-fitting riding outfits that highlighted their lean, muscular structure. Combined with the distinctive facial structure of their kind, this made them seem scarily alike when discounting their more obvious gender differences.

They appeared to be no more than ten years Eve's seniors and she was shocked to discover that they were in actual fact over twice that amount older than her. She could not keep from wondering if her own fate was to age as slowly as they.

They revealed they were members of Artora's household, distant relatives who held positions of no great significance. Eve realised with a smile that it also meant they were distant cousins of hers.

They spent the early evening eating around their campfire and telling small tales of Ednor, the surrounding land and most dearly to Eve, stories of their family, who were, albeit distantly, also her own. They had been well educated and traveled across Caledan before as scouts and envoys and, as Eve was sure she would find their tales much more exciting than they found hers, she was keen to listen. Luke sat beside her and listened as Nolwen and Nelda shared tales in undulating voices.

So it was that by the time they came upon the Great Lake a couple of days later, after several discussions as to their course of action, Eve felt at ease with her new companions. Even Luke had begun to emerge from his shell and speak to them, his mixture of fear and reverence ebbing.

TWENTY ONE

Jem scrambled for his horse, but Edmund rode to cut him off and dealt a stinging blow across the back of his shoulders with the flat of his sword. Jem yelped, causing his horse to bolt. He futilely sprinted after it whilst Edmund gave chase.

With his accomplice suffering, Al rushed towards Soren, who was forced to turn Miri out of harm's way as Al raised the axe. Al moved forward and grasped her rein, but Soren could not swing his sword; Al had moved to the opposite side of Miri's head. Quick as a flash, Soren grasped his hunting knife and plunged it into the man's outstretched arm.

With a howl, Al dropped the reins and crumpled, cradling his bleeding arm. Miri threw herself away from him. Her eyes rolled and her stride lengthened as she fled. Soren forced her to turn back and brought down his sword on Al's axe as the man stood before the charging mare. The weathered wood was not fit to stand before a royal blade and it shattered, the axe head spinning away into the undergrowth. With nothing but a shortened stick to defend him, Al turned tail and fled.

Soren turned back as Edmund returned. "Shall I kill him?"

Edmund shook his head.

"Why not?" Soren asked, surprised at his response.

"They are not worth it," said Edmund, his voice heavy with contempt. "Pathetic. They do not even deserve to be called men."

"What if they should tell someone we are here?" Soren persisted.

"I would not worry about that," Edmund replied, dismounting to check his horse over. "I would imagine if they did not confront us in Harring, it was because they did not wish to share the bounty. Saying that, we should go. There may be more of these folk about and I would not care to meet them."

All seemed calm as they moved on, but it took a while for the hammering of Soren's heart to quiet. Before they had gone far, they came upon the still form of Jem, blood upon his brow.

"Tripped. Hit his head upon the ground," said Edmund in response to Soren's enquiry. Soon they passed the bandit's horse quietly grazing, and after that they were alone. To their relief, there were no more encounters in the desolate place. When they came upon the fisherman's house that afternoon, it was such an unobtrusive place that if not for the boat bobbing up and down by the shore, they would have entirely missed it.

A rocky cliff rose up from the shore and out into the sea to form shelter and natural harbour for both boat and dwelling. Behind the cliff a wooden shack, grey with weathering, blended into the rocky wall and a similarly colourless, aged gangway extended into the water from the beach.

The craft moored there seemed the most well cared for thing of all and Soren recalled seeing similar boats at the main docks in Pandora. A large lean-to, a shed, and a cart sat against the cliff next to the house. The place seemed deserted as they scouted the area.

Their horses' hooves clattered on the rocky ground as they rode down to the dwelling. When they dismounted some yards away, a disembodied voice rang out.

"Oy! What d'yer want?" it shouted.

Soren and Edmund scanned the area. No one was there. A clatter drew their attention to the small craft. A man's head popped up over the rail, wild-haired and bearded.

"We mean no harm," called Edmund. He raised his hands in a gesture of peace. "Do you know where we may find Garth Storrsson? We have a business proposition for him."

"Aye," said the man, after a pause. "Yer looking at him. A business proposition yer say? I ain't had one o' them in a while. Hang fast, I'll be a moment." He ducked out of sight, and after more clattering, swung himself over the rail and onto the gangway with a resounding thud.

With a slap of his hands and a quick stride up the pebbled

beach, he stood at his door looking them over. He was not a tall man by any standards, but his stocky build and confident gait made him an impressive figure. His chin held high, he stared at them with wrinkled eyes and ruddy cheeks.

"And who might you be?" He folded his arms as he faced them.

Soren's eyes flicked to Edmund.

"My name is Erik," said Edmund in his usual measured tone. "I'm a merchant looking to expand into trading on this coast line. My servant here accompanies me. You were, ah, recommended to us in Harring for the quality of your fish."

Garth squinted suspiciously.

"Very well then, yeh may come in to talk but I aren't making no promises," said Garth.

The distinct smell of fish outside formed an offensive sensory barrier, but as they ducked through the low door, they were surprised. It was clean inside and tidy, although sparse and small. There were two rooms; a living space and what appeared to be a bedroom, kept warm by an aged stove, but Soren was glad it was summer. It looked like one winter gale would blow the place down.

"Sit down," said Garth.

They backed onto a wooden bench and placed their swords down beside them; their crossbows and everything else outside with the horses.

"To business then. What're yeh interested in trading?" Garth leaned against the stove.

"Well, it depends what you catch," improvised Edmund. "I was hoping we might accompany you the next time you go to sea?"

"Hah! What kind of merchant are yeh if you don't know what yeh looking to buy?" snorted Garth. "What do yeh want, trout, pike, sturgeon, or somethin' else?." He fired the names at them. Soren had no idea what any of them were.

"Any of those would be perfectly adequate if they're the best you catch," replied Edmund.

Soren noticed Edmund's agitation and shuffled nervously.

"Well, I can't magic them up out the sea!" Garth slapped his hand against his thigh in frustration. Soren jumped. "They're all freshwater fish; any merchant hereabouts with a grain o' sense would know that! Now I'll ask yeh again what kind of merchant are yeh, if y'are one at all, and if you'd stop wasting my time! I got a tide to catch and I ain't wasting it on the likes o' you."

Soren's heart pounded in his chest as his body flooded with panic. A bead of sweat rolled down Edmund's forehead next to him. Neither Edmund nor Soren answered. Edmund flexed his hand, but did not reach for his sword.

"Well?" Garth demanded. "Yer filthy and no offence to yeh, but the pair of yeh stink to high blinking heaven; I dunno what swamp yeh've been bathing in! Even so, I ain't seen no strangers before riding such fine horses, dressed in such fine clothing, wi' such nice weapons, nor talking so proper neither. I aren't stupid, so why are yeh here and what do yeh want wi' me an' my boat?" His hand toyed with the handle of the knife stuffed through his worn belt, and his brow was dark with suspicion.

Soren and Edmund shared a look, resigned to the truth. Soren stood. Edmund remained seated.

"We're no merchants, you are correct. I apologise, but we desperately need your boat. We must travel to the Isles of Kotyir. It's a matter of life and death and we could find no other sailor who would dare venture even half as close as you do."

"Yeh want to see the dragon isles?" Garth seemed confused by their role reversal and glanced between them.

"Not to see them, we want to land on them," said Soren.

Garth's bushy eyebrows rose. "Land? Why on earth would yeh want to land there? D'yeh know what's out there?"

"Yes," said Soren, "and it is for that reason we need to go. We need to find the dragons."

Garth's mouth fell open. "Who are yeh?" he wheezed.

"Prince Soren, son of the late Queen Naisa and rightful king of Caledan. I travel with Sir Edmund, advisor to my late mother. My throne has been taken from me and Caledan is in peril. I am forced to desperate measures to right the wrongs that have been done. I *must* travel to the islands of Kotyir."

Garth sat down on top of a barrel. His mouth gaped. "Bloody hell," he said at last.

"Will you help us?" Soren said. "We can pay you."

"I dunno what to say," murmured Garth almost to himself, his eyes downcast and his brow furrowed.

Soren waited with bated breath.

"It ain't every day I get a supposed king to be riding up asking me to show him some dragons." Soren shared a look with Edmund. It was clear Garth wasn't convinced; yet he had no idea what to make of them.

Eventually, Garth sighed, sat back, and folded his arms. "I migh' be crazy, but I'm tempted. However, I'm not about to believe I'm in the company of the righ'ful king of Caledan and some all-important lord. Yer don't seem very kingly to me! How do I know if I can trust yeh?"

"I suppose you don't," replied Soren. For the first time, he felt anonymous. He realised that, although everyone in the capital would recognise him, here, where people had never seen the king or queen, he would be just another face amongst everyone else. "We'll leave the horses here though, as our guarantee."

"Oh, righ', so I'm only worth two horses am I? Thanks!" replied Garth. "I dare say that ain't gonna convince me!"

"No! That's not what I meant." Soren tried to rectify the misinterpretation.

Edmund interrupted. "We mean to prove ourselves trustworthy. Of course we will pay you handsomely as well. We will leave the horses and money here. As for giving you some confidence that we are who we claim to be, you will know the royal crest?"

Garth raised an eyebrow and nodded once.

"Here." Edmund took from around his neck a long, gold chain that had lain hidden under his clothes. He tossed it to Garth, who caught it one-handed with sharp reflexes that Soren had not expected him to possess. Soren saw attached to the swinging chain a yellow gold signet ring. Standing in sharp relief against the shape of a shield and upheld by golden arms, inlaid with polished rubies, was the dragon and crown that was his mother's crest.

Garth held in his hand a priceless piece, worth more than he could ever hope to earn in ten lifetimes and he clearly realised it. He weighed the heavy ring in his palm and ran his fingers along the finely crafted chain as he absorbed with reverence the treasure that lay in his hand.

"Do you believe us?" Soren was eager to know where they stood.

Garth paused before he answered, and his eyes wandered over the fine hilts and scabbards of their swords. He glanced at the door, and Soren knew he was thinking of the fine horses they rode, the weapons and supplies they carried. "I'm startin' to." Silence fell as he thought. "Even if I believe who y'are, why on earth do you need to travel to the dragon isles? It doesn't make no sense."

"We need to find the dragons and speak with them," replied Soren. "They may be the only hope of me regaining the crown."

"Yeh speak as if yeh believe in them," said Garth guardedly.

"I do. I know they exist," said Soren.

"So yeh wouldn't think a man was mad if he said he'd seen them?" suggested the fisherman.

Soren smiled. "No, we wouldn't, and we would appreciate the man who saw them telling us everything he knew about them."

"Well," said Garth thoughtfully, "I can't say whether I saw them or I didn't, but I've sailed close to those islands and I've heard a roar as what couldn't have been made by the sea, or the rumble of the islands as they make themselves anew. I've seen winged things that were so far away yet so big I don't think they were birds and I swear I saw one breathe fire. Unless I'm goin' crazy, I'm sure I wasn't mistaken.

"Surely you've heard the tales of them, though? Child-snatching, livestock-stealing, giant, winged terrors? Why on earth would yeh want to go and try talk to one? Especially when they live in such an awful place as them islands. They're hard places to get to and the earth belches out hot, glowing, melted rocks that makes the sea steam an' the sky dark. Yeh could be killed! If the islands don't kill yeh, the dragons damn well migh' before yeh can say so much as 'good day'!"

Edmund shifted in his chair. "It will be dangerous, but worth the risk. We must try."

"Yeh more determined than most then, to seek me out. Never before in my life have I heard of such a venture." Garth shook his head.

"Will you help us?" asked Soren.

Garth did not respond.

"Think of it this way." Edmund joined Soren in their efforts. "You can go on an adventure that no one else will have lived through, and I'm sure it would entail no more danger than your fishing trips do. If we succeed, you will have the most fantastic tale to tell and a bag of gold to tide you over.

"Even if we fail and die, you still have a fantastic tale and the bag of gold and we wouldn't be needing our horses back. Either way, you can move up in the world if you choose. Time is of the essence and we need your decision. What say you, fisherman?"

Garth looked out of the window and huffed. "I've missed mi' tide today now."

"Will you take us on the next one?"

Garth did not reply.

Clattering awoke a stiff Soren. He rested for a moment, cheek pressed against wood, before he came to his senses and sat up. He had slept on the shack's floor, with his pack as a pillow and his cloak as a blanket; relative luxury compared to the bare earth yet just as uncomfortable. Edmund was nowhere to be seen.

Soren rushed out, not caring he was half-asleep and dishevelled. Edmund and Garth were loading various caskets, barrels, and bundles onto the small boat. Edmund paused to smile at Soren as he drew closer. Soren grinned as he realised why Edmund was so cheerful.

"You decided to take us!" Soren exclaimed to Garth, who paused with a sack in his arms.

"Aye," said Garth. "It's a foolish and dangerous venture, Yer

Majesty, but I'm not one to turn down the most interestin' offer that ever came my way. I could use the money to give my Lindy a better life than what she's gonna get otherwise."

Soren noticed a girl with bushy brown hair and baggy shapeless clothes working in silence on the boat. Soren thought with a stab of sadness that she looked much the same age as his own sister. He forced himself not to think of Irumae as he greeted her. She did not reply, only gazed at him with wide eyes before turning back to her task.

Who knows what is in his mind, thought Soren as he glanced back at the fisherman. *At least we have a boat.* With that, he ran his hand through his hair in an attempt to comb it, before joining Edmund in loading the craft with renewed vigour.

It took a further hour to finish. They loaded boxes and sacks and containers of varying sizes and shapes, with contents from food to fishing equipment; everything the three of them would need to reach the Isles of Kotyir and everything Garth would need for fishing along the way. The deck remained clear but the cabin was crowded; there was just enough space for one man to bunk, let alone three. Soren was so glad to be on a boat heading for the dragon isles that he had no regrets about having to sleep on the deck under a makeshift shelter.

Edmund and Soren gathered up their things. They unpacked every single saddlebag they had with them, repacked anything they did not need and kept out the necessities such as food and weapons. They bundled their things in blankets, packed those in saddlebags that were small enough to carry as satchels, and stored the rest of their possessions in Garth's house.

Their horses and tack remained in the lean-to and they said goodbye to their mounts with a final pat. The horses nickered as they walked away. Grey ocean mirrored dull sky as they boarded and hoisted the sail to catch the slight breeze.

Their fee, which cost almost every single coin they had, they left on Garth's table in a glittering pile for Lindy to hide. She untied the mooring ropes and hopped off the boat with the agility of a goat, after wriggling free of a scratchy kiss from her father and his beard.

The breeze and slight current tugged the craft out until the wind threw some might against the sail as they cleared the headland. Soren had not yet thought about the return journey; now he was within a couple of days of reaching the ancient home of the dragons, he had little room in his mind for anything else.

His thoughts spun on a repetitive loop, imagining a myriad of possibilities; what the dragons would be like in body and spirit, how he could find them, how they could communicate, how he could introduce himself, how the first encounter would play out, and what he could say to convince them to give him the crown or tell him where it was. His mind gave him few answers. He had no idea what to expect.

He spent hours sat and stood by the bow of the ship, straining his eyes for the first sight of their destination as Edmund helped Garth, interested in the workings of the small boat and learning how to fish and crab with lines, nets, and pots. The east coast of Caledan passed by to their left as they sailed, always in sight of land. Garth insisted on pulling in to anchor nearer land that first night, much to Soren's frustration.

"If we sail through the night, we'll make much faster progress!" Soren protested.

"And dash ourselves on the rocks or Gods know what else," replied Garth ominously. "The only reason I've managed to keep meself out of trouble is because I've enough sense not to go sailing off in any old direction at night. Always stay in sight of land when yeh can an' always drop anchor at night. Yeh never know what lurks in or above these waters at night. I'd rather be a slow man than a dead one." He folded his arms and glared, as if daring Soren to challenge his decision.

Soren nodded reluctantly and turned away. Edmund put a warning hand on his shoulder and looked at him with a cautionary glance. "I know you're impatient, Soren, but we must trust that he knows best," Edmund muttered to him as he passed. Soren acknowledged the comment with an uncharacteristic grunt and resumed his position at the bow.

He soon became glad of their night time stops; their slow

progress and the intolerable pitching of the small vessel on the larger waves was not leaving him in the best of moods. He realised his unreasonableness and felt guilty, but another pang of seasickness smothered it as it rolled over him. He scrambled up to vomit yet again over the railings and into the sea.

Garth's booming laugh rang out and he disappeared into the cabin. He reappeared a minute later with a small, twisted thing resembling a root. He took his knife, shaved several small slivers from one end, and deposited them into the prince's limp hand.

"Eat."

Soren pulled a face as he chewed the strange substance. "Ginger?"

"Should cure a turnin' tummy." Garth cut some more peelings and gave them to the prince, who ate them without question. The ginger did help, but Soren was still glad when they steered towards shallower, calmer waters to anchor for the night.

The Isles of Kotyir rose into sight the following day. Mounds loomed in the haze as they drew closer in a chain of islands that led eastwards from the mainland until they faded into the distance. Garth, who they had gathered was quiet at the best of times, was even more taciturn and tense as he began to steer his precious boat away from the mainland and northeast towards them

The sound of seabirds had disappeared that day, leaving nothing except the slap of waves upon the hull and the swirling of the sea around them. As they grew closer to the islands, deep, low rumbles permeated through the air at irregular intervals.

"The fire mountains," called Garth quietly, in reply to Soren's enquiry. He stood by the wheel of his ship, seeming to grasp it for comfort and reassurance rather than purpose.

Soren felt a rush of excitement and fear turn his stomach upside down.

The nearest island drew steadily closer and Garth rushed to lower the sail and hoisted a smaller one in its place. It brought the craft to the slowest crawl so Garth could avoid hazards. When Soren stuck his neck over the edge of the boat, he could see how shallow the grey water was. Under the surface, dark rocks stood like teeth in the darker sand. He shuddered.

The waters were clear and calm as they inched around the first island. It was eerily quiet. A vague breeze rustled around them as they waited and watched, silent as ghosts themselves. There were no beaches on this part of the island; tall, black-grey cliffs formed an impenetrable wall barring their way, until at last they came to a small cove that allowed them somewhere to stop.

The cliffs diminished and receded to beaches of fine, black sand and it was just within their shadow that Garth dropped the anchor. They could see waves crashing over a hidden barrier out to the open sea. Garth explained to his passengers that they were in a lagoon, which sheltered them from the main brunt of the sea's force. A ridge of rocks that almost broke the sea's surface at low tide formed a calmer channel between the sea and the islands, however it was tricky to navigate to the safety of the lagoon.

"That there is why so few return from the Dragon Isles," the fisherman said sombrely. "At high tide they're treacherous at best, at low tide, suicide. Even I've only come this far twice and I'd not have dared to a third time, I dare say, had yeh not appeared."

After standing for a moment longer, they turned to face land. The black beach bathed in its shallow waters was bare. It gave way to rocks as dark as the cliffs and then higher to vivid greenery, a wild tangle of dense forests rising out of sight to culminate in the dormant volcanic peak that had once built the island. Although the chatter of life—hidden birds and animals—floated faintly on the air, it seemed an unnerving place.

Soren felt dwarfed by the task ahead. They were at just the first island in a chain of several. *How do I find the dragons?* he questioned himself.

"Should we try here?" Soren asked.

Edmund frowned. "Were your sightings here, Garth?"

"Let's try the next island and maybe past that un' too," suggested Garth. "It's not that much further round and I've never had any sightings this close to the mainland."

Soren agreed with relief. He did not fancy the thought of having to explore such a wild and unknown tangle of forests without even an inkling of whether they were heading in the right direction.

The second island proved much the same as the first, but as they sailed past it after a unanimous decision, the third came into view. It was smaller and much rockier. Trails of black destruction cut stark swathes through the greenery.

"That's what a live fire mountain looks like then?" Edmund asked Garth.

Garth tipped his head to one side, neither agreeing nor disagreeing. "Well, it's living rather than dead, but now it slumbers an' thankful we should be it does."

Another rumble emanated around them.

"Long may we hope it sleeps whilst we're here," Garth muttered, almost to himself. "We'll be coming to islands that are more live than asleep or dead if we keep on," he cautioned. "Choose wise an' quick or we'll have to turn back for our own safety when night falls."

"It just doesn't feel right," Soren said. He looked at Edmund in desperation, as panic rose inside him. "I don't know what to look for now that I'm here. There are so many islands and time is not on our side to explore them all!"

"Perhaps then, we ought to summon them?" Edmund said.

Soren did not understand. "How so?"

"Garth, perhaps you have something that could make a loud, carrying noise?" Edmund asked.

"I have a horn and the boat has a bell, though both are small," the sailor replied.

"Anything might help," said Edmund. "It is certainly worth a try. Perhaps we are being watched this very moment without realising, but we cannot see what is before our eyes. It might draw something out."

Garth shivered; perhaps at the thought, or maybe because the insidious breeze was becoming chillier. Edmund and Garth began to create the loudest din possible using horn and bell, whilst Soren beat his sword unceremoniously against a metal bucket.

Pealing bell fought discordantly against baying horn and clanging metal. It seemed like they continued for an age, until they were sore with effort and their hearing dulled. Even deafened, they could not fail to hear the huge roar that drowned their din.

It rumbled and reverberated around them and through them, a low, disembodied sound so large it came from everywhere. The three men fell silent. Shivers crawled up Soren's spine. The roar ceased, echoing, and as it faded, he heard a repetitive thud, like a giant heart beating.

From behind the island, a great, black, winged beast arose, its wings the source of the dull thuds. Flying low against the horizon it sped towards them, huge and growing more monstrous by the second. They froze in fear and indecision, but it pulled up short to alight some distance away on the nearest cliff edge.

Although so far away, its size was beyond estimation. It roared its terrifying dominance at them, unleashing a huge, spurting jet of flame in their direction. Soren flinched. It did not reach the boat but sent a wave of heat roiling across them.

"God save us," whispered a dumbfounded Garth. Edmund and Soren stood, rooted to the spot.

TWENTY TWO

Eve and Luke awoke on their final morning before reaching the lakeside town to the great shock of two unfamiliar faces staring down at them. Nolwen and Nelda's sharp features had rounded and most distinctively, both their hair and eyes were now brown.

"A necessary disguise, these days," said Nolwen with a wink. Their voices had not changed at all, which reassured Eve that they were still the Eldarkind siblings, before she was able to see the slight resemblance remaining in their faces. Luke was spooked, but Eve observed the effort he made to act as though nothing had happened.

Dwellings crowded the side of the great lake; the busyness of the place was a shock after the peace of the wild. Chivvied on by Nolwen, they bought passage on a boat to Pandora. As Eve opened up the purse containing her savings and a small allowance given by her father for the trip to count out the large fee for herself and Luke, she noted how much her funds had been depleted. Just a few coins remained in what had been a bulging bag.

The docks were a flurry of motion in the predawn. The four led their horses on foot through the weaving net of people to the huge wooden barge that awaited them.

Soon, the shore was hazy in the distance as it floated southeast across the Great Lake and once it had disappeared altogether, there was nothing save water and sky in all directions. Although Nolwen and Nelda seemed content staring into the distance and occasionally talking in a mix of languages, Eve and Luke were frustrated and bored by the evening.

They had spent the day in relative solitude; tending the horses, or sat with their thoughts, and were glad to come together for the evening meal, however meagre. They could light no fire and there was no galley, so it was cold, and in the looming darkness, their light was a solitary lamp. There was nothing more to do afterwards save sleep and so they set the usual watch and attempted to bed down for the night with the horses.

"I think I prefer sleeping on tree roots," Eve said with an almighty yawn as she awoke the next day. The four were bleary-eyed, stiff, and dishevelled as they ate breakfast in the fog to which they had awoken.

It was a strange contrast to the clear though overcast day before. Steely grey waters swirled around the boat, wavelets slapping against its side as it ploughed through the thick, clinging mists. The bow and aft were barely visible and the chill of the fog resisted the morning's warmth.

Huddling close together in the shelter made them colder and stiffer, so they rose and raced each other back and forth across the ship; even Luke cast off his reservations and joined in. Once warm and red-cheeked, they collapsed laughing in the piles of hay, feeling far more enlivened. The energy soon passed however, and even Nolwen and Nelda seemed subdued, but Eve, feeling emboldened, nudged Luke and mouthed to him to follow her.

Curiously, he rose to trail her across the boat into the mist. When Eve turned to find Luke standing next to her with a questioning look on his face, her heart leapt into action, beating fast in her chest, and she began to question herself.

It is not too late to turn back, not yet, the thought crept into her mind. She looked into his open face, wondering if she were right to trust him, and he gazed back, nonplussed. After a long pause, he moved slightly, as if to withdraw, but she reached out to grasp his sleeve. She dropped it almost instantly, her cheeks burning.

"Please stay," she said.

He leaned on the railing and shifted his focus from her out into the unending white as he waited. Her heart would not return to its resting rate and hammered as nerves rushed through her.

"How long is it since we spent time together as children and friends?" she asked him.

"At least seven years now," he replied. "Although we've trained together with the guardsmen since I joined their ranks."

"It's not the same though," she muttered.

"No. It's not."

"I miss it, you know." She dared to confide in him as he remained silent. "Our friendship. We used to be close, once upon a time. Things aren't the same without you. There's not been anyone else I felt so at ease with." Her mouth curved in a small smile.

"You were right, that night before Ednor, to try and help me, but you must understand, my mother's identity is something I've never shared with anyone before." She peered at him anxiously, but could not gauge his reaction. "I hope I didn't offend you by concealing it. I hoped that our friendship counted for something."

"Is that why you kept me on, and not Nyle?" he asked.

"Partly," she said. "You and I were closer. I would have kept Nyle too but there's something in him I can't trust. I'm frustrated with myself for not noticing it before. I might as well tell you and then you can decide for yourself whether you still trust and believe in me or whether you wish to follow him home." She trailed off.

"Tell me what?" Luke frowned.

"In hindsight, perhaps I should have told you before you got on this boat and then at least you could have had the chance to ride off if you had chosen. Perhaps that is what I feared…"

"Tell me what?" Luke repeated.

Eve looked at Luke with dread, biting her lip, but the moment had come and she could put it off no longer. She closed her eyes, as if to protect herself, and turned away, burying her chin into her shoulder.

"Eve?"

"I might have magic." She forced out as if it were a swear word. "Because my mother was one of the Eldarkind, she had magic. Queen Artora said it is practically certain that I will inherit it too. I don't know if or when or how it will happen and I'm not sure what it means. I was scared to admit it even to myself at first, and especially to you.

"I wouldn't blame you if you refused to come with me. I know the prejudice held against magic; Nyle made it clear enough that it still runs deep. I appreciate your efforts in being so courteous towards Nolwen and Nelda. I won't ask you to stay if you don't want to." She rushed over the words, dreading the response.

"I already know."

"I beg your pardon?" Eve's voice was shrill with surprise.

"I already know," he repeated softly to her amazed silence, as she comprehended the reason for his secrecy at last and tried to understand his decision to stay with her. "When Queen Artora took me aside at our leave-taking, she told me. I think she wished to test me, for your sake."

"Are you leaving, then?" Her fists clenched around the rail.

"No," he replied after a pause. "I'll do my duty."

She recoiled, indignant. "You don't have to stay for duty!"

"That's not what I meant." He was hasty to placate her, but he stopped speaking and huffed. One hand struck against the rail whilst the other ran through his hair. "I don't have the same way with words that you do," he said. After a moment's silence, he continued.

"I didn't lie, that night in the mountains. I stay because I wish to do my duty and protect you, but I also miss our friendship. I'll be there for you whenever you wish to call on me, as a guard, a friend; whatever you should require. My lady." He turned and bowed before striding away into the mist.

She watched Luke go, stunned as she turned around and sunk to sit with her back to the rail. A warm relief blossomed in her stomach. The tense knot of anxiety and anticipation, which had been so immovable just minutes before, dissipated.

She let out a great sigh of release, knowing she had been right to place her faith in him. In the same instance however, she still could not pin down his character. He seemed forthright and friendly and yet distant and formal, and she could not understand why.

It was some while later when she arose to re-join the others. The mist was burning off and pale light filtered through it, though warmth was still lacking. As she returned and seated herself on a bale of hay, there was the slightest tension between her and Luke as they exchanged faint, polite smiles and this did not go unnoticed by Nolwen and Nelda, who shared a look of their own.

Suddenly, Nolwen leapt to his feet. "Come! Let us train," he said. They regarded him with slow comprehension. "It is cold, I am stiff, and it would do us well to warm our muscles and our wits." He smiled at them. "Come, Master Luke. I wish to see the proficiency of the men of Arlyn."

"And I wish to see the skills of the Lady of Arlyn, Mistress Eve," Nelda said, with a mischievous smile.

Eve grinned. Luke got up and retrieved his sword. She fished around in her pack for the sword that had lain so carefully wrapped up in its sheath and belt since the day she had left Arlyn, leaving her armour concealed.

It had been weeks since she had trained, and she noticed with regret the heavy weight of her sword, which felt less than familiar. *At least against a woman I should still be a fair match*, she thought as she cast an eye over her weapon to check it was in working order.

They stood, two pairs facing each other, spaced out on the empty deck. Eve gripped her slim blade whilst Luke experimentally whirled his hand-and-a-half broadsword in a figure of eight. Nolwen and Nelda drew almost identical, razor thin, long blades covered in the same swirling patterns that adorned the dagger that Artora had gifted Eve.

Heads were inclined as the humans saluted with their swords and the Eldarkind made a flourishing gesture with theirs, then the siblings leapt into action with inhuman speed. Eve clumsily brought up her blade just in time as the ring of metal clashing on metal sounded.

The speed and force of the attack was astounding and unexpected, and Eve had not even a moment spare to see if Luke was as surprised as she. The jarring impact radiated pain up her arm and she danced backwards out of the way to buy valuable seconds, but she had no time.

Before she could breathe, Nelda was upon her again. Eve defended better this time, having forced her stiff legs into action and dodged to one side. Crew members spilled onto the deck from the cabin to see the commotion and settled down to spectate.

With the distraction, Eve spared a glance at Luke and Nolwen, who seemed much more closely matched; Luke, at least, was holding his ground better than she could manage against Nelda. They sparred for twenty minutes with Eve struggling to attack and forced to defend, before Nelda flicked Eve's sword aside with relative ease and drew close to rest her blade against Eve's neck.

Her eyes bored accusingly into Eve, who realised with guilt just how complacent she had grown in her training. With a sudden spark of inspiration, she dropped her sword with a clang and wrenched out her dagger to point it at Nelda's stomach. Nelda looked down at the noise, raised her eyebrows, and let out a single, clear peal of laughter that stopped Nolwen and Luke in their tracks several yards away.

"Well, Mistress Eve," she said with twinkling eyes. "You are a rough gem, but resourceful!"

"Your skills are amazing!" Eve's breath came heavily as she regarded Nelda with awe.

"Years of training." Nolwen dismissed the compliment. "Maybe we could train together when we can as, please take no offence, Lady Eve, perhaps you need to challenge yourself further."

Eve was glad for the colour already in her cheeks from the exertion as she blushed from embarrassment for her poor form, agreeing gratefully to Nelda's proposal.

Nolwen sauntered over with Luke in tow. Eve was glad to see he was as breathless as her. "I find the soldiers of Arlyn to be good fighters amongst men. What say you, sister?" Nolwen said.

"And the lady must be counted as a good fighter amongst their women," said Nelda. She was generous and Luke smiled at the praise. Eve winced as she caught the undertone of their meaning; amongst humans they were somewhat proficient, however against Eldarkind, they were no match.

They lent the rest of the day to amicable discussion about weaponry and fighting techniques and manoeuvres, with Eve volunteering first watch that night. The fog had vanished and the sunset was glorious, setting lake and sky on fire. As it sunk below the horizon, they set out their bedding and, wrapped in a blanket, Eve perched on a bale of hay and stargazed as she waited for her companions to fall asleep.

Some hours later, when Eve was sure they were unconscious, she reached into her bag to pull out the box that had been a gift from the fey queen. As she opened up the dark container, the pearls and reflective surface of the mirror gleamed faintly in the starlight. She breathed the incantation of far-seeing on the mirror. "*Leitha Soren!*"

Nothing happened. She frowned in annoyance, about to repeat the incantation, until the faintest flicker of light across the surface of the mirror stalled her. There was nothing more however, just roiling darkness with faint swatches of light passing across the mirror's dark surface. With an internal curse, she released the image, annoyed with herself for assuming that, despite the late hour, she would still be able to scry her cousin.

She tried to scry Irumae. The room was in darkness. Last of all, she tried to scry her father—to no avail. "*Lessa.*" Not even the faintest flicker of light crossed the surface as she released the seeing spell. She packed away the mirror and, when the moon was high enough, rose to wake Nolwen for the next watch.

Eve next awoke to the loud cry of, "Land ho!" She scrambled out from underneath her blanket and peered out into the bright light. As her eyes adjusted to the familiar blue, she spied a faint smudge on the horizon. With a rustle, Nelda stood beside her.

"The mount that marks Pandora," Nelda answered Eve's enquiring glance. "We are close."

Even so, reaching the horizon and making port took a great deal longer than Eve anticipated, to the extent that there was ample time for more sword practice. This time, instead of a relentless pace, Nolwen and Nelda—who had swapped charges today—went through battle motions in exaggerated slowness to correct poor technique. A short and intense full speed practice fight followed this, cheered on by the crew, until once more Luke and Eve found themselves outmatched. Eve had the niggling feeling their partners were holding back.

By midday, they had sailed into Pandora's harbour to dock. The great castle on the hill loomed above them to the north over the rest of the city and the lake. The docks bustled, full of people and a barrage of sounds, sights, and smells that assaulted them almost physically as they disembarked and dove into the overwhelming maelstrom.

Towering city walls rose close to the docks, but Nolwen steered the group away from them and southeast around the outskirts of the city within the walls so they could stay in the city outside the fortified ramparts, buried deep within the churning chaos of human comings and goings.

The Rose and Crown Inn became their cover of choice, so they stabled the horses there and retired to their room to discuss strategy. They decided Nolwen and Nelda, who blended in well with their disguises, would trawl the city for a way into the castle, as they knew the city far better. Luke was to remain with Eve as her protector and they were to remain as low key as possible, roaming around the local precinct to see what news they could glean from the lower levels of the city, which were rife with gossip.

Pandora was a bustling and vast human population compared to the much quieter town of Arlyn and the loud clamour of people and animals and carts was initially indiscernible. Despite the recent upheaval, there was no clue of any fear or ill feelings on the surface. Rather, everyone seemed to go about their daily business as normal.

The sole hint of change was the flag that flew from every flagpole. The crown and dragon of the queen on a blue and gold field was gone, replaced by the crown and sword on gold and black belonging to Zaki. Soldiers patrolled every street.

With her hair hidden under a shawl, Eve and Luke wandered up and down the roads and side streets, losing themselves in the higgledy-piggledy arrangement of buildings, but here the city wall proved of some use. Although the buildings were several storeys tall in places, creating shadowy alleys, the wall was visible in the gaps between them and gave some clue to determine their position.

From the inn to the docks they wandered and back without success. Snippets of mundane conversation and haggling were all they caught in the commotion. Feeling disheartened, they returned to the inn before sundown, as agreed, to reunite with Nolwen and Nelda.

The room was just large enough for four and overlooked the busy street below. They perched by the window, but it was dark and some hours later before the two Eldarkind slipped into their rented room, startling Eve. Eve and Luke had eaten without them; cold, salted slices of meat, bread and cheese and strange tasting local ale to wash down their meal. Eve didn't mind—it made a refreshing change from the travelling biscuits, which she was beginning to despise.

Nolwen and Nelda's portions lay untouched on the plates and when the two returned, they consumed the food before speaking.

"I gather you wish for our news first?" Nolwen said.

Eve and Luke nodded.

"We have been into the city proper through the east gate and circled the castle. From all angles, it is well guarded. The main entrances of course would be no sensible way to enter and all of the side doors we found are guarded more than I would expect to see.

"We were not able to check the parts of the castle inaccessible to the city—that is to say, those parts that lead into the walled gardens. Unless we scale the walls into the castle gardens and perhaps find a way in there, and mind, this would have to be at night to avoid detection, I do not see how we can gain entry. The fortress is well protected, as Zaki well knows, and he has ensconced himself well."

Eve sat up, startling Luke, who was slumped on the window-seat next to her. "I may have found something useful!" she said. Luke was nonplussed beside her. "I thought our day was quite fruitless until you said that, but I'm positive I heard today that Zaki may not even currently be in the city. I'm sure as we were at the docks I recall someone mentioning preparations needed to be made for his return."

"Perhaps the guards are for show," murmured Nelda, her eyes narrowed.

"We cannot count it for definite if we are to be cautious."

Nolwen bit his lip. "We can make enquiries tomorrow. Do you have any other news?"

Eve and Luke shook their heads.

"No matter. We have something to start with. If Zaki is not here, it may greatly help us."

TWENTY THREE

"Before I kill you, insolent humans who trespass in my territory, explain your din!" a fierce, guttural voice that was not his own sounded in Soren's head. He exclaimed as one with Edmund and Garth.

"You heard it too?" he asked.

They nodded. Even Edmund was wide-eyed.

"Is it..." Soren trailed off and they gawked at the dragon on the cliff.

It flexed an onyx paw, crushing stones into pebbles with ease. They dropped into the sea a long distance below. It roared again, a column of fire erupting from its mouth.

"ANSWER ME!" the voice growled.

As one, they flinched.

"Dragon," called out Soren, but his voice faltered. He coughed and cleared his throat. "Dragon!" he called again as loudly as he could.

The dragon raised its head. Even from so far away, it's bulk was so large that he could see its glittering eyes fix on him, and a tremor of primal fear shook his body.

"I- I am Prince Soren of Caledan, son of Her Majesty Queen Naisa. I come to seek the Crown of the Dragon Kings, which I believe to be in the safekeeping of your kind, brought here by the great dragon Brithilca."

There was silence as the breeze fell and without warning, the dragon leapt off the cliff to fly closer. It battered them with gusts of wind as it circled around the small boat, which pitched upon the water as the displaced air caught the sails. It did not land on their boat, which was fortunate—for the dragon was several times the larger and would have killed them all and destroyed the boat in the attempt—but Soren noted that neither did it land in the water.

"I am curious of the human that knows of our ancestor Brithilca," the dragon replied. It circled low. Its vast wingspan was terrifyingly enormous; it covered the entire boat and more as it blotted out the light with each pass above.

Its long tail snaked behind the wings, and they could see that great plates of a strange material, neither skin nor scales, covered its stomach. It alighted on a large rock that broke through the surface of the water much closer than before and settled itself so not one inch of it touched the sea.

If any of them had paid attention to the others, Garth, Edmund and Soren would have noticed that they all shared the same expression of fear and wonder. Tightly aligned scales covered its body from head to tail, leaving no visible gap uncovered, and the edge of its face was covered in long barbs that made its streamlined head even more intimidating. Golden-amber eyes with a long, vertical slit-like pupil glared out above smoking nostrils and its ajar mouth revealed a glittering white maze of sharp teeth.

As it coiled its tail around itself and hid its clawed feet from view, Soren could see that from the top of its head to the tip of its tail it had sharp spikes at regular intervals; some of which, judging by the size of the beast, must have been as long as the prince's entire leg. Its wings, much like those of the bats that Soren had seen in Pandora only much more beautiful, folded to its body. They were covered partly in armoured scales but mostly in a smooth membrane that gave the wings the required surface area to lift the dragon's huge bulk from the ground.

In its entirety, it was a beautiful creature, designed with such perfection and precision that they were left in no doubt it was a fearsome and successful hunter.

"Will you release the crown to me?" Soren called after a long silence. Once more, he felt the strange brush of an alien presence against his mind, but no voice sounded this time.

"I have been waiting for you, princeling. I know why you are here, however that is not for me to decide alone," replied the dragon. It exhaled a huge puff of smoke. "You shall return to my brethren with me and we shall confer." It was not a question.

Soren looked to Edmund for guidance, but he had none.

"Out of the frying pan and into the fire," Edmund said.

"Or the dragons' nest," replied Soren. "Is it safe?"

"Who can tell." Edmund shook his head. "I fear we have no choice left now but to go forwards."

"You're right, of course," admitted Soren. "Where are your brethren?" he called to the dragon.

"Over the mountain. You shall soar with me. Your floating tree is too slow. Come to the sea shore and we shall fly together."

"I shall join him," Edmund spoke up.

"So be it," the dragon replied indifferently. It uncoiled and jumped into the air; powerful wings carried it back to shore as it let out its greatest roar yet.

Seconds later, the roar was answered in the distance and as Garth steered the boat closer to land, a red dragon, far smaller than the black dragon but still far larger than Soren, Edmund and Garth, appeared. It alighted on a beach that became visible as they rounded the tall headland that obscured the rest of the island.

Garth brought his flat-bottomed boat as close as he dared to the shore so they could disembark and then dropped the anchor. "How long should I wait?" he said.

Soren and Edmund, who were busy fetching their possessions, paused for a moment.

"Don't. Get yourself well away from this place. We cannot guarantee our safety, let alone yours," Soren answered.

"Yeh'll be fine, I'm sure," muttered Garth, but it seemed more for his own peace of mind. He seemed uncomfortable with the parting. "Thanks for showing me real dragons though." His weathered face broke in a lopsided grin. "I know I'm not crazy now!"

Soren chuckled. "You weren't imagining things at least, but perhaps your sanity could be questioned for agreeing to chase them?"

Garth guffawed. "Well, I'm as close as I'd want to be now; rather you than me getting closer still, I'll admit."

Soon enough their small pile of possessions was laid out in

several bundles on the shore. Garth stayed on his boat and waved as they emerged dripping from the water.

"I hope I haven't just sent the King of Caledan to his death," he muttered to himself. He raised anchor to take his boat back out to deeper waters before the tide stranded him - or winged beasts snapped him up for lunch.

Flying was disconcerting and Soren returned to solid ground with great relief. He had ridden upon the black dragon's back and Edmund the red's, nestled between and clinging to the huge spikes. The two dragons had gathered up the bags of possessions in their great claws to carry. Garth's small boat soon disappeared behind them as they flew low and quick over the ocean. Wind raced past them as they circled up on thermals, before gliding back over the island and out of sight of the fisherman's craft.

Soren's stomach lurched every time he looked down at the dizzying distance between them and the ground. Instead, he concentrated on looking ahead at either scenery level with them, or better still, the intricate detail and repetition of the dragon's scales. It was not much easier, but he could steady himself enough this way.

At least, he considered, *I am too busy being frightened of the great drop to worry about flying into the midst of a clan of dragons.*

As they rose through the air, the main features of the island became visible. Although one peak was visible from the sea to the south, the island had two volcanic cones: one active and one dormant or extinct. The evidence from minor eruptions in the very recent past dominated the landscape in the form of destructive black trails, which carved through the remaining sparse greenery of the first peak.

The second, inactive peak stood in sharp contrast. Vegetation clothed it almost fully from bottom to top, showing that it had not been subject to any recent disturbances. It was the rocky summit of this cone that the dragons had made their home.

They rose higher than the peak itself and Soren dared to look down at this point, clinging even more carefully to the dragon as the wind rushed past and buffeted him unevenly. His hands were frozen against the ridged scales.

Laying sprawled below was the entire island laid out just like a map, but in colour and very real. Beaches, bays, and cliffs defined the boundaries of the island in a beautiful display of natural forces at work, but the real sight lay at the peaks of the two volcanoes.

Nearby, the northern side of the first volcano had great oozing vents of hot, molten magma, which expelled ribbons of slow-moving lava. The heat and noxious fumes as they flew over this area were almost unbearable, and Soren was glad they did not linger long. They passed over the taller inactive peak at their highest altitude yet before descending towards it.

For a few precious minutes, sunlight broke through the clouds and dropped piercing golden rays onto the ground and water below. A flash of brightest blue caught Soren's eyes as they flew over the old volcano; in the enormous crater lay a huge pool of the calmest, purest blue they had ever seen, with a tiny island in its centre.

The two dragons angled their wings and glided down in ever-smaller spirals. Soren just managed to keep his eyes open as they hurtled down. His stomach turned with the nauseating motion, but his watering eyes were unable to look away from the intoxicating perspective offered to him.

As they plummeted, the crater opened beneath them. It was huge, Soren realised, and the island in its centre not as tiny as it had first appeared but hundreds of metres wide and long. The black dragon roared; it was deafening this close and Soren clapped his hands over his ears as the sound penetrated deep into his head, holding onto the dragon with just his legs.

"*Come all, I summon thee!*"

Soren braced himself for landing with closed eyes, hugging the spike in front of him with both arms as he was rocked back and forth by the powerful downward beats of the dragon's wings and jerks of its body as it slowed to touch down. It landed and stopped in a few paces with a series of giant, shock-absorbing steps that jolted Soren, who almost lost his grasp.

He opened his eyes. The dragon had folded one wing to its side and left the other laid to the ground for him to climb down. Edmund emerged from behind the red dragon, looking shaken by the experience as the black dragon folded in its remaining wing and turned to face Soren. The dragon lowered his head until one of his great eyes was level with the prince's own.

"I have called my clan and they will come." The great dragon spoke with authority. "You shall follow me to our most sacred place and there we shall have our meet." Soren shivered, half with nerves and half with cold, still drenched in now ice cold water.

The dragon turned and strode away, tail slithering on the rocky ground, to the highest point of the small island, which by Soren's best judgement stood about ten feet above the surface of the lake. Their possessions were left in a jumbled heap by the lake as Soren and Edmund hurried to follow.

There was not one tree on the island. It was barren and rocky in the centre of the calm lake, though bathed in light as the crater walls extended not so far up as to darken it. As they climbed to the very top of it, a hollow became visible. It seemed odd to Soren; it was no wider than he was tall and almost circular, and strange gouges he could not account for covered its rim. It took him a minute to realise that the strange gouges were of similar spacing and depth as dragon claws, and he wondered aloud at it.

"We heated the rock with our breath and scraped out the molten stone with our claws," the dragon explained.

Soren's eyes widened in awe, and he moved closer to peer down into it. A shallow pool of still water almost filled the depression. At the bottom, he could see the swirling patterns of claw marks frozen in the stone.

"What is it for?" the prince asked tentatively.

The dragon puffed a small column of smoke from its nostrils. "At the beginning of our time, this was the first nest of the first dragon. In this nest, the mother of our race spawned us all. And now, this nest forms our seeing pool," he said, leaving Soren none the wiser. "With it we can see events from afar and speak with the Eldarkind as we will it." The dragon paused and his eyes flicked skyward. His nostrils twitched.

Faint at first and becoming louder, great wings flapped in the air. Soren raised his eyes from the pool to see dragons approaching from all directions. Some flew directly to land on the island with a tremor that Soren felt through his feet; some spiralled down as they had. All were fearsome and impressive. Soren fought back an instinctive flight response at the sight of their teeth, and claws, and predatory eyes.

Dragons of many colours, shades, and sizes converged; black, grey, brown, red, green, gold, amber and even a few blue dragons. Soren and Edmund stood by the pool, slack-jawed as the clan landed around them, battering them with wind. Hundreds of dragons crowded onto the small island. The red dragon that had borne Edmund, Soren noticed, retreated some distance away.

Once the clacking of claws on stone and the rustling of scales and wings had ceased, the black dragon extended his neck to survey all who gathered about him. The largest and most magnificent of the dragons gathered themselves around the pool, with the smaller dragons craning their necks for a glimpse from further back. It seemed to be a system of classes, where the strongest took precedence.

Soren and Edmund found themselves the focus of hundreds of pairs of glittering eyes belonging to faces with smoking nostrils, slitted pupils, and sharp teeth. Standing on the only clear piece of land he could see, Soren felt like he was on a dragon's dinner plate, and hoped very much that they were not thinking the same thing. His heart pounded deep and fast in his chest and perspiration sprang from his brow.

"I, Myrkith-visir, clan master, have summoned you here with such urgency for a meet of significance that has not been seen for many seasons," rumbled the black dragon, finally naming himself. "Before you all stands a human who comes to claim the Crown of the Dragon Kings."

Soren stood up straighter.

"If it is here, human, why should we pass it to you? What have you done to earn it?" A silvery dragon snaked its head forward from the front row.

"Silence!" snapped Myrkith-visir and the dragon snatched its head back with a hiss. "Our pact with the Eldarkind requires us to act and we must act with caution if we are to keep the peace of the world. If we should fail to make the right choice, the world shall fall into the endless fires. Caledan and its peace is the keystone to the security of the world and we are bound to its fate. Younglings," he said and stood on his hindmost legs to survey the smaller dragons at the rear of the gathering, "you will now experience the true majesty of our aged and unique race."

He lowered himself to the ground with a grace that belied his great bulk and turned to the pool behind him. Uttering a low, continuous moan, echoed by the oldest of the dragons encircling him, a strange melody began weaving itself, ebbing and flowing in volume and tone. Soren gazed entranced at the pool, barely breathing and frozen in anticipation.

As the dragons sang, the water began to ripple and expand upwards, impossibly increasing its bulk. It swirled into a flowing form that had no set definition as it grew to the height of Myrkith-visir and then more, spreading outwards. After what seemed like minutes, though it had in fact been mere seconds, the flowing contortions grew finer as the shape settled into the form of a dragon, whose feet remained tethered to the pool.

Soren stood still, covered in goosebumps with the hairs on the back of his neck rising as he felt the strange power of what they witnessed. It shimmered with the glinting light that caught the forms of the moving water, and he could pick out scales, teeth, and a blinking eye as it swung its head to regard them all. The dragons' song faded and as one, they lowered their heads to bow to it.

"*Wise one*," Myrkith-visir greeted the form. It regarded him and swung its head to Soren without seeming to reply.

"Soren Rasirsson," a strong voice echoed.

TWENTY FOUR

"Zaki is absent," Nolwen said, "and we need to leave. At once."

"Why?" asked Eve, but she scrambled to her feet at his tone, as her intuition tingled with premonition.

"Questions are not welcomed of your new king, it would seem."

"His peace and power is precarious, and he challenges anyone who questions it," Nelda chipped in. She set to packing their meagre possessions, grim-faced.

"That's good for Prince Soren though, no?" Luke asked.

"In a way. If he were here, perhaps he would have a chance. For us? Less so. We've barely beaten the city watch here and I'd guess have seconds to leave before we're hauled out and taken goodness knows where. I'd rather not dilly dally answering questions of them."

Eve quickened her pace, shoving the last of her things into the bag, as Luke swung his own onto his soulder.

"Ready," they said in unison.

"Good," Nelda said. "With me, now. The horses await us out the back."

They crept downstairs and sidled through the back door just as the booted feet of the city soldiers drummed on the floor in the bar at the front of the pub. Muffled voices came from the front, harsh and demanding. Nolwen chivvied them out bodily, latching the door behind them and moving a few choice obstructions in the way, before he joined them on horseback and they left with as much haste as they dared without arising suspicion.

Eve's heart hammered in her chest as they rode, a beat for every hoof that pounded on the road. She checked and double checked her bright, unusual hair was tucked in the shawl that she had tied around her head to cover it, wondering how much the soldiers knew of them. "Where are we going?"

Nolwen sped them up as they left the city without, onto the open road of the country.

"South. The Royal Forest. We'll be safe there." There was no punishment for passing through the forest, but as hunting was prohibited, few locals bothered to stray beyond its borders; preferring instead to set up small rabbit snares on its edge where trapping was legal.

Nolwen, Nelda, Eve, and Luke slipped into the forest at the earliest opportunity. They guided their horses off the beaten track and let them trot into the forest until all signs of habitation behind them were gone.

The forest completely extinguished the noise of the city, even though they were still in easy reach of the city gates, a deceptive illusion that lulled Eve into thinking they were in the depths of the countryside. Even though she knew it not to be the case, rustling leaves and muted birdsong helped her relax after Pandora's hustle and bustle.

Since landing in Pandora, the irresponsibility, rashness, and implications of her actions were dawning on her. *I must not have doubts now. Irumae needs my help.* She resolved to scry the princess again that night, regretting the lack of privacy she had had since Ednor and feeling guilty that she had not yet managed to scry her father, Soren or Irumae.

By the time they had scouted the area and made camp, it was almost too late to venture back into the walled city. The gates closed every day an hour after sundown until dawn the next morning. The exception was the dock gate, which shut later and opened earlier for business to commence.

Nolwen and Nelda decided to return to the dock front anyway to lurk about in the public spaces in the hope of seeing or hearing something useful. Eve agreed to remain behind. She cursed her conspicuous appearance, which the Eldarkind refused to disguise. Luke would not leave her alone in the woods, so the Eldarkind departed without them.

Eve was glad he remained behind, so she did not have to be alone in the unfamiliar place, but a little frustrated as it meant that she would not be able to use the scrying mirror in his presence. Although she was sure she could trust him, she was reluctant to show him its power; he already seemed unnerved by any display of magic.

As they waited for Nolwen and Nelda to return, they sat with their backs against the bank and talked freely as they watched the horses graze on long tethers. Eve felt at ease in his presence, as she always had done when they were children. It felt to her just as it had then and filled her with a warmth, knowing she had one friend in the world that would follow her so far.

Luke was surprisingly open in return; since finishing in the town school at the age of eleven, she had returned to her father's care for private tutelage whilst Luke, who was slightly older, had already joined the ranks of the guards. He had started at the lowest rank, working his way up to just below captain before they had departed.

Until he joined the ranks of the household guard with Nyle, the only contact they had were brief encounters, mostly in the training ground where the guardsmen trained daily. Eve had also trained with them at her father's insistence. Lord Karn had never believed in mollycoddling his daughter; she was the heir to the county and he wanted her to succeed him, rather than have Arrow county ruled by an outsider. It was a wish that was now becoming his demise. His desire for her obedience could not match the level of independence and free thinking he had allowed her.

Now, she was halfway across Caledan. She knew it would be against her father's wishes. For the first time she felt concerned her actions might not pay off and what the consequences might be. In a world ruled by laws and politics, her actions might have consequences beyond herself—consequences that could affect her father, her home, and the land she loved, which would one day would be hers.

She shared all of this with Luke and the moments of her life that he had missed and in turn, he shared such moments with her.

They laughed together into the sunset and beyond as darkness fell. They lit no fire, but the darkness did not feel as intimidating as it first had to Eve when they set out from Arlyn, now she had acclimatised to the night time sights and sounds.

Eve lay down that night as they awaited the Eldarkind's return, whilst Luke took the first watch, feeling happier than she had in a while. She bid him a warm good night, but could not settle. She must have slept, for the next thing she knew, she was shaken awake with a hand hovering over her mouth. She struggled, about to cry out, when Luke whispered to her.

"Eve, shh, it's me! I'm sorry." He apologised and removed his hand hastily as she stopped squirming. "I didn't want you to make a sound. There are horses nearby; I don't know who they are."

She sat up. It was nearly pitch black. They could see the faint glow of the moon through the trees, though it offered little light to them. She could indeed hear horses nearby – and the pounding of her own heart – but the tramp and rustle of their hooves came from a different direction to where their own horses rested. Adrenaline coursed through her, her heart pounding.

"Lady Eve? Luke?" The faint cry came and she sagged with relief.

"Nelda!" Luke called and scrambled to stand up. From behind the bank, the Eldarkind emerged, each holding a lamp that illuminated the trees and forest floor. "Are you alright?"

Eve shook off her thin blanket and stood to greet them. She was not sure whether it was due to the poor light, but they appeared tired for the first time since she had met them.

"What time is it?" Eve asked, disorientated by her sleep.

"The second hour of the new day," Nelda replied as her brother tethered their two horses by the beck. She sank onto her blankets.

Eve waited for her to speak.

"We think we might have found a way. We shall talk when we awake. Can you keep guard tonight?"

Eve agreed despite her disappointment. Nelda thanked her, before she descended into her blankets, closely followed by Nolwen.

Light snores soon rose from their still forms.

"I'll stay up," said Eve. She held out her hand for the second lamp.

"Wake me when you tire," replied Luke, before he too lay down to sleep.

Eve set up her blankets between Luke and Nelda, who were a metre away on either side, placing both lamps by her feet and extinguishing one. Before she woke Luke for his watch, she thought he muttered her name, but in her tiredness, she could not be sure. Once she was certain he was awake, she passed him the lamp and fell asleep.

Nolwen and Nelda still slumbered peacefully when she awoke. She yawned, and Luke glanced down and smiled at her.

"Morning." They greeted each other as she rose to wash her face and hands in the brook. She felt stiff and grimy that day. Splashing the cool water over her face, she longed for the luxury of a bath and could not remember how many days it had been since Ednor and her last proper wash. A hot bath, she decided, was her target; however she might procure it.

As she stretched and wandered back to camp, Nolwen and Nelda stirred. They too washed and broke fast as they explained their ventures the previous night.

"We passed up and down the docks," Nelda said, "stopping off in the inns along the way. We found one tavern, close to the dock gate, that seemed to be a favourite of the off duty city guardsmen and so we lingered there the longest, until turning out time at midnight."

"I have a sore head this morning." Nolwen grimaced. Nelda buffeted him on the shoulder.

"That is your own fault, brother! You should have kept to water like I." She admonished him, though not harshly. She turned back to Luke and Eve to continue. "In any case, we heard many an interesting thing. Zaki left the city after the seven days of mourning for Queen Naisa, riding north as if the very devils of the earth were after him and taking a large contingent of men. He returned days later with nothing to show for it.

"He was crowned not two days after his return. However, his coronation was not after the fashion of old. There was no blessing performed by the abbot, who seems to have vanished—imprisoned or dead are the rumours—and the dragon guardian did not release the throne to him. The archbishop crowned him with a simple ceremonial crown, though he maintained the rest of the usual pomp. The people rest uneasy at this. It does not sit well that he is unblessed by both abbot and great spirit and does not even possess the traditional crown, as all good kings and queens must if Caledan's history and lore is anything to judge by.

"There are already mutterings that Soren is alive and has fled not as a coward and a criminal, but to gather men and rightfully take his throne by force. There are whispers—and only whispers, for anything louder would be certain treason—that the king is not so innocent as he would have his subjects believe. I have reason to suspect that should it come to it, some, perhaps many of the guard and the city folk would support the prince if and when he returns.

"A few days ago, Zaki rode south. Apparently, he shall meet with a small force of his father-in-law King Harad's soldiers, who will return to the city to ensure the successful transition to his rule. I am not certain how credible the source is, but we can be sure that he is absent for now."

"I hope that will help us," said Luke. "If he is absent, few should remain to guard the palace."

"We can be hopeful it will be favourable for us that he is away," Nelda said.

"Did you find anything that may help us enter the castle?" asked Eve.

Nolwen nodded and then groaned. "You had best continue, sister. My head betrays me."

Nelda rolled her eyes. "We cannot hope to acquire any plans of the city or castle, but there is one way we might be able to access the castle in broad daylight without being seen."

Eve was not convinced and Luke seemed cautious.

"Magic?" he asked.

"No, that would be much too complicated," said Nelda. "The

castle has its own private dock."

Luke and Eve remained nonplussed.

"This dock," Nelda said, "is underground and can only be reached by a channel that flows from the lake right into the hill and under the castle itself, ending in a large chamber where boats can moor. It is how all provisions destined for the castle arrive. Rather than carting them into the city from the common docks and up the hill and then through the castle itself, it is much easier to sail them up this channel, moor the boats at the pool within, and then offload the goods. For all we know, it could be the route Soren took to escape from right under Zaki's nose."

"How could we access it?" Eve asked.

"It still may not be our best option," said Nelda. "We still do not know where Irumae is held; we are assuming she is in the castle at all."

"I think I can shed some light on that," said Eve. She regretted having to reveal her secret possession but knew that it would be necessary to convince the others. She retrieved the black box containing the scrying mirror from her saddlebag and sat down again. She took out the mirror and placed it down before her on top of the box so it did not touch the dirt.

"Ah! Good idea." Nelda smiled.

"*Leitha Irumae*," she whispered to it. The mirror's surface distorted and swam with colours, until once more she saw the room that contained Irumae. It was the same room, darkened with no visible windows, and she suggested that it could mean the princess resided within the dungeons. Irumae remained still on the bed, unconscious, as Eve had last seen her.

"She could be drugged," murmured Nelda, with pity in her eyes, "but she seems to be alive, which is something, and we can hope that she has been treated well."

"Do you agree she could be in the dungeons though?" Eve said.

Nelda frowned. Nolwen did not react. His hand still cradled his head and his hair fell forward over his face. Luke remained impassive with a troubled gaze.

"It may be a good indicator," Nelda replied, "though of course they may simply have closed and barred the shutters on her window. The dungeons should be easiest to reach if we enter the castle by the docks. Shall we?"

Silence fell. It was time to make their decision; to attempt to enter the castle, or to abandon the idea altogether.

TWENTY FIVE

Soren gasped and his mouth fell open with astonishment at the strange being that knew his name. He felt a great weight and everything around him seemed to fall away as the figure scrutinised him and he could do nothing but gaze back. Transfixed yet unsettled, shivers crawled over his skin.

"I am Brithilca," the ethereal dragon rumbled, confirming Soren's guess.

Soren bowed low to the watery figure. "I am honoured to meet you, Great Dragon."

"I know why you are here. I cannot give you the crown, though it is within my power to bestow it."

"Why not?" asked Soren, forgetting manners and courtesy and stepping forward in his surprise.

"You are yet to prove yourself and the true nature of your character," the dragon explained. He growled as Soren began to protest. "Peace, youngling. I know of your circumstances, I know of what you have endured to reach this place, and I know of your legitimacy through your bloodline; it is not enough. Before you can inherit the Crown of the Dragon Kings, you must prove your worth, prove that you are worthy to ensure the peace of the realm."

"My uncle has already seized the realm under false pretences and if I cannot claim the crown, the kingdom will fall to him!" exclaimed Soren. "I cannot let that happen! His madness, cruelty, and self-serving nature would do irreparable damage to Caledan!"

"Peace, youngling," said the great dragon once more. His voice swelled in magnitude. "Zaki sought to take the crown by force from its resting place, without earning the privilege of possessing it. For that and other reasons, it will never be his to hold."

"If you will not give me the crown to prove I am the rightful heir," replied Soren, subdued, "then how am I to prove myself at all? Zaki already holds the kingdom in name and by force of military might. There is no one else but he and I who could hold a claim to the throne and I have nothing to back mine with, though I am certain I would make a more just guardian to our people than he. How can I overcome that?"

"It will not be easy, yet the seeds of his downfall are already sown. He has already been crowned, but not with the true Crown of the Dragon Kings, and he extends his hands holding the keys of the realm to the men of the south, who have long desired Caledan as their trophy.

"Thus, the people know him for what he is: a fraud. He has no love for them, save for the fruits of their toil helping him meet his own selfish ends, and they see this and do not trust or serve him well him for it. You have but to extend your hand to them. If your true nature is that worthy of a king of Caledan, the people will flock to your banners. You will have victory and you shall prove you are worthy of lifting the true crown onto your head."

"How do you know this?" wondered Soren, distracted from the disappointment of being denied the crown.

"I am at one with the world," Brithilca said. When Soren did not reply, he continued. "The dragons have had a long standing pact with the Eldarkind. It is our duty alongside them to safeguard Caledan and through its peace, the rest of the world. Caledan is the keystone. Thus I, and we, know of the world as we watch it to ensure peace reigns. Although my body rests beneath your citadel, my spirit roams free, and although the Eldarkind remain in their secret realm, they see the world through their hidden eyes."

Soren pondered Brithilca's answer. He wondered what he meant by roaming spirits and hidden eyes, but pushed aside his curiosity.

"If you and yours guard the peace, as you say you do, then surely you will invoke the old alliance to help me cleanse the kingdom of Zaki's illegitimate reign and any claim his father-in-law might stake to Caledan," Soren said more boldly than he felt, hoping it would pay off.

Brithilca did not reply immediately. "You make a daring request of me," said the dragon spirit. "Already the world moves at a fast pace with dangers greater than Zaki growing and I fear our involvement will be needed in some way. I must speak with the Eldarkind first. You shall leave me now and return here in the morning at first light. I will tell you our decision."

Soren and Edmund bowed to Brithilca. The dragons lowered their necks again, all except Myrkith-visir, who held Brithilca's gaze as if in a private conversation of their own. Finally, Myrkith-visir too dropped his long neck in submission and murmured a faint "Brithilca-visir" in parting. The sound of rushing, trickling water filled their ears. Seconds later, Brithilca was gone. The pool settled to rest again.

Dragons departed around them with great leaps into the sky. They battered and buffeted those who remained with gusts of air. Soren felt as if he were in the midst of a jewelled flock of birds as they took off and scattered into the sky. During the appearance of Brithilca's spirit, the sun had deigned to shine and blue skies dominated, illuminating the crater lake and causing the dragons to glitter fiercely as they passed overhead and out of sight beyond the crater rim in all directions.

Soon, three dragons remained: Myrkith-visir and two others dwarfed by his size. Both were shades of earthy brown and Soren was sure that if they curled up, he could mistake them on a murky day for gnarled tree roots. Myrkith-visir entrusted the care of Soren and Edmund to the two dragons, Feldloga and Feldith.

The flight to their overnight shelter was much rougher than their previous journey with Myrkith-visir, requiring more laboured flapping to gain enough altitude to fly over the crater rim, which jolted Soren about as he clung to a spike on Feldloga's back trying not to vomit. Compared to Myrkith-visir's bulk, the smaller dragons, although still towering above Soren and Edmund, felt insubstantial beneath them.

Once they landed, Soren sat with his head between his legs until the nausea subsided. As he recovered, he lifted his head, hair tousled, to notice the two dragons sat close by. They regarded him with tilted heads, like a dog or a cat might.

"Is this your home?" he asked them.

One answered the affirmative, which one he could not tell.

"Feldloga," the dragon reminded him. "It's easy to tell. I'm the handsome one."

His brother growled and swiped at him with his tail. Feldloga rumbled in laughter.

Soren stood unsteadily to survey his surroundings. Vegetation obscured his view to the right; trees and shrubs he did not recognise, though the patchy grass beneath his feet that petered out further up the peak looked familiar enough. He scanned the rest of the panorama.

The cave behind him was nothing more than a deep impression partly formed naturally from the rock beneath an overhang and partly scraped out by the dragons to offer some shelter. He saw dried grasses lined it, forming a thick layer of insulation from the cold stone. Structured piles of rubble to either side of the entrance extended the barrier against wind and weather.

The most impressive view, however, lay before him. The land swept away and, except for one large rise which obscured the beach, he could see all the way to the sea. From here, the shallows were azure. As he gazed further afield, he could see the stark contrast of the steely grey-blue waters out to sea that swirled under matching clouds.

"It's beautiful," Soren murmured. They were so high and so far north that the weather had a noticeable chill to it despite the bright sun, and when the breeze rose, Soren shivered.

"It's cold this far north, isn't it," Edmund remarked.

"Not for dragons," Feldith said, and ruffled his wings. "But, if you're cold, fetch some wood, and we'll light you a fire."

Soren scrambled to his feet and rushed down the hill a ways to fetch some wood from the gnarled bushes that grew thereabouts. When he returned, Feldith stirred, snaking his neck forward. Opening his jaws just a fraction, he rumbled, and a jet of white hot flames shot out, licking at the wood and catching it ablaze in a second. Within minutes, the fire roared hot and strong, and Soren warmed his front and back on it gratefully.

"Thank you."

"Our pleasure, princeling."

"Call me Soren."

"Soren."

"How long have you lived here?"

"Our clan has been here since the dawn of the pact."

Soren raised his eyebrows. *So long? A thousand years?* "Do… do you like living here?"

"I don't understand."

"Well, would you live elsewhere?" *Maybe it's not so unpleasant for the dragons, if they cannot feel the cold here.*

"The pact forbids it."

"Oh…" *That doesn't seem fair.* Soren realised he knew very little of the pact that man, Eldarkind, and dragon had made; a pact for peace that clearly had more subtleties than he knew.

The two dragons and the two men spent the rest of the day in conversation, each race curious about the other. Other young dragons, overcome by curiosity, continued to arrive, until there was hardly any space left around the two men. It became apparent to Soren that the dragons could tell them apart as poorly as Soren and Edmund could differentiate between the two brown dragons. This caused some amusement to both sides, although all parties were adamant that the differences between them were obvious.

Soren and Edmund were the first humans that the young dragons had laid eyes on; they were curious to understand how such small, scale-less, wing-less, claw-less and to their eyes teeth-less creatures could hold dominion over most of the known world. Edmund and Soren showed the dragons their swords and small knives; the dragons remained unconvinced.

A black dragon put it to them with derision, "How can you do anything with one claw?"

"Well, what if you had just one claw to fight with?" asked Soren, emboldened.

The dragon growled in response, as his companions let out strange rumbles that seemed to be laughter. "I am Myrkdaga, son of

Myrkith, and I am a dragon, not a mouse!"

Faced with a row of glittering teeth so close to his head, Soren reconsidered. "I meant no offence," he said contritely.

Myrkdaga, Feldloga, and Feldith were the boldest of the dragons, Soren discovered, although Myrkdaga seemed dominant and the others deferred to him.

Although still awed by their size, several feet taller than Edmund, who was no short man himself, they discovered that they were the younger dragons of the clan. Feldloga and Feldith were brood-mates of twelve years old, sired by Myrkith-visir's younger brother, and Myrkdaga slightly older.

So young, thought Soren, *yet so huge!*

Both Feldloga and Feldith, though this was not immediately apparent to Soren or Edmund, were males, with fierce attitudes and each strove to dominate the other. The sibling rivalry was almost comical in their attempts to outwit each other and take the last word on a matter, but Soren sensed that he did not want to be in the middle of the more physical expressions of their disagreement if he could help it.

The two brother dragons lived together because they were still too young to fight with either each other or larger dragons for a more prominent position in the clan. According to Feldith, the lifespan of a dragon was so long that it would be at least another twelve years before they would be big enough to fight or seek a mate. Soren did not dare to ask how old Myrkith-visir was.

Their sharp minds were impressive; despite their youth, they seemed to be wise and witty beyond their years and Soren would have sworn, had he not been able to see their bodies, that he was conversing with another human. It was bizarre to experience the contrast of their predatory bodies—perfectly designed for fighting, hunting and killing—and their minds, which possessed astounding intelligence.

As the sun set, and Edmund dumped more wood onto the dying fire, the dragons challenged them to a game of wit. Soren shared a glance with Edmund, who gave him a small smile.

"Alright," said Soren, emboldened. "Outwit us."

"Riddles first, methinks." Feldloga's eyes half-shut in what Soren could have sworn was a look of smug pleasure.

He held his chin high. "As you wish."

Feldloga began, shooting his brother a mischievous look. "A dragon bathed a warrior in flame. No being came to help him, and yet he did not die. How is it possible?"

Soren gaped. "Uhm… he was immortal!" he blurted after a minute of silence.

Feldith snorted with laughter.

"No; he was already dead!"

"Well… he could also have been immortal," Soren defended himself. "Technically."

Feldloga rumbled. "Fine. Another riddle. Your turn."

Soren cleared his throat. "You buy me to eat, but never eat me. What am I?"

Feldith conferred with Feldloga for a good long while. "We do not know," he admitted grumpily.

Soren beamed. "Crockery, of course!"

"What is 'crockery'?"

"Oh. I… well I suppose you don't use it. We place food on crockery—plates, bowls and the like—to eat it."

"What a silly riddle," Feldloga grumbled. "No dragon needs 'crockery'. Give us one we shall know."

"Ah, but isn't that the point?" Soren asked with a wicked grin. "They're not meant to be easy!"

"I fly without wings and cry without eyes," Feldloga fired back, with narrowed eyes that glittered with annoyance.

Edmund stirred excitedly. "I know this one! Clouds! Clouds!"

"Well done," the dragon said grudgingly. "Your turn."

Edmund pondered. "Ok, I have one. If you desire me, you must share me, yet if you share me, I am no more."

"A secret," Myrkdaga chipped in after a while, rumbling with satisfaction at his cleverness.

"Well done," acknowledged Edmund, dipping his head.

"My turn…" Myrkdaga said gleefully. "I stay by you all day; you cannot be rid of me. Yet, at night, I am nowhere to be found.

What am I?"

"Light?" Soren rushed.

"No!" Myrkdaga pounced on the incorrect answer. "Try again."

"I stay by you all day…" Soren murmured the riddle to himself. He glanced at Edmund, who frowned and shook his head, deep in thought but with no answers too.

"Do you yield?" Myrkdaga loomed out of the darkness with a terrifying, toothy grin.

Edmund sighed, and shared another look - this time of a man defeated - with Soren.

"Fine," Soren admitted. "We yield. What is it?"

Feldloga reared up. The fire cast flickering light across his shining scales, and cast a monstrous sized version of him in shadow on the cave wall behind him. "Shadow!" he said gleefully.

Soren groaned, and rolled his eyes. "Now it makes sense."

That night, after being outfoxed in games of riddles by the wily dragons, Soren fell asleep to dreams of sweeping away Zaki under a storm of dragon fire as he descended with the entire might of the dragon clan behind him.

The following morning dawned bright as the rumbling of stirring dragons woke Soren with a start. He had spent the night on a pile of dried grasses in the dragons' cave, whilst the dragons laid underneath the stars. It was sheltered and had retained enough heat to keep them warm despite the altitude and the latitude.

Soren dressed, wishing for a hot bath. Every inch of him was caked with dirt despite yesterday's dunking in the sea. He wore his other set of clothes, which were marginally cleaner, wrinkling his nose with distaste at the state of the last as he scrunched them up into a bundle. They were covered in grime, fish slime, and probably worse.

Next to the magnificent dragons, who cleaned themselves with barbed tongues, scraping each scale until it shone, he felt disgustingly inferior. Half-asleep, he wondered if they despised his scent and was glad that he had grown unable to smell himself.

Eager to hear the dragons' judgement, they returned to the small island in the crater lake where they found Myrkith-visir waiting by the pool. This time, without the power of the entire clan's summoning, Brithilca's face swam beneath the surface of the tiny pool as if it were a reflection. They knelt by the poolside, with Myrkith-visir lowering his neck so it was level with their heads. Feldloga and Feldith waited some distance away, beside Myrkdaga, who had insisted on accompanying them.

Soren addressed him today as 'Brithilca-visir,' understanding now from Feldloga that 'visir' was a special term of respect for the highest of the clan; applied only to Myrkith, the clan chief, and Brithilca, the great dragon spirit.

'The decision has been made," Brithilca said.

Soren froze, not even breathing.

"One of the clan will escort you to Pandora."

One... thought Soren. He closed his eyes in dismay. *What can one dragon do?* His dream of sweeping Zaki away under a mighty assault now seemed impossible.

"My kin will take you to Pandora and return henceforth. The clan will take no part in your affairs."

Soren opened his mouth to protest, but Brithilca did not pause.

"It is you who must unite the kingdom. Only then can you claim the crown of your forebears and then will it be your right to do so."

Soren bowed to the ground. Disappointment rendered the words hollow as he tried to thank Brithilca. He was not sure if the dragon sensed his insincerity or not.

"I also bear you a message from Queen Artora of the Eldarkind. She bade me tell you this to give you hope in a dark time." Brithilca's voice ceased, and there spoke into Soren's mind a different voice; one that made his heart quicken.

"Prince Soren, you stand out of favour and luck with life," the rich, warm voice of Queen Artora said. Soren saw the flash of a disembodied smile in his mind's eye and felt a strange sensation of a hand upon his head as she spoke. "Fear not, for although you face perils beyond your imagination, if you cannot unite the kingdom, no one can. This I have foreseen. Go with confidence to Pandora and speak to Caledan's people of your hopes and desires for their kingdom and they will rise up and follow you. Ride into your city not with an army, but with honesty."

He saw the smile again as the light touch faded. The voice disappeared and a tear sprang to his eye at the sadness its departure left him. The voice was loving, soothing, reassuring. He longed to hear it again.

Silence fell. Soren did not speak to break it and pondered what he had heard. Myrkith stirred.

"You should depart immediately, Prince Soren," he said. Any hope Soren had that Myrkith would lend him more support than Brithilca had allowed was crushed.

Dragons were not subject to the long drawn out partings and ceremonies that Soren was accustomed to. They exchanged a quick farewell with Brithilca, although Soren would have longed to stay and talk with him for days if he could, wholly fascinated by the spirit and his knowledge. Brithilca faded from the pool and Myrkith too departed with few words or ceremony.

Soren was delighted to learn Feldloga and Feldith would fly alongside them part of the way to return Soren and Edmund to the mainland, unbeknownst to Myrkith-visir, for they longed to stretch their wings. However, he was apprehensive when he learnt that Myrkdaga would be the one to carry them to Pandora; it meant flying all the way and after their disagreements the previous day.

The journey would take a few days, instead of weeks sailing back to land with Garth and travelling the remainder of the way on horseback. This was advantageous for Soren, who realised that speed would be of the essence, but the thought of flying such a long distance when the two short journeys he had previously embarked on upon dragonback had been so nauseating, was less than welcome.

Soren felt overwhelmed by the dragons as they gathered up into bundles his and Edmund's few possessions to transport in their giant clawed feet. Ever practical, Edmund had noticed how sharp the dragons' scales were and laid, with their permission, one thin blanket over each back; it was all they had that could suffice as a makeshift saddle and protective layer.

Soren appreciated Edmund's quick thinking. Even riding a horse saddled was sore enough. He did not want to imagine flying all the way to Pandora seated on razor sharp scales. As he watched, Edmund punctured holes in two corners of each blanket and passed through a length of cord to tie around the dragons' bellies.

To their credit, the two dragons were tolerant of what must have seemed to them a very strange practice. Soren, having an appreciation for the great status of the legendary creatures, felt guilty about having to treat them as if they were pack horses and made an effort not to call the makeshift contraption a saddle, for fear of offending them. He thanked them for agreeing to bear them and the other dragons for carrying their things, before he climbed up Feldith's leg.

Once mounted, there was one more addition to make to their makeshift riding gear. Both Soren and Edmund tied a short length of rope around one wrist, passed it around the spike in front of them and then tied it around the other wrist.

They did not tie these too tightly, but it would mean that, if they lost their grip on the spike when buffeted with wind, they were more likely to be able to right themselves without falling off. Soren resolved to devise an easier way to ride a dragon.

All too suddenly, they were flying. Myrkdaga took a running leap into the air and rose with strong wing-beats. Feldloga and Feldith, having things grasped in their claws, crouched and with the enormous strength of their haunches, jumped into flight.

Soren held onto the spike and hugged it close so his face touched the smooth, almost warm, bone-like material. Then Feldith jumped, jolting Soren again and again as he flapped to gain altitude. A wingspan to his side rose Feldloga.

The island fell away beneath them until they could not see the small pool where Brithilca's incarnation had risen. The crater lake dwindled as they left it behind and then they were over the rim of the crater, returning the way they had come. They soared down the heights of the rich green inactive peak, gliding around its black and scarred but now sleeping sister peak.

"Take us down please!" Soren shouted as he noticed the tiny boat waiting for them in the bay. He was surprised Garth had waited for them, and he smiled, feeling sudden warmth for the stranger they had roped into the hare-brained mission.

"*Why?*" questioned Feldith.

"The man who brought us here is just down in the bay, still waiting for news of us. I would like to go to him to thank him for his support and release him from his service."

Feldith conferred with Myrkdaga, who grudgingly agreed to land on the beach where his father had first appeared to Soren and Edmund. Feldith roared to announce their presence as they circled low over the ship. Within moments, Garth stumbled out of the cabin in panic, with a pan on his head, clutching the most pathetic makeshift bow Soren had ever seen. Soren burst out laughing. Garth looked up, open-mouthed, as the three dragons soared over him and landed on the beach.

Soren untied his hands and slipped down from Feldith's back as Garth swam to shore with short, efficient strokes. He emerged dripping from the water as Soren met him at the shore, the prince grasping forearms with him. Garth looked over Soren's shoulder at the three scaled predators, who crouched on the beach with their glittering eyes fixed on him.

"Some escort, eh?" Garth gulped, half-frozen in the scaled behemoths' gazes.

Soren chuckled. "Thank you for waiting," he said to the fisherman. "We won't be sailing back to Pandora, however," Soren admitted. "We'll be flying."

"All the way from here to there?" Garth gaped. "Gods, aren't yeh scared you'll fall off? I beg yer pardon." He backtracked.

"I can't say it appeals to me, but the speed would hold a great advantage," Soren said with a grim smile. "Can I ask a favour of you though, Garth?"

"Of course," said the fisherman.

"Our horses will have no way to return with us, except in the stomachs of my new esteemed companions." One of the dragons behind him snorted in a rumbling laugh. "I regret I hold greater affection for them than that and wouldn't wish to leave them behind either if possible. Would you send them to me in Pandora by any means as soon as you land? I will reward you handsomely."

Garth considered it for a moment. "It should be possible," he said slowly. "I'll see what I can do." The prince thanked him and then they bade each other farewell. The fisherman swam back to his boat whilst Soren remounted Feldith. Edmund had already climbed back into Feldloga's makeshift saddle.

With a run and a leap, Myrkdaga took to the air again and his companions followed in quick succession. They soared upwards in wide circles; over the small bay, over the boat where Garth stood with his hand raised, over the cliffs and then out to sea and south. The islands soon faded behind them as they climbed higher and higher, and soared further away. Soon, there was nothing below them but an expanse of blue.

TWENTY SIX

"Yes," said Eve. She examined the image of Irumae in the mirror before her. "It might be our best chance and for now, it's our one chance to help her. That's what I came for. I'll go even if none of you join me." She felt nervous at the prospect of going alone, unprepared as she was, but knew she could not ask the others to follow her.

"I'll go," Luke said, though he stared at the mirror with a furrowed brow.

Eve met his sincere eyes and a beaming smile crossed her face.

"I shall come," Nelda said serenely. "I would not have come so far to leave you now."

Nolwen was last to speak. "As will I. I have not had a good fight in many years." He grinned at his sister, who tutted at him.

"Thank you," said Eve. "I appreciate your support beyond words." She studied Irumae's image one last time. The young girl remained prone, stretched out on the bed. "*Lessa*," she murmured and Irumae faded away as the mirror returned to reflecting the web of leaves of the forest canopy above it.

"There's just one more thing," Eve added. Nolwen and Nelda looked at her. "You need to disguise me. I stand out like a sore thumb as I am, and I don't have the power to do so myself. I won't be left behind." Her mouth set in a line that brooked no argument.

"It will be dangerous," said Nelda.

Eve glared at her.

"And it is against etiquette to change another's features," said Nolwen.

"I'm asking you to. Etiquette be damned."

The siblings shared a look, and Nelda's mouth tweaked in a hint of a smile. "Very well, Eve, if you insist."

As they muttered and passed their hands over her, Eve felt a tingle rushing through her, though otherwise, she felt no difference.

"Wow." Luke gawked.

Eve scrambled for the scrying mirror and peered into it. Her eyes widened; now they were brown, her skin more tanned, and her hair dark brown. "I look so…"

"Exactly. You'll blend right in," said Nolwen with a grin.

The sun was already high in the sky, and so they made haste for the city in their disguises - save for Luke who needed none. Nolwen still felt the effects of his drinks the previous night an grumbled the entire way at the ride, which jarred his thick head, but Nelda allowed him no sympathy and pushed him all the harder for it, to Eve's amusement.

They spent the day frequenting the dockside taverns and markets in pairs. Nolwen and Nelda wove through the throngs of people, listening for anything useful, whilst Luke and Eve moved from tavern to tavern, watching the comings and goings of all the vessels in the bay, large and small, with a mind to which went to the royal docks.

They met that evening as the sun set in a rowdy tavern that stunk of crab and fish. The four perched in a dingy corner on rickety stools so old and grey with weathering it felt as though they would snap under their weight, with a mug of the local brew each. Eve could not drink hers; she took one sniff and gagged. Luke forced his down, tight-lipped. Nolwen and Nelda ignored theirs.

"By what we saw, there would be no way to procure passage on one of these boats; foot passengers are not accepted into the castle, especially by such a vulnerable route," said Nelda. "Nor could we hope to gain entry to the boats on a working basis; I doubt they accept any old stranger from the docks to man boats at the drop of a hat. Even if they did, it would be too slow, and too much would be left to chance."

"Luke may have found a way." Eve looked to Luke to continue.

Luke cleared his throat. "I noticed the marina doesn't have gangways large enough for all the boats to moor at. It means some boats have to drop anchor in the lake itself and row in and out of the marina in small rowing boats, which the city keeps for communal use. It's such a busy place that no one seems to take any notice of who uses them. One would just about fit the four of us in it; if we could happen to borrow one for the night, we could slip unnoticed out of the marina and into the royal dock."

"That's brilliant," said Nelda, surprised by the simplicity of the solution.

With nightfall approaching, they rode from the city once more and tethered the horses with their possessions just outside it in a small, secluded dell away from the road, for Nolwen wisely suggested they may need a quick escape route.

They dressed in light armour pieces in silence. Eve wore hers for the first time, slipping the chain mail over her top and strapping the greaves and bracers onto her shins and arms. She braided her hair in a long plait as Nelda had, which flowed down her back, and double-checked that her helmet fitted well. The weight of the armour was noticeable, even though it was not a full suit and the Eldarkind smiths had somehow made it light enough to not hinder or burden her.

Eve flexed her arms and legs, trying to move in all directions to check she had full mobility and blushing when the others laughed at her strange movements. On her left hip, she hung her sword in its scabbard from her belt and on her right, the Eldarkind dagger, and she checked she could draw both without hindrance. The routine felt familiar, as if she were dressing in light armour for a training session at home.

Lastly, she regarded her bow, which had hung disused from her saddle since she left Arlyn. It would not do for the confined spaces inside the castle. She stroked its smooth wooden limb fondly and left it atop her pile of belongings, next to her quiver, hoping they would still be there when she returned. Once finished, she saw Nolwen and Nelda similarly attired, although they retained their brown-haired and dark-eyed disguises, like her.

Luke had donned the traditional style of armour Eve wore to train in at Arlyn; chain mail shirt reinforced with thick leather plates on the front and back, bracers that extended to protect the back of his hand and the first joint of the fingers, greaves that extended up to protect the kneecaps. On top of that, he wore a formal helmet that protected the back of his neck and carried a small shield—more of a buckler than a true shield—which he hung from his hand, and a half broadsword handle that sat in his belt.

They ate what they could to give them strength through the night and concealed their armour beneath cloaks. Keeping to the wooded borders for as long as possible before venturing out onto a road in pairs, they kept their heads down and their armour hidden below their cloaks, blending in amongst the many other users of the road.

By the time they reached the docks on foot and retired to yet another tavern, this one with the distinct aroma of smoked mackerel, the moon had risen, and the last dregs of sunlight were fading from the sky, along with the hubbub of activity from the docks. When life had faded around them—having moved inside either the taverns, ships, or city—they stirred with nervous excitement.

Nolwen sprinted onto the northernmost gangway and wove between crates and mooring ropes until he found a rowing boat tied up between two larger craft that hid it from the dockside. Once he had untied its mooring, he signalled to the others to join him.

They piled into the boat, which sunk low into the water under their weight. There were two sets of oars resting in the boat across its two benches, so they took one each and coordinated their strokes to move through the marina, keeping behind large boats wherever they could to remain hidden from shore.

The night was clear and large clouds drifted across the sky, obscuring the small amount of moonlight available; it helped conceal them, but hindered their movement through the maze of crafts. Eve could not be sure how long it took before they made it unseen to the mouth of the cave, although it seemed like hours.

The void-like opening swallowed them in oppressive darkness. The pitch-black tunnel was not long, and they could see a dim glow ahead from the underground dock. Even so, it was a disconcerting journey, moving through the darkness and gliding over still, black water.

As they exited the tunnel, the cave broadened out to huge proportions. They could see no one, although they could hear the faint sounds of talking coming from the guardroom. The water was still here, being so sheltered, and there were small barges moored.

The cave had formed naturally, though an entrance had been bored down to it from above many centuries ago. A small guardhouse guarded the way, next to a gate with a portcullis that could be lowered to protect it; a strange sight in an underground cave. A raised stone floor had been constructed by backfilling part of the cave so that there was a wide area to offload goods; this also meant that there was an open area for them to cross that would risk their discovery.

The floor level was almost high enough to hide them in the shadows as they sculled across the water. They stowed the oars with a tiny clunk and the rowing boat glided to the wall with what was left of its momentum.

It came to the wall side-on and Luke and Nelda stretched their arms out to touch the wall first and push against it to slow the boat to a stop before it bumped against the stone. Nelda jumped out, quick as a flash, and was gone, whilst the other three waited in silence as they had agreed earlier. Within minutes, she had returned.

"All clear," she whispered. She reached down to pull Luke up and out of the boat, and then Eve, whilst Nolwen climbed out on his own. They made for the guardroom in single file led by Nelda, who ushered them in and then closed the door. Two guards lay sprawled out on the floor.

For the first time, Eve looked at Nelda with a tingle of fear; she knew her distant cousin to be well trained, but Nelda's carefree personality hid colder skills that she did not understand. Not for the first time she began to feel out of her depth and fought to keep the unease buried.

Nelda saw her consternation. "They are not dead, cousin." Nolwen drew Eve aside. "I merely sent them into a deep sleep from which they will not awaken for many hours. However, the next men we meet we shall probably have no option but to kill. They are traitors and will not show us mercy; we must show them none in return if we are to accomplish what we came for."

Eve nodded, though she had no idea if she were capable of that, as Nelda turned back to her brother and Luke, who had finished stripping the tunics from the limp guards. The two men donned these over their armour and belted their swords over the top. Once more, they put on their cloaks. Nelda and Eve put their cloak hoods up to obscure their faces and the four left the guardroom, Nelda grabbing a lamp on the way out.

The portcullis led to a wide, spiralling ramp that felt far too conspicuous, so they chose instead the original spiral staircase next to it to ascend to the inner castle. The single-file stairs climbed several storeys up before ejecting them onto a wide corridor joined by the ramped road. There were no windows, just lines of dully-burning torches to illuminate their way, and so they crept along its length until the way bent up and down.

They followed the downward arc to an iron gate. A locked, iron gate. Luke and Eve shared a look of despair, but Nelda crept forward. They made to follow her until Nolwen cast his arm out to halt them in their tracks. Nelda crouched by the gate, whispered, and the gate clicked open.

They filed into a corridor that could take four men walking abreast. Doors lined the corridor on each side and Eve's heart quickened. However, they discovered no prisoners, just dusty bottles of wine in racks towering above them on tall shelves. Nolwen huffed in disgust at the wasted time and they retreated.

There was no choice but to follow the wide corridor up. The further they went, the better lit it was and the more chance they would be discovered. Yet the castle was unnervingly empty. Eve wondered whether the late hour of the night, combined with the king's absence, meant that the guard was minimal. Silent and tense, they crept on.

The ramp led to a second closed portcullis set in the high-ceilinged corridor. The small wooden gate next to it also lay shut. Beyond, they could not see anyone; it was not a well-defended part of the fort, for who could send an army the way they had come, through a small cave and two portcullises, without being noticed in the heart of Caledan first?

Nolwen unlocked the gate, pushed it open, and they crept through. They were on the lower levels of the castle now; the servants' quarters, the kitchens, and service rooms would be hereabouts and somewhere, the dungeons.

Before they could discover the kitchens and servants' quarters, they came upon what they had been looking for: the dungeons. Another locked gate barred their way. Nolwen opened it without a hitch. They followed the corridor down a gradient to a closed wooden door on their left whilst the corridor stretched ahead and bent right.

On the other side of the door they could hear talking and laughter; Nelda raised her eyebrows at Nolwen and held up five fingers. He frowned, listened, shook his head and held up six. They tiptoed past and began to examine the doors. Eve's body coursed with nervous energy, feeling electrified and alert.

From the scrying they knew the door was solid; it did not have a hole barred by iron as the first few doors did and so they passed these by without stopping. The corridor bent right and suddenly before them were two guards standing sleepily by a door matching what they had seen in the scrying mirror.

The two guards stood no chance. Nolwen and Nelda leapt forward, swords drawn, and cut the soldiers down before they could even notice the intruders. Almost in synchronisation, they lowered the men in slow motion to rest them on the ground with the smallest scrape of their armour on the stone flags. Eve dared not look at either of the bodies let alone her two companions as they all hurried into the room. The smell of blood caught the back of her nose and she held in a retch.

Irumae lay on the bed, just as she had done in the mirror, the folds of her long dress falling about her legs and slippered feet. Nelda rushed over with Eve and though blood-stained, bent close to examine the girl. Her face was pale, made more so by the dark hair tumbling across her. She was twelve and her small form was frail in the dull light. She did not wake to a gentle shake, but did not appear to have any injuries.

"I think she's been drugged," said Nelda. "We will have to carry her out like this."

"So be it," said Nolwen. "Let's go." He scooped up the girl in his arms as if she weighed no more than a leaf. They froze at a noise outside.

"Which idiot left the gate open?" a man's voice called some distance away. "Rouse yourselves and check the prisoners!"

Nolwen swore and passed Irumae to Luke so he could draw his sword. "Stay behind us," he said to Luke and Eve, as he and his sister led them from the room with grim faces. Once out, they ran— around the corner and straight into a group of six soldiers who had spilled out of the guardroom in confusion in front of a seventh figure, who had his back turned to Nolwen and Nelda.

Some of the guards already had swords drawn and they leapt forward with snarls as they beheld the intruders. The seventh man joined them as Luke passed Irumae to Eve, who stumbled under the sudden weight. Luke stepped in front of her to meet the onslaught as Eve drew her sword with difficulty, frozen in the face of such peril.

The metallic clash of swords hammering against each other filled the corridor with a din that jarred Eve's ears. They had a slight advantage, as the corridor was too narrow for all the guards to meet them at once. Even so, it was difficult to fight in such a confined space. With their long swords, the Eldarkind were at a disadvantage to the guards who were equipped with shorter blades, even though they had far greater skill and a longer reach, and Eve heard Nolwen's growl as they nicked him.

One guard and then a second fell, and Nolwen, Nelda, and Luke pushed forward, but as Eve turned around, several feet behind her companions who were engaged in the other direction, a soldier was barrelling towards her from behind with his sword drawn. She was forced to almost drop Irumae to the floor and raised her sword just in time to meet his.

Where did he spring from? He was strong, far stronger than she, and she felt his determination to best her through the sheer force of his blows. Back and forth across the corridor they danced, but she could not beat him although somehow she managed to escape his blade's scything swings by darting out of reach.

Once more she sprang at him and once more he parried her sword thrust. The clash of steel rung in her ears as her arm seared with pain at the force of his block. She whipped the blade away and slashed at his side. Once more, he was there to stop her cutting open his unprotected abdomen. She had the smallest opening to slice deeply into his leg, but something within her caused her to hesitate and his sword met hers.

The edge of his blade slid along hers until they were hilt to hilt and then it was his turn to surprise her, pushing her away with such force, she reeled for a moment, lost her balance, and fell to the ground, crying out with the pain of the fall. Her sword bounced out of her hand and came to rest over an arm's length away in the shadows, as she laid semi-stunned on her back.

His footsteps approached and her dazed senses heard his heavy breathing and the clang of steel as he kicked her blade away. She saw his shadow over her, black against the dark vaulted ceiling. He circled her, sword still drawn, until they were face to face. He looked down, lifted his broadsword and rested the point on her collarbone. The cold of the steel seeped into her, but it did not dull the erratic heartbeat in her chest, the only sign of her fear. She could not move, could not speak.

"Do you yield, traitor?" he asked her coldly.

"No!" she heard Luke scream. She could not see him behind her, struggling to cut down the soldier in front of him to reach her. All she could see was Irumae slumped against the wall next to her. She did not answer the man, lost in her blank thought and staring at her cousin's still form. He kicked her with contempt. As she cried out, he raised his sword to strike her.

Fear gripped her as she lay powerless and frozen against the stone, until something else flooded through her, energizing her body as though she had been struck by lightning.

"NO!" she screamed and threw up her arm. The world turned white and unbearably bright as energy flooded through her. She was

207

catapulted bodily off the ground and struck the wall. The world turned black and silent. She heard nothing more.

TWENTY SEVEN

Soren was glad for the cord that tied his hands to one of Feldith's spines. It kept him upright and stable when the wind plucked and tore at them, or Feldith shifted beneath him. As well as the wind, it was also cold despite the summer month. The single redeeming quality was that, flying above the low clouds, they remained in the sun and although the wind snatched away any warmth it could give them, Soren was grateful at the very least to be dry.

The day passed swiftly and engaging in such an unusual perspective was captivating. To be able to see blue waves crashing thousands of feet below him and clouds drifting past forming various shapes and apparitions was unlike anything Soren had witnessed before. It felt so abstract that his fear of heights receded. Exhilarated, he felt like he was a bird. *Is this what it is to be free?*

They passed over the shoreline in the early evening, far north of Harring and even Garth's tiny shack, and so none but animals witnessed their passage as they flew low over the land. The mountains ahead barred their way to Pandora, although they already flew higher than some of the clouds.

The dragons flew between peaks rather than over them. It was because, as Feldith explained, the air was so thin at the top of the mountains that there was not enough breath for them to fly on. Soren regarded the glacier-capped peaks; he would never have guessed the deadly secret of their deserted heights.

They crossed the entire chain of mountains before stopping for the night. It was dark when they landed in a valley sheltered by foothills. Mountains hid in the darkness above them, their silhouettes visible against the starry sky. Soren and Edmund lit a fire from discarded branches and huddled around it and ate their meagre fare, longing for meat and a proper meal. The dragons flew off to hunt; the air was quiet after the sound of their wing beats had disappeared into the distance.

Soren and Edmund remained on the banks of a small river, although they could not see much in the small firelight. It snaked back and forth across the valley, leaving a flat valley floor free of the forests that clustered thickly upon the hills. Around them the landscape rustled as hidden animals moved.

By unspoken agreement, they set out drawn swords on the ground and sat alert and focused, almost back to back next to the fire, just in case a wolf or large animal should chance upon them. They were east of the protected central lands surrounding Pandora and here, on the other side of the plains, roamed greater predators than they; brown bears and grey wolves that were never to be trusted.

The dragons soon returned, bringing their protection along with the scent of fresh blood on their breath. On edge, Soren felt reassured by their presence despite this going against all instinct and intuition.

"Forgive me," Edmund said. "I did not think you were to accompany us so far," he addressed the two brown dragons.

Feldith snorted.

Feldloga snaked his neck out to stretch as he lay down. "We were not intended to." His reply was short, though it did not seem curt.

"Why did you come, then?" Soren asked.

"Because islands are tedious, and the sea is cold and tedious!" complained Feldith. "We tire of it; we wish to see the world!"

"What if the world should see you?" said Edmund. "Your islands, as dull as you may think them to be, may no longer be the haven they are now."

"My sire did not say I could have any of my clan with me," Myrkdaga said, "yet neither did he say they could not come with me. I will not send them away if they wish to fly with me."

"I suspect Myrkith-visir will not be happy once he learns of your absence," murmured Edmund.

Feldith growled; a deep rumble full of warning.

"I am glad you came, though," Soren said earnestly, though he received no response. He pondered the dragon's words, wondering if they were to come all the way with him and crucially, whether they would defy Brithilca's words to help him take back the throne. He and Edmund tried to settle for the night, but in the wild, surrounded by dragons, sleep did not come and Soren had a restless night filled with twisted nightmares.

They were beyond tired when they glimpsed Pandora on the horizon, but the sight of their home cheered Soren. As they drew closer, he marvelled at the view of the city they received from so high up; an unrivalled sight impossible to recreate from ground level. By this point, he had become accustomed to flying and swayed instinctively with the wind and motion of the dragon's bodies. Myrkdaga now bore Soren and Feldith, Edmund, whilst Feldloga transported their possessions tied to his belly.

The castle dominated the city, built on the great hill that fell away into the lake behind it and surrounded by the city within the walls. The city crowded onto the hill; larger buildings nearer the top were the official buildings of the city and the richer districts. These gave way to smaller buildings which formed the rest of the city and poorer districts.

They were arranged in an orderly fashion nearer the main roads of the city, but within their depths, the alleyways dove higgledy-piggledy: a labyrinth of passageways through the city. The great, fortified ramparts surrounded what was known as 'the city within,' but these alone could not contain or sustain the population of Pandora, and so 'the city without' grew. Dwellings clustered close to the walls, spreading out and clinging to the lakeside.

Outside the walls were the docks of the city, a vital artery of trade that fed into the city mainly through the southwest gate. Here also, in the city without, was the farming might of Pandora. The plains around the city were ideal farming. As the dragons flew nearer, they began to cross over the sprawl of patchwork fields and open lands where the people farmed animals and crops for the residents of the city to consume and trade. Seeing the city in its entirety left

Soren feeling proud of its beauty, order, and peace. Yet, it seemed so small and fragile, he felt even more protective, knowing it was his duty to preserve it.

By prior agreement, they angled for the south gate, circling in great, descending loops over the city. It took surprisingly long before they were noticed; cries and screams rang out over the city, as the three dragons were low enough to leave yawning shadows under them. Guards on the wall began to raise a clamour, bells rang out, and everywhere they could hear the sounds of the city stirring. The portcullises clanged as they shut and the gates boomed as the city was sealed. The dragons at last announced their presence, roaring as one, deafeningly and joyously.

Myrkdaga landed some few hundred metres from the city gate, out in the open, followed by his brethren. Soren untied his hands and slid down from Myrkdaga's back, as Edmund dismounted from Feldith. Feldloga shed their possessions so they could retrieve their swords and armour from their bundles.

Shielded from view of the walls by Myrkdaga, they donned the light armour, though Soren wished for something far more substantial. Belting on their swords, they stood and regarded each other for a moment in the calm before the unknown ahead of them. Soren tried to smooth and flatten his tangled hair to no avail. The action was a small comfort, insignificant as it was.

They took a deep, simultaneous breath, turned to the gate, and began to walk forward. Soren knew longbowmen stood hidden upon the walls and prayed they would not shoot. The city fell quiet as the people crowded on the walls alongside the soldiers watched them advance. As they moved, the ground shaking weight of the dragons shadowed them and their scaly tails slithered on the dry earth.

Watched by the thousands of people craning for a glimpse of him, Soren felt miniscule in comparison, despite having three of the most fearsome predators he knew any of his people would ever have laid eyes on flanking him. He tried to keep in his mind the words the strange Eldarkind woman had spoken to his mind to give him confidence and strength in the face of the adversity before him.

"Fear not, for although you face perils beyond your imagination, if you

cannot unite the kingdom, no one can." Her voice, so hard to forget, swam into his mind. Her words had etched themselves into his memory. "*Ride into your city not with an army, but with honesty.*"

"Name yourself and declare your purpose," the booming voice challenged him.

Soren stood as tall as he could before the gates of his city. The walls loomed over him, crowded with people. In his dishevelled state, he appeared no more than a pauper, but he knew he and his scaly companions would at least be an interesting sight.

"I name myself Soren Rasirson, rightful heir to the kingdom, and I challenge the unlawful rule of Zaki, who I name guilty of regicide, high treason, and murder! I return to claim the throne that is mine by right. I return to remove the usurper Zaki, who murdered my mother in cold blood, amongst many others, all for greed; all for a throne which is not his to sit upon. I demand his immediate abdication and arrest," he shouted to the men on the gate. The silence on the walls turned to instant noise; wondrous murmurs overtaken by cheering from the population. A horn blew and silence fell.

"You have been declared guilty of those same crimes," the voice called. "An order has been issued for your capture, dead or alive. You will be arrested and held awaiting trial until His Majesty King Zaki returns."

"I think not!" Soren spat, baring his teeth. "Where is he?"

"Kings do not answer to traitors." The mans voice dripped with disdain.

"He cannot answer, for he is not here. Even now, he marches to our border to meet with forces of King Harad of Roher. I will not see him hand over our country to the rule of the southern king, to see our great nation subjugated and ruled by cruelty!"

An outcry rose on the wall, and soldiers clamored to quiet it.

"I have the support of the dragons for my cause," Soren called, striding forward as Myrkdaga advanced behind him. "Yet, I cannot succeed alone. You must all stand too; stand and be counted in the battle to come, for us all to restore the peace and stability we enjoyed under my mother's reign, God rest her soul. Who is with me?" Soren drew his sword and raised it high in the air, gleaming, as the outcry behind the city walls arose once more.

TWENTY EIGHT

"Eve!" cried Luke. He threw the soldier in front of him aside bodily to rush to her, as Nolwen stabbed the man Luke had engaged with through the back. Nelda dispatched the very last soldier. The gurgles of the dying faded. Silence fell. The scene was carnage. Bodies lay strewn over the corridor. Blood pooled around them and spattered over walls and rent armour.

Bruises, grazes, and cuts covered Nolwen, Nelda, and Luke. Nelda, pale-faced, had suffered a long and deep gash on one arm, which Nolwen bound for her with a rag torn from the bottom of his borrowed tunic. They rushed forward to join Luke, who knelt with Eve cradled in his arms. He felt for a pulse and listened for any sign of breath. Her skin felt boiling to the touch as if she raged with fever.

"She's alive," Luke said, weak with relief.

"We need to go," said Nolwen. "Now."

Luke picked up Eve as gently as he could whilst Nelda shouldered Irumae and together, swords still drawn, they raced as fast as they could out of the dungeons and locked the door on their way out to conceal the destruction. Back down the corridors they fled, fear making them run faster than their sore bodies ought to have allowed.

Shouts rang out in the distance and they sped up, not knowing the cause. Luke hoped they were not about to be set upon. His priority was to make sure Eve was safe. Back down the round staircase they jogged. They reached the bottom. All was silent. The portcullis remained locked. The guards remained on the floor, sprawled where they had fallen.

They chanced it, barred the gate behind them, and darted across the open area into the boat. Nolwen climbed in. Luke passed Eve to Nolwen, clambered in himself, and then received Irumae as

Nelda followed. There was not enough room for five of them in the boat. It sank dangerously low in the water, but desperation fuelled them.

Quickly they were away, back through the tunnel and its clinging darkness, out into the fragmented moonlight. They rowed past the marinas, not daring to stop so close to the city, until their limbs shook, their mouths were dry with dehydration, and the pain began to take control of their bodies as the adrenaline faded.

Finally, they pulled the boat to shore on a small beach outside the city. The three sat in silence for a few minutes to catch their breath, before continuing on foot carrying their still companions with them.

It was still dark when they stumbled into the woods and it was the last spark of their energy that enabled them to find the horses. The horses nickered and strained at their tethers in greeting. Nolwen and Nelda mounted up, balancing Eve and Irumae before them, whilst Luke led the spare horse. He led them away from the city at a fast trot and back into the royal forest until he shook with exhaustion and they could go no further.

Nelda rolled out blankets and they set Eve and Irumae down, side by side, removing her glamour as she removed her own and Nolwen's. Irumae lay unresponsive, though faintly warm to the touch. Luke felt Eve's forehead in concern. She was still consumed by fire; her skin seemed too hot to be possible. Nolwen and Nelda hovered over both of them, muttering to each other and checking both over for injuries in more detail.

Luke, who knew he could not help Eve, tried to distract himself by packing the horses. They nuzzled his hands for treats, but he had none to give them. As he finished, Nolwen and Nelda stood up.

"We do not think it will be safe to venture out on the roads at this time of the night; we could be seen. Do you agree?" Nelda said to Luke, who nodded.

"Good. Instead we shall move deeper into the forest; we are too discoverable here. We do not know what scale of search they will mount for the princess, but our reckoning is that it will already have begun. We need to be as far away as we can before we may chance some rest."

It took hours of leading the horses on foot through the wood south and east away from habitation, whilst Irumae and Eve sat propped up on horseback. The sun had almost fully risen when they stopped in a depression that led to a small valley with steep sides.

It was the ideal place to spend a few hours, their position hidden from the forest above. Nolwen volunteered first watch, having had more sleep than the others the previous day, and without bothering to so much as undress or lay out bedding for themselves, his sister and Luke sprawled out and fell asleep.

Exhaustion trapped them there that day, unable to go on and unable to go back. Nolwen washed his cuts and nicks in the brook at the valley floor to clean them and said words of healing in the old tongue over them. Nelda healed her own wounds in the same fashion as her brother, though her arm took much longer for her to repair. Luke cleaned his cuts in the running water and bound a large gash on his shoulder with a strip of fabric, refusing the help of the Eldarkind.

The two men kept a distance as Nelda checked over and bathed the two unconscious young women by hand. Luke found himself tempted to turn around to watch whatever Nelda was doing and so stormed out of sight but not hearing, so he could not give in to the temptation. Eve had various cuts and bruises over her body that needed cleaning, including a patch of matted blood on the back of the head where she had struck the wall. Her raging fever had subsided and as Nelda beckoned the men back over, she said one word to her brother.

"Soon."

Luke didn't understand, though Nolwen seemed to. He knelt by Eve helplessly, thinking about the strange events of the night before, whilst Nelda and her brother sat by Irumae and discussed how to cure her. Luke did not comprehend most of it, though they were courteous enough to speak in his tongue.

"I have sourced the cause of her ill," began Nelda. "Deep within her blood there is some strange substance. The rest of her body is healthy, however these tendrils seem to have slowed her body to a sleep-like status. Her mind is closed and dormant. I think it will take both of our skills to remove this from her body; I have not encountered this before."

"Nor I," mused Nolwen. "Very well, how do you propose we perform?" They continued to throw ideas back and forth as Luke grew more frustrated.

"Stop!" he cried in exasperation. "Aren't you going to explain anything to me?"

They paused, confused.

"What happened last night? The light that I saw, was that real? Why won't she wake?" Luke gestured at Eve.

Nolwen returned Nelda's cautious glance.

"The light you saw was real," Nolwen said slowly, "yet it is not for us to explain it. Eve will have that choice when she wakes. Worry not, though. She is fine, excepting the obvious knocks from last night. Does that ease your worry?"

"In part. I just wish I understood." Luke felt foolish for his outburst. "I'm sorry for being rude. I know you are trying to help the princess, I just..."

"We know," said Nelda with a faint smile. "Try not to worry. She'll be fine."

It was several minutes later when Luke, focused on Eve's face, gasped. The Eldarkind paused once more. Eve's eyes flicked open as she breathed in a great gulp of air, as if she had just surfaced from swimming underwater.

"Eve!" Luke bent over her.

"Luke," she said, more strongly than he was expecting. "You look...different." Her voice was thick and here eyes unfocused. "Everything looks different..."

"Different how?" said Luke, worrying that the knock to her head had caused more damage than Nelda had realised.

"Everything seems... I'm not sure. Brighter." She continued

to look around, drinking in the sights around her, which seemed brighter and richer, when she felt it flicker through her mind like a light caress. All at once, she realised why, as the night before rushed back into the forefront of her mind.

"What happened last night?" she addressed Nolwen and Nelda. She propped herself up on an elbow. "The light, what was it? I thought I was about to die. I thought I did die. What happened?" she repeated, confused and not daring to accept the dawning realisation.

"Perhaps we might explain to you alone," Nolwen said. He glanced pointedly at Luke.

Eve looked between them. "Alright."

Luke stood and withdrew from hearing, without a word.

"Last night, we think you awoke magically," said Nelda. "You must have been so desperate to survive that it unlocked the way to your power. You threw up the barrier of white light; it was pure energy. It threw you back into the wall, and the knock to your head combined with the dramatic cost to your energy caused you to collapse. You'll be pleased to know that your opponent was thrown about twenty feet away into a wall. He broke his neck."

"I killed a man?" she said almost stupidly. She could not comprehend it.

"Well, yes, but it meant you kept your own life and that of your cousin," replied Nelda. "Do not dwell on it."

Eve still did not understand, so for the moment she set the thought aside.

"Do you feel anything different inside you?"

"I feel it in my head," whispered Eve after a pause. For indeed, she could feel something there. Lazy tendrils that tingled across her mind.

Nelda and Nolwen broke out into broad smiles.

Why are they smiling?

"Then we are right, cousin," Nolwen addressed her informally for the first time. "You have awoken. Congratulations!"

"What does it mean?" she asked, as they drew her up to each kiss her on both cheeks.

"It means you are who you were born to be," replied Nelda, though that made little sense to Eve. "However, it is a big responsibility. You now have access to the force which sustains the world and our power. You have the power to change life for better or worse, and you simply have to reach out to that power and voice your intentions in the old tongue to access it. Do not fritter it."

Eve realised that not only was the strange caressing touch there, but also a whole new language, hovering over her own in her mind as familiar as her mother tongue.

"*I think I understand,*" she said to her companions in the old tongue, as easily as if she were speaking her mother tongue, and they laughed in pure delight. A sense of warmth and belonging settled over her. *I'm one of them.* She felt a tentative sense of reassurance.

"You need only ask us for guidance should you want it, cousin," said Nolwen in the old tongue.

Eve thanked them. She went to find Luke, leaving Nelda and Nolwen to begin their healing of Irumae. He was not hard to find, but appeared a little restrained and there seemed to be awkwardness between them.

"I'm so glad you're well," he said after a long pause. He stepped forward, gathered her into a tight hug, and buried his face in her hair. She froze, taken by surprise, and rested her hands on his sides until he released her.

She saw he had tears in his eyes and looked at him in concern.

"I'm sorry, I'm just so glad you're alright," he laughed and wiped his eyes on the back of one hand. "I thought I'd lost you; it was a black moment."

"It's alright. Are you well?" she asked him. "How did we escape?"

They perched upon a fallen tree and he recounted the night's events to her. They fell into companionable silence when he had finished.

"Thank you for getting me out of there," she said once he had finished. "I cannot imagine how hard it was."

"You're not that heavy," said Luke, wrinkling his nose, "but it was hard. I still feel tired even after a sleep. I ache everywhere, especially my shoulder." He explained how he had been slashed on his upper arm from behind when he had raised his sword arm to strike.

"I might be able to help you," said Eve. "I'd have to check with Nolwen and Nelda first, to see if it's possible."

"What do you mean?" said Luke.

"Nolwen and Nelda explained the light to me just now," said Eve. Luke tensed, unblinking. She repeated much of what they had said, but she struggled to describe how everything appeared slightly different, the strange language in her head, and explain how perhaps she would be able to heal him with her new abilities.

Luke was stunned. "I can barely believe it, but it would explain why the pair of them haven't got a scratch on them after last night," he said after mulling over her words. "How did you kill a man like that?"

"I didn't mean to. It just burst out! I feel so conflicted!" she admitted to him.

"Well, talk to me then."

She hesitated for a moment, but realising she had no one else to confide in and did not trust anyone else as she trusted him, spoke quietly, feeling dismal.

"I couldn't kill him," she said. "I feel so ashamed. I saw his desire to beat me and I knew he would not spare my life given the chance. Even so, I had an opening to best him and I could not take it, although he tried to kill me a second later. I did not want to take his life. I never thought it would be possible to feel that way about someone who wished to kill me."

"You're too kind-hearted," said Luke, after a long pause. He slid his hand along the tree trunk to squeeze hers and she did not withdraw from him. "It's not a bad thing, but it doesn't help you now. Sword practice at home is a long way from fighting for your life."

"How did you do it, though? You killed last night," asked Eve.

"I did it because you needed me and the man in front of me was stopping me helping you. I would have killed a hundred men if it meant I could keep you safe," Luke said, more open in that moment with her than he had ever been before. "I would do anything to protect you."

Eve's stomach fluttered as she tried to comprehend the depth of what he had just said. "Truly?" she met his eye.

"Truly."

"Will you stay with me?" she asked.

"Now? Of course I will, why?"

"No, I mean after now. I mean, do you trust me? Now that what Artora suspected has come to pass?"

He hesitated as he tried to find the best way to reply. "I won't pretend. I don't understand it, Eve." As he said her name it sent a thrill across her. "If I'm to be honest, it scares me a little. Maybe a lot. I don't know if it will change you, but I know you and I trust you and that is what I will hold on to."

She dared to lean into his arm briefly and he took her under it in a warm hug. "Thank you," she murmured to him, though the words seemed to express her gratitude inadequately.

Her heart beat faster as she studied the wood around them with her fresh eyes, admiring the beauty that seemed to leap into new focus from everything her gaze touched. Her senses seemed invigorated and infinitely sharper; the colours brighter, the sounds more diverse, the touches against her skin tingling. She lost herself in the moment, feeling invigorated, as Luke sat with her in quiet contentment, resting his head atop hers.

Eventually he moved, infinitesimally. Eve sat up straight. Luke released her, his touch lingering across her back. He looked at her with eyebrows raised and his cheeks flushed, as she stared searchingly at him.

"Do you think you can help me become more ruthless?" she asked.

"I'm not sure if it can be taught," Luke said. "Besides, it's not all about being ruthless, or heartless or cruel. Sometimes you just have to be able to do what is necessary."

"Well, can you show me if we practice together?" He agreed and she went back to camp to collect their swords and check on Irumae. Nolwen and Nelda were still hard at work over the immobile girl and looked up with a cursory glance as she left the camp with the two blades.

She returned to Luke and tossed him his sword in its scabbard. They drew blades and circled each other.

"I need you to beat me," said Luke. He flung the empty scabbard to one side. "And instead of being polite about it, you need to push me to the edge. Show me you're the best; be hard."

"Fine, don't go easy on me though," she said. "I want it to be fair."

"Done."

They came together with a smash of steel, both going for the head-on attack. Luke had the advantage; he was taller and heavier, despite being aching and exhausted. *I'll have to play a cleverer game*, Eve realised.

They danced back and forth and around the trees, always keeping the fallen log in sight so they would not get lost. Each gained and lost the advantage, but Eve never pushed when she could have bested him and Luke grew frustrated.

"You're not trying hard enough!" he growled at her, red-faced after he called a halt. "You've had at least five chances where you could have caused me damage and you didn't press it far enough!"

"We're just practising!" Eve replied, as red and out of breath. "I'm not going to try to stab you, am I!"

"Again," said Luke. "I'll show you what I mean. I apologise in advance, but you told me not to go easy on you."

He flew at her again in his head-on style and as she stepped to sideswipe him, he surprised her by sidestepping too and slashed at her. She raised her blade to meet him, surprised by his ferocity, and parried, but he caught her on the back foot and she could not gain the advantage. He beat her down and forced her towards an old tree.

Knocking into her, he tripped her backwards over a gnarled root. As she fell, she dropped her sword and he pinned her with the full weight of his body against the ground. One of her wrists held in his hand, the other arm pinned to her side by his knee as he half-straddled her, he rested his sword across her chest, near her throat.

"That is what I wanted from you," he said between catching

his breath. "Don't just drop your sword and start a new round when you feel you've won. Push as far as you can."

She lay under him, winded. She was not sure whether it was the lack of breath affecting her or the heat of the fight, but she felt a strange stirring within her as his warm weight pressed down on her. She had not been this close to him before, mere inches from his face. She could see for the first time that intricate lines of amber traced through his bright, warm, brown eyes, framed with dark curling lashes.

He was attractive. She had always known it, yet never realised that she might be attracted to him, nor just how comfortable she felt around him. Their close contact and sparring had lowered her defences. His mouth was so close to hers. She felt a sudden desire to kiss him and opened her lips. He must have felt it too for he bent towards her until they were almost touching, their eyes locked.

The only sound was of their laboured breathing until Luke gave an agonised groan.

"Don't," he said. He rolled away and sat up. To her surprise, he slapped himself around the face.

"Don't?" she questioned. He ignored her.

"Again. We'll fight again," he insisted. He grabbed her hand and pulled her to her feet. "I want you to be that ruthless with me. If you can do it to me, I'm sure you can do it to someone who's really trying to kill you." He turned and stomped away, vigorously swinging his sword as he walked back to the fallen tree. Puzzled, she followed him, confused by what had just happened.

It took a few minutes of sparring to distract her. Luke pushed her even harder than before and she had to give it her all to keep up with him. Eventually, she bested him by ducking his guard and, to her shame, using what seemed like the only option of kicking him between his legs. He went down in a chorus of swearwords.

"Oh my goodness, I'm so sorry! I'm sorry!" She panicked around him and dropped her sword, full of regret.

"No, don't apologise," he spat out in between curses, "that's perfect. Not for me. That's exactly what you should be trying to do; win in any way possible. I think we'll halt there if you don't mind."

Their timing was perfect, for Nolwen's voice rang out in the distance. "Eve!"

Luke, still on the floor, waved her away.

"Go on, I have some pieces of my pride to find." He forced out a smile.

She laughed and apologised once more, before running back to camp, where Nolwen beckoned her.

"We're about to wake her." Nolwen gestured to Irumae behind him, "and we need you to be the first face she sees; we don't want to scare or panic her after whatever she's been through." Eve hurried to kneel by her cousin, feeling tense as she held one of Irumae's hands.

"*Awaken.*" Nolwen imbued the word from the old tongue with power and a second later, Eve felt Irumae's hand twitch against hers. The young girl's cheeks reddened to a healthy hue as she breathed deeply and her eyelids flickered for a few seconds before she opened them.

"Cousin Eve?" she said, confused, as she saw Eve. "Where am I? Why are you here?"

Eve glanced across Irumae's head over to Nolwen, who had retreated. He shrugged and stepped further back to give them privacy.

"We are in the woods south of Pandora, Irri," Eve said. She tried to smile. "We rescued you from the castle. What happened?"

Irumae sat up and gazed around their small camp—Nelda and Nolwen had now vanished—before replying.

"Men came in the afternoon, just before high tea," she began. "I did not recognise their crests. They did not knock and forced their way in. I have no idea where my guards were. I tried to fight them and I tried to escape, but there were too many of them! They held me down and made me drink a foul-tasting liquid, and that is the last I remember. What day is it?"

Eve paused, trying to work it out. "I fear I have lost count!" she admitted. "I believe we are a week into the sixth month of the year."

"So late?" Irumae exclaimed. "Then it has been weeks!

Perhaps some of my dreams were reality; I woke again and again in a small stone room. Pandora Castle? Why was I held in the castle?" She frowned. "What has happened?"

A feeling of horror swept over Eve. *It is my duty to tell her that her mother is dead*, she realised, chills creeping down her spine. *I cannot avoid it.* She closed her eyes and took a deep breath to compose herself, moving to kneel opposite Irumae.

"Your uncle took the throne from your mother. He took it by force; he will have commanded the men who captured you, no doubt. As far as I know, he also took your mother's life in the process. I am so sorry, dear cousin," she said, aching with sorrow as her cousin's face registered mingled confusion, shock, and sadness.

Before her eyes, Irumae seemed to shrink even further into herself. Eve reached out to embrace her. Her cousin did not resist and fell into her arms. Irumae clung to her and buried her head into Eve's shoulder.

"What of my brother?" Irumae said, her voice still muffled, turned into Eve's chest.

"As far as I know he lives."

"Yet he has not come for me?"

"No, but Sir Edmund said that he wished to—greatly—and was most reluctant to flee without you. He will not have forgotten you," Eve promised Irumae.

Her cousin fell silent. She did not weep. Instead, she seemed altogether emotionless. However, that night, despite being introduced to Luke, Nolwen, and Nelda, who had all tried to distract her as best they could, the four of them could not fail to hear her stifled sobs as she lay in the dark. Eve rose to comfort her, but she was beyond consolation and so Eve lay down with her and held her close until the fits subsided and she drifted into broken sleep.

TWENTY NINE

Boos and jeers from the crowd accumulating unseen behind the city walls drowned out all else. The cries rang out from within, taken up by many voices: "The true king has returned!" "Long live the king!" "Loyalty to the dragon king!" "Down with the imposter!"

It sounded much like there was a riot unfolding within the city; the mood had turned sour and angry shouts rang out. Clashes sounded within the walls and Soren stood before the gates, unable to see what was happening within the city. At last he heard the faint cry calling "open the gates!" and unseen men drew up the portcullis. Soren watched the gates inch apart, opened by the efforts of the city folk themselves.

Soren tensed, his sword in hand, ready to leap onto a dragon should he need to flee. Yet the people before him were no soldiers, but ordinary, unarmed Caledonians. He was welcomed with cheers by the people, who surged out to line the way to invite him into the city.

"Ride me," said Myrkdaga into his mind. "You should make the grandest entrance with what you have; let it be one the people remember."

Soren was surprised. The great black dragon had seemed distant and aloof in their brief time together and he had not expected him to offer such a submissive gesture. He bowed to the dragon and thanked him.

Before he could climb up onto Myrkdaga's back, a small figure broke from the rest and hurried towards him. The man prostrated himself on the ground a safe distance away from the dragons. As the figure rose up, Soren saw it to be the city's steward; a middle-aged man with greying temples and deep wrinkles set into his face.

"You're alive!" Soren said.

"Zaki could not kill me, Your Royal Highness," said Lord Behan, beaming at the prince. "I obey different laws. Even he must abide by those, despite my loyalty to your mother and to you."

"I am most glad that you are well, Behan." Soren strode over to grasp his forearms in a formal embrace. "Is it safe to enter the city?"

"Not safe, as such," said Behan, "but the city is certainly with you, sire. The people forced the soldiers loyal to Zaki to retreat into the castle; many of them even threw down their arms, declaring themselves no enemy to you. It would appear that many have been waiting for you to return."

"Zaki is not here though?"

"You have missed much," admitted Behan. "It would do well to update you on the events in Pandora, however yes, he is gone for the present time. Now please, it is time for you to return home. Whilst the castle is held against you, you may reside with me."

And so it was that Prince Soren returned to Pandora on the back of the black dragon Myrkdaga, flanked by two of his kin, with Lord Behan the Steward and Sir Edmund leading the way through the crowds of welcoming city folk. The enthusiastic welcome he received—and riding through the city streets on dragonback—felt altogether like an out of body experience.

Soren retired to Behan's dwelling; a grand, detached townhouse, gated with its own guard, where he bathed and changed into spare clothes donated by the household. The dragons rested in large gardens under Behan's pruned trees. Behan set out all the guards he had at the perimeter of his land, though there seemed no need. The people of the city took up their own vigil outside and the excited babble and occasional rousing song filtered through the walls. Soren listened as he dressed in the soft, finely woven, and most noticeably cleaner fabrics, savouring the feel of the smooth materials over his newly scrubbed skin more than he ever had.

He met with Behan and Edmund to dine, plot, and find out what had occurred in his absence. As hungry as he was, the food before him lay untouched. Behan described what had happened from the day everything had changed, including Zaki's movements and those of his men outside Pandora. Soren stepped in to fill in the gaps in Behan's knowledge, relating in a few breaths how Zaki had destroyed the northern monastery in his quest to procure the crown for his coronation.

"What a monstrosity." Behan's eyes widened. "I had hoped that was nothing more than a rumour. It explains why he was crowned by his deputy and with a lesser crown. The abbot did not attend and the throne did not reveal itself at the opportune moment. By rushing to crown himself, he could have doomed his own rule.

"Since that day, and perhaps even before, there has been discontent growing. The number of disappearances and strange deaths of nobles grows daily; those who were open supporters of your mother, or who are less than discreet in their displeasure at the regime change. Zaki ordered the entire city be locked down in the week of mourning, so that it could be searched to weed you out.

"Of course, since the coronation fiasco, every tongue in the city is wagging with the most colourful rumours imaginable. On the surface, it is business as usual, although Zaki is keen to show himself as a strong ruler and has doubled the city guard with men loyal to him, but in the shadows, the people know that something is afoot."

"Which are the most likely rumours?" asked Soren.

"Well, perhaps you can tell me the truth about what happened the day that you fled and I can judge," replied Behan. He sat back in his chair, food forgotten. "I hope that my faith and trust in you is not misplaced, sir. Despite the advantages of my independence in this position, Zaki will have my head for taking you in, if he can."

Soren inclined his head in thanks for the risks Behan was taking and told the steward what had happened to both him and Edmund on and since, starting with the attack in the royal forest. Soren pulled from under his shirt, where he always kept it, the letter still covered in his mother's blood which Edmund had discovered from his spies. Behan read the letter. His mouth was agape by the time he had finished absorbing its contents.

"You must keep that as safe as your life," Behan urged the prince, "for it will see him proved guilty more than any word of any man. I see he is more devious and ruthless than even I thought.

"In any case, the rumours of his guilt are truer than the people know. They certainly mutter that he cannot be the true king after such a poor coronation. I have also heard rumours echoing the sentiments of that letter. King Harad may indeed by sending forces as we speak. From the evidence we know, I suspect Zaki has gone to meet them at the border or perhaps even past it, so that he can guarantee them safe passage to Pandora."

Soren, Edmund, and Behan sat in silence for some minutes, digesting their realisation of Zaki's plan.

"We cannot act if we do not know what opposes us. We should send out scouts to determine the size of any force," proposed Edmund.

"Consider it done," said Behan. He summoned the head of his household and charged him with overseeing a reconnaissance mission.

"What course of action should I take now, in any case?" asked Soren. "Here I sit, in the city of my enemy, alone. I fear they will sweep out from the castle and that will be the end of my attempt to restore the monarchy."

"Nay," answered Behan. He regarded Soren through veiled eyes. "The people have not risen up as they did today in living memory. On the wind already we can hear them singing of bravery and honour and hope. I think they will be your greatest allies."

"They can be my army," said Soren.

Behan scoffed. Soren silenced him with a sharp glance. "See what a force they can be, Lord Steward; see how they repelled what remains of Zaki's supporters. Yes, they are people of the city, but every man and woman outside is there because they have faith and hope.

"I have no army and I can call on few to support me as they would. They shall be mine and with them, I have some hope of sweeping out Zaki from Pandora whether we fight with swords or farmers' hoes. If King Harad sends forces north against us, we must at the very least hold Pandora, if we are to have any hope of surviving or triumphing against him. I must call the city's people to my aid."

With that, Soren excused himself from the table, his mind made up. *It's a desperate plan, but the best I have...* Edmund and Behan scrambled to escort him as he belted on his sword and strode out to address the crowds, who cheered his appearance. In the small square in front of Behan's house, there was no room to move. People backed up into main roads and alleyways alike, hoping for a glimpse of the prince.

Soren realised there was no way that he could speak to enough people in the small space. He ran to find Myrkdaga, who consented to bear him to the main square outside the castle; a much larger space where he could gain a bigger audience.

As the steward, whose duty it was to oversee city announcements, Behan emerged with a large hand bell and rung it until the crowd silenced.

"Hear ye, oh hear ye, citizens of Pandora," he cried.

Soren drew his sword from its scabbard, from where he sat erect on Myrkdaga's back, and raised it in the air. He cut a striking figure in his fine new clothes with his gleaming sword pointing straight up.

"I fly to Castle Square and I summon you all to an audience the likes of which you have never known," he cried out. The crowd roiled as people made the mad dash up the hill through the city streets to Castle Square, whilst Myrkdaga took a great leap into the air and took flight from the open space before Behan's house, battering all below them with gusts of wind.

He landed in the large square that led to the castle and sat after the prince had dismounted. Soren climbed up on a great plinth bearing the statue the first king of Caledan, King Beren, to gain a vantage point as people spilled into the square to gather before him. When the space was full, he held up a hand and the people quietened.

Behind him, set back from the square, the castle lay closed and silent, though flashing glints of light bounced off the armour of soldiers on the battlements. The great mass of people before him stood eerily silent.

"People of Pandora, I return to claim the throne that is mine by right. I come to remove the usurper and murderer Zaki from it and restore peace and order to our city and our land. Even now, Zaki, who dared to murder my mother—"

Gasps rang out from the crowd.

"—and is responsible for the disappearance of my sister, many others, and murders of the most heinous nature, seeks to hand over our country meekly to the rule of King Harad of Roher, who marches here with an army now."

The biggest outcry yet rose up. The people shouted their defiance for minutes until he could speak once more, his confidence emboldened by their response.

"I say no to the subjugation of our great and historic land! I say no to the fear and instability his rule will bring to Caledan, and the selfishness and cruelty with which he will rule. The truth of this you know in your own hearts! I say no to the false king who could not even crown himself with the blessing of his people or the great dragon spirit," Soren roared out to the receptive crowd, who cheered his every point. He paused as they cheered and held up his hand to quiet them again.

"I cannot do this alone. I have the support of the dragons for my cause. I also need the support of you, my people, to ensure Caledan is protected. I call you all now, every man and every woman, to take up arms for this just cause, to protect your city and your country from invasion and enslavement.

"I call every man and every woman to protect what is theirs, as is right and proper. I promise in return to safeguard every one of you until my dying day and punish those who have wronged us all. I promise to restore the peace that ruled this kingdom under my mother's reign, God rest her soul, and rebuild Caledan if you should choose to follow me. Stand up and be counted so that you can restore the course of our nation!"

The crowd erupted in roars that did not subside for many minutes as he smiled and waved at the crowd, surprised that they were following him so willingly and wondering why. *Perhaps Zaki has been especially neglectful or cruel to their wellbeing already,* he pondered, *or perhaps they loved and respected my mother even more than I knew and it has passed to my shoulders.*

His reverie was broken as the steward's bell rang out again. Red faced, Behan made his way through the square. Unable to reach Soren at the far side, he paused at the fountain in its centre and climbed onto its rim, followed by Edmund.

"Hear ye, oh hear ye." Behan sounded his bell. "Go now to your houses now should you support this cause, inventory your armour and your weapons, be they swords or bows or spades or rakes, and sign notice of your service at the steward's quarters to count yourselves amongst those fighting for our true king! Even if you have no armour or weaponry, stand up and be counted and you shall be loaned what is required."

His speech was less evocative than Soren's, but the people dispersed with excitement. As they exited the square, members of Behan's personal guard entered it to form a protective circle around the prince, Behan, and Edmund.

"Sir!" said Behan. "What were you thinking? You could have been killed! I cannot protect you if you fly away on dragonback into the midst of the city—it is not yours to call your own yet!" he hissed, unwilling to cause a scene in front of the few city folk that had lingered in the square.

Soren felt a twinge of regret as he glanced at Edmund, who gave him a look of poorly suppressed disapproval.

"My apologies, Lord Steward," Soren apologised. He realised he had to placate Behan. "It shall not happen again."

"My presence alone is sufficient to protect the prince," growled Myrkdaga into the minds of those who were present.

Behan's face went white as he gazed up at the dragon. "Quite, great dragon," he stammered in reply.

"Come," prompted Soren, who stifled a grin. "We must return to your dwelling. Myrkdaga—" He gestured to the dragon behind him. "—and his kin are hungry and tired after our long journey and we must be ready to take on the service of any city folk willing to assist me."

That night as he lay down to sleep, Soren was restless. The bed, the first he had been in for some time, was sumptuously comfortable by any standards, but he could not find peace in the enveloping mattress from the thoughts whirling around his head. He had checked every guard position, trusting no one, until he was satisfied that the security of Behan's house with the extra guards laid on was reliable enough to protect him through the night.

He hoped the show of strength from the people earlier would cause his enemies to cower in the castle until he came for them. Behan had reassured him this would be the case, adding, "that it would not be prudent of them to act in Zaki's absence on this matter."

Nevertheless, despite his locked and guarded door, Soren lay naked under plump covers that night with his sword by his bed and a dagger under his pillow. He was unable to sleep and shuffled at every noise. He was right to be cautious. In the early hours of the morning, his window on the first floor, which had remained ajar due to the high temperature, emitted a tiny creak.

Soren's eyes flicked open and he waited and watched, immobile. The air was hot, but still. *That was no breeze…* A dark form blended in with the shadows pooled around the curtains. Soren froze, not even breathing. The almost imperceptible sound of someone else's breath filtered into his ears and he worked the dagger free from under his pillow as silently as possible, manoeuvring his arm under the duvet so that he could throw the covers back.

The shadow detached from the curtains after some minutes of waiting and crept across the carpeted floor. Soren had resumed breathing, to give the illusion that he still slept. Something flashed in the gloom and Soren's heart rushed into life, pounding so hard in his chest it deafened him. The figure had a blade. If there had been any doubt of the stranger's intentions in Soren's mind, they vanished now.

The shadow drew close enough. Soren threw back the covers with a mighty cry for the guards and launched himself at the man with his dagger pointing forward. The man drew back, but Soren's dagger found him in the gut and he cried out as shouts from outside the room sounded and keys scrabbled at the door to unlock it. Soren cursed himself for bolting the door from the inside, as thuds emanated through it from those outside throwing their weight against it.

Soren saw the shadow of the man's head turn at the noise. He must have realised the suicidal nature of his mission then, for he assaulted Soren with renewed aggression, who held his dripping dagger in his left hand as he dragged his sword out of its scabbard with his right.

The man's dagger fell upon him and Soren roared in pain as the blade slashed his left shoulder, and continued its downward momentum to slice through his chest. Sword now in his grasp and his left hand in spasms, Soren threw the dagger behind him and advanced with grim determination on the man, still fighting a shadow.

The man backed off now that he knew Soren had armed himself with a longer blade than his own. The battering against the door crescendoed with the thud of something hard and heavy, but the bolts and hinges held. Frantic shouts outside barely registered in Soren's mind as he forced his opponent towards the door, away from the window. Stood by the curtains now, he wrenched them open, flooding the room with moonlight.

Black clothed the man from head to toe and Soren guessed that he did not have any armour weighing him down from how little noise he made and how easily Soren had stabbed him. Cloth covered his face, obscuring his features, but Soren could not mistake the gleam of bloodlust in the man's eyes. Soren stepped to the side so his silhouette would not reveal him and rushed forward.

Just behind the man, the door shattered, sending splinters everywhere as men battered their way through it to reach the prince. It distracted the assassin for a moment, which was just enough for Soren. The assassin's guard went wide and Soren stabbed, up through his stomach, to bury the blade deep in his torso.

The man's face contorted in pain and hate as he struck out at the prince, who was now within his grasp. However, before the dagger fell, arms grabbed the man from behind, pulling him off the sword still held by Soren and roughly onto the floor, forcing the dagger from his hand.

The man coughed up blood, now choking. Soren's guards rolled him onto his side. It was too late. His lungs must have been punctured for he was struggling to breathe. He made a rasping sound and his face turned a mottled shade. As blood seeped out from his wounds and his mouth, he shuddered and was still. A guard checked for a pulse and shook his head.

Soren stood there; still, naked, and dripping, sword in hand, tensed and not breathing. Edmund barrelled through the door in night robes, took one look at the wild-eyed prince and the dead man on the floor, and cursed. It seemed to break the spell, for Soren stopped tensing and breathed once more. All at once, pain besieged him as he noticed his torn shoulder and chest. The gaping wounds stung angrily as boiling blood scalded his stomach.

If not for the creak at the window, he would have had no warning of the man's presence. If not for the creak at the window, he would be dead. The reality of the situation crashed down upon him. He sunk, dazed, onto the edge of the bed.

The following few hours passed in a blur of pain and tiredness. A physician cleaned and stitched his wounds in a neat process that seemed even more painful than procuring them. Soren left the physician after thanking him with gritted teeth as he pressed pain-killing medicine on the prince to take over the coming days. Behan rushed about his complex in a hive of activity.

Every room glowed with all available lanterns and candles as his men scoured every inch for more intruders. Recovered by sombre colleagues were the corpses of five guards; four of their throats were cut and one had been strangled. The path of their bodies showed beyond reasonable doubt where the assassin had entered, though no one had determined how he had found the prince.

It was clear to Soren that despite the heavy and obvious security, he would find no sanctuary here. He was glad it was so brightly lit, for every shadow he glanced at twice and every man thrice, trying to determine if one would turn on him.

By dawn, a tired-looking Behan called Soren and Edmund to the breakfast room. Soren realised how ravenous he was and ate until he could burst before realising that Behan had sat in silence the whole time, his hands clasped under his chin. Edmund had barely eaten half of his plate.

"I apologise most humbly for the events of this night past," said Behan, whose face was haggard. "Never did I think that this could occur. There were nearly three hundred men on my property last night. I do not understand how it is possible."

"It cannot be attributed to you, I am sure," said Soren, though in truth he had no idea whether Behan could have been involved in some way. "It would seem others cannot be trusted. Have you any word on how he managed to find me, or who he was?"

"None whatsoever," replied Behan, frustrated. "The man bore not one identifying mark on his body, his clothing, or his blade. For all we know he could have been acting on his own."

"I doubt it, given the situation, but that is a possibility," said Soren. "Perhaps I should become accustomed to such attempts now that I place myself in harm's way."

"In any case, we do not know where he originates from," Behan said. "The fact that he came directly to your window from the perimeter would suggest that perhaps he or whoever owned his service compromised someone within my very household, which worries me. Until I can perform a head count of my full staff and their whereabouts, I cannot guarantee to know them all innocent or safe."

"In light of this, I don't think it safe for me to remain here or within the city," said Soren. He looked to Edmund for guidance. Edmund agreed. "I would rather be outside it, where I can better see my enemies approaching."

Behan protested until Soren held up a hand to forestall him. He winced as his stitches tugged.

"My mind is made up. I'm well aware that poor sleep clouds judgement, however after last night, I shall not sleep at all here. I'd rather sleep surrounded by three dragons than three hundred of your men, Behan. I thank you for your hospitality, but if I remain, I may be a dead man and that is not part of my plan."

"Sire," Behan bowed his head. "I shall accompany you with men whose loyalty I can guarantee, in that case. It is the least I can do if you insist on leaving."

The steward made quick preparations for them to leave within the hour, having procured a large pavilion tent as a favour from a local guild and spread the word, following Edmund's advice, of the assassination attempt and Soren's stand outside the city. Soon, every tongue wagged with tales more fanciful than the last, of how Soren had singlehandedly fought off one, then three, then ten men.

Within hours, Soren had set up a lavish camp half a mile outside the city's south gate on a small hill by the royal forest, joined by throngs of people who flocked to see him and offer themselves, their men or their goods in his service. His solitary tent, surrounded by the three dragons, became one of many as first Behan and his soldiers set up tents nearby, and then makeshift tents sprung up all around as more people joined him.

Behan inventoried everything; every man and woman, every set of chainmail, every horse that joined them, and reported regularly to Soren. Soren, despite his tiredness and wounds, rode about the camp on a spirited stallion, loaned to him by Behan with his personal guard, also loaned by the steward, to meet and thank as many individuals as he could for their support.

He was surprised to find some of the great houses there, though more shocked by how few men they brought. When he spoke to them, they reported themselves still loyal to his cause despite many of their men already lying dead, killed in the fighting following Zaki's seizure of the throne.

Soren did not know whether to be disheartened at the fact that so few men from the houses he had expected to be loyal were signing up in his service, or gladdened that any true fighting men had joined at all. Hiding his troubled feelings, he thanked their captains and lords for their support and promised rewards and revenge for their help—hoping he could fulfil his words.

The most surprising contribution to his ranks was the swelling group of women from the farmers' guild. As hunter-gatherers, they were strong and skilled in a wealth of useful talents from spear-throwing to archery, in addition to having a bank of knowledge regarding local natural remedies and poisons. He found himself gladder for their pledges.

Many more ordinary citizens had joined his cause, including more women than he had expected; they seemed to relish the thought of having the chance to help. Despite his invite for women to fight alongside him, Soren turned away many a young boy eager to fight, specifying to Behan that he would not allow any boy under the age of sixteen nor girl under the age of eighteen to sign up. Soren returned to personally oversee his new recruits' skills-testing after a few hours riding around the growing camp, which Behan's men conducted on a patch of land kept clear from tents and other people.

By sunset that day, the camp had swelled with people joining from the outlying lands of the city, those who lived in the city beyond the gates, and men from the great houses that were within the walls. Nearly three and a half thousand men and women signed up promising their service, with Behan assigning them tasks from fighting to cooking, and healing, knowing there would be casualties to come.

Night was fraught with anxiety for Soren. After the previous night, he did not much feel like sleeping. Edmund remained with him, as did Behan and a large personal guard within the tent. As awkward as it felt trying sleep surrounded by men, Edmund's relaxed presence helped soothe his nerves and before he knew it, the sun had risen once more before he woke.

"Sire, wake up!" Behan called to Soren, who sat bolt upright at the noise and cast around for the source. "Riders approach from the city!"

Soren scrambled to dress, smoothed his hair down, and rushed from his tent to find Myrkdaga stood before it, facing the city. The dragon huffed as he smelled Soren, turned around to greet him, and paced with the prince towards the north of the camp, which had grown even more since the day before. Men and women in a hive of activity paused with various expressions of astonishment at the prince and the dragon walking through the camp; a murmur followed them as they went.

A crowd of people stood behind the prince as he emerged at the edge of the camp. Fifty feet away a nervous rider stood. The horse's anxious prancing mimicked its rider's discomfort. He had good reason to be nervous. Several men had openly drawn swords and arrows already to the string on bows were ready to be drawn.

"Speak your business, rider," stated the prince. The rider briefly regarded him, but did not dare keep his eyes off the glittering black dragon crouched beside Soren. The horse had its ears back, the whites of its eyes visible as it too fixed its wild gaze on the dragon.

"I come under the white banner of parley bearing a message from the council, who rule the city in the king's stead," said the man, whose voice belied his youth. Although he wore the crest adopted by Zaki, Soren himself did not recognise the young man. His words made Soren swap a knowing glance with Edmund. *They admit he is not here, then.*

"The council order your immediate peaceful surrender and that of any armed man with you. You will all be taken into custody and charged appropriately for such treasonous rebellion against his majesty. Should you do so peacefully, the king will show greater leniency and mercy to all those but Prince Soren. The Lady Irumae will also be shown greater mercy if you comply, Prince Soren."

He was jeered at then by those behind Soren and struggled to continue. Soren had stopped listening. *They have my sister. She is alive.* His eyes were wide and he was glad none of the men behind him, or the rider in front, could see his shock.

"I demand the safe release of my sister before I will so much as consider your requests," Soren shouted out in desperation. "If you have harmed her..." He left the threat unfinished, but the envoy knew his words were empty as he did.

"You are in no position to demand such things. Should you choose not to comply with the demands laid forth," the envoy carried on as loudly as he could, "you will unleash the wrath of the king, who will sweep down upon you with no mercy.

"Every house supporting you will be razed to the ground, with property and land being forfeited to the king. He will execute every man, woman, and child of those families for treason. Your life and that of your sister will be forfeit, Prince Soren. You will also consent for your dragons to be restrained so that the king can deal with them as he wishes."

"His dragons?" Myrkdaga rumbled with anger. "We are no dumb beasts to be possessed, you insolent rat!"

The rider's horse squealed, an ear-piercing sound, and bolted towards the city. Its rider clung on for dear life, as Soren's men mocked him and cheered Myrkdaga. Myrkdaga's two clan members dropped from the sky in front of him, as he roared as loud as he could in defiance, joining his voice with their own and creating a din that forced the men behind them to cover their ears and retreat some distance away before the noise was bearable.

Soren stood with his fingers in ears before his allies as he watched the south gate open and close for the horseman. *I think he can guess our answer*, the prince thought, distracted from thoughts of his sister.

Myrkdaga was quite literally fuming with anger; smoky tendrils twisted from his nostrils as they strode back to Soren's tent. In the space around it, Behan's guards cleared the area so that Soren could hold a small, private council with Behan, Edmund, and the dragons.

They unanimously decided to reject the surrender and with that formality over with, discussed what their course of action should be. Behan and Edmund advocated a swift attack with the element of surprise, and marching up through the city, which as yet appeared to be barely fortified; the majority of men were barricaded in the castle according to the hourly reports from informants within the city. The dragons supported this, much more in favour of action than inaction.

"I saw we burn the castle to the ground with them all inside," growled Myrkdaga.

"We cannot do that!" protested Soren. "Remember, we need

the city and the castle intact… it must be defensible when Zaki arrives."

Myrkdaga glowered, but did not retort. Soren dithered over what to do. *I must attack soon, but I cannot risk Irumae's safety…*

THIRTY

The din was overwhelming—a roaring they could not identify. It broke over the camp, startling Eve and her companions with various exclamations. Nolwen sprinted off in the direction of the sound.

"Where's he going?" said Eve, confused.

"To find out what that noise is," said Nelda, her eyes narrowed as she watched him leave.

"He's going towards a noise like that? That doesn't sound wise! We should leave as soon as possible, surely?" Eve replied.

"Hmm," replied Nelda noncommittally. "We should pack." Nolwen soon returned, crashing through the trees, his face flushed and his eyes alight.

"*The dragons are here!*" he crowed to his sister in the old tongue, who replied with exclamations and questions in the same language.

"What?" Eve exclaimed, open-mouthed. "It cannot be!"

Luke and Irumae burst out in a babble of enquiries, for they had not understood Nolwen's words.

"The dragons are here, he said," Eve relayed to them, distracted as she tried to listen to their fast-paced exchange. "What does this mean, Nolwen?"

Nolwen related what he had seen in the common tongue: a great camp outside the city and three dragons at its centre by a large tent. His companions plied him with questions about what it could be. It was Nelda who answered.

"Take out your mirror, Eve. Scry the prince and I think you shall have your answer."

Eve did as Nelda bid her to and the mirror revealed an astonishing sight. In the company of men and dragons was her cousin. Irumae cried out, and fingered her brother's image on the mirror as if by doing so she could touch him.

"We must go to him at once!" Irumae said.

"Could it be a trap?" asked Luke, his brow furrowed with mingled confusion and suspicion.

"It is unlikely. Dragons are cunning. They are not creatures to be tricked," replied Nolwen.

"Are they on our side?" Luke said.

"Undoubtedly. I believe Lady Eve will know I speak the truth?" Nolwen raised an eyebrow at Eve.

"*The pact?*" she guessed in the old tongue, knowing it to be a secret she should not reveal.

Nolwen nodded, grinning.

"I believe Nolwen to speak the truth," Eve said with a little shrug to Luke, who didn't look any less confused.

"It seems counterproductive to return from where we've just fled," he muttered, not convinced, but the opinions of his companions outweighed his in number and rank, giving him no choice but to agree.

They rode to the eastern edge of the forest through the thinning trees and were greeted by the sight of the camp outside the city, nearer to the forest than they had realised. The camp thrummed with life. Men and women went back and forth on their business. Randomly picketed horses stood chewing grass and straw, whilst armoured men wandered about.

Eve rode first with her arms clasped around Irumae, who sat in front of her on the saddle. Behind them rode the Eldarkind, now undisguised and followed by Luke. They were worn and dirty, but Eve hoped they would be able to gain entrance with Irumae.

Guards exclaimed as they broke the cover of the forest, rushing towards them with weapons drawn and calling for them to halt. Irumae stood up in the saddle, half-supported by Eve as they drew near.

"Lay down your weapons," she said with an authority that did not match the stature of a girl of twelve. However, as her face became visible to the men, they dropped to the ground and bowed, lowering their weapons and murmuring greetings to her.

More and more people approached and cheered when they recognised the princess; her absence in the capital had been notable and many had feared for her life. The din soon brought more attention as they made their way into the camp. Around the corner of a tent, Prince Soren himself ran towards them, his eyes glittering with hope at the news of his sister's arrival, which had spread like wildfire to him, despite being in a private meeting.

Irumae threw herself from the horse and rushed to embrace him with tears flowing down her face. He picked her up and swung her around before setting her down and kissing her on both cheeks.

"Dear sister, I have missed you so! I cannot believe I see you before my very eyes!" Soren's smile could not widen any more across his face as he hugged his sister close once more. "How on earth did you come to be here?" he asked incredulously, still clasping her hands. Eve smiled at the sight, Soren's joy infectious.

Irumae turned and gazed at her companions, who had dismounted behind her. Soren followed her glance. His expression caught when he beheld her strange company, recognising Eve under the grime and in her masculine clothing.

"Cousin Eve?" he said, incredulous. Eve guessed that he was trying to reconcile the grubby young woman in men's pants before him with the polished and lady-like image he had last seen at the royal court.

"Your Majesty," Eve replied. She dipped her head, conscious of the strangers surrounding her; their attention and crowding presence stifled her after so long in relative isolation.

Soren caught the undertone implied by her formal greeting and swept his eyes around the crowd gathered by them. "Come, sister, cousin, and your companions, to my pavilion."

Soren led the way back to his pavilion, flanked by guards. At the base of the hill, in the wide, open area kept clear of other tents, waited the dragons, Behan, and Edmund, in heated discussion. Guards held the gathered crowds at bay, far enough away to allow some privacy. Behan and Edmund froze, mid-sentence, as Soren strode back into the open space, followed by the rabble of strangers and horses.

Silence reigned for a moment and then chaos erupted. Behan and Edmund greeted Soren and his sister with delight, welcoming her and expressing their joy at her safety and good health.

Nolwen and Nelda bounded into the grassy knoll to greet the dragons in the old tongue with delight and offer them strange bows that were mirrored by the dragons themselves; bowing as low as they could and then, rising back up and arching their heads

245

backwards to offer their necks to each other. Eve entered the space with Luke close in tow, making a mental note to ask Nolwen or Nelda the significance of this, but before she could take in anything else, a thunderous voice broke over her head.

"Eve!" Edmund's eyebrows and the corners of his mouth slanted dangerously low as she froze and regarded him like a rabbit caught in a hunter's gaze. He stormed over. "What in the blazes are you doing here?" he hissed so just she could hear.

"I came to rescue the princess," Eve said as bravely as she could. She stood tall and tried to appear more confident than she felt, facing Edmund's wrath. Edmund frowned and glanced at Irumae, who stood huddled under her brother's protective arm as he and Behan spoke.

"Be that as it may," he said, seemingly put off by the unexpected answer, "you were supposed to return at once to your father after your visit to Ednor and promised to me that you would do so."

"I promised to you I would neither follow you nor seek out Soren. I didn't say *when* I would return," she dared to correct him. "I'm old enough to make my own choices and I felt strongly about my cousin's plight. I felt she needed my help and look, I and my companions managed to secure her release from the castle, which wasn't without its risks and dangers. If there's to be an issue, let it be between my father and myself. I know I'll have to answer to him."

"I do not wish there to be enmity between us, Eve," sighed Edmund. "I shall not pretend to be satisfied with your choices, but nevertheless, I am glad you are well and that Irumae is once more safely with us. It will help our position having her here." He enquired as to how they had managed to rescue her, but at that moment, Soren called them over to introduce his companions and for Eve to introduce hers.

Nolwen and Nelda seemed at home with the dragons, but Eve felt more hesitant and she could tell that Luke was resisting the urge to draw his sword from the way he kept tapping his fingers upon its hilt. She had heard of the dragons from Artora and her Eldarkind kin, but the tales did nothing to convey their impressiveness and imposing presence. She admired them with wide eyes and managed a steady curtsy and greeting in the old tongue, after prompting from Nelda, with a slight squeak to her voice.

Soren allowed everyone save Luke and Irumae to sit in on the council; he was of too low a rank and she too young. Eve looked apologetically at Luke as a guard chivvied him away, but he regarded her with an indecipherable expression before turning away. The dragons crowded in around them, forming an impenetrable barrier to the outside world and the meet re-convened with its extra guests in a circle on the grass.

Eve recounted her journey right up to the previous night. In halting tones, she explained how they had rescued Irumae, though she omitted details about the fight with the dungeon guards. Finally, Nelda picked up the tale of Irumae's recovery, stressing that she was fully healed and would suffer no ill effects from her captivity or drugging. She finished with the moment that reunited brother and sister.

"You surprise me, cousin," said Soren to Eve, his voice coloured with respect. "I cannot say how much I thank you and your companions for rescuing my sister. I find myself on the brink of warring with my own people and having her safely with me makes my position much more straightforward."

Soren briefly explained the current state of play for their benefit before returning to his earlier discussion. The decision of what course of action to take seemed far simpler now Irumae's fate had been determined, but there were still issues to account for.

"He has no personal leverage to use against you," said Behan, "so our advantage would be in the surprise attack. We should sweep through the city and press them back into the castle. If we can contain them there, it will be easier than them holding the city."

"And if they should run, through the royal dock for example?" replied Soren.

"Not many would chance it, fewer should make it, and I dare say it, good riddance to the dogs, for there will be less for us to deal with." Behan slapped the grass in front of him to emphasise his point.

"Are we not opening ourselves up to a vulnerable position in the city, though? The people of Pandora will surround us. Many have joined my cause, but there are still a significant number of people left in the city. What of their intentions?"

"I believe you should be heartened by your warm reception into Pandora," said Behan. "Yes, many have joined you, and yes, many have not. However, my reckoning is that many are too scared of the consequences and wish to continue with their lives. I feel that if they do not support you, most of them will be at least neutral towards you."

Soren considered this but had no definite decision as to the truth of Behan's words, and invited Edmund to share his view. Edmund agreed with Behan. Behan's knowledge of the city guard suggested that there were few left of those serving under Zaki to guard the city; many had gone with Zaki and he had sent out many more to guard the roads and search for the prince and Edmund. Behan's sources within the city reported a skeleton guard left on the walls and gates, with the small remaining bulk of forces holed up within the castle.

They lapsed into silence as Soren deliberated. *If I don't take the city now, Zaki may return… If I do, I might be able to hold him off…* "I think we should take the city before Zaki returns," he said at last. "Now that Irumae is safe, I have nothing to hold me back. We must not leave ourselves vulnerable inside the city, though. How can we achieve this?"

As the sun sank from its zenith, Soren led a body of men and women containing all of his forces on foot and horseback to Pandora's great south gate in a thin, long line that streamed from his makeshift camp. He rode on horseback in shining armour polished by Behan's men and looked every inch as grand as he ought to, despite the plates being slightly too big. As agreed, nobles and captains took charge of ranks, organising them on the flat plains outside the city as they arrived in battalions of hundreds of people apiece.

The dragons volunteered for the task of breaching the gates with relish. Nolwen and Nelda stayed with Soren at the front of the force for their part in unlocking the gates. The dragons wished to burn the gates to the ground and tear apart the portcullises; Soren refused without hesitation.

If he were to take the city and hold it against Harad's forces, Soren would need the fortifications to remain intact. There would be no guarantee of any time to repair anything once he had taken the city before the invasion arrived. This battle would take great skill; they had to defeat Zaki's forces whilst damaging as little infrastructure as possible.

Instead, the dragons flew around the battlements to harry the soldiers upon them and, judging by the screaming, crunches and thuds of impacts, and crackling of fires started by spurts of dragon fire, killing some as well. As they did this, Nolwen and Nelda dismounted and walked as close to the main gates as they dared, protected by the bows of the farming women who trained arrows on the battlements in readiness.

Holding hands, the two Eldarkind raised their arms and chanted in the old tongue. A wind began to rise and the earth shuddered. The gates groaned and creaked. Soren's forces were still with awe as they watched. It was minutes, though it seemed like hours, when the gates began to shudder open as each individual locking bolt slid open and the great beam of wood holding the gates shut could be heard dropping, with the loudest thud yet, to the ground. The ratchet controlling the portcullis gears clicked away, and Soren knew it would be raising itself seemingly of its own accord.

Myrkdaga dropped like a stone from the sky inside the gates, his great bulk shattering the paving behind the gate and sending small shards of stone flying out from under him. With the strength of his shoulders, he pushed open the gate as his kin landed to help him. Soren, on his horse behind Nolwen and Nelda, watched as the grass browned and withered around their feet. The opening gates revealed the dragons occupying the empty square behind them.

His forces erupted into loud cheers and Soren raised his sword, allowing them to move forward into the city. Ranks filed in through the gates, peeling left and right to comb the city from bottom to top for soldiers and spread Soren's message of peace to the city's inhabitants, warning them not to take up arms against his forces and assuring the citizens that they would not come to any harm. Even so, clashes erupted around them.

Soren observed Nolwen and Nelda. Their shoulders sagged with exhaustion, but they insisted they were fit enough to continue. He rode through the gate with his sword drawn, driving at the head of his forces through the heart of the city to the castle. Soldiers met him and a fierce exhileration swept over him as he joined the frey, at last able to vent some of his frustrations on the soldiers who stood before them.

His sword danced through the air, as Nolwen and Nelda's sang next to him, and behind and around him, his men drove forward. Up they fought, closer to the castle, up winding ways to the castle square, where Soren at last stood before the castle gates to declare his terms.

Small skirmishes had erupted across the city, but Soren was unconcerned. Myrkdaga and his kin offered him a bird's eye view of the city and the unfriendly forces within it, relaying events across Pandora to him.

After the assault on the walls by the dragons and the impressive size of his force, despite it being made up of common folk, the few soldiers left opposing him were in a panic. They fled in disarray to their homes, the castle, the other gate: anywhere they could.

Soren's satisfaction and relief grew as each captain relayed that they had swept and cleared their sections of the city. As planned, their men set to work emptying the armoury for his own forces in case they could not secure the city in one attempt.

The castle loomed above him and he could clearly see guards within the gatehouse. Once more, he called forward the women archers to cover him. Nolwen and Nelda also insisted on stepping forward with him. It was not clear why until after he had demanded his terms: the immediate surrender of all those loyal to Zaki and the return of the castle and city to his possession, or their capture and trial for treason.

An arrow whistled towards him from a slit above the gate as he finished speaking, but before he could react, it stopped dead in the air four feet away and dropped to the ground with a clatter against the cobbles. He looked at his two companions.

Nolwen winked at him conspiratorially. "We really can perform some extraordinary and useful tasks with magic."

"Fascinating," murmured Soren, unable to discern a physical semblance to their barrier. "First rank, shoot!"

A volley whooshed over his head and bowstrings twanged as his archers released a line of arrows over the castle wall and into its first courtyard. The clatter of arrows on stone sounded, though some found their intended targets and cries broke out. Once more, the dragons proved their infinite usefulness; they soared over the courtyard in a blaze of fire and bathed the courtyard in blinding light and heat.

They landed, wreaking havoc with their teeth and claws, as Nolwen and Nelda chanted even faster than they had before to open the castle portcullis and gate in the same manner with the help of the dragons. After the second wave of exertion, they were almost grey.

Here, Soren executed the riskiest part of his plan. Mingling in with the rest of his forces that massed around a wide part of the city's highest levels, Nolwen and Nelda made their way around to where the high castle garden wall met the city at a point that was largely undefended due to its lack of weaknesses.

Soren ensured his forces avoided this area, attempting to give his enemies a false sense of security. The royal garden had never been defended unless the need arose, and Soren was determined to make use of the vulnerability, however small it was.

Whilst he concentrated the main bulk of his forces on fighting their way into the castle, Nolwen and Nelda slipped inside the castle itself to open as many gates and doors as they could, allowing Soren's forces easier access when they breached the main castle. Soren was well aware that without the dragons or the magic and skill of the Eldarkind, this was an attempt that would take much time and cost many lives, but by using their unique skills, he hoped to save an impossible amount of both.

As dragons gleefully rained down from overhead in spiralling, somersaulting dives to pick off archers and guardsmen, Soren kept up his assault and sent waves of archers and infantry until no more could go forward. They kept this up for hours until the forces opposing them fell back another level into the castle and allowed Soren access to all grounds but the private walled royal garden through which Nolwen and Nelda had entered.

The castle's main door, made of heavy, thick wood and reinforced with metal, stood barred before his forces. Nolwen and Nelda were nowhere to be seen. Soren had no choice but to begin the assault on the home he loved. His heartstrings quivered every time a precious stained glass window was smashed and every time a dragon landed on a battlement and crunched the carved stone into pebbles and dust with their bulk and strength.

Arrows rained down upon them, some flaming, to bury themselves within his forces. Screams of the injured and dying lay before and behind him as the battle raged on. Soren felt as if he was in a bubble and separated from it all, as he concentrated on organising his forces.

One by one from his left, he heard his captains signal with horns that the way lay open before them, made possible by the Eldarkind. Soren kept up the pretence, delaying allowing his forces to surge inside the castle until the last possible moment. The alerts came close and closer until Nolwen and Nelda themselves appeared through his forces.

"It is done! We could go no further!" shouted Nolwen over the noise. He shook with tiredness.

Immediately, Soren grabbed a horn from the nearest source and winded it himself; three short bursts that signalled permission to move forward. With renewed vigour, his forces cheered and his captains swept into the castle on foot to lead his forces surging through it. Their orders had been clear: once within the castle, show mercy to those who could be captured and kill those who would not submit.

THIRTY ONE

"It already begins! You must flee, my queen!" Ambassador Delgado begged her.

Pale-faced, Demara shook her head as her ladies in waiting paced nervously around them. It was daytime and yet dark. Demara had ordered them to shutter the windows and light the lamps. The sturdy castle now felt paper-thin to her, as if her enemies could tear through the walls with their hands at any minute.

"I cannot flee, Tomas. A true queen does not flee," she said, though she could not convince herself to feel as brave as she tried to sound.

Ser Tomas made to speak but she continued.

"How can I leave in any case? Look at me! I am unfit, I am tired, and I cannot come so far to lose everything now. What if I were to flee and lose my child?"

"What if you were to stay and lose the child?" he said, impassioned.

"There is no way to leave." She shot his suggestion down. "Look at them. They crowd the castle like ants. Stay your cowardice, for we will win!"

"I am no coward!" Ser Tomas recoiled. "There is no one here to defend you, my queen. We cannot win and will not last the day. I cannot let you come to harm, I wish to save you!"

"Be silent, Tomas! I will not go. I forbid you to go. You will stay and do your duty. We will triumph. Leave me now. I tire." Strong-backed and stern-faced, she stood before him.

He searched her eyes, but they were impassive. Without a choice, he bowed and left without meeting her gaze again.

Demara waited until he had left before she collapsed, sobbing. Her ladies rushed to her side to fuss over her and guide her to bed where they lay her fully clothed. Seline draped a cold cloth across her forehead.

"My lady?" Seline asked, as the other maids dispersed to a distance.

"Seline, I am so frightened!" Demara confided in their native tongue, unwilling to show the full extent of her fears to her Caledonian maids.

The girl grasped her hand.

"I even wish my husband were here to protect me. I fear Tomas is all I have and he has turned to cowardice!".

THIRTY TWO

Soren's forces swept through the castle like wildfire. Nolwen and Nelda remained with him; they were spent but refused to give up. Soon, the gate was unbarred and opened from within. Soren made his way to the great hall where prisoners were already being assembled, sat crammed together on the floor. It was the same, and yet different. Under Zaki's banners, the hall seemed darker. Filled with stinking, bloodied men, it was overcrowded; an assault on the senses.

Soren set Behan's men, whom he trusted more than most, to guard the gate, having ordered them to deny anyone exit. Behan stayed with him to help supervise his forces, whilst Edmund oversaw sweeps across the castle to search for anyone who remained.

Many soldiers surrendered to them, but many of their leaders did not. As such, there were numerous bodies to lay out in the courtyard; some of whom had been prominent figures in the councils. Soren felt an unexpected twinge of relief at the large number of corpses; their deaths had at least spared him the decision of what to do with them.

Soren was forced to imprison those who had surrendered. He could not turn them free, but nor could he kill them in cold blood when they had willingly given their lives into his hands.

His most prominent prisoner came as the greatest surprise to him. Draped in the finest silks and glittering with jewellery appeared Demara, his uncle's wife and the daughter of the King Harad. She entered, surrounded by guards who dared not restrain her, and held her head up as she surveyed the great hall with disdain.

She was beautiful in her own way, with bronzed skin and sultry eyes, but pride marred her face. Soren's eyes widened as he beheld her. In none of his plans had he expected her to be here, but a blind fury overtook his surprise as he saw his mother's favourite crown upon her head.

Soren struggled to suppress his anger as she glided forward to greet him where he stood upon the raised dais, in his armour, stinking and covered in dirt and blood. The hall fell silent as all, prisoners and his own men alike, turned to watch her entrance.

"Prince Soren," she murmured, her words accented.

"It is rightfully king. Princess Demara."

"It is rightfully queen."

He jumped from the dais in a single leap, furious with her beyond words. He raised his hand, wishing to strike her, but snatched his mother's crown from her head instead.

"How dare you," he snarled. The crown trembled in his shaking hand. To her credit, she did not flinch, but stood regarding him through narrowed eyes. Soren stepped back and tried to suppress his temper, when he realised something was different about her. His eyes narrowed as he took in the curve of her stomach under the draped fabrics.

"You are with child," he stated. She did not reply; she did not need to. Her bulging stomach gave away that she was close to giving birth. Now, the timing of Zaki's actions made perfect sense to him. Zaki was securing his future upon the throne in time for the birth of his child, replacing Soren as king even as he fathered a child who would replace Soren's own line.

Soren felt sick. Here was a life he could not in good conscience end standing in front of him, though she carried within her the life which could be his downfall. *I cannot kill Demara and provoke war with her father, yet I cannot let her live and bear her child to adulthood, for it will challenge me should Zaki fail.* Soren was filled with dismay, unsure what to do with her.

A grim-faced Edmund emerged from behind Demara. Edmund must have seen the indecision in Soren's eyes, for he took charge and arranged the detention of the princess within a small apartment in the castle. There, she would stay in seclusion, with guards and women companions handpicked to watch her every move. It left Soren with a sour taste in his mouth, though he knew keeping her prisoner gave him a useful bargaining chip.

Pandora thrummed with life, a hive of activity since Soren's return to the castle. The city itself was not badly damaged from the fighting and little looting or vandalism had occurred. Nevertheless, repairs were needed and so he sent out the city's finest smiths and masons to repair all damage, funding the costs from the royal coffers. He felt too guilty to make Pandora's residents pay for the damage, which he blamed himself for causing, and it inadvertently curried him greater favour amongst the people.

The castle was worse for wear. Smashed windows and shards of glass lay forlornly about, tapestries and works of art were torn, and priceless treasures in the vaults had managed to vanish altogether. What Soren felt most bitter about, however, was the defacing and vandalism of his mother's apartment. When he visited it as part of his routine examination of the entire castle, it filled him with such sadness that he had it sealed off.

The first thing Soren did, when he had a moment of reprieve, was visit his mother's grave. He took Irumae with him. Naisa lay at rest in the castle cemetery under a stone carving of herself asleep, crowned with a stony mantle and everlasting youth on her face. They ran their hands over her hard cheeks and across the flowing forms in the stone, which had been roughly carved in the haste of its need, both wishing she had a grave more fitting for her. Compared to the graves of her forebears, it was shoddy.

Soren still could not reconcile that his mother lay under the impassive stone. Every moment he spent in the castle, he expected to hear her voice and smell her perfume, but all had faded. Out in the wilderness, under the urgency of his tasks, the grief was something he had managed to lock away and so he thought, come to terms with. However, coming back to the home they had shared brought everything back. Soren had never felt less at ease. In every corner lurked more grief. Brother and sister huddled by the grave for the entire afternoon, lost in their sadness as the city repaired itself around them.

The reprieve could not last forever and Soren soon threw himself with renewed determination back into overseeing the fortification of the city. There remained a fraction of the nobles and captains who had served under his mother; Soren used them all to try to ready the city.

In place of those who had perished, their sons and nephews stepped forward. Some oversaw improving the defences outside the city, clearing away debris close to the wall, whilst others concentrated on building siege engines from plans in the armoury.

Two trebuchets were constructed just inside the south gate by utilising the city's many carpenters, who worked day and night. Many more, smaller catapults on wheels were produced that could be relocated anywhere in the city they were required. Soren gave special permission for them to cut wood from the royal forest itself for the purpose of restoring and fortifying Pandora.

Most were constructed on the top of the walls themselves; Soren noticed a great disadvantage of the city walls was a lack of ramps, only steps, leading to the broad walkways on top of them. Ammunition in the form of stones and rubble stood heaped in piles along key roads in the city and by the walls, with residents of the city invited to add anything they had that would prove useful missiles. No one knew what size host Harad might send.

The camp outside the city dismantled as swiftly as it had sprung up, with residents cheerfully relocating themselves back within the city and taking up the defensive work with vigour. Normal trade had stopped within the city, with many shops closed as the people gave their efforts to Pandora, but Soren ensured the markets and dock remained operational, as well as the healers, so the city remained well provisioned and functioning. The farmers returned to their holdings, to reap all the crops and grain they could from the fields and send it to be stored inside the city in case of siege.

The dragons settled in the castle grounds, and took to basking in the summer sun on the terraces in the private walled garden. It was here that Soren hosted his meetings with Edmund and Behan also and at Edmund's suggestion, Nolwen and Nelda, who represented the dragon's counterparts.

THIRTY THREE

Eve found herself at leisure; not involved in the councils, the running of the city, or the battle to come. At first she was angry about being ignored and discounted, but as Nelda mentored her in the art of magical and non-magical medical treatments, her frustration disappeared, replaced by a fascination with healing.

There were many to heal after the taking of the city, both enemy and friend alike, and Eve healed anyone she could, regardless of their loyalties or status, soon becoming immune to the stench of blood and worse bodily odours, and the squeamishness of blood and gangrenous wounds. Nelda taught her how to alter the wording of her incantations slightly but significantly, so she could choose where to draw the energy required to sustain the magic from; herself, the patient, or the surroundings.

It gave her a feeling of greater satisfaction to mend lives rather than take them; after her near death experience, she understood the limits to her own boldness, and they did not include killing another, even to save herself. Her father would be disappointed, she knew; she was not the son and heir she knew he wished for, but if nothing else, it resolved her determination to keep her own independence. Outside his control, she revelled in being able to choose her own path freely.

Experimenting on many patients with a variety of ailments helped her broaden her understanding of anatomy and the rules of magic. Eve found she learnt quickly and could soon manage to heal many more people in a short time with better results and less of her own energy than it had taken to heal Luke, by using the magic in a different way; its subtleties fascinated her.

Luke accompanied her everywhere, insisting on ensuring her safety despite Pandora now being under Soren's control. He observed her work, now more intrigued than intimidated by magic. After each session, which lasted a few hours between mealtimes, he would question her about a certain task and listen with interest as she explained what was required in order to fix or relieve the symptoms of the ailment.

Sometimes he could listen to Nelda's tutelage, but sometimes not, as she chose to speak to Eve in the old tongue about matters of magic and the secrets of their shared race. Eve found satisfaction and fulfilment in the simple act of helping someone else that she had not experienced before. So it was that after an afternoon at the healing houses, an idea began to form.

"I think I'd like to be a healer," she said as she wandered through the castle with Luke. "I always assumed I'd have to become my father one day, to fight and defend Arrow county and the country, but after what happened in the castle when we rescued Irumae, I don't think I can be that person.

"Working with Nelda has been so rewarding," she continued. "I think I'd rather heal people, rather than dealing out death myself. Why should I pass judgement on others who I do not know? How is that fair?"

"I play devil's advocate, I hope you understand," Luke replied, "but what would your father say? Who would defend the county in your name?"

"I'm not sure," said Eve. "On the one hand, he would be glad that I was safe. On the other hand, I think he'd be disappointed to have no proper heir. I don't think he'd like me to fight, but I think he'd see not fighting as a weakness, which would be exploited by others."

"I think many others would share that view," Luke replied, "and that it would plague you for however long it took to prove them otherwise. Who would defend Arrow, if you don't take up the sword?"

"Well, my father wishes me to marry," admitted Eve reluctantly.

"Marry?" exclaimed Luke.

"Yes. I'll be expected to marry. I dread it."

"You dread it?"

"Wouldn't you? Who would enjoy spending their life with someone they didn't choose?" Eve sighed. "I suppose it would leave someone to defend the county as long as Arrow remained under my guardianship. I won't give Arrow to an outsider."

"You'll marry an outsider?"

Eve met his eyes, which were troubled under his wrinkled brow. "I have no inkling," she said, uncomfortable. "Father hasn't pressed the idea, but he soon will; I'm of age, as much as he doesn't want to admit that. I don't know where he'd find a suitable match, though."

Luke was silent. Eve did not speak as she brooded. The idea of marriage induced many sources of trepidation and fear of the unknown in her and she sought comfort in the fact that her father was not seeking her marriage then.

"You should seek Nelda's advice," Luke said. "See what she thinks about you becoming a healer. I think it's a fine idea. You're much better at healing than you are at fighting. Although you're skilled with a sword or bow, it's not that which gets you through a real fight. I haven't seen you so calm and at peace as you are when you're healing."

She answered his smile with her own. "That reassures me. Thanks for your ear, Luke. You're a good friend." She clasped his hand between hers briefly to communicate her appreciation. They walked around the first floor of the castle once more in companionable silence, before Eve bid Luke farewell and slipped into her chambers to bathe.

Nelda supported her idea wholeheartedly. "Taking life and causing injury is a grievous task that should not be lightly done. If you feel that your efforts are lent better to healing, then I shall support you in this. I fight when I have to, as you have seen, but I too much prefer to heal and nourish and tend.

"Perhaps you should apprentice yourself to one of the traditional healers in the city to gain some knowledge of non-magical healing techniques. Go to the prince and ask him if this is possible."

Eve followed her advice and that evening, after dinner in the great hall, approached her cousin for a meeting. Soren seemed withdrawn, and she surmised the demands upon him were taking their toll. His sternness softened when she explained her reasoning and once finished, gave his answer.

"I give you my blessing, cousin," Soren said. "It's good that you see the value of life. I wish I could preserve, rather than take it too. I'm glad I now have a reason not to ask you to fight, as is your right; your father would never forgive me for placing you in such danger.

"You may have the freedom to do as you wish whilst you are a guest here. The healers would appreciate any help you can offer them. I need to be better informed about my casualties in any case; you may report to me with anything of importance."

Eve returned to her apartment with a beaming smile, although she was disappointed that her cousin seemed so distant with her. She knew she would still have to broach the subject with her father. Eve dreaded the moment, not least because there were other things that they would speak of first, but it was time for her to make use of Artora's gift.

Her apartment door closed with a snap behind her and Eve turned the key in the lock before retrieving the mirror from the bottom of the wardrobe. She rested the mirror on the dresser and stood before it, taking a deep breath and then two more before feeling for the magic and uttering, "*Leitha Karn.*"

The mirror surface shimmered and rippled, but did not show her father; just the ceiling of his study. The magical link was complex enough to be above Eve's ken, and it did not show him directly as any other scrying would, instead revealing the true reflection of his own mirror, wherever it sat.

"Father!" she called to the mirror.

There was silence.

"*Let our voices pass through the mirror.*" Faint sounds emanated from the mirror before her; background noise from her house. The familiarity of the sounds made her smile as she recognised them. She could discern the faint rustling of trees; the windows must have been open for the light was bright and she could hear the neighing of horses and the blackbird's song that woke her every morning.

"Father," she called again.

Footsteps sounded and her father appeared over the mirror looking down into it, askew. She must have appeared upside down to him too, for he turned the mirror around until he could gaze at her eye to eye.

"Eve, where in God's name are you?" His mouth tightened as he bent close to the mirror, gazing at her and about her as he tried to discern where she was. "Why did you not return? Are you well?"

"Father, calm down," she said, holding a hand up to halt his tirade of questions. "I'm quite well. I chose not to come back."

"I ordered you to return immediately, Eve! It was not your choice!" said her father. "How dare you disobey me and then vanish like this with some garbled message passed on to me. Have you any inkling of the worry and frustration this has caused?"

"I had many good reasons to justify my decision," replied Eve. Colour rose in her cheeks. Could she have seen it, the slant in her eyebrows matched her father's.

"That I doubt," retorted her father, his eyes narrow.

"Firstly, Princess Irumae was being held against her will, so I decided I would rescue her, which I have done."

Her father's expression turned and his eyebrows rose from anger to disbelief. "Do not lie to me, Eve."

"I'm telling the truth!" said Eve, feeling hurt. "With the help of my companions, I liberated her from Pandora's castle dungeons some nights hence. I lose track of the days."

"Companions?" said her father.

"Yes, Father. I have travelled from Ednor to Pandora with Luke, who has remained my faithful protector, and two of the Eldarkind, who Queen Artora handpicked to accompany me."

Her father covered his face and rubbed his temples with a frustrated sigh. "This becomes worse and worse," she heard him mutter. "So now, Eve, I find that you have been traipsing across the wilderness with a man and two strangers not even of this race? How is this a respectable preoccupation for my daughter and heir?"

"You forced me to this, Father," said Eve in a brittle tone.

"How the blazes have I?" Her father exploded into rage once more. "I ordered you quite clearly to give my correspondence to Artora and return immediately!"

"Why would I," Eve said, "when you have lied to me for all these years? Why did you not tell me about my mother?" She raised her hands in the air in frustration. "Why did you hide from me what I ought to have known?"

Her father stepped back from the mirror until Eve could no longer see him.

"Father!" she called out, thinking he had abandoned their conversation, as more pent up frustration stirred in her belly.

"I am here," Karn said in a muffled voice. Part of his forehead reappeared, but there was a long silence before he spoke. "I assume you now know of your mother's heritage, her status and her...skills?"

"Magic, yes."

"I did not tell you because I wished to protect you," Karn said. "Magic is a thing I do not understand, despite my years with Freya, for she hid it amongst our race. I always wondered if she died because she practised it, or because she lived too long amongst her people to be immune to whatever killed her. I had many ideas, but I never understood why the sickness took her." His voice coloured with sadness.

"I did not want that same fate for you, daughter. I thought that if I raised you in the traditional way, as my parents raised me, you would be better protected."

"Your views nearly killed me, father," said Eve. "Magic isn't something you can learn, it's in my blood and you can't protect me from it. It's awoken. By shielding me from it for all these years you have ensured that I am not equipped, as I should be, to manage it." She saw her father's eyebrows crinkle, the rest of his face still not visible.

"Neither of us has acted perfectly in this," her father admitted. He sidled into view again. "You must return home at once; we have much to discuss."

"I can't come home yet. I'm needed here," said Eve

cautiously. She did not want to provoke him to anger again.

"Where is 'here'?"

"I'm in Pandora. Much has happened since I left." She summarised the events in the capital, including her own deployment in the healing houses as her father's eyes widened.

"I had heard nothing of this. I assumed that Zaki had cut me off from the capital over recent weeks. I have been expecting an assault on Arrow, truth be told."

"Soren is expecting a battle here. Can you spare any men? There are few enough who are well trained and I'm sure Soren would welcome more skilled soldiers."

"Consider it done," said her father. "I shall marshal my men and send as many as I can spare, on one condition."

"Yes?" said Eve hesitantly.

"I expect that you come home to Arlyn with them once the capital has been secured."

After a pause, Eve agreed.

"I shall tolerate no more disobedience on this matter," warned her father. "Do not test me further."

Eve did not reply to that. After exchanging awkward pleasantries, she called an end to their meeting, feigning that she was required elsewhere. Her father's troubled face faded from the mirror until it reflected her own. She sat staring at herself for some minutes, before packing away the mirror and writing a message to Soren to notify him of Karn's assistance. Agitated, she returned to the healing houses. It was late, but she needed the distraction.

Karn's forces arrived days later and Soren gratefully received the five hundred extra men into his ranks. Eve was glad to see that her father was not present; he had sent his deputy to command his men.

The captain greeted her with a show of deference but after the formality was done with, he sought immediate council with Soren, bypassing her authority. She was relieved not to have to manage them in matters of war, of which she knew very little. Karn had taught her the ways of managing Arrow county: not the ways of a kingdom, or of war.

That afternoon, Behan's scouts also arrived, exhausted, and declared Zaki to be less than a day's ride behind them. The city sprang into action as the news spread like wildfire and Soren ordered all forces to be ready and marshalled.

The city glowed that night; every inch of it lit by thousands of lanterns as men and women toiled to ensure all fortifications were completed and in working order in time. Had the city folk been able to see Pandora from afar, they would have been able to see it in its greatest glory; a city glowing gold and amber in the night.

THIRTY FOUR

Soren rose early after a sleepless night. Knowing Zaki approached filled him with nervous energy. He could not eat, drink or rest and took to pacing around his apartment, relentlessly reviewing and rehearsing the strategies, though he could not improve upon them.

Day dawned cloudy and stiflingly warm, not ideal conditions. Such weather would hamper both sides and cause more injuries than were necessary due to exhaustion and heatstroke. Soren hope there would be no need to fight, but he knew Zaki would not surrender.

Soren had visited Demara daily without fail since the taking of the castle; to quite what end he was not sure himself. Nevertheless, he deemed it a priority to try and understand her motives and provoke her to share any knowledge of her father's or Zaki's strategies, as any information she divulged could aid him.

Despite his attempts, she remained uncooperative and denied any knowledge of her father or husband's plans. Soren did not know whether to believe her or not. She appeared to be an innocent and delicate woman; a pawn of the men in her life. Nevertheless, the prince knew he could not trust a woman with such dangerous connections, however harmless she seemed.

Impatient after the early visit, he abandoned the castle to ride out in the city, to check and double-check the defences with Edmund and a small company of guards who rode around the city with him. Finally, he was sure he could prepare no more and climbed up to the watch post on the south gate to join the surprised guards in their vigil and watch for the coming of his enemy.

The first sign of Zaki's approach was a small dust cloud far to the south; the dried, powdery earth shook loose from the passage.

Soren's heart leapt in his chest and nervous energy coursed through him. Soren sent runners to every corner of the city to rouse and amass his forces. At his word, the dragons retired to the castle, to be his secret weapon, should he have need of them.

As the group of men drew nearer, it solidified into a dark band on the horizon and grew larger by the hour, until in plain sight a vast force of riders galloped towards them in a wide line with their armour flashing in the sun. Soren and the guards on the wall watched them approach.

When they were a mile away, the sound of a grand, trumpeting tune floated towards them. The sound was strange and haunting, a southern instrument, he presumed. Soren signalled for his men to blow the horns in response as normal; he wanted Zaki to think he was riding triumphantly home until the last possible moment, so that he was within range to take alive or dead if possible. One horn rang out, and then another, until they sounded from every gate.

Zaki's forces led the group of men and also brought up the rear in their silver armour, whilst the men of Roher were sandwiched between, armoured in golden metal that shone, even in the cloudy weather that morning. Before the bulk of the forces rode two figures, whom Soren deduced would be Zaki himself and King Harad.

They were almost close enough for Soren to make out faces under helmets and hands on reins when two standard-bearers and a herald came forward, raising their standards. One showed Zaki's coat of arms, which had fluttered on flags around Pandora until Soren had had every single one ripped down and burnt. The other bore the coat of arms of King Harad; a rampant red lion and rose on a golden field, which Soren recognised from the wedding of Zaki and Demara two years previously.

The herald charged forward and blew his horn with all his might. "Open the gates!"

With a smile, Soren gave the signal he had so long been waiting for in response. He stood to look over the south gate crenellations at Zaki and Harad, who were slowing to a trot two hundred yards away.

At Soren's command, giant flags were raised and allowed to

unfurl in the slight breeze to reveal his mother's coat of arms, which he had adopted as his own. The herald stopped dead at the sight of the billowing flags, before turning his mount and charging back to Zaki and Harad.

Silence fell. Not a man spoke on the wall, and no murmur arose from the forces amassed so close to the city. All stood to attention and it seemed every man held his breath. Soren too waited in silence as the herald turned once more to return within shooting distance of the gates.

"His Majesty King Zaki commands the gate to open and for all non-authorised standards to be cast down at once!" the man called authoritatively.

"I reject his command, for he holds no authority here!" Soren called back.

"Who are you to speak so?" the herald replied pompously.

"I name myself Prince Soren, son of Queen Naisa and rightful heir to the kingdom of Caledan. I call for Zaki, the false pretender to the throne, who I name murderer, treasonous usurper, and kidnapper, to surrender himself to trial by a jury of the people to attest for his crimes.

"The city and its people stand with me in this and you cannot hope to succeed against us. To King Harad, who I know to not be innocent in relation to these matters, I bid him take the most sensible course of action and retreat peacefully beyond our borders to his own kingdom."

As recognition flashed in Zaki's eyes, and his uncle lifted his gaze to meet Soren's, a thrill of emotion Soren could not name rushed through him. To see that face in the flesh after all he had endured: he could not fathom what that meant to him.

"You dog!" shrieked Zaki. "Seize him, I command you! I will double the reward for his capture!"

Not a man on the wall moved. Soren released his pent-up breath in relief. Zaki sunk into his saddle as it dawned on him that he had lost the city.

"If you will not surrender him to me, you shall all burn!" With that, he turned his horse away, shouting indistinct orders to his men.

A large group broke off riding east and north around the city whilst Zaki rode himself with the main bulk of his men west towards the city without and the docks.

His intentions soon became very clear; fires sprung up in the hamlets and farms surrounding the city and the sound of fighting and screaming came from the docks as Soren's men poured out from the dock gate to meet him. He made to join them, but King Harad's herald called to him from before the gate.

"My master bids thee open the gates and speak with him under the banner of parley," cried the herald.

"How can I know his intentions to be honourable?" Soren called back.

"He will approach alone if you will do the same. Come and speak to him before the gates, where you are still within the safety of the city, if you will."

Intrigued, Soren made his way to the gates. His men opened them with reluctance and crowded there with weapons drawn, should he need them. King Harad ordered his men to retreat a little further, whilst he himself advanced into the shadow of the walls, dismounting his horse and accompanied by the herald, who quickly took his reins.

Soren strode out to meet him, presenting as confident an exterior as he could, mindful of the danger he was placing himself in and relieved to have hundreds of men covering him from the city. He found himself wishing for Edmund's reassuring presence, but Edmund covered the defences of the southwest of the city, far from his side.

Soren and the king greeted each other cautiously and coolly. Soren waited for Harad to begin, and observed what he could as Harad passed his feather-plumed helmet to his herald. Harad stood tall and proud, a little shorter than Soren and on the decline into the corpulence of middle age, although his physique was stocky and his armour had been shaped to complement and enhance his form.

He had thick black hair, greying at the temples, and a dark, trimmed beard flecked with greying hairs. Patterns too detailed for Soren to pick out weaved across his armour, recording untold hours of careful tooling. He must have been sweltering in the humidity, stifled by his ceremonial dress, but he betrayed no sign of discomfort.

"My daughter is in the citadel, yes?" Harad asked in a rich, deep voice. He glared at Soren with dark, inscrutable eyes under bushy eyebrows.

"Yes."

"Is she well, and being treated as befits her rank and current health?"

"She is well and I treat her with the greatest privilege."

"I am gladdened to hear this. Now that her husband and I are now here, will you release her into our care? It would be fitting, of course, given the delicate nature of her condition." Harad smiled at Soren, seeming sincere, but his eyes were sharp.

"She is my prisoner," said Soren flatly. "I will not relinquish her for any reward. I hope that her continued stay with me will ensure your good conduct."

Harad's mask faltered then with his surprise, before he returned to an impassive expression. "I have many daughters and sons," said Harad. "What makes you think that I would value the life of one enough to cause me to retreat like a coward?"

"I would hope you would not be so callous to your own kin," replied Soren, "though I know such things happen. However, given that she carries within her a babe that under my rule would be third in line to the throne of Caledan after my sister and uncle, I doubt that you would throw such a thing away."

"It seems that I underestimate you." Harad bowed his head to Soren. The gesture felt insincere and mocking, which riled Soren.

"You do," Soren replied. He immediately regretted his words and took a breath to calm himself.

"You are however correct," conceded the king. "Consider my forces neutral to you for the time being. I will cause you no harm if none is brought to my daughter or her unborn son. I will make you an offer you think worthy of consideration. If you release my daughter to me unharmed and a free woman, I will give you Zaki in chains to do with as you will and leave your land."

Soren's eyes widened in surprise. Here was a development he had not expected. "Why should I strike this deal with you?" he asked slowly. "I can crush Zaki myself without your help." The sound of fighting came from the docks, where smoke rose from many fires.

"You may, young prince, but the cost in the lives of your own men would be a great price to pay and I will be forced to react hostilely if you refuse to release my daughter. I do not think you could hope to defeat my entire army in your present state." The king smiled, satisfied with his position.

"If I am to agree to this, you will sign a treaty swearing never to invade my kingdom."

"I will do no such thing," refused Harad. "A life for a life is a fair trade."

"Technically, I am to trade you two lives for my uncle."

Harad shrugged. "The life of the babe is not guaranteed. Childbirth is a dangerous undertaking, thus it should not be used as a bargaining chip. That is my offer. Take or leave it as you wish."

Soren paused and did not reply, struggling with his conscience.

"The clock ticks," murmured the king insipidly. "Every moment you dally a man dies."

"I consent to the terms you have laid out," agreed Soren. He sensed he had little other choice. He could see but two options laid before him; he could crush Zaki himself to then be faced with Harad's might, or take Zaki with much less bloodshed and begin immediate preparations for the fortification of Caledan in the hope that he could repel Harad. In either case, he was sure that Harad would want to make a claim for Caledan's throne.

Harad smiled at Soren's answer, looking self-satisfied.

"It shall be done. Meet me at sunset at the gates with my daughter; you shall have Zaki then," said Harad.

The horse squealed and sprung forward as Zaki dug his spurs into its flanks. He gave a great howl of anger and screamed for his men to follow him. To his surprise, the city without was deserted and the west gate closed and barred.

Buildings were burning before long as he charged through the empty streets, smashing windows and taking pleasure in destroying everything he could reach to vent his frustration at being outwitted.

Through the smoke he rode, straight into a line of pikes. The men in front of him screamed as their dying horses collapsed under them, and men darted forward from behind the pikes to cut them down. Zaki retreated as his men continued to pass him, battle cries in their throats as they met their foe.

The air cleared. Standing tall in stirrups under the gate he saw Sir Edmund, grim-faced and shouting commands. An inhuman growl rose in his throat as he charged forward, but a horse drew beside him and the rider forced him to a halt, daring to grab hold of his reins.

"Sir, stop! Stop, sir!" Reynard called, as Edmund met Zaki's gaze, distracted by the call. "We lose the fight badly, sir. We must fall back!"

"I will do no such thing!" replied Zaki, his eyes still locked upon Edmund's. "We cannot be losing. Our numbers must be greater!" He broke eye contact with Edmund and realised the armour about him was all silver. "Where is Harad?" he demanded.

"He did not come," Reynard admitted. He refused to release Zaki's reins. "We must fall back, sir!" he repeated in desperation. "We will be overcome without Harad's men."

Zaki twisted away. Edmund had vanished. The tide of battle was turning as his men were pressed back step by step from the gates. "Sound the retreat." He cursed Harad.

By the time Soren returned to the city, news reached him of Zaki's outnumbered forces being routed by his own. Behan had swept out of the east gate and decimated the men who were attempting to destroy the outlying lands, whilst Edmund and the main concentration of Soren's army were busy defending the most vulnerable area of the city by the docks. Soren gave orders for Zaki's forces to be allowed to flee and efforts concentrated on putting out the fires in the city outside the walls to save as much of the area as possible.

Harad's forces pulled well back from the wall and dallied almost at the spot where Soren had held his own camp. As Zaki rode out to meet them with what few men were left in his forces who were fit to ride, Soren knew Zaki would be furious that Harad had not joined him. He did not know how Harad would take custody of his uncle, nor was he sure about trusting the Roherii king, but he suspected foul play would be involved.

In the ceasefire, Soren reunited with Behan and Edmund, who brought their reports of the fighting. Losses had been significant, as had injuries, but not enough to cripple Soren's chances of success if the fighting continued, given the numbers they were up against. Soren admitted the deal he had struck with Harad. Behan was surprised, while Edmund was annoyed that he had done so without consultation.

"I know the stakes, Edmund!" Soren replied to Edmund's curt comments. "I'm not a child. I have made the best with what I have; I would rather have Zaki in my custody and Harad's army at my door in the future, than not have him and have Harad's army at my door today!"

Edmund acquiesced, deferring to him in a way Soren had not seen before. He realised that his mentor, friend, and ally would always be forced to defer to him. It saddened Soren, who knew the cost could be their friendship. He could have offered a concession to Edmund then, to soften the blow, but he could not think what to say.

THIRTY FIVE

The horns rang out as Zaki charged alone, ahead of his men, across the plains towards Harad's camp. The King of Roher reclined under the shade of a pavilion when Zaki found him. Zaki leapt from his horse and flung his helmet away.

"What in God's name are you playing at?!" Zaki shouted at him.

"You would do well to compose yourself," Harad remarked in a benign voice, but this infuriated Zaki further.

"Compose myself! You abandoned me to a humiliating defeat! With your help we could be sitting in that castle—my castle—right now! You told me to crush them without mercy and yet you will not follow your own advice!"

Harad rose from his recliner, more swiftly than Zaki expected, and stood in front of him with fists clenched. "You will not address me thus," Harad said, his voice iron. "You were too hasty in your attack. I will not suffer my men to die to satisfy your trivial ego when there are better ways to achieve our goals."

Harad turned away and dismissed him with a wave as he strode into his tent. Zaki made to follow, but the tent flap closed and guards barred his way. He kicked the recliner in anger and stormed off to take his frustration out elsewhere.

Just before sunset that evening, Harad and Zaki, backed by a hundred of Harad's men, approached the city gates where Soren still waited. He made his way down, flanked by Behan and Edmund. The gates opened as armoured cavalry waited in the courtyard where they would be visible to Harad.

"Greetings, Prince Soren," said Harad, as Zaki dismounted to stand beside him. Their horses were led away to the side. Soren could see how close Harad's men stood to Zaki in neat formation and could see the trap that would soon spring into motion, if Harad was to keep his word.

"I trust that my daughter is awaiting our arrival, yes?" Harad questioned, after Soren had greeted him in return. Soren and Zaki did not acknowledge each other. Soren refused to look at his uncle. He signalled Edmund, who gestured to the men by the gate to reveal Demara.

Demara was dressed simply, shadowed by her maid and carrying no possessions. She stood in silence as she saw her father for the first time since she had married. Not a flicker of emotion crossed her face. Soren admired her courage. He allowed her to approach closer so Harad could see she was in perfect condition.

Harad smiled, a cold smile that showed no emotion at the sight his daughter. "She is well. I am glad. Seize him."

The trap sprang into motion. Harad's men overpowered Zaki, who had no time to resist. A man to each limb, they forced him to the ground as he hurled abuse at them. When he rose again, supported by guards, his clothes and face were smeared with dirt where he had been pushed into the earth. His hands were bound behind him and his ankles tied together.

He continued to swear at Harad, but his father-in-law gazed around at Pandora's walls as if admiring the fortifications. Last of all, a guard moved forward to shove a rag into Zaki's mouth. The guard recoiled with a suppressed cry as Zaki bit him.

"Give up," said Harad disdainfully. "You have lost." Zaki stopped moving and glared at him with malevolence instead. "Take comfort in knowing your wife still lives and bears you an heir, and be done with it." Harad turned away.

Zaki responded with insults and curses, which were nothing more than muffed, indistinct sounds. He struggled against his bonds but he could not free himself. Soren dared to look him in the face as Zaki looked between Harad and Soren with such hatred that Soren was taken aback.

"My daughter, please," requested Harad. He opened his arms.

"Zaki first," Soren said, his eyes narrowing.

"As you wish." A click of King Harad's fingers and the guards dragged Zaki forward and sent him sprawling across the ground in front of Soren, where he lay writhing. Edmund gestured and five of Soren's men ran forward. They grabbed Zaki bodily and rushed him within the city gates.

"My daughter," said Harad. When Soren paused, the king glowered. "Do not double-cross me, for it would be a grievous mistake."

"I would do no such thing," replied Soren, stung. "I wish you to reiterate your promise that you will leave my land peacefully and immediately, as we agreed earlier, in the hearing of all those present, before I release Demara to you."

Harad surveyed the wall towering above him that bristled with armoured soldiers. Soren knew the king would be calculating his chances if a battle commenced. The prince stood tall to portray confidence he did not possess. He hoped the bravado would cause Harad to retreat.

Slowly, Harad inclined his head. In his deep voice, he stated what he had promised earlier loud enough that those present could hear it. Without further hesitation, Soren signalled for Demara to step forward. Her maid scurried behind her. Demara stood opposite her father, who helped her mount Zaki's now abandoned horse. Without a backward glance, he mounted and rode swiftly off.

Soren called for the word of victory and the capture of the false king to be spread everywhere throughout the city, and he sent riders to share the news further afield. A great guard was set on that night, but when dawn broke, there was no sign of Harad or of his men. More worryingly, Zaki's men had also vanished, though Soren could not spare much thought for them.

THIRTY SIX

It took weeks of labour to make the city good once more; days flowed from one to the next as Soren oversaw the restoration. He could do nothing to save the lives that had been lost, but he was determined to help salvage what was left.

At first, the people were apprehensive and avoided him, unsure how to react to his presence amongst them. Yet as his perseverance shone through, their affection and familiarity for him grew, for taking his time and spending his money freely to help them. In return, Soren found himself rewarded by their appreciation and his own satisfaction, not to mention a growing confidence.

The prince had not spared a moment of time for Zaki since his detainment, happy to be distracted by more pleasing things. His uncle's trial had yet to be arranged and although the shadow of his fate hung over Soren, he buried the decision in the business of helping Pandora's people, until the city was restored and he safely enthroned. He was glad to have what his senior advisers would agree was a reasonable cause to divert his attention. He still felt unable to confront the man, who was a monster in his mind.

He relied on Behan for support and guidance; the steward was a respected and reliable figurehead for the people, with connections spreading like a spider's web throughout the city. In truth, Behan's wealth of contacts unnerved Soren. The man was powerful to be sure, but the prince was so desperate for allies that he grasped the opportunity.

Behan offered his help so freely for the present, which Soren appreciated, but there grew a suspicion that he would have a debt to pay to others, mostly Behan, sooner rather than later as a reward for their loyalty. Edmund also provided a source of constant morale, though in contrast to Behan, after their adventures and ordeals, the prince trusted Sir Edmund far more and spent much more time confiding in him than anyone else.

From the noble houses sprung up the sons of now-dead lords to take up his cause; with their youth they brought inexperience, but also vitality. Soren was glad that members of the older generation remained. Although few, they knew the ways of the world far better than their sons. To Edmund's great delight, his son Dane appeared from the wilderness, emaciated and bedraggled—but alive—having traveled all the way to Pandora on foot after escaping his father's occupied estate.

For all their enthusiasm, the naivety of the young lords saddened Soren; a few months ago, he had been identical to them in hopes and dreams, and their lives in a sheltered environment. Now he saw what a disadvantage that upbringing had been.

I am not one of them anymore, he realised. No more could he hunt and jest in ignorance and bliss after what he had endured, and the responsibility he now found himself with.

Once Pandora had been restored, there was one event remaining to prepare for and it sparked joy in the city: Soren's coronation. Pandora was cleaned and decorated from bottom to top, flowerpots and troughs liberally adorned buildings and streets were swept whilst homemade bunting, strung from roof to roof, fluttered in the breeze. Each citizen seemed more house proud than the next and the further into the city and the wealthier the occupants, the more extravagant the displays of flowers, exotic shrubs, and other shows of celebration.

Guests and revellers poured in from all corners of the kingdom to join in the celebrations. Before Eve had had a chance to consider returning home, her father arrived from Arlyn. She had been dreading their eventual meeting, but her father greeted her with an unexpected embrace and betrayed no hints of anything other than genuine affection and relief she was well. For this, she was glad.

They dined and drank together as they always had at home, until it seemed that no time had passed and they had not ever parted. There was the slightest awkwardness in the occasional lull in the conversation that betrayed what remained unspoken between them. Eve knew they must soon have a reckoning, but the thought of it sparked dread in her heart.

To Soren's surprise, Garth also appeared with his daughter Lindy in tow, atop Soren's own horse with Edmund's riding alongside. Soren greeted them with delight, astonished that the fisherman had returned the horses himself. He invited them to the coronation and gave them the freedom of the city for their help.

Garth, typical of his gruff nature, which Soren had come to be fond of, shook off the thanks, uncomfortable with being made such a fuss of, but he seemed genuinely pleased that Soren appreciated his efforts nonetheless.

With the city returned to business as usual, Soren's mood lightened, as though he had been relieved of a huge burden. In the small family meals that he shared with Irumae, Eve, Karn, and a few chosen others amongst his extended family and cohort, he almost seemed to return to his former self. He appeared carefree and witty in his conversations, although the dark shadows under his eyes, which had not quite faded, betrayed his continuing stress.

He was increasingly nervous about his coronation; he required both Eldarkind and dragon blessings to ensure his success. Neither race had yet graced the capital with their presence, although Soren had made sure that Nolwen had conveyed Soren's invitation to his queen. Myrkdaga and his kin had departed weeks before; bored once the battles had finished, but able to carry news to Myrkith-visir of what had passed, and request Brithilca's blessing.

A small group of the Eldarkind, sent by Artora, arrived two days in advance of the coronation and were welcomed into the city by its people, to Soren's relief on both counts. East of the great lake, the Eldarkind were regarded with intrigue and reverence, being ingrained in royal history and folklore.

On the morning of the fifteenth day of the seventh month, the great cathedral in Pandora played host to the great event, bedecked in colourful decorations. Lords, ladies, clergymen, special guests, and all those who could fit packed into the huge building to see the spectacle of coronation as it should be.

Queen Naisa's standard hung from rafters and balconies wherever it could be draped, spreading blue and gold across the grey stone and complemented by flowers woven into ornate structures adorning the columns and altars. They filled the vaulted space with colour, matched by the ceremonial capes of scarlet and white, fine fur adorning the shoulders of the highest-ranking parties there who occupied the front rows of seating.

The Eldarkind stood in flowing robes of white along the central aisle that ran the length of the cathedral's nave, as Soren entered dressed in simple but smart trousers and doublet, wearing the crown of the heir to the throne. Hador met him at the head of the aisle. As the new abbot, it was his duty to preside over the ceremony. Soren was glad for his presence. He felt a bond with the monk after their shared experiences.

The Eldarkind sang as Soren entered and their melody floated into the heights as the ceremony began. Hador passed the crown of the heir from Soren to Irumae, who sat in a smaller throne by her brother atop the huge dais. The abbot charged Soren with the fair running of the country and treatment of its subjects, and Soren promised to govern it so. Two pages draped the purple mantle of kingship over Soren's shoulders as he stood before the dragon throne.

Impassive, silent, motionless, it towered before him. He accepted the royal ceremonial sword that represented honour and chivalry. Then he took the golden sceptre and promised to rule in line with the law and knelt to accept the blessing of the abbot upon his brow. Soren prayed under his breath. This was the moment he had been waiting for. Nowhere had he found the Crown of the Dragon Kings and he wondered whether Brithilca watched over him.

The Eldarkind's song increased in complexity; harmonies emerged through the melody that flowed through the summer air, bewitching their audience. Eve felt a shiver down her spine and her hair stand on end all across her body as she listened to the magic-infused words of the old tongue.

They sang for prosperity, wellbeing, good harvests and all manner of things to the sky, blessing the coronation of King Soren and calling their allies, the dragons, forth to do likewise. The sun brightened in the sky and flowers blossomed spontaneously, called forth by the magic of the song, and radiant joy was mirrored on the face of everyone who listened.

As they sang, repeating the verses again and again, a piercing crack split the still air and then another, and then a rumble. All looked up in wonder as the stone dragon rose and spread its wings. Soren dropped to his knees before it.

"You have proven your worth, young prince," Brithilca judged to Soren privately.

Soren breathed again and a great smile crossed his face as the unrealised tension pent up in him released; he had been so terrified the dragon would not bless him that he had not slept for days.

"All hail King Soren," Brithilca rumbled for all to head, and released a column of spectral flame into the air, before a great flash of light split the sky. Soren felt a sudden weight upon his head, and as he opened his eyes, he knew that he had not found the Crown of the Dragon Kings; it had found him. Brithilca the great dragon was once more immobile, now standing guard over the dragon throne with open wings. Soren knelt on the steps, with the ancient crown pressing down on his head as the citizens of Caledan erupted into raucous cheers and applause around him.

"All hail King Soren!" roared the crowd as one. "All hail King Soren! All hail King Soren!"

In unison, the crowd bowed low to their new king. Soren sat on the throne as the nobility paid homage and swore their allegiance to him in a great long line, before proceeding onto the brightly lit steps of the cathedral where it seemed the entire city's population was trying to cram into the square to see him.

The ceremony was not finished yet, however. The crowds parted way for Edmund, who had slipped off to fetch a horse and now rode, proudly dressed in full armour on a black stallion, into the square, bearing aloft Soren's standard and a black leather glove. He rode to the very centre of the square, where there stood a thin, square plinth raised to waist height.

"I name myself Sir Edmund Arransson, champion of His Majesty King Soren. Let all those who seek to challenge him fight me in his stead. Take up the gauntlet if you dare!" He cast down the gauntlet on the plinth where it lay, an open invite. Not one person moved; all waited in eager anticipation, until a man's voice called from the back of the crowd.

"I'll challenge you if you will give me the other glove, good sir!"

A ripple of laughter spread out amongst those in hearing and Edmund grinned and shook his head as he turned away.

As was customary on coronation day, the new king, adorned in his robes and crown, rode to the very gates of the city before walking all the way back up on the main road, to view his subjects and press a coronation coin into the hand of anyone who came to pay homage to him. There were so many people in the city that the prince required bags of coins, drawn in wagons behind him by horses sweating in the sun under their burdens.

Soren enjoyed the task of meeting his people, tiring though it was. It took all day to reach the castle for his coronation dinner, as he stopped to talk with many of the residents: his grand crown tucked under his arm like an armful of scrolls. He was surprised at how many people he now knew by face or name, and even more so by how much he could relate to many of them now; be it the carpenter who had a similar sense of humour, or the smith's apprentice with a fascination for swordplay.

Last of all that day, Nelda drew him aside, still dressed in the robes she had worn to his coronation. She led him to the castle gardens in the fading light until she reached the wall covered in honeysuckle ready to flower that led to the castle cemetery. He hung back with misgiving reflected in his eyes, but she beckoned him with a knowing smile. Through the gate, a dozen of her kind, identically adorned, stood waiting for her and barring the way.

"Your Majesty," they murmured. They bowed and parted like water to allow him past.

"Our gift to you," Nelda said.

As Soren stepped towards his mother's grave, he saw that the tombstone had been replaced or reworked by their magic. Where there had been rough stone there now lay an intricate, lifelike carving of his mother. Veins and flecks ran through the stone and it was rose-hued, giving the statue a warm glow. Soren drew closer. He searched the face and gasped when he realised how perfect a likeness it was. Her eyes lay shut and her face was peaceful. Her hands clasped across her belly. Detail of lace and gold leaf inlaid in the form sprang out as Soren absorbed each minuscule detail.

When he could look no more, he turned around. Nelda's kin had vanished, leaving only her. He had not heard them leave.

"Thank you," he said, though the words seemed unworthy. Tears pricked his eyes. "Thank you so much. Please tell them thank you."

Nelda bowed her head and slipped away. After a few more minutes in solitude, tracing details of the statue with his fingers, he returned to the great hall to re-join his coronation supper. Sadness ran through him, with the unexpected thoughts of his mother's death creeping to the forefront of his thoughts, but he was glad she had now been given a resting place far more appropriate and deserving than he could have provided for her.

The rest of the night passed in a whirlwind of food, drink, dancing, and conversation that he could not remember much of later. When the new king retired to bed in the early hours of the following morning, he felt dazed by the experiences of the past months; a feeling not helped by the copious amount of alcohol he had drunk that night.

His last thought before sleep enveloped him from atop his wave of euphoria was that everything must be a dream. However, the blinding headache that greeted him as he awoke many hours later dispelled any notion that that could be the case.

THIRTY SEVEN

"You agreed that it's worthwhile returning to Ednor for training, so why won't you let me go at once, Father?" said Eve.

"Because you must return home to take care of everything else that has been neglected in your absence." Her father's thunderous expression would normally have caused her to back down, but her confidence had grown enough to assert herself since last she had been in Arlyn.

"Why, for you to never let me go?" retorted Eve.

"I am a man of my word," said her father in a brittle voice. He was in a dangerous mood, not helped by her persistence.

"Well, what other responsibilities do I have aside from my education, which is complete, and my training, which is a constant undertaking? You give me no other responsibilities from your own pool of duties, despite the fact I am of age and able to take them on! I am not a child anymore, and it's time you stopped treating me like one!"

"Do not disrespect me, Eve!" thundered Karn. "Why should I give you such duties when you run off so lightly? Flightiness has ne'er been the quality of a good leader!"

"I was trying to do what was right and that has *ne'er* been a poor quality for a good leader." She scowled.

"You need to grow up and settle down," her father said. His eyes narrowed at her mockery.

"What's that supposed to mean?" retorted Eve. "I am settled, and maturity comes with age. Will you make me wait until I am old before you deign to let me help you?" She folded her arms.

"No. You need to settle down and marry. I have already begun searching for a suitable match."

"What?" cried Eve. "You can't! I won't!"

"I can't? You won't?" Karn's eyebrows slanted in a dangerous 'v' shape. "It is my right to make such a decision, as your father and your lord, for the good of our county and you will do as I say."

"Father, I don't want to marry! I'm too young, I'm not ready, and there is no one suitable!"

Her father softened at the panic in her eyes, but he remained firm. "You are well of age and there are plenty of suitable matches. Worry not, I will find you a good man. I would not give away my only daughter to a man who did not deserve her."

His words did nothing to placate Eve. She paced in front of him, wringing her hands together and folding them close as if to protect herself. The thought of being in the power of a man she did not know terrified her. She knew what her wifely duties would be and the thought was revolting. Marriage did not factor into her plans of independence.

"I cannot, Father. Please do not make me," she asked him with desperation.

"I can make you, whether you will it or not," said her father. "However, I do not wish to be that kind of man. Eventually, you will see I act in your best interests and eventually, you will thank me, Eve, although I know it will be hard at first to see that I am right. I will make you a deal."

Eve paused and turned to him.

"I will permit you to go to Ednor and spend as long there as you need to train you to control your magic, with not one word of complaint."

Eve held her breath for what came next.

"I will do this, if you will marry the man of my choosing."

Her breath whooshed out of her lungs, but they tightened and she could not breathe back in as panic flooded through her. She stumbled to a chair and fell into it. "What if I say no?" she choked out, hunched over with her hands to her chest and her loose hair tumbling about her.

"Then you will return home with me regardless and I make no promises about if you shall go to Ednor, or when, or for how long I will permit your visit to be."

"I am not your game piece to play as you will." Her voice was muffled as tears began to roll down her face. She covered them with her hands.

"You will have to marry a man of my choosing sooner or later," said her father. He turned away. His tone was level. From under her fall of hair, she could not discern his expression.

"You married for love! Why do you deny the same for me?" Eve's voice caught as more tears fell.

"You will grow to love him," said Karn, "and that should be enough. Who else would you choose? Who else would be good enough for you?"

Eve stayed silent and did not answer from within her cocoon. Luke flashed across her mind. He was as close a friend as she had and she would not hate to be his companion, as she would anyone else's. At least he was not a stranger. At least she knew him well and though she barely dared admit it to herself, she did find him attractive. She did not reveal that to her father, knowing he would be angered by such an unsuitable union. She feared that if she frustrated him further, he would withdraw his offer to let her go to Ednor at all.

Karn took her silence for a no, and turned around to leave. "I shall give you time to think on this. I expect your answer by the time we are returned home."

It was the following day, a week after the coronation of Soren, that they departed, much to Eve's growing dread. After a sleepless night, she had come no closer to a decision. The prize of going to Ednor for as long as she pleased dangled before her, but its worth was equal to the horror and despair of agreeing to her father's deal.

She scrutinised every man she saw in the castle who seemed to be her own age or older, wondering if they would be the man her father chose. Luke, who still accompanied her everywhere, enquired about her agitation. She shook him off and told him she did not feel well.

With a heavy heart, she bade farewell to the healers, who had become dear to her in her time there. They were sorry to see her leave. The head healer thanked her for her help, wished her well, and invited her to return to help, expressing that she would always be welcome there.

As they said goodbye to the new king and his sister, Soren and Irumae embraced them, with words of parting as affectionate as always, despite the blankness in their eyes that seemed etched there. Now that the festivities and whirlwind of events surrounding the restoration and coronation was over, they seemed to have slipped into a depression of sorts. It would take time for the grief to pass and Eve bid them good health and wished fervently for their happiness to return.

She smiled at Edmund as they parted. She had grown up with his presence from a young age and her father treated him like family. Eve was glad that Soren and Irumae had such a good man to guide them at the beginning of Soren's reign. Her father shared a few muttered words with Edmund before embracing him.

Nolwen and Nelda also chose that day to depart. Eve parted with them with reluctance, as her father and his men waited to be off. They took leave at the castle gate; the Eldarkind were to travel north, whilst the easiest way to Arlyn lay along the south road. She would have much rather travelled with them, but her father refused to dally and take the longer road.

Nelda and Eve embraced and Nolwen bowed low to her. She replied with a curtsy. She could not bow in return to him, not least because her father was observing her, but because he had also insisted she ride home in a ladylike fashion: in a dress and worse, a carriage. To placate him, she had agreed. As Nelda and Nolwen mounted their horses and rode out of sight, Eve could not delay climbing into the four-wheeled contraption any longer.

A seat wide enough for two people was affixed within it, though no companion joined her. It felt like a prison. Painted black within and without, it had a covered top, solid front and back, and a small window set into the doors on either side. It had been made with no thought for comfort or decoration, save the dismal seat pads that had been added later. The driver sat on a bench affixed to the front.

Eve would have much rather joined the men on horseback, where she could see the world flowing by her and have the wind running through her hair and reddening her cheeks. In contrast, she resigned herself to a miserable return journey home as the wheeled cart jolted her from cobble to cobble and ditch to ditch and the clatter of hooves jarred her head.

She did not know where Luke rode within the group. From within the confining carriage she watched the small panel that was the world outside pass by through the window, agonising over her choice.

THIRTY EIGHT

The halls of Pandora Castle fell silent as guests who had flooded in now poured out to return home. For the first time, Soren had time and leisure on his hands and fell to brooding and apathy in the absence of other driving tasks.

Now that the council had been restored and its numbers lifted again with younger men of the various houses, Soren found that much of the menial day-to-day running of affairs was accounted for, with Behan overseeing operations and managing the city. The steward was invaluable, but it did not help Soren stay busy.

Consequently, although Behan had accounted for everything else, it meant that one task remained a priority for Soren above all others, nagging and chewing away at his thoughts. It was time for him to deal with his uncle and he could not afford to put it off any longer. He sent orders for the trial to be scheduled the following week and held in the courts of law, before filing his evidence with the clerks.

The bloodstained letter had been with him, tucked inside his clothes, since his flight from Pandora; he had even worn it within his robes during his coronation, such was his reluctance to leave it anywhere. It felt strange to part with an object he had kept so close for so long, but as Soren unwrapped the silk napkin he stored it in, he was glad he would not have the constant reminder of what had passed so near to him anymore.

"Guard it with your life and release it only to those who bear my seal," he warned the young clerk, who nodded uncontrollably and looked at the letter before him as if it would bite.

Not one hour later the courts had confirmed the date of the hearing to him and, feeling grim, he sent a messenger to inform Zaki of his impending trial, still unable to face his uncle. Butterflies leapt in his stomach when he thought about what was to come.

That night, after consuming copious amounts of beer with the young lords who kept him constant company at the evening meals, Soren stumbled to bed in a heavy stupor. He was too intoxicated to hear the clamour that arose within the castle in the middle of the night, until alarm bells themselves sounded, a discordant clanging of metal on metal and metal on wood as men raised the alert to every corner of the city.

Soren awoke, groggy and slow, clambering out of bed and dragging on a dressing gown. Outside his apartment, there were at least two dozen extra guards crowding the corridor. All had drawn their weapons, including the two guards who stood either side of his door.

"What's the meaning of this?" he asked.

The guards looked fearfully at him and one dared to speak up.

"A prisoner has escaped, Your Majesty," he stammered. "We were sent by Sir Edmund to guard your cham—"

"Escaped? Who?" Soren questioned. His mind cleared as anxiety rushed through him, but his heart sunk before the man had spoken, because he knew the answer. *Why else would Edmund send so many to guard me?*

"Zaki," the man whispered.

"What happened? When?" Soren questioned.

The man turned to his colleagues. None volunteered an answer. "I— We do not know, Your Majesty. Sir Edmund ordered us to guard you and told us no more."

Soren barrelled through their midst, his dressing gown flapping as he passed them and raced barefoot down the corridor. The guards leapt into action, sheathed their weapons, and ran after him in full armour, clanking and grinding metal with every step as they fought to keep up with him; taken by surprise.

The king ran to the great hall, where lights blazed, illuminating every single inch of the huge room. People came and went, scurrying like ants.

"Where is Sir Edmund?" Soren shouted. Every single person halted in their tracks and scrambled to bow low to their dishevelled king, with his tousled hair and red eyes, as they realised who he was.

"Your Majesty!" Behan bounded forward, having just jogged into the hall. He was red-faced, out of breath, and seemed to have travelled to the castle in his bedclothes. As he bent double, wheezing, Soren waited for the steward to catch his breath, leaning forward with impatience.

"Yes?" he prompted.

Behan ushered Soren aside as noise picked up around them and people once more resumed their tasks.

"He's gone, sire—Zaki. You need to see this." He gestured at Soren to follow him, and they started towards the dungeons, with Soren's heightened guard in tow.

"What happened?" asked Soren in a low voice, not wanting their conversation to be overheard.

"I haven't the foggiest idea, sire." Behan was frank. "Every man you have is out looking for him now, including Edmund. I hope they find him, after what he's done, but we don't have any leads to start with."

He glanced at Soren to gauge his reaction and mood. Still intoxicated from the previous evening's antics and feeling numb and tired above all, a dull, glazed look seemed fixed on Soren's face as he stifled the urge to yawn.

As they arrived at the dungeons, Soren understood why Behan had been so apprehensive. The entire area was crawling with officials and soldiers alike, who trawled for evidence and clues, and a few unfortunate folk who cleaned up the wreckage.

Zaki had been held in the depths of the dungeons, in the furthest, hardest to reach, and most secure cell available to the castle. It was impenetrable; buried under thousands of tons of earth deep in the hill under the castle and accessible by one, windowless door. It was exactly why Soren had imprisoned his uncle here. Yet the door lay in pieces around the fractured frame. Black marks spread across wood and stone.

"He appears to have used some type of incendiary device, sire." Behan looked about, his mouth set in a thin line. "We have no idea how he managed to procure or use it, but he made short work of his guards." He gestured at the forlorn remains on the floor.

Two bodies lay on the floor, face down, burnt and covered in debris. As Soren leaned closer, daring to turn over the bodies himself, he retched and stumbled back. They had been hacked, stabbed, and sliced multiple times in what appeared to be a frenzied attack. Soren eyed Behan in horror. Behan met his eyes with trepidation.

"He is a monster," said Soren in hushed tones. *And he could be anywhere...* an insidious voice whispered from the darkest recesses of his mind. A chill settled over the prince. Weary and intoxicated, his mind remained slow. Listless, he gazed into the cell, which men had turned upside down in the fruitless hunt for a clue.

Everything he had fought for, all that he had gained and the price he had paid for his successes, seemed worthless and frail. Even when his uncle had been in his power, Soren had been outwitted. He did not even have the ability of thought at that moment to curse himself for underestimating his uncle; that would come with the harsh, grey light of dawn.

Despair filled him.

THE
BROODING
CROWN

ONE

Talons pinned Soren to the bed, gripping his flesh. He twisted, crying out as he thrashed, but the claws did not relinquish their grasp. With great shuddering gulps, Soren surfaced from sleep to his dimly lit bedchamber.

Cautious faces loomed over him. The hands, not talons, which had held him down loosened. One of the hands stroked his own in comfort, whilst the other soothed his forehead with a cold cloth, wiping the sweat from his face. His clammy nightclothes clung to him, constricting his movements.

Soren's breathing slowed to a weak flutter as he lay back into his pillow, his eyes slipping shut once more.

"Another nightmare?" Edmund's voice sounded from his side.

Soren did not nod; the answer was obvious.

"The usual," Soren murmured. "Zaki's searching for me, hunting me through the castle dungeons. I try to run, but I cannot. It's as if the air has turned to water and I'm drowning, but then all of a sudden everything turns to light and pain and fire searing through me. In that moment, I know he's found me, and I know I'm dead."

Soren opened his eyes as Edmund gave his shoulder a reassuring squeeze. Edmund's face was ashen with his own exhaustion. He sat with Soren, guarding him through the inevitable torture that returned every night.

"This will not last forever," said Edmund.

Soren rubbed the sleep from his eyes. "I hope you're right. I cannot last on nightmares."

Edmund did not reply, but Soren had a feeling he would be thinking the same. He had tried to send Edmund away for the man's

297

own health and sanity, but every night, when Soren awoke hyperventilating and in a blind panic, Edmund's presence was the first thing he noticed.

With a flick of Edmund's hands, the servants dispersed, though it took an extra shoo for the physician to retreat.

"You are safe here, Soren. Zaki is most likely dead, but if not, he would not be able to reach you." Edmund shuffled to an armchair and sank into it with a sigh of relief. "It has been over two months since your uncle escaped. Rest easier in the knowledge that all of Caledan knows him for a traitor, a usurper... and a murderer," Edmund added softly, his eyes flicking to Soren. "Zaki will find no shelter here."

"I tell myself that daily, yet now I know what he's capable of. The worst thing is not knowing where he is. I almost expect him to jump from behind the curtain or under the bed. Ridiculous, I know. And yet I cannot dispel the fear. I was so close to returning true peace and security to Caledan. He escaped so easily—what if he returns?"

"Zaki is long gone. The hundreds of armoured men crossing the border heading south, bearing no banner or crest, could only be him fleeing with his last supporters. The deserts will claim him before he reaches anywhere that he could survive."

Soren could not help but question otherwise. Every shadow held his uncle waiting to leap out and kill him. Even at night, Soren insisted on the room being lit to give an extra shred of peace to his mind, for what it was worth, but the nightmares came as virulently as ever.

"What is it you fear the most?" Edmund's hooded eyes regarded Soren thoughtfully.

Soren stirred, pulling the cover closer around him, despite the insufferable warmth it created. His eyes drifted closed again. They ached with such a fierce throb that it hurt to open them. "I'm not sure." *He's a monster, and his absence only makes him grow more terrible.* Soren could not think of his uncle's face, nor his name, without flinching.

"I fear that he will never give up, that he will return, that he will hunt me down and that there is nothing I can do to stop it. I fear that he will kill me—I fear death." Soren shivered as he thought of the blackened and contorted bodies left behind by his uncle. "I fear how he will kill me, what dark weapon he would use against me. Castle walls feel as thin as air when I know that he could escape from such a prison."

"The entire kingdom hunts for him, Soren. He could not pass our borders, let alone reach Pandora or you. You have nothing to fear."

"Yet Roher supplies him with military technology—so how sure can you be that he will seek to come alone?" Soren's voice rose in pitch as his breathing quickened again.

Edmund paused. "I do not understand it myself. Lord Behan's intelligence suggests that the incendiary device used in your uncle's escape was almost certainly developed and produced within Roher's borders, yet we cannot be sure Harad supplied it. Harad has remained true to his word: he left peacefully and has not returned."

"Yet," Soren said. The word hung ominously in the air.

"Perhaps Harad will return. However, think of the journey Zaki would have to undertake to even reach Roher's borders, let alone its capital city. Why would Harad assist him, after trading him with us? Surely, he is a lost cause."

Soren did not answer. His gaze drifted from the stone walls of his chamber to the flickering light of the candle on his side table. Once more, he wondered how fire could break stone. "I don't know what to believe anymore, Edmund."

TWO

The golden-domed watchtowers of Arrans, capital of Roher, blazed on the horizon under the punishing sun. Zaki ached. A deep-seated, dull, pulsing ache that encompassed his entire being: his bones, his muscles, even his head. *At last...*

Beside him, Reynard sank to the ground. "Thank you, Lord God, for blessing us with your divine intervention, by showing us the way to our salvation." Reynard murmured fervent prayers to himself, his bobbing head bowed over shaking, clasped hands, and his eyes scrunched shut.

Zaki looked at him through narrow eyes, disdaining the wreck of a man kneeling at his side, but Reynard was still in a better state than most of the others who had survived the torturous journey. *There is no God, you fool. After all 'God' has done to me, he cannot be. If he exists, then he has wronged me and should be damned to hell himself.*

His eyes flicked back to drink in the vista before him. Where they had tramped for endless weeks through desert, now grass grew beneath their ruined feet. With every step they took, the land became lush, green and hopeful.

Before them stood the red stone walls of Arrans. Topped with triangular crenulations, they stretched into the distance, encircling the vast city within their protection. They snaked over the five hills on which Arrans was built, even spanning the river that carved through the city's belly.

On each of the five hills stood a great watch-tower, a hundred and fifty feet high, an unlit yet blazing beacon reflecting the light from gilded brickwork and mosaic patterns. He could not see the detail he knew to be there—they were still miles away—but the flash of colour atop the closest towers was visible. Below the golden sun of Roher flew the banner of his father-in-law: the red rose and

300

rampant lion of King Harad the Third.

Zaki's only other visit to the city—to meet his bride-to-be and formalise their wedding—had been a grander and more pleasant occasion. Instead of a harsh journey through the desert, they had sailed to Bera, the sea-port and travelled at leisure to Arrans from there. The men had ridden in upon horses, with the ladies riding in palanquins, fanned by servants. All had been cheered into the city by rich and poor alike who lined the streets up to the royal palace at the top of the tallest of Arrans's hills.

In contrast to the well-fed prince entering Arrans in triumph, Zaki was now a pauper and passed for a different person. His eyes had sunk into his burnt and weathered cheeks under unkempt, shaggy hair, and his soft skin had been hardened by the long duration of rough travel. His clothes hung off him—he and his men had long eaten all the horses, surviving on nought for days—and his body, which had been so well trained and fed, had melted away to a toughened, wiry frame.

They had little left—no money between them, nor armour. In the blistering heat, it was an unnecessary burden. Even Zaki's royal armour, worth more than the annual earnings of all his men put together, had been dumped. Instead they survived like bandits, thieving food, drink and luxuries like blankets from those they passed, either through force or by silent theft in the night.

The sight before him made him forget the weeks—or it could have been months, he had lost track of the endless cycle of night and day—of hardship. Spurred on and reinvigorated by the sight he had so longed to see, he drove his men on, commanding them through cracked and dried lips.

His men followed in silence like sheep behind a shepherd. They had little energy to talk and no desire to rejoice after everything they had lost. More than one had died along the way through illness, starvation, dehydration or because their mutinous words and discontent had reached a ruthless Zaki's ears. But Zaki was no shepherd. He watched them all like a wolf over prey. *I will not let them betray me.*

The hard, dry earth pained Zaki's feet; they tingled and

spasmed with every step, but he pushed on. It was still hours before they reached the gates. So huge were the towers and walls from afar that they seemed closer; a cruel illusion. But when he stepped under the cooling shadow of the gate at last, it was no vision.

The gate was open, but men barred the way with a makeshift barrier across the entrance to the city.

"Quis est iste?" one of them asked him. "Vade, pauper!" The man shooed him away, but Zaki stood his ground.

"Caledan," Zaki said. "Do you speak Caledonian?"

"Caledonian?" The guard sneered. "Nulla. Non Caledonian."

"I must see King Harad," Zaki emphasised, wishing he could speak some broken words of their language, or they his. "King Harad—take me to him. I am King Zaki of Caledan. King Zaki."

"King? Regis? Quod homo petit esse rex!" The guards burst out laughing, taking great pleasure in their amusement.

"Regis Zaki!" One bowed mockingly to him, sweeping his hand before him in a grand gesture, as the others continued their raucous laughter behind him. His balding head gleamed in the sun.

Zaki stepped forwards in anger, drawing his sword, the one weapon remaining to him.

At once the merriment ceased. The Roherii drew their own blades.

"I am King Zaki of Caledan. I command you to take me to King Harad immediately, or I swear upon my crown I will kill you all where you stand." His sword point wavered before him as his arm shook with the weight of the blade, but Zaki's blood boiled with fury at being so treated. After all he had endured, he refused to be turned away at the gate like a commoner. He stood, glaring at them, with his legs planted upon the ground and his free hand clenched.

Their leader looked him up and down, frowning, his eyes lingering over Zaki's sword and the gold signet ring, which out of vanity Zaki could not bear to part with. Zaki tilted his ring so the gold flashed in the light, revealing the imprint of his crest upon it. The man turned to his companions, his expression one of doubt.

"Non certus sum... sed ut homo vera praedicat... Vide annulum? Vide viri eius?"

Zaki looked between them, but he did not understand their words. The man pointed to his hand and Zaki lifted it, showing his ring to the men, who were quieter and shifted upon their feet whilst sneaking uncomfortable glances at each other.

"Yes," said their captain in accented Caledonian. He beckoned Zaki and his men forward, firing a rapid babble of orders at the Roherii men who scattered, their eyes wide. One returned, leading two horses—one for the captain and one for Zaki. He was thankful they had a mounting block, but even then he struggled, trying to conceal his involuntary grimaces beneath his hair.

His men remained on foot, limping along behind him, as they passed along one of the main avenues, bustling in the pre-evening rush. Men, women and children rushed about, some with baskets and packages, others with guards in carriages, but most on foot, weaving in-between each other.

The guards cut a column through the maelstrom before them. Zaki worried they were causing a spectacle and he slouched, flopping his hair across his face. He did not want to be recognised, but he need not have been concerned. Few batted an eye-lid at their passage—fewer stopped to stare. Zaki glanced at his dirty skin and tatty clothes. *I look just like one of them.* His lip curled with distaste.

The noise and smell of the city was overwhelming after weeks of near silence and nothingness. Zaki's ears filled with an unbearable level of sound, worsening his pounding headache. The smells turned his stomach, especially the stench from the sewers and waste piles, and even the scent of food made him gag.

At last Zaki entered the palace compound, stopping for a moment at the gate as their guide spoke in hushed tones with those guarding the way, throwing many glances back towards the Caledonians. Zaki was beckoned through the gates, which clanged shut once his men had entered.

Peace returned. On the hill, away from the poorer districts of the city, the wealthy lived in quiet contentment, overlooked by the sprawling royal palace. Vast gardens opened up, and although the wealthier district's streets on the slopes were more spacious than the crowded roads through the valley-bottom slums, the space in the

303

palace grounds was most freeing.

Fountains babbled amid birdsong. Thirst rushed to the forefront of Zaki's mind. He licked his lips in frustration, longing to dive into one of the gurgling ponds to drink, cool himself and cleanse the disgusting amount of grime from his body and clothing. It felt so ingrained Zaki feared he would never be purged of it.

They were led to Harad's throne room, announced, and ushered through the golden doors. Zaki ignored the frescoed walls, the metal-plated and gem-studded marble carvings, and the rich tapestries. He did not even look up to the high ceiling, painted with scenes of the creation as told by Harad's religion: it was a practice that worshipped many deities, which was strange to Zaki's mind. Instead, his attention fixed on the figures at the far end of the room. Servants surrounded the king, who sat upon his grand throne.

They had last met in what felt like another life. Unbidden, Zaki recalled the moment when, stood before the gates of Pandora shoulder to shoulder with Harad, his father-in-law had betrayed him. Subdued and shackled like a common prisoner, though he tried with all his might to break free, Zaki had been handed over to Soren in exchange for the freedom of Zaki's wife, Demara, and her unborn child. Instead of ascending in victory to Caledan's throne, he had fallen to the deepest dungeon. Despite Harad's assistance in Zaki's escape, Zaki had not forgiven him that.

"Your Majesty." Zaki was forced to greet Harad first, though he longed to stride up to the man and stab him in the gut for his betrayal.

"Your Royal Highness." Harad returned the greeting.

Zaki felt a hot stab of anger. *He dishonours me in public!*

"Welcome to Arrans—at last! Let us refresh you," Harad continued before Zaki could react. He clapped his hands: a sharp, short sound that reverberated around the large space.

At once his servants dispersed, returning moments later carrying trays piled high with sweet and savoury morsels and small glasses of pale yellow liquid.

His men fell upon them, so desperate were they for sustenance. Zaki longed to do the same, but forced himself to stand, waiting, until he was offered something, trembling as he suppressed his desire to move. He waved away the food, not trusting himself to eat with reserve, but he could not refuse the drink. *I need a feast, not these pathetic scraps.*

Zaki took—with meticulous steadiness—a glass between his forefinger and thumb, tipping its entire contents slowly down his throat, all the while with his eyes fixed on Harad. The liquid swirled around his mouth and swam down his throat, cool and refreshing. Zaki took another glass, and then a third, touching his lips with shaking fingers and savouring the wetness there. He waited for Harad to speak, to make the next move.

"You do not look well," the king remarked, regarding him with veiled eyes.

Zaki could not control his temper any longer. "How dare you! How dare you betray me—abandon me to my death and pretend all is well!"

"I welcome you, do I not? I offer you good food and drink, no? What is past is past."

"I nearly died! Look at me! I have travelled for who knows how many weeks or months through that God forsaken desert trying to stay alive—we ate every last damn horse and it wasn't enough," Zaki raged, storming around with frustration. The delicate glass shattered in his clenched fist and he paused, swearing. He dropped the shards to the floor and sucked his bleeding palm before he continued, his hand throbbing.

"My men are dead. My hopes are dead. You have crushed everything. You have stolen my future when it was there for me to take. I have nothing—and it is all your fault! And now, when I arrive here, starving and a wreck, you have the nerve to offer me sweets?" Zaki slapped a tray from the hand of a nearby servant. It smashed upon the floor, food and glass cascading everywhere.

Harad stood, snarling. Thunderous eyebrows sunk over narrowed eyes as his guards moved forward in synchronisation. The king waved them away with a slash of his hand and they melted into the shadows.

Around Zaki, a flurry of servants crawled upon the floor,

picking up every last morsel in blank-faced silence.

"Take these men away to bathe, eat and rest," Harad commanded, gesturing at Zaki's ragged band. They were led away. Harad stepped down ever so slowly from his throne, though he kept a distance between himself and Zaki.

"There was no successful outcome for us that day," Harad said as the door shut behind the last of the Caledonians.

Zaki didn't need to ask which day. *Us?* Zaki noticed Harad's choice of word.

"I made the best decisions I could based on the moves we could have made. You are lucky that I helped you to escape."

"This is not a game, and your fire device almost killed me in the process!"

"Then you are lucky; I admit it is not perfected. However, I disagree. It is very much a game—of strategy—and that day, whatever had happened, we would have lost had I not acted thusly. I would have lost—and Roher does not lose. Roher is strong and Roher is feared. And why do you think that is?

"Because I always choose the battles we will win. We could not have won with the men we had that day. Yet, if I had retreated with you, my daughter and her babe—the heir to your claim—would still be in Pandora, and Roher's reputation would be ruined."

Zaki looked up, his eyes wide and mouth open. "I have a son?"

"No. You have a daughter."

Zaki growled, an inhuman sound. "I did not risk my life for a daughter!"

Servants scurried away from him in fear.

"You have much to learn if you dismiss the value of a daughter," said Harad. "In any case, you still have a wife to give you many sons. Stay, and recover. There is nothing to say that Caledan's throne will not someday be yours."

Zaki was thrown by the offer. He regarded Harad with suspicion. The older man seemed genuine and caring in his offer, which made Zaki more distrustful. *Harad never gives something for nothing.* But there was little to consider; no man in his right mind would choose to turn back into the desert, away from such a haven. "How do I know I can trust you?"

Harad shrugged. "You do not. I helped you escape with a gift of our newest and most expensive warfare technology, experimental as it may be. Make what you will of that. But you have my assurance that you will have a chance to redeem yourself here in Roher. I am impressed that you have made it so far."

Zaki splashed absentmindedly in the bath; it was a huge depression carved in the floor of his room and lined with polished stone—a novel concept compared to Caledan's wooden tubs. The warm water filled with oils soothed his aching body, and he could have fallen asleep there, drowning in the enticing scents and the sheer comfort of such luxuries.

He ate from the snacks offered to him by the tiny serving boy next to the bath for the sake of it. Despite gorging himself on a meal after his meeting with Harad, he felt the need to eat after his enforced starvation, as if the supply of food might soon cease again.

Not concentrating on what he consumed, Zaki chewed upon the latest bite whilst contemplating his father-in-law's plans.

Why would he have me incarcerated only to then help me escape in order to come all the way here? The device was a brilliant contraption. I wish we had such technology in Caledan. Perhaps he knew I would escape, that I would reach him here. Perhaps he seeks to help me regain the throne of Caledan with all of Roher's might, not that poxy guard with which Harad and I returned to Pandora.

He relished the thought, but it was not satisfying. He still did not feel confident that he had a grasp of Harad's plans. *All I know for certain is that he uses me for his own ends. I must work this to my advantage. It may be a game, but it is not his. I must use his resources to take back my kingdom.*

As he hauled himself out of the cooling bath, a maid hurried to wrap a towel around him. Neither the woman nor the boy spoke. Zaki took a moment to appreciate her slender form as her uniform pressed against his skin for a moment. It had been a long time since he had remembered the existence of women, let alone enjoyed one. Her dark skin fascinated him. His was burnt from the harsh sun, but hers glowed.

Thinking about the woman reminded him of his wife: a much less tempting prospect. Zaki sighed. *A wife and a daughter. What use are women? I suppose I must visit her.*

It was mid-afternoon by the time he had dressed and followed his guide to Demara's chambers. He wore Roherii clothes, far different to Caledonian attire and better suited to Roher's hotter climes. Loose fitting, the finely woven, light material slithered across his clean skin, sending it tingling with pleasure.

To have new shoes upon his feet pleased him more than anything. The soles were so soft that he sunk into them, his newly scrubbed and tended feet relishing the relief. All of his old clothes had been disposed of; they were not even worth cleaning to salvage the fabric.

The palace was as different to Pandora's castle as the garb was to his own. Pandora's castle was spacious, yet it held a darkness to it that daylight could not shift. It was a true castle, built for war and only later converted for living in comfort. In contrast, Harad's palace had been constructed purely for luxury.

Spacious, high corridors linked the various quarters and private apartments within the building, which were given over to various branches of the family. The palace sprawled over a wide space, and in places was several stories high, extended as needed.

Instead of windows were giant openings with drapes hung on the inner wall and shutters outside to protect against sun or rain if needed. Arrans had certainly never known the same winter snows as Pandora.

The palace was constructed from the red stone that had built most of Arrans, but most of the surfaces were marble or polished stone. Floors were laid in patterns, some even made of the tiniest coloured tiles to depict scenes. Wooden floors were all of the highest quality, laid in intricate designs—all far from Pandora's simple stone floors or wooden boards.

Open dining areas, large courtyards with fountains and greenery, and frequent open mezzanine levels held up by the columns that seemed to be a staple of Roherii architecture offered chance glimpses at the scenery over the city, the countryside or parts of the palace and grounds.

Zaki shook his head at such opulence in disbelief that such a place could exist, but he was also envious of the lifestyle Harad surrounded himself with. At last his escort gestured towards a door.

"Hic est. Demara." The man knocked on the door, which was opened by the tiniest crack. A young woman's face peered out.

Her maid. Zaki recognised her in a flash, though he had never bothered to learn her name.

Her eyes widened as she looked him up and down, her mouth ajar. The escort must have introduced him, for he heard his name amongst the babble of Roherish, but instead of being admitted that instant, the lady withdrew her head and called into the apartments within. A muffled voice replied and the door opened, the lady moving to the side to allow him to pass. Zaki strode in, his guide following.

Before open doors that led to a stone edged balcony sat his wife. Demara held a babe swaddled in layers of colourful fabric and gazed into its face adoringly. As she looked up, her smile faded and her face closed.

"Husband," she greeted him.

"Wife." His reply was just as awkward, yet it was as if nothing had passed between them, that he had not endured the last months and she had not ridden away and left him to his fate. Her face showed no emotion at his unexpected return. *Does she care?* he fleetingly wondered.

She gestured for him to sit and he perched on the opposing chair. Silence fell.

"Would you like to see your daughter?" Demara asked him after the lengthy pause, shifting the babe in her grasp.

Zaki nodded curtly. *If I must.*

Without a word Demara passed him the girl. She was tiny, made huge by the cloths swaddling her, and so young he could not tell her gender. *Would that you were a boy,* he wished. He stared at her, but could not see the attraction that had caused Demara to gaze at her with such open love. *It's a baby. Unremarkable.* He sighed.

Tiny eyelids fluttered open, revealing brown eyes matching her mother's. They bored into him.

"She is called Leika," Demara volunteered, shifting in her seat with agitation as if she wished to take the child from him again.

Zaki looked down at his daughter and thrust her back at Demara.

"Do you not love her?" Demara asked, indignant. She clutched Leika to her chest, stroking the cloths.

"She is a girl."

"She is your daughter."

"Yes, a daughter. What need do I have of daughters? None. I need a son. A daughter is nothing more than an insult."

Demara's mouth fell open at that, and her eyes flashed with rage. "You dishonour me with your callous words. Get out!" She stood and turned away, dismissing him with her body too.

"I will not," he replied, incredulous that a woman should give orders to him.

But the maid stepped forward to add insult to injury. "Please, this way, sir." She gestured towards the door.

Zaki stood. He prowled towards the girl with menace.

With no fear in her eyes, she clapped.

From seemingly nowhere, several guards appeared.

Zaki's eyes flicked around the room.

"Please, this way, sir," the maid said again. Her next words must have repeated her sentiments to the guards in Roherii for they crowded Zaki, forcing him from the room.

The moment the door shut in his face, he struggled against the guards, but to no avail.

"She is a woman! How dare she order me about! I command you to let me back in."

The guards moved him along, blank faced, as if they could not hear him.

When he was alone in his own chamber, he stood white-faced, his entire body shaking with fury. *How dare she! My own wife, ordering me around and throwing me out!* He stormed around the room in a chorus of curses.

THREE

The door opened before her without a sound and her father beckoned her in. Eve entered with deliberate slowness, wishing she could be anywhere else.

"Have you made your decision?" He sat forward in his chair, his eyes fixed upon her expectantly.

"Yes, Father."

"And?"

She took a deep breath in and exhaled. *There's no going back from this.* The decision made her miserable, but there was no outcome she would be happy with. *At least this way, I'll get to go to Ednor.* There, she could practise controlling her magical abilities, which had blossomed a few months before in a confusing incident while she had been rescuing King Soren's sister Irumae from captivity. She could also visit her mother's—and her own—ethereal kin: the Eldarkind.

Eve swallowed. The deep breath had done nothing to still her jumping heart or her shaking, sweaty hands. "I'll do it."

Her father raised an eyebrow, but did not speak.

He wants me to say it. Ice cold shivers crawled down her spine. "I will marry the man of your choosing," she forced herself to say. It came out in a monotone, but she could not have managed any more. To say it was torture enough.

Her father broke into a wide smile, relaxing back in his chair, and then stood to embrace her. He clasped her to his chest, but she was wooden in his grasp and he soon released her. "Good, I'm pleased. I already have some suitable matches in mind. I will begin preparations."

Her father's uncharacteristic excitement was tempered by her growing feeling of nausea. *I have to leave.* She bade her father a quick farewell and rushed to the stables to saddle Alia, knowing a ride would calm her and clear her head.

Alia whinnied in greeting as she entered the stable. It was cool and quiet—a reprieve from the hot summer sun—but the darkness and enclosed space did nothing to ease Eve's discomfort. As she fumbled with the saddle's buckles, someone entered the stables behind her. She turned, expecting it to be one of the stable boys.

Luke. Damn it. She had avoided him in the days since returning to Arlyn. Her heart quickened.

"Eve," he said, moving towards her. "Are you well? I haven't seen you for ages. I've been worried."

"Thank you, I'm fine," she said. "I'm going for a ride."

He scrutinised her face. "I can tell when you're lying," he said after a pause. "You know you can talk to me."

I wish I could tell you, she thought to herself, leaning her cheek against the cool leather of the saddle.

"Eve?"

I suppose he'll find out anyway.

"My father is arranging my marriage," she said.

"No! It cannot be true."

"It's true." She sighed. "I had to promise him. It's the one way he'll let me return to Ednor. I either agree to marry the man of his choosing, and he will permit me to go to Ednor to train, or I do not agree, but he will make me marry anyway, with no certainty of visiting Ednor."

Luke frowned, shaking his head. "Lord Karn would never—"

"I don't know anymore, Luke. At least this way he's promised me that I may go—for as long as I need to—to be trained in controlling my... skills. I don't understand them well enough. Sometimes I worry they'll burst out of me again. There's no one I can ask for help here. If they discovered my abilities, they'd shun me."

"Please don't do it," Luke pleaded. "There must be another way!"

I wish I didn't have to, she wanted to say, but instead she answered, "I don't have a choice, Luke." She made to move away, but he reached out to grasp her hand. She flinched as he touched her, but did not pull away. His hands were warm and clammy, matching her own.

"If you have any feelings for me, Eve, please don't do this. We'll find a way to make it work."

She did not answer, closing her eyes to block the world out. *Don't make this harder for me, Luke!*

Even the few days apart had left her feeling lost after they had spent so much time together in the months before. His sudden appearance had removed any notion of indifference. Nevertheless, her feelings did not mean she could change her father's mind.

Even so, she still found herself stepping forward to lean upon his chest. He took her in an embrace, his warm arms surrounding her and hers encircling his waist.

"I know that you have feelings for me too," Luke said, "even though you don't want to admit it."

Tears flowed from Eve's eyes. *This is so unfair! Why can't I make my own choice, like Father did!* "I wish things could be different," she croaked.

"I'll ask for your hand instead." He leaned back, catching her eye before wiping the tears from her cheeks with a soft touch of his thumb. "If you don't marry whoever your father wants you to. I will save every penny I have to raise a house and provide for you."

"There's no way he would agree to that. He wants me to marry at least a sir, if not a lord," she said, and the tears poured from her cheeks as she held back sobs.

"I'll try anyway," Luke said. He brought her hand to his lips and pressed a warm kiss to her knuckles.

Eve pulled away. Grabbing Alia's reins, she ran from the stable without a backwards glance.

Her father had invited her to dinner; a worrying sign that meant something serious was afoot. *He never eats with me. What does he want?*

Eve slipped into her chair, opposite Karn. They were not in

the main dining room, which was too large for the two of them, but instead in the small dining room, which gave beautiful views of the forested mountains.

The smallest smile flitted across her lips as he greeted her with unusual cheer, but it did not reach her eyes. She tried to covertly scrutinise him.

"I have something to discuss with you, Eve," he said at last as they finished the main course.

It was her favourite meal—chicken breast wrapped in salty bacon rashers and served with sweet, roasted potatoes and vegetables—but she had not been able to enjoy it, worrying what her father would say. *Please don't let it be about marriage, please*, she prayed.

Her father cleared his throat. "I have found a suitable match for you."

No! Her heart sunk and her face fell in dismay.

"I am happy to announce that you will be betrothed to Dane Edmundsson of House Arendall. It is a good match, do you not agree? A familiar face to you—and Edmund, of course, is like family to us."

Eve was silent. *Dane Edmundsson?* She couldn't remember him well. It had been many years since she had last met him.

"What do you think?" her father prompted, his smile fading.

"Isn't he really old?" She wrinkled her nose in distaste.

"Eve!" Karn stifled a chuckle. "You should not say such things! He is older than you, yes, but he is not old. I believe he is about thirty-two. I forget when his birthday is. A fifteen-year age gap or thereabouts is not so great, and not as large as it could be! Despite what you may think he is still young, but well established upon his lands and from a good family."

Eve had stopped listening. *Fifteen-years different! That's almost double my age.* She tried to imagine his face, but her memory of him was so incomplete that it was Dane's father Edmund's face she visualised.

She stared at her plate, which was still half full. The vegetables were growing cold but the chicken steamed. The meaty smell wafted into her nose, but she felt nauseated and pushed back her plate, taking a great gulp of water to empty her mouth of taste.

"Aren't Arendall lands far from here, in the south?" Eve asked, realising the implications.

Karn nodded.

"Then we won't see each other much?"

Karn frowned. "What do you mean?"

"Well, I'll be here and he'll be there, won't he?"

"Oh, Eve." Karn shook his head, smiling with a tinge of sadness. "You will be expected to accompany him wherever he desires, perhaps to his own lands, to Pandora, or even elsewhere, should he so choose."

"I'll have to leave? No! Please, can't I stay here?" *Please don't make me leave Arlyn!* Eve's heart pounded with the force of a horse kicking a stable door, and her mouth dried as though parched for days.

"It is the way things are. You will return. After all, these are to be your lands, but it may not be for some time."

Eve swallowed, wetting her lips. "Is there no one closer?"

Her father shook his head. "You are worth far more than all the lordlings hereabouts combined. I would not have considered any of them."

Eve slumped in her chair, wishing it would somehow swallow her up and take her to a land where she did not have to marry a stranger, and an old stranger far away at that. However, its wooden surface was hard and unyielding, offering her no comfort.

Karn continued to speak, but Eve's eyes had glazed over as her attention drifted.

"Eve, pay attention," he admonished. "Did you hear what I said?"

She straightened in her chair.

"I take that as a no. Within the month you will be betrothed at Arlyn chapel. The marriage will then be arranged at Pandora, or perhaps on Arendall lands."

So soon. Eve's belly lurched in fear. "Please may I be excused?" She stood up before he had finished giving his permission and ran to her bedchamber as swiftly as possible. She threw open the shutters, which the servants had closed, breathing in great gulps of the cooling evening air.

The room lay in the shadow of the March Mountains, and the familiar scent of pine wafting through the window reassured her. Her breathing slowed but her pulse was still erratic, and the fear coiled in her stomach refused to dissipate.

What have I agreed to?

Before long, the day of the betrothal was upon her; no amount of dreading could delay it. The dawn matched Eve's mood. The weather was miserable. It was one of the first days heralding autumn. A deep mist clung to the ground, smothering everything with dew and coldness, permeated by drizzle.

It was dull, the sun too low in the sky and too weak yet to break through the haze, so daylight came late to Arlyn that morning. Eve woke, thick headed in the faint light, feeling as if she had woken in the eleventh month of the year, not the ninth. Shivering under the cooling water as she washed with deliberate slowness, she tried to steady herself for what was to come.

In the weeks since her father's announcement, no amount of thinking and rethinking had managed to give her a solution. There seemed to be no honourable escape from her predicament. The fear she had felt that night over dinner had not vanished, instead returning with malicious glee to torment her again at whatever waking moment it could.

A dress had already been laid out for her. It was pretty, she could not deny it, but knowing what it symbolised made her want to burn it rather than wear it. Her skin crawled as the maid's cold fingers buttoned it from the back. There had been no time to send for fabric to have a new garment made. Instead, an older dress had been altered, fitted with lace trims and resized to fit with perfection. *I preferred it how it was.* She fingered the lace with dislike.

Although the dress was not optional, breakfast was out of the question thanks to her roiling stomach. She turned away the plate, instead going to the stables—taking care not to catch her dress in the mud—to see Alia. Alia never failed to calm her, and, as usual, the horse moved to greet her with a gentle whinny, nuzzling her shoulder and nibbling at her palm for treats.

"Nothing for you today, girl," Eve mumbled, leaning against Alia's neck and closing her eyes.

Eve stayed there for as long as she could, until the inevitable occurred.

"Eve!" her father's voice rang out in the distance. "Eve!"

"Wish me luck, Alia," Eve whispered.

FOUR

Myrkdaga somersaulted through the air, crowing his return. His joyful roars split the silence, overpowering the gentle sounds of waves lapping upon the Isles of Kotyir and startling birds into squawking flight below him.

"I return!" he shouted, searching the skies for his father's presence as Feldloga and Feldith laboured to keep up with him. *He will be proud of me for this! I have blooded myself in battle and restored the throne of the dragon kings to the rightful heir of House Balaur.* He recalled with relish his part in the battle for Pandora.

A black dot rose from the horizon, growing larger as it approached.

"Sire!" Myrkdaga greeted Myrkith-visir as he drew close, expecting his father to slow or stop and hover in the air upon his gigantic wings. But the great, black dragon did not reduce his speed. By the time Myrkdaga realised his father's intentions, it was too late.

Myrkith-visir slammed into him, crushing the breath from Myrkdaga's chest and knocking him out of flight. Myrkith-visir's clawed feet, each large enough to wrap around an entire limb of Myrkdaga's, gripped him, as strong and unyielding as the volcanic rocks of their homeland.

Myrkdaga's wings were useless as he and his father fell from the sky, crumpling against the rushing wind each time he attempted to open them. Myrkith-visir's wings were tucked into a perfect diving position: sleek, streamlined and built for speed.

At the very last moment, Myrkith-visir's wings snapped open and began to flap. Their speed slowed, to Myrkdaga's relief, but then his father released him.

Myrkdaga plummeted from the sky and crashed into the ground. The impact felt like it had shaken him apart. Black beach sand, tasting of destruction and fire, choked him. He coughed and sneezed to expel it and rose on shaking limbs, but his father's claws pinioned him to the ground by his neck. Their sharp points dug into the softer flesh under his chin, constricting his airways.

Myrkdaga did not struggle. To do so would be to challenge his father, and he had learnt long ago not to be so foolish. From the corner of his eye, Myrkdaga could see Feldloga and Feldith prostrated on the ground, the ultimate position of submission, but his eyes flicked back to his father, who growled with a low, deep rumble that made his head vibrate.

"You disobeyed my orders!" Myrkith-visir pushed harder on his neck.

Myrkdaga tried to breathe past the obstruction. "I worked around your orders, I did not break them! You said tha—"

His father's growl turned into a sharp roar. "Enough! Explain yourself before I expel you from the clan!"

Myrkdaga choked, his speech prevented by his father, who pressed even harder on his throat.

Myrkith-visir reduced the pressure to allow Myrkdaga to speak.

"This is of my choice and doing. Feldloga, Feldith and I flew Soren and Edmund to Pandora. There, we discovered Zaki, the false king, absent. He was to return with many more men sent by the king in the south. Our presence intimidated the humans sufficiently to allow Soren entrance and welcome into the city.

"Later, we helped Soren breach the gates and secure Pandora. Those who resisted gave us good sport, but were no match. By the time Zaki returned, Soren's strength was too great and the fortifications of Pandora were a deterrent to the pathetic amount of soldiers who came. It was easy—for us—but without our help, Soren would have failed.

"Had he returned alone, he would have been too late to take Pandora. Zaki would have already reinforced Pandora with the extra humans. I swear, without our aid, Soren would not be king of Caledan. Peace would not be restored."

Myrkith-visir's growl diminished.

"You do not lie?"

"I swear on my blood."

Myrkith-visir slapped his tail against the ground. Loose twigs and debris rattled from nearby trees as he tossed Myrkdaga aside with ease. The young dragon choked back his pain and stood, a little unsteadily, watching and waiting. Myrkith-visir paced the beach before him.

"You fool! Do you understand what your idiotic decisions could mean for us? Not only have you disobeyed my orders, you have shown yourself to humans. We could be revealed to the world!"

"They would not find us here. We saved Soren and put him back upon his throne. We restored peace in Caledan, and without us, he would have failed. Does that mean nothing to you?"

"Silence! That is not the worst of it! By straying from our territory without due permissions, the pact could fail and it would be your fault!" Myrkith-visir punctuated his words with his loudest growl yet; it pained Myrkdaga's ears.

At that, Myrkdaga fell silent, a cold rush overtaking him as his father continued. *Surely not...*

"Everything we strove to create, the peace we have maintained for thousands of years, all ruined because of the actions of one foolish young dragonet who longed for a fight. It is not just us who will be unbound. I could banish you for this. I could kill you; I have done such a thing for far less."

Myrkdaga swallowed past the lump in his throat. His heart wanted to beat out of his chest, but he stood up, straighter and taller. Dragons did not beg. He would not show fear, if that were to be his fate.

"And you—how do you explain your actions?" Myrkith-visir's attention snapped to his two companions, still laid flat upon the ground.

Their reply was directed at Myrkith-visir and Myrkdaga could not hear it. He glanced between the two parties until Myrkith-visir turned away from them and paced once more.

"You are dragonets, it must be said—not full dragons yet. I am glad of that, as you are of my blood. My punishment will not be as severe, but you will be banished from the clan."

Myrkdaga, Feldloga and Feldith cried out simultaneously in protest.

Myrkith-visir growled, smoke curling from his nose, and they ceased. "Henceforth, you and your companions are exiled to the northern edge of our territory. I will not expel you forever; you are my son, Myrkdaga. I do not want to see your faces until midwinter."

"But that is months away!"

"You brought this upon yourselves. Go, before I change my mind to a punishment less kind!" Myrkith's rumble was full of warning.

Myrkdaga wanted to argue, but he knew it would be futile. Anger boiled within him. Without another glance at his father, he took to the wing.

FIVE

Arlyn was bustling as Dane rode into the town with his father by his side. As a newcomer to Arrow County, he observed it all with curiosity. His own estates were far quieter, containing villages, no towns. Arlyn in comparison was much larger, much grander and far busier, its population matching that of his entire county.

Everywhere traders hawked their wares, and women and men marched and idled with laughing children weaving though the mix.

Dane sneaked a sidelong glance at his father. Edmund's smile grew with every hour and mile they drew closer to Arlyn. Now they were here, it stretched across his face. *He is happy, at least.* Dane still had no idea what to make of the arrangement.

He could not fault his father's choice, for he had at last grown to respect the wisdom his father possessed. *House Arrow is a good house, with good lands.* They had seen plenty of sheep along the road into the town—their wool and meat one of the staple incomes of the county, alongside metal ores from the mines hidden in the mountains and timber from the plentiful forests. He glanced around as he rode with continued interest as people moved off the street to let them pass.

They were welcomed by a flustered Lord Karn who greeted Edmund with brotherly affection.

"Dane, it is my greatest pleasure to welcome you to Arlyn." Karn beamed at him.

Dane bowed in return. "I thank you for your hospitality."

"Please, come in and make yourselves comfortable."

They took refreshments in a vast dining room, Dane enjoying the vista over Arlyn town and Arrow Lake in the distance, visible through the diminishing mist. He shivered. It was unseasonably cold, but at least the rain had ceased.

Before long it was time to ready for the ceremony. Dane had still not seen his bride-to-be. Her father called her impatiently as they stood upon the front steps waiting for her. She slunk from the stables, her eyes downcast.

Dane recognised her, but he could hardly reconcile the woman before him with the young girl he had last seen. He appreciated her willowy form, although with her hunched shoulders and down-turned face, she seemed delicate too.

"Lady Eve." He smiled at her.

"Lord Dane." She flashed the briefest glance at him, curtsying.

"You have grown much since I last saw you," he remarked, a vision appearing in his mind of a tiny girl hiding behind her mother's skirts.

She did not reply, but then he could not fault her. *She probably feels some nerves or shyness too,* he mused. Even he felt anxious, though he was careful not to show it. In silence, they walked the short distance to the family chapel over crunching gravel and rough cobblestones.

Dane had to stoop, as most of them did, to fit beneath the doorway and into the small space. Pews lined the interior, so narrow they sat only a few people each. At the front, there was a small space to stand by the altar and a priest waiting in his white robes.

Minuscule windows—more like glazed arrow slits than church windows—set high in the walls allowed in the smallest rays of light. Combined with the dark morning, it made the space oppressively dim.

Dane was thankful that the priest had lit a multitude of candles to brighten the place up. The scent of burning string and wax was a pleasant overlay to the invasive smell of damp rising from the stone floor.

His gaze returned to Eve, stood next to him at the altar, but his smile faltered as he beheld her. She was rigid, her fists balled and her face pale. Even her lips held a bluish tinge. *She's terrified...* He tried to catch her eye, but she stared at the wall in front of them, her eyes boring into it without even a flicker.

"I consent," he replied to the priest, returning his attention to the ceremony.

"And do you, Lady Eve of House Arrow, consent to this betrothal, committing yourself to Lord Dane of House Arendall?"

Beside him, Eve did not reply.

The pause yawned into a long silence.

"As her father and lord, I consent on her behalf," Karn replied in her stead.

Eve shifted beside him, her hands shaking so slightly it was almost imperceptible.

"May I speak with my betrothed?" Dane asked as they filed out of the chapel.

Their fathers exchanged mutual grins.

"Of course," Karn said.

Dane thanked them, motioning for Eve to follow him as he drew her aside.

"You need not fear me, Lady Eve," he said gently, bending his head to try and meet her gaze.

She raised her face to look at him from beneath creased brows, her eyes wide, but did not speak.

Is she so fearful she has turned mute? Dane tried again. "I appreciate that an arranged marriage is perhaps difficult, but I will treat you well and we shall be happy together. You will love my estates. It is warmer and richer there. Everywhere is green and pretty, we have beautiful gardens and the food produced there is of the most appetising in all of Caledan. Does it not sound lovely?"

Eve did not reply.

"We do not have mountains there, but many green rolling hills. You would be able to have your fill of riding there too," he added, guessing that she might like to ride after their meeting by the stables earlier.

Eve nodded, biting a lip. "Thank you," she said, but then swallowed and said nothing more.

He smiled to himself, a thin-lipped grimace of frustration,

before moving away to speak with his father as they strolled back to the manor.

"Congratulations, my son," Edmund greeted him with cheer.

"Thank you, Father," Dane replied. "I wish my bride-to-be were as happy though." He lowered his voice before continuing. "She is altogether emotionless. I have barely managed to squeeze two words from her!"

"Be sympathetic, son," Edmund cautioned as Eve marched past them.

Dane had not realised that she stood behind them so close and flushed, hoping she had not heard his words.

Edmund watched her stride through the front door. "Have patience. Think of it from her perspective; the poor girl must be terrified, having to marry a stranger and leave her protected world along with everything she knows. Be kind to her. She will soften."

SIX

Eve's breath came in shuddering gulps, her entire body shaking with anxiety and fear as she barred herself into the sanctuary of her room. Now she had seen Dane, her fears had been realised. *This is real. There's no way to escape.*

Eve had never given much thought to marriage before, but the vague notion that one day Luke would be her companion had lingered in the recesses of her mind. The notion of being taken away to an unfamiliar place by a stranger was bad enough, but it was the first moment she had realised in fullness: *I will never have that now.*

Dane described his estates as pleasant, and he seemed kind enough, but in her mind's eye she saw a dreary and dismal place, devoid of all she loved and far from anywhere she knew. It would be a prison, nothing more. *How will I learn to control my magic there?*

Her room was darkening again so she strode over to one of her lamps, fighting down the tingle of fear in her belly. *Father will keep his promise and let me return to Ednor, I'm sure.*

"*Fang fram brun,*" she commanded the candle to light. Nothing happened. "*Brun leioss?*" The candle remained dead. Eve growled in frustration. "*Leioss fram brun!*"

Still nothing. Eve had last accessed her magic weeks ago; her connection to it had been severed. The language of the Eldarkind still sat in her mind as familiar to her as Caledonian, but no amount of wishing the words alive had made them become so. The language fell dead upon her tongue.

Eve collapsed upon her bed, covering her face with her hands. *What mess have I gotten myself into? I should have run away with Luke whilst I had the chance. Hang being honourable!*

The sound of loud laughter rose through the house. Men's—

of the raucous kind she heard when they had drunk too much. It was louder and more wanton than before. A tingle of fear shot through her.

"I can't go through with this. I can't lose my home, my family, everything I know." *And Luke*, her mind whispered. "I'll go. They can't stop me in such a state. I'll never have to get married in Ednor. They can't force me. Once I'm there, I can access my magic again." *And send for Luke.*

She packed without much thought, taking the barest of essentials. She stole along the back corridor to purloin food from the larder and a knife from the kitchen. Her next stop was the armoury, where she collected her sword and bow with half a dozen feather flighted arrows. Had she not known the house so well, she would have stumbled and attracted attention, but she had spent years playing hide and seek, honing skills that proved useful in the dark.

Alia will be the trickiest thing, she judged, peering across the courtyard towards the stables from the servants' door. Night was falling, with clouds obscuring the moonlight, but the gravel was pale against the sky.

I'll go around the edge. Beneath the walls she skulked, moving as smoothly as she could from one shadow to another, wincing and freezing every time her feet crunched on loose stones.

She made it to the stable unhindered, but she knew the night stable-hand slept upstairs to protect the horses and saddle them in case of any emergency. Eve was determined that no one should see her leave. *They'll be sure to follow. I must have a good head start.*

It took what felt like hours to saddle Alia up in relative silence, with only the tiniest chink of metal on metal as she buckled the leather saddle across the horse's belly. It boded well that the doors always remained well maintained, for they let her enter and leave without a sound. She had brought rags to quieten Alia's hooves and was thankful she had, for their sound would have woken the sleeping man upstairs.

The silence overwhelmed her ears as she strained for any signs of life, hesitantly leading Alia around the courtyard. The silver mare seemed to emit her own light in the darkness. *I wish I'd brought a dark cloth to hide her coat.* Every sound of Alia's hooves jarred Eve's already fraught nerves.

After far too long, in Eve's opinion, they entered the rear gardens. Eve mounted and let Alia progress up the hill to her usual exit from the town at its highest point. She paused at the boundary, already enveloped by the protective shadow of the forest, to scan her surroundings.

Silent. Deserted. Still. She turned into the woods and, trusting the mare's agility, let Alia race north through the woods.

The end of the following evening saw her halt for the first time. Her heart still rattled against her ribs—a bird trying to free itself from a cage—and nervous energy rushed through her without pause, but she felt calmer, reassured that she had covered such a distance. Exhaustion rolled in waves over her, but nerves held it at bay.

They had not used the north road, instead following game trails through the woods. By always keeping the mountains on her left, she was sure they were heading in the right direction, but she could not be certain how far they had ridden.

Eve dismounted in the shadow of an overhanging cliff and tethered Alia, but she was not relaxed enough to unsaddle her.

Alia whinnied.

"I know girl, I'm sorry," Eve murmured, patting her neck. "I'll give you an extra rub down when we stop properly." *Who knows, we may need to move on.* Eve looked around. The forest stood still around her, the slightest breeze rustling the treetops far above.

She sat down, nibbling on some cheese from her pack. Her limbs refused to relax and her eyes roamed around, darting at every movement or sound.

Night fell, but she could not sleep. Alia was content to rest after her hard ride. Her presence was a constant reassurance to Eve, even in the dark. Even so, she dared not start a fire, for fear of what she would attract. Instead, she sat with her back placed square against the rock face.

She must have slept, for a cracking twig awoke her. Immediately her eyes opened, scanning the pitch black wood. Alia's pale form standing nearby in slumber was all that was visible.

Her ears strained for any sound. It was quiet. *Where are all the animals?* Her gut stirred, clenching. Unnerved, she shifted, overcome by foreboding. But when the whisper of a command came, she knew it was too late.

"Now."

Men sprang forth from the foliage, tearing covers off lamps, which flooded the small space with light. Alia awoke, neighing in fear and treading about, almost trampling Eve, who struggled to stand. Men grabbed her arms and legs, some trying to pin her down, others to lift her to her feet, until she cried out in pain from being twisted and pulled around.

"Eve, we mean you no harm." She knew Nyle's voice even before he stepped from the darkness, yet she did not trust it. He had not forgiven her for her actions months before—he had been punished the last time she had run away. The grudge was easy to see in his closed body language and curt, sharp voice when he spoke to her or saw her. Even so, she ceased struggling, knowing that her father had found her.

"Is my father here?" she dared to ask.

"No," Nyle replied after a pause. "He still entertains your visitors from House Arendall. Why did you run away?"

Eve did not answer.

Nyle sighed. "Sure. You wouldn't tell me such a thing. I suppose you thought you would make it to Ednor? You were too easy to track! We know your patterns, Eve. Worry not. Your father is aware, but your betrothed and his are not. They think you're ill in your bedroom."

Eve shifted her balance. The men holding her forearms tightened their grasp.

"We must return to Arlyn. We can travel no other way, so I will permit you to ride, but you must promise not to break free. Do you promise?"

Eve sighed, her posture drooping. "I won't." *I won't promise.*

"Release her," Nyle said, misunderstanding her intentions.

Eve considered running then, but she would not have made it past the men, who surrounded her. In the dark, she had no idea how many Nyle had brought with him. There could be more hidden in the darkness. Instead, demure, with her gaze averted, she remounted Alia without a word.

Nyle led her for a while before they all dismounted and set up a camp for what remained of the night. The chase had been long and hard and the horses flagged.

Eve would have been glad, but her adrenaline levels still ran too high for her to even consider sleeping. Despite the short amount of rest she had had, she felt alert.

The men bedded down around her as Nyle, with an apology, bound her feet and hands. "I cannot take the chance." To her surprise, he did seem sorry.

He was courteous enough to help her lie down, offering her a supporting arm to lower herself to her knees and then onto her side. She had forgotten how uncomfortable laying on the ground was. Roots and stones poked her everywhere, even through the thin blanket under her, which had been folded twice.

The camp fell into silence. Horses had been tethered in a wide circle outside the ring of men, with Eve in the centre. Slow burning candles in the shuttered lamps illuminated the camp with dim light.

Eve forced her breathing to slow. She still couldn't sleep, but she heard those around her falling into slumber, the night air split by a rumbling snore, a lone snort, or the shuffle of someone twitching or turning in their sleep.

After a while, she opened her eyes a crack and watched them through her eyelashes. Nyle's glittering gaze was fixed upon her from where he sat, several feet away, with his back against a tree. Eve closed her eyes again, hoping the movement had been imperceptible.

She had to wait hours before all of them, even Nyle, were asleep. Despite setting himself on guard, sleep had called him. Cautiously she looked around, moving only her eyes at first and then her head. All but one of the lamps had died. The men were barely visible in the dark.

Under her thin blanket, Eve wriggled with deliberate slowness, making no sound as she tried to work her arms free of the bonds. It was to no avail. The knot was too tight and would not slide over her hands.

"Nyle," she whispered. Across from her, his eyes flicked open in an instant. Though she could hardly see him, his eyes gleamed in the darkness. "I need to relieve myself."

Nyle rose in silence, untied her legs, hoisted her to her feet and walked them past the edge of the clearing.

"Here will be fine."

"You'll need to undo me," Eve said, keeping her tone as normal as possible. "I can't relieve myself like this and I won't have you undress me."

Nyle sighed. "Fine." He complied and stood, arms folded, watching her.

She paused, waiting, but he did not move. "Turn around at least, or go over there and turn around, for the sake of decency!"

"Do not run away," he warned her.

But no sooner was she sure that his back was turned, she tiptoed off in another direction. After a minute, she heard his shout, still too close for comfort, and froze. She could hear him, crashing around in the dark, but couldn't tell quite how close he was. Shrinking into a tree trunk, Eve shook, mouthing a silent prayer that he would not find her.

"Boys, rouse yourselves! She's gone!" she heard him call, and he crashed through the foliage again, this time in the opposite direction. She forced herself to move, taking one quiet, deliberate step at a time away from the sound of his voice.

Before long she was jogging, and then running—a slow run with her hands outstretched before her, for she could not see. The moon had risen and the clouds cleared, but in the dense woodland, darkness still held sway.

Eve's limbs shook, the adrenaline ebbing as exhaustion took its place. Each footstep became less controlled than the last. She did not see the hollow, landing so hard upon the ground her knees jarred, and in the next step she had collapsed upon her ankle.

It bent, she could tell even in the darkness, in a way it should not have under the full weight of her body. After a moment of shock came the pain, lancing up her entire leg, an internal scream from her body. Eve cried out, stifling sobs. She could not even move the ankle or try to remove the boot, let alone put weight on it. Even hauling herself up onto one foot using the tree before her proved too much.

Sinking back to the floor, she knew she could not go on. *I've failed. It's over.* Tears spilled down her face as she sobbed into her hands.

It did not take long for them to find her, but she did not care anymore. She said nothing as Nyle hoisted her up onto her feet, but screamed in pain and fell once he removed his support.

"Where does it hurt?" His voice was quiet—with anger, not sympathy.

She replied by pointing with a shaking hand at her ankle.

"Fetch me some cloths, some sturdy twigs, and find me a crutch," he said to his men.

Eve almost fainted as he loosened her boot and had to bite down on her sleeve to suppress her cries. Foul tasting dirt filled her mouth. Nyle was not rough with her but neither was he gentle as he fashioned a makeshift splint.

The grimace upon his face seemed to be one of concentration, yet Eve had no doubt that he was furious with her. He did not speak to her, nor did he look at her as he offered her his arm to get her to her feet. He passed her a large branch to act as a crutch.

She was glad not to have to bear his scrutiny.

It was dawn a full day later that they arrived in Arlyn. The town was deserted, as was the manor, for which Eve was thankful. She did not want to bring any further shame upon herself or her family. It had been a torturous ride home.

Every jolt made her ankle shoot pain up her leg and through her body again, but Nyle refused to slow the pace. She was tired too, having been kept awake every minute by the punishing, unceasing pain, and was glad to reach home, despite whatever fate awaited her there.

The moment they reached the courtyard, Eve was whisked off horseback and rushed to her bed-chamber by two maids. A physician waited there, ready to examine her. He tutted, shaking his head as be beheld her poor state and then her ankle. Prodding and poking it, he muttered to himself, ignoring her discomfort.

"It is broken, but will heal," he said after his examination. He bound it up, but after the initial unbearable increase in pain, it did feel better for having the support. He bowed and left, allowing her maids to bathe her by hand.

Eve lay in bed, numbed by her experiences, but before she could fall asleep her father strode into the room, emanating fury. His white face took in her poor state and he shook his head in disgust, regarding her through narrow eyes, his mouth thin lipped.

"What were you thinking?"

She did not reply. There was no need to.

Karn huffed. "I cannot decide whether I am furious with you, or glad you are safe, if not well. That is your own fault. In any case, you are confined to your room until further notice. You are lucky you have not disgraced our family with your actions. Be thankful Edmund and Dane remain unaware of your transgression." He turned to leave.

"Can I still go to Ednor?" Eve managed to croak, still clinging to the hope.

Her father halted, twisting to meet her eye. "You are not travelling to Ednor under my authority. You may not, and you will not, leave. The commitment has been made for you to marry. You will do so and follow your husband wherever he commands."

Without waiting for her response, he left. For the first time, she heard a key turn in the lock on her door. Part born of exhaustion, pain and despair, tears leaked from her closed eyes.

I've ruined everything.

SEVEN

Soren awoke to a still morning. He blinked, clearing his eyes of sleep, before he realised. *I slept through the night.* A relieved smile crossed his face and he closed his eyes, leaning back into the plump pillows once more. He calculated the dates. For the first time in months, he felt well rested.

Soren was grateful to no longer be waking up several times each night drenched in sweat, struggling to breathe or, even more embarrassing, screaming or crying in panic. The worst embarrassment was the need to have a physician and Edmund keep him safe from injury during his thrashing and watch over him as he slept, ruled by his inner demons.

And all for fear that Zaki will return and kill me in my sleep. He's dead, Soren told himself again, as he did every day. He had not managed to convince himself it was true yet, despite the improbability of Zaki surviving to reach safety.

Reassuringly dry, still wearing his bedclothes and with the covers laid over him, not tangled around him or tossed upon the floor, Soren savoured the comfort, idling as shafts of morning light beamed through splits in the curtains. He did not rise until a soft knock on his door roused him from his daydreams.

Petitions were to be heard that day and he could not be late. He left the sumptuous bed with reluctance.

After a hasty breakfast, he sat straight backed upon his throne in the royal courts. Pews of noble subjects and law readers lined the long walls. Near the far end of the hall, where petitioners entered, was the standing area for the commoners to look on, but it stood almost empty. Autumn's arrival meant the harvest was in full swing, and there was no time for dawdling.

To either side of him upon the dais sat those members of his council who were able to attend. Edmund had returned, but most of the other chairs were empty. *He never rests*, thought Soren as he greeted his most trusted advisor.

Aside from Edmund, Lord Asquith of House Bryars, a convert to Soren's reign who Soren did not trust in the slightest, and Lord Willam of House Walbridge, also of dubious allegiance, were present.

The secretary called for quiet and Soren turned his attention to the great doors, which had been opened to allow the petitioners to stream in. They had already been organised by rank—most important first—and queued behind the man who wore what Soren thought was a pretty ridiculous plumed hat. *Dyed peacock feathers, honestly.*

Soren sighed, feeling self conscious, as the secretary turned and bowed with everyone as one to him. *Will I ever get used to being the centre of attention?* Being under so much scrutiny was an unpleasant experience.

"Petition number one, sire. Lady Varan."

A lady stepped forward. She was not old, but worry had prematurely aged her. Thin lines carved permanent sorrow upon her face. Her hair was pinned back and she wore a demure, almost simple, black dress. *Mourning whom?* Soren wondered.

Lady Varan motioned behind her. Two young boys moved forward. The smaller, just a toddler, hid behind the folds of her skirt, peering up at Soren with wide eyes and a thumb in his mouth. The older boy stood next to his mother, inching forward at her prompt, to stand staring at the wall behind Soren's head, chin held high.

"Your Majesty," Lady Varan said, curtsying as her elder boy executed a neat bow. "I petition you today to recognise the rights of my sons and legal heirs to the lands and titles of House Varan, whose inheritance has been taken by the crown."

Soren frowned, looking between them. "The lands and titles

of House Varan were seized due to their father's and kinsmen's treasons."

Now he could place them. *Their father tried to kill me.* He recalled the moment his life had shattered, stood beneath the portcullis of Pandora castle, when the men of House Varan had attacked him without warning. *One of them must have been her husband.*

"The action taken complies with the law that all those guilty of treason have their assets and titles frozen, claimed in the name of the crown."

"I understand, sire," Lady Varan replied, but she wrung her hands together, her eyes worried under a creased brow. Her desperation was clear to see. "I only mean that I am penniless and cannot provide for my children. We reside with my own kin, of House Orrell, by their kindness and generosity. Yet I fear that when my boys grow older, they will have no means to live themselves.

"Would you see the noble House Varan destroyed and two boys' futures ruined for the treasons of their father? I beg that you consider them." She dropped to the floor then, kneeling and dragging the younger boy from behind her. He stood, quivering, with wide eyes fixed on Soren.

The older boy dropped beside his mother onto one knee, his head bowed.

Soren regarded them. He paid little heed to the younger boy— too young to know what was happening—but was impressed by the elder. *He's well composed.* "Boy," he called to him upon a whim. "What is your name?"

The older boy looked up, surprised. "Your Majesty. I am Ricken Ivorsson, of House Varan."

"How old are you?"

"Ten."

"Rise."

The boy stood without question.

"I have heard your mother's requests, but I ask you—what do you wish for?" Soren tilted his head, his eyes fixed upon the boy.

Ricken looked to his mother.

"Answer him," she hissed at Ricken, her voice barely audible to Soren.

Ricken looked back toward his king. "I wish for my mother to be happy, Your Majesty."

"A noble desire. Be that as it may," replied Soren gently, "your father committed treason against my mother, the queen. How can I be certain that, in time, you would not do the same thing?"

Ricken looked to his mother, unsure how to answer. She stepped in to fill the gap.

"If I may, Your Majesty. Please allow us to serve you. We will prove our loyalty with deeds, not words." She clamped her mouth shut as Soren shifted in his chair—the throne hard and uncomfortable—as if fearful that she had spoken out of turn.

He turned to his councillors and asked for their opinions. Asquith and Walbridge's views he cared not one whit for—after all, he felt that such hypocrites should not pass judgement on one of their own who had fallen from grace—but Edmund's whispered view he listened to keenly.

"I will offer a solution, Lady Varan."

She looked up, her eyes filled with hope.

"I will grant your eldest son, Ricken Ivorsson of House Varan, some of his hereditary lands and titles upon examination of the records, in return for the fealty of your family, his unswerving loyalty and his service in my household from his eleventh birthday. What say you to this?"

Her face faltered at his last condition. *She does not wish me to take him from her, yet she will know it to be necessary.* Soren waited for her response.

She stood once more. "I thank you, Your Majesty, for your clemency and generosity. It would be my greatest pleasure to agree to your terms." She pushed Ricken forward and he knelt upon the steps of the dais to swear fealty to Soren in front of the court, repeating the words of the secretary.

While Lady Varan and her boys left, Soren instructed the secretary to bring him comprehensive lists of all property and titles held by the house so that he could decide what assets to release.

After that, commoners came in to petition, and Soren found

himself distracted, reminded more than anything else just how crucial mending, making and strengthening alliances with the twelve noble houses was.

When he could take no more of farmers' arguments and traders' disagreements, Soren stood, relishing the relief in his numb bottom, aching back and sore shoulder as he stretched his stiff body. He beckoned Edmund to follow suit. Lord Behan, the steward of Pandora, was summoned to continue proceedings, as Soren left, taking a curious Edmund with him.

"We need to discuss the restructuring of the court, Edmund," Soren said, massaging his forehead with a hand as he sighed. "I'm concerned as to who I can rely on."

The desk before him was covered in piles of papers, all requests requiring something from him: approval, money, favours, time. *I don't know where to begin with all this.* He swept some papers to one side to create a gap, shivering in the disruption of air. His clothes were dampened with drizzle from the brief walk to the castle, which had permeated his collar and cuffs enough to chill his skin.

Soren waited for the serving boy to set the fire before he spoke. As the youngster left in silence, Soren shook his head. "Where to start," he muttered, turning to warm his hands in the feeble blaze.

"Well, let us think in terms of houses, perhaps?"

"As good a starting point as any." Soren raised his hands in a wide shrug. He stood to rummage through piles of books and parchments, coughing through the dust clouds.

"You need to let the servants sweep your study out more," Edmund said, wafting the cloud away from him.

Soren ignored him, instead dropping a framed map onto his desk with a thud. It showed Caledan split into land owned by the twelve noble houses of the realm.

"Well House Balaur is of no concern," Soren began, glancing over his own family's territories that followed the Lowen River south from the Great Lake to the sea. His mother's cousins and their relatives governed the southern Balaur lands from Lowenmouth.

"Lord Andor is a great support, though distant. House Arrow is loyal, though it is too small to be of any difference politically." *Thank goodness my own relatives support me.* Soren was relieved to have some semblance of an alliance within his family, though he did not dare probe too far into their actions during Zaki's takeover of the throne.

Edmund's agreement reassured Soren. "My son's house also." Edmund's son Dane had inherited the titles of House Arendall through his late mother. "I do not think any of the lesser branches would disagree; they benefit too much from a close royal association."

"Kinsley is also of unquestionable allegiance, which makes four houses."

"Excepting Sir Loren," Edmund interjected.

"Mmm. But a loyal house cannot be responsible for one dead traitor, and we need their lands to remain open to us for the trade routes south. Varan no longer concerns me." Soren traced his fingers to territory bordering both Arendall and Balaur lands. "They are too small to be a threat and now bound to our cause. Perhaps we can use their copper mines more to our advantage from this strengthened alliance." Soren's fingers drummed upon the desk. "What else do they produce?"

"Little, but the ore is lucrative enough," Edmund said. "What of Rainsford?" Edmund's eyes narrowed as he stared at the border lands on the southern edge of the map.

Soren continued tapping his fingers on the desk, frowning. "I cannot decide. They seem all for the monarchy, but I would not count them amongst my friends."

"I think you may be correct there," Edmund replied after some thought. "Lord Bron goes to no great lengths to prove allegiance to any one cause, but rather fades into the background. Perhaps he cares not, as long as he may continue to extort taxes from land trade coming across the border under the protection of the crown."

Soren let out a hollow laugh. "We shall have to watch him. Lord Verio too; House Denholm is most definitely our enemy." Soren rested his chin on steepled fingers. "I confess, I don't know what to do with Verio."

Edmund snorted with derision. "That old pretender. A few hills yielding some half decent silver and lead and he thinks he should be king. Verio is ambitious and full of his own self-importance, and his sons are no better. Disregard it. Pay him respect—but not too much, for it will inflame his ego. Buy his metals and praise the quality of his region's seafood. That is the best way to keep him happy."

"I don't think I'd be happy if I had his lands—metals and fancy fish or not." Soren grimaced as he remembered how dull, damp and miserable the lands east of the Grey Mountains were.

"Verio's land to the south is not so unpleasant. He does not have to live as they do in Harring."

"Even so. I think I would rather visit Harring again than Verio himself!"

"You may one day be required to do both," said Edmund wryly. "Be careful what you wish for."

Soren dropped his gaze to the map, hoping he would not have to do either.

"Oh, here's another tricky one. House Walbridge, Lord Willam; what do you think?"

"One to watch," Edmund said, scowling. "An altogether untrustworthy man. The family has never been on the losing side of any battle, and for good reason. Walbridge is always clever enough to side with the obvious winner, or wait until such a time that it becomes clear who will succeed before declaring his position. Treat him warily."

Soren regarded him from beneath raised eyebrows, surprised at the strength of dislike in Edmund's voice. "Do we have need of him?"

"Definitely." Edmund's voice was grim. "As much as I hate to admit it, the man does have an impressive, well-trained retinue and his forgeries are of the highest class."

"He keeps that hidden well," said Soren, troubled. *I regret assuming he farmed only sheep for textiles. I should have paid more attention when my tutors taught me of the houses.*

"He neighbours Balaur and Duncombe however, so do not be disheartened. Andor and Finihan's son would not see him grow too big for his boots."

"I suppose not. Lord Finihan was a reliable advisor to my mother."

"Indeed. His son is still of excellent use to the crown."

"On the other hand, he is bordered by Lunder and Bryars, who are both not friendly to my reign."

"Well, Lunder may not be receptive, but Bryars is a tangled family with opinions as divided as their lands. Many of them recognise the benefits that trading their assets with the crown brings—no matter who wears the crown. They too suffered under Zaki, and I'll wager have lost their taste for war."

"And last of all, there is Orrell," Soren said. "Unquestionably against us after the fall of their brightest star."

"Aye. If Reynard is not dead, he will never be welcome or successful in Caledan again. They waged much on his success, to their regret."

Soren leaned back in his chair, worried by both the dwindling perceptions of his allies and the prospect of Zaki's right-hand man, who had also disappeared without a trace. His fingers rattled on the chair arm like rain hitting the floor. *That's an awful lot of Caledan that is unfriendly to my rule,* he thought, totalling it up. "Five loyal houses, four not so and three of questionable allegiance. That does not bode well."

"I would disagree, with respect." Edmund tilted his head, sucking on the inside of a cheek. "If we say you have six loyal houses—Balaur, Arendall, Kinsley, Duncombe, Arrow and I would include Varan—then there are Denholm, Orrell, Lunder and maybe Bryars to oppose you. Rainsford will not care either way but will support you as long as you sit on the throne, and Walbridge does not matter unless we have a war on our hands, so he is yours for the time being."

"So. I need to favour Denholm, Orrell, Lunder and perhaps

Bryars and Walbridge too?"

"Yes, but you do not want to disenfranchise your supporters by just favouring your enemies. You could risk their loyalty—even those whose support for you seems unwavering."

I have so much to learn. Soren sighed, propping his head up on his hands and elbows.

"You will soon handle these things with little effort, Soren." Edmund caught his eye and smiled to reassure him.

"I hope so," replied Soren, feeling glum. He exhaled loudly. "So the gist is to give favours to everyone fairly, within reason, even if such boons are not earned, all for the sake of keeping smiles and peace that are most likely fake anyway."

"There—you're learning already."

"Without somehow offending anybody, provoking discord of any kind, or emptying the coffers."

"Naturally." Edmund laughed. "You can use alliances to strengthen your position, as you have the power to arrange marriages over and above anyone else, should you so choose. The Orrell's for example, however despicable, seem to be a veritable spring of beautiful young ladies, just as the Walbridge's are blessed with strong sons. Choose their marriages well and you can bind them to your causes."

"How... devious," said Soren.

"Politics."

"Can I trust anyone in this?"

Edmund paused. "No," he said frankly. "The sons of your enemies could be your friends, yet the sons of your friends could well be your enemies. Judge each person on their own merit, but be careful in whom you place your confidence."

That sounds far too much like a riddle.

EIGHT

Since his humiliation at Demara's hands, Zaki had struggled to reconcile with the role reversal of having less power than his wife. He was already fed up of Roher and its hot climate, strange customs and, most of all, the unfamiliar language, which isolated him from everyone.

For the fifth time, he sat in on the petty court listening to the day's petitions. He had hoped that by doing so, he could discover the power players in his new court and glean useful information on who wanted what. Yet it was as useless as before. *These damn Roherii speak too fast. Why can't everyone speak Caledonian?*

He had learnt one phrase of Roherish, "regis mendicus", which had been uttered many times by many mouths around him until he demanded that someone reveal its meaning to him. "The beggar king," he had been told. They did not say that in his hearing anymore. One had made the mistake of doing so since he had learned its meaning, and Zaki had taught him a painful, humiliating lesson for his mockery.

He did not turn when Reynard sat beside him; no one else would choose to sit with the beggar king, so he knew who it would be.

"Sir, I have someone you should meet," Reynard whispered into his ear.

Interest piqued, Zaki twisted in his seat to see a small, dark-haired young man. He was of slight build and, with his eyes cast to the floor, a timid figure. *He cannot be anyone of importance*, Zaki judged, scrutinising his plain clothes.

"Tobias Collado," Reynard said.

The man looked up at Zaki, executing a short, sharp bow in his direction before replacing his gaze upon the ground. "He is a translator who speaks Caledonian."

Zaki regarded him with refreshed interest. *Good, my window onto this world of Harad's, at last.* "Well done," he praised Reynard, impressed at his ingenuity.

"Tobias, you shall begin now. Translate their words." Zaki gestured towards the lone figure standing before the king in the centre of the throne room.

"Yes, ser. This man, he is the Ser Mertillius who is working in... How you say... Buying? Selling?"

"Commerce," said Reynard.

"Yes, yes, commerce. He wants to reduce his taxes." Tobias paused as Harad burst into laughter. "To thirty parts of every hundred from fifty, because he works so hard to keep the valuable ports at Bera open and they cost much money to do so. His Majesty does not wish this to be the case. His Majesty decrees that his taxes may be reduced to forty parts on account of his good work and invaluable services. You see that Ser Mertillius bows and leaves, but he is not happy. Ah, and here is a farmer—"

"I do not care about farmers," said Zaki, his eyes following the unconcealed scowl upon Ser Mertillius's face.

"As you wish, ser."

A man prostrated himself upon the floor, of so low a rank that he was not even allowed to raise his head to address the king. Zaki turned away from the view before them.

"This was a brilliant notion," Zaki muttered to Reynard. "We can have eyes and ears within the Roherii court. However, I will need money—and plenty of it—before I can hope to be of any influence here or in Caledan."

I refuse to be a beggar king, but I need more power here and money before I can be anything else. Demara's dowry and income—his by right—was not enough. He turned to Tobias with a spark of inspiration. "You will teach me the Roherii tongue."

It was weeks before Zaki saw his wife again; in his

stubbornness, he refused to submit to her authority. However, eventually he relented, knowing that, with his insecure position, he needed a son.

He visited her in the nursery whilst she played with Leika. He was gradually becoming more comfortable around the two of them. *I will admit, the babe is not uncomely*, he thought one day as Leika stared at him with bright eyes, her rosebud mouth pursed open.

Wispy hair was beginning to find purchase on her head, hinting at curls. Her warm, honey skin glowed with good health, whilst her red-tinged cheeks gave her a seemly hue.

Her minuscule nails intrigued him most. Tinier than even the smallest jewel he had seen, they sat upon the ends of her kicking toes and wiggling fingers. He caught himself daydreaming with a tut. Demara looked up at him from the floor where she tickled the babe, but he did not speak to her.

I grow soft in the company of women. He felt irked with himself for being so pathetic and was glad neither Reynard nor any of his men were there to see him at that moment. *I need some prospects to occupy my time lest I turn into one!* He regarded his daughter again. *At least she will be a useful bargaining tool in the future. I will make a good marriage with her. Would that I had a son.*

He stood to leave, Demara rising with him, Leika in her arms. She stood in silence, waiting for him to speak.

Zaki forced down his pride. "Will you come to my chamber tonight?" The feeling of asking, of submitting to her authority, was repulsive. He had to make the words march from his reluctant mouth.

She looked at him, not quite blank-faced but with an imperturbable expression, her eyes seeming to analyse him. After a pause, she replied. "I will come." She turned away with Leika, handed her to the maid and motioned to the door with no hint of emotion.

Dismissed again! Swallowing, Zaki strode to the door before his anger could get the better of him.

After that night he did not see her for another week, but for that he was glad. It was a duty and a chance for a son, nothing more. On the other nights, he revelled with the other younger lords of Roher, finally included in their circle with his increasing knowledge of the Roherii tongue.

Tobias was the best asset he had, accompanying him anywhere. The young Roherii lords had even learnt some Caledonian—though Zaki was careful not to educate them too well.

"After all, they must not know when we talk about them!" he said to Reynard through a fake smile as they gambled on the cards in his favourite tavern. His new friends mirrored his grin as Reynard murmured his agreement, but his Caledonian men took care not to react to his words.

Zaki bet again—it was easy to deduce the Roherii were fond of gambling. Behind him, Tobias praised him in Caledonian.

"This is a good hand, ser, and a large bet. You will not be a beggar king if you can afford so much!"

Zaki smiled smugly, his eyes not leaving the playing surface as the cards were dealt. This was his strongest game and he always won at this table. *If only my wife had brought a larger dowry, I would be even richer still.*

NINE

"I've tried to be lenient," said Nyle, looking at Luke pityingly. "I really have. But I'm going to have to issue you a final warning if this keeps up. This is no fit behaviour for an Arlyn guard."

Luke stood before him, but instead of being straight backed, he slouched, fixated upon the floor.

"What's gotten into you?" Nyle tried again.

Luke did not answer. He had stopped listening, in any case. Nothing mattered.

Nyle huffed, shaking his head. "Look, Luke. I can't keep allowing this. Turn up on time, in clean uniform. If I smell beer on your breath in the morning again, you're done." He turned away and marched off.

Luke started at his departure. After a pause, he turned and headed for home.

"You must try to accept it, love," his mother said to him, as she did every day. "The daughter of a lord, the cousin to a king, would never be able to marry someone of our standing."

Every day his reaction was the same. With hot tears burning at his eyes, he would storm off to the public house to drown his sorrows so far they could not see the light of day. It never worked, though. The best he managed was to feel nothing for a little while.

I still want her as much as I always have done. Luke sat in the corner of the public house, at what had become his usual table, given a wide berth by the other patrons there who had learnt he was in no mood for laughter or jest. One hand grasped the handle of a tankard half-filled with frothing beer, the other held his face as he heaved another

348

deep sigh.

He sat up to drain the tankard and wiped his mouth with a filthy sleeve, not troubling to subdue the resulting belch. Within minutes the barmaid had whisked away his empty tankard and replaced it with a full one, swiping a few more of the coins he had abandoned on the table as payment. She did not bother to speak to him anymore.

He did not have many coins left, and after his conversation with Nyle it sounded like he would not have a job for much longer either. Yet he felt nothing when he considered it—no sadness or worry or anger at the thought of losing his position.

Luke stared at the wooden vessel, tracing a thumb across the surface worn smooth by years of handling. He was glad he could not see his reflection anywhere. It would be a mess. He had not bothered to shave or trim his beard or hair in weeks. Luke knew he was being difficult and should feel guilty, but he could not force himself to care.

A wave of laughter erupted from the bar. Luke did not glance up—it would be one bawdy joke or another and he was no longer amused by such trifles. It was only when he heard Eve's name that his ears pricked up.

They make jokes about her honour! He stood, knocking the table so hard in his rush that his tankard jumped of its own accord. It crashed to the floor, spilling its contents far and wide.

Luke lurched towards the men, clutching tables and chair backs for balance as he stumbled. His head swam. They were laughing so hard they did not notice him—until Luke shoved one in the back, almost pushing the man forward into his own drink. "Oi!"

The man turned, slow and deliberate, fixing Luke with beady eyes.

Luke was dwarfed in his presence. He did not feel afraid, but further emboldened.

"What's up, boy?" the man sneered at him, looking him up and down with disdain. His friends, who had turned to see the challenger, chuckled amongst themselves.

"How dare you speak of the Lady Eve thus," Luke growled at him.

"I will say whatever I please, boy." He pushed Luke back as his friends crowded around. Luke stumbled, overbalanced and fell backwards. He hauled himself upright with the aid of a table to the laughter of those around him.

Using his momentum, Luke lurched forwards. "You will not dishonour her!" He lashed out with his fist, connecting with the man's temple.

The man crumpled to the floor.

A moment of astonished silence fell as those around him absorbed the change of events. Hands grabbed Luke; he swung his arms and flailed his feet as they carried him outside and threw him to the floor. Then they set upon him, punching and kicking his prone body.

Each blow paralysed him. They seemed to come from every direction, but the numbness brought a relief from the pain. In the dark street, he could not see his attackers and was in no fit state to defend himself.

He fell into unconsciousness where he lay.

Cold water drenched Luke and he awoke with a gasp, sitting up. He groaned and lay down again, closing his eyes. It hurt far too much to move.

"Boy, wake up."

Constable Sameth appeared, peering down at him, as Luke opened his eyes again.

"I didn't expect to see you in trouble, young Lucan," said Sameth, disapproval radiating from his thin mouth and accusing stare.

"Where am I?" Luke swallowed and licked his lips. He looked around. It was still dark.

"Exactly where you were. In the middle of the street, like the drunken idiot you are." Sameth bent down to pull him into a sitting position.

"Off to the cell for you. You'll be there until the man you

assaulted decides if he'll be pressing charges, but seeing as you received a lot worse than you gave, I doubt he'll think it worth it. You need to sober up before I'll let you leave. Can you walk?"

Luke struggled to keep up, his head moving at too slow a pace to decipher the man's words. Before he could answer, he sunk into blackness again, to the sound of Sameth's cursing.

When next he awoke, he was inside and propped against a wall. His surroundings were warm, dry and dimly lit. He could not see out; there were no windows and the door had a covered peephole. *What time is it?* he wondered as he clutched his pounding head.

He looked up at the door as the grille opened. Eve's face peered through it, sending a shock across Luke's body. He shook his head.

"Leave me alone, let me sleep," he mumbled. "Stop haunting me."

Her reproachful face disappeared, reappearing moments later when the door opened.

"You're not dreaming, Luke," she said sadly. "Your mother sent me. She's worried about you."

He was awake in an instant, as if another icy blast of water had drenched him. He staggered to his feet, clutching the wall for support.

"Please don't marry that man, I beg you. See what this torture has made me?" he gestured around the cell helplessly. "I cannot eat. I cannot sleep. I cannot work. All for love of you. Please don't choose him. Please." He gaped, open mouthed, not knowing what else he could say.

She stepped back, betraying a slight limp. Beyond her, Luke could see daylight. Her posture was drooped and she clutched her cloak about her.

"My feelings and what must be are two separate things, Luke," she said, not meeting his eyes. "I am honour-bound, and I cannot break that. When you leave here, forget me." Without looking at him, she turned and left.

Luke's head lolled onto his chest. The door was shut and locked once more. The stone floor was so cold it pained him, searing against his skin, but he did not care.

TEN

The shutter rattled. Eve glanced at the window, annoyed. "Go away, wind!" She concentrated on her sewing, her fingers struggling with the needle.

"Argh, why must I learn how to use this stupid thing!" she exclaimed as it pricked her finger and she stitched in the wrong place again. She stabbed it into the cushion and tossed her project aside in frustration.

At the sound of a knock Eve rose to answer the door, wincing as her ankle twinged with pain, but no one was there. She paused and glanced around the hallway. It was empty. Another knock sounded and she froze. *Someone is outside my window.*

She rushed to the fireplace, grabbed the poker and held it ready before she approached the shutters with caution. After opening the window from the inside, Eve unlatched the shutter, pushed it and retreated. As it swung out, the poker wavered in front of her and her mouth dropped open.

Luke grasped the sill, red faced with effort as he struggled to keep his grip, feet lodged in the trailing ivy and upon the rough stone brickwork. Without thinking, she flung the poker onto her bed and rushed forward to grab his arms and haul him in.

"What are you doing here?" she hissed.

He stood, closing the window behind him.

Eve was glad, for it let in a cold, pervasive wind that chilled the warm room, though her own shivering had not entirely been caused by it.

She looked over him. He was a different man to the Luke stewing in the gaol cell a few days prior. He wore his best clothes, which had been patched in places and meticulously cleaned. His hair had been trimmed and his beard too. He stood with ease—no hint of alcohol upon his breath or in his movements.

Realising his effort, her face coloured and her pulse raced as she met his bright, glossy eyes that were fixed upon her.

Luke fiddled with his collar, smoothing the fabric on his sleeves as his own cheeks reddened. He took a deep breath and crossed the room to take her hands in his own. This close, she could smell the fresh, woody scent of the soap he had used to wash.

"Eve, I had to see you. I'm sorry you saw me in such a state the other day, but it made me realise why you left so quick."

She made to reply, but he held up a hand to stall her.

"Please. I was in no fit state to ask for you then, so I shall do it now. Eve," he said, raising a hand to brush the hair from her face and stroke her cheek, sending thrills across her and causing her breath to catch. "I love you. I'm not ashamed to say it. I can tell that you have feelings for me too, and I know that the betrothal is not what you want. It's so clear to see. You know I'm right." He searched her face.

She could not respond, captivated by his touch and his words. Her breathing stalled.

"Be mine instead. I'll provide for you, keep you safe, and together we'll be happy. We don't have to stay, if you fear your father's disapproval. I can turn my hand to other trades and find a job elsewhere, but I promise I'll keep you well." His hands jumped to smooth his hair again. "Will you marry me?"

She stilled, taken aback by his unexpected question. Her eyes flickered as she faltered, knowing that she could not say yes, however much she might wish to. She couldn't resist the urge to draw nearer to him however, though her eyes closed as if denying the action. Her move betrayed her feelings.

All of a sudden, he gathered her in his arms and kissed her so hard that she could not breathe. She savoured his lips upon hers until she pulled away and they broke contact.

"I want to, Luke, but I cannot! I do not want this betrothal, but I cannot escape it—my father has proved that." Eve explained her previous attempt to run away. "I failed in my bid for freedom, and I bear the consequences of my choices."

Eve froze with surprise when he embraced her.

"I thought you had been avoiding me. I felt so miserable that you would hate me so." The relief in his voice was clear. "I would keep you safe. Your father would not find us," Luke promised, kissing her again, softly this time.

"He would," she replied, miserable. She rested her forehead against his shoulder, exhaling. "I couldn't do that to him, and there's no one else to keep Arrow county—just me."

She pushed him away. All emotion stilled within her in a few moments of clarity. It was easier to bear if she could not see him, so she turned away. "I can't be with you, Luke. There's no way for me to escape from this. I wish there was, but it's my own fault; I agreed to it." She shook her head, more at herself than him. *You're such a fool, Eve.*

"Is that your decision?" Luke asked in a low voice.

She did not dare turn around. "Yes." Her voice caught. "Yes," she repeated more strongly.

She heard Luke swallow behind her. "Very well," he replied, but there was a strange tone in his voice she could not identify. "I'll leave. You won't see me again."

She turned around full of sorrow, but his eyes, fixed on hers, seemed empty.

"Goodbye, Eve."

"Goodbye, Luke."

He opened the shutter and clambered out of the window without a further word. She heard the thud as he dropped to the ground, and then his footsteps as he stole away in the dark.

It was his mother she saw next, at the market-place as Eve rode past.

"Lady Eve," she hailed.

Eve reined in Alia, looking down from the horse. "Good morning, Nora," she said, trying to smile.

"Good morning, my lady. I'm sorry to bother you, but I

haven't seen my Luke in days, and I wonder have you seen anything of him? He's not been home and I worry. He's not been so well lately."

Eve froze. "No, no I haven't, I'm sorry. If I see him, I'll let you know." Her cheeks felt aflame as she shifted in the saddle, uncomfortable.

Nora's face fell. She looked to the floor, biting her lip. "Thank you, my lady. Sorry to bother you. Good day."

Eve rode off, geeing Alia along. Shivers crept across her skin. *If she hasn't seen him, he didn't mean to avoid me. He meant to leave.*

ELEVEN

Leika smiled, a sight Demara could not bear to tear herself away from. It was a new ability for the little girl. Demara stood, excusing herself to use the privy.

Seline raised her eyebrow. "For the third time today?"

A knowing grin flitted across Demara's face.

Seline broke out into an excited laugh. "Mistress! You are not?"

"I believe so, and the physician is confident it will be a boy this time."

Seline leapt to her feet and hugged her with joy, a gesture she would not have accepted from anyone else. "Congratulations, my lady!"

When Demara returned, Seline greeted her with orange cakes—her favourite. Demara favoured Seline with a kiss on the cheek and hauled Leika onto her lap. She shared the treat with her daughter, letting her try a few crumbs of the tangy sponge.

"This is wonderful news, mistress. I wish you had told me!"

"I did not want to presume." She shrugged, smiling.

"It will be wonderful for your husband to have a legitimate son too. At last he may leave you in peace."

Demara paused, frowning, her mouth open with a question. "A legitimate son? What do you suggest?"

Seline bit her lip, eyes wide. "Nothing, mistress! As I said, it will be good for him to have a son."

"No." Demara's voice was flat as her eyes probed the young woman. "I know you well enough to know when you are hiding something from me, Seline. Tell me."

Seline squirmed in her chair, her hands clenching together. She looked at her mistress from under lowered eye-lashes, a worried expression upon her face. "I wish to protect you, my lady, but I have ever done as you commanded. There are rumours that your husband is less than faithful to you. I hear that he often visits certain… establishments with his men."

"You mean that he seeks the company of courtesans." She was blunt.

Seline nodded, her lips clamped shut as though she did not want to admit it.

Demara swore. "Take Leika. I will go to see him. I am a princess—a queen in his country. I do not want him, but I will not share him!" Fury rose within her.

"Mistress, please do not go," Seline begged her. "Calm down for the sake of the child. You must remain restful."

"I did not ask you."

His chambers were deserted when she reached them. It was early evening and she had no idea where he could be. She dithered on the threshold. Within, his rooms were pleasantly cool, though darkening in the fading day. He had not been given the nicest chambers, she noted; they did not face much daylight. *Good. He deserves it.*

She sat on his long couch, waiting, fidgeting and listening for any sound of his return. After a while, she had to admit that her anger had cooled, replaced by misgivings.

Perhaps Seline was right. Am I wise in confronting him? I never would have dared to do so in Pandora. She knew his temper and feared it. Nerves stirred in her stomach.

The sun must have set, for she sat in the dark gloom, ages later. She chewed on a nail, playing with some beads on her clothing in agitation. *I will go. This is of no use.* She stood to leave, but froze at sounds outside. The scrape of a boot upon the tiled floor. The twist of the handle. The click of the door opening.

He's here! Blood and adrenaline rushed through her. Her cheeks felt at once as if they burnt red hot, and her hands shook with a tremor. Fury had ebbed during the long wait, replaced by doubt, but even so, Demara knew she must not appear weak. She smoothed down the folds of her dress, bead fringing rustling and clinking against her bangles.

"Hello?" Zaki stopped as he beheld her. His gaze paused on her one fist.

She blazed determination at him, wishing she felt as confident as she must have looked.

"Leave us," Zaki said to his companions.

His entourage shuffled outside and closed the door. A round of muffled laughter filtered through.

Demara had not moved. Her eyes followed Zaki as he used a taper to light some of the lamps around the room. He motioned towards the bed, assuming her purpose.

She huffed in disgust. "I would not touch you." Her mouth curled with distaste. "I hear where you spend your time! I will not share a man with courtesans."

His hand dropped to his side. Understanding crossed his face, before anger seized it. "It is none of your damn business where I go. I shall do whatever I like, whenever I please, with whomever I choose."

"You would shame me? You would shame our children, our family, even my father?"

"You shame me by not bearing me a son!"

Demara opened her mouth, but indignation made her pause. *May he rot. I will not tell him.*

He took her pause for his victory. "Get out."

"You presume to order me?"

"I am your husband; you will do as I command."

"You have no authority here. I will not leave." She raised her chin in defiance, standing taller. She struggled not to shrink into herself as he approached. He was more powerful than she, of that there was no doubt.

Zaki stood in front of her and looked down upon her—a deliberate intimidation. "You will get out, or I will make you leave. Your choice."

She did not move.

He swore. It was Caledonian—he never deigned to speak Roherii with her—but she did not need to understand the meaning to know his feelings. "Fine. Forget it. Stay. I will go." He shouldered her aside.

In a moment she had lost her balance and, within the folds of the dress, could not gain it again. She crashed into the table, its corner burying itself deep in her midriff. Crying out in pain, she scrabbled at the structure in a failed attempt to right herself. She thudded onto the floor.

The door slammed. The room fell into silence. Moaning, she curled into a ball and wept.

That night, she tossed and turned for hours. The cover constricted, catching her at the throat and pinning down her limbs, yet the faint breeze stole all warmth from her skin and left her shivering.

Not even Seline's presence next to her was reassuring, though Demara was often glad for the company of her bedmate. When she did manage to sleep, her slumber was haunted by twisted nightmares filled with Zaki that woke her.

After he had pushed her into the table for what seemed like the tenth time that night, Demara woke again. She turned over, trying to get back to sleep, when the pain stabbed at her.

Her eyes snapped open. *That was no dream.* She stroked her stomach, which had already bloomed in bruises. It was sore and the pressure of her hand worsened it. *In fact*, she slowly realised, *it cramps...*

With a gasp she tore back the cover and sat up, whimpering at the pain. Even in the night, she could not miss the dark stain on her pale bedclothes. She screamed.

Seline awoke next to her, thrashing in panic.

"Mistress! Are you alright?"

Demara jumped from the bed, tearing off her nightgown, and stared at the dark stains upon it and the bed sheets with horror. Seline fumbled with the oil lamp, lighting it. Colour and light flooded the room.

Red. It's red. Blood.

Seline swore and shouted for help. The door burst open as the guard tumbled in. "Fetch the physician!" she screeched at him before he could speak or even look around the room.

He ran as if the devil himself pursued him, whilst Seline leapt over the bed to Demara's side to support her as they made their way into the bathroom.

"Come mistress, come."

"It's gone, I think it's gone!" Demara mumbled to herself in shock, shaking.

"Your skin is so cold, mistress," Seline said with alarm, feeling Demara's arm and then her forehead. She ran a hot bath. "Thank the gods and goddesses that the furnaces burn all night. Worry not, mistress, I will tend to you."

Demara let Seline sit her in the bath—it felt at once too hot and too cold. She stared blank-eyed, unthinking, at the blood upon her thighs as Seline gently dabbed it away with a dark cloth. The water took on the faintest pink tinge.

Within minutes the physician burst in. His hair was a wild mess and his beard uncombed. "I came as soon as I could."

He took one look at the bed, the discarded bloody garment and Seline's tender ministrations of her mistress and tutted, sighing.

"You must describe your symptoms, mistress. Any pain or discomfort? Where?"

Demara answered his questions in a dull voice.

"Have you suffered any accidents of late?"

She replied without thinking or caring. The physician's eyes were hard as he listened.

"Why did you not tell me!" Seline's face was aghast as she grasped Demara's hand.

"I must inform His Majesty of this transgression," the physician said.

"What of my son?" Demara forced out, leaning forward.

The physician paused, but could not find any kind way to phrase it. "I am afraid that there is but a slim hope he will survive, my lady." Demara slumped back in the bath, not caring what he said next.

All for nothing.

She did not listen as he spoke with Seline, prescribing her bed rest and constant care, nor did she protest when Seline drew her from the bath, dried and dressed her, and put her to sleep in a clean bed. She lay, staring into the distance far past the ceiling, unthinking and unfeeling.

TWELVE

Myrkdaga's jaws crushed the goat's neck with ease, snapping the brittle bones. He tore out the flesh, hot blood spilling from the wound and dribbling down the scales on his chin. Behind him, Feldloga and Feldith waited for a moment before diving in to each rip off a limb.

Meat was scarce this far north. Birds were barely a bite and anything bigger was few and far between. The dragonets were too hungry to waste energy bickering over their share of the meat. They all ate as much as they could: bones, fur and all.

"This is ridiculous," said Myrkdaga with a growl as he cleaned his claws with a barbed tongue, still starving. "It's too cold this far north, there's not enough food and it worsens as winter creeps upon us. I like it not."

Feldloga huffed. "It's no fun, but I cannot imagine that returning to Kotyir under banishment would be either."

"I don't care. I'm going south at least, where there's better hunting. Are your wings with me?"

His two companions shared a look—the identical dragons mirroring each other's movement.

"We will come," replied Feldith.

Still on the northern edges of the clan territory, Myrkdaga, Feldith and Feldloga dropped out of the air the moment they saw dragons in the sky, landing and crawling under foliage to hide themselves from view. It would not do them well to be seen by any of their kin.

They waited in silence, eyes watching the skies, for them to pass by.

The dragons flew low and with no hurry in a northern direction. Their conversation was unguarded, shouted over the distance between their wheeling forms, but it was too far away to distinguish.

Myrkdaga hissed, flexing his claws as they crossed overhead.

"The silver dragon must be Cies. There's no other as large as that in the clan."

"What business does he have here?" Feldith wondered aloud.

"I'd like to find out." Myrkdaga's narrowed eyes watched them pass. "I know my sire distrusts him."

A slight tremor shook the earth nearby.

"They've landed," Myrkdaga said, slithering towards the vibrations on his belly as his two companions followed suit.

Cies basked upon a rocky outcrop for what little warmth there was in the light. He was joined by a red dragon Myrkdaga did not recognise. Myrkdaga and his companions retreated well out of sight, lying without a sound upon the forest floor.

The wind threw most of the conversation between the two dragons elsewhere as Myrkdaga strained to understand.

"We shame ourselves by following one so weak."

The wind changed direction, and Myrkdaga twitched as he heard their last words, his mouth open in a silent hiss. *They speak of my father?*

The other dragon replied. "It may be so, but you would have to challenge for clan chief position. Are you ready to do so?"

"As ready as I will ever be," Cies replied. "I have my methods, and many to support me."

"What will you do?"

The wind blew north again, wiping out the conversation. Myrkdaga heard nothing further. He was forced to retreat in silence, but he longed to roar his anger. Feldloga and Feldith slunk behind him like shadows until they were all well out of sight and sound of their elders.

"I'm returning to the clan. I must warn my father." Myrkdaga paced, kneading the ground with his claws and leaving furrows in the earth with each step he took.

Feldloga stirred, glancing at his brother.

"What of the penalty? Would you risk that to tell your father of Cies's malcontent? It could be nothing."

"And it could be something. I won't let my father down again, and I won't see that traitor become clan chief." Myrkdaga rumbled, smoke falling from his nose and ajar mouth.

Feldloga shared a long look with his brother.

"We cannot come with you. The price is too high and the need not great," Feldloga said, averting his eyes from Myrkdaga.

Myrkdaga looked between them. "Fine. Do as you will. I will not be allowed to stay in any case, and I plan to arrive in the dark. If I am lucky, only my father will encounter me. I cannot ask you both to risk yourselves too in this."

The crescent moon shone through hazy clouds as Myrkdaga flew low over the Isles of Kotyir. It felt good to smell his home, tasting each scent in his mouth. He moved with silence, gliding where possible. Dragons by no means slept at night, but he was counting on his father to be alone at his usual haunt: Brithilca's pool.

Sure enough, Myrkith-visir stood, keeping his night-time vigil over the water.

"Father," Myrkdaga called out in a low voice.

Myrkith-visir's head snapped round to fix the young dragonet in a penetrating stare.

Myrkdaga was certain the only reason his father did not kill him upon sight was their kinship, but even so, Myrkdaga backtracked as he landed, pressing himself to the ground in submission as Myrkith-visir reared onto his hind legs.

"Wait, I don't seek to return. I bear news you need to hear."

Myrkith-visir paused, low rumbles emanating from his throat. Myrkdaga took this as a sign to continue and explained all that he had seen. Myrkith-visir lowered himself onto four legs.

"I thank you for your warning," Myrkith-visir said, his rumble changing to a lower frequency as he stared into the distance; Myrkdaga knew his father was pondering his news. "Cies is ever discontent, but never has he dared to challenge me. Perhaps that time has come."

"You can defeat him," Myrkdaga said.

"Of course I can," Myrkith-visir replied, almost arrogant in his self-assurance, but Myrkdaga knew him to be speaking the truth. His father was far stronger and faster than the silver dragon, though who had mastered slyness and cunning most could be argued. "Thanks to you, I will be on my guard henceforth."

Myrkdaga rose from the ground, unfurling his wings to leave, but a warning growl from his father halted him.

"You know the penalty for returning from banishment is death," Myrkith-visir said, surprisingly softly.

Myrkdaga froze.

"Yet I cannot help but falter when it is my own blood, who returns to warn me of this."

Even Myrkdaga's breath had stopped in anticipation of his father's judgement.

Myrkith-visir turned away from him. "Go; tell no dragon of this and be seen by no dragon, for you would weaken my position beyond repair. If you are caught, I will be forced to act. I did not see you—you were never here."

Myrkdaga-visir did not question nor thank his father. Instead, he took a running leap into the air, flapping at twice his normal rate in case his father changed his mind.

THIRTEEN

As usual, the guard refused to allow Zaki immediate entry, but his behaviour seemed even more unfriendly that day. He stood in front of the door, his chest and chin jutting out, glaring at Zaki.

Zaki shuffled on his feet, impatient to get his apology over and done with. *I was wrong to push her*, he had to acknowledge, but he was still angry that she presumed to lecture him. Reynard had persuaded him to apologise, for diplomatic reasons, but he was having a change of heart.

Her maid glared at him with open hatred as he entered. He was surprised to find Demara abed. She did not greet him or look at him as he entered.

"Is she unwell?" Zaki looked at the maid with confusion, but was stunned into silence at her insubordinate reply.

"Thanks to you," she snarled at him.

Zaki looked at her, his eyebrows rising. He barged past her without a word.

Demara turned her head, regarding him with no expression upon her face.

"I have come to apologise for my actions yesterday," Zaki said, stiff backed and staring at the wall above Demara's head. "I was wrong to act thus."

Demara watched him still, but her face filled with dislike. "You pushed a pregnant lady onto the floor—your own wife—and left her there alone in the darkness. You cannot make up for that with an apology!"

Zaki's heart stopped for a second before it kicked back into life and hammered against his chest, blood rushing to his head. *What did she say?* "I beg your pardon? You are with child?" A smile widened upon his face as he processed the information, but before it could fix there, she replied.

"I was." Her tone was scathing and she regarded him with pure loathing, her lip curling. "I was. Now I am not, and it is all your fault!" Her voice caught and he could see her eyes glisten with tears.

"I do not understand," he forced out, bewildered.

Tears spilt onto Demara's cheeks as she recounted her experience, but her face remained a mask of anger. "My baby—my strong son, for I know he was a boy—is dead, and you are to blame! No apology could ever repair that."

Zaki's mouth became a parched desert and speech failed him. He stood transfixed. "We can make a new son," he said, but that enraged Demara.

"I do not want your murdering, lecherous hands anywhere near me!" she screeched at him.

Her maid moved between them and batted him away. "You are upsetting her. I will not have it," she said, her own anger blazing at him. "Out! Leave!"

Zaki stumbled backwards, turned and fled as he tried to understand what had happened. His feet carried him out of the palace, through the grounds and outside their boundaries by one of the lesser gates.

The guard let him pass without question.

Zaki took the usual turn down one of the smaller alleyways of the wealthy districts. It soon ejected him into the less affluent area where seedy businesses hawked their services down shaded back alleys.

It was still light when Reynard found him, but Zaki had already downed more tankards in the past hour than he would on a night.

"Thank God I found you!" Reynard exclaimed, dropping his voice as the other patrons in the dingy bar turned at his entrance. "Come, we must leave. This hole is no place for you." He gestured to the door, not daring to lay a hand on Zaki, but Zaki did not move and remained hunched over the grubby wooden cup. Reynard fished the vessel out of his reach, gagging as he smelt the contents. "Piss would taste better than this," he muttered. "At least let us find a place more savoury to drown whatever ails you, sir. I do not like the look of this place."

Zaki leaned forwards to snatch back the cup. He downed the contents and tossed the vessel onto the table, where it rolled onto the floor with a clunk. "Get me another one."

Reynard bowed and strode to the bar without a word, returning with another wooden cup. He perched upon the stool opposite Zaki, his lips pursed in distaste.

Zaki scowled at his right-hand man. "You won't join me?"

"No, sir."

"Join me or get out. I have no need for anyone's judgement tonight, least of all yours!"

"I would prefer not to leave you in this district, sir. It seems unsafe."

"I can take care of myself. Go." Zaki waved him away. "And get me another drink on your way out."

He did not look up as Reynard left. His corner of the bar grew duller. Candles burnt out and left him and his growing collection of drinking mugs to the darkness until even the bartender had had enough of him and threw him onto the street with the rest of the late night drinkers.

Zaki stumbled out into the air. It was barely fresh, the heat of the day still sweltering between the crooked buildings, but the breeze caressed his skin and he drank it in.

Staggering through alleyways, Zaki was soon disorientated with a swimming head. He sagged against the wall for support.

"Oi!" he cried with slurred indignation as he was jolted by someone shouldering past him. He tripped forwards, but his feet did not find the ground fast enough and it rushed up to meet him.

The blinding pain of his elbow breaking the fall was blurred by his intoxication, but his entire arm jarred from the impact. Zaki rolled over, groaning. He propped himself up on his other shaking elbow only for it to be kicked out from under him.

Laughter circled Zaki as he fell back to the ground once more, sodden in the stagnant contents of the gutter. In the darkness of the alley, lit by the faint light spilling from windows far above him, he saw dark shapes looming over him, silhouettes against the stars.

His mouth tried to frame words, to tell them who he was, to command them to assist him to the palace, but an unintelligible sound came out.

The laughter started again, but this time a blow to his side joined it, and then another and another, until they rained down upon him from all directions.

Hard edges dug into his soft flesh or crunched against his bones as he hunched into as small a ball as possible to avoid them. Feet stamped on him, heels driving the wind from his lungs and toes crushing his hands into the hard stone, twisting them without mercy until his fingers cracked.

He had no weapon, nor the coordination or even the consciousness, to respond. Hands grabbed him, prised open his closed form and slammed him against a wall, which trickled dust and debris into his eyes from the impact.

Eyes gleamed beneath the hood of the figure before him, but the fist smashing into his face shot his gaze to the floor, and then the other way as another blow made his teeth crunch.

He spat out a globule of blood, the rest dribbling down his front. They dropped him. Zaki cascaded to the floor, limp.

Several disjointed kicks later, the torture ended. He sunk into oblivion, away from the pain and the overwhelming smell of the gutter's excrement smeared upon his face.

Pain greeted Zaki before light did. He moaned, wincing and whimpering as he uncurled, each movement sending hurt searing through him. His eyes opened, or tried to. One was fixed shut by blood and swelling. The other fared little better. His nose pulsed upon his face—an angry, red mess.

What happened?

Through the tiny slit of vision left to him, Zaki saw that the fine fabrics of his robes were ruined: torn and soiled by waste part-solid and part-liquid, and by dark burgundy splatters of his own blood. The night before rushed back to him, or what little he could remember.

Who did this?

"Unnhhh…" he groaned, trying to sit up, but this made him more aware of his pounding head. He gingerly touched his crown with hands contorted like claws, but everything hurt and filth matted his hair. Zaki could not tell whether the pain was due to head injuries or hangover. Swooning dizziness did not help answer.

His mouth was parched. Zaki wished for a cooling drink, but he did not know where he was, let alone how to reach the palace. He turned his head with care, up and down the street, and began crawling uphill towards where he hoped the palace would be, feeling grateful that the city had not yet awoken.

It was cold in the new dawn, colder than he had yet experienced in Roher. It did not help distil the stiffness and chill infused in his body. He was more glad than he dared admit that the streets were empty.

The quiet did not last long. The city awoke around him, to his great embarrassment. Thankful that no one would recognise him in his pitiful, humiliating state, he continued to inch uphill until his knees bled and his palms were cut from the debris upon the ground.

Zaki tried to rise to his feet and walk, but after a few staggered steps he fell down again. People avoided him as if he were a rabid dog or a plague-bearer. The hardness and contempt in their eyes frightened him more than he cared to admit. *I will find no help here.* His will pushed him on, for his body had little left to give.

"Help me," he said to the guard upon the side gate, when at last he reached the palace garden boundaries, collapsing onto the ground in relief. The smooth paving was clean here, and pleasantly cool and soothing upon his tender, overheated body.

Zaki looked up when he received no response. The guard stared out over the courtyard. His eyes were visible under the shadow cast by his ornamental helmet.

"Succurro," Zaki said, repeating his request in the Roherii tongue.

The guard's eyes flicked down, but caught before they met him, returning to their forward gaze.

"Regis ego sum." *I am the king.* Zaki attempted again, gasping with every breath. "Regis Zaki. Vos opem!" *You must help me!* "Ego praecipio tibi." *I command you.*

The guard shifted and took a small horn from his belt. He winded it in a trilling pattern. The sharp, rich sound carried and was met with another identical to it.

More men soon appeared. They stopped when they saw Zaki upon the floor and raced out of sight. They returned with a palanquin and helped him into it with as little effort as they could.

Zaki's cheeks burned with the shame of being carried like a woman, but as he sat in the soft, pillowed chair, his eyes closed in sweet relief.

The pain was both soothed and unbearable as he soaked in a scented bath. "They did not rob me," Zaki mused, staring at his cleaned signet ring. *My pockets still had all my effects and money, so they were there by intent or malice.*

"Too skilled in thuggery to be petty thieves in any case." He tapped the side of the bath, chewing on his lip. He stopped as his stiff, battered fingers sent lancing warnings up his arms. *They must have been paid to target me. Perhaps someone tires of the regis mendicus.*

The physician had bathed his wounds with care—and a stinging liquid to ward off any illness or bad spirits—and reset his broken nose. He could do nothing for Zaki's bruised and battered body, cautioning rest, as if it were not obvious enough. Zaki glanced down his black and blue form. Not an inch seemed to have escaped notice. The hot water helped lull his form into a relaxed state. However, his mind remained keen.

He had yet to see anyone—not even Reynard had called upon him, though the hour was still early—but for that, he was glad. It gave him time to reflect, though the more he did so, the more suspicion gnawed at him.

It is too convenient. He thought back to the events of the previous days. *Would she order such a thing?* Zaki shook his head, dismissing the idea that his wife could have hired the strangers to attack him. *Where would she know such people? Could Harad have done so?* He would not put such things past his father-in-law, knowing well the ruthless streak within the Roherii king.

Surely he would not know so quickly. Would she even tell him what has passed? Who else could be my enemy? He sighed, unable to solve the riddle, his head still pounding. Both his eyes were open, but even looking around was painful.

As usual, the boy stood nearby in silence, ready to tend to him. Zaki tried to scowl in disgust, fed up of the hostile servants, but he winced instead. "I'm done," he said, rising from the bath and grimacing with every movement. The boy unfolded a luxurious soft cloth to dry him by hand, yet every soft dab poked yet another bruise. Zaki waved him away with a growl, snatching the towel from him and finishing the job as briskly as he could bear.

He chose robes looser than usual, holding his breath as the smooth fabric slid across his skin, but the fabric was of such fine quality that it did not aggravate him.

A rap on the door heralded Reynard, who charged in wide-eyed. He swore as his eyes raked over Zaki's pitiful state. "Thank God you're alive." Reynard sagged against the wall and let out a rush of breath. "What happened?"

Zaki recounted everything since his meeting with Demara the day before. Reynard's frown deepened as he spoke.

"Are you—are we—safe here?" Reynard whispered, glancing around the empty chambers.

Zaki scoffed. "Of course not—we never have been. I need to discover who dares to target me."

"Demara? She has the motive."

"She's a woman." Zaki looked at Reynard scornfully. *Though I would not put it past anyone of Harad's blood. Could she have arranged it?*

"Harad?" Reynard's voice distracted him.

"I doubt it. He does not notice my existence, it seems." Zaki huffed as he belted up the outfit and slipped on shoes of soft, patterned leather. "Let us talk no more of this. Come, I have a mind for pleasure tonight." *I am sick to death of bowing and scraping to these foreigners!*

It was early evening by the time they wended their way out of the square filled with market stalls and a colourful array of Roherii that paraded through the upper districts. Zaki was content after a lazy meal sampling some of the finer delicacies that had travelled the world to reach Arrans.

He hobbled along, turning down Reynard's support just as he had refused to make use of a walking stick. Every step sent jolts of pain shooting through him, but he was determined not to appear weak. Alcohol with the meal had helped to numb him somewhat, to his relief. As a result, he had drank generously.

They stumbled through the door of his favourite courtesans' house. It was a discreet establishment tucked behind an arch draped in exotic flowers and lit by a single lamp, the light of which was blocked from the street by the hulking doorman whose eyes followed them.

"Good evening, sers!" greeted the mistress of the house, Meera. A gleaming smile fixed upon her face as always as she swept into an exaggerated curtsy. "How good of you to visit us again. Please, this way."

No extra words were needed. Reynard handed her the usual purse, already counted out, and sidled off to try his luck whilst Zaki made his way to the bar where the free ladies waited for custom. The house was as tastefully decorated as could be expected, though Zaki would not have lived there. The lady of the house had added the finest ornaments and decorations she could afford in a show of wealth.

A small flurry of motion greeted his entrance; the ladies shifted from slouching to lounging provocatively, or stood to show him their best features, which they had not even attempted to hide under strands of gauzy material and strings of tacky beads. Some could not conceal their revulsion at his appearance.

It was the olive-skinned beauty in the corner who caught Zaki's eye most of all, for she made no effort to put herself forward to him and regarded him almost insolently. She smiled at his attention, but it was not the smile of a woman won, more the smile of a challenge to be accepted.

"What is her name? Over in the corner," Zaki asked.

The mistress regarded him with twinkling eyes. "This new gem is Tulia. Feisty. Most satisfying."

"I'll take her."

In response, Meera beckoned Tulia with a sharp motion. Tulia rose, unhurried, her eyes still fixed upon him, but imperturbable as she moved across the room with the languid grace of a predator.

"I will make you feel nothing but joy," she purred at Zaki, transfixing him with green eyes half hidden by shaded lids. Her plump, painted lips parted as she reached towards him.

FOURTEEN

Snow gripped Caledan, bringing light dustings in the south but impassable ways in the north. It purified the land, shrouding it in a cleansing white layer. Even the lake froze near to the shore, heralding a harsh winter.

The great hall thrummed with life. Caledan's nobility packed into it for the ten day midwinter celebrations of feasting and revelry, whilst across the kingdom, Caledan's citizens indulged too.

Soren enjoyed such things, but it was the first Christmas since his mother's passing and his first time sat in the throne upon the dais that she had made for the celebrations. Carved from one single piece, the wood flowed around him, yet he could not find comfort and fidgeted, memories of prior winter festivals involuntarily drawn forth from his mind.

The warmth and noise was almost overwhelming; outside the chill permeated a body, but great roaring fires, combined with the heat of so many people, made the vast space too hot for Soren's liking.

In the hall, it was simultaneously darker and lighter than usual. Candles and lamps burned everywhere in an endless carpet of twinkling light before him, yet dark greenery above him and decorating the walls and trestle tables absorbed their light. Holly sprigs, evergreen boughs littering needles, and clumps of winter berries somehow found room between dishes of all shapes and sizes crammed upon the table. Scraps falling to the floor were snapped up by the dogs; they slunk and dove between tables, occasionally snarling and fighting to snatch food from each others' jaws.

The smell of the fires and food clogged the room, both intoxicating and inviting, yet cloying and overpowering. Once Soren had had his fill, he waved the rest of the dishes away, grateful for the ice-cold water that kept his nausea at bay.

Many came to present themselves to him throughout the course of the evening. Soren could not remember all their names but, since they sat in house groupings, it was easy to see which of the houses attending were the largest.

He had not realised in his prior conversations with Edmund how large House Walbridge was, or how withered House Varan. *I must have new family trees drawn up.* His eyes swept across the hall again, calculating. *There doesn't seem to be enough of a margin for me to be safe upon the throne.*

Even so, the houses' oldest men were well outnumbered by youths. *Such was the price paid for my uncle's actions.* Again, he wondered just how many had died when Zaki had usurped the throne from Soren's mother. Soren still could not decide whether to be glad for the bounty of young, strong men to swell up through the ranks or disheartened from the loss of their fathers' irreplaceable experience. There were notable absences of those still incarcerated in the dungeons for their part in events, but their kin seemed to have no shadow of this upon their mood.

Edmund's words had stayed with him. "The sons of your enemies could be your friends, yet the sons of your friends could well be your enemies. Judge each person on their own merit, but be careful in whom you place your confidence."

Edmund is right, I cannot afford to discriminate against those whose fathers were against me, or supported Zaki. This must be a clean slate for us all. Soren sighed, his fingers tapping upon the table. It would be more than difficult to determine who was loyal, he was certain. The only other man close to his age that he knew well was Edmund's own son, Dane, but he was too busy to attend this year's festivities.

Before he could sink further into his own company, the musicians struck up a bright tune and, as one, the crowd rose obligingly and wheeled about the room in time with their partners. Edmund hauled Soren to his feet, ignoring Soren's protests, and placed his hand into that of a blushing young lady.

"Lady Elsa of House Bryars," Edmund introduced them.

Soren bowed as the girl sank into a curtsy, giggling. He danced around the room with her, using the space in the centre of the hall that had been kept clear of tables and rushes. Their feet tapped with many others upon the stone floor as they weaved amongst the other couples.

She was pretty, albeit a few years too young for his liking, Soren acknowledged, but that made him worry. *Soon I'll be expected to wed and produce an heir. Twenty-one and not even betrothed is not a good thing for a king.* He dreaded picking a consort. Whoever he chose would aggravate at least several of the houses, and he did not relish a political marriage of any kind—to an allied house or not.

Then there was the small matter of his sister, for whom he was also responsible. *She could hate me, whatever I choose for her.* A small sigh, lost in the noise and movement, escaped Soren's lips.

After Lady Elsa, Soren danced—or was forced by Edmund to dance—with seven other eligible ladies, until at last he found himself with his sister. Her eyes sparkled over rosy cheeks, and her mouth was open in a permanent grin of joy. It was so infectious that Soren smiled too. With two hands around her waist, he picked her up and placed her feet upon his own to lead her in the dance as he had done since they were young children.

"You're enjoying yourself?"

"So much!" Irumae's reply increased her smile. "I've danced with all of our cousins from Lowenmouth, though Uncle Andor was too busy drinking to join in, and did you know cousin Ilyas's new wife was so beautiful? She has told me all about the most fashionable gowns, and she promises she will teach me some new dances!"

Soren chuckled as his sister babbled on, filled with quiet contentment at her open happiness. *It has been far too long since I saw her smile this much.* "She will be one of your ladies-in-waiting, if you desire it," Soren promised his sister.

He retired to his chair with relief as his sister galloped off to ask Ilyas's wife to wait upon her.

Edmund answered Soren's glare with an unapologetic grin.

"You know it is your duty to entertain your guests," Edmund said, winking.

"Hmm."

Edmund's voice dropped to a murmur no one else but Soren could hear. "You sister is well, in any case. I am glad to see her so recovered."

Soren also lowered his tone. "So am I, Edmund, but I still fear for her long-term health after all that she has endured."

"We must hope for the future to be as bright as the present."

"I hope that she will still be so happy when I find her a suitor."

Edmund's fixed him with a sharp gaze. "You think of this already?"

"I think I must consider it so soon, for both of us—though I'd rather not. There seems too much else to do. However, my own betrothal fell through after my uncle's actions and I'm not secure until I have an heir."

Edmund paused before replying. "An heir would help strengthen your position somewhat, yes, but marriage brings more immediate alliances. Have you given any thought to potential consorts for either of you?"

"Not in any detail. As both our marriages will have to be beneficial for our house, I wonder which houses are best to ally with. There are still a few to choose from. Which is the better house: Arendall, Kinsley or Duncombe?" Soren picked at a dessert, plucking off glazed fruits and eating them one by one, sucking the sweet sticky mess off his fingers after every bite.

"I would caution you to widen your choices," Edmund replied, glancing around them. "Perhaps it is best that we talk of this further somewhere more private. Suffice to say, strengthening alliances is crucial, but especially with those most alienated to your rule. Consider those options too. Perhaps your cousin Ilyas's choice was, in fact, most wise."

Soren glanced up, searching for his cousin. Across the hall, Ilyas twirled his wife back into her chair, both breathless and laughing. *Of course, Lady Nance is of House Orrell, how could I forget? Famous for producing beautiful daughters, and an old house with wealth and good lands.* "Maybe Ilyas has secured House Orrell for me," Soren mused aloud.

"Indeed," said Edmund, a satisfied smile upon his face.

"Walbridge is of dubious alliance and blessed with sons—perhaps one of their boys could be a suitable match for my sister."

Edmund started to reply, but was cut off.

"I beg your pardon!" Irumae's shrill voice sounded behind Soren and he twisted in his chair with haste. She stood with her hand upon the back of his throne, her mouth open and eyes accusing.

She overheard us.

"Irumae, you should not eavesdrop," Soren chided her, but he felt guilty. *I should not have spoken of this here.*

Her voice had carried to those nearest, who looked up with piqued interest. Soren signalled the musicians to increase their volume and turned back to his sister.

"We will talk of this later. I promise you I won't rush into anything, but it's something that I, as your brother and your guardian, need to arrange." He stood, reaching out for her, but she shrunk from him, her lip trembling, before turning and fleeing the hall.

Edmund said nothing. Soren sunk back into his throne, but knew Edmund would be biting back a comment.

"I'll go and speak to her tomorrow," Soren said, knowing it was his duty to stay, though he would have rather followed his sister. He fixed a fake smile upon his face for the benefit of his guests, some of whom were less than slyly observing him.

"Wise choice," Edmund murmured. "Don't forget to greet those at the table over there." He pointed discreetly. "Some more of House Bryars have come to sup and eat your winter stores, by the looks of it."

Soren sighed and rose to mingle.

"Do you see why I'm concerned?" Soren finished.

"I do," Behan, Pandora's Lord Steward, replied.

As usual, Soren's office was a mess. Soren dumped his desk clutter upon the floor, which resembled a paper maze, in favour of twelve large parchments, which he shuffled between.

Each detailed the current family tree of the twelve noble houses, but Soren had not expected some to be so sizable.

"I realise both myself and my sister need to somehow strengthen ourselves from our betrothals, but how do I begin to choose the houses, and to whom should we promised?"

"How is your sister?" Edmund asked.

"Better." Soren grimaced. "She didn't appreciate the surprise and was worried I would sell her off to the highest bidder—can you imagine that! I know our alliances must be well chosen, but she is my sister and I want her to be happy above all else."

"So she is open to the idea?" Edmund asked, leaning forward.

"Unexpectedly so. I think she's rather taken with how well married life suits Lady Nance, who it's clear she adores. I must be careful that Nance doesn't influence her too much—after all, she is of House Orrell—but it seems she has inspired my sister to become a 'great lady', as Irumae says."

Edmund chuckled. "She is a girl who loves finery. Give her a pretty dress and she will love you, but give her a new jewellery piece and you will be forgiven anything."

Soren let out a small laugh. "I don't think that's true of all women," he replied, thinking of his mother, who had been the opposite. "In any case, I feel that whatever I choose, the effect of the alliance will be but a drop of water in the ocean. How can I possibly ally myself with all of these people?" Soren gestured at the maps, feeling helpless as he slumped back into his chair.

"Moreover, there are so few of them actually here at court. How can I know what any of them are doing with their time? This makes me worry that there is far too much of Caledan plotting against me whilst I sit here in complete ignorance."

Soren also worried whether or not one of these houses hid Zaki—he saw how it could so easily be done, now he knew the vastness of their families—but he did not say that aloud.

Edmund and Behan shared a look.

"What?"

"There is a way for you to know what is happening in each noble house in every county, every day," Behan offered.

"I don't follow." Soren's brow creased. *Short of flying on dragon back—and it's not as if I can do that anyway—there's no way to travel so fast!* The dragons had appeared out of myth and legend to help him regain the throne and vanquish Zaki, before disappearing. He had not seen or heard of them since, but that did not stop him wondering if and when they would return.

"A network of informants."

"Oh? Oh!" Soren's reverie was broken. "You mean to spy on my own people?" Soren shook his head at the thought. "I couldn't do that—it's immoral!"

"It depends how you look at it, sire," Behan said, his expression neutral. "You would not be using the information gathered for your own ends, per se, but more for safeguarding the good of Caledan—to prevent strife in your own kingdom."

"And to ensure my own position upon the throne is secure." Soren regarded the older man through narrowed eyes, but Behan remained unruffled and shrugged.

"I do not wish to alarm you, sire, but do not mislead yourself into thinking your noble stance the same as any other man's. The other houses use informants of their own—part of my duty remains weeding them out."

"There are spies in my own household?" Soren said, stiffening.

"Not at present, but yes, these things are commonplace. Do not be alarmed!" Behan added, raising his hands. "My men monitor such things well and are proud to say we are excellent at what we do. You are in no danger."

Even so, Soren looked around the room with shivers creeping up his spine, wondering if the walls had ears—or the floor, or the tapestries.

"Behan is correct," Edmund added. "There is little reason for you to abstain on the grounds of morality or to respect others' privacy. They do not have the same consideration for you."

"Because others do it, does not make it right for me to."

"Of course not," said Edmund, "yet there are benefits for you. Think of the peace of mind you will have knowing that if anything amiss occurs you will be the first to know, not the last. Your forewarning and swift action could curtail treasonous plans that threaten the safety of Caledan and its people." Edmund lowered his voice. "If your uncle is still alive and in hiding in Caledan, we may also yet find him."

Soren's hands tightened upon the chair arms, his knuckles whitening. He swallowed, persuaded more by the fear of that than anything else. "Say, then, that I did agree to this; is it not an impossible feat to infiltrate every single house worthy of note in Caledan?"

"Not at all," Behan said. "Your mother sanctioned such actions, as her forebears did before her. The network I managed under her reign is intact, though inactive. It would not take long to reinstate it and recruit extra bodies for those I have lost."

"I struggle to believe that people are happy to spy both for and against their own king." Soren massaged his creased forehead.

"Every person has their price," Behan said.

Soren stood, drawing closer to the fire to rid his body of the chills that had overtaken it, as he considered what to do. His eyes were fixed on the mesmerising flames dancing in the grate, but he was not watching them, instead lost in his thoughts.

A breach of privacy, but safety for the kingdom… and safety for me. Are they one and the same? He bit his fingernail as thoughts of his uncle resurfaced. *He could be here still, hiding somewhere. Who would shelter him if that were the case?* Soren glanced at the pile of family trees.

There are so many places he could be. The fear of his nightmares returned and his breathing started to quicken. Before another thought could cross his mind, he turned round and met Behan's gaze.

"Do it." He sunk back into his chair, the cold tingles still not gone, not listening to what the Lord Steward said to him as Behan bowed and strode out.

"You've made a good choice, Soren." Edmund nodded with approval.

Yes, but at what cost?

FIFTEEN

Their eyes met across the courtyard, and Demara paused with shock at her husband's appearance. She moved towards him, gliding down the stairs and across the turf, fascinated though she did not want to see him. Zaki met her at the fountain in its centre. *He limps...*

"What has befallen you?" Demara asked, her face crinkling with confusion. *He looks like he has been involved in a brawl. If it is so, my father will not stand for it! What an insult to his hospitality.*

She was surprised by the scowl he returned her.

"You would know, *wife*." He almost spat the word at her.

Demara stepped back, affronted.

When she did not respond, he continued. "Do not plead innocence! The day we have a major... disturbance"—he seemed to struggle to find the right word to describe what had happened between them—"I am set upon by professional thugs, beaten senseless and left for dead! I see no coincidence there!"

Demara's mouth gaped. "You dare accuse me of such a deed?" she said, her voice quiet and incredulous.

"You are the spawn of Harad. I know you all to be capable of such things."

Demara drew herself up, standing tall and proud, with her chin raised. "I have wished you harm—and worse—for your misdemeanours, but I would not act upon it. It would be beneath me, and you are still my husband."

Without waiting for a reply, she strode away. Zaki did not follow. Upon reaching a secluded corridor, Demara leaned against the wall feeling cool relief against her palms.

He was covered in cuts and bruises. She wondered what other injuries his robes hid. *And that limp. Who would do such a thing to a man under the protection of my father?* Suspicion stirred. *If the physician informed my father of Zaki's transgression, would my father act upon it?* Harad was famed for being ruthless, even to his own kin when he saw fit.

She dashed to her father's quarters, slowing to a sedate walk as she turned the last corner and requested admittance, out of breath.

"My daughter!" Harad greeted her as she entered, rising with a smile to kiss her on both cheeks and enquire after her health.

She greeted him in return, adding her own kiss to his signet ring as she dipped into a curtsy. Before he could turn to sit, she stood to address him.

"Zaki was attacked in Arrans this previous night."

"Was he?" Harad sounded bored, with no trace of surprise.

"You knew?"

"Hmm."

Demara waited.

Harad sighed. "Yes, I knew. I know many things, my daughter, such is kingship. I must know everything to remain safe and secure."

"If you know everything," Demara began, clasping her shaking hands and taking a breath to still her nerves, for she had never been so forward with her father before, "then you will know who committed the crime."

Harad inclined his head, but did not comment.

"Who?"

"Demara, my dear, you need not concern yourself with these things. Such is the ugliness of life and such is my burden to deal with it, whereas you are lucky enough to live under my protection in bliss and ignorance."

"Did you order it?" Demara asked, glaring at her father.

Harad looked at her, eyebrows rising in feigned innocence before he met her hardened glare and abandoned his false surprise.

"You are my daughter," he muttered, eyes narrowing at her. "Yes, he deserved a lesson for his insolence. I will not have anyone assault you—or any other member of my family—as he did. I was merciful to let him live after his deeds, was I not?" he said.

Demara nodded. It had been enjoyable to see him in pain, a small, dark part of her was forced to admit.

385

"You must make more strong sons and then we shall have no need of him."

I wish that were not my duty! He is a vile man. But Demara did not voice her thoughts and instead curtsied again. It was her place to obey her father and husband. *One day, at least I will be free of Zaki,* she hoped.

With her father's words occupying her mind, Demara waited for Zaki that night with trepidation, passing the time with Seline in her chambers. It had long since grown dark, even though the nights had not yet lengthened to the peak of midwinter, yet he had neither come himself nor called for her, as she worried he would.

The coil of tension and nerves in Demara's stomach diminished with each passing hour until, at last, she surmised that it was not to be. She smiled at Seline in relief.

"Come, let us to bed. Thank the Gods, he has no need for me tonight."

"Long may it be so!" Seline replied, extinguishing the lights one by one until a only few candles remained scattered about the room.

Demara settled into her sumptuous bed with a sigh of pleasure, closing her eyes as the fabric enveloped her. Seline clambered under the covers next to her, pulling an additional thin throw over them both to ward off the autumn chill. The weather here was nothing compared to Caledan's harsh autumn gales, permeating fogs and driving rains, but they had both reacclimatised to the much warmer, drier autumn in Roher, glad to have returned to their homeland.

A week later, Demara had neither seen nor heard from Zaki. Her days were spent with Seline: playing with Leika, walking around the vast palace in conversation or recreation, and visiting the nicer areas of the city with guards to attend shows or markets. She steered clear of Zaki's chambers, not wishing to cross paths with him even in passing, but even so, she grew curious about his disappearance.

"He should at least come to visit Leika," Demara said to Seline as she bounced the baby on her knee. She held Leika's podgy hands safe within her own slender grasp.

"It is a shame." Seline frowned, offering Leika mouthfuls of sweetened yogurt before laughing as it dribbled down her chin.

Demara deftly switched her arms, catching the mess in a silk napkin. Her face darkened. "I would, however, like to know how Zaki spends his time and, no doubt, my dowry.

"Glad though I am that he chooses not to spend it with me, he should see his daughter more. I worry his actions will sully our reputation, if it is not already tarnished enough, being the women of a kingdomless king!"

"I can arrange to have him followed, if you wish?" Seline suggested, reaching out for Leika to wind her.

Demara stilled, her eyes flicking to Seline's. "You would do this for me?"

Seline dipped her head, lowering her eyes.

"Underhand, admittedly," murmured Demara, "but necessary. Arrange this for me and I will be most grateful, Seline."

Seline took messages daily from her source—a small rap on the door, a whispered conversation and the clink of coins—with Demara craning her neck, eager to hear news.

Yet every day Seline would say the same when she returned. "He has done nothing much today, it seems."

After the third day, Demara was impatient for more. "This cannot be it! The man seems a hermit! Surely there is more—do you have him followed at every minute of the day?"

"Yes, of course," Seline answered. "My man is very good at his job."

And yet you avoid my eyes at all cost when you answer me, thought Demara. "I doubt that very much. He must be going out at night-time, at the very least."

"He is."

"But this you do not report to me?"

"Well, no ma'am. His business is not fit for your ears."

Demara stiffened. She transfixed Seline in a glare. "He still sees courtesans."

Seline twitched.

"Do not lie to me. Do not seek to protect me. Is that the truth?"

Seline nodded, her eyes filling with tears. "I'm sorry, I did not want to cause you further pain."

"You do not cause me hurt." Demara rested her chin on steepled fingers. "It is he that does so, yet I feel anger that he insults me thus. Not only does he squander my dowry on gambling and drink, but fornication too? By the gods, I wish him dead more than ever. Will they not rid me of him!" She took deep breaths to calm her racing pulse and paced out onto the balcony, shivering as the cool evening breeze stole the warmth from her skin.

"Do you have any more news of him? More details of his transgressions?"

Seline stole up behind her, slipping her arm into Demara's to link up with her. "If you wish me to tell you."

"Tell me already!" Demara's voice carried a snap, growing impatient. "I apologise," she added. *I know she seeks to protect me.*

"My source has reason to believe that he visits the same place and the same woman each night. The House of Cherished Flowers, it is called. He also said that it is impossible for any other man to have relations with this woman."

Demara stiffened, turning to look at Seline, aghast. "He has made her his concubine? So soon?"

"They do not live together as such. But it would seem so."

"Find out more about her. I want to know everything!" Demara snatched her arm away from Seline and stormed back into her rooms. "I will not share my husband with a concubine," she muttered angrily to herself as she undressed for bed. "Nor my dowry!"

Zaki sighed in bliss, uncurling beside Tulia, who surfaced from underneath the sheets.

She smirked at him, capturing his gaze with her sultry, dark eyes. They were always so lazily half-open and framed by long, curling lashes.

Irresistible.

Around them the city moved as it always did, but in that room was stillness and peace. Draped fabrics hung from the walls, covered the window and dressed the four-poster bed, made up with gold-embroidered linen and silken pillows, though many of them slumped on the floor where they had fallen or been tossed.

Recovered from his beating—in part due to Tulia's tender ministrations of nightly massages—he could at last sleep through the night without waking in pain from leaning on one sore spot or another.

"You have been good to me," he murmured.

She snuggled up to him, her hand sliding across his chest. "And you to me, my king." She kissed down his throat, tracing his collarbone.

"How would you like to leave this place?"

"What do you mean?"

"Exactly that—leave this house, leave this life behind."

She stopped tracing patterns upon his chest with her silky smooth fingers and propped herself up on an elbow. "Why do you ask?" Her tone was guarded, her eyes hard.

"Would you like a house of your very own, full of servants and fine things, to be mine alone there?"

Her lips parted. "You jest?"

"I would do no such thing to you, my queen." He caught her still hand in his own, gathered her fingers and kissed them one by one. "Would you like this?"

"Such generosity would be a gift beyond anything I could want or deserve." Her expression softened.

"Then it will be so. By the end of the week, you will be here no longer. You will be mine alone, and I yours."

Tulia threw her arms around his neck, kissing him on the lips, before wriggling back under the cover to show him her gratitude.

The house he led her to was a two-storey dwelling plastered in cream with ornate shutters covering the windows and a ridged, terracotta roof in the heart of the higher districts of Arrans. Set back from the cobbled road, it hid in its own sanctuary of green behind high walls. Their plastering matched the building, and a row of citrus trees peeked over the terracotta tile-topped boundary.

A wrought gate under a stone arch opened onto a path paved with shaped stones slotted together like pieces of a jigsaw. It led to the front door through green gardens stuffed with blossoming flowers, such was the generosity of Roher's winter clime.

Tulia, hand entwined with his, pulled him inside, delight and awe evident upon her face. A row of five servants standing in a line within the hallway, men and women of varying ages, bowed to her in unison. She exclaimed in delight.

"These are your servants, Lady Tulia," Zaki said to her, smiling. "They shall tend to your every need."

Tulia flashed a smile at them before rushing around to explore the many rooms.

Zaki followed her at a slower pace.

Light flooded in as she opened the shutters, leaning out of the window to cast them wide, revealing well-proportioned rooms filled with luxurious furnishings.

"You have somewhere to live that befits your beauty and your importance to me," Zaki said.

"You will not live here too?"

"My place is at the palace, but I will visit as often as I can. You will not care—you will have more than enough to keep you entertained, running a household."

It was weeks before he did return to his own bed in the palace; her company was so appealing he did not wish to deprive himself of it. Each morning he awoke feeling carefree and refreshed, though in the back of his mind grew a niggling guilt that he strayed from his true path.

Even so, he was relieved to be away from the political mire that was the Roherii upper class: their petty squabbles, power games, the language that he still found impossible to master, and the still poor state of his own affairs. He had been in Arrans for months, with still no prospects of regaining Caledan's throne on the horizon.

By the time the new year arrived, he had not seen Demara in many more weeks, nor visited Leika in her nursery—both of them long forgotten, a distant memory and someone else's family—yet his return to his wife came about far sooner than he had anticipated.

"How could you do this to me!" he raged, storming around the room and kicking over a potted plant in his anger. "You were supposed to be careful!"

"I'm sorry, my love!" Tulia wrung her hands, regarding him through wide, tearful eyes from the cushioned couch upon which she sat. "I am sorry for failing you, yet shouldn't you be happy? The love I bear for you has created a child, and you will gain a son from me that you will otherwise never have!"

Zaki paused. "How can I be sure that it is mine? Who knows what you did before you met me."

"It can be no one else's, I promise you," she said. "You do not see your wife anymore. She has not given you a boy. I will give you the strong son you need."

I will not find an heir elsewhere. The thought plagued Zaki, as it had often done before. The room felt warm and stifling all of a sudden.

Zaki loosened the collar of his robe with a tremulous hand and strode from the room, away from the house and through the gates, ignoring Tulia's imploring wails behind him.

I need space! God, what mess have I gotten myself in to?

SIXTEEN

Soren paced around the room with his hands clasped behind his back. Each lap he stopped, sat, and rose again, unable to still himself.

A rap on the door announced his visitor.

"Come in."

Behan slipped through the opening and bowed. Soren gestured towards the chair and Behan sat.

"Your Majesty, thank you for your time."

"Welcome, Lord Behan. I received your note. What's your news?"

Behan sat up straight in his chair, and presented Soren with a thick wad of parchment. Soren glanced across the outermost pieces. All were covered in a tiny script that he had to squint at to decipher.

"My informants send me word from certain houses—those are their more detailed reports."

"And?" Soren froze, even his breath stilling.

"Orrell, Walbridge and Bryars conspire against you."

Soren's breath escaped in a whoosh as he sunk onto the corner of his desk for support.

"Only some members of the houses are responsible, you understand, sire. This is the perfect time to nip it in the bud, before it becomes widespread."

"Before what becomes more widespread?"

"They plan to restore Zaki to the throne."

Soren clutched the edge of the desk, his eyes widening. "He is alive?"

Behan nodded.

"In Caledan?" Soren's voice rose an octave.

"He resides in the Roherii capital, Arrans, under the

protection of Harad. Certain members of those houses have been supplying him with funds and working towards reprovisioning their arms to hasten and support his return. Asquith of House Bryars, most notably."

Soren heaved a sigh of relief. *Thank goodness he is not here.* "And you are certain of this—beyond any doubt? I don't understand, Asquith swore loyalty to me; he renounced his support of my uncle in public!"

"Unfortunately so, sire. It was not difficult to discover this. They have grown complacent, thinking themselves safe or above such notice. Here are the names of the key conspirators."

Behan passed Soren a list of about a dozen names. "They had tried to be thorough, squirrelling money away under false ventures, but their deceptions were not skilled enough to stand."

So many... Soren's heart sank. *Asquith of Bryars, Harl, Lord Willam of Walbridge's own brother, Lord Royce, the heir to House Orrell, brother to Reynard...*

"I cannot ignore names of such power," Soren said, biting his lip. "Nor can I forgive them." He took to pacing once more, the list rumpled in his fist. "This treason cannot go unpunished—yet how do I prove their guilt and set a fit punishment without destabilising the court?"

"Every monarch has to deal with at least one such plot," Behan said, shrugging. "These people understand the risks they take, even if they are so cocksure that they will escape detection or punishment. The best thing to do is to make an example of them, swiftly, before this escalates. Others sensing any sign of weakness may perhaps question your rule and choose to join these rebels."

"How can you prove their guilt?"

"The documents I gave you earlier show sufficient proof—copies of correspondence, household accounts, witness accounts of conversations, meetings and so on. Any court would find them guilty with the weight of evidence."

"And you think I should try them in public rather than private?"

"Most definitely. A show of strength, if you will. They will perceive any private attempt to meddle as insecurity, which will spur them on."

"The penalty for treason is death." Soren stared into space.

"It is," Behan replied. After a pause, he added more. "It is unpleasant, yes, but necessary for Caledan. Think of that, sire."

Soren gave him a hesitant smile. He thanked the steward, who left, before departing himself, hurrying to find Edmund.

Edmund's views were much the same as Behan's, but even so, it was with reluctance that Soren called for the trial of Lord Asquith of Bryars, Sir Harl of Walbridge, Lord Royce of Orrell and some of their less noble supporters.

That night he lay awake, pondering his choice. By the small hours, he was exhausted and no further decided in the best course of action. *I can see the sense in making an example of them,* he considered again, *but I balk from taking the lives of men I have known since I was a boy.*

Yet they are traitors and would betray me, given the chance—have already betrayed me. They need to be punished, as the law decrees to be fair and so that others will also be dissuaded. However, should I go so far to make an example of them? Is that not selfishness? Soren growled, punching the pillow beside him with a soft thump.

"What else can I do?" he asked the ceiling, heaving a great sigh.

When morning arrived, Soren threw back the covers, dressed in a hurry and sent messages to summon Lord Behan, Sir Edmund and Lord Heligan. As they arrived in his office, he rose to greet them.

"Sire, you look well," Lord Behan said.

"Much better than yesterday," murmured Edmund.

Soren flashed him a quick smile. "I have a solution that is amenable to both the law and my conscience. All those so accused will stand trial for the deeds which they may have committed. Those deemed to be the leaders in any such plot will be sentenced in line with the law, by its harshest penalty, to serve as punishment—nay, atonement—for their crimes.

"Those who are also found guilty, but could be mistaken for being ill-led by their liege lord, will instead surrender members of their households as surety of their commitment to Caledan's future of peace and prosperity. I see this as a fair punishment that will ensure the ringleaders of any rebellion are crushed and an example set to others. What do you think?"

Edmund nodded, looking surprised. "I would see that as a very reasonable solution, Soren. Neither too harsh, nor too light-handed."

Soren looked to Behan and Heligan, who gave their agreement.

"Lord Heligan—may I charge you with managing the trials?"

"Yes, sir," said Heligan, sweeping into a deep bow. He collected the packet of evidence from Soren's desk and departed.

Winter worsened much more before the trials began weeks later, though it had abated by the time they concluded. The snow still drifted deep about the walls of Pandora, but the streets had begun to thaw and the winter storms had turned to sleet, heralding the spring rains to come.

Soren shivered with fever, his nose and eyes streaming, but he sat in the freezing courthouse nonetheless, perched on the throne and glad for the furs that shrouded him, protecting him from the deathly cold of the stone. Lord Heligan stood before him to deliver the verdict. Those accused knelt to one side of the vast room, their heads bowed. The court was warmer than usual, the lofty room stuffed to the brim with everyone who could fit in, and louder as their murmurs accumulated.

"Your Majesty." Heligan sunk onto one knee, casting aside his ceremonial cloak. "Lords, ladies, sirs, men and women of Caledan, we gather here on the fourth day of the second month to learn of the verdict in the trial of these men before you." He gestured to the subdued men.

Standing, he pulled a scroll from within his deep sleeves, the lips of which trailed upon the floor. "Lord Asquith of House Bryars, stand."

A bedraggled figure struggled to its feet and moved forward. Soren was surprised to see the poor state of the men before him. They had not been maltreated within the royal dungeons as far as he knew, yet they seemed haunted, with dark shadows upon their faces. *Perhaps they know their fate and fear it.*

"You are charged with high treason, for instigating rebellious thoughts and acts and leading others to follow. You are found guilty on all counts. You are sentenced to death by beheading in three days."

"Mercy!" cried Asquith, crumpling to his knees. "I pleaded not guilty—I appeal!"

Soren looked away, feeling nauseous. *This is no easy thing,* he still thought, yet the cowardice of the man disgusted him.

Asquith had already crumpled to the floor. Royce made no sound as Heligan read his charges and verdict.

"You are found guilty on all counts and sentenced to death by beheading in three days."

Royce bowed his head and his shoulders sunk.

Soren felt a twinge of respect. *At least he is honourable in his defeat.*

"Sir Harl of House Walbridge." Heligan waited for the next charge to stand. Harl rose, a hulk of a man compared to his peers. "You are charged with treason, for conspiring with others to overthrow the king."

A murmur arose within the court before fading as Heligan opened his mouth to deliver his verdict.

Soren's interest had also piqued at Heligan's charge. *Not high treason? Still, House Walbridge could yet ally with us. I fear our bridges with Orrell and some of the Bryars are well burnt.*

"You have been found guilty of treason, and by the graciousness of His Majesty King Soren have been sentenced to house arrest under the care of your brother until such time as is deemed fit. Lord Willam, do you accept this charge?"

Willam stood, his face bereft of expression. "I do accept this charge." He executed a short bow towards Soren and sat once more, regarding his brother with a thoughtful stare.

Heligan progressed onto charging and sentencing the rest of those standing in the dock, reading from the long parchment before him that held the courts decisions after much deliberation of the evidence. Almost a dozen others from lesser houses were charged, and all but one found guilty of, at the very least, following others in treasonous acts. The punishments ranged from hangings to whippings and imprisonments, which would be carried out in the castle dungeons on the decreed dates.

Last of all, Heligan retired with Lord Behan, Sir Edmund and Soren himself to discuss which strategic wards should also be exchanged to ensure good conduct from the houses.

"I prepared a list of possible candidates," Heligan said, offering it to Soren, who took it.

Soren read through it, placing each name on its respective family tree. "This is most thorough," he said to Heligan, impressed, before reading out those he most preferred.

"Two daughters from Orrell to serve under Irumae—Lady Nance is already a fast companion to my sister, but her family is hostile to us. Lady Elsard might yet see the value in allying with Balaur, if she can further her daughters' positions.

"A son, but perhaps also a nephew, from Walbridge could shore up our alliances. One man each from Harl and Willam's broods. A few Bryars, definitely including Asquith's sons. They must be under our watch henceforth in case they are anything as untrustworthy as their father.

"A son from House Denholm too, though there are not many—I will not have Lord Verio think he is above reproach or beyond my reach for this. Perhaps a marriage can also be arranged there, to bring him into the fold. Do I have any Balaur cousins who would suit a match with House Denholm?"

Edmund tugged at his beard as he thought. "One step at a time, perhaps. Let us see how they first respond to the summons."

It was with relief that Soren learnt of Asquith's and Royce's deaths three days later, after an anxious morning of pacing around his apartments. They had been beheaded upon the new scaffold Soren had inspected that morning, but he could not bring himself to watch, though he questioned the wisdom of that decision. Soren hoped this would not set a bad tone for his rule and mar his subjects' opinion of him, but Behan informed him the event was well attended and the crowd enthusiastic to see the traitors' punishments.

He ordered both bodies to be given over to their families. Some of their co-conspirators had already been punished and released, some were still to be hanged the following day and others were beginning lengthy sentences in the dungeons. Harl had departed and was travelling south along the River Lowen to be confined on his estates. Behan had already promised Soren to monitor his every move. Soren would not be naive enough to trust a Walbridge again.

The day did not bring the closure Soren sought, however. No sooner was the evening upon him, than he had already turned once more to thoughts of Zaki. A sleepless night followed, as he worried about this uncle. *Is he a broken man? Does he gather his strength? Does he march here at this very moment?*

The following morning, hollow-eyed, Soren ordered Behan to discover as much about his uncle as possible.

SEVENTEEN

Reynard waved the parchment above his head as he crossed the flower gardens to join Zaki, who sat basking in the sunshine of the palace grounds. Spring had long since arrived in Roher, the mild chill of winter dispelled and the sun strengthening daily.

Zaki had returned to the palace, distancing himself from Tulia and working without rest on plans to retake Caledan. This included reconciling with Demara in the faint hope of securing an heir to his yet-to-be-gained throne. Their relationship was still full of tension and wariness, but at least he had a husband's rights. He suppressed any guilt at cutting off his mistress.

Zaki's spirits rose as he noticed Reynard. *More news from Caledan!* He knew Reynard carried correspondence of how Asquith's plans progressed apace—no one else wrote to him. He slipped the letter from between Reynard's outstretched fingers, tore through the seal and scrabbled to open the parchment, eager for the weeks old news. This letter would detail when forces would be ready for him to join them in Caledan to retake the throne, but the breath that had caught in his chest with anticipation escaped in a gasp of horror.

"No!"

"What news is there?" Reynard leaned forward.

Zaki stood. Rage rose within him. He re-read the letter, pacing around. "We have failed." He tossed the letter to Reynard, unable to read its contents aloud, and stood silent as Reynard scanned it.

It was not from Asquith, but from his son, describing his father's death at the hands of the king for high treason. No detail had been spared of what had passed in Caledan. Soren had dealt with his discovery as he would have done, Zaki thought with grudging respect. But now, Zaki hated Soren more for spoiling what he had believed to be a flawless plan and his best hope of retaking Caledan.

Discontent lurked in the pit of his stomach as Zaki realised how hopeful he had been that this plot would succeed.

"This is grave news, sire," Reynard said in a subdued tone, frowning as he looked up from the letter.

"We have lost yet again, Reynard," Zaki said with a scowl. "Not only are my hopes for regaining the throne gone, but we will have no supply of funds from Caledan." *I will be the regis mendicus, the beggar king, once more—whether I wish it or not.*

He sunk onto the stone bench, cradling his head in his hands. Reynard joined him in silence, staring out over the lawns.

"I must go to Harad," Zaki said at last, with a sigh of reluctance.

His father-in-law seemed unaffected by his news—as imperturbable as always. Zaki watched him, as distrustful as ever towards him, masking his own frustration.

"Will you assist me in this?"

"No," replied Harad. "It is the perfect season for a campaign, but I have my own affairs to manage. My neighbours in Ladrin seek to rise above their station and I must teach them a lesson. Janus, my eldest son, leads my banners. If you are short of things to occupy your time since your latest plans have failed, you may accompany him and see how the Roherii battle. You will learn something valuable. Perhaps if you return successful, I may reconsider."

Zaki, about to refuse, paused and thought of how unfamiliar Roherii weaponry and technology was. *I could find here the weapons that will help me take back Caledan.* He thought of Harad's incendiary devices. *If I had even ten of those, think of what I could do...*

"I would be honoured, Your Majesty," Zaki answered, sinking into a low bow.

Zaki retired, with Reynard in tow, feeling cheerful as he explained his motives.

"You are happy to not even be in the chain of command, though?" Reynard said, his eyebrow raised.

"For once, yes. I will see how the Roherii operate. I confess, Harad is a force to be reckoned with and I am curious to see how he manages this."

Zaki met Janus the next day as preparations to leave were made. He expected Janus's resemblance to his father—albeit a taller, slimmer, younger version of his dark-haired, dark-eyed, imposing sire—but was surprised by the severity of his disposition. A scowl was etched upon his face, and he snapped with no provocation at those about him.

Even his greeting to Zaki was brusque and impolite. The servants scurried about him without a sound, averting their eyes as if to escape notice.

He is feared, Zaki thought, eyeing him with caution. *I wonder if it is with good reason.*

Reynard was to remain behind to manage his affairs, so Zaki was to travel along with his remaining men, who had grown soft in their stay in Arrans and longed for the excitement of a battle and the chance to regain some status. Janus accepted their company, though from the scorn upon his face it was clear he thought they would be of little use to him.

Before Zaki departed, he bade farewell to Demara—though not to Tulia. Demara seemed surprised to see him leave, as he had not told her of his planned trip, but she seemed impressed that he was making something more of himself and said as much to him.

"Return triumphant," she said, without any sentiment in her words or warmth in her voice.

He bowed and left, his glance lingering for a moment on Leika, who played on the rug near her mother's feet.

The journey to Ladrin took weeks, riding on horseback southeast from Arrans. Once outside the lush river valleys, the green land gave way to arid terrain. It was, though dry to the point his lips cracked and chapped, far better than Zaki's travels to Roher, given that they had the comforts of horses, foods and fine supplies to make camp with. Despite this, Zaki still missed his feather bed. They stopped to camp and water at oases on the way—brief jewels of humidity and life—but these were few and far between.

Janus invited Zaki to dine each night, but only out of politeness, it seemed. Janus took no interest in his brother-in-law. Zaki, on the other hand, was far more curious about the next king of Roher and took the opportunity to glean all he could of the man.

He could not deduce much, but it was easy to see that Janus was an unlikeable person—too feared by those around him for any reproach about his manner. He was ruthless and efficient, effective in everything he did, yet perhaps this was why he seemed so arrogant.

He probably thinks himself far above me, Zaki thought, irked by the younger man's complete lack of respect for him.

The edge of Roher was signalled by a ridge of low mountains that rose in dry desolation to the sky. As they crossed the horizon, the land fell away. Ladrin sprawled before them: green and fertile lands stretching as far as the eye could see. In the distance, Karan, the jewel of Ladrin, stood. A city older than even Arrans, it lay in the river-rich land, protected on three sides by water. Once glorious, it had crumbled into decay, and its once bright golden stone was faded to dirty ochre.

Each village they passed was empty—their inhabitants visible in the distance, fleeing before Janus, who had made no secret of his presence, blowing the Roherii horns to carry over the wind. Janus burnt the villages, devoid of any mercy towards his fellow human beings.

Zaki observed the results as he passed. *He seeks to send a message. These people already have nothing, yet he takes it from them anyway.* As he rode past, a shack collapsed in a whoosh of sparks and a puff of smoke. Zaki liked to consider himself ruthless, but Janus seemed unnecessarily cruel.

As they drew closer to Karan, emerging from the woodlands and marching across the plains with renewed vigour, Zaki saw how the fortifications had been weathered by wind and rain. Their carvings and sharp edges had been long lost to the elements and the grandeur of the entire place muted by a sense of tiredness. Even the gates were old, their metal frameworks and studs rusting into their wooden surfaces.

"Who visits our gates with weapons?" a voice shouted down in accented Roherii.

It seemed Janus intended no terms were to be made, nor greetings exchanged. He ordered the Roherii to form up, and set about bellowing commands to be passed back through the ranks.

With nothing to do and no one to command—for his men had been given the humiliating task of manning the baggage and weaponry trains—Zaki stood about with Janus and his command in nervous anticipation.

At last, the mysterious waggon that had travelled with them from Arrans was unveiled, revealing hundreds of the fire-devices that Zaki had used to escape Pandora. They were each the size and shape of a lemon, one of Roher's speciality fruits, and hollow, filled with powder that would explode once exposed to a naked flame. A fuse of thread, sealed by wax, fed through to the deadly contents. They were handled with extreme care.

At once, men distributed them to the front ranks, where the men had already begun digging holes set a few feet apart into the ground. The strange items on their back became apparent to Zaki as giant slingshots, which they stabbed into the earth. They were staked deep and packed in with tamped down earth.

Each man worked as a pair, one stretching back the fabric of the slingshot almost half his own height, whilst the other, with steady hands and a grim face frozen in concentration, used flints to create sparks to ignite the small wick extending from the single fire-device each pair had. It seemed the line of men moved in synchronisation, the second man loading the device into the hands of the first man, who strained to hold back the material.

After a quick adjustment to aim the contraption over the walls of Karan, each pair released with not a moment's delay. Men grasped each other's forearms in celebration, grinning with unconcealed relief, before plugging their ears and watching expectantly.

Arrows and then stones began to fly from the walls, but fell short of their position.

Have they no longbows? Zaki questioned.

The Roherii men stood in rank, armoured and unmoving as they waited for their command.

Zaki covered his ears, remembering how loud one device had sounded at close quarters and expecting this to be a thousand-fold worse, but he barely heard the explosions, shielded as he was from them by the stone walls of Karan.

They punctuated the air as a hail of booms, some striking the walls and exploding upon impact, some finding targets behind it and out of sight. Tendrils of smoke arose. Zaki had expected a great wall of fire, smoke and debris, but the result was underwhelming.

Janus appeared to agree, for he punched the unfortunate man next to him, howling swearwords, causing the man to crumple to the ground without a sound.

"They must have been damaged on the journey! Damn it all! I will gut whoever is responsible!"

"They still contain the fire powder, though?" Zaki said, leaning towards Janus. "If we shoot fire arrows, we could yet ignite them."

"I can manage my own siege!" Janus snapped, wheeling on Zaki.

Zaki narrowed his eyes, but stepped back without another word, not intending to become Janus's next casualty.

"Next wave!" Janus ordered.

The pairs of men repeated their tasks, setting off the second wave of incendiary devices. These fared little better than the first, to Janus's evident anger, for he paced with a dark face whilst muttering a continuous string of curses under his breath.

His nervous men paid the price for their fear; two devices exploded when they were loaded into the slingshot. Men were torn to shreds with the force of the blast, dying in that instant, others mutilated but clinging to life.

Zaki averted his eyes as those moaning on the floor were killed by their comrades for mercy and the honour of a quick death, glad that it was not his job to risk his life using the experimental weapons. He looked up as Janus addressed him.

"Sometimes these things happen!" Janus smiled, as if jesting.

Zaki hastened to smile back, though he felt disturbed by what he had seen. *These Roherii are barbarians. At least in Caledan we give men a chance to fight with weapons and honour.*

"Archers, ready the oil!" Janus shouted.

A flurry of motion sprung up as barrels of oil were rolled forward and unsealed. Arrows, pre-made with rags wrapped around their points, were unbundled, dipped in the oil and passed along the lines.

Zaki could not help but be impressed by how organised Janus was, though he was frustrated to dither about doing nothing.

Bows were strung and arrows set alight and shot at will into the city. Archers ran forward into range, loosed their arrows and ran back to their rank out of danger of Ladrini missiles. Janus seemed unconcerned about a synchronised attack. At last, he turned to Zaki.

"Do you wish to fight?"

"Of course," replied Zaki, certain it was a trick question but desperate to prove himself to Harad on the faint promise of gaining men to retake Caledan.

"Take the north section, by the river. Do not let any pass. You must kill all in your way—men, women and children. Do you understand?"

Zaki nodded.

"If I see anyone escaping, I will hold you responsible. You would not wish my father to hear of this."

Janus knows what is at stake for me here. The thought concerned Zaki. Usually he was the manipulator, not the pawn. Nevertheless, he was relieved to be given any command—it meant something to do as much as a chance to prove himself.

Zaki relieved his men of their dull duties and they marched around the rear of Janus's ranks to watch the unguarded northern side of the city. He repeated Janus's instructions to his men.

"Our lives will not be worth living should we fail in this," Zaki added with a scowl.

Night fell as they waited, watching the walls and the numerous small gates and window holes set into them, separated from the main body of Janus's men, who had continued their assault. The west side of the city burned high into the sky: a funeral pyre for those trapped within, for there were no gates out over the land.

Instead, inhabitants had taken to the water. Numerous small crafts dotting the darkening river were easy targets for Janus's men, who delighted in picking them off one by one with arrows, flaming arrows and well-thrown rocks that tore holes in the delicate crafts.

Zaki longed for the Caledonian longbow his own countrymen took for granted—here, they were non-existent. The Roherii favoured shorter bows that could be shot from horseback, but their range was pitiful. The Ladrini seemed to have no better bows, instead using slingshots. It was too easy for Zaki to remain outside their range.

It seemed as night fell that the Ladrini had decided to make their stand. The main gates opened and men poured out. Zaki saw them spilling into the empty zone between the walls and Janus's men, before he was distracted with those emptying through the smaller gates nearer to him.

Their poor state was an extension of their city. Few were fully armoured, some not at all, and the weapons shared between them were anything from swords and pikes to shovels and hoes. He called his men to engage and ran forward with his sword drawn. The first man he cut down came at him wearing a helmet and brandishing a stick with a nail in it.

These people are fools!

Some were younger than he cared to think about—boys poured out with their fathers, wide eyed and skinny legged, flailing their weapons about them. Zaki cut them down with the rest of the men, blocking out the horrors he committed.

The Ladrini outnumbered his men by several to one, but before he knew it, silence fell. In the sick, flickering illumination from the growing city fires, he could see a sea of dead before him.

"Leave them," he commanded. "Find our own." There would be no picking to be had from these poor souls, Zaki knew, and he did not care to count how many they had slaughtered.

Despite the difference in numbers, few of his men had perished after being overwhelmed. The rest had survived, due to their superior equipment and training, Zaki was sure, though they all shared the same look of dull-eyed exhaustion. His men carried their comrades reverently out of the piles of bodies, setting them down by the river in solitude and murmuring a prayer over them.

"Who's there!" cried one of his men.

Zaki looked over to see him pointing towards the city, where shadows skulked by the wall.

"Fetch your bows and shoot at will," he commanded.

His men hurried to pick up their borrowed weapons. Many of their arrows missed, but enough found their mark. Soon one person remained standing, a young girl a few years old. The last man standing with an arrow nocked and ready to draw hesitated.

"Do it," urged Zaki.

The man paused. "I cannot."

"She will either die with mercy at your hands, be burnt alive in the city, or worse still butchered by Janus's men. Give it here." Zaki stepped forward. "Never let it be said that I ask of you what I would not do myself."

He took the bow, drew it back to his cheek and, stilling himself for the moment of aiming, released. Well practised, his aim struck true. The girl crumpled to the ground without a sound. He thrust the bow back at the man, who looked at him with revulsion in his eyes.

"Do not judge me," said Zaki. "If we are to meet the dawn alive—nay, if we are ever to set foot in Caledan again and call it home—this is what we must do. Be glad these people had a kinder end at our hands. At the very least, we are not barbarians."

Morning arrived, but the blaze of Karan was brighter than the sun itself, which skulked behind the veil of black smoke still belching from the city. It brought a slight illumination to the carnage of the previous night. Zaki had done battle before—had seen death—but not to this extent. Bodies carpeted the ground, twisted, bloodied and blackened.

Exhausted, Zaki sat a distance away with the rest of his men where they could watch the wall but not smell or see the bodies before them. He could not help but contemplate on his actions that night. *What in life has led me to this godforsaken place?*

From the smoke, Janus approached on horseback the most cheerful Zaki had seen him yet.

"A good night, brother!" Janus said with a gleaming smile.

Zaki grinned back, playing along.

"I can see that you had great sport last night." From his high vantage point, Janus surveyed the carnage. "Come watch for the finale!"

Zaki grinned and nodded, but as Janus rode off, he turned to his men with a grim face.

"Come. Watch when you are told, do what you are asked without question, fear or repugnance, smile or laugh as the others do and soon we will be free of this madness." He looked at the men surrounding him. Their eyes held fear, doubt and exhaustion. "I promise to lead you home," he vowed.

They met Janus before the main gate. Zaki rode forward, away from his men, still armoured. Janus had removed his. *Is he so confident?*

But then Zaki realised why Janus was so cocksure. The gates had been destroyed and the burning city no place for anyone living.

Janus saw Zaki gazing into the city. "We had much to do! We ransacked the city before the dawn—wherever was not burning, in any case—and took what we pleased. We killed anyone we saw and spoiled their food and water stores. Anyone left will not find sanctuary in this nest of rats."

"So the city is empty?" Zaki dared to ask.

"Oh no, the principal rats are still alive, having hidden in their little ratty holes all night," Janus chuckled. "Let us see them run for the light. Come, look at them!"

Janus beckoned Zaki to follow him, to where they had gathered a pitiful group of aged and bearded men before Karan's gates. Sandy coloured robes, blackened with soot and ash, garbed them. Their dark skin swam with sweat. Huddled together, they were surrounded by a group of Roherii, each with swords drawn and pointing towards them.

"I believe you wished to discuss terms," Janus said brightly as Zaki watched on.

This is a sport for him, no different to hunting animals, Zaki realised.

One man stepped forward, but was prodded back into place by the sharp end of a sword, which tore the belly of his tunic. He winced, stepping back.

"We wish to be left in peace. You have no right to bring such devastation on our people—what have we done to you?"

A soldier strode forward and struck the man with a backhanded blow to the face.

"You are in the presence of High Prince Janus, First of his Name, son of His Supreme Majesty King Harad, Third of his Name, King of Roher, Ladrin and all the lands of the West."

The old man shrunk from the force of the strike, but his eyes sparked with defiance at the man's last words.

"We have no king in Ladrin. We are an independent nation and we will not be enslaved and exploited by your barbaric king!"

Janus nodded to his soldier, who sprung forward, stabbing the man in the gut with a long knife that had a cruel, twisted blade. It drew out with a squelch as the man sunk to his knees, crying in pain.

"You shall die a slow, agonising death for your insolence," promised Janus. "As for the rest of you, the so-called leaders of the Ladrini, the free peoples of the West, know this. You have lost. Roher is victorious and we will have our prize. You can choose— you may surrender, or you may not. Karan is lost to you regardless of your choice—she has been utterly spoiled and destroyed. I will give you a moment to choose your path."

He fell silent. The men glanced at each other, fear flickering in some of their eyes. Their comrade lay curled on the floor, cradling his bleeding stomach in his hands as he wept and moaned.

"I will surrender," said the first, a middle-aged man with hooded eyes.

"As will I," croaked an old man, so hunched he was almost half the height he should have been.

Janus nodded, gesturing for them to move to one side.

"I cannot surrender the freedom of my people," said another man. His eyes bored into Janus with an expression Zaki recognised as pity, to his surprise.

Over half of the men surrendered in the end, with the others remaining in a sombre huddle. They were aware of their fate, but stood tall, ready to receive it, though Zaki could see their chests heaved with deep breaths and their nostrils flared below widened eyes. Hands clasped in brotherhood.

Janus turned to those who had surrendered to him. "You chose wisely. Go, you have a chance to find your freedom."

Janus's men parted behind him, offering a clear passage through their ranks. They stood silent as the men walked, at first, before breaking into a nervous jog and then a run, with the old bearded man getting left behind in moments as he struggled to keep up.

"Shall we shoot them?" Janus's deputy asked.

Janus cocked his head as he watched them retreat, contemplating. "Hmm. I feel merciful today. Let them live. They will be dead within the week. How can those old, fat cowards survive in the wild?" He turned back to those who had not surrendered to him. "You, my friends, can run for your lives. Archers, ready."

Without a backwards glance, the men scattered. Some ran the same way as their freed fellows, others made for the river. Some stumbled and fell before picking themselves up. Those who made it first dove without any thought for their safety into the river and tried to swim either across it or downstream as fast as they could.

"Loose!" came the command from Janus.

Screams erupted as Janus's men peppered the fleeing Ladrini with arrows. The Roherii rode alongside the river picking off their targets from horseback with ease, trusting their well-trained horses to find sure footing. Soon, there was silence.

Zaki forced himself to watch, unblinking and unthinking, trying to neither see nor hear anything before him.

Janus clapped his hands, breaking Zaki's reverie. "Bravo, bravo! That was well done." He laughed. "We shall have the spoils. Douse the main way and we will see what treasures we can find in this pitiful palace of theirs to show off to the people of Arrans and my father when we return."

He turned to Zaki, clapping him on the back. "I will battle with you again, brother. Take what you wish." He gestured towards the city.

EIGHTEEN

Demara scooped Leika up into her arms and blew wet kisses on the girl's belly as she attempted to wriggle free and resume her adventures. The babe was crawling, pulling herself up onto furniture and babbling away in indecipherable noises. She was growing rapidly too; even her hair was beginning to form more solid curls.

"She is the most beautiful," said Demara proudly. She handed her to Seline.

"She will make a lovely big sister to her brother," replied Seline with a glance at Demara's once more growing stomach as she took hold of Leika, who stopped squirming to take the bribe of a candied apple piece to suck and chew upon with her single tooth.

They emerged from Demara's room to begin their daily walk around the complex, soon finding themselves outside Zaki's apartment having promised to bring Leika to see him at some point. Since his return from Ladrin a few moons ago, he had been much more tolerable.

Seline raised her hand to knock on the door, balancing Leika on her other hip, when Demara thrust out her arm to stop her.

"Listen!" she hissed. They tiptoed closer to the door and leant their ears against it.

"Get out! Be gone!" Zaki's voice said from within.

"I will not leave until you recognise your son!" replied a woman's voice. It was unfamiliar to Demara, but the woman was crying. "Look at him!"

"He is no son of mine," Zaki said, his voice so cold that Demara shivered. She knew that cruel tone.

"He can be no one else's and you know it! Every inch of him is you—pale skin, dark hair, blue eyes. Recognise him!"

"He is base-born. Mongrels are not recognised by kings. I

have a wife, and she bears me a legitimate son—what do I have need of yours for?"

"I cannot go!" Her voice was plaintive as she begged him once more to recognise his son, to care and provide for him, and asked why he had neglected to visit her for so long.

"What does it matter?" was his snappy response. "You are your own mistress—you have a house, servants and luxuries beyond your wildest dreams, paid from my pocket, as I promised you. Why do you care?"

"Because it is nothing without you," said the woman, sobbing so hard that Demara could not understand her next words. She crushed her ear closer to the door. Her breath held in suspense as Seline mirrored her, bouncing Leika on her hip to keep her quiet. The smooth wood was cool against her face, but the action did not help the conversation within come into sharper focus.

Zaki gave an indecipherable reply.

The woman burst into a long wail—of happiness or despair, Demara could not tell—but her voice was cut off by Zaki.

"Silence, woman! Would you bring the guard upon me! Leave, before you compromise my position and reputation more than you have done! No one must know about this. You are to tell no one that this boy is mine."

Seline tapped Demara on the arm and motioned for her to move, lest they be discovered. Leika had begun to gurgle again, her mumbles getting louder.

"Come, mistress!" Seline whispered, backing away.

Demara took one last look at the door and, with Seline, ran down the corridor and out of sight. Her heart hammered as she returned to her chambers.

The pair of them collapsed onto a plump couch in the peaceful warmth of Demara's rooms. A light breeze ruffled the translucent drapes shading the room from the mid-afternoon sun. Leika hauled herself around the room on unsteady feet, clinging to furniture as she tottered about.

After a while, Seline spoke. "Are you alright, mistress?"

"No," said Demara dully. "It is worse than I feared." She rubbed her forehead.

"Please do not go to speak with him," said Seline, leaning forward to grasp Demara's hands.

"Worry not." Demara extracted her hands. "I know what he is capable of—I would not risk my child again."

"What will you do?"

"I do not know. But it would appear that he has a son—illegitimate or not. What if I have another daughter? Would he recognise a base-born child over his daughters, over any sons we may yet have? I cannot see it of him—he takes great pride in his pure lineage—yet I know he seeks to secure his future with an heir."

"I am sure he would not recognise the child—can you imagine the child of a courtesan being acknowledged as the heir to a kingdom, especially by Zaki?"

Demara chuckled, though her face was grim. "When you describe it like that, it does sound ridiculous. Perhaps I fear nothing. I should instead be angry that he tarnishes my own reputation alongside his. As if it is not bad enough; I was once a queen and now I am nothing. Though I much prefer living in Roher, I know he gambles my dowry away and spends it providing for a courtesan. Even worse than all of that, he has fathered a child with her! How can I rid us of this nuisance?"

Seline had no answer.

Demara pursed her lips as fury rose in her. "I refuse to be humiliated like this."

NINETEEN

The sun grew in the sky as the season passed from winter to spring. Its welcome energy allowed the dragons to return to strength after the cold, harsh months when they were at their weakest, when the fires within them burnt slow and dim and their prey diminished.

Myrkdaga, Feldloga and Feldith had returned from their exile and Myrkith-visir was pleased to see that they now followed the rules of the clan with fresh vigour, no longer straying further than the coast of the mainland.

Nothing had come of Myrkdaga's warning about Cies, who had not spoken to him since long beforehand, but the silver dragon was more distant than usual from the clan core and Myrkith-visir, living a secluded life on the northernmost of the Isles of Kotyir.

Myrkith-visir soared above the islands on his daily patrol of the dragon territory. The colder air forced him to fly low, in the more sheltered pockets around the islands. The seething sky was dull and threatened rain. Master of all he surveyed, he enjoyed the view regardless.

Turning south as he wheeled in the sky, he noticed a dragon rising to meet him. The gleaming silver scales could only be Cies. Myrkith-visir roared in greeting, but Cies failed to answer in kind, instead replying with the low, carrying snarl of a challenge.

"Do you seek to contest me?" said Myrkith-visir, gliding towards Cies.

Cies roared in reply with a gout of fire springing from his mouth.

Smoke oozed from Myrkith-visir's nostrils with relish. *I will put you down once and for all, worm.*

'Let us settle this!" Myrkith-visir changed direction, making for the crater lake that was the cradle of his species and where any challenges for leadership of the clan were conducted.

It was clear that Cies had no such intention, for rising ahead of Myrkith-visir were two other dragons: a red dragon half the size of Myrkith and a blue dragon almost the same size as Cies, slightly smaller than Myrkith-visir. Cies, behind Myrkith-visir, crowed to signal the attack.

Myrkith-visir growled in anger. 'Dishonourable, underhand, scaleless coward! You bring shame on your clan, Cies!"

He had no choice but to meet the attack. Myrkith-visir kicked out at the small red dragon, catching him in the back as he rose to snap at his belly. It bought him moments of extra time. He roared as loud as he could before engaging with the blue dragon.

"Cease this madness, Arun!" Myrkith-visir said, recognising the dragon, but Arun did not reply, instead opening his jaws to snap at Myrkith-visir. Myrkith-visir dodged out of the way, raking his claws along Arun's side as he flew past. They skittered off the hard, smooth surface, not finding a point of weakness.

Arun's snaking tail glanced Myrkith-visir's cheek and he snarled before somersaulting in the air to catch the tail in his teeth. Arun tumbled many dragon lengths from the air before regaining his balance as the red dragon rose to meet Myrkith-visir.

Myrkith-visir kicked out, but the red dragon—Brun, Myrkith-visir remembered—avoided the attack, dodging through the air. He was fast, Myrkith-visir acknowledged, but for one of his size, a minor annoyance. Myrkith-visir lunged forward and grasped him with all his claws, clamping his jaws on the smaller dragon's neck.

Brun shrieked, a piercing sound that carried far—ear-splitting to Myrkith-visir. He struggled in Myrkith-visir's grasp. Myrkith-visir tightened his teeth a fraction and the young dragon ceased moving, except to continue flapping his wings in a desperate attempt to remain airborne.

Myrkith-visir released Brun and kicked him away with contempt. His legs pushed so much force onto Brun that the young dragon fell from the air and smashed into the ground hundreds of lengths below with a crash.

Cies must have decided the odds were less in his favour than he preferred at that point, for he joined the fray as Arun re-engaged with Myrkith-visir. They became a flashing, writhing ball of blue, silver and black scales. Myrkith-visir roared and keened in pain and wrath as claws scrabbled into his scales, nicking into the softer flesh underneath, and teeth clamped into his tail and his vulnerable wings.

He lashed out, his claws extended, his eyes shut to protect them, building the fire in his belly until it grew too great to bear. He bathed them in a great swathe of fire; they were forced to release him. Raining hot drops of blood, he pumped his wings harder than he had ever before, driving into the heights with the rush of the battle upon him and a red mist before his eyes.

Members of his clan appeared on the horizon, speeding towards him as the clouds above them dispersed. With every ray of sunshine Myrkith-visir flew through, he became more energised, his rage fuelled.

Myrkith-visir dove from the sky, through the clouds, tucking his wings in to create a sharp dive. He descended on Arun in wrath, knocking him from the sky with a sharp blow to the base of the skull. Using the other dragon's body to push off from, he propelled himself towards Cies with a howl of rage.

Cies turned to flee before him. With more energy, the silver dragon outstripped Myrkith-visir with ease.

"I banish you from the clan, coward, oath breaker, Cies of the silver scales! Never return, unless you wish to meet your doom!" Myrkith-visir roared after him before dropping to the black sand for a brief reprieve.

He was greeted by a barrage of questions as clan members surged forward.

Myrkith-visir answered them in little detail, his voice grim as he flew towards the crater pool. His body was sore, but that was nothing compared to the pain in his punctured and rent wings, which would take several weeks to fully heal.

Landing with a painful thud upon the unforgiving stone, he summoned Brithilca's spirit, the fury still burning within him. The image of the blue dragon swam upon the face of the still pool.

"Brithilca-visir," Myrkith-visir said, lowering his gaze

respectfully.

Brithilca rumbled. "I know why you seek me," he said. "But I cannot find the silver dragon. I no longer possess the power."

Myrkith-visir raised his head, opening his jaws to question Brithilca as his anger ebbed away and was replaced by curiosity.

"The pact is broken," Brithilca said.

Myrkith-visir stilled. He couldn't put his claws on it, but something had felt different for a while.

"I can no longer move beyond our lands—I have not the energy needed—but you will be able to stray. The bonds that once held you here are gone."

"Is that not a good thing?" Myrkith-visir asked. "We can expand our territories as we need, for these small islands become too crowded, and I can hunt down the coward Cies myself."

"No," replied Brithilca, with a low growl. "For there are also other, less fortuitous consequences. We are unbound, as are the Eldarkind. Unbound, we are also alone—isolated from each other. We can no longer contact each other, unless by meeting physically. Our two races must remain united to protect all others from those who sleep. You know of whom I speak.

"If they—if He—should awaken, the balance of power will shift in the world, and not in our favour. The breaking of the pact has already begun this process. Already, magic seeps into the void. For the good of all, they must remain asleep. *He* must remain asleep."

TWENTY

Aside from the annoyance caused by his mistress, Zaki had enjoyed returning to Arrans at the head of a victorious army, riding in pride of place beside Janus, the king's own heir.

He had reaped the rewards, taking a cart of treasure as his spoils from the destroyed city. A satisfied Harad had bestowed more gifts upon him: Roherii titles and land near Bera, on the coast, promising it to be some of the most beautiful land in all of Roher.

Zaki was under no illusion that he and Janus were companionable, nor that Harad had no agenda involving him. However, he was content to enjoy the favours at last, not least because it meant escaping from under the watching eyes of the palace to his own residence.

No longer the regis mendicus, he was pleased to confirm.

Zaki had retired to his palace chambers on the day of his return with a spring in his step, glad that he had done what was needed to secure Harad's support for a campaign in Caledan. Harad was, for once, in favour, agreeing that he had proved himself in Ladrin, pleased with Janus's reports on him.

Demara, however, was another matter. It was clear she thought little of their success was attributable to him. Though she did not say it to his face, her views on his return to Caledan were clear.

"It is a foolish idea!" Demara said when Zaki informed her that he would not be there for much longer. "Autumn will be coming soon, and then winter—the weather becomes too unfriendly for you to travel all that way and fight your way to Pandora."

"All I must do is defeat Soren's army."

"Nonsense. I know how your people would react to an army of foreigners entering their kingdom, for they would do the same in

Roher. They would fight to the very death to keep you out."

"I am their king," said Zaki, scowling at her, "whether I have a borrowed army or not. Your father has promised me twelve thousand men, and I am sure I can count on thousands more joining me in Caledan. I will return victorious."

"Must you go so soon?" she asked.

There was no warmth in her tone. He dismissed any notion that she said it out of sentiment. He raised an eyebrow, inviting her to continue.

"I worry for your safety, as it also means my own safety and the safety of our children. Will you rush to go before you should even meet your son?"

"What son?" he said, his mouth drying and his heart leaping in his chest.

"Ours," she said, her eyes narrowing.

Good. She does not know. He nodded, relief flooding him. "Oh, of course. The longer I wait, the stronger Soren grows. I must oust him before he becomes too secure in my throne, before he has time to turn my allies to his cause. He will not expect an attack in this season, which makes it even more advantageous. He will be unprepared—I can sweep through Caledan before there is even an army to defend it. I cannot risk waiting to attack until the spring. But I will admit, I will sleep a great deal easier once I have an heir."

"I will call him Thai," Demara said in a tone brooking no disagreement. "It means 'unyielding' in my tongue."

Zaki smiled, satisfied. "It is a good name. Thai." He tested it on his tongue. "His enemies will cower before him. But you are wrong to be concerned. I will succeed."

"I beseech you, if you bear any love for your children, not to go yet."

"I have no choice. Even if I did not wish to go, I would be duty-bound to. I was born to be the king of my country, not to languish in exile in someone else's court, living as a pauper. Now I have money, influence in court and your father's support in men and arms, I must try."

Men were mustered, armour and weaponry allotted, and Zaki stood at the palace gates ready to ride in a grand procession through Arrans and all the way to Bera to board the fleet of boats conscripted to take him and his men to Caledan via sea.

As was her place, Demara waited at the palace door with Leika and her woman servant attending her; Janus stood in place of Harad to bid him farewell and success.

As he left, he paused first to bow to Janus and accept his token of a royal Roherii sword, an extravagant gold and jewelled piece. Ceremonial or functional, he was not sure, but it was a beautiful weapon nonetheless.

"Do not leave," Demara said as soon as he turned to her. She spoke in a low tone that Janus, retreating back into the cool gloom of the hallway, could not hear.

He sighed. "I have already spoken of this with you. I am going to reclaim my throne."

Demara raised her chin, her mouth set with defiance as she stepped forward, looking up into his eyes with blazing determination.

"If you leave, I will kill your mistress."

Half surprised that she knew, half amused, he laughed, incredulous that she would threaten him. "No you will not." He smiled at her, as an adult would smile to a naive child, but that seemed to anger her more and her cheeks blushed.

"Then I will kill your bastard boy."

Zaki's amusement turned to shock as a cold rush overtook him. *How does she know?* His surprise turned to anger as he realised how she intended to manipulate him. He stepped back, glaring at her. His fingers twitched. But he would not strike her and cause a scene. Not here, not on this day.

"I will do far worse if you lift so much as a finger towards that child."

Demara turned and stormed inside the front door. The maid, carrying Leika, followed. On silent hinges, the doors slid closed with

421

the smallest thud as the guards stood to one side.

After a moment's pause, Zaki unfroze. He fixed a glowing smile upon his face, turned and walked down the steps to mount his horse and join the front of the parade.

From the sweeping balcony of her father's quarters overlooking Arrans, Demara watched her husband leave, standing in seething anger with Seline beside her. As the great column of men wended its way down the hill, disappearing between the tall buildings, she deliberated, drumming her fingers upon the balustrade.

As if reading her mind, Seline moved forward to stand beside her. "Will you do as you threatened him?"

Demara shrugged. "I dislike him—nay, perhaps I still loathe him in parts—for he is as selfish and self-serving as always. I feel a fool for ever thinking otherwise, for ever softening towards him. He thinks of his own goals—Leika and I are nothing but pawns to him. Yet perhaps I spoke in haste. Should I punish another for his sins? Especially a child?"

Demara fell silent for a moment. "If I know anything, it is that a child should never be held responsible for the choices of their parents," she muttered. Her own mother had been banished by Harad when he grew tired of her and desired his fourth wife—Demara had never seen her again. It was not something she liked to dwell on.

"A child he may be, but he is a threat to you and yours," Seline replied.

Demara knew she was right, but it was impossible to condemn another babe to death when the comforting warmth of her own was cradled against her chest. She handed Leika to Seline, folded her arms and turned away.

"I know I cannot tolerate that, nor appear weak by not carrying out what I threatened. I fear I have backed myself into a corner."

"When Zaki returns, if he finds you have not raised a finger, your strength will be lost. You must follow through on your promises, or he will never fear you again, nor take you seriously. If you wish, I can make the arrangements—it will wash the guilt from your hands in some part. Would you like me to do this for you?"

Demara considered. *How easy would it be to be rid of this faceless woman and her babe?* But the face that swam in her mind was the face of the son she yearned for, with her own eyes, skin and hair. She ground her teeth in frustration.

"I cannot do it. But I will be rid of her one way or another. Let me consider it."

It consumed her that day. She was unable to go forward with her threats, but unable to distract herself either. At last she found a solution.

"Seline!" she called her maid, who ran from the other room.

"Yes, mistress?"

"Come, sit! I have an idea. I do not have to kill him. Her I worry not for, but I would save the child from his parents' follies if I could. I can ensure they are no longer a threat to me." Her eyes glittered and her smile was wide with enthusiasm.

"I will exile them," Demara said with a smug smile. "What think you? I will confiscate all her goods—as they are doubtless paid for with my dowry, they are mine by right anyway—and cast her and the babe out of Roher altogether. Then, her fate is in the hands of the gods."

Seline did not answer, but Demara could tell that she pondered something.

"What?"

Seline frowned. "She will die—they both will. I do not criticise you, lady, but how is this any different to having them killed? If anything, perhaps it is more cruel, as they will both suffer at your hands—and you wish to avoid harming the boy. Will your conscience be clear?"

"The gods have been good to me," explained Demara. "Their blessings brought me—us—back to our homeland. They have given me a beautiful girl and a boy soon to follow. Why, they have, in a strange way, even rid me of my husband. Perhaps they have given me everything I could dream of.

"Praying every day to the Mother to protect me has brought me what I sought—if this woman is as devout as she should be, then she will survive or quickly perish. I have asked for the Mother's understanding and blessing in this difficult matter. I am sure that She will continue to favour me."

And if She does, then this woman and her babe will die by the gods' own hands, not mine. Who could survive outside Arrans with no food, water, money or shelter, and with a babe? Even the gods could not grant her that much favour, unless by a miracle. If they are of a mind to be merciful, they will grant her a swift end.

"As you wish."

"I cannot wait another day—ready the guards."

The translucent veils of fabric shrouding the palanquin and hiding Demara from view rippled in the light breeze as she sat up for a better look, peering through the fabric.

Before her was the house Seline had spoken of—the maid accompanied her upon horseback, mounted in silence to her right— but Demara had not passed it before. She looked over the tall, painted walls topped with their clean, ridged, terracotta tiles and draped in green, leafy boughs with a twang of envy. It was far more pleasant than she had expected.

Guards blocked her view as they opened the gate and barged up the path. Minutes later, servants fled in a ruckus, running this way and that in confusion as they encountered the still and silent rank of soldiers upon the street, without a glance in her direction.

Demara saw a green garden space through the gate and the hint of a beautiful house within. Annoyance surged within her that she had not been able to enjoy such a nice home with her husband and had instead been shut up in a cold and dreary castle in Caledan.

So, this is what my dowry has been squandered upon.

Demara watched, all sympathy lost, as a woman was dragged

out by several men. The moment they released her, she threw herself back through the gate, ran to the house and tried to shut the door. Before she could, they were upon her again, with grim faces this time as they marched her out.

She was beautiful, Demara begrudgingly admitted, but that, she had expected. She was almost naked too, for Demara had ordered that all of the woman's possessions be taken; they belonged to her since she owned the coin that paid for them.

As the men pulled the woman onto the street, they ripped the few remaining fabrics from her figure. The clothes were damaged beyond repair and Demara would not have touched them in any case, but that was besides the point. It was the principle. Demara smiled in cold satisfaction.

Hunched over and shrunk into herself, the woman tried to conceal her modesty with her hands. Demara heard her wailing, begging the guards to stop.

The head of the guard stepped forward with a scroll of paper and read from it in a loud, carrying voice so that all around could hear.

"You, of the name Tulia, belonging to no house or family, are hereby exiled from all of Roher and its territories with immediate effect. You may not reside in any place within the state henceforth and must exit the country immediately, never to return. You may take your possessions with you, but any land and property you hold is forfeited to the crown."

"You would not even let me have my clothes?" Tulia shrieked. "You would rather tear them off me than see me wear them?"

"These possessions are not your own but bought with the coin of another, and no doubt tricked from that person. Be glad that you are not charged with other crimes for which you are most likely guilty! I'll have your jewellery too. Your earrings—give them to me before I rip them out."

Demara could not see the man's face, but his voice was flat and altogether un-compassionate.

Tulia paused for a moment, her mouth gaping as she looked at him with wide eyes.

He started towards her, but she edged back, holding up her arms before extracting her dangling earrings—gold and jewel studded, Demara noticed—with shaking hands and handing them to him along with the matching necklace and anklet.

Another man stepped forward, thrusting the naked child at her.

"Take your mongrel and get out."

She cradled the babe to her chest, sinking to the floor, but as the men drew their swords she cried out and ran away barefooted, disappearing down a side street. Several guards gave chase to make sure she left the city boundaries.

Demara heaved a deep sigh of relief, reclining back onto the sumptuous, plump cushions. Coldly satisfied, she gestured for her bearers to return her home. Seline remained behind to ensure nothing went missing from Demara's new house.

TWENTY ONE

Since Asquith's deposition, Edmund had taken charge of the royal accounts. They were well kept; for all Asquith's shortcomings, he seemed to be an excellent accountant. As Edmund presented the finances to Soren, he pointed out the lone error that had outwitted his problem solving.

"Every month, the same amount—yet I cannot figure out where it goes," Edmund said, frowning.

"Forty-seven silver coins. By no means a small amount," Soren relied.

"No. Such an error is of no matter to the crown, yet it piques my interest that it is an identical amount and has been taken every thirty days for over half a year."

"No receipts or notes of any kind to explain its purpose?"

"None at all, sire. I have been through the records with a fine comb several times. Not a trace to be found, except in one case, where a paper details the money's passage south—nothing more than that."

Soren tapped his fingers upon the desk. *South. South of here could be anywhere, for anything.* "Who has access to that fund?"

Edmund paused before he answered. "Behan."

Soren's eyes widened.

"I cannot fathom it. He has no need of this money, if he is indeed responsible," Edmund mused, worrying his beard with a hand. "Theft seems unlikely."

Soren ordered for Behan to be summoned, but a messenger returned bearing word of Behan's absence and with no idea when he would return or where he could be. Soren gritted his teeth, frustrated after the wait. "As soon as he arrives, send him to me," he said. Once the man left, he continued. "Have you the note?"

Edmund flicked through the sheaf of papers, slipping one out from their midst. "Here."

Soren scanned its contents. "'T. Collado. South, by hand of' ... scribbled out 'to'... scribbled out... 'by order of'... that is blacked out too. Hmm. What does 'Collado' mean?"

Edmund chewed his lip, staring at the rough script. "Perhaps a name, as it's capitalised. T. Collado," Edmund said, sounding the name out. He froze. "If I am not mistaken, that name is Roherii!"

Soren's head snapped up. "Does this mean that our own Lord Steward sends funds to Roher—to Zaki?"

"It could, I suppose," said Edmund, but he fell silent, staring at the note.

"We crushed any hope of Zaki regaining the throne with help from Caledan. Why would he do such a thing? He has status, power, wealth. What more can he want?" Soren's breathing quickened.

"I do not know. Perhaps more of the same. Men can be greedy. Or perhaps he believes Zaki should sit the throne."

"I would believe it of others, yet not of him." *What are his motives?* Soren tapped his foot upon the floor without thinking. *Would he betray me too? It seems I can only trust those in house Arendall, or perhaps everyone crosses me. No, it's not healthy to think like this. What do I do?*

"Without Behan here to answer for himself, it is difficult to say."

"Call the council," Soren said with a heavy heart. "Perhaps someone else knew of this."

Edmund glanced up from his reverie. "Are you sure it is wise to share this?"

"My council is there for times of crisis. Perhaps they can shed light on this before we rush to conclusions—I cannot wait with the burden of this knowledge." *I cannot bear to think that the person I trust most after Edmund could deceive me.*

Everyone besides the Lord Steward appeared at the council. They listened without a sound as Edmund explained his findings and asked them for any knowledge they had of the matter. Blank faces exchanged glances; shoulders were shrugged.

"Collado *is* a Roherii family name," said Lady Felra with confidence. She represented her mother, Lady Elsard, the head of House Orrell, on the council.

Beside her, Lord Heligan nodded, murmuring his agreement but looking troubled.

"So he is sending money to Roher, then," Willam of Walbridge said.

"Well, we cannot be sure," answered Edmund. "Perhaps the recipient has an unfortunate sur—"

"No Roherii would be welcome in Caledan," Felra cut in. "He is betraying the crown."

As you would know how to, Soren could not help but think as his eyes flicked towards her. He was about to speak, but Heligan's mouth opened first.

"Lord Behan is a great friend to the crown, as you should all know," he said with indignance. "Throughout Soren's absence, Behan remained loyal and was the first to welcome him home, even putting his own life in danger to do so. He may have many different agendas, many different responsibilities, many different purposes, but he remains throughout all of them devoted to Caledan."

"Devoted to Caledan does not infer devotion to our king," Felra said snidely.

"He shall, however, be given the chance to explain," Soren said, glancing around the table to each person. His voice was quiet, but Felda's words had riled him. *So eager to condemn others when your own house was guilty!* Heligan's devotion to his friend Behan had reassured Soren that he was not wrong to trust the steward, though Behan still had questions to answer before Soren could be sure his confidence was well placed.

At that moment, as if fate had summoned him, Behan burst in, red faced and wheezing, his apology for tardiness punctuated with many gasps. Behan seemed surprised to find the mood of the council sour, though as Edmund explained again for his benefit what he had found, he became more unfathomable. He watched Edmund though half-lidded eyes and with his hands clasped across his belly as he sat listening.

Edmund invited him to speak.

"The council will know nothing of this, for I acted alone," Behan said without fear or shame.

Felra sat forward in her chair, a predatory smile upon her face. "You admit treason!"

"I admit no such thing," said Behan, glaring at her. "If you will listen." He made a point of waiting until she subsided back into her seat before he continued.

"I have been sending funds every thirty days to a man named Tobias Collado, a Roherii national residing in Bera, outside Roher's capital. A gem of a find, he is one of my finest spies in Roher. Collado sends me word of Zaki's movements and any plans of Harad's that he can discover. He is situated within Zaki's household, acting as his interpreter."

"I knew you were not guilty of any scheming," said Heligan, beaming at his friend.

Soren frowned, however. "Be that as it may, why did you not tell me of this before? Why have I heard no news from Roher?"

"There are problems with the line of communications, in the first instance," said Behan. "News often goes amiss or arrives weeks later than it ought to. The Caledonian ambassador sends news back monthly, but I know his words are censored as his letters are checked on Harad's orders and, as a result, never contain anything of real use. We dare not use codes.

"Tobias is far more open—hence why we pay him so well, for all the risk he takes—and sends us monthly reports by sea, which arrive more reliably than the land caravans do. I have not spoken to you thus far as there has been little to report.

"Zaki is well, and has been away campaigning with Harad's eldest son in Ladrin of late. I have yet to hear of his return, safe or otherwise, though I expect Tobias's next correspondence any day. I'll admit that I did not wish to disturb you with any news of your uncle," Behan continued, his voice dropping in volume. "I do not wish to cause you distress."

"Your consideration is appreciated, Behan," Soren replied after a pause, "but unwarranted. Please keep me informed henceforth."

"Yes, sire."

Soren let the council go, keeping Behan back for a quiet word, feeling guilty about his handling of the matter.

"We did try to summon you to speak in private," Soren said to Behan, feeling as though he needed to make amends. "I did not mean to escalate this, but discover if the council had any information to support you, though it becomes clear some of them wish to harm others to feather their own nests. I apologise for ever doubting you and hope that this will not cause any ill feelings between us."

"Well, I must confess I feel somewhat stung to be thought a traitor by some, but I know you act in Caledan's best interests. I understand the pressures you are under to surround yourself with strong council," replied Behan. His tone seemed cool and his glance veiled, with little warmth, but Soren took his words at face value.

"Thank you, Lord Steward, for all that you do."

Behan bowed and left without another word.

"Your Majesty!"

Soren heard Behan's voice before he saw him. The old man ran up the corridor as fast as his short legs would carry him, his beard bouncing on his rounded stomach with each step. Behan stumbled to a halt before him, bent double as he caught his breath. All Soren could see was the top of his bright red scalp peeking through his thinning hair.

"Your Majesty, urgent news," Behan forced out, straightening up. "Zaki is coming."

An icy coldness flooded Soren's body. "W-what?" he stammered.

"Zaki is coming, Soren," Behan repeated, aghast. "Tobias sent word—but it is weeks old—we must act! Harad sends men with him—many thousands—travelling by sea all the way from Roher.

Zaki plans to land near to the border on the isthmus to open the land route and hold the town of Braith and, with it, the border."

Soren swore, sinking into the wall for support. Its cold stone made him feel worse.

"Assemble everyone," he said as his belly lurched. "I will ride out tomorrow with whatever company we can make. Muster everyone who can fight and have them follow!"

Soren did not sleep that night, plagued again by the nightmares he had been so glad to be rid of. When the dawn came, he was already dressed and about his business organising supply trains, armour, weapons, men and mounts—everything he would need to reach Braith and the border before Zaki.

I'm not ready for this. The thought taunted him. It had, he realised with a jolt, been almost a year since he had been crowned. *A whole year and still I feel no safer, still I am not rid of Zaki.*

His mind drifted to members of those houses who were less than supportive. He feared their actions, though all had agreed the previous night at an emergency council meeting to accompany him and pledge men, arms and provisions.

At least they are with me—where I can watch them.

It was a long march south, hindered by those on foot and the slow, oxen-drawn waggons of supplies. But with every town they passed, more joined to swell Soren's ranks as the news of an impending Roherii invasion spread. If nothing else, his enemies would be united with him to repel an invasion by foreign soldiers, even if led by Zaki, Soren hoped.

His small company of hundreds of men from Pandora grew to a host of thousands; Arendall, Varan, Walbridge, Duncombe and even Lunder joined him as they followed the River Lowen through Edmund's county.

Soren looked back at each high point they crested to see a line of men trailing into the distance beyond the horizon through the sleepy rolling downs that were hazy in the heat of late summer. He could not help but feel a twinge of awe that they followed him.

As they crossed the hills into Balaur land, approaching Lowenmouth, Lord Andor himself rode out with a force of almost a thousand men drafted from his county, leaving the same amount to keep Lowenmouth, which was to be their strategic retreat if needed.

Heartened by the support, Soren marched on, feeling somewhat reassured about his chances of repelling Zaki and the Roherii from Caledan, but they had taken too long to muster and too long to travel. Andor confirmed his worst fears.

"I have been watching, as have all my vessels in the bay. Zaki will have already arrived at the border. I have no news from Braith this week, but I suspect it will not come."

"Perhaps they can hold him off."

"Perhaps." Andor said no more, but Soren knew what remained unspoken. Zaki brought a great host upon a small town, possibly from their own side of the border and without the safety of the wall that closed off the isthmus from the mainland.

They have no chance of victory if Zaki attacks.

Within a few more days they were close enough for Soren's mounted scouts to bring back news of Zaki's forces—sighted at last—as the main bulk of Soren's nine thousand men made their way up and over the last high hill pass into Rainsford's border county.

The news was grim. They were too close for comfort. Soren halted his men and gave word for them to retreat. Here, there were no bridges to destroy, such luxuries reserved for more well-travelled routes. The fords would cause Zaki little hindrance, Soren knew.

Beyond that the scouts could give little detail, but the column of smoke rising high into the sky told its own story. They were many miles from Braith, but its fate was clear. Soren's heart sank at the sight as he watched it bloom, stony faced, with Edmund as ever beside him.

"The border has fallen," said Soren. "We must make a new one that he cannot cross."

"The passes," replied Edmund as Soren thought it.

"Is the one we came down though the easiest, largest and most direct?"

Edmund nodded, his eyes still fixed upon the smoke.

"If we direct Zaki to that pass, then we will have the best chance of holding the hills, and Caledan. Have everyone fall back to the valley. Who shall hold it?" Soren asked Edmund.

"Give me the charge," said Edmund. "I will see that Zaki does not pass."

TWENTY TWO

Eve's ankle had long since healed, but she was more ill than ever before, bedridden and wasting away with depression. Her father had given up on trying to rouse her each morning, and left her in quiet solitude. The maid came in to open and close the shutters, set the fire, light and douse the lamps and feed her, but Eve was so unresponsive that even the maid had stopped talking to her.

Her days were spent inside, in bed, and she rarely rode Alia anymore, having become fed up with being followed everywhere she went by her father's men, who called her back if she strayed too far from home. Gone were the solitary trips to the moors and beyond that fed her joy.

Her marriage loomed ahead, first months away, then weeks. A dress had been made, the ceremony and feasting afterwards planned and paid for. There was nothing left but to travel to Pandora for the celebration—not that Eve associated that word with her upcoming nuptials.

It was the best news she could have hoped for, hearing of the coming invasion, for it meant that all events were cancelled. Eve struggled not to smile when her father informed her with a drawn face, but her relief faded when her father revealed he would be going to fight.

"Must you?" Eve had never experienced battle, but she knew enough to understand it placed her father in grave danger.

"It is my duty to protect king and country, Eve. I wish it were otherwise—I'm too old for this—but I cannot ask my men to fight when I do not."

"Am I to stay here?"

"Of course!" Karn seemed shocked that she would think otherwise. "I am most certainly not allowing you accompany me.

You are my heir—the only heir—to house Arrow. I must keep you safe."

"Perhaps I would be safer in Ednor?" Eve dared to suggest, holding her breath as she waited for an answer.

Her father scowled. "I thought we had put this to bed," he muttered. "Who would run Arrow county and oversee Arlyn?" he said in a louder voice.

"Your steward—he knows far more than I do and can manage everything in your absence." Karn remained silent, so Eve pushed on. "I need to go there to train. How else will I manage my skills? Artora warned me they could be dangerous if I remained uneducated," she improvised. "Please?"

"I worry that you will become someone else if I let you go there again."

"Consider it, Father—please."

Karn nodded and left. Eve jumped out of bed and punched the air, a wide smile fixed to her face. *This is the best day! Please, Father, please let me go.*

She did not have to wait long for her reply; her father summoned her that evening.

"I will let you go," Karn said with no preamble, though his voice was less than enthusiastic, "because I sense I have no choice. The moment I leave, I have a feeling that you will be upon a horse riding north whether I like it or not." His accusing glare penetrated her.

Eve coloured. *I had considered that,* she admitted to herself whilst widening her eyes in feigned innocence.

Her father had mustered in two days, and so it was then that they parted at the gates of Arlyn. Karn was not dressed for battle—to ride so for weeks would be too tiresome—but his saddlebags bulged with his armour, freshly polished and maintained. His newly sharpened sword hung from his waistline—a long, slim blade in a scabbard of new blackened, tanned leather.

Karn had trimmed his hair and beard for the occasion and rode in his finest outdoor clothes with a light cloak to keep the late summer morning chill away. A silver arrowhead, the mark of the family, clasped his cloak close about his neck, glinting as it caught the sun.

Eve rode similarly outfitted, her armour—gifted to her by Artora on her previous trip to Ednor—stowed in her own panniers. Her bow and quiver hung from the pommel; it had been months since Eve had used them, but it felt wrong to ride without them. Belted at her own waist was Artora's dagger, and hidden at the very bottom of her baggage was the scrying mirror in its dark case.

Eve drank in all the details of her father before her. Time seemed to slow. Reluctant to part, they stood there as Arlyn's men assembled around them, women and children milling around as they said their farewells, passed on last messages and gifted tokens of luck onto their loved ones.

Yet they could not delay forever. Karn called for his men to assemble and rode to the front of the column, Eve beside him upon Alia. Karn leaned across to clasp her in a one-armed hug, kissing her upon the top of her head.

"Be safe, my little dove. I will return soon. Make the best of your training, for we do not know where the coming weeks will lead us."

Eve said goodbye to her father, feeling unsettled, and watched as they left. The column marched past her for ages: a long line of men—some mounted, some not—followed by donkey-led carts of provisions that rattled as they rolled along. Despite still being cut off from the powers of the old tongue, she could not help but mutter a blessing in it.

"*By all the powers that be, keep him safe.*"

Soon, there were two left beside her: Nyle and another guard, Olly, whom she knew by sight, to accompany her to Ednor and then return to Arlyn. Eve had not been anticipating this.

Nyle had suffered a demotion at the hands of her father after her last Ednor adventure. Despite her setting things right by reversing this, Nyle had not forgiven her, and the incident in the woods after her betrothal had served to anger him further. Nyle, ever professional, was never rude or improper, but his icy demeanour towards her was unpleasant to bear.

The ride to Ednor was spent in silence. Eve was glad when, days later, they crested the hill onto the secret valley. Nyle halted at once, unwilling to set foot inside the place, a shadow upon his face at the view, whilst Olly stared in open-mouthed awe at the unexpected sight before him.

Somehow, it had already been over an entire year since Eve had bid farewell to her Eldarkind kin at Pandora, and even longer still since she had set foot in Ednor, met Artora, the queen of the Eldarkind, and learnt of the significance of her kinship to their race.

She thought of Ednor most days, but her memory of this place had faded and the sight of it before her so brilliant and vivid she could not help but stare with Olly. Her recollection did not do Ednor justice.

"We will leave you here?" said Nyle, breaking her reverie. It was veiled as a request, but Eve knew that Nyle would go no further with her. It did not matter, in any case. Free of them, she could race to Ednor and her kin. Her safety in the valley was no issue.

Eve nodded with a wide grin. "I thank you for your services and release you both to ride home. Watch Arlyn well for my father. Please send word the moment he returns, if I am not already there myself."

As Nyle and Olly trotted back down the mountain following the trail they had arrived by, Eve urged Alia on and thundered over grassy meadows that rolled all the way to the forests across the valley. As she drew nearer, excitement shot around her body, sending nerves tingling as her anticipation grew.

Eve could not decide who she was more eager to see: Nolwen and Nelda—the sibling Eldarkind who had accompanied and safeguarded her on her quest to rescue Soren's sister Irumae from the hands of Zaki—or Artora, the queen of the Eldarkind.

Her fondness for Nolwen and Nelda, after their shared adventure, was tempered by her desire to ask Artora for help in restoring and honing her magical abilities. Whilst she had spent most of her life without them, their loss was still a great and bewildering blow she could not understand.

The grass rolled under her feet as she raced through fragrant flower patches, birds wheeling high overhead and calling out as if to greet her. The further Alia cantered, the more Eve could feel the tingle within her head growing—the faintest connection to her magic returning. Whether it was her own relief at her changing fortunes or perhaps some resonating presence within the valley, she did not know or care, such was her joy.

Her fear that she had lost that part of her forever had been as great. She whooped in relief, startling Alia, but things fell quiet when she met the deciduous woodlands at the other side of the valley some hours later, and her excitement tempered. There was little bird song here. Eve was sure she remembered a cacophony of choruses when she last passed through.

When she reached the first of the sprawling buildings that marked Ednor, the sense of wrongness grew. The light had faded, the brilliance and vividness of the colours drained, though the end of summer was still a while away.

Perhaps autumn comes early here, Eve mused. The word *sombre* sprung to mind as she rode up and through Ednor. At last she met some of her kin, but they did not laugh and converse in lilting voices as they had a year ago. Now they were subdued and quiescent, watching her pass with inscrutable faces.

Eve's excitement waned, draining with every length she rode Alia, until only a sense of foreboding remained.

To the Eldarkind guarding the way at the height of Ednor, she held up her hand in greeting before sliding down from Alia.

"Good day, sir," she said in the Eldar tongue. "I am Lady Eve of Arlyn. I request the pleasure of an audience with the queen, if I may."

He looked at her, frowning. "Have you not heard, sister?" he said. He executed a smooth bow. "Forgive me, I do not mean to speak out of turn. Follow me." He whistled and called for someone to lead Alia to the stables before marching through the gates of Artora's abode with Eve in tow.

Eve hurried to keep up with the tall Eldarkind's large strides as she thought over his words. *Have I not heard what?* she asked herself, feeling apprehensive.

Despite the strange feeling lurking in the pit of her stomach, Eve expected her distant aunt to greet her, but when she at last arrived at Artora's office, the guards stepped forward to bar her way.

"None may pass," said the first.

"I beg for audience with the queen," said Eve. "I am Lady Eve, come from Arlyn to seek the refuge and training she once offered me."

"None may pass," said the second.

"Let her through," a low voice called from within.

In synchronisation, the guards bowed and parted before Eve.

As she entered, Eve saw the tall, airy room that she remembered, with high glass-paned windows looking out over the alpine meadows, but a diminished figure sat in Artora's place, hunched over the desk.

The person looked up—limp, pale hair trailing over her shoulders—as Eve entered. Her face rose from the shadows, and Eve realised with a jolt it was Artora who sat before her. She sunk into a deep curtsy before the queen.

"Your Majesty," she murmured, pausing in the curtsy to compose herself. Her voice was steady, but her heart pounded. *What has happened to her?*

"Lady Eve." Artora smiled, but it was a weary smile that soon faded from her face. Artora rose with care from behind the desk and shuffled forward to greet Eve, but her usual languid grace was lacking, and instead Eve could see that each movement pained her.

The once radiant glow of Artora's skin had gone. It was now sallow and pale, almost grey in pallor, sunk into her cheeks and eye sockets. Her bony fingers reached out to clasp Eve's hand. Her skin was cool to the touch—too cold, sapping Eve's own warmth away from her—and hard, the healthy plumpness of the queen's figure gone.

Even her eyes seemed to belong to another—no longer wells of light and laughter, but pits of weariness and something else Eve could not identify. Pain? Fear? Despair? Eve struggled not to stare at her in morbid shock and fascination.

"Eve, you are most welcome." Artora kissed her upon the forehead.

They sat, Eve supporting Artora back as they made their way to her desk first, and Artora rang a small tinkling bell at her fingertips. Moments later a tray of food materialised upon the desk, forming from nothing, and next to it, a steaming pot and two cups.

Eve would have revelled at the sight of magic once more, after so long, but her jubilance was drowned with concern for her sickening relation.

Artora enquired after her health and that of her father, picking at small morsels on the tray of caramelised nuts and small cakes. Eve answered her, but did not dare ask Artora after her own health. Eve explained why she had come, and Artora reiterated her offer of help.

"You are free to stay as long as you wish. I will see to it that you have the training you need to manage your skills," Artora said. "I would oversee this myself, but as you can see—and as you are far too polite to mention—you do not find me in the best health of late."

Eve held her breath, not daring to comment one way or the other.

"I have been ill a while, alas," Artora murmured. "It began almost a year ago, though I did not notice it at first. It grows worse each passing week." She shook her head. "None could have foreseen, of course. The pact has broken and the consequences manifest." She looked up at Eve, her gaze full of sadness.

"How did it happen? What does it mean?" Eve asked, confused. *Surely it is an agreement, nothing more?* She could not remember what Artora had said about it the year before. She dove into her memory for any recollection.

"The dragons strayed too far from both their territory and their agreement not to intervene in the bloodline of the throne's business. It began with Brithilca's removal of the crown from Pandora, but the young dragons leaving their lands to restore Soren without permission were its death knell, though he would have failed without their assistance. The pact unravels as a result. All our magic, in place to protect our own races, the humans, and others in the world, crumbles.

"The consequences are more dire than can be imagined. If I thought I felt a darkness growing within the world a year ago, it is nothing compared to the desolation I see before us. Things are waking which should have forever remained asleep," she said, her voice so quiet that Eve had to strain to hear her.

Artora shivered, clutching at her cup for warmth. "Our old enemy rises; He waxes as we wane. His kith and kin will grow stronger as we fail."

"Who is He?" Eve could not help but ask, unable to imagine a person more dangerous or powerful than the Eldarkind, or even dragons.

Once more Artora turned her baleful look upon Eve. "He is Bahr of the fire, a being of pure energy and magic from the days of the formation of the world itself. An elemental, we name His species to be."

Eve's lips parted as she heard the word. *An elemental.* That word she remembered from her last visit to Ednor. *The creators of all upon the earth. But wait, Artora said the elementals diminished to unknown places.* She repeated this thought aloud.

"Not all elementals were as noble as those who gave their energy to create life," she said, her tone dark. "Some were dangerous—too dangerous—but with the power to kill them by magical means gone with the fall of Death, who had not limited the life force of the elementals themselves, only the power of binding remained. And so we bound them, together with the aid of the dragons.

"Into the pact we sung their binding—forever were they to

sleep, unrising, unless the pact itself were broken." Artora shook her head. "The breaking of the pact was something we had never considered could happen, such were the wards and guards we put in place—but the dragons have doomed us all.

"As the keeper of my people, I bear this burden the greatest, but my people begin to weaken and fail too, and there is nothing that I can do to prevent it."

"Can you not replace the bindings—remake the pact?" said Eve.

"If we remained at our full strength, then yes—but alas, we do not. Our magic has faded over time, but with the breaking of the pact it seems what remains spills away. My ability to scry outside Ednor's borders wanes, and I cannot contact the dragons anymore. Every member of my kind that I send to pass word to them, to scout in Caledan or to confirm that Bahr still remains bound does not return. I fear the worst."

"What will happen if he—Bahr—rises?"

"It sounds like a prophecy of the worst kind, but it would mean death and destruction for us all. His retribution will be swift and terrible, yet we cannot stand before him, though we must try. The Eldarkind and the dragons will be gone forever. I fear who will catch his attention next, for they will also be doomed."

"Is there no hope?" Eve said in a small voice, wondering why Artora had chosen to share this with her.

"There is always hope," Artora said, favouring her with the warmest smile she could muster.

Eve remained unconvinced.

"If we can prevent him from rising, it will go a great way towards protecting all of us," Artora added. "Perhaps, if we are fortunate, we may yet even prevent the entire loss of our powers."

"How can that be done?" Eve latched on to the idea.

"I cannot be sure, though I have my ideas. The binding needs replacing, but those with magic cannot venture near Him. We have already tried and failed. If my theory that our magic is our undoing is correct, then one of mortal blood could succeed where we have failed," said Artora. She shook her head. "Yet who would undertake such a great task for us when few humans know of our existence? And how can a mortal stand before Bahr and live? I have even thought of asking you in the hope that your human blood would be enough, but I shrink from asking you to risk yourself."

"If I were to volunteer," Eve said slowly, "what would I need to do?"

"First, we need news of Caledan."

"I can give you that with ease," Eve said, and reported recent events to Artora, who looked more troubled as she spoke, which Eve did not think was possible.

"If Caledan is once more in danger from war, it is more urgent that Bahr be stopped so we do not face perils on two fronts. Bahr sleeps far in the north. The snow and ice lessens his power, you see, but that is not enough to keep him in slumber should his bonds weaken too far or break.

"We need information—does Bahr still sleep? How deeply? Then we could use that to try and find a solution." Artora stilled for a second, a light flickering in her eyes. "Perhaps your magic could aid us as much as your mortal status. If indeed your human blood protects you from weakening as my kin do, your magic might also remain undiminished. Perhaps you could deepen the bindings upon him."

Eve hesitated as Artora looked at her with expectation. "I haven't been able to access my magic for many months," Eve admitted.

To her surprise, Artora smiled. "And you are afraid that it will never return?"

"Yes." Eve chewed her lip. The faint tingle was still there, but it felt so remote it was as intangible as smoke.

"Never fear," said Artora. "I can feel it within you. It is strong and very much alive. You will have to coax it forth again; once we commence your training, you will feel it blossom once more. Worrying about it will not help you."

Eve's stomach unclenched, the knot of worry that had built within her for months, becoming heavier and heavier with its burden, easing. It did not disappear—for Eve did not dare hope too much at Artora's words, after her own failed attempts to reconnect with her magical abilities—but she trusted in Artora enough to entertain the possibility.

"Do not decide in haste," said Artora, perhaps mistaking Eve silence for thinking about Artora's need for information. "You may of course stay here. You require much training before you are ready to harness your powers, let alone to lay a binding."

TWENTY THREE

The fleet stretched to the horizon and beyond as crafts of all sizes carried Zaki's twelve thousand men to Caledan. Zaki was glad when the isthmus, the land bridge linking Caledan to the continent, was at last sighted stretching north, for it meant the end of weeks of unpleasant sailing on rough waters. His own ship—the finest of them all—stunk of the vomit and excrement of hundreds of men, and the fresh water had long since run out, meaning that many of the men drank brewed drinks, which caused no end of fights on board. The food was terrible—they had no fire, so all rations were cold and, by the end of the journey, soggy too. All combined, Zaki felt permanently nauseous.

Zaki could not have been happier to put his feet on land—but it felt even better to step onto Caledonian land, even if for the first few steps he stumbled, still swaying with the motion of the ship, although he was no longer upon it.

His men marshalled with what little they had as the vessels withdrew. Zaki did not allow them a comfort stop. They had been doing little enough on the voyage, and he counted rowing as menial work that only some of the crew could do at any one time. The weather was colder than Roher and made him loathe to tarry. Zaki had grown soft in his time away, forgetting how biting the winter winds could be.

It took a day's slow march to reach the town of Braith, which guarded the border, but Zaki was in no rush. After Janus's successful use of the strategy in Ladrin, Zaki planned to attack under cover of night, and he wanted his forces fresh. It would be an easy task with so many men—he would require but a fraction of them—but even so, they had a long road ahead of them and battle after that, and he could not afford to fail again. It weighed heavy on his mind.

Waiting for the early sunset and concealed behind nearby hills, he sent scouts out that afternoon. In the distance, the dark grey band of the border's wall was visible. There marked the narrowest point of the isthmus, where the seas had gnawed the earth away over the many years until the wall sat upon deep cliffs that, near the edge, were at a terrible risk of erosion. Parts of the wall were at the bottom of the sea; in the hundreds of years since its construction, the pounding waters had claimed some of its length.

What remained guarded the way: a tall wall, several men high and thick, which would require an army with siege warfare to break. It had not fallen yet, because on the other side of it lay vast plains and then deserts that would not support even a man, let alone an army, as Zaki had discovered from his own experiences.

There was a single entrance—a series of three gates guarding the way—but Zaki did not need to concern himself with them. He had already foiled their defences, for they were meant to prevent a land approach from the south, but could not stop him landing ships far to the north of the wall itself. Braith, on the other hand, lay defenceless before him. To the southern side of the town a stone wall rose—the predecessor to the border's defences and shadow of their glory—but on the north side, as the town expanded, a series of wooden palisades was all that defended Braith.

It was too easy for Zaki, who after sunset set out with two thousand of his men armed with bows, rag-tipped arrows and small barrels of oil, in addition to their short, thick swords. He wasted no time. They set the palisade afire with flaming arrows as soon as they were within range. Some kindled, though much remained smoking, too damp to catch. Where it didn't catch, they battered it down to force a way through, instead setting the thatched roofs on fire.

Swords out, his men advanced through the town, sacking it as they went and cutting down anyone they encountered who resisted them, indiscriminate of age or class. Zaki ordered his men to allow women and children to flee. After the cruelty he had witnessed in Ladrin, he was loath to deliver more.

Civilians streamed across the countryside, fanning over a wide area in their desperation to escape. The element of surprise was key, but Zaki knew they would be of little harm or consequence to him. *They won't make it past the next village.* He watched them disappear into the darkness beyond the glowing area lit by the growing fires.

When the morning came, the town was gone; a charred wall and the blackened remains of buildings were all that remained. Those with stone walls had survived, but they were few and far between.

Zaki had already left. After a brief respite for those who had marched, he led them north.

Zaki rode towards the pass, which rose as a cleft between the two hills. There were many that he could have chosen, but this was the easiest—the lowest, the widest and the most travelled, though not in the winter months—and would allow quick passage into mainland Caledan.

Of those who had fled before them the night before, he had seen nothing, but the few villages they passed were emptied of people, livestock and possessions—in hiding, Zaki presumed, but he cared little either way. Every avoided delay was an advantage to him of speed and surprise.

The pass was unguarded to his knowledge, but he sent men before him, for which he was glad, for they returned with word of others in the hills. He pressed them for details but they were few—they could approach little closer before being spotted.

Reynard was quick to panic. "Do they know we are here? Does Soren already send an army to meet us?"

Zaki shook his head. "It is impossible. It could be those we let free from Braith, those fleeing from the villages, or a small guard in the hills. At worst it could be Rainsford or perhaps Arendall men—we outnumber them. I guarantee that Soren is sat ignorant in Pandora. How could he know we are here? And if he does, he would not have made it in time. Even if he did—we would have met him at the border, no doubt. Worry not."

"Should we at least change our path?"

"Why bother? A detour would cost us valuable time and the other ways north are harder than this one. No wonder they watch the easiest way; Rainsford does so like collecting his tolls. To go further by sea would be an intolerable exercise and even more time consuming.

"The men need to be blooded in battle. Winning so easily will serve to motivate them, and in any case, if we have been spotted, we need to eliminate those who have seen us so that news of our presence does not travel. The more unaware Soren is, the simpler this will be."

Upon his command, the vanguard surged ahead, led by Reynard, overtaking the body of his forces as they went to dispose of the men up in the pass. Zaki was content to wait in the valley bottom, but their return came much sooner than anticipated.

"Sire, there could be as many as a thousand in the pass. I could not see, but they hold the best positions. I fear they will pick us off at leisure. What are we to do?"

"Damn it!" Zaki swore. He leapt upon his horse—one of the few which had travelled with them—and rode to see what he faced. It was clear to see that, without a leader, his men were already becoming disorganised.

"To me! To me!" Zaki shouted, forcing his way forward. He drew his sword and held it up in the air for all to see: a beacon rallying his men towards him. As he drew closer to the pass, the gradient of the hill becoming steeper and steeper and the valley sides closed in around them. In the surging mess of men around and before him, he spotted arrows flying down from upon high where archers, concealed upon the ridge, shot them one by one.

He yanked the reins of his horse, stopping it so suddenly he had to brace backwards in the saddle to stop himself tumbling forwards over its neck. "Reynard, move the rest of my men on. If we cannot defeat them with tactics, we will overwhelm them by number."

Without a backwards glance or a reply, Reynard bolted down the hill winding his Roherii horn. Its twisting sound echoed around the valley as he blew it once, twice and thrice. He held the third blow as long as he could before it trailed off into silence.

Zaki scanned the heights around him. He could not see a trace of those who shot down upon his men, but before him, some way up the hill, lines of pike men held the pass, stretching across the entire valley. Behind them the banners of Arendall, Kinsley and Varan fluttered in the growing breeze surrounded by many mounted men. Highest of all, he was dismayed to see the royal standard rippling. Zaki barked a choice curse. *Damn it all to hell! How is this possible?*

He searched those on the hill for any sign of his nephew, but he could not find him anywhere. The men before him were indistinguishable in their grey armour—though many of them wore incomplete suits and some leather-made fittings—but he would have been able to spot that made by a royal smith. Instead, his eyes fell on a rare, bare-headed man. *Edmund!*

Zaki bared his teeth in a snarl. *I will kill you!* He was filled with hate and frustration at the sight of the man who had helped to foil everything time and again.

"Charge!" he bellowed at his men, who were beginning to lose enthusiasm. Together, they ploughed forward as one, reinforced by those rising from the valley behind them. Zaki leant down from his saddle to grab one of his men's bows from his hands—a bow meant for those on horseback, though its wielder had no animal to bear him—and an arrow from the quiver on his back. He pulled back on the string before he raised it to his eye level. Used to the heavier draw of a longbow, the bow snapped in his hands, shattering into pieces. The string narrowly missed his face as it snapped back from the force. Cursing, he flung it away and yelled at those around him.

"Kill him above all others!" He pointed towards Edmund, whose green surcoat was visible from this distance. With a knot of men around him, including the lucky few also to have horses, he pushed forward again as his men at last broke the line of pikes. They were through, fighting hand to hand as Caledonian men swept through their ranks. The wave of silver water crashed against the swell of golden fire in an overwhelming cacophony of metal screeching and clashing upon metal as weapons met.

The longer Caledonian swords outreached the shorter Roherii blades, but in the confined space they were unwieldy, giving advantage to the Roherii warriors. Those on horseback fared best, having the room to sweep their swords down upon those below them. The Caledonian men had the upper hand, being on higher ground, so they pressed down upon the Roherii, forcing them back, as the Roherii dodged under their reach and undercut them.

Back and forth they swayed, in a sick dance, as men fell to the floor dead and dying to be replaced with more who stepped in to fill the gaps. Soon the ground—grass and stones bound together with moss, offering firm footing—was dangerous and seemed determined to trip men up as they stood on the fallen and lost their balance or slipped on the slick blood washing down the hillside. The cliffs hemmed them in from both sides, offering no chance to encircle the Caledonians.

The men on horseback around Zaki fired arrows up the hill towards Edmund whilst those on foot protected them with shields; his own was raised too, an impenetrable barrier. Some unfortunate souls were shot from the saddle from those on the clifftops—easy targets for a well-aimed arrow or bolt—falling into their saddles. They were dragged off in short order, others jumping up to fill their places—a horse was a valuable asset in a battlefield. Zaki knew the Roherii placed their own lives above the dignity of their dead in such a situation; as he would do.

He turned back to face the hills. The world slowed. An arrow whizzed past his face, as if he had shot it himself, and dove straight into the shoulder of Edmund's horse. The animal reared. Edmund struggled to keep balance, and his shield arm flung wide to expose his body. The horse crashed back to the ground, jolting him in the saddle.

"Again!" Zaki shouted, meeting a blow from his right hand side. Without thinking, he stabbed down, so driven to reach Edmund, who was temptingly close. It was as if his men could read his mind, for more arrows followed in quick succession before the word had even finished leaving his mouth.

Once more, they struck the horse, but as it turned, presenting side on, one struck Edmund's unguarded thigh before he could raise his shield again, another glanced off his shoulder and a third nestled into his side, finding a chink of weakness through his armour. Zaki saw him cry out, though above the noise of battle—Zaki was sure he was deaf—he could not hear the sound. Edmund retreated, those about him pressing close.

Filled with impatience and reluctance to see him escape, Zaki grabbed the bow from the man next to him, demanding his arrows too. Careful not to draw too far back with this bow, he loosed an arrow. It went wide. In quick succession he shot several more, snatching the arrows from the man's trembling fingers, until at last one did not skitter off Edmund's back.

With the force of this blow, Edmund rocked forward in his saddle, but the arrow held, lodged in his lower back with its barbed point. Zaki's men were still shooting, almost out of arrows. The men around Edmund fell down from their horses or slumped in their saddles as they were hit instead. And then Edmund was out of range, but Zaki could see that he was worse for wear, trotting away up the hill surrounded by others and leaning forwards in his saddle with his head bowed low.

Zaki's shoulder and arms throbbed; out of practice, with bad technique and overexerting unused muscles, he had no doubt he had torn or ruined them, but he did not care. It was worth it to see Edmund suffer, and worth it ten times over if it killed him.

He pressed forward. Those before him crumbled with the loss of their leader, but before him another man stepped up, wielding the Arendall standard. He was armoured and helmed, his voice ringing through the mouth hole.

"To me! For Caledan, to me!"

The Caledonians rallied, but it was to form an orderly retreat back down the pass as darkness fell. Stood at the head of the pass as the Caledonians fled before him, some in panic, Zaki looked down from the horizon with glee that turned to surprise when he beheld the army before him in the valley. It sprawled further than he could see, meandering around the base of the hills.

Reynard rode up beside him.

"What orders, sire?"

Zaki looked him up and down. Reynard was dirty, grubby and looked exhausted. Zaki realised his own poor state. A sudden wave of tiredness overtook his adrenaline.

"We cannot press them through the night. Not with forces that size. Soren is here. The royal standard was raised." He explained what had passed, including his wounding of Edmund.

"May his wounds rot," said Reynard, spitting upon the ground.

"Indeed. I will set men up in the pass overnight—you are to oversee them. We will retreat to the valley. In the morning, we advance."

TWENTY FOUR

Eve was to be housed in a different wing of Artora's sprawling dwelling on this visit, in a secluded room on the ground floor overlooking one of the many meadows carpeted in flowers whose heady scents floated in through the open window. Before she had the chance to rest too long, two familiar figures burst in.

"Well met, cousin." Nolwen grinned, enveloping Eve in a one-armed embrace before passing her to his sister Nelda, who squeezed her tight and kissed her upon both cheeks.

"Nolwen, Nelda, it's so good to see you," Eve replied in the old tongue, realising she had forgotten how infectious their warm personalities were.

They chatted, sharing all their news from the past year. Eve was as surprised to learn that Nolwen and Nelda had not even set foot out of Ednor as they were to learn that she was betrothed to marry someone she did not know—a bizarre notion to the Eldarkind, who, they explained, did not believe in such concepts.

"We were waiting for you to return," said Nelda.

"Not that staying here was a punishment," Nolwen chipped in, winking at Eve.

Eve looked at them with a raised eyebrow.

"We are to teach you the ways of the Eldarkind," revealed Nelda. "Of course, we don't have to be your tutors, you can always ask for someone else, but our offer is there."

"Yes," said Eve before Nelda had quite finished speaking. "You're going to teach me how to use my magic?"

Nelda nodded, her eyes warm. "Artora wished to teach you herself, which is most unusual, but, well… her health of late does not permit that, as you have seen. In her stead, we hope that we will suffice."

"When do we start?" Eve said, her eyes wide in anticipation.

Nolwen and Nelda shared a look. "Well we have nothing else to do today so—now?"

Eve grabbed them both in an excited hug. "Yes please!"

In the middle of a gently sloping meadow far away from any buildings they stood amongst the swaying grass and nodding blooms.

"First, we would like to see what you can already do," said Nolwen.

Eve faltered. *Of course, I haven't told them.* She explained her lost skills to them and the reappearing sensation of her connection to the energy stream within her.

"We can help you," said Nolwen. "Until you come back into your powers, we can emulate them. Even our presence working magic near to you will stimulate its return. See?"

He muttered under his breath something Eve could not hear. In the palm of his hand a spinning flower grew from thin air, its delicate petals blooming and pulsing open and closed. As he did this a tingle overtook Eve, racing from her torso out to the extremities of her body and leaving her fingers and toes fuzzing and warm. She gasped at the unexpected response.

Nolwen gave his usual lazy grin in reply.

They joined hands at Nelda's instructions and Eve ran through what she could remember. She had learnt much of healing with Nelda the previous year at Pandora in addition to a little of making and growing, but not much of the knowledge remained.

"You have remembered a surprising amount," Nelda acknowledged. "Little used is oft forgot," she added with sympathy in her voice. "We shall practise such things once more, cousin. I am to train you in my strength—magery. You will learn much more than you already know or remember about energy, magic and how to use it with skill and precision."

"Meanwhile, I am to train you in my strength—physical

endurance," said Nolwen. "I will show you how to build your physical strength to aid your use of magic. We shall train together as we once did, though this time, little cousin, your sparring partner will show you the full potential of your body."

Nolwen insisted then that she present her sword. He examined it at great length, turning it this way and that.

"How do you find this blade?"

"It's good," said Eve, not understanding. "I've practised with that one for a couple of years."

"Hmm." Nolwen stood and drew his own sword—which Eve could have sworn appeared from nowhere—before returning Eve's to her. "Let's practice."

Eve was confident she could do better this time, but it was not to be, for she had lost much of her good health in her time spent languishing. The meadow provided good footing beneath her, despite the sloping surface and long grass covering the ground, yet Nolwen was too skilled and too strong.

Soon she was sweating and red-faced, with an aching arm and sore leg where he had stung her with the flat of his blade after a poorly defended attack.

"It is as I thought," Nolwen said. "That blade is not fit for you."

"What's wrong with it?" Eve asked, regarding it with raised eyebrows. It looked fine to her—one sword was the same as another at Arlyn, where the forge turned out identical iron blades that were either one-handed or two, with a straight edge, a fuller, a rain guard and a leather wrapped grip under the cross-guard. Eve had customised hers with new leather: now well worn in. Only her father had a steel sword with precious metals in the hilt—that had been forged elsewhere and was an heirloom of the house.

"It's too heavy for you, too short and too wide. It does not suit your balance, your weight, or your reach," said Nolwen. "No, this will not do at all. Come with me."

He marched so fast that Eve had to jog to keep up with him whilst Nelda followed at her own more unhurried pace. He led her into Artora's home, which Eve still did not know what to name. Too large for a house, yet too humble for a manor, mansion or palace, it was an abode the likes of which she had not seen elsewhere. Through it Nolwen walked, down corridors, staircases and across balconied walkways until Eve was lost.

He pushed open the last wooden door to reveal a cellar. It was an unremarkable room with vaulted ceilings and its contents piled up on shelves wrapped or covered in cloths. It was the one dusty room in the place that Eve had seen. Everywhere else was spotless—without even a fleck of dust Eve suspected—but here spiders were permitted to weave webs.

Nolwen grabbed several of the wrapped long, thin objects—swords, Eve realised—picking one up and either replacing it in a puff of dust or keeping it in his arms. Dirt smeared over his embroidered shirt, but he did not seem to mind or notice.

He passed the bundle onto Eve, who stumbled under the sudden weight and sneezed as the dust shot up her nose. After a few more caught his attention, Nolwen chivvied her outside, back through the door, up the stairs and outside into the sunshine. Blinking in the bright light, Eve found herself in a stone-floored courtyard. Ivy covered walls surrounded them, punctuated with windows: some open, some shuttered.

Nolwen took from her the bundle of objects and placed them with care upon the ground. He unwrapped the first—it was indeed a sword—and offered it to Eve. It was the same length as her own, but slimmer.

As she took it, she felt the weight difference in her hand. "So light!" she exclaimed. She moved the blade and it glimmered as it caught the sunlight on it's pale grey blade. "There are ripples in the metal. Is it broken?" *These are like the patterns in the dagger Artora gave to me.*

"Ha, no." Nolwen laughed. "It is stronger than any blade you will have ever seen—the match of ours. Our craftspeople have a different process of working, but our swords use folded steel. We can make them much lighter because they are so much stronger than conventional steel or iron blades."

"They're beautiful," said Eve. She trailed the sword through the air in a loop. Despite the tiredness of her arms, it sailed through the air with almost no effort at all. The bound handle seemed moulded to her grasp.

"They are, but that one is not for you," said Nolwen, frowning. "Give me it. Here, try this one."

The second blade he handed her was even slimmer, but longer. Again she tested it, cutting through the air.

"No. Next."

In total she tried six blades, but though each felt much lighter and easier to use than her own, they dissatisfied Nolwen. The seventh one he gave her was a little shorter than the last.

Compared to her own sword, it was a hand longer but thinner and much slimmer. The blade was a stormy dark grey, highly reflective despite the fact it had laid wrapped in a cloth and left for a length of time. The same ripples flowed down its length like the other blades—some darker and some lighter. The cross guard was small on this sword, though large enough to cover her hand and the grip one handed, wrapped in plaited black leather. The pommel was shaped like two ivy leaves meeting and set with green enamel that once rubbed to clear the dust, was smooth and unblemished.

Eve felt the edge—razor sharp. She raised it once more and moved around the courtyard as she parried invisible enemies: blocking, lunging, stabbing, and defending. The blade sliced through the air with no resistance.

"That is the blade," Nolwen said and clapped his hands together. Eve held it out to return it to him, but he stepped back and held up his hands to refuse. "It is a gift from Artora to you. Keep it."

"I cannot," Eve said, her mouth agape. "This is worth more than I could imagine—it is far too good to give to me!"

"It is already done," said Nolwen. His easy grin emerged. "We have no need to fight with swords anymore. We create them as a labour of love to keep the art alive. The owner and forger of this blade has long since had no need of it, so you are to enjoy it instead. Does it not feel perfect in your hand?"

"It does," Eve admitted. She fingered the leather grip in her hand and slid a finger over the glossy surface of the enamel pommel.

"Much better than your current blade?"

"Without a doubt. It's so much lighter! The length is better too—I never realised how short my blade was, but I've always had to overreach. It will take some getting used to though."

"All blades do." Nolwen shrugged. "Give it a try with me—if you like it afterwards, it is yours and I promise you—you will like this blade. It will become an indispensable extension of your own body, as any good weapon should!"

Impressed, Eve returned the blade to its green scabbard, which was bright, vivid, woodland green in colour. She had no idea how the Eldarkind had managed to make it such a beautiful colour, but then it looked like no material she had ever seen before.

Nelda stirred from where she had stood in silence. "Are you quite done bashing each other with swords?" she said to her brother in mock disdain.

"I suppose so, you can have her," Nolwen replied. He scooped up the unwanted swords in his arm and bumped into Nelda on purpose as he passed her. She shoved him back—almost sending him sprawling—and skipped out of his reach. Eve could not help but laugh.

"Come with me," Nelda said, her eyes gleaming with mirth. She led Eve through the building until they reemerged on the meadow. Eve followed as Nelda climbed higher, past a ridge of trees and onto a secluded hillside that overlooked a small valley dotted with copses. On the other side of the valley, a goat herd grazed.

Eve watched them, captivated by an even more beautiful sight of Ednor until Nelda caught her attention.

"Nolwen will teach you combat and physical strength," Nelda said, "but I will be teaching you endurance of a different kind. With me you will learn to be at one with the world and to use its strength as your own.

"I will teach you how to safely extract energy from the environment to fuel magic greater than you are capable of alone but also how to respect what is around you so that you do not abuse it and as you gain strength, you also gain the knowledge of how to use it well.

"Let us begin." Nelda cast her eyes around until she saw a boulder, large enough for them both to be seated upon. She leapt onto it, beckoned Eve, and seated herself cross-legged at its peak. Eve clambered up and sat. She fidgeted as the sharp, unyielding surface dug into her thighs.

"As it is your first day here with us, I will be easier on you than my brother was!" Nelda smiled at Eve and folded her hands in her lap. "I will start to teach you magery tomorrow. Today, we shall meditate."

Eve cocked her head to one side, but did not dare question Nelda. *Meditate? What's that?*

"Contemplation, deep thinking, joining ourselves to the world," explained Nelda, catching her look. "Close your eyes." Her voice changed to a softer volume. "Breathe deeply in, slowly exhale. Breathe deeply in, slowly exhale."

Eve took a deep breath before expelling it all until it felt like her chest would crumple from lack of air. Her bottom was sore and her legs and back ached from sitting so awkwardly on the uncomfortable surface. She could not help but feel impatient, but tried to refrain from moving. *What's the point of this?*

They continued until Eve lost track of time, before Nelda's instructions changed.

"And be still. Open your other senses, keeping your eyes closed. What can you hear, feel, touch, taste?"

A really hard rock! Eve thought to herself with annoyance. She straightened up and her back cracked each time she moved. Without opening her eyes she leaned back and propped herself up with the palm of her hands.

In the late afternoon, the stone's rough surface was warm beneath her hands—pleasantly so—and pitted. Her hand slid over its crumpled form, feeling in nooks and crannies, caressing the soft mosses that found purchase upon it and crumbling dead lichens that crawled over it.

A breeze picked up, sighing up the valley. Grass rustled, a feather-light sound, whilst the tree branches bent and creaked in their own dance. The air smoothed her skin as it passed by, a cooling touch that broke the warm sun baking her skin and brought with it the scent of the coniferous trees intermingled with the sweeter notes of the meadow's flowers. Small birds soared past in a joyful cacophony of chirps and if she strained, Eve thought she could hear the loose stones being dislodged by the grazing goats at the other side of the valley.

Its beautiful even without looking, Eve reflected, *but all I can taste is my own empty mouth.* Distracted from the moment, she sighed, reminded how long and demanding a day it had been. *I'm starving.*

"And open your eyes," Nelda said in such a quiet voice that Eve was sure, had her eyes been open and her other senses as unobservant as usual, she would not have heard. "Come."

Eve unfolded her petrified legs and they strolled around the clearing twice in silence. Eve's limbs loosened—though the aches of her sparring earlier with Nolwen would not fade—but this did not distract her from the newfound beauty in the place.

As if reading her mind, Nelda said, "By freeing all in your mind but the awareness and needs of your body, your capacity to sense and use magic also becomes greater and keener. The more that we practice this, the easier you will find it to reconnect to your powers." Nelda offered her hand to Eve, who stretched out her own. The moment they touched fingers, a jolt of energy leaped between them, travelling as fast as a flash through Eve and leaving her breathless.

For a second, Eve felt as alive as she had ever been, full of energy, free of pain and most importantly, tingling with the power of magic flowing through her veins. She drew herself up tall, exhilarated, but the instant passed through her and outside her skin with the weirdest sensation. All that remained was an empty, aching shell. Disheartened, she faltered.

Nelda smiled at her and motioned for her to sit down again. Eve sank onto the soft cushion of the grass, which rose about her to head height in places: a comforting wall of stalks and hidden blooms. Nelda's face appeared before her as she parted the grass and peered through the gap.

461

"Try again. Familiarise with your surroundings and then I would like you to reach out with your mind and sense what other living things surround us."

Eve did not understand what Nelda meant in the slightest, but the Eldarkind had already withdrawn behind the curtain of grass. Eve shook her head and shrugged. *I might as well try.*

She stilled for a moment and focused on her breathing. When it steadied, she concentrated on her other senses. Once again, she heard the birds, the trees, the goats, the breeze. She threw all her attention towards the goats, the most obvious and noisy signs of life—of Nelda she could feel nothing and the birds had not yet wheeled round for their next pass over the valley—but to no avail.

They didn't seem any closer or any louder and she could not feel them with her mind. She scowled and cast her attention elsewhere. The trees were silent. The grass had no presence. When her hand tingled and she opened an eye to see an insect crawling over it, she could no sooner feel it with her mind than shrink herself to its size.

Frustrated, she scowled. "It's not working. I don't feel anything!" Her frustration welled up into her eyes, which stung with un-shed tears.

Nelda's disembodied voice sounded from her right. "It's alright," Nelda said. "Don't become angry or disheartened. It's a very difficult task. I doubt that anyone ever achieved this on their first attempt. Like anything worth doing, it requires time, patience and persistence to achieve. Perhaps I push you too far in any case—I forget how long your day has been. Come, let us rest until tomorrow."

They returned to Artora's abode, where Eve found a steaming bath awaiting her in her chambers. She sunk into it, embracing the scalding water as it stripped the scum from her skin and the aches from her body.

The sun was on its descent towards the horizon and they had missed the evening meal, so Nelda had promised to have food sent to her. Eve's gurgling stomach had little patience and she fell on the meal as soon as it arrived, devouring it in a most unladylike manner within the privacy of her room.

Warm and full, Eve sat on the cushioned window seat. The mountains darkened above her, the flaming sky behind them shedding its colours as the light faded to lilac. She reflected on the day—a strange one, to be sure. She did not know what to make of Nelda's instruction at all—still an enigma—but the sword she had received from Nolwen was a thing of beauty. It lay on her bed, the river-like blade hidden in its green sheath.

Training with Nolwen had brought back memories of the last time she had raised a sword in true combat the year before in Pandora, the night she had almost died and the night her magic had awakened. Inspiration struck her and she slid off the seat to fetch the scrying mirror that Artora had gifted Eve on her last visit to Ednor.

"Enchanted to work without my magic!" She remembered with a smile. Extracting it from the case with a steady hand, she wiped the surface with her sleeve to clean it.

"*Leitha isa,*" she said. She shivered at the slight tingle that ran through her on uttering the words.

Her father's face swam onto its surface. It rippled until the image fixed itself. Karn still rode, despite the late hour, and seemed in good spirits: laughing and jesting with someone Eve could not see. *He is still safe yet. I should check every day, to make sure.*

"*Lessa,*" she murmured and the mirror faded to reflect her own shadowed face.

Next, Eve scried Soren, who appeared to be in some kind of shelter surrounded by other men she did not know in a huddle over something on a table. *He looks grim*, Eve reflected, *and so much older*. It had been an entire year since they had last met. He looked even more haunted. The night light did not help: shadows pooled under his eyes and in the creases of his worried face.

Irumae could not have been more different. She appeared to be at Pandora surrounded by ladies—her ladies in waiting, Eve presumed—laughing and talking. Unlike Soren, she seemed to have no cares. Eve was glad to see at least one of her cousins in good health.

The image disappeared at her command. Each time she spoke, the tingle passed through her. *Perhaps I begin to reconnect with the old tongue at last! Who can I scry next.* Inevitably, Luke sidled into her mind. *Should I? Should I not?* Eve deliberated. She clutched the mirror to her chest. *It's been so long since I saw him and I do miss him... but I dread to think where he is.* Unacknowledged thoughts raced through her brain as she chewed her lip. *Maybe it's better not to know.*

"*Leitha Dane,*" she said instead. He appeared on the other side of the same huddle as Soren. She shook her head with confusion, for her cousin had come into sight as Dane leaned forward and the mirror's image moved with him. "*Lessa.*" She felt strange all of a sudden, her emotions jumbled. "It's been a long day," she muttered. "Time for bed."

Eve awoke well rested the following morning having forgotten her scryings the night before and full of anticipation to begin her training with her Eldarkind cousins.

Nelda knocked on the door to take her to breakfast. Eve was so excited that her stomach quivered. Was the tingling upon her skin anticipation or magic?

TWENTY FIVE

Soren suppressed a huff of impatience as the young squire's fingers slipped in the buckles and clasps again.

"Careful, Ricken," he chastised. The young boy nodded, wide eyed and still too awe-stricken in his presence to speak. "Take your time, there's no rush."

It was ridiculous, Soren reasoned, to be dressing in armour when he was not even to to do battle, but all of his advisors, Edmund most of all, had insisted he be prepared.

"Just in case," they cautioned. Already, he grew hotter under it. It was winter, so at first he had been glad to wear the padded undercoat. The leathers over it were not a burden, until the restrictive chain-mail was placed on top.

It dragged him to the ground and he found himself wishing that he had thought to bring a vest instead of a knee-length tunic. The weight of the plate armour on top was unbearable. With every step, Soren felt like he would step right through the earth itself, he was so heavy, or that his legs would snap with the weight of it.

"Take it off," Soren said with a scowl. "I draw the line at wearing the full thing for no damn reason," he muttered to himself. With deft, practised fingers, he helped Ricken remove the plates where he could reach and stomped out of the tent once he had been divested of them.

Weak sun penetrated the leaden sky, though it did not seem to reach the valley bottom. The colours were bleached as if life itself had been sucked away from the place.

Miserable.

Soren far preferred the leafy lands of home—and the comforts too for that matter. He was one of few to possess a tent. Most of the men slept rough on the heathers and mosses of the low moors with a blanket if they were lucky, a pillow of anything they could find—a rolled up jacket, or a rock—if they were exceptionally so, or in complete misery if they were not.

There were at the very least plenty of rocky outcrops to shelter behind and hollows to sleep in. The same terrain that made for dangerous riding off the road was the best they could find short of cover in the woods, but the nearest forests were far away from this windswept land.

He searched up the valley, but could see nothing of Edmund and his men who were at the other side of the hills. They had had to move quite far down from the pass to find any sort of shelter and space. Soren wondered how Edmund fared. Nerves gnawed at the pit of his stomach as he contemplated that Edmund and a thousand men stood between himself and Zaki. *Zaki and his army*, he reminded himself. As he turned, a flash of colour caught his eye—a white speck moved upon the hillside.

A grey horse. A rider in green. House Arendall. He bolted towards his tent and called for Lord Andor.

The other noblemen, too nosy not to interfere, poured out of their own shelters whilst Soren explained what he had seen to Andor.

"Best saddle up, we'll ride out to meet him. It will do us no good to fret here waiting," said Andor.

They met the messenger far from camp and rode with him down the valley as he relayed his message.

"Sir Edmund sends word that Zaki advances towards the pass. The size of his forces are still unknown. We have engaged on the front line and expect to hold the pass."

"We should send extra men in case," Soren said.

Andor agreed.

"Assemble the cavalry from Kinsley and Lunder and send them up to the pass."

Andor sped away as if Zaki himself gave chase whilst Soren quizzed the messenger on all he had seen. The man relayed what positions the men had been arranged in, the arrangement of those they faced, and the brief sightings of Reynard.

Soren was surprised at that, for in Behan's reports there had been no mention of Reynard, so Soren had assumed he had died, though he was aware some of Zaki's Caledonian men had made it to Roher alive—if not well. It kindled the apprehension rising within him, though he suppressed it with positive thoughts and a dose of denial where his insecurities were too large.

When Soren returned to camp he consented to be strapped into his armour again: wearing the blue and gold surcoat of House Balaur over the gleaming metal surface. He was sweating—an unpleasant feeling that gave him chills as it cooled on his skin, even though he was hot enough to perspire in the first place. He had not eaten for hours, but was far too full of nerves to do so. His belly cringed at the thought of food and roiled as the scent from small cooking fires wafted past him.

It took far too long in Soren's eyes to assemble the men, most of whom had assumed they would be staying there for a while. Soren's frustration grew with his impatience, but Andor counselled him not to ride off without the support of his men behind him. Instead he paced around the camp, chivying men along himself and lending a hand to prepare horses. All nerves were forgotten in his annoyance at the delays.

At last they were off and Soren cantered ahead of the others, who struggled to keep up. It had been hours since the messenger had been sent, but no more had come. It was only when Soren began the final ascent to the pass in the narrowing, steeply rising valley that he encountered another man in great distress. He wore no identifying marks or arms and his armour was poor, but he spoke with a southern accent.

"Sir, sir, send for the king at once!" he cried out to Soren, before pulling his horse up short and leaping from his saddle to bow low to the ground when he saw Soren's surcoat. "I beg your pardon, I mean no offence, Your Majesty, sire!"

"What news have you?" asked Soren, unsettled by the man's distress.

"Sire, Sir Edmund has fallen in the battle."

"But he lives?"

"No, sire, dead. Lord Dane leads in his stead."

Soren swallowed. The ground seemed to fall away from him. *But he cannot be dead. He's always there. I need him...* He steadied himself and clutched at his reins. "It cannot be. Take me to him at once. What has passed?"

The exhausted man struggled to remount. Andor rode up beside him.

"Sir Edmund has fallen," repeated Soren in a hollow voice, not looking at him.

As they made for the head of the pass, they were met by Soren's own forces retreating: a straggling line of men and horses streamed down the hill.

"Where is Lord Dane?" shouted Soren. His voice carried enough to be heard by all those nearby. They bowed to him, but continued to move down the valley.

"Sire." Lord Dane rode forward through the ranks of his men. "They have taken the pass." His eyes were red.

Soren grasped forearms with him. "Where is he?"

"He follows." Dane did not need to ask who he spoke of. "We had no time nor the materials to make a bier so he is slung over a horse like a sack." Dane's voice cracked.

Leaning between their horses, Soren pulled him into an embrace.

"I would not ask it of you if it were not urgent, but I must know the situation. Why do we retreat?"

Motioning for Andor to join them, Soren turned and rode with Dane down the hill.

Dane spoke in a dead monotone. "When my father fell, our men faltered. Zaki gained the upper hand even when I stepped in to command. We could not regain our position. He held the best part of the pass. I thought it better we retreated rather than died. He has thousands of men. I could not see an end to them.

"I had hoped we could also save my father, but it was not to be. His wounds were too deep. When we drew out the arrows that had pierced him, their barbed heads caused more damage. Those Roherii are barbarians." Hate filled his voice. "Zaki did it. I saw him from up the hill. With a cluster of men, he shot arrow after arrow at my father until they had no more."

"We will avenge him," replied Soren grimly.

They rode in silence thereon, each consumed by their own thoughts. Soren still could not believe his mentor dead—the man felt like his last connection to his upbringing, his parents and the comfort of childhood—but the body upon the horse was indeed Edmund. Soren had told himself not to look, but could not help himself. He did not have to see the face to recognise Edmund's clothes.

"What is to be our strategy?" Lord Andor interrupted his thoughts.

Soren struggled to pull his thoughts back to their present predicament. "If we have lost the pass then we must retreat to a more favourable location, I suppose. We cannot hold our position here."

Soon they entered the camp amid a sombre mood. News had already travelled ahead of them with those at the front of the retreat. Soren met with the rest of the noblemen, each responsible for leading their houses. The sun had almost set—the grey skies fading to black above them—and the tent was dull in the limited lamplight.

Soren explained what he knew of the retreat to save Dane the pain. They stood as the horse bearing his father came forth, led by two men, who lowered the body to the floor. They laid Edmund on a borrowed blanket to save him from resting in the churned mud.

In the torchlight he looked asleep, albeit with a sickly pallor upon him. His face was slack and his body limp. The dark stain of blood—already bloomed and dried—coated his green surcoat. A lump formed in Soren's throat.

A man stepped forward to kneel before Dane and offer him his father's sword.

Dane's lips disappeared as he clenched them tightly together to suppress his emotions, before he took the scabbarded blade and held it in limp hands.

A poor substitute for a father, Soren could not help but think. Soren's rested his hand upon the handle of his own sword, which had belonged to his father many years before.

469

"Come," Soren said in a low voice to those around him. They filed into his large tent, to allow Dane some time alone beside his father, whilst they discussed their next move. Soren longed to be out there with Edmund—after all Edmund had accompanied him through, he was as dear as a father to Soren too—but it was not his place. He looked up, to find himself fixed in everyone's gaze. *I am needed here whether I like it or not.*

Last of all to enter was Andor, clutching three sticks. On closer inspection they were arrows, but not made by Caledonian hands. Each arrow head had three barbs carved into it. They were covered in blood—Edmund's, Soren realised with a shock—and their cruelty was clear to see.

Soren held a shaking hand out for them.

Andor hesitated, but passed them to him.

Soren clenched his fist around them. Seeing the arrowheads made him angrier. "These Roherii do not build clean weapons of war, to put a man out of misery fairly, but devices of torture." With an impulse, he snapped them over his knee and threw them to the floor.

"I will not stand for this! My uncle was ousted from Caledan and has the gall to come back with foreigners to claim a throne that is not his. Caledonian lives are being lost to prevent him from doing so, yet unless we end this here, many more must die. I will not stand for it!"

At that moment Dane slunk into the tent, his eyes downcast.

Soren turned back to the lords stood before him.

"We cannot remain here—our position is too weak—yet I cannot allow Zaki to advance into Caledan as he pleases and I will not draw him further in unless I must. Far too much is at stake and we have already lost more than what we ought to have done by his hands. It ends here. We will assassinate him. Tonight. If we cut the head off the beast, it cannot survive. The Roherii have no place here in Caledan by themselves."

"Are you not concerned that without a leader they will run rampant over our lands, taking what they please and destroying what they will?"

"I would rather conquer them divided, than united under one cause."

"I think it a fine idea," said Andor.

Soren flashed him a quick smile, grateful for his support.

"I also agree," said Lord Willam. "It is a winning strategy."

Soren bowed his head in thanks to the Lord of House Walbridge, not at all convinced of his sincerity.

But the others counselled against it, until Dane at last spoke up.

"We owe it to my father and those who died with him today to avenge them. I will not see that murderer enjoy another day alive. If none of you should support this, I will see it done myself."

"You have my support," said Soren. "I'll go with you."

An outcry arose at his words.

"You cannot risk yourself, Soren!" exclaimed Lord Karn. "Caledan needs you to remain safe."

"Edmund was as good as a father to me, Lord Karn. How can I not share Dane's feelings, when Zaki is also responsible and unpunished for the death of my mother and so many more people whose names I will never know. I will go." His tone brooked no argument, but the men shuffled.

Andor watched him with keen eyes before he spoke. "It is clear we all think it unwise that you go yourself. You are our king and commander. But if you are unyielding in this, we cannot stop you and I beg of you to take more men with you—the finest that we have—to protect you and aid in this."

Soren nodded. "I will consent to that. I do not wish to fail." In his mind, he knew it was rash, unwise and downright foolish—and Edmund would not approve—but grief fuelled his decision, and he was determined Zaki would pay for taking yet another crucial person from his life. *Enough is enough. It ends tonight.*

The lord discussed amongst themselves who would go, comparing their strongest, fastest and most skilled soldiers and all the while trying to persuade Soren not to endanger himself—but fruitlessly. Eventually, they decided on eight others to accompany Soren and Dane; few enough to escape detection, yet enough to protect the king whatever happened.

The men were soon assembled and briefed on their mission—Soren had met two of them before, though not well enough to know them by name—and set off without delay. They dressed in light armour and in the darkest clothes they had—borrowed and begged where needed. Armed to the teeth with daggers, swords, knives and bows, they mounted horses as dark as the night to bear them.

As they rode up another valley, for there were many ways through the hills, Soren could see their own camp in the darkness: a mass of fires stretching out like a glowing lake of stars across the valley floor. He was unprepared for the scale of Zaki's forces.

A terrifying sight awaited them when they crested the last horizon before the land dropped down onto House Rainsford's county. Before them a sea of fires sprawled. In the dark, they could not see what else lay before them, but the campfires spread far into the distance and to either side.

In synchronisation, they halted.

"By God, how many are there?" asked Soren in hushed tones.

"Many thousands," answered a voice from his side. "I would wager more than ten thousand."

Humbled and unnerved by the vastness of Zaki's forces, the anger which had been sustaining Soren faltered. It shrunk away to be replaced by apprehension.

What am I doing?

TWENTY SIX

"What is it?" asked Eve, her mouth open in awe as she felt the invisible barrier.

Nolwen stood before her grinning.

She held his sword in one hand with her other feeling the blade—or trying to. Yet for all she tried, her fingers could not touch the metal, instead finding an unseen barrier a finger's width away from it on all side. It was the same temperature as her skin and hard to the touch and when she pushed, gave way with a slight amount of cushioning.

"Your protection!" Nolwen chuckled. "I have created a block on the blade—it will not slow it or weight it down, but it means that the cutting edge is rendered useless."

"How is it done?"

"I make the air around the blade compress into a barrier to allow nothing else to touch the metal. Once you know how, it is simply done, though it does take some practice to achieve the correct thickness and hardness. You cannot make it too hard you see, or if you hit someone with it, it will crack their bones even if it does not cut them! We want to avoid that, of course."

Eve nodded. *Definitely no broken bones.*

He took the blade back and muttered some more words to it that she could not hear, cradling it to his chest as if a precious bundle. "Try it—this block is the hardest to achieve and maintain. We will not use it, but it amuses me to no end. Touch the blade."

Eve took the blade with a frown. *Is this a trick?* As her hesitant fingers brushed upon the surface, she yanked them back, but nothing happened. Eve touched them to the blade again with more confidence. The folded steel felt cold and silky smooth beneath her hands.

"I don't understand," she said, wrinkling her nose.

"Feel the edge."

Eve gave him a quizzical look. The blade was sharp—of that she had no doubt. She touched her finger to the edge, but pulled it back before she felt it cut into her skin.

Nolwen tutted. "You can trust me, cousin. I would not sever your finger off!" He beckoned for the blade and, when Eve passed it back to him, offering him the handle first, wrapped his hand about the blade instead.

Eve gasped and her hand rushed to her mouth.

Nolwen snorted with laughter. "Look! There is no damage, see?" He spread his hand wide before her and indeed, his skin was unblemished and uncut.

Eve's face screwed up with bafflement. Trusting him, she reached out to touch the blade by its edge. It felt like she pushed her hand into butter—dry, not wet or sticky—as the edge of the blade gave way to the pressure from her fingers, but when she pulled her hand back, the blade was whole again and its cutting edge straight and true.

"That's amazing," she said.

"You need to ask the blade to help you and help you it will. We need to incant in the old tongue as follows. 'Make a shield of the air so that nothing else may touch the blade.' When you speak, picture the barrier you have seen and felt—the thickness, the texture, the hardness, the consistency."

He placed his hand on the blade, asked her to do the same and told her to say the words with him. As she placed her hand upon the sword, his fingers inched to touch hers at their tips. At the moment of contact, like the day before, Eve felt a whisper of energy rush through her. She closed her eyes and threw the weight of her mind out-wards, searching for the energy stream.

"*Efla rond a lofti sa att ingeth annao kan sverd taka,*" they said together.

The blade seemed to move of its own accord underneath her hand. It pushed her away with unyielding force as she sought to keep contact with the metal. In a few seconds it stilled.

Nolwen ran his hand up and down the blade. "Not bad at all. Of course, you had my help, but not a bad block at all, well done."

They sparred with the two blocked blades all morning, until Eve ran with sweat and shook with tiredness. Nolwen at last allowed her to leave the courtyard, barely out of breath to her frustration and showed her a refectory where she could eat. She was thirsty more than anything and gulped down two delicate glasses of water before diving into her plate of thin bread, butter and game meats dressed with what looked like leaves.

"Eat them," Nolwen said. "We call it salad—it contains many nutrients to help keep you strong."

Eve wrinkled her nose but ate them despite her doubts. She was too hungry to argue and in any case, had already learnt that life in Ednor was far from ordinary.

After she had eaten, it was time for meditation with Nelda again. Eve felt relieved by this—she was tired and longed for a rest—but Nelda would not let her sleep. They sat again for the whole afternoon in solitary peace with Eve no closer to feeling the energy stream by herself than before.

For two weeks Eve continued in this routine. She rose early to spar with Nolwen and spent her afternoons in the meadows and forests with Nelda. Time seemed to flow faster in Ednor where it had dragged in Arlyn, but Eve could not be sure whether this was due to some strange magical phenomenon or because she enjoyed every day in fullness.

The sparring had become easier. It was clear that she was still no match for Nolwen. Still, she was quicker, more accurate and more effective with her new blade than she had ever been before. After each session she ached a little less and for the next session, had a little more endurance.

Because of the hours of meditation she had also begun to feel the pull of the magical energy at last, which grew stronger every day though her powers were still weak. Despite this, she was relieved to have any kind of abilities again; it felt like a part of her once lost had returned and with it came her own deepening sense of satisfaction and contentment. Her concentration was also greater and she found herself not irritated, bored, or tired.

As her connection with her magical abilities grew once more, she could at last feel what Nelda had spoke of: pulses of energy dotted in the river that marked the life energy of creatures and Eldarkind around her. Before, the new rush had been so exhilarating that she had been overwhelmed with the force of its power, but Nelda taught her how to find other things within it.

Nelda was pleased with her progress and promised her that they could soon move onto working with magic. "If you can sense things you can learn to identify them, to analyse them and to harness their energy or choose not to."

They visited the same clearing every day at first. Eve became quite familiar with her surroundings even when she closed her eyes. The slow, sonorous, looming life force of the trees surrounded them, interspersed with much lighter, brighter, faster and more energetic bursts of energy as other creatures moved. Without looking, she could feel things around her though she could not sense what they were.

Next, Nelda moved them into new environments. Sorting through the deluge of new information was impossible at first— despite her surroundings being not much different to what she had seen before with open eyes and ears—until she managed to slow her breathing and look through what surrounded her in a meticulous order.

Eventually she was able to do this with ease and so, as promised, Nelda allowed Eve onto the next step of her training. Eve grinned with excitement when they paused from their wanderings amongst the trees.

"Here will be sufficient, I think," said Nelda with a glance around. "You can already heal well—I will not discuss this again with you for there are other skills you should master first. But I am glad that you already know how important the wordings you utter are. You recall how specific you need to be?"

Eve nodded. Her excitement was tempered with solemnity as she recalled those she had tended to at Pandora—some with horrific injuries and wounds. She had healed many of them with great success, but not without making the mistakes of a beginner too: healing the wrong layer of skin or muscle first, forgetting to numb the area, setting bones incorrectly and taking on tasks far too demanding for her skills or energy levels. She suppressed a cringe at the memories.

"You remember, I see. Lucky for those you healed, the energy to heal them came from your own. If you had happened to draw too large a reserve from them instead and not ceased your enchantments, they would have perished."

"I would never have allowed that," said Eve.

"Not knowingly but still, you must see the consequences to understand what destruction this wreaks."

Eve did not understand, but there was no time to question her mentor.

"To use the life force of another thing, you can name it in your incantation, or you can feel for it in the energy stream to draw down from its energy. Initially you will use worded incantations, moving to the latter, for it is far more effective—you can draw down precisely what you need, not a drop of energy more, for it is easier to feel what is remaining. Try this, here. Lift this stump from the ground adding to your instructions 'with the energy of this sapling'."

"*Risa frama a feld yta a ethera ro a ungr etre,*" Eve said and focused her energy on the fallen log. It was far heavier than she could have picked up with her own hands and should have required all her energy even try to lift it, but to her surprise, just a trickle of energy leeched away from her once she finished speaking. "*Sitya!*" she commanded the log to stay as it rose in the air. It floated upon nothing: still. "This is so easy!" she turned to Nelda, surprised and impressed.

But when she turned back, something had changed. It was autumn, so the leaves were already beginning to turn, but she watched them change hue before her, from pale green to yellow and orange, and then a dull, papery brown. A few seconds later, they began to fall from the tree and tumbled through the air in an almost silent dance.

"*Lessa!*" she said to release the magic, aghast at what she had done.

The log fell to the ground with a mighty boom that echoed around the still hillside.

Eve ran to the tree and reached up to touch a withered leaf on one of the lower branches. It fell off and tumbled past her outstretched fingers.

"What have I done?" Eve turned to Nelda in concern.

"You took too much from the tree," replied Nelda. "That was my intent. I apologise."

"Will it be ok?"

"Nelda stepped up to the tree and placed her palm upon its surface. She closed her eyes. Her mouth moved in silence. Before her the tree grew new buds, flowered, grew leaves and within minutes had returned to the same state it had been before Eve's incantation. Nelda stepped back. She sagged with exhaustion. "There are no ill effects."

Eve would have been furious had she not seen Nelda's own sacrifice to the tree. "Why did you have me do that?"

"You cannot imagine what you cost another living thing until you see it with your own eyes and it is necessary to know so that you understand the balance between all living things, for it is fragile and once disturbed, hard to remake."

Eve was relieved that she had somehow not managed to overexert herself to the point of danger before.

Nolwen's sessions were much simpler in a way, because the sword practice was much more familiar to her. However this did not mean they were any less frustrating at times. Nolwen was a good tutor and an expert at all he taught her, but he was a perfectionist and insistent on her mastery of everything he showed her.

Every day they practised fighting positions and moves, sequenced them together in slow mock battles and then forgot all semblance of alliance and fought for real. Eve had had more than one blow from Nolwen's protected blade. She was glad it did not cut her, though she still flinched each time it touched her from the expectation that it would, but she could testify that the blows hurt. She had the bruises and stiff, sore limbs to prove it.

Even so, her precision and strength grew. Muscles were hard beneath her skin where it had been soft in their absence and her stamina had improved. Even if she never needed her physique to be so well exercised or used her fighting skills, which Eve hoped she would not have to do again, Nolwen insisted that it was a necessary part of her progress and training. He lived by his principle of having complete control over one's own body.

Her mentor was pleased with her progress too. Nolwen was never over generous with his praise, but always doled it out when deserved. Her blade blocks had become more effective, especially since she could draw magic from the environment to sustain them and she had already shown promise at spelling her blade to renew and strengthen the enchantments that stopped it from dulling, chipping and breaking.

Nolwen had even taught her minor ways to spell the blade so it flew true to its target. It did not work every time, for spells could not overcome poor form, he explained to her, but such things had helped him over the years in tight spots.

He also helped to enhance Eve's archery skills, though she would not let him replace her beloved bow with one of Eldarkind make. Her magic helped in this, for he taught her how to enchant her arrows to always find their mark.

Eve found archery much more enjoyable than sword fighting and the novelty of being able to shoot in any direction and have her arrow bend through the air to bury in its target a fascinating occurrence. It drained her energy, the further the arrow had to change course, but she could not resist the temptation.

Whilst it amused her at first, she did however slink off in the evenings after Nolwen's mentoring to shoot—just her and the bow—with no magic. With magic making the perfect shot every time, the fun had been taken out of it as well as the skill and she missed the calm moment of true aiming before the release and the satisfaction of hitting her mark, knowing that years of practice honing skills were behind it.

"I've not lost my skills," she said to herself with a relieved smile. "Perhaps I won't use magic in this unless I must."

TWENTY SEVEN

"Where will Zaki be? How can we reach him?" Soren said to distract himself. His eyes were transfixed on the scene before him.

"If I were him I'd place myself right in the middle," replied Dane.

They scanned the camp again.

"See there." Dane pointed—but in the dark, Soren could not see his hand. "There, not quite in the middle, a little to the right, a little further, yes there, where there is a concentration of fires? I'd bet that he is there."

They gave the camp a wide berth and picketed their horses on the south side. Soren reasoned this would be where they would be least expected. It was impossible to spot the guards, even though the entire camp was ringed by fire, but in the shadows it was easy for the ten of them to pass unseen into the tangled maze. They could not use the stars for guides, covered over as they were by the dark clouds which even deprived them of moonlight to ride by and instead had to guess as best they could which way to go.

Soren moved as one with the group over uneven ground and between dark and silent mounds that were men sleeping rough under the winter night's sky. The flickering light illuminated their path, but they still had to move carefully. Debris littered their way: discarded boots, cooking pots and travelling paraphernalia.

On several occasions Roherii men loomed out of the darkness. Soren's companions leapt forwards to silence them. They were chillingly effective assassins. Soren could not help but think back to when he had been the victim of such an attack—and lucky to escape with his life. A shadow of doubt crossed his mind, but it was too late to turn back now.

His heart pounded and he moved with care. The low lying

smoke stung his eyes and the stench of it, mingled with the body odour of the thousands about him, made him see men in every shadow or twisting tendril of smoke. Whilst he and Dane watched, their companions one by one slunk into the uniforms of their victims, shrugging on Roherii tunics and wrapping Roherii cloaks over their shoulders. In the dark, they abandoned helmets—which would restrict their already restricted vision—but they were glad for the night that added to their cover.

As they moved closer to the centre, pockets of the camp were still alive—throngs of men raucous in the night. Guards changed and soldiers ate and drank. It was hard to stroll past them at such close proximity with confidence. Soren's hands shook and his breathing was unsteady.

They pushed towards the cluster of lights ahead. In a clear area, backed up against a rocky outcrop, lay a single structure so large it could only belong to one person. Every instinct inside Soren cautioned him to run the other way.

"He travels in style," muttered Dane.

They sneaked to the back of the tent for the front was guarded by two still forms and, squeezing between the rock and the fabric, lodged themselves out of sight.

"Here," breathed Dane. He looked through a small slit in the fabric below eye level. In silence he worked his knife free and cut the fabric from the ground up. He struggled not to bump against the side of the tent in the confined space. Soren caught a glimpse of the warm glow of lamplight within—it shone through the widening hole—as one of the others watched and signalled for Dane to stop when they heard a sound.

Dane stood at last, but kept his knife in hand. A hand belonging to someone Soren could not see peeled back the flap and Dane slunk inside without a sound. Soren followed. His eyes darted about. His knife was ready in his hand. Their companions waited outside, ready to follow should they be needed.

Inside it was dimly lit. A single space—not like Soren's tent which had a separate sleeping and living area—was stuffed with equipment and spoils—from Braith, Soren presumed—right down to a chamberpot, a luxury even Soren did not have.

Halfway between where they had entered and the front of the tent was a figure rolled over in slumber. It was impossible to see who it was, they were so bundled up in blankets. Soren's breath caught in his chest as adrenaline rushed through him. They crept forwards.

A shock of dark hair came into view. Soren was sure his breathing was too loud, but when he held his breath, the rasping sounds emanated from the sleeping figure. Distracted, Soren bumped into the chamberpot with a clang.

The figure moved. Dane and Soren froze. The man rolled over—with his eyes closed.

Zaki!

Zaki's eyes opened as if Soren had called his name aloud. Before he could open his mouth, Dane leapt upon him, clapped a hand over his mouth and wrapped him in a stranglehold. It was not tight enough. Zaki worked free enough to bite Dane's hand.

Dane grunted and refused to release him. He readjusted and tightened his grasp on Zaki's neck. Zaki battered Dane with his hands. He clutched and scrabbled for release until his eyes locked with Soren's.

Zaki's eyes widened in recognition and at that moment, he gained a breath and some freedom. A cry escaped his lips. The sound was indistinguishable as a word, but it did not matter.

Two men burst in, took one look at the scene, and charged. Soren's companions rushed to meet protect him. In the close confines it was a mess of flailing limbs and noise.

The guards were soon dispatched, but Zaki was already stumbling through the rippling tent flaps. Dane sunk to the floor. His eyes glazed over. He rolled over onto his back to reveal his own dagger plunged into his side.

Outside Zaki cried out in a tongue unfamiliar to Soren. A furore arose.

"We need to leave," said one of Soren's companions. He grabbed one of Dane's arms and hoisted him upright with the help of another.

Dane groaned and his face contorted with pain.

"Nothing for it, Lord Dane," said the man. "If we stay here, we will die. We must try to get you to safety before we see about that wound. Stay with us, you'll be right."

Bolting away as fast as they could, they left the way they had arrived whilst the camp awoke around them. In their uniforms, the men carrying Dane blended in. Soren hoped he was nothing more than a moving shadow. Men stumbled around them. They headed the other way, stupefied.

They somehow managed to find the horses and mounted, but Dane was limp and unconscious. Soren mounted behind him and clung onto his friend with grim determination as they fled. He could not see or feel if Dane breathed and with the jolting motion of the horse, his clumsy fingers could not detect a pulse.

West and north they rode—back into the hills and through the passes. It took far longer than Soren hoped, for they had to be careful since the moon had forsaken them. Winter's frost was already reclaiming the earth and with every hoof beat, the ground crackled and crunched with their passing. They no longer held caution, determined to get Dane home alive.

One of the other men had also obtained a nasty slash on his forearm in the attack, but he bore it with silent determination much to Soren's admiration. With every yard they rode more recklessly into the darkness. Soren prayed their horses would not stumble. A growing fear masked all other emotions within him as he wondered if he had lost his mentor and his friend at once.

You fool. How could you be so stupid?

When Soren and his men returned to camp they were faltering with weariness. Soren's arms burned from holding Dane's weight onto his horse and he had not drunk in so long his mouth felt as parched as a desert. His eyes stung—though from tiredness or smoke from the fires, he could not tell.

They rode into the centre of the camp to the hollow eyed lords who awaited their return and were welcomed with cheers and praises. The merriment ceased when Soren halted. Dane slumped forwards upon the horse's neck. Hands lifted him from the horse and supported Soren as he dismounted.

They laid upon the floor. Andor bent down. His face was deep in concentration as he placed his hand above Dane's mouth and then two fingers to his neck. Back went the hand to Dane's mouth—and then the fingers pressed upon his neck once more. Andor frowned. He lifted Dane's hand up, clasped it within his own, looked up and shook his head.

"He is not…?" Soren could not bear to say 'dead'.

"I am afraid so," said Andor lowering his eyes.

Soren swallowed past the lump in his throat. His vision blurred with tears. Exhaustion did not help his composure as a wave of despair and sorrow rolled over him.

Andor stood and grasped him in a one armed hug. "Do not blame yourself," he murmured in Soren's ear. "Dane chose to do this and Edmund died a good death on the field of battle. We have no choice but to continue. We will mourn later."

Soren nodded. He knew Andor was right, as much as it pained him. "We must retreat," he said, managing to keep his voice from breaking.

Soren left it to one of his companions to describe Zaki's camp. The council was shocked by the size of the forces opposing them.

"How did he come to obtain so many men?"

"How did they all travel here?"

"Can this be true?"

Soren held up his hand—even that tired him—and the hubbub ceased. "We must retreat. We'll not hold this valley against any force as large as our own—or larger as it seems to be. If we had retained the pass it might be a different tale, but we did not. If we remain here, we'll be at their mercy whilst they pick us off from the higher grounds. Where can we go? Where can we defend ourselves?"

"There is nothing hereabouts but more of the same: hills, moors, valleys, rivers," said Kinsley.

"Lowenmouth," said Andor. "It is the closest defensible location. The terrain is favourable for attack and defence, I can promise you, and the city can withstand siege for months. We will certainly succeed if they have no seige weapons."

"You are right," said Lord Willam Walbridge in a voice so quiet all others had to still to hear him. "But we should not retreat yet."

The others turned to listen to him. The Walbridge's were famous for their winning strategies after all.

"If we fall back, this will become a chase and we will fall into chaos as they nip at our heels. We should retreat tactically. It will cost more lives but it may save more and allow us to reach a more defensible position where we will be at our leisure to take advantage of our surroundings.

"We should send a company back up in a feigned attempt to retake the pass. In engaging Zaki's forces there, we will allow the rest of our men to begin the journey to Lowenmouth. By the time Zaki realises we are gone, it will be too late. He will follow the last of our rearguard—straight into our trap—but far enough behind so we may manoeuvre ourselves first.

"If we have men in position to engage them by dawn, we could be a day ahead of them. If our men can hold the pass until dark we could gain even more time."

"How?" Soren could not help but ask.

Walbridge smiled: a crafty smile with narrow eyes, that gave Soren a chill. "Did you see all of Zaki's ten thousand men?"

"No, of course not. It was dark."

"Then how did you know they were there?"

"All the fir—" Soren halted. His eyes flicked to meet Walbridge's. Willam's sinister grin widened.

"Exactly. I doubt he is clever enough to think of this strategy himself, but who knows! He may have a few thousand men for all we know, though what we have already seen makes that unlikely. But there is no reason that we cannot lead him to believe where we are. If we build the campfires before sunset and set them ablaze, for all he knows we could be here until dawn. It is of no matter whether he advances on our current position then. By the time he finds out we are no longer here, it will be too late."

Soren pondered Willam's words along with those others in the tent. The man had never spoken so much to him before. *Usually he dismisses my presence. Perhaps I have earned some of his respect at last—better to have it than not if so. He might remain on my side.*

"How many men would we need to leave as the rearguard to hold the pass?" Soren asked. He was reluctant to lose more men.

"Two thousand," suggested Andor. "Whilst you were absent we sent scouts into the hills. A small force commands the pass. If we take them unawares before dawn, we could have success with that portion of our men."

So many. "But how many would return alive?" said Soren with concern.

Andor could not answer.

"I believe Lord Walbridge's strategy is sound," said Lord Karn. "The sacrifice of a few will save many more of our men—and in turn many more Caledonians. It will give us the best chance of fighting Zaki on our own terms—and winning."

Others nodded along to his words as Soren glanced at those around him.

"Very well. We shall do as Lord Walbridge suggests. Arendall, Varan and Kinsley have already served well. Let Balaur men stand with Walbridges to execute this."

"I beg leave to remain in the vanguard," said Andor. "I offer my son in my place to manage our rearguard so that I may ensure we have favourable positions surrounding Lowenmouth when we arrive—if you will trust our arrangements to me."

"Of course," replied Soren. If so much had not been at stake and the past day not been quite so devastating, he would have been enthusiastic to learn about positioning their troops and which strategies to apply. He yawned as another wave of exhaustion stifled his senses for a moment.

"Get some sleep, Soren," Lord Karn suggested. "We will see to the arrangements."

Soren gratefully agreed. Despite the noise of the camp

awakening around him—the shouting, crashing and banging of men packing up and moving around, greeting their fellows and marshalling—Soren sunk into a dreamless slumber.

Soren's snatched few hours of rest still left him feeling out of sorts. The camp disappeared around him: the area left flattened and muddied. Whilst Soren dressed and ate, his shelter was also dismantled around him until only he remained, sat on a stool in the middle of his rug, eating dried meat strips and drinking fresh tea so hot it scalded his mouth with every sip.

Fires were built around him as far as the eye could see using everything available—small twigs upon the ground, dried mosses and heathers, small bushes and even broken arrows and pike staffs.

The morning fog lifted into the grey skies, which threatened snow and rain, but held it at bay. It would not do well if their fires were too sodden to light. Soren hoped Walbridge's idea would work to allow them a safe retreat.

Karn reported to him that Andor's men had gone into the hills with Walbridge's. Soren hoped that Walbridge would return on his side and not with Zaki. He did not trust Walbridge's oath of fealty in the slightest, given the man's dubious, evasive character and his family history of treachery. A betrayal would also do far more damage than the loss of men, he knew. *I pray I have done enough to keep him.*

His thoughts turned to Walbridge's brother, still under house arrest, and then to Behan. Soren had heard no news from the capital—but then, it would be impossible for Behan to know where he was. He made a mental note to send word to Pandora the moment they reached Lowenmouth.

At the very least he will need to know of our movements and Zaki's, but there are also the dead to report. Unbidden, his mind settled once more on the loss of Edmund and Dane. It opened the yawning void inside him again as a dull ache settled in his chest.

"Cannot dwell on this," he muttered to himself. He finished

the last of his tea. It had cooled in the winter air and was lukewarm. Soren's feet were already frozen blocks of ice, so he walked around the camp with Lord Karn.

There were far fewer men than before, because the exodus had begun. Already, a long line of men trailed down the valley led by Lord Andor. Those on foot led the way whilst those on horseback dallied to bring up the rear.

There was little left to do but wait for news sent back by scouts who described the scene at the pass. It was a bloodbath, by all accounts. Balaur and Walbridge had indeed taken the advantage. They had surprised Zaki's forces and pushed them back down the pass. They succeeded with heavy losses, but it was not long before the main body of Zaki's force roused to join their fellows. The Roherii attacked—savage and relentless—and wore down the defence. The pass was holding, but only just.

"It's time," said Soren as the light began to fade in the mid-afternoon. The boredom was frustrating, but he did not want to leave. He felt as though when he did, he would be forsaking all those who remained behind. The few mounted men who remained set to the giant task of lighting all the fires.

It was not the first time Soren wished for a dragon to make the task easier. He thought back. He had had neither sight nor sound of a dragon since Brithilca's apparition at his coronation. Yet again, he wondered how they fared before Karn distracted him.

"We're ready, Soren."

The rest of his men were already hours in front of them, but on horseback they could catch up with the marching men overnight. It would be a long, dark ride, but at least they had the road.

With a last look back towards the pass and a muttered prayer for those up in the hills, Soren mounted and led his men away.

The valley burned bright behind them, spotted with fires and ringed with large pyres that would burn long into the night. Soren hoped their ruse would succeed.

TWENTY EIGHT

Eve scratched the dried wax with her nail, to add another identical mark to the others. This was how she kept track of the days in Ednor, for each merged into another.

There seemed to be little routine here. Each person came and went as they pleased and completed whatever tasks they wished to. Once more she sat at the window seat, as she did every night, to watch the stars above the mountains and daydream.

Her scrying mirror sat on the small table nearby. Before each bedtime, she scried those that she cared about, in their special order. She abstained from thinking of them as her loved ones, for Dane was also on the list and she scried him more out of curiosity than anything else. Today, it was far later than usual. She had lost track of time wandering in the woods, to find sticks suitable to make new arrows with, and then she had had to eat her supper late too.

Hopefully it isn't too dark yet. "*Leitha Dane,*" Eve said. She always scried him first to get it out of the way. Today though, the mirror remained dark. She tilted it to catch some of the lamplight from her room. The surface, which had reflected her own face back at her moments ago, was an inky blackness with nothing in its depths.

"*Lessa. Leitha isa.*" Yet the same held true of her father—no image came to the surface of the mirror. "I cannot believe they sleep already," she said.

"*Lessa. Leitha Soren.*" Again the mirror plunged into darkness. This time however, a faint light emanated and she could see her cousin's face.

Soren seemed to be moving through the darkness, his face lit by a small flame, but other than that she could not tell. A tingle of apprehension crawled through her.

Last night, the three had been together with many stern-

490

looking, armoured strangers.

"*Lessa. Leitha Irumae.*" Her cousin revelled in the royal palace at Pandora. The sight cheered Eve as it did every day, for the young girl seemed so much happier of late. "*Lessa.*"

She held the mirror in her hands and contemplated what she had seen. Her sights of recent days had been worrying. They were harrowed: more tired, worn and grim than she had seen them before, even her father. She was glad he thought he was to be in the rearguard and hoped that was where he found himself. *No harm will come to him there. What of Edmund?* She had not scried him for days. But when she spoke, the mirror sunk back to black. She looked outside again. Clouds marched across the skies, hiding the stars from view.

They must be asleep, she decided. *It is well past sunset, after all. I should not have tarried so long outside.*

She undressed and sunk into her soft bed with relief, for she was exhausted from her long day.

Her eyes snapped open in the early hours of the new day. She lay immobile for a few seconds, confused and wondering what had awoken her. Silence. She turned over, but could not get comfortable. A niggling feeling burned at her.

For the remainder of the night she tossed and turned until at last she dragged herself from the bed after dawn. Instead of leaving for breakfast, she sat once more on the window seat with the mirror clasped between her hands, still unnerved by her scryings the night before.

She scried them all in quick succession again. Once more the mirror remained blacker than the night when she commanded her father, Dane and Edmund to appear. Shaking, she commanded her cousins to appear. Irumae was asleep in her chambers. Soren slumbered in what looked like a tent.

A third time, she called the images forth. Her breath caught in her chest. *It cannot be.* She knew what it meant—her first meeting with Artora had told her that no one could see beyond the black veil of death. *They were alive yesterday. They cannot be gone.* On an impulse, she called Luke forth on the mirror—something she had avoided so far, for fear of what she might see. *There has to be someone left.* Nothing but darkness appeared. The fear that had taunted her unidentified all night solidified into tears that slid from her eyes and spattered on the mirror. *They cannot all be gone!*

"*Leitha isa! Leitha Luke! Leitha Edmund! Leitha Dane!*"

But the mirror revealed nothing. She dashed it onto the floor with all her might and it smashed, shattering into thousands of pieces. The frame broke too. The cascade of pearls scattered across the floor.

Eve opened the window, slipped through it, and fled into the hills. She ran until she could run no more and collapsed upon a cushion of grass on the fringe of an unfamiliar meadow. Sobs heaved her chest. She buried her face in her arms and shut the world out.

It was almost dark again when she wended her way back down the valley again. The window to her room was ajar, hooked from the inside. She undid the catch and climbed back in.

A cold jug of water awaited and a slab of fresh bread with cheese. Her stomach rumbled—she was starving—but her appetite had deserted her. All traces of her smashed mirror had vanished. Instead she washed from the ewer and brushed her hair. The rasping sound of the brush and the cold shock of the water did nothing to ease bleak emptiness inside her.

Sleep would not come. The sheets stifled her body. Eve cast them off, to be overcome with chills. Miserably, she went and sat by the window once more with her head propped against the cool pane of glass, until she fell asleep at last.

Nelda woke her with a soft touch to the hand. Eve opened her eyes. Her head was dull and slow. She blinked blearily.

"What has passed, cousin?" said Nelda softly. "I scried you yesterday to see you far from here and in great distress."

Eve welled up and hot tears spilled from her eyes once more.

492

"I scried my father and others. They're dead," she croaked. "The mirror was black."

Nelda pulled her into a tight embrace.

"Can it be wrong?" Eve said into her shoulder, her voice muffled.

Nelda held her tighter. "I am afraid not, dear cousin. I am so sorry for your losses. My heart aches for you."

"Would you like to train today to distract yourself?" Nelda said after a long silence.

"I don't want to train. I want to leave, but I don't want to go home! There's nothing there for me."

Nelda stopped to make sure she ate and drank something, before she left.

Eve nibbled on her food to be obliging, but she did not taste it, nor did it stir her appetite. On an impulse, once Nelda had gone, Eve pushed back her plate. She opened the door and turned the opposite way from her cousin, to seek Artora.

Artora's grey skin fell from her in folds, creased and wrinkled upon her face, which frowned, even in sleep. Eve faltered on the threshold, taken aback by the sight. Artora no longer worked it seemed, but was bedridden instead, confined to her chamber by her growing infirmity. It was cool and dim—a perfect resting place. A window open by the tiniest measurement let in a small breeze that dispelled the cloying, moist heat of illness that suffocated the room.

The queen of the Eldarkind stirred as Eve entered.

"Your Majesty," Eve said, trying to keep her voice level. More upset brewed as she beheld her distant aunt's frail state.

"Welcome, Eve. It is good to see you. How do you keep?"

They shared small talk, but Eve did not dare enquire after Artora's health, for the answer was easy to see.

"Why have you come?" said Artora. She regarded Eve through alert eyes.

Eve told her of what she had seen in the mirror—hoping that

Artora would tell her that it was a mistake, a fault, and reveal to her her father and Luke safe and well. Their loss would be too great—and what would come next. *I don't want my father's place. I don't want to rule Arrow County. I'm not ready, and father knew it. There are many others who could do a better job; the captain of the guard, anyone.*

Artora's eyes softened. "There are no lies in the mirror. The magic will spell true."

Eve nodded past the lump in her throat. It had been the faintest hope in any case.

I have nothing left. She stared at the floor. *My father is gone. Luke is gone. Even Edmund is gone—and Dane. At least I won't have to marry him.* She would have felt sad for his death too, had it not been eclipsed by that of her father and Luke. *I thought I'd see them both again. I thought there'd be a chance to make amends.*

"I can offer you little comfort," said Artora, "only our companionship here."

"I have lost all joy," said Eve, her eyes cast to the floor. "I came to ask if you still sought a volunteer to journey north. I will go if you wish."

Artora's eyes widened. She sat up with much effort and reached for Eve with bony hands. Artora clasped Eve's hands in her own. Her skin the feel of paper against Eve's.

"Thank you, Eve." Her voice was filled with fervent gratitude. She coughed and her face scrunched in pain. The rasps subsided and she sagged back into her pillows dragging her hands from Eve to tuck them back under the coverlet.

"Nolwen and Nelda have told me of all your progress," she continued in a weak voice. "They see that I am updated each day. They are most impressed with you—it would seem you have progressed much since I last saw you. I am glad that the connection to your magic waxes once more.

"You are welcome to stay and train for as long as you like, but if you wish to undertake the journey to see if our fears are founded or not, there is but one more thing that you may need to learn. I will have to teach you how to place a binding upon Bahr of the fire. Please return tomorrow—I have no energy left for the present. I will send someone for you."

Eve bid her goodbye and left, unnerved by how sick Artora was. *Will I have no one left?*

She spent the rest of the day in solitary confinement. Each moment was a torture spent drifting from contemplation to blank thoughts. Nolwen and Nelda both knocked on the door at different times and called to her, but she had locked it and did not answer. To talk made it true.

Artora had reached a chair the next day, thick blankets tucked around her lap as she sat by a gentle fire. The window was closed and rain lashed against it heralding the true autumn's arrival. Eve sat before her on the shaggy rug, her back warmed by the flames.

"You will journey to the east first," began Artora, who sounded much stronger, "with some of my own kin—Nolwen and Nelda, amongst others. At the northern monastery you will gain more men and provisions for protection along the way. The abbot will not refuse us in our hour of need."

"Continue east along the tracks through the forest with the Helm Mountains always on your left shoulder. Eventually, the forest will end and you will come to the northernmost edge of the great plains that sweep through central Caledan, but your path will take you further north still. This is where you need the expertise of my kin and the monks; we know where Bahr is located, but you will need their help to reach him for the north is a harsh and inhospitable place.

"It is better to travel in numbers for there are great wolf packs that roam the frozen tundra, little food and no shelter to be had. We are expert hunters and can source all that we need to sustain ourselves, but as you draw closer to Bahr and the power of my kin fails, the mortal men will be your protection.

"When you have journeyed for many days and nights, you will at last sight the white peaks of the Kirkus Mountains on the horizon. The smallest of them is Juska. In her bowels sleeps Bahr of the fire.

All I ask of you is that you journey close enough to see if ought stirs. Venture into the mountain only if you must. Lay the binding if you are certain that Bahr slumbers—an extra hold upon him will help us. If he stirs, or worse if he roams, leave with all haste. Return to me at once so that I may do what I can to stop him. It may require the sacrifice of many, but I would not ask you to do this. I wish to keep you from harm's way if I can." Artora paused and glanced at Eve.

Eve nodded.

"I will give you the words of the binding. You must not speak them in the Eldar tongue unless you utter them in all sincerity for they are such powerful words they will draw the magic forth from you whether you intend it or not." Artora slipped a small scroll from her pocket and gave it to Eve.

"The binding will restrain Bahr if he awakens. It will still his thoughts and his movements. If he slumbers, it will deepen his rest. Long may he sleep." The words were intoned almost like a prayer.

"If you can give us news of him, perhaps we will find a way to send more of our strength and reinforce the binding in greater numbers if it is needed. It may yet hold. You must use all the energy available to you, should you use the binding. I have a gift which will help you. It took many years in the weaving, but it is yours."

From her other sleeve, Artora pulled a bracelet. At first it looked to be made of a strange metal unlike anything Eve had seen before, for it emitted a strange light. When Artora held it out to her, Eve could see that the smooth surface tumbled over itself, rippling like water driven by a current.

The moment it contacted her skin, she gasped. It felt like she had fallen into the river of energy itself. She blinked and the bright dizziness cleared. Artora returned to view before her. In her hand, the bracelet seemed to buzz against her skin—it hummed with vitality. On closer inspection, it seemed to be made out of no solid substance at all.

"It is pure energy, woven together."

Eve watched the band without reply. The raw power of it set her nerves on edge—though she was not sure she was frightened of it. If she closed her eyes and looked to the river of energy, she was sure she would not see it, blinded as she would be by the overwhelming power of the bracelet.

"The north will be cold," Artora said with a shiver. "Colder than you could ever imagine and many times worse than the harshest of our winters. You must take care on your journey not to let it take your limbs from you, nor to sap the energy from that source. We cannot make another. If you use it, use it well and if you do not, return it to us whole."

Artora gestured for her to put it on, so Eve stretched it over her hand and onto her wrist where it contracted to fit her. Next she looked at the parchment. It had been written in a flowing script using the Caledonian alphabet, but the Eldar tongue. Eve read it out in Caledonian.

"Bahr of the Fire spirit, I command you to sleep, unmoving, unthinking, unchanging, unyielding in the ice. I bind you with this, my energy and the energy of all living creatures everywhere until the end of time."

"The simplest wordings are sometimes the most effective," Artora said. "You must memorise this exactly as it is—in the Eldar tongue—in case you need to use it. It will be easier for you to do this if it remains short."

Even in her own tongue the words sounded ominous. Eve stared at the handwriting and held the paper at a distance as if it would bite her.

TWENTY NINE

Tired and aching after a ruthless march and days in the saddle, Soren sighted Lowenmouth upon the horizon. To their left the cliffs and grey sea disappeared into the hazy distance. To their right a low line of hills crowned with thick forests hid the mainland. It had been a miserable ride. The rain had begun on the first night of their travels and had not ceased since; it could have been snow, but Soren thought the freezing, driving downpour far worse.

Soren longed to sleep upon a soft bed, wash in hot water—or in fact, wash at all—and eat fresh meat and vegetables, all of which had been nonexistent since they had left Pandora. It was not to be. There was too much to do to idle and the city was to be their last retreat, though Soren did not intend to use it. There had been no word from the rearguard, who had not caught up with them yet. Soren feared than Zaki would soon be upon them.

They rode close to the coast where the cold sea winds stole the warmth from their skin. It numbed their faces and stung their eyes, but they endured it; to move inland was folly. Andor had already warned Soren that the ground there was marshy, so they were forced to stick to the coast road and made slow progress. It was even worse than Andor had described; an inhospitable mess after the fresh rains, however given the part it was to play in their plans, Soren was glad.

A straggling trail of men announced the rearguard's arrival. Andor's son and Walbridge himself rode at their helm. Their ranks had been decimated to Soren's distress. Soren had never been gladder to see anyone of House Walbridge. Only those who were on horseback remained; Soren knew that meant there were no more to follow. He could not believe that thousands had left and hundreds returned.

Andor had already left his men to destroy the last bridge to Lowenmouth. The rearguard arrived just in time to cross it. The bridge's destruction was key to luring Zaki away from the easy passage of the coastal road.

The wooden structure floated in pieces down the river to the sea, battered and chopped to pieces by hand. It was a regrettable loss, for it had taken a year to build not that long since, but it would force Zaki to ford the river to the north, where the direct approach to Lowenmouth would draw him straight into the clutches of the marsh.

Andor had intended they fight upon the plains to draw Zaki into the bog, but had realised upon seeing its state that they too would be mired and stranded in it. The swamp could be their own downfall—a risk too great to take. Instead, upon reaching the city, Soren and Andor directed and led men out into the hills to fight around the valley.

Men lined up on the hillside and retreated into the woods for cover. Here, Soren stationed all the archers and many more came from the city to join them—local hunters who used the woods to feed their families. The mix of deciduous and coniferous trees blazed with colour before the bleakness of winter and offered his men dappled camouflage.

Cavalry also positioned here, though feed stored in the city had to be brought out for them because of the sparse grazing in the woods. The remainder of the infantry waited in the rain upon the gentle slopes, with the protection of the swamp before them and the city behind them.

Soren and Andor stayed with them whilst their ranks were swelled by the guard from Lowenmouth. Meanwhile, Walbridge went to join what remained of his men in the woods and command the cavalry. Karn accompanied him to manage the archers: many of whom were from Arrow county.

The rearguard gave valuable news despite their sad return. Zaki was hours behind them and with the delay caused by the broken bridge, at best guess half a day away. Soren's stomach somersaulted at that. His nerves needed no encouragement to build. The time seemed to drag and race by at the same time, because they seemed to have waited forever and yet no time at all before Zaki's men arrived from the east.

The rains had lifted and weak sunlight filtered through the clouds, but it was still cold. Soren shivered along with the rest of his men, who could light no fires in the damp conditions to warm themselves. The flash of gold in the distance was the first clue and whispered word soon raced from the tip of the forest, where Caledonians lay concealed, all the way along its length and through his men to Soren himself.

"Good, they come from the right direction," said Andor. He smiled a grim smile of satisfaction. "He will know not to use the road—it leaves his forces too thin, too vulnerable. He will use the plain."

Zaki's forces fell into the trap. The mounted men rode forward, specks in the distance, past the arm of the forest. Soren could not believe their luck, but success was not his yet.

"Where are the rest? There must be three thousand men there, if that?" Soren was surprised at how many had horses.

"They will be the first. I think the rest will follow sooner than we like," replied Andor.

Feeling agitated, Soren mounted his horse. Andor did the same. "Now?"

"Not yet." Andor's eyes remained fixed on their foes. The tramp of their feet could be heard as a deep rumble—so many passed upon the land. "A little further." They waited. "Now!" He raised his arm and waved it twice.

A horn rang out to his right in two short blasts and all of a sudden, arrows rained down from the north to pepper the Roherii.

Their ranks roiled in confusion and turned to face this new challenge even as they strove to face Soren's front.

"Now." Andor grinned at Soren. A maniacal smile that was almost a grimace crossed his face.

"Charge! For Caledan!" Soren bellowed at the top of his voice.

"For Caledan!" The reply was roared by thousands of voices

around him.

The horn rang—long and clear and strong. Soren surged forward with his ranks. To ride forward brought a strange sense of exhilaration as he lowered the visor on his helmet, even though he knew he should have been terrified. Andor kept pace beside him. The Roherii cavalry were forced to meet them by riding through the mire.

They floundered as the wave of Caledonian men and horses crashed into their midst and cut through them left and right. Men fell from horses, which bolted riderless, as a new wave of men—this time on foot—crested the hill.

The clash and clang of weapons meeting, men screaming and shouting, horses shrieking and mud squelching overpowered all as Soren stayed with his knot of men with Andor to his left hand side and his standard bearer behind him. He did not get much chance to fight, whilst those around him surrounded him in a protective shield, but as their positions changed, he was able to lash out and deliver blows to the Roherii before him.

Three short blasts of a horn sounded, cutting through all else. Soren searched for the source. He swore as he saw the solid front of men running towards them.

"Come on Walbridge, where are you!" he shouted, though it was useless. No one could hear him over the deafening sound of battle. "Damn it, he had better not betray us!"

A frisson of fear and doubt gnawed at his anticipation and exhilaration. *Will Walbridge fail me? Instead of rallying to my banners, would Willam watch us fight and lose? Would he rally to Zaki's cause?*

Soren and his men floundered in the mud with their enemy. The scene had grown even more terrible as the already sodden grounds were washed with blood and the men grouped around Soren grew fewer.

Although the slight valley had forced Zaki's forces into a thinner band, they still seemed to be never ending, bolstered by their infantry reserves, though Soren's own ranks were helped by their own reinforcements who joined the chaos. Soren could not have counted the seething mass of men about him, but he knew they numbered many thousands. Again, Soren looked to the trees. Arrows flew from disembodied bows to bite into Zaki's arriving ranks.

At last, and not a moment too soon, Willam answered his call. A line of riders emerged from the trees. They descended from the hills in a streak of movement. The charge was swift and effective.

Zaki's men scattered. They fled to the sea, where the sneaky sinking sands of the beach and icy water of the high tide awaited them. Some retreated to the east, their organisation in turmoil from the attack, as Walbridge's command cut into their ranks and broke what little formation remained.

Many became stuck in the mud as Soren's forces drove forward with renewed vigour. Soren felt buoyant with relief that Walbridge had not failed him. What remained of Zaki's cavalry was destroyed, the riders powerless and abandoned by their comrades as their mounts floundered.

The Roherii infantry fared little better. Many of them threw up their arms in surrender with fear in their eyes when the line of horses surged upon them. They were rounded up, weapons confiscated and sat in well guarded huddles, whilst Soren congratulated the men about him.

Andor clasped arms with him as they circled together. "Well met, Soren."

"Well met, Andor."

"I have not seen or heard sign of Zaki yet," Andor said. He wiped blood and grime from his forehead with his sleeve—but it was so dirty it smeared more across his face.

"Myself neither," replied Soren. It was a troubling thought.

"We have broken the first wave. I think Zaki may have spent more than he realised there." Andor glanced around them. "By the looks of it there are thousands dead, hundreds fled and hundreds our captives. He cannot have many more, surely."

"Can we survive if he does?" Soren's relief and exhilaration at their success was tempered. It faded when he looked about and saw the extent of devastation.

Andor shook his head. "I cannot say, but we can withstand

whatever he has left. He would be foolish to come at us again."

They turned back to where Caledonians guarded Roherii prisoners. Soren was about to command that they be taken and held within the city for the present time, when a foreign bugle rang out from over the horizon.

Andor swore. "He attacks again, perhaps with all his remaining strength. You—ride out and scout."

At his command, one of the Balaur standard bearers handed his banner to another and rode as fast as he could across the unstable ground. He soon returned, with wide eyes. "M'lord, I can see many footmen marching towards us. They stretch all the way back to the river and beyond. There could be as many as eight thousand! There seemed no end to them and they filled the width of the valley."

Andor met Soren's concerned gaze. "Eight thousand? They outnumber us by far. We must regroup."

Soren nodded, but he frowned when he looked at the Roherii sat at their feet. "What are we to do with them? There may not be enough time to escort them to the city, and we cannot leave them here." The answer had already manifested inside his head, though he refused to admit it. "Summon my council with all haste."

"The rest of his forces advance—who can count how many we have already defeated—if he has as many as eight thousand men, can we succeed?" asked Soren. "We started with barely more than that and think how much our own ranks have been decimated by our battles thus far. We have five thousand men left at most, according to your estimates."

His counsellors remained silent, stood in a ring around him on the mud. They were at the furthest point in the valley away from Lowenmouth and vulnerable to Zaki's approach. Soren shifted, agitated by this, but he was unwilling to move until they had a solution.

"I do not speak from cowardice, but common sense. How can we win against almost double our number?"

"With difficulty," Lord Karn answered. His voice was as grave as his expression.

"We could withdraw to the city," Andor suggested.

"I would rather not bring war upon our citizens if it can be helped," replied Soren. "In any case it could become our prison not our sanctuary. I will withdraw to before the city. Perhaps we can operate the same trap upon Zaki's approaching forces? They may not know of our strategy."

"It would be difficult to do so," said Willam. "I have near no cavalry remaining to me for the charge. We could round up the horses that roam free and allocate them to other riders, but I would estimate that we do not have the time."

"Our archers have already exhausted their arrows," Karn added.

"Well then. It would seem that we have few options left to us," Soren replied. A flutter of panic rose through him. "We will regroup before the city and draw Zaki across the mire. We will wait for him to exhaust himself coming to us before we charge out to meet them. A retreat into the city will be our last resort. I hope that it will be our triumph, rather than our last stand."

At that moment, a scout interrupted. "I beg pardons, Your Majesty, Lords, Sirs." He bowed. "The Roherii draw close. We have little time remaining before they are here. I would urge that you reposition."

"That's settled, then. Let us away," said Soren.

"What of the prisoners?" Andor asked.

Soren paused. "Ah, yes. Do we have time to see them inside the city?"

"It does not seem so."

Soren paused. "What else can be done with them?" His heart sunk—there was one outcome.

"I think you know the truth of that, sire," said Walbridge. "We cannot take them with us. We cannot free them. We cannot leave them here. They must be… removed."

"There must be another way. I cannot slaughter unarmed men in good conscience."

"So you would give them arms, do battle to the death instead and call it honourable? We have neither the men nor the time for it, sire."

Soren did not reply.

"You know it would be folly to release them," Walbridge said as the foreign bugle sounded, much louder and closer this time.

Soren's heart palpitated in his chest at the sound.

"You must decide quickly, sire," Walbridge urged.

Behind them a scuffle broke out. One of the captives broke free and hurled himself at his guards.

"Roher!" he cried. He had no weapons—it did not stop him head-butting a guard. He bit another and used his hands and feet to batter through their ranks.

The sharp blades of Caledonian swords cut him down where he stood and he dropped to the mud, dying and then dead. His comrades rumbled in discontent, with dark looks and spat curses at their guards, but when they attempted to move forward, they too were faced by drawn blades.

Soren stared at the man's body, transfixed. *We may yet still win or lose. But against eight thousand? We do not need these extra mouths to feed, if it comes to siege, if we can get them into the city before Zaki arrive. There are too many 'ifs'!*

Frustration filled him, followed by stress when the Roherii bugle sounded again. He could hear the Roherii—an approaching rumble. Panic rose in his body.

"Do it," he ordered. "Kill them or we shall all die here and Caledan will fall! Mount up. Sound the retreat!"

The dying cries of the first man were multiplied by hundreds as his orders spread and they were cut down. It filled his ears and burnt itself into his memory. He rode from hearing as fast as he could with bile rising in his throat. Their bodies carpeted the ground. Soren wished he had not looked back.

He was soon before the city once more, with what remained of his men behind him in a great wall of armour. They were fewer than before, but their ranks built up by the remaining men of Karn and Walbridge who had joined them from the woods.

They had formed up when the Roherii crested the horizon. They advanced at an unrelenting pace.

Soren watched them with a heavy heart.

Andor leaned over. "You did the right thing for Caledan," he whispered and gave Soren an encouraging smile. "That was no easy decision."

But Soren felt no better. Guilt multiplied within him. "As long as it will save Caledan," he replied more confidently than he felt.

Zaki's army spread the entire width of the valley's opening: matched by Soren's at its opposite end, spread before the walls of Lowenmouth. A nervous tension hung in the air as the last of Zaki's men crossed the horizon.

Soren frowned and glanced around at his own men to compare. "They cannot have eight thousand men," he said to Andor.

Andor shook his head. "Nay, they do not. It must have been some ruse, or our scout made a grave calculation error. There can be no more than our own number of men there, but I am sure we may still have more."

They watched as Zaki's men halted, and a party swarmed by those slain on Soren's orders.

"They will see the carnage," Andor said. "I doubt they will engage—not with the stronghold of Lowenmouth behind us, unless they have many more men on the way."

Contrary to his beliefs the Roherii charged forward despite the fact that they were outnumbered. The vanguard remained upon the hillside. Soren presumed they waited for their orders to advance.

Soren sent his own forces forward to meet the Roherii with reluctance—it seemed such a waste for more to die in vain, when he was certain the Caledonians would prevail—but from within the eye of the storm, a small pond of calm in a raging sea and surrounded by his protectors, he saw the rearguard turn tail and vanish. Nowhere could he see any sign of Zaki, or a standard bearer of any kind. He yelled at Andor, who joined him within the circle of blades.

"They flee!" Soren pointed at the Roherii vanishing over the horizon.

"Then Zaki flees with them, I would wager!" Andor replied

with a growl. "Coward." He spat on the ground and scowled. "I can see no sign of him anywhere. I think he knew that he could not win upon seeing our strength and so sent his men to die for him and delay our pursuit."

"Can we give chase?" Soren said, but he knew he was too hopeful. There were still a thousand men upon the battlefield to defeat first.

"We cannot until our foe here is vanquished," said Andor. With a great cry, he charged forward into the fray.

Soren nudged his own horse, drew his blade and joined in with a howl of frustration. *Will he ever answer for what he has done!*

Darkness had fallen by the time they had slain the last foe. Many had surrendered upon seeing the remaining Roherii flee. Soren ached from head to toe and was dizzy with exhaustion. He had no choice but to stay awake. He rode with Andor and many others across the battlefield to search for injured friends amongst the dead.

Any Roherii they came across, they helped. Soren was indiscriminate in his aid, too full of remorse for his earlier actions to deal out more death. He sent the injured back to Lowenmouth, carried or supported as needed. Healers in white robes—that were soon blood and mud stained—moved amongst them to tend to those they could.

Moving amongst his men, who all shared the same grey face and slouched posture of spent energy, Soren knew that none of them were fit enough to pursue Zaki. It already burned in his heart that he had been so close to the man who had caused to much strife, harm and grief, but could not put an end to him.

If Zaki has learnt his lesson he will not return, Soren considered. However, it was hard to believe that the man who had been captured, miraculously escaped, survived and returned stronger than ever—like a weed that refused to die—would not return again.

Soren was welcomed into the city of Lowenmouth by cheering men, women and children who packed onto streets that were flooded with light from those who held burning brands and lamps. He smiled and waved as he rode at the head of the procession into the city—as was his duty—but he longed to scream at them all to be silent instead.

You should all be filled with sorrow, grieving for your lost kinsmen, he wanted to say. *You should even grieve for those fallen Roherii.* For when he recalled the moment he had ordered their deaths, every face he observed in its dying moments was no monster, but a man. A man fighting under the orders he had received.

It is the orders that are evil, not the man, realised Soren—but it was too late. The actions—his actions—could not be undone. As the false grin widened on his face, his cheeks ached even more from the gesture and his mind threw self-loathing at him. *You're a monster.*

That night he dined with Balaur cousins who he had not seen since his coronation well over a year before. It was hard to celebrate along with them, for he felt the payment required for their victory was too great to justify laughter and joy. His own actions haunted him too, so out of character that he found it hard to believe what he had done. His extended cousins did not share his troubled thoughts, for they feasted and revelled until late into the night, whilst Soren drifted to sleep in his chair, jolted awake by raucous laughter and shrieking.

THIRTY

What is the boy doing? Zaki wondered as he forded the river, annoyed by the hour's detour they had been forced to make because of the broken bridge. His vanguard were already upon the battlefield, but when he crested the final hill, Lowenmouth was revealed before him. He paused in shock.

Not a man of his remained upon the battlefield. Instead, the area swarmed with Caledonians and worse, a sea of the dead.

"Good, they are almost spent," Reynard said from his side. "Let us attack them at once!"

"They are not so," said Zaki, "merely disorganised. Do not forget that they have the city to fall back upon if they need to—we would starve before they did." *Campaigning in winter was a poor choice,* he reflected. *What a miserable affair without the element of surprise.* He thought he had missed Caledan. Now he found himself longing for the warmth of Roher. *I'm sick of being cold, tired and wet.*

They rode closer at the head of his men, none of whom had horses, for all the cavalry had gone before.

"Wait," said Reynard all of a sudden. He stood in his saddle. "They have Roherii prisoners. Hundreds by the looks of it."

"The cowards surrendered?" Anger flared within Zaki. "I did not come all this way to be let down by cowards!"

In the next moment, a flurry of motion occurred and the Caledonian men fled towards the city.

"They flee before us as they should!" exclaimed Reynard with satisfaction.

"Will you be silent!" snapped Zaki. "They do not flee—can you not see? They have slain every last man." Zaki stilled for a moment. "They would not have done that had it not been ordered by Soren." *I did not expect such ruthlessness from that sap of a boy.* Zaki felt

509

a twinge of very grudging respect—he was even a slight bit impressed—but it did not reassure him. *If Soren can make such decisions, he is not the boy that I last faced.*

"I have a new plan." He surveyed the scene before him. The last of the straggling Caledonians joined their comrades in a huge block before the walls of Lowenmouth, which were as grey as the sky and the sea and dulling in the early evening.

"We do not have the numbers to defeat them. These Roherii are cowards—I fear we have lost almost a thousand to desertion already and the cravens could have made the difference. I hope they die and rot. As it stands, we will not see success and I am not prepared to die this day in vain, or at all.

"I will send in what Roherii remain and hold back a small rearguard. When Soren is engaged with our men and unable to stop us, we will retreat."

"To Roher?" asked Reynard in a low voice.

"To Roher. We do not remain in any number great enough to be a threat and I will not find support here, after Walbridge has betrayed us. I had expected him to rally to my cause, but it is clear he has lost his mind and supports the boy instead. I hope he has paid for his treachery."

"Why would he not support your cause as he always has done?" asked Reynard. His face scrunched in confusion.

Because he did not believe I would succeed, Zaki's thoughts replied. "He is a traitor, nothing more and he will pay with all the rest of them!" he snapped instead, to silence his own doubts as well as reply to Reynard.

"We will retreat to Roher," repeated Zaki, "where I will bide my time and campaign again next season. We will return in the summer, when I can live off the land. Soren will not be able to rally this number again. We have exhausted his support. He will retreat within his poxy castle and I will starve him out and grow fat from his land whilst he withers away." Zaki laughed, a short bark of satisfaction, at the thought.

"Will Harad support you in this?"

"He will have no choice. I am his son-in-law and the closest he will get to Caledan's throne. He is no fool. I am confident he will appreciate how close we are. One more push and Caledan will be mine and through me, his. It is a prize too great to refuse."

Zaki signalled for his men to advance and they rushed past him in a wave that rolled down the hillside and over the valley bottom. Their golden armour was covered by dull, brown mud as they ran into the arms of their death-dealers. He saw how the silver armour of the Caledonians mixed with the gold until the scene was a mess of mixed men. Yet, his mind was already elsewhere planning the quickest route back to the isthmus, where he could steal boats— for he doubted those who had brought them to Caledan would have waited—and how to sail back to Roher. The desert route was unthinkable. He was lucky to survive it the first time and he doubted his fortune would hold a second.

With a silent gesture, Zaki signalled the retreat. His rearguard, made up of those Caledonians who had survived with him all the way to Roher and back, moved with him as he rode over the horizon. For all they had endured with him, he cared not at this point if his men lived nor died—not even Reynard, after the disappointment his second-in-command had proved to be—only that he himself would reach safety..

THIRTY ONE

After two days of preparations, Eve left Ednor accompanied by four of the Eldarkind; Nolwen and Nelda, and two others that she had not encountered before: Iara, a burly, muscled hulk and Tolthe, as tall as Iara but much slimmer. She said her farewells to Artora early that morning, for they had to depart swiftly to outrun the storm clouds that chased them over the pass. It was with a heart growing in heaviness that Eve departed.

The smell of sickness upon the queen was sweet and cloying, a scent that would not dissipate from her nostrils until well after they had left. Artora could not rise from bed that day, so Eve instead leaned down to kiss her on the forehead in farewell. Her skin was as hot as fire and clammy to the touch.

Several days later, they reached the monastery and were admitted through open gates. The weather was cooler outside Ednor's valley. In the mornings and evenings, the air became bitingly cold—painful to breathe—and a frost had begun to creep upon everything about them when they awoke. Eve was glad for the warm clothes she had been outfitted in—woven fabrics that were spelled so wind and water could not penetrate them. Fur lined boots adorned her feet. They kept her toes toasty warm and she even had mittens made from a hide with fur so fine her hands felt like they were cushioned by silk.

The winters in Arlyn were snowy and cold enough, but they did not warrant such measures and Eve was beginning to think what they were to encounter would be far more severe than she expected. She realised that it was the worst time of year to travel north, now winter marched south and worsened in the extreme heights of the world.

That morning, Artora had impressed upon her the need for

haste. "There is no time to waste!" she had said with such a fervent determination in her gaze that Eve was frozen in her glare.

The abbot soon appeared to meet them, though he did not rush. He was a tall and thickset man: a dark haired, dark eyed match of Iara it would seem.

Iara, their natural leader, greeted him and introduced their small group and purpose.

Hador welcomed them inside what appeared to be a new gatehouse, out of the rising wind that nipped at their exposed faces. He was worried by their news, but reluctant to become involved.

"The winter is no time for a man to be away from his home—or her home," he added with a glance towards Eve and Nelda, "and a journey past the gap is more treacherous. Would you have me send my men to icy deaths, never to return? Besides that, we are already so few after the attack last year. You have not seen the fullness of our graveyard and the emptiness of our beds. We cannot even rebuild with any speed, because there are not enough men to quarry, lumber, build and eke a living. We will see our second winter though without the protection of our home."

"We would not ask unless the need were great, abbot," Nolwen said, leaning forward. "This is a threat far beyond any of our ken, but if the worst is to pass, your brothers will not be safe here. The devastation shall not spare you. We must work together to ensure our success."

"You mean to kill the beast?"

"He is no beast," said Iara in his deep voice. "He is the very essence of life, of fire, of energy. Bahr controls unimaginable power that no man could stand before. No human—not even an army of you—could destroy him."

Hador sent them to eat whilst he deliberated. Eve enjoyed the first human meal she had eaten in weeks. The Eldarkind's food was exquisite, but she had missed game meat, potatoes and vegetables drowned in a hearty gravy and accompanied by a crusty bread roll for dunking and mopping up the remainder of the plate.

After they had eaten, they returned to hear Hador's judgement.

His brow was creased and his arms folded as he stood before them. "I will not order my men to do this for you. I cannot ask such a great thing of them. I will however, let any volunteers who wish to go accompany you. I will send some of my brothers to ask if there are any willing to journey with you, with instructions to gather by dawn to leave. We will aid you with provisions—you will need more horses to carry shelter and fire materials and food too. Those things we will gladly give you in your time of need."

"Thank you, abbot," said Iara. He bowed low—the others copied him.

With the rest of the pre-evening free, they were able to explore the walled compound of the monks. It was a pleasant and green place, even in the winter, with lawned gardens well kept, though the flowerbeds were bare and the trees stripped of their leaves.

The patch of greatest disturbance was the extended cemetery, where bare earth ruled kept free of the grass by careful tending and adorned with green wreaths and small tokens of remembrance. It was a peaceful place, but full of sorrow and empty too. They rarely saw large groups of monks anywhere and the brown-robed men were few and far between.

There was no denying that the monastery itself was a shell of its former self. The canteen they had eaten in was a wooden cabin and the monastery a set of broken stone walls, almost like a large drawing on the ground that had never been made into the full sized model. From what they could see, log cabins were the only completed structures.

Rubble was piled near the walls: a giant mixture of pieces large and small, some seeming too huge to move. Reconstruction projects had begun on the central chapel first and foremost, but it seemed to have newly begun, or not progressed. Eve suspected the latter.

Buildings took lots of men to construct she knew, and there were not enough here. She could see from what remained that the building had been huge. *They spend too much time trying to live from the land, as they must,* she observed. Men moved in silence in their duties: gathering winter root vegetables and chopping firewood on large stone flagged courtyards that were out of place with nothing to surround them.

A week later, the warmth had deserted them as they crossed out of Caledan into the wild lands of the north that were unmapped by men, who could find no use for their presence. They had left the last of any shelter behind with the wood's end and the days and nights merged into one as they rode under the vast white sky that had begun to snow daily upon them. It turned the land into a white mirror of the sky that stretched in all directions. They used the Helm Mountains to their west and then to their south for navigation. The peaks soon shrank behind them, until they too had disappeared in the distance.

The nights were the worst. At least upon horseback during the day's travels, they could stay warm from the exertion of riding, or run where they needed to stretch stiff limbs. But at night, all they had for shelter was a large canvas made from several hides sewn together and propped up by a series of sticks. They huddled under it each night, wrapped in their blankets, still fully clothed. They had to lay on the folds of the skin to keep it flat to the ground. It was unpleasant to say the least, sleeping on hard ground in such close proximity to each other. Eve had lost all thoughts of grief, her sole concentration being to gain warmth and stay warm: a constant battle of a different sort.

The horses had to be dressed for the weather too, with skins, furs and cloths wrapped around their legs and neck, especially at night, where they tried to huddle out of the wind behind the tent in misery, their heads down and tails between their legs. Each morning, the company would awake to find snow banked on one side of the skin tent, with the world whiter than it had been before.

Eve thought snow was beautiful in Arlyn. Here, it was a menace that would not leave them alone.

The Kirkus mountains rose in the distance: a brilliant white against the rare blue sky that dazzled them that morning. They were already coated in snow and ice from their highest peak to the lowest.

It had been a long, hard week of riding in a direction-less landscape that was flat and white as far as the eye could see, broken by low rolling hills. There were no woods, it seemed, in this part of the world, nor life, for they had not seen another living being or sign of life—smoke rising, dwellings—and even struggled to find animals to eat.

It was said that the north men of old, a hardy but primitive race that had not survived, came from beyond these mountains. The original reason the northern monastery had been constructed was as a defensible position to keep them out of early Caledan and defend against their raids. No one lived north of the gap any more.

They had resorted to rationing the dried meat strips given to them by the monastery, together with flat, round travelling biscuits from the Eldarkind. Their water was found from melting the snow over their small fires, made from the fast dwindling supply of wood, for there was nothing to be found here, not even the smallest bush.

Eve was glad for the horses, for without them their progress would have been too slow, and for her warm attire, which trapped her warmth next to her skin in a way she had never before appreciated. One of the older monks had already shown them his several missing toes, claiming that the frost had eaten them many years ago.

The monks prided themselves on quiet solitude and rarely spoke to Eve or her Eldarkind companions, who were much more sociable.

"Why did you come?" she asked them one morning.

"To see the wonder of God in places new," said one, who Eve took to be very devout.

"To explore the world," said another, whose youthful face lit up at the prospect of discovery.

"For the greater good," said a third, who seemed troubled. "Our abbot insisted this was a task of vital importance for the safeguarding of all humanity."

Eve had begun to question her own belief in God. The

revelation that magic existed and dragons—amongst greater forces—had turned her away from the idea of an all-controlling deity. Not to mention, the loss of her loved ones. What God would do such a thing? She feared the answer. It was easier to believe in what she could see. But she held her doubts to herself and nodded politely at their words.

They could already see Juska—'the little spur', Nelda told her it once used to mean. A dark line ascended from its base: a tear in the side of the mountain that led to the secret within. Unanimously they decided not to camp near to the peak for its presence already fostered an unnerving fear upon them, like the atmosphere itself held evil. The sun was not yet near to setting, but they did not want to venture closer.

Eve sat with her Eldarkind companions on rocks brushed clean of snow, observing Juska whilst the monks behind them sung their daily hymns. A narrow cleft hundreds of yards high, was visible from where they sat, shrinking into itself until it closed.

"That is where He sleeps," Nolwen muttered in a dark tone, nodding towards the cavern.

"Who is Bahr? I don't know much of him," asked Eve.

"Do not speak His name so close to the mountain," warned Nelda. "In itself, it carries power."

Eve shivered.

"He of the fire is one of the oldest and most potent elementals that we know to still remain," Iara said. "Those that do are all bound as He is, in the element most debilitating to them, to sleep through all time in many far flung locations across the world."

Eve wondered how big the world was. Caledan was all she knew and even its borders seemed huge and distant.

"Yet of all the others, He has awoken. Perhaps because He is the closest to the pact's breaking point, its weakness aids him first. Who knows what His counterparts do in their shackles. We believe in no Gods, but even we pray for their unending slumber.

"He of the fire was, in legend, a cruel and vindictive spirit, of a fiery temper and quick to judge and condemn others. He delighted in playing tricks and hurting others if He could for his own amusement.

"Elementals are witty, clever and sly, creatures to be wary of, careful around and never trusted. They are ones to twists words and muddle meanings and promises. Never give an elemental your word, it is said, for you will never have it back.

"They are powerful too, more than you could begin to imagine. Even we would struggle to conceive of such might, had we not the memories, magically retained, to see for ourselves the devastation they can wreak.

"Bahr had to be bound by the first of the Eldarkind. He was too dangerous, too unpredictable, and too selfish to risk remaining free. He burned for sport all in his path. In those days, He was so powerful that He had to be bound by an entire race, as all the elementals did, a collective gathering of magics from all mouths and minds, focused in one task."

"How can we bind him, if He is so powerful?" said Eve, scared by Iara's words.

"We do not bind Him starting from nothing. Asleep, He should be much easier to re-seal. He will have lost much of his power in slumber—or it will be suppressed, at the very least."

"He may yet sleep," Nelda whispered to her, squeezing her in a one armed hug and smiling to reassure her, but Eve could not help but wonder if Bahr slept at all.

This may not have been a good idea.

She struggled to sleep that night. It was like she could feel the chasm as a baleful pressure over her and a presence behind her. The skin of the shelter seemed no protection at all that night. By the morning, she was exhausted and plagued by growing doubts.

Why am I here? I cannot presume to succeed.

THIRTY TWO

The robes itched against Luke's sweating skin. They were too big, made for his wide shoulders but drowning the rest of his body. Luke suppressed a loud curse, muttering it into his own hearing instead. He wiped his ruddy face with a hand, hitched both sleeves back up his arms again and took a fresh grasp on the axe. The rhythmic thock of chopping firewood dulled his mind as it did every day.

He had been out with the brotherhood in the woods collecting firewood for a week. It was almost time to return and he was anticipating a softer bed that night and a proper hot meal in his stomach. Being as young and strong as he was, he was often volunteered for the most demanding tasks.

The previous week, he had been further up in the hills, quarrying what rock they could from the mountains. It was a dwindling hoard. They needed more men and warmer weather to succeed. They had returned with not enough to show for their hard work and the unwelcome news that the mountains would soon be closed to them for the winter.

The horses were loaded with panniers of wood, with most going into the precious two carts that had been repaired time and time again. The wood clattered as the carts bumped over the ground, a happy tune to accompany them back home as he chatted with his brothers. His smile grew when the familiar wall appeared through the trees.

As the most junior brother, it was his duty to care for the horses before himself. Luke turned them free in the paddock once he had deposited their load in the carpentry station, fed them and reported back to the abbot. At the carpenter's bench, the wood needed to be sorted into that fit to be crafted, and that fit to be firewood—but that was a job for another day.

Luke clambered up the wooden steps into the dormitory, where a pail of water sat in the corner. It was cold, but he was grateful to be able to have a brisk wash, even if he had to put the same robes back on again. He no longer smelt himself—or his brothers—for which he was glad.

"Aaahhh," he groaned as he stretched out his muscles. *Time to eat, at last.*

The dining hall—a grand name for a poor place—was too small to hold everyone at once, so he joined the freezing queue and waited for his turn. Soon he was in the warm, dry space, with a piping hot bowl in his hand. With the other, he collected a wooden beaker and scooped up a cup of home-brewed ale: the monastery's special brew and his ration for the week. He looked around for a space and slotted between two of his brothers with a grin.

"Well met, brother Luke."

"Good day brother Ormund."

Luke muttered a small grace over his meal before he ate, sinking his spoon into the bowl as the last word faded from his lips and replacing it with a mouthful of hot meat and gravy. He ate in silence, half listening to the chatter about him. It was good to return. The monastery was a simple place, but homely and full of kindness; they had taken him in in his hour of need and cared for him since.

His ears pricked up at the unfamiliar chatter—normally his brethren spoke of little else but the rebuilding of the abbey, but today many spoke also of the strange visitors they had received that week. Luke paled as he put the pieces of the puzzle together.

Blond hair... inhuman beauty... special mission... Could it be the Eldarkind? He could not help but interrupt and leaned across the table.

"Eldarkind? Lady?" he said to a brother several seats down from him.

"Well aye, did you not see them? Ah, apologies brother Luke, I forgot, you have been elsewhere. Aye, we had visitors, the Eldarkind from beyond the mountains—straight out of myth if you please—and with them a Lady of Aryn.. Alana..."

"Arlyn!"

"Yes, something like that."

"The lady of Arlyn?" *It cannot be.*

Aye," replied the monk, his tone growing more disgruntled from Luke's questions. "That's who she said she was."

"Where are they?" said Luke. He stood and struggled out from the trestle bench.

"What's your hurry, brother Luke?" asked Ormund. "They're long gone."

"Gone? Where?"

"Off up north on secret business. Dangerous, we heard, but nothing more. Volunteers was wanted for the journey to safeguard them on the way. Not surprised too! Two slight ladies and some weedy men. On'y one of them had any look of strength about him. They wouldn't have lasted alone in the north."

Luke knew the skills of the Eldarkind better, but he did not say, preoccupied with thoughts of Eve. He closed his eyes for a moment. *She was here and I missed her.*

"Do you know anything else?" Luke said.

Ormund shook his head. "That's it."

Luke sunk back onto the bench, before gobbling down the rest of his food and gulping his drink. He no longer wanted any of it, but to leave it would be an insult to the cooks and committing the sin of wastefulness.

He rushed out after washing his wooden plate and mug and handing them to the next man in line and made his way to Hador's hut. The abbot had a cabin of his own: a small space for him to work in. It was crammed with books upon crude shelves. Most of their precious resources were stored in the cellar, but with winter's approach, the books had had to make way for the food stores: the meagre amount of grain they had bought and bartered for and the years worth of cured and dried meat.

Hador answered his frantic knocks upon the door. His eyebrows rose when he beheld Luke.

"Brother Luke, is all well? Come in." He stepped aside to let Luke out of the cold and paused when he saw Luke's troubled face.

"Was the Lady Eve of Arlyn here?"

Hador regarded him with keen eyes. "Yes, why do you ask?"

"I… I knew her, once."

Hador pursed his lips. "It is not for me to comment upon such things. Each man's past is his own before he enters our sanctuary. But on your entry into our brotherhood, you should have forsaken all former ties, forgotten and erased as you dedicate yourself to God, king and country. I feel that it may not be wise to rekindle memories of your old life by discussing this with you."

"I beg you," said Luke. He explained in halting words what had passed before he had entered the monastery, all the way from his part in helping rescue Irumae to his feelings for the lady and how they had caused him to cast off his old life in an attempt to escape. "But if she needs assistance, I would give it all over again. I could not see her come to harm. It would torment me for the rest of my living days if I could have helped her and did not."

"You forsook women when you entered this place, Brother Luke," Hador said, his eyes serious as they probed Luke. "Do you wish to break that?"

"No, father, though I still bear feelings for her. Regardless of those, I feel a great duty to her after so many years in her father's service. Please let me aid her."

Hador turned away from him, his hands clasped behind his back and his head bowed forwards.

Luke waited, in absolute silence. He did not dare move though his agitation grew. *What if he says no? What will I do. Would I run away? I would have to steal to succeed. I could not do that in good faith. He must say yes…*

At last, Hador turned to face him once more. He sighed. "You may go. I cannot deny you in good faith as I allowed your brethren to volunteer themselves, especially given you are so driven to help. I can guess the distress that it would cause you if I denied you. Are you sure you wish to risk yourself? Travelling alone is foolish beyond belief. You might not return."

"Yes." Luke nodded, filled with determination.

Hador sighed. "We cannot really afford to spare one more

horse for we are already short of them from our generosity to those who travelled north—but I will support you, brother. I will send you with what provisions we can afford to give you, with warm clothes too and I will draw you a map for your direction. Perhaps you can catch up to them. They are two days ahead and may be riding more slowly than you, as burdened as they are with supplies. Leave at dawn."

"Please may I leave now, father?" said Luke. *I cannot stay another minute!*

"What use it setting out in the dark? You could become lost, or hurt. Get a night's sleep—for I suspect it may be your last good one in a while—and set out at dawn, refreshed."

Luke bowed his head, though he did not agree with the abbot. "I will do as you say, father—thank you."

THIRTY THREE

Vomit sprayed across the snow as Nelda grasped her brother for support. Her face was an off shade of grey, but her brother fared little better. He bent over double and retched. Eve halted in concern.

"It's alright, go on," said Nelda. She staggered behind them, but vomited again and sunk to the ground in a heap. Soon her brother was on his knees too and Iara—even Tolthe.

Eve regarded them with consternation—she was unaffected, as were the monks. She halted the monks and retraced the footprints in the snow back to Tolthe so she could help him to his feet.

"Thank you," he murmured.

"What's wrong?" Eve's brow furrowed.

"I feel so unwell," said Tolthe. "Waves of... nausea." He paused and clamped his mouth shut for a moment. "A headache so strong I can barely see. And the taste of metal in my mouth, hard and tangy."

"I feel this also." Iara shuffled forward.

"And I," Nolwen called in a low voice from where he sat in the snow.

Nelda, still retching, did not respond.

Eve felt fine—though when she concentrated, there did seem to be a pressure upon her, almost like the fuzzy beginnings of a headache, but nothing on the same scale as her companions.

"Do you feel any of this?" she asked the monks.

They shook their heads in bafflement, their faces blank.

"The closer we travel to the mountain, the worse it seems to become," Iara growled. "I was of good health this morning." He turned around and walked away with a grimace. "I fear there is more to this than meets the eye. Let us retreat."

The Eldarkind retreated in their tracks, shuffling with

hunched shoulders and heads down. Eve followed in silence, though she was bursting with questions. They walked for hundreds of yards before they halted.

Iara closed his eyes and his face filled with relief. "It is as I thought. I feel much better. How fare you?" He turned to his companions.

Nelda nodded. "I feel improved, but though much has been taken from me."

They rested awhile before attempting the approach once more. This time however, they were even further away when the nausea started. This time it brought stomach cramps with it.

Again, they drew back.

"It is like something weakens us," Nolwen said. "I feel worse for doing less."

Nelda had once more sunk onto a rock for support, not even bothering to clear the snow from its surface.

"What could cause it?" asked Eve.

"Perhaps this is His effect," Iara replied. "Perhaps He strains against his bonds, waiting, poisoning them. The energy of this place feels wrong."

Eve realised that he was right.

"It's darker," she said, after probing the depths of the river of energy.

"Corrupted." Iara scowled.

"I feel a malign presence sitting upon my shoulders like a dead weight," said Nelda. She seemed short of breath.

"What should we do? Should we approach?"

"I must," said Iara, gritting his teeth. "For my queen, for my people, I must do what I set out to, as was promised. I will return with news of Him. If this is His evil will, I will triumph." Iara set off again. They passed where they had stopped before and pressed on.

Eve could see from their scrunched faces and erratic movements that they were being overcome. When they were within a stone's throw of the cavern, Nelda collapsed for good. Nolwen bent to help her up, but fell down himself. The pair sat shuddering with their eyes closed. Tolthe was even quieter than usual, which was something to be said.

As before, the monks followed them, unaffected and perturbed by their companions ailments. One muttered prayers under his breath whilst glancing about with suspicious, narrowed eyes.

Iara almost made it to the very entrance before he too fell, unconscious upon the ground. The men rushed forwards to support him. They carried Nolwen and Nelda away from the cave. Eve helped to support Nelda, whose face felt burning hot to the touch. Tolthe waved away their support and shuffled away by himself.

"You fainted," Eve told Iara as they revived him with a trickle of water between his blued lips.

"It cannot be done." Iara said. He cursed in a language Eve did not understand. "If we are to succeed, you must go ahead, Eve. You are the only one of us who is unaffected and possesses the magic to protect themselves inside Juska."

"I'm scared," Eve admitted.

"Eve." Nolwen leaned forward to grasp her hand in his. He smiled at her and though it was warm, it was also wan and without his usual vitality. "We have come so far, for this. Artora asked you for a reason. Eldarkind have failed in this—and now we know why—and these men cannot hope to understand what they face. It must be you. Remember the binding Artora taught you, but do what you must. Do not take unnecessary risks and do not perform any magic. Find him and make sure he sleeps. Do nothing more unless you have no choice."

"We will come with you for a way," said one of the monks. They broke from their separate huddle as their muttered conversation ceased. "Brother Sirus wishes to see inside the mountain and others are curious too."

"But it could be dangerous," said Eve, not understanding why they would volunteer. *Do they not understand? Even I cannot fathom the true peril of this and I already wish to leave this cursed place.*

"There is a creature in the mountain," said the monk, "but it sleeps and with God's will it will continue to do so. With the protection of our Saviour, nothing can harm us unless it be His will."

Eve nodded. "As you wish. Thank you," she added.

There seemed no reason to delay. She embraced Nelda and Nolwen with fondness, taking confidence and comfort from the contact. Iara and Tolthe bowed to her with grave faces.

The yawning presence of the cave loomed over her. Its pitch black depths wanted to swallow her up. Eve shivered, unsettled. She swallowed and looked around her for support. The monks surrounded her. They were serious—solemn faced as always—but not as grim as Iara, who looked at her with an imperturbable expression. Their solid presence reassured her as she stared up at the fissure. It rose far out of sight above them.

Eve turned around to see her Eldarkind companions well out of the way across the snow. They raised their hands to her and she replied in kind. She paced forwards, her steps slow, deliberate and reluctant. Darkness swallowed her.

The blinding light of the sunlit snow behind Eve was in great contrast to the void they had stepped into. Daylight shrunk behind them with every step, until it had almost vanished and any helping hand it gave them was lost. The blue stone, flecked with silver and glistening with ice, reflected golden light back at them as the monks lit brands, prepared with the last of the wood and material torn from all their clothes.

It revealed a flat path—that Eve reckoned had been formed with magic, for there were no marks of working upon it and it bore straight into the mountain with not a single twist or turn—guiding them forward between two uneven walls that rose out of sight and into darkness above their heads. The way was three men abreast in width. At once, it felt constricting and huge.

Eve fingered her bracelet. Its warmth was reassuring and touching it was a bond to the pure energy stream she knew, not the darkened version that flowered about her. Her nerves hummed with energy.

She kept her hand upon the bracelet as they continued. The monks muttered and whispered amongst themselves, amazed by what they were seeing, but each word was magnified a thousand fold and each footfall was an advancing army, echoing many times over.

Every sound made her wince.

There was no hint of day in Juska's bowels. Their barrier to darkness was the warm, comforting glow of the torches. With each ragged breath, clouds plumed before them. The air was still, with no hint of a breeze, but not stuffy. Rather, it was a freezing air that was so cold it sapped the warmth and life from them.

If Eve had been there by herself, she would have panicked. She was not afraid of the dark, but in a place this confined and lifeless with that strange sense of pressure growing the further they went, her instincts screamed for her to run. Even the presence of strangers reassured her, though they halted here and there to look at strange formations and features in the rocks, which forced Eve to stop too. It gave Eve the chance to try and feel ahead with her senses, but Juska was unwilling to reveal her secrets yet it seemed. Dark, empty silence awaited them.

As they progressed, other ways began to snake off the main passage. Up and down they tunnelled into the mountainside—some wide, some narrow, some tall, some so small a man could not fit through them. Yet none were made by nature, but some device of man or magic, for the surfaces were smooth-faced, almost polished in appearance. Each time they passed one, Eve's chest constricted and she held her breath. But nothing stirred in the darkness and no sounds emanated from within these new passages, not even the whisper of a breeze.

She continued with her torch—having taken it from one of the monks who wished to examine the rock—but could see that already it had begun to dim. She had no idea how long they had been in the mountain—it could not have been hours yet, but their progress was slow and time lost in there without the passage of the sun to mark it.

Eve looked back at her companions and froze. She was alone. A whimper escaped her as her body locked in place, rigid with fear. Eve strangled a cry. She dared not move. Her eyes darted about her and above her. There was nothing there—that she could see—but the darkness taunted her with spectres.

Eve sunk onto the floor and tucked herself into the wall,

trying to stop hyperventilating. She tucked her head between her knees and squeezed her eyes shut. At last, her breathing slowed as her internal monologue rolled over her fears.

You're fine, you're fine, you're fine, you'll be fine, you're fine.

Eve forced herself to move on. She touched the wall for comfort and stayed close to it, whilst the torch burned lower. With every few steps, she glanced behind and around herself with agitation. She walked sideways with her back scraping along the wall, reluctant to turn it on empty space. Ahead, a light grew.

Have I made it outside again? she wondered, feeling a twinge of relief at the prospect. It was blue, the colour of the sky, but it seemed to lack the same intensity of the day she had left behind. Nevertheless, it drew her towards it. *It could be the way out.*

The fissure narrowed ahead, to the width of a single person and then thinner still. Eve had to squeeze through. It was so tight the stone tugged on her furs. It spat her out into a huge space. She hovered at the entrance to a grand chamber that was illuminated of its own accord in an icy blue.

It stretched hundreds of yards above her and seemed almost circular. The floor was polished smooth, but it seemed to be glass, not stone. On closer inspection it was ice, frozen over the stone in swirling patterns.

But when her gaze circled from the blue, glowing walls, to the dizzying heights, to the intricate floor, it fell on the single subject of the space. The sight of it gripped her. Eve was unable to look away. A dark figure sat upon an icy throne at the far end of the cavern. Three times the height of a man it sat, gripping the arm rests of the stone chair. Its legs and arms were rigid and its head looked forwards, unmoving.

Eve's breath caught. It was no human. Its skin was almost pure darkness and yet full of light, emitting an eerie, red glow that countered the blue of the chamber as if eating away at it. The skin—if it was skin—was so dark that she could see no features upon it—no lips, no nose, not even eyes.

Vestments shrouded it, but they seemed to be made of darkness, rather than cloth, for they fell as wisps of translucence to the floor and clung in places, like armour, to its torso. Atop its bald head soared a pointed crown—both there and not there, it disappeared as she squinted—made of no metal she had ever seen, but a substance that sapped the light from around it into its tall, cruel spikes.

When she squinted, ethereal chains also sprang into focus, bright silver bonds much stronger than any forged links that held their captive in place. It was terribly beautiful she thought, yet harsh and brutal looking. *It is Him.* She shivered—part with cold and part with fear. Relief welled in her that he still slept. She shuffled backwards and prepared to leave.

With a sound like breaking rock, his head snapped around to look at her. He fixed her in his penetrating gaze with eyes burning like fire. Now she could see his face. His black lips split. Heat roiled out.

"Welcome, daughter of the Eldar race," he said to her in the Eldar tongue, in a voice that sounded like the roar and crackle of a thousand fires.

Eve froze with dread, paralysed.

"Goodbye, foolish one, who dares to look upon the face of Bahr."

As he said his name, the energy around her surged and buzzed.

I need to bind him! Eve wet her lips, about to speak, but unsure whether to communicate with him or launch straight into the words Artora had given her. She was deliberating when he spoke again.

"Come forth." His commands cracked like a whip over her. "Submit yourself to me, sacrifice your life energy, that I may come yet closer to my day of freedom."

A strange tug grabbed her, like someone had grabbed her arms and was pulling her forward, whilst pushing her from behind. However, it was not a powerful enough compulsion to obey, though she stumbled forward involuntarily, almost tripping, before she caught herself.

Bahr paused, surprised by her resilience. "You resist me," he pondered aloud. "Are you a daughter of the Eldarkind, or an impostor? I command all magic, all guises to fall from you." He waved his hand. Nothing happened. To Eve's surprise, a wide grin split his face, revealing the hot, orange glow of his inner fire.

"Ah! Here you stand before me as I foresaw! Daughter Eve," he said. His eyes narrowed with menace, though his words overflowed with glee.

"How- how?" Eve's mouth opened.

"Throughout time, I have known that one would come to free me. I foresaw your passing and when your life changed course, I tricked you here." Bahr's grin widened further. His mouth was an inhuman maw upon his face. "I shrouded your magic with my own. Where is your father?" he asked. A lighter note of innocence entered his tone.

Eve paused. She did not understand, however she did not wish to speak before him again, mindful of Iara's words not to arm Bahr with information.

"Come," Bahr said with sadness. "Will you not speak with me?"

"He is dead." Eve replied.

Bahr waved his hand across the floor, transforming it into a living mirror. On a huge scale, she could see her father. Karn feasted with Soren and many others she did not recognise. "I had you think your most dearly beloved had fallen into the void. Only then would you despair enough to follow your path here." A note of pride crept into his voice. "Even though I sit here in chains and weakened, I am all powerful."

"You lie," she said. Anger curdled in her stomach.

Bahr shrugged. "As you wish. Believe me, do not believe me, I care not. All I did, I did to draw you here, to me. Like a spider in a web," he said. Bahr clapped with excitement. The harsh sound echoed.

Eve did not know whether to believe him. The sight of her father had stirred up emotions she had buried—albeit without resolving. She turned to leave on an impulse, but an invisible barrier held her back.

"You cannot thwart me," said Bahr, angry. "My freedom has been long planned and longer awaited. I will not be denied!"

THIRTY FOUR

There were horses ahead, stamping and champing in the snow with their breath pluming white. Luke hurried his own horse along: a stocky, hairy cob called Sam that he had managed to beg and borrow from the smith. Sam was perfect—unrelenting even in the harsh surroundings—though Luke himself felt exhausted, starving and worse of all, frozen. The abbot had allowed him provisions and warm clothing, but no fires or warm food only helped the cold creeping through him.

He had not seen anyone in days since crossing the Caledonian border at the great gap. He knew that he had not turned back on himself, because the stark mountains before him were nothing like the forested Helm Mountains he had left behind. As he rode closer, a flash of relief coursed through him.

Brown robes. It is them!

They seemed to be in a huddle. When he drew closer, dismounted, and ran forwards to meet them, they turned in surprise.

"Nolwen! Nelda!" Luke exclaimed. He saw them prone upon the floor. "Where is she?"

The men turned towards him, drawing whatever weapons and blunt, heavy things they had to hand, but relaxed as they saw him. He did not hear his brothers' greetings—they exchanged looks of confusion, as did two other Eldarkind that Luke did not recognise.

"Who is this?" said one sharply.

"This is our brother Luke," said Sirus.

"You're a monk?" said Nolwen, confused, but he remained unheard by the others.

"I do not understand, Luke," said Sirus. "Why are you here? Is all well?" His eyes filled with concern.

"Don't worry, Brother Sirus, our brothers and the monastery keep. I come to aid the Lady Eve. Where is she?" he repeated.

His brethren swapped looks, but did not answer.

"She is inside the mountain," Nolwen said. He struggled to prop himself up on an arm. Nolwen looked terrible, Luke realised, like he had been ill for a week, but then he noticed Nelda, who looked much, much worse. Their skin was a deathly shade of white, their lips blue and their eyes pale. Nolwen's hand shook as he reached forward to grasp Luke's. He took it, afraid of how weak Nolwen's grip was.

"In the mountain?" Luke said.

Nolwen nodded.

"I don't understand. Why?"

"There is something in there that the Eldarkind seek. We cannot enter—the place repels us. Your brothers accompanied her inside, but they returned without her. In the darkness, they became separated."

"She is lost in there?" said Luke, gaping at the cleft in the mountainside.

"We fear so," said Sirus.

"I must follow her," said Luke without a moment's hesitation.

"I must caution you Luke. What she seeks in there is a creature of incredible danger," Nolwen said.

"All the more reason for me to go to her," Luke said. "She may need my help. I would do anything for her," he added in a low voice.

"I know that," said Nolwen. "I do not doubt you. I know that you will not be swayed, not where she is concerned. Take my sword—it will be unfamiliar to you, but it is spelled by our people and much stronger than any blade you may carry. It will help protect you."

Luke took it, thanking him. He weighed the blade in his hand. It was indeed light, and the make unlike anything he had ever seen before, but he trusted Nolwen's choice. He looked around at his brothers, who stood, subdued. They did not seem enthusiastic about joining him.

Luke snatched one of his brother's walking aid, a carved piece that had taken years of whittling and tore off a rag from his own hem. His brother looked set to protest, but Sirus gave him a sharp shake of the head and he stilled, looking disgruntled.

"I will return."

Nolwen and Nelda and their Eldarkind kin murmured good luck and farewell to him. Without another word he marched into the mountain, his borrowed sword drawn and his makeshift brand lighting his way.

THIRTY FIVE

It has to be now!

Eve took a deep breath, before Bahr could speak again and shouted out the binding. Her eyes were scrunched closed with concentration as she held the parchment in her mind's eye and read every word from the paper.

"Brun anda Bahr, ia kaskea uan att aslura, inge flytte, inge tenkir, inge endra, inge eiende i a isen. Ia sinuar uan yta detthe, mina ethera ja a ethera ro navan lifanti kaperur kallikkiala asti a lok ro timi!" She shook with huge, jolting motions as energy rushed through her: her own and that from the bracelet. It arced across the gap between her and Bahr with a blinding light.

Into the energy she sunk, until she could feel nothing more. The dark stream was not devoid of life. Through the vortex swirling around her she sensed another power: Bahr, whose energy resources were so vast that it felt as deep and vast as an ocean.

Too late, she realised that hers was an impossible task. Her concentration wavered, for Eve was nothing more than a speck of light against the overwhelming blot that was Bahr. Even the extra power of the bracelet, which contained thousands of times more power than her at the very least, was insignificant.

She pushed power towards Bahr with all her might as she cried the binding again, but failed. Exhausted, drained of magic, she severed her ties to the energy stream and dropped to the floor. It was as if a blanket had been thrown over her, smothering her magic.

Eve's breath came heavy from the effort. She had failed. There was nothing left—no other energy to command, save for his, which was far too powerful for her to wield. The magic faded into dark and silence. From her position, drooped, Bahr looked to be sleeping, but she knew she had failed. As if to answer her thought, he opened his eyes and fixed them on her once more.

"That was well tried," he said, "but of no consequence. One so small as you should never presume to trouble Bahr of the fire. But I admire you your fortitude. Perhaps you and I can aid each other. Would you like that? I could give you powers greater than your wildest dreams."

His voice lowered, his tone persuasive. "Come, daughter of the Eldarkind. Together, we could be great rulers, she of the lightness and I of the darkness, together as one."

Eve was too exhausted to resist or rebuff him, though she was sure he was toying with her. She lay still on the floor as it froze her.

Suddenly, a figure burst in. Eve craned her neck to look up and her heart stopped. A man paused, frozen in Bahr's glare, but there was enough of the sickly blue light to recognise him.

"Luke?"

Luke looked down and cryed out as he saw her. He rushed over and bent down to her. "Eve, thanks be to God that I found you. Come on, I need to get you out of here."

A thunderous laughter rolled around the cave.

Luke paused, still trying to lift her up. Fear flashed over his face as he turned to face the elemental.

"How quaint," said Bahr, the volume of his voice rising. "A gallant rescuer here for his lady love."

Unbidden, tears slid from Eve's eyes. "What new trick is this?" she said.

Bahr laughed. "No falsehoods!" he promised. "I told you that I manipulated your magic. You thought your most beloved dead and yet here one stands. Now do you believe me?"

Eve looked up at Luke. He looked real enough. She reached out to feel his clothes and then his hand. He felt real enough. Coarse fabric slid under her fingers. His skin was smooth and warm to the touch.

"Is it really you?" she asked in a whisper, hope rising within her.

Luke nodded.

"Touching," said Bahr. His voice faded into boredom. "We

536

have dallied long enough. Shall I kill you both? Shall I see one suffer whilst the other is forced to watch on? Oh, the choices." Bahr tutted. "Young man, your arrival has complicated matters," he chided Luke.

Luke bared his teeth and placed himself between Bahr and Eve, his eyebrows furrowed with determination. "You will not harm her."

"Do you know who I am, human?" said Bahr.

"No and nor do I care, dark spirit. We're leaving."

Bahr relaxed back in his chair as Luke backed towards Eve and waved his hand as if inviting them to go.

With his eyes never leaving Bahr, Luke scooped her up in his arms.

As he did, Bahr began to speak in a language that Eve did not recognise. Older than the Eldar tongue it felt and even more potent.

Luke stumbled backwards. He tried to find the crack in the wall, but the light distorted around them. In a moment, a flash of the purest darkness spread across the cave and plunged them into the void.

When light returned, Eve and Luke found themselves in the middle of the vast room.

"I demand that you release us," Luke said. He drew his borrowed sword.

"You may demand nothing," said Bahr. Anger crackled in his voice. "You presume to challenge me?"

"If that is what it takes, then I will."

Bahr laughed incredulously. "What a fool! He has no idea of the danger he places himself in," he said to Eve.

"Luke, go," said Eve. "This is not your cause. He cannot be defeated. I have tried and failed. There is no reason for you to lose your life on my account."

Luke looked at her with a strange glint in his eye, before he turned back to Bahr. "I beg that you release her, then. I will stay in her stead if you desire it."

"Begging, good. Much more appropriate," praised Bahr. "But see, you have revealed your weakness to me in its fullness." He grinned with relish. "Your simple human mind amuses me, boy."

MEG COWLEY

Bahr flicked his gaze to Eve.

"I will not kill you," Bahr said.

A flicker of relief surged through Eve, but she still did not trust Bahr's word.

"I will not even kill the human. His life is worth nought and below the effort. But a daughter of the Eldarkind is too pure, too good to waste. I will not sacrifice you needlessly." His tone was honeyed and dripped with softness. "I took much of the energy I needed from your little display, your misguided attempt to bind me anew. I thank you for that."

Shivers crept through Eve. *What have I done?*

"I require only a minuscule amount more to be free. So I will take my due and leave you here in the dark with your pet human, to see how your love helps you to survive." His voice rang with cruel glee and a jarring laugh escaped him.

"What does he mean?" Luke hissed at Eve, but she did not know. A growing sense of foreboding and danger rose.

All of a sudden, she was plucked from the ground to dangle in mid-air, as though seized by an invisible giant. She resisted the urge to vomit as she was moved through the air, thrown by the empty space beneath her, her balance and any control over her body gone. She writhed, unable to right herself.

Luke cried out and jumped up. He could not reach her—as if to make sure of it, Eve was jerked yet higher from the floor.

She squeaked in fear. She drifted towards Bahr as deafening cracks and rumbles emanated around them. Bahr's arms were already free, but as she watched, with morbid horror, his legs tore free of the throne, fracturing the stone beneath them. He wrenched himself forward to free his back from where he had become one with the stone.

He reached out towards Eve. The heat from his open mouth scorched her face and the brightness from within caused her to close her eyes. She threw up her arms to shield herself from him, but it was of no use. He plucked her from the air, almost cradling her in his giant arms. The heat coming from him was unbearable. Her furs singed and caught alight, sparks stung her skin and smoke choked her lungs.

Eve could see nothing but the fire glowing around them, an angry, fiery red light that consumed her, mixed with a warming honey that soothed her burning skin. Eve felt the strangest tug as dizziness overcame her. In a moment, darkness and absolute silence fell. All her senses were extinguished.

When light returned, she was all the way across the cave and high up. *Sat down*, she realised, *on Bahr's throne*. Dread grew within her. *NO!* She tried to move, but could not. Every inch of her body from the strongest muscle to the softest strand of hair was frozen. Her blackened clothes seemed fused to the stone. Panic fluttered in her chest.

A stain of pure darkness occupied the centre of the chamber. She could not see Luke. Bahr flexed and stretched his limbs sensually, the smile wide upon his face and his eyes closed in bliss as his movements threw shadows and light against the contours of the room.

"Free," he crooned. "At last…"

THIRTY SIX

It was strange to walk through the gates of Arrans to such little response, Zaki considered. They had commandeered a large trading vessel on their way home by terrorising the crew. It had taken weeks of poor sailing from Braith to Bera filled with seasickness as winter raced in from the north. Zaki sent word from Bera to the Roherii palace the moment they docked, so Zaki was more than surprised that they had no welcome party.

Once more he returned with no horse. They had eaten the few beasts remaining to them on the voyage, for the ship's food stocks were soon decimated by Zaki's men. It was not the return he had expected or hoped for; at the worst he had hoped to return with half the men he had set out with and at best triumphant, already crowned king at the head of a victorious army of Caledonians and Roherii.

Nevertheless, he was glad to have returned alive, though malnourished and ill, not to mention dirty and travel stained.

When they reached the palace he was taken in to meet Harad, but this time his welcome was less than warm. No refreshments awaited him, though Zaki was parched and starving, just Harad's clear, radiating disapproval.

"Your Majesty," Zaki said. He bowed low and deep.

Harad did not greet him in return. "I expected better news from you." He glared at Zaki. "I hear that you return with nothing—that you have lost twelve thousand men!" His voice rose to an unrestrained shout. "And now, you have the nerve to return to me here and greet me, like you have not destroyed everything Roher stands for!"

"We lost this time," said Zaki, scowling. "Campaigning in winter was foolish, but we are so close. The next time we will—"

"There will be no next time!" Harad's booming yell blasted across Zaki's voice. "If I ever give you anything again, you will be lucky! Count yourself the most fortunate man alive that you are my son-in-law, or I would kill you where you stand! You escape with the gift of your worthless life!"

540

Harad's rage was in full flow. He stormed about the room, his hands taut claws as he shook them at Zaki to emphasise every word.

"Roher will be a laughing stock the moment this news travels! The nation who lost twelve thousand men to a boy king wet behind the ears! How many other countries will step up to face us, emboldened by the fact that a child has defeated us? The nation whom no one dared challenge, whom no one could triumph against, is ripe for the taking! You have given them a taste of weakness and though it was your own, because you led my men, it will be mine. You leave my reputation in tatters!

"In the time you have spent dallying on your return—"

Zaki's anger flared, for it had been another hard journey to Roher, but Harad was in full flow and would not be broken off.

"—I have already had word from King Soren with demands for an affirmation of peace between our nations. I have no option but to accept! Roher, accept equal terms with another nation! How ridiculous! He talks of a peace treaty—promises not to invade, tax bargains—you would not believe the humiliating concessions he would have me make.

"With Janus squandering my most precious weapons in Ladrin and you spending my men's lives as if you gamble at the casinos with my daughter's dowry, I have nothing left. It will take years—YEARS—before I can return my weapon stocks and men to such great numbers! It may not happen in my lifetime. As it is, I have barely enough left to defend my own borders. I blame you entirely." Harad stopped and fixed Zaki in his piercing, chilling gaze, before continuing his tirade.

"You have exhausted my patience. I have been nothing but generous, understanding and supporting of you, for the sake of my daughter. I gave you my blessings. I handed you Caledan on a plate and you could not even prove yourself in that.

"I am of a mind to grant Soren his deepest wish and hand you over as a hostage of goodwill," Harad finished. He glowered with anger.

Zaki stiffened. "You would not."

Harad's eyes narrowed. "I can offer him others in the hope it would placate him, but he has requested you for good reason. I doubt he will be denied. You did kill his mother."

"You were not blameless."

"No, I am not. But I am not his uncle and I did not commit the act."

Zaki's breath stalled. He waited for Harad to speak again. *Will*

541

he send me? I have not journeyed all the way here to be betrayed. His heart stopped in his chest at the thought. After seeing Soren's actions upon the battlefield, he had no doubt what would happen to him if he returned to Caledan as a captive. A cold chill settled over him. His clenched hands became clammy.

"I may yet agree to his treaty. It will give me perfect cover to restock my weapons and perfect my incendiary device technology with fewer of his spies in court."

"He does not have spies here! He is a boy."

"Your translator worked for Caledan, sending messages back to his master. I had him tortured and killed," Harad said, with no emotion in his voice.

Tobias was a spy? Zaki could not believe it. But then, when he considered, where did a lowborn Roherii learn almost fluent Caledonian? *What a fool I have been. Soren knew everything.* Anger filled him at his own shortsightedness.

"Without me, Caledan will never be yours! You do not have the right," he snarled at Harad.

Harad laughed, to his surprise, a hard laugh of someone who knew better. "Who needs right when you have might? Remember Ladrin, Zaki. Right means nothing. In this world, in this life, you have to earn or take what is yours. Even money is but a tool. Power is everything."

Zaki received the summons with surprise.

"Harad has not admitted me into his presence since I returned," he mused aloud. He had laid low for weeks, not even leaving his rooms.

"Perhaps all is forgiven," Reynard said. You know Harad's temper, but after all, you are the heir to Caledan's throne and you are gifted with your own son."

Zaki smiled. He had forgotten about Demara and Leika on his travels, but was pleased to find he had a son at last. Unlike Leika, who had her mother's brown eyes, Thai had inherited deep, sea blue eyes from him. "Thai is a strong boy, he takes after me. We will weather this together—perhaps this is a new start."

Zaki had not been impressed to find out of Demara's poor treatment of his mistress, but a legitimate son ruled out any need for an illegitimate one. *Tulia will be fine,* he told himself.

"This could be the welcome back into the fold, the pardon

you have been waiting for." Reynard's smile matched his own—for Reynard's success rose and fell with Zaki's. Zaki knew Reynard was aware of that.

Zaki nodded. He looked himself up and down in the mirror to double check he was impeccably dressed. He thought of how disdainfully Demara had treated him since his return, filled with the same resentment and brooding disappointment as her father, but Zaki was confident. *My station is so high they cannot desert me. Thai's birth has strengthened me—I am safe with an heir.*

When he reached the open chamber where Harad managed his affairs, the throne room was packed with rows and rows of seated men. They sat as silent and still as statues, but for their eyes, which followed him as he walked through their midst to face Harad upon his throne. If he had not known better, it would have looked like a trial.

Reynard walked a pace behind him and guards shadowed them. Zaki glanced behind, moving his head fractionally to observe them, before his eyes slid back to Harad, who sat impassive upon his throne before them. His face was shaded. His eyes loomed from the darkness. A tingle of fear stroked Zaki's spine. He quickly suppressed it.

"Your Majesty," Zaki greeted with respect. He held a bow for several seconds. Behind him, Reynard knelt upon the floor with his eyes cast down—too unworthy to look at the king of Roher.

"I have made my decision regarding your fate," said Harad.

Zaki could tell nothing from Harad's face nor his voice, both of which which were impassive and emotionless. He stilled, waiting for Harad's next words.

"I will yield you to Soren. I have no further use for you."

Zaki held himself for a moment, sure he had misheard. "I beg your pardon?"

"Soren has demanded you as a hostage and I consent to his wish. You are to be returned to Caledan with all haste."

"You cannot do this!" shouted Zaki, his eyes wide with shock.

"I can do what I please and I will," said Harad through thin lips. "I have already expressed my immense disappointment in you and I realise that, since you have an heir, I no longer need you for me to have a claim to Caledan's throne. Thai shall be brought up in the Roherii way, to become a strong and fearless warrior who will succeed in everything he does. I will win Caledan's throne on his behalf and rule until he is of an age to succeed to the throne."

"Caledan will never be ruled by a foreigner," said Zaki. His lip curled with contempt. "There is no surer way to fail than to raise him as a Roherii prince."

"You think I am a fool!" Harad laughed. "He will be educated in fluent Caledonian, the ways of their court and all else he needs to know. To them, he will appear to be their perfect king, ready-made and waiting to ascend to the throne."

"They will know—you think they will be satisfied by your offer of peace? A Caledonian will never trust a Roherii, as sure as the sun sets each day."

"It matters not. They will be trapped by their own promises and by the time we rise, it will be too late for them. I will have perfected my incendiary device and rebuilt my forces. They will stand no chance—I will make certain of it."

"I could tell Soren of this, to bargain for a pardon."

Harad chuckled, a strange sound that Zaki had never before heard him utter. "You are a fool if you believe he will ever pardon you. Go and say farewell to your wife and children. You will leave today."

"Am I to take my men with me?"

"No. They will remain here and serve me."

"I doubt that."

"Well, your servant here can set an example for them to follow. Will you serve me as faithfully as you serve him?" Harad asked Reynard, who looked up to meet his gaze.

Reynard looked to Zaki. His face was far more drawn than when they had feasted together in Caledan and toasted to their success, all that long time ago. "I would not forsake my king," he replied. "I have travelled through through hells and back to serve him."

Zaki could not deny that he had been faithful and for the first time felt grateful for his unending support. *I wonder where I would be without you, friend.* He smiled at Reynard with open appreciation.

Harad shrugged. "That is noble, but a shame." He flicked his fingers.

Reynard was hauled to his feet and stood before Harad in the grasp of two burly guards.

"The other choice is death." He flicked his fingers again.

"No!" cried Reynard, but it was too late. A curved blade had already crossed his throat. He gurgled as they dropped him onto the floor. Face down, he convulsed. After a few moments he was still.

Zaki's face had paled as if his own blood had been drained. "That was unnecessary," he said. Hate bubbled inside him.

"I do not care," said Harad in a patronising tone. "I tire of you—get out." Zaki stood his ground, so the guards dragged him all the way to the door, outside and then to Demara's chambers. They escorted him inside, jostling him.

"Get away from me!" he snarled at them, but they ignored him. "Have you heard what your father plans to do with me?" he asked Demara.

She nodded but did not speak.

"Tell him to undo this madness! I am the rightful king of Caledan! I will not be treated with such disrespect."

Demara shrugged—unresponsive, like her father. "Goodbye husband."

Zaki paused, his mouth agape. "You care not?"

Demara regarded him as if evaluating whether she should answer. "No," she said. "I thank you for my beautiful children, but in all else you have brought me misery." She left the room. The two children remained with the maid—who refused to look at him.

Leika had grown visibly in his absence. Her hair had grown and darkened yet further and she could speak, stringing nonsense words together with Roherii words and snatches of phrases. She did not come to him, but looked at him like he was a stranger. Her pudgy hand clasped one of the maid's fingers.

The boy, Thai, looked up with liquid eyes from his regal crib. He stared at Zaki with curiosity as he chewed on his hand, spit dribbling down his chin and arm.

Zaki felt a hard lump in his throat. *This could be the last time I see them.* His gaze hardened. *My own children. My prince and princess.*

Zaki moved forward to pick up his daughter, but she hid behind the woman's skirt.

She bent down to comfort the girl, but did not offer her to him as she should have done.

I have no influence here. Struck by inspiration, Zaki searched his person for something of his to leave her.

He undid the golden bracelet on his left wrist. It was borrowed, like most things of his were, but it was the one thing he had left to give her. The maid took it from him and showed it to Leika. Leika grabbed the shining object, distracted from her apprehension towards him.

Tuning to Thai, he scooped the boy up in his arms. Zaki savoured every detail of his face and appreciated the handsome beauty of dark blue eyes against his deep olive coloured skin. Thai gurgled at him and Zaki smiled. Placing the boy in his satin bedding, he removed his most precious remaining link to Caledan—his golden signet ring. It was so large that Thai would take many years to grow into it.

"Make sure this is kept safe for him," he said to the room at large, his eyes still fixed on the boy. He tucked it into the bedding and turned away, steeling himself for what was to come.

This will not be the end of me. I will return to take you away from this monstrous place.

THIRTY SEVEN

Bahr clapped his mighty hands above his head and vanished in an instant. He left nothing behind but the fading smell of smoke.

Disorientated, Luke struggled to his feet. He was still for some seconds whilst he tried to comprehend what had happened. He looked around for Eve but she was nowhere to be seen on the ground. His heart leapt in his chest when he saw her, yet even as he watched, her head slumped forward onto her chest.

Luke rushed forward to the great seat, which rose above his head. He could barely touch her boot. She looked like a doll sat upon a human chair, so huge was the throne. He tried to grasp it to tug her from the seat, intending to catch her as she fell, but her frame was immovable and rigid.

A golden glow seemed to illuminate her. Then it faded to nothing and she was lit only by the cold blue surrounding them.

"Eve? Speak to me, Eve! What do I do?" he asked her. He tugged upon her feet again. He glanced around for anything that might help him, but the space was empty.

She is so pale and still. Luke chewed on his lip. *What do I do?* He deliberated leaving her, but in this cold, dark space, he could not think of her remaining here whilst he sought their companions. It would feel like he had abandoned her. *I did not come all this way to lose.*

Luke grabbed hold of the stone chair, which seemed hewn from a single block, and climbed up onto the seat, finding plenty of handholds to haul himself up on. Using his weight, he tried to move her and then, shoving with all his might, but to no avail. He cried out in frustration, slapping the stone.

With a sigh, he sat beside her. His legs dangled off the edge. Eve's face was still and her eyes closed as he looked at her. Her skin was ice cold to the touch. Luke murmured in her ear, but there was no response. No breath came from her mouth or nose even when he waved a hand before her face.

547

She cannot be dead. He said he would not kill her. What good would it do to bind her here dead?

"Magic," he spat the word out like a curse. *I need help.* He leaned over to Eve for one last time. "Forgive me," he whispered in her ear, and squeezed her still hand. "I will return."

With that, he jumped down from the seat. The impact jarred his knees and he slipped onto his side when his feet found no purchase on the icy surface. His hip crunched. Luke pulled himself up and limped away. As he slipped through the crack, he allowed one last look back. The blackened bundle of furs and pale flash of skin were tiny.

He dove straight through the mountain in as straight a line as he could with his arms outstretched before and around him so that he did not bump into anything. Before long the black faded to grey and then red as up ahead the fissure came into view. It revealed the beginnings of a glorious sunset. But as he left the cave, he paused for a moment blinking in the light. *Where is everyone?*

"Sirus? Nolwen? Nelda? Brothers?" he called. There was no answer.

He moved away from the opening, towards where he had last parted with them. As he approached the site, it appeared as if the snow had been melted in a great trail, right down to the bare earth beneath, and refrozen again in smooth, swirling ice patterns. *Footprints*, he realised. Their scale was terrifying to behold.

He stopped dead in his tracks as he crested a small horizon. Laid out like the rag dolls the girls of Arlyn played with, were all those who had accompanied Eve. There was no sign of the horses. Mingled amongst brown robes were the fair-haired Eldarkind. As he paced through them in shocked silence, nothing moved. He bent down to check them. They all held the same, wide eyed look of fear—or the men did at least. There were no traces of blood, but they had no pulse or breath either. It was as if they had died of fear. *Bahr did this*, Luke realised.

He paused at the Eldarkind, but they had no life in them. Their glassy eyes held a different emotion—anger, Luke thought. *How could Bahr kill them so easily?* Luke wondered. They seemed invincible to him.

Last of all and furthest away lay Nolwen and Nelda. He cradled his sister in his arms. Nelda looked to be sleeping against him, but they were so still that Luke assumed the worst. A lump formed in Luke's throat, but he inhaled when Nolwen stirred.

"Nolwen, you live!" Luke rushed forward to kneel in the slush around them.

"Not for long," Nolwen regarded him with half open eyes. Pain was written in the lines upon his face.

"What happened?" Luke asked.

"We tried to fight him—to stop him. It was foolish of us. He is gone. The pact is broken."

Luke did not understand. "Nolwen, I need your help," he said, but as he said it, he realised how foolish he was. They were in no state to move. No one would be coming with him back into the mountain. "Eve is trapped in the mountain, upon a great stone chair. Bahr was sat upon it, but he's gone and she is and I cannot free her." His message was garbled in his haste.

Nolwen closed his eyes. "I cannot help you free her. I used what little energy I have left to try and heal my sister, though it did her no good. I will not rise again." His face was sorrowful.

"I can help you," Luke offered, but the tiniest shake of Nolwen's head stopped him.

Nolwen opened his eyes again, this time looking at his sister's still form, tucked against his chest. "I am dying. It is cold and painful, my body is broken. You can help by easing my passing. I can do one thing for you. My sword."

Luke fumbled at his waist. He pulled the blade from its scabbard and handed it to Nolwen, handle first.

"I will give my remaining life energy to the sword. Touch Eve with the blade. Perhaps she will be able to free herself." He was unable to clasp the sword. His hand fell into the snow beside him with his fingers trailing upon the pommel.

"Goodbye, Luke," Nolwen said. His blue eyes pierced Luke's. He closed his eyes as glowing energy trickled down his arm and sunk into the blade. With a sigh, the last life of Nolwen left him. His head tipped sideways to rest atop Nelda's.

Fighting back tears, Luke surveyed the scene. He knew he should try to bury his fallen brothers and pay respect to the Eldarkind, yet the earth lay frozen, packed beneath ice and snow. He had nothing to dig with but his hands and besides that, Eve waited for him, alone in the darkness.

The sky blazed red as the sun slipped towards the horizon. The first stars already revealed themselves in the sky between the gathering clouds. It would have been beautiful were it not for the devastation surrounding him.

He looked to the sky and asked God to guide him—the only reason he had managed to survive so far was his faith. As his cheeks turned skyward, flakes of snow settled upon his skin. They were cold kisses that brought no answers.

Aching, exhausted and demoralised, he clambered to his feet with Nolwen's blade in his hand. His eyes were downcast to the snow and he tramped back to the door into the mountain with his shoulders hunched against the deepening flurry.

Eve awoke to the blue light. Her eyes flickered open, but though they rolled in their sockets and blinked, the rest of her body could not even twitch. Her chest rose and fell with each breath, though she could not take a full breath, her paralysed form stopping the expansion of her lungs. She could hear the silence of the mountain around her. Its empty bowels reflected solitude towards her.

The faint smell of burning lingered in her nose. She strained her eyes towards her body and saw with great relief that the blaze was extinguished. Her clothes were ruined and blackened. Strands of hair falling across her face were singed. With every breath, she could taste ash on her lips. Eve recalled the fire. She was cold now, but not pleasantly so. The chill was numbing as it wormed its way through her still body.

What do I do? She strained but it was of no use. Her body did not move. Eve concentrated on bending a finger with all her might, until she growled with frustration. Nothing. *I don't want to stay here. Will I die here? I don't want to.* The cold would kill her if she didn't suffocate or starve first. It was already a painful burn creeping through her. Eve could see the dark slit in the wall that taunted her with freedom, yet she could not reach it.

Magic. Eve licked her lips—or tried to, but her tongue was frozen. Her lips were dry and chapped. A moan of annoyance escaped her lungs, though she could form no words.

Instead she built a spell in her mind, picking and choosing words with care from the Eldar tongue that might free her, comforted by the light touch of the energy and the stronger pulse of the bracelet. Its remains were pitiful—she could see it faint and thin upon her skin with a small glow to it, like it had disintegrated—yet it held enough energy to bring her hope.

Maybe, just maybe.

Nevertheless it was a dangerous idea, for the spell could free her—or drain her of her remaining energy, which would result in certain death. As she strung the spell together and rehearsed it, she filled her mind with fervent hope that she might succeed.

A clatter at the cave edge distracted her with a jolt. The world, that had disappeared before her in her focus, reappeared once more as she saw Luke standing before her.

For a moment there was a lull. Time froze whilst she blinked her eyes several times, trying to determine if what she saw was real. The sight of his face brought a warm relief that blossomed inside her, fighting back the cold a little. She was surprised that he had returned, but a part of her did not understand why anyone would choose to come back to this cursed place, or follow anyone so far on the promise of nothing.

The spell dissolved before her and in its place she conjured up one to free her voice. Her mouth remained silent as she screamed it inside her mind. At once, pressure lifted from her chest and movement returned to her head and upper torso. She breathed deeply for a few seconds, not caring that the freezing air burnt her lungs with an ice-fire. The bracelet buzzed against her wrist.

Luke crossed the cave to stand before her. He exclaimed as she moved her head up to look him in the eye.

"Luke," she said, her voice hoarse. "You came back."

"I promised I would," he replied with a smile stretching across his face. He held out his hand to her. "Jump, I'll catch you."

Eve shook her head, the movement slow and laboured. *So tired...* "I cannot move."

His smile faltered.

"How did you find me? Why did you come back?" Eve asked.

"When I found out that you had passed the monastery, I couldn't think of anything else that I needed to do more."

Eve looked at him and frowned. *Brown robes.* "You're a monk?"

"I was. Well, yes I suppose I am. I'm not sure, but I'll have to go back."

"You don't want to?"

A rueful smile crossed his face. "I've found you again—not a chance. I'd forgotten how beautiful you were. I'd forgotten how sweet your voice sounds. Seeing you again makes me feel everything that I sought to escape."

Eve spoke—or tried to—but her throat was sore and it came out as a bark that turned into a fit of coughing. *So thirsty.*

Luke scrambled up onto the throne beside her and offered her a drink from his water skin. With little movement in her body, she tilted her head awkwardly as he held it before her. Much ran down her chin, but a sweet trickle slid into her throat and relieved her scalded mouth and lips.

Silence fell as he put the stopper in the the gourd and hung it from his belt once more.

"It's been so long since I saw you, I don't know where to begin," said Eve.

"There's nothing much to say," Luke said with a shrug. "I ran away. I thought I could escape my problems—but as it turned out, you followed me." He grinned at her before returning his gaze to the polished floor. "I didn't know where else to go, so I wandered, and one day I turned up on the doorstep of the monastery. I've been there ever since, helping them to rebuild."

"Are you happy there?"

Luke paused. "In a way. It is a simple life. What about you? I thought you had big plans."

"They didn't work out," Eve said. "War came first, so father sent me to Ednor so that I could be safe." She told him what she had found when she had reached the home of the Eldarkind.

"May she recover soon," said Luke, when she mentioned Artora. "You did not marry, then?"

"No. I managed to escape that."

"Won't you have to when you return, when the war is done with?"

Eve froze. *What if Dane isn't dead? What if it was another cruel trick of Bahr's?*

"*Leitha Dane*," she said without hesitation, thankful for the polished floor, which acted like a giant window into the visions. The surface shimmered in colour and darkened, but nothing else happened.

"*Lessa. Leitha isa*," she said.

The black faded. Her father appeared, almost transparent upon the floor.

Luke gasped upon seeing the giant image before him.

"He's alive!" Tears pricked Eve's eyes. "Thanks be. *Lessa. Leitha Edmund.*"

Once more the surface faded to darkness.

"*Lessa*," she said.

"What is it?" Luke said, his forehead creased. "I don't understand."

"My father is safe," Eve said. She closed her eyes and sighed with relief. Her eyes opened as a tinge of sadness returned. "But Edmund is not. Neither is Dane. They are both dead. I do not know how, but I cannot see them anymore. In truth, I thought you dead also, but Bahr played a cruel trick on me from afar."

Luke shook his head. "I don't follow. But Edmund is dead? How can it be so?" He sat in silence with her for a few moments. "Wait, if Dane is no longer alive, does that mean you are no longer to be married?"

"I consider it so." Eve shivered, remembering how she had felt. "I will not be put in that position again."

She could sense an awkwardness between them as once more they lapsed into quiescence. *So much has passed since we last met*, she considered. *Do we even know each other anymore?* She could not deny it was a relief to see him, especially since she had believed the worst after scrying him to find darkness in the mirror. But hope was slow to come, even though he had travelled so far to see her. She knew that she could not return to the childish naivety of assuming anything between them would flourish.

After a while, when she had begun to notice the cold creeping through her again, Luke spoke.

"How can I help you escape this place? Nolwen gave me his sword to free you."

Eve's heart sunk. "You cannot. I'm stuck fast and I don't have enough magic to escape. The sword will be of no use." She could sense the weak energy within it; far less than the bracelet, and that had been of no use either. "The solution is to do as Bahr did and switch my place for another. There's no way to leave." She hung her head.

"What if I stayed?" Luke said in a low voice.

Eve turned her head and fixed him with a stare. "You would do that for me?" she said, touched.

Luke sighed. "You know I would. I've come to what feels like the end of the world to find you. What does that tell you?"

"I wish I'd run away with you," said Eve.

"No, you don't. You'd never leave your father, you know that."

"I can't ask this of you, though."

"You don't ask me—I choose this."

"But what if I try to free you, but it's impossible?"

Luke shrugged. "I trust you to do the right thing, like you always have done."

"I haven't always done the right thing," Eve admitted. "I never should have agreed to father's proposal, for one."

"You thought it was necessary—don't be angry with yourself. We all make mistakes. Mine was not asking for your hand sooner, first." He placed his gloved hand atop her own, but Eve could not feel anything.

Not for the first time, she wished things could have been different.

"Are you certain you want to do this?" Eve said. She searched Luke's face for any sign of uncertainty.

"I am," he said. He met her stare without a flicker.

"Alright." She took a deep breath. "I'm going to put you into a deep sleep, one that you won't waken from. The sleep must be undone by a spell caster, or the breaking of the original bonds that bind a sacrifice to the chair. Are you ready?"

He nodded and his eyes softened. "Promise me you'll return," he said.

"I will." She strained, leaning as much of her upper body to him as she could, to plant a soft kiss on his lips.

He gathered her in a tight hug of warmth that she savoured, unable to move to embrace him back.

"I love you," she whispered, feeling a thrill as she admitted it for the first time.

"I love you more," he murmured, before drawing back. "Make it quick."

Eve closed her eyes and sunk into the stream of energy that was faint about them to draw from the remaining power of the bracelet. After seeing Bahr perform it, she understood what she had to do. Bahr was cleverer than she had realised. The energy cost of breaking the binding was so huge it was impossible without more support.

To switch places however, required much less energy, because the binding remained true though the subject was substituted. The energy was not broken: it was bent. *It might be possible and then I can return with help to free him. Maybe with Bahr gone, Nolwen, Nelda, Iara and Tolthe will be able to enter this place and use their magic to help me free Luke.*

The spell complete in her head, she met Luke's gaze. Without a pause Eve ordered the switching of their bodies. Light grew around them until it was so bright that she was forced to shut her eyes. It grew even further until it pierced through her eyelids. It felt like she was shaking herself to pieces. And then with a sudden snapping feeling, like she had hurled herself through a window into a calm place, it was over. The light vanished and she opened her eyes. She still sat upon the throne, but she could move. Next to her, slumped against one of the giant arms, was Luke in a breathless, dreamless slumber.

She fixed his face into her memory, before she clambered down from the high seat and raced across the chamber, whilst conjuring light to lead her from the dark place, fuelled by the fast dwindling supply of energy from the bracelet. Eve could not help but feel guilty and selfish as she fled, haunted by sacrificing Luke's freedom for her own. *It will not be for long,* she promised. Her limbs were stubborn to obey and she shuffled across the cavern, forcing her body to coordinate and shuck the cold that had seeped into it.

It was still dark when she reached freedom, so much so that when she stumbled from the cave entrance, she did not at first realise she had left the cover of the mountain. As her eyes accustomed to the little light, she made her way from the mountain. On an impulse, she grabbed a handful of snow and swallowed with delight the water it formed when it melted inside her mouth.

Progress was slow as she searched around for her companions, until dawn at last arrived to banish the darkness. The clouds remained, making the atmosphere dull and seething. Discovering the devastation, Eve stopped in her tracks. Her companions' bodies lay crooked, like discarded rubbish on the ground. She swallowed. There was no life here—she could feel it—not in Iara and Tolthe, who had died grim-faced, nor in the monks, whose empty gazes stared into forever. Pain cut through her heart when she found Nolwen and Nelda.

"No!" she said and rushed forward, but it was of no use. They were cold and frozen, in a sleep from which they would never awaken. Eve shivered herself, her damaged clothing no shield to the freezing temperatures and biting wind. Yet she would not take the clothing of the dead. It was too disrespectful to bear contemplating, even if they had no further use for it.

Tears rolled down her face and froze in trails upon her cheeks as she stood. *I cannot stay here.* She glanced around, but there was no sign of the horses. No food. No shelter. No water. Eve swallowed.

I have to get to Ednor and warn them that Bahr is free. It's my chance to survive and free Luke. I cannot forsake him.

She touched Nolwen and Nelda's hands one last time, muttered a blessing to them from her childhood, and shuffled away. Her limbs were already stiff from tarrying.

Away from Juska Eve walked, one footstep after another, until the mountain dwindled behind her and the day had spent itself. When darkness fell again, she spied ahead a bulky shape in the fading light. As she squinted, it moved.

A horse! she realised. With renewed energy she strode forward. Drawing closer, she realised that it had far too many legs and was in fact two. She could have cried with relief, for they were oddly shaped—still carrying saddlebags. As she caught them and held onto their slack reins, she stroked their noses, thanking whatever power had led her to them.

She rummaged through the bags to find some spare furs and a little food. The furs would not give her a new outfit, but she could at least replace her burnt hat and gloves. It was a start. The food was nothing more than some cracked biscuits and the remaining dried meat strips.

Eve ate one, but had to stop herself falling upon the rest—she knew well enough to save them. She was a long way from help and with no certain idea about where to go. There was no wood, nor water, but one empty skin lurked at the bottom. She packed it with snow and put it back in the bag, in the hope that it would melt.

The horses were as listless and starving as she when they first sighted a dark smudge on the horizon days later, but Eve was overjoyed, for it, along with the receding snow, meant that she had found the Helm Mountains once more. She forged south east to the great gap with all the vigour she could muster. That night she stopped to rest on mossy ground, not snow, and the horses ate to their contentment.

It still took her days from there to plod to the northern monastery, the closest point of human contact. Eve trembled with weariness as she passed under the shadow of the gates, still atop one of the horses, whose necks drooped with tiredness.

Brown-robed men rushed towards her. Hands lifted her down as she staggered on her feet and leaned upon them for support. Her head swam. They plied her with questions, but she could not answer, not least because she could not distinguish the words.

She noticed the absence of the winter air and looked around as they sat her in a comfortable, padded chair, in a warm room, peeled her hat and gloves off and called to each other to fetch this and that. Before long a meal steamed before her and a drink of refreshing cordial.

Without a thought she tucked in, eating as ravenously as she had ever done. Her stomach was so full afterwards that it hurt, but she did not care. It felt so good to be warm and content, even if she was still exhausted. When she looked up, there was one person left in the small log cabin with her—the abbot himself.

"Welcome, Lady Eve," he said. "Where are your companions?" he asked.

Eve's lip trembled. Her fatigue left no energy to keep her emotions under control. "They're all dead," she croaked. "I am the last."

Hador sunk back into his chair and closed his eyes for a moment. "That is ill news indeed, mistress."

"Luke survives," she said. "But he is trapped. I must reach Ednor, for they are his only hope of freedom."

"Lady, please forgive me, but you are in no fit state. You must rest!"

Tears spilt from Eve's eyes. "I cannot abandon him, sir."

"We can send a message on for you, if that should ease your troubles. It will reach Ednor quicker than you will."

Eve sniffed, wiping her eyes. A sudden thought had struck her. "Do you have a mirror? Or a smooth surface of some kind? Anything will do. I can contact them from here. Please, I beg you, too much time has already been lost."

Hador frowned at her, but nodded his head and sent someone to fetch something from the stores. They soon returned with a small shaving mirror. It was made crudely, and was small, but it did not matter.

Eve whispered the command to scry the queen of the Eldarkind, but instead of Artora's face, another Eldarkind appeared in the mirror.

"*Let our voices pass through the mirror,*" Eve commanded. "Hello?"

He turned, unable to see her, before conjuring a mirror to levitate before him from nothing. "*Who speaks to me,*" he said to the empty air, in the Eldar tongue.

"Lady Eve of Ednor."

He muttered an enchantment and the mirror's surface rippled. His face appeared: he had linked the two scryings.

"Who are you?" Eve asked. "I meant to contact Artora, I have grave news that she must hear."

"I am Tarrell," he said, replying in Caledonian to match her. "I am the keeper of the Eldarkind. Artora passed away nine days hence."

Eve stilled. *No! No more sorrow! It cannot be—but he would not lie.*

"Then it is to you that I must deliver my news." She swallowed past the lump in her throat. Artora's face was strong in her mind—

558

as she had been the first time Eve had seen her, not the last, when she had been sickly and unrecognisable. *She gave me so much. I should have shown her far more thanks for it, returned her kindness. It is too late to repay it...* "But forgive me, I must ask. How did it happen? I cannot understand it."

"We could do nought to heal her and she could no longer hold on," Tarrell said. "We made her as comfortable as possible," he added. "She felt no pain at the end. I am tasked with continuing her duties. You are still welcome here, Lady Eve."

Eve did not reply. She closed her eyes. It did not ward off the wave of fresh grief that threatened to crush her.

"What news do you have Lady Eve? Where are your companions?"

At that, Eve burst into tears. "They're all dead." Eve saw the obvious question upon his lips. She did not want to talk of it but knew she must. She fought back her tears and told him what had passed since they had left Caledan's borders in as few words as possible.

"That is terrible to hear. May Iara, Tolthe, Nelda and Nolwen rest in eternal peace for their sacrifice." After a lengthy pause, he continued. "I will send a party to find them. They shall be brought home, for a proper farewell and a resting place that befits them, under the stars of their homeland.

"Will you return to stay with us?" he added.

Eve shook her head. "Please, I must go north again—will you help me free Luke? I cannot leave him to the mercy of Bahr, if he returns, or to spend eternity in that awful place. Please help me!"

But Tarrell also shook his head. "It is with a heavy heart, but I must say that it would be almost impossible to do so. A binding of this magnitude, on an elemental no less, is hard to undo. The combined power of our race and the dragons would be required, and even then it might not be successful. The only certain way to break the magic is for its original subject to die. As you well know, we have no way to kill Bahr. I apologise with all my heart, but I cannot help you in this."

"I'm begging you, please! I will not give up after he has sacrificed so much to help me."

THIRTY EIGHT

Sheets of fire soared into the sky as they advanced from the north. Smoke clogged the air and shielded the sun, plunging the Isles of Kotyir into darkness.

Myrkith-visir watched the approaching flames with the tingle of premonition and nerves mingled.

"What is it, sire?" Myrkdaga asked him.

Myrkith-visir turned to his son, regarding him gravely. "One who could be our doom, my son." *And there is not time to prepare.* Myrkith-visir glanced up at he sky. *Would that this happened in summer, at our full strength.*

He let out an urgent, bellowing roar to summon the clan and launched off the heights of the peak. His keen hearing could already detect the crackling and spitting of the burning vegetation miles away as the fire leaped from the mainland to the first island, an impossible distance away. A new column of black, acrid smoke spiralled into the sky as it burnt.

Trying to ignore rising trepidation, Myrkith-visir wheeled down in gentle circles to the crater lake, where dragons were already arriving amid much commotion. Myrkdaga landed behind him and dived through the throng to take his place with the smaller dragons at the back of the gathering.

"We have no time, be silent!" Myrkith-visir ordered.

The dragons before him subsided and turned to face him, though many could not help but keep glancing at the smoke that encroached upon them.

"The pact is broken. He of the fire, whom some name Bahr, is free. I do not understand his enmity, but it is clear he bears us no goodwill. We must repel him, for he will destroy us all if given the chance." Myrkith-visir's words subsided into a growl, for the earth beneath them shuddered from some great force.

Destruction surrounded them as the entire peak seemed to erupt in flames. The fire bothered the dragons little—Myrkith-visir instead felt refreshed from the light and heat—but the smoke was suffocating. The temperature soared so high that the lake bubbled and boiled around them, disappearing into thin air as it escaped liquid form.

Materialising from the smoke and flames, Bahr stepped from the air into the shallows of the lake, which hissed and evaporated around him with each step. Dragons backed away from him.

Myrkith-visir held his head tall and showed no sign of submission. With any other, he would have shown aggression, but Myrkith-visir was aware of Bahr's far superior strength and wary as a result of his conduct so far. Already he could feel the thrum of Bahr's powerful magic vibrating through the air and earth.

Bahr moved forwards with predatory grace to stand before him. His face was twisted in a sinister grin. Behind him, a silver dragon of gigantic bulk thudded into the earth. To Myrkith-visir's surprise, Bahr did not flinch or show any reaction at all. With a shock, Myrkith-visir realised it was Cies who had landed, though twisted in form.

"We greet you and extend welcome, Bahr of the fire." Myrkith-visir lowered his head into a bow, before raising it to offer the softer, fleshy underside of his jaw—a sign of friendship and mutual vulnerability—but for the briefest moment, before he returned his eyes to watch Bahr. It was a gesture of mutual trust, though he had none for the elemental. He had even less for Cies, though he felt safe here, surrounded by his clan.

"You are not welcome here, outcast," Myrkith-visir said to Cies. "Begone unless you wish to die."

To his surprise, Cies roared defiance at him in response as his wings snapped open.

He is changed, thought Myrkith-visir, confused. It was as if Cies was a different dragon, no longer light, sleek and powerful, but bulging with corded muscles that did not balance his form. Myrkth-visir wondered how Cies's wings could even support him.

Bahr did not reply. Instead he smiled lazily with half lidded eyes. He toyed with a fireball, rolling it in and around his palm with ease, where it lit up the dark surface of his being—for he had no skin—with embers.

"Why do you burn our lands?"

Bahr's face soured. "All should burn," Bahr hissed," for the wrong that you have done unto me."

"We wish you no ill will, Bahr of the fire."

"And yet you bound me in ice to lie for millennia." Bahr's scathing tone cut Myrkith off.

"That was not of our doing," retorted Myrkith-visir. He suppressed his rising temper.

"It was the doing of your ancestors and as their blood, you must pay my price!"

"Unless you offer our great lord Bahr your allegiance," Cies said in a carrying voice so loud that all the clan could hear him. He drew up with pride. "Let me be the first to offer him my support as the true head of our clan." He bowed before Bahr before raising up his chin and holding it there.

Cies stood fixed for a length of time so great that others muttered to each other, shocked at such a gesture of submission.

Myrkith-visir growled. "Do you hear yourselves? Cies is a banished coward, drawn to a power that raises him to be greater than he is, nothing more. Bahr has shown that he is in no way inclined to befriend us. Would you trust him with your lives?

Kin of Arun and Brun, the two dragons who had also been banished as a result of their part in Cies' treason, stepped forward.

"Your leadership has brought us nothing but shame and sorrow," their matriarch said, before moving to stand before Bahr and pledge their support.

"You brought your dishonour upon yourself," snarled Myrkith-visir. "Let it be know that any who join Cies and Bahr of the fire will be forever excluded from our clan, cast out until the end of time! You will never be welcome to set foot in any dragon-held lands across the world."

"There is a new clan," Cies said with a grin that revealed rows of gleaming, sharp teeth.

"I have heard enough of your treachery, dishonourable worm! I will not suffer my clan to be destroyed by the guiles of one so low as you, even if an elemental lies in my path. You die here, Cies, I promise you that. I call you all, my clan to me, to rid us of this coward and this evil!" Myrkith-visir bared his teeth as he crouched on his haunches. As he prepared to launch himself at the silver dragon, Cies mirrored his movements.

Faster than he could move, a swirling mess of flames engulfed them all, to the tune of Bahr's maniacal laughter. The fireball did not hurt Myrkith-visir as such, for in the fire was their life, but the power it burned with was so potent it was painful it sent his body tingling. Each scale ached from the force of it and Myrkith-visir was forced to shut his eyes to shield them, for even his protective inner eyelids could not withstand the fireball.

"To your wings!" he called and thrust off from the ground to escape the storm. "Cast down our enemies!"

Myrkith-visir broke free of the fire and roared with relief as the pains subsided. The smoke surrounded them still, but the higher they rose, the more it dispersed.

As he rose, his clan soared with him. They wheeled through the sky, but the darkness shrouded their glittering scales and instead, they were a maelstrom of blackened teeth and claws, fighting with their clan members. Myrkith-visir dropped from the sky to where the fireball subsided and bathed its location in a spurting jet of flame whilst wishing death and destruction upon Bahr and Cies.

From the flames rose Bahr, untouched, on the back of Cies. At last, Myrkith-visir understood that he must have enchanted the silver dragon, for there was no way that his wings could lift both their bulks, though Bahr was perfectly sized to ride upon Cies' back.

Other dragons copied Myrkith-visir and descended in to bathe Cies in fire before darting away—some daring to come in close enough to rend him with claw and tooth, or buffet them with gusts of wing. Others had the strength to carry and drop projectiles onto them.

Cies flew unmarked. The sharp points skittered off his tough scales, though he shook from the turbulence and impacts of small objects dropped and thrown at him. Those who got too close or flew too slow received a painful punishment from Bahr and retreated yelping to a distance.

As Myrkith-visir dove into the fray, intent on defeating Cies, more fighting erupted around him in pockets as dragons changed allegiances back and forth, swayed by one power show or another. Worrying numbers had already defected to follow Bahr. As a collective body they drifted south, away from the Isles of Kotyir and over the steel-grey sea. Dragons fell from the sky. Some recovered and flapped with all their strength to regain the heights.

Others not so fortunate could not save themselves and plunged into the depths. With a hiss, the water turned to steam around them. Their death was almost instant. Others were already dead when they hit the surface of the ocean with a crash and sunk, never to be seen again. Myrkith-visir shuddered as he saw their fates. Death by water was the worst fate a dragon could endure.

Bahr was in his element. He flung fireballs in all directions, which incapacitated or killed those they hit. When his aim was true, dragons dropped from the sky like a flock of birds roasted by dragon-breath.

Myrkith-visir gave chase. He avoided Bahr's deadly projectiles with years of practised agility, though at times, Bahr's attacks grazed his scales. Already he began to tire from the constant weaving and ducking, but anger from the deaths of his clan-mates fuelled his attacks.

Myrkith-visir spiralled up at Cies from beneath and dived at him from above with his wings tucked in to achieve maximum speeds. He nipped Cies and tore at his wings, tail and legs until they were rent and scored with wounds. Myrkith-visir did not notice his own growing injuries, so focused was he.

It seemed to be of no use. The further they flew, the more tired Myrkith-visir and the dragons became, yet Cies continued to fly with strength, despite blood raining from his many wounds. He should have been incapacitated. To Myrkith-visir, it was more frustrating that Cies cheated than Bahr's attack. Bahr's anger he could understand, through reasoning. Cies was a coward and a bully.

The sun had emerged once they were far from the blackened islands. Smoke still rose from Kotyir in the distance, like a great beacon. Myrkith-visir felt the boost to his energy and was spurred on as the rest of his clan found renewed vigour. Unfortunately the same effect was true on those he struggled against. Cies roared with joy, almost basking mid-flight in the heat and light.

Thinking with a clearer mind, Myrkith shouted the order. "Swarm Him!"

Myrkith-visir dove forward to tackle Cies in mid air. His clan-mates did likewise, forsaking their other foes, for there could be only one that Myrkith-visir referred to. Their weight buffeted Myrkith-visir and for a moment, dislodged him from flight, but he suppressed the automatic response to re-stabilise and instead folded his wings away. It was against all instincts.

Do what must be done. Myrkith-visir was resolute. No trickery would defeat him. He gripped Cies with claws, teeth and tail from his belly. Other dragons did the same, until Myrkith-visir was almost smothered with their weight and mass. He could not see Bahr, but he knew his clan contained them in a living prison. He could hear their punishment—yelping and snarling.

A moment came, when the entire bundle wobbled. Myrkith-visir knew he had achieved his aim. Not even Bahr's magic could keep them flying under the combined weight. Myrkith-visir's stomachs lurched as they plummeted with no control. They fell for seconds that felt like minutes and yet an instant, before a great impact shook them. With a force great enough to blow a mountain apart, Bahr scattered the dragons.

Myrkith-visir alone remained latched onto Cies, who regained controlled flight. Cies kicked Myrkith-visir off whilst they were both still falling towards the sea, but Myrkith-visir dropped back onto him, this time wrapping his great bulk around both Bahr and Cies.

The heat from the elemental was enough to cause him pain. It was hotter than any fire he had encountered, even the heat belching forth from the molten fire rocks of the earth. Howling through the searing agony he clung on whilst Bahr clutched and grappled with his bulk.

They were mobbed again by dragons, but Myrkith-visir could not tell whose side they were on, for the biting, clawing and heavy blows indiscriminately rained down upon him also. Once more they had begun to fall—much closer to the sea. Myrkith-visir now knew that he would not survive, but was determined to end Bahr and Cies so that his clan could live on. There would be no good leadership from Cies, he was certain.

At the last moment, for he could see the ocean rushing up to meet them, he ordered his clan members to release them. Many of the dragons released, though a few stayed clung on, attacking both him and Cies.

As the inevitable end came, Bahr gripped Myrkith-visir's head with iron like strength, forcing the dragon to meet his fiery gaze. He grinned at the dragon and bared his own pointed teeth. "You think you have saved your pitiful lizard family but far worse comes for you and yours, dragon."

Myrkith-visir did not know whether Bahr's threat was empty. He struggled and tried to free himself to fly away, to kick off, but Bahr's grip upon him was unyielding. The world turned upside down as Cies somersaulted, turned upside down and snapped his wings open to brake.

NO! Myrkith-visir panicked, for the first time. Cies had tricked him.

Bahr fell from Cies' back with a scream like a thousand sword blades screeching over each other and Myrkith-visir fell with him.

They plunged into the sea.

THIRTY NINE

His world was nothing: devoid of both light and dark and empty of senses, where a second before, she had been with him, frozen upon the throne as he beheld her. In the dim light he could see that he sat alone atop the icy throne, but Eve was nowhere. Had it been moments? Or had it been minutes, hours, weeks, years? He forced down panic and breathed, in and out, and repeated the motion until his heart quietened.

He waved his hands before him, because lights danced in his eyes and he could not be sure if they were real. Sure enough, his mitts crossed his field of vision, paler than the darkness around them, in light that had a blueish tinge. Luke wondered with a jolt, was he old and wrinkled?

Luke paid no heed to the cold that already bit at his face, tore off his mitts and searched his cheeks and forehead with his fingers. His beard still covered his chin, but it did not feel long. He cheeks were smooth and his forehead also, once he had uncreased it from wrinkling with worry. Luke sighed with relief. Perhaps no time had passed at all.

"Eve?" he called.

"EVE, EVE, EVE, Eve, Eve, Eve," the echoes answered, before fading into whispers, but he could not hear her voice in the replies.

I have to get out of here.

Using the advantage of the high seat, he examined the dark nooks and crannies of the cave, but he could not see an exit. Luke shuffled to the edge of the chair and prepared to leap down. With both hands, he searched his belt for his equipment—if it could be called that for he had Nolwen's sword and little else. As his hand grazed the sword's handle, warmth flowed from the blade, replenishing him with energy. He paused for a moment appreciating the feeling. *Thank you, Nolwen.*

After a pause, Luke jumped into the dark void. His feet slammed onto the cold, hard surface. Bones juddered and knees crunched from the impact. Suppressing a howl of pain and a string of curses he straightened up, stretched his legs out and hobbled to the wall. With one hand trailing upon the cold stone, he walked around the edge of the giant space until at last the wall vanished into a breath of air. Luke wobbled, almost falling into the hole. He had found a way out, though he did not know where it led to.

Nevertheless he followed it without question and crept forward as he searched through the darkness with his hands. Time ran without end or measure. Thirsty, hungry, tired and weak, he faltered and eventually fell to the ground unable to continue. He lay upon the floor, panting. The cold seeped into him.

So cold. So easy to fall asleep and never wake up. But as his eyelids drooped to send him into slumber, the cold tickled his skin. *Air… A breeze!* Luke staggered to his feet and used the last of his reserves and followed the minuscule current of air, pausing here and there to feel it upon his face.

Before long he found what he sought. Pale moonlight bathed the land in an ethereal glow. After the completeness of the darkness, if was so blinding and bright that Luke's eyes watered as he emerged from Juska. With aching legs, he stumbled away from the mountain, towards where his companions lay. He soon found them and, abhorring himself for what he was about to do, prayed that he might be forgiven.

With a deep breath, Luke rifled through their robes, bags, pockets, whatever they had, to find food. He managed to find a full water skin and some remnants of biscuits, but nothing else. Muttering apologies to the dead, he swapped his damaged mittens for theirs, took a fur scarf that would cover his face and a hat that had flaps to cover his ears better.

Luke's cheeks burned with shame, even though he took no more than he needed and what they no longer had use for. His skin crawled in the darkness, as if others watched him, so he finished as quickly as he could and walked away with many a backwards glance, unable to shake the feeling of a baleful glance upon him.

All around the landscape was identical and stretched away in unbroken rolling hills of white in all directions. He struck out, always keeping Juska at his back and hoped that it would lead him home, if he could survive that long. He didn't want to sleep near the mountain—or near the dead. He would walk all night to escape their presence.

Luke trudged all through the night and the next day, because there was no reason to stop. The movement became ingrained. He was unwilling to halt, knowing that if he did, it would be many times harder to start walking again. Juska was already lost in the white behind him. Luke had no idea whether he was still heading true, but his two choices were to continue or to die, and he would not give himself up to the latter yet.

Red pricked the snow around him. His feet stopped. He brushed the snow, swiping it away with his mitt. Red berries shone before him, their glossy surface gleaming and boasting juicy prizes. Luke swallowed. *I'm so hungry, but they're probably poisonous.* With a great effort, he turned away from the berries and resumed his plodding march.

That night, a fire burnt in the distance. Luke was almost spent, but it spurred him on. Impossibly far away, it seemed to never draw closer, and it was almost morning again by the time he reached it. It had almost died, a tiny ball of warm light against the overpowering darkness.

Still forms slumbered around it. They were so close. He needed to move another few yards, but his feet could go no further. Luke tripped and fell. Try as he might, he could not rise again. *So close.* He moaned in frustration and exhaustion, before slipping into the void.

FORTY

Back at Kotyir, the fires had burnt out. The lands were desolate and scorched, scarred by the fire. What life there was had deserted the havens or died in the blaze.

Myrkdaga flew with Feldloga and Feldith by his sides. All three were in silence. The moments kept replaying in Myrkdaga's head of his father's brave actions and his sacrifice to protect the clan, yet how he had been tricked by Cies.

At least Bahr is no longer a threat.

The silver dragon led them all. He crowed his success to the skies as he alighted in the crater lake—or what remained of it—taking the place of the clan head.

"You have no right to that place!" Myrkdaga began.

Cies leapt upon Myrkdaga and pinned him down with his great bulk. His teeth closed around Myrkdaga's neck and shook him like a prey animal, before tossing him aside with ease. Myrkdaga gulped in deep breaths after his choking and struggled to his feet.

"I am clan chief," Cies said. He growled his dominance as he surveyed them all.

Farran, the sire of Feldloga and Feldith, stepped forward. "I agree with Myrkdaga. You have not the right. You won through trickery and deceit—we are a clever race, but we are an honourable one. We do not use magic to achieve our means. Besides this, you were banished from the clan. You have no place here at all. May Myrkith-visir's flame burn long in our hearts to remind us of his sacrifice to save our clan from Bahr of the fire."

Dragons all around rumbled in agreement.

"In light of present circumstances, I assert my claim as clan chief through kinship with my brood-mate Myrkith-visir. I am strong and fierce, but honourable." Farran glared at Cies. "I will lead our clan well—back to a flourishing homeland." He surveyed the devastation around them.

Myrkdaga took a place behind his uncle.

Some of the elders rumbled behind him. "What of the present?" one said. "We need to widen our hunting grounds in order to survive—there is nothing left for us in Kotyir. The pact is broken, so there is nought that prohibits us doing so."

Farran bared his lower jaw in agreement. "Be that as it may, we cannot stray too far, especially into human territory. We do not want to start a war."

Cies laughed and a roar escaped his throat. "Farran, you worm! You fear the humans? We cannot allow this coward to lead us!"

Farran snarled at Cies. "We may not be bound by the pact, but would you, the remnant of a race, start a war with one so huge it could wipe us out?"

He was both cheered and booed. Some stepped towards Farran to support him, whilst others sidled towards Cies.

Cies barged past him into the centre of the ring of dragons.

"I challenge you all!" Cies said. He puffed out his chest and flexed his wings. "I challenge you all to be dragons, not sheep. Dragons should hunt, burn and take what they want, when they want—so we shall! We have grown feeble and soft. I tire of living off tough mountain goats, wiry horses, bears at best. I want to taste well fed, plump sheep, cattle and fowl as and when I choose. I want to roam free, not be confined to a miserable island at the corner of the world. I want humans to fear me, to respect me—us. Who chooses to be a dragon?" He roared at Farran in defiance.

Farran roared back. "Listen not to this madness! We can move, but we should not act without cause! The humans and Eldarkind have long been our allies. I will not forsake them on a whim! By earning their trust and friendship, we can earn greater rewards than by stealing and burning."

But many of the clan had sided with Cies and formed an impressive line before him of teeth bared and claws extended.

Myrkdaga stood behind his uncle still. *I would rather die than serve Cies*, he thought.

Farran must have realised what he faced, yet he stood taller and prouder. "I will not suffer this madness. Those who wish to continue as we have, living in peace and harmony for millennia, ally yourselves with me. We leave. I will not associate with oath-breakers, outcasts and cowards."

He turned, ran, and leaped into the air. Myrkdaga hurried after him, flanked by Feldloga and Feldith. Many other dragons rose with them; they were flashing jewels in the sky as the sun ricocheted off their scales. Many more remained behind on the ground and roared their challenge into the sky.

"Worms!" Cies' parting shot followed them.

FORTY ONE

The crowd looked towards Soren with stern faces, huddled together in the cold. It was silent. Only a breeze blew through the courtyard with a disrespectful whistle. Snowdrops lined it, bulging out of flowerbeds where elsewhere, the bare stone was covered by patches of dirty snow.

Soren shifted so that his cloak would fall further around him, glad for the fur lining around the neck.

"We are gathered here today to see the passing of the sentence deemed justified by our highest court of law. His Royal Highness Prince Zaki, son of King Thoren the second of Caledan and her fairness Queen Solana has been found guilty of high treason, regicide, the murder of his sister, the murder of many unnamed others, ordering the murder and unjust imprisonment of many unnamed others, embezzlement..." The list continued. "He has been sentenced to death by public beheading. Bring forth the prisoner."

Soren moved to the side of the dais and swept his cloak around him as he turned. He had not seen his uncle since they day Zaki had been returned to Pandora a week earlier under heavy armed guard. Even then, he had watched from afar, behind a drape from a high part of the castle as his uncle was handed over to Caledonian soldiers to be sent straight to the dungeons.

Messages had been sent by Zaki; he begged for an audience, but Soren had denied him on every occasion. The requests became more frequent and more desperate, claiming of a plot by Harad to break the peace treaty. Soren took no heed from the words. He already knew Harad was not to be trusted.

It did not redeem Zaki in his eyes, who asked for his life to be spared. He did not beg in that regard, Soren acknowledged, but Soren did not understand how Zaki would expect him to fulfil the request after all that had passed. In a rare moment of what seemed total clarity, Zaki had promised he did not lie and would not see Caledan be destroyed by Harad and fall to an outsider. Soren reckoned that it was one of the few truthful words uttered to him by his uncle, but it would not save him.

Zaki stood before him. It was the closest they had come to each other since Zaki's had last been in chains before the gates of Pandora, handed over by Harad in exchange for the safe passage of Demara. *Should he have expected that Harad would betray him again?* Soren wondered. His uncle seemed a changed man. He was white faced— the first sign of fear that Soren had ever seen from him.

The crowd were agitated. They booed and called for Zaki to be punished. But it was as if Soren had gone deaf. All his body and senses were frozen but his eyes, which were fixed upon his uncle. Soren's heart pounded as if it wanted to leap out of his chest, though he wasn't sure why. Residual fear lurked—Zaki had become a creature of his nightmares, after all—but they were both surrounded by armed soldiers. Soren was as safe as he would ever be.

There was anxiety too, in his tremoring fingers that refused to be still. Soren was glad his cloak concealed such a sign of weakness brought out by the culmination of the years since that fateful night of his mother's death. It had been a long journey to get here, but never had Soren played through this scenario in his mind.

What did I imagine would happen? Who knows.

Soren could not decide how he felt towards his uncle at that point. So much had happened and yet a man, a simple man, stood before him. There was hate and contempt for Zaki's cowardice, but in that moment it faded to indifference, like Soren watched a stranger—not the man who had murdered Soren's mother, kidnapped his sister, and caused irreparable damage to so many other lives including Soren's.

Time seemed to slow when the black-hooded executioner stepped forward. Up onto the wooden stage he climbed. It creaked under his weight. A new wooden block had been prepared with a place for the chin crafted from the solid lump of wood.

The executioner was a hulk of a man made of pure knots of muscle. Zaki, thin and diminished, seemed puny in comparison. Soren was glad that he did not have to wield the sword himself, for he would have faltered and done a terrible job. He did not embrace that feeling and shrunk away from the cowardice, but it seemed wrong to kill an unarmed man, even if it was justified by the law—and all that Zaki had done. It seemed more of a performance than a carriage of justice. The pathetic form before him looked so pitiful.

Nevertheless, Soren felt a twinge of relief, glad that in moments it would be over. Soren would be king beyond doubt. He would have avenged his mother and all those who died or suffered under Zaki's orders. Peace would be restored for certain in Caledan, and a truce with Roher binding. It had cost a great deal to get to this place, but it would not be wasted. Not for the first time, his thoughts turned to Edmund and those nearest and dearest that he had lost. He swallowed. It was too hard to think about them.

The roar of the crowd cut through his reverie as the guards drew Zaki forward and pushed him to his knees. The collar of his shirt was loosened for him, because Zaki's own hands shook too much to untie the knot at his throat.

Zaki glanced at Soren and paused.

Does he still think I'm bluffing? Soren wondered. It was as if Zaki expected that it was a charade and for Soren to call off the punishment. Soren betrayed no emotion—but his face was frozen, whether he liked it or not.

Zaki did not bow his head to pray, as the executioner muttered a swift blessing, echoed by most of the people assembled before them. Instead, he held Soren's gaze and searched his face. Soren realised with ironic humour that all that had happened had cost them both their faith in any higher power. They had both realised the score; those in power did as they pleased, whether it was right or wrong.

Zaki shuffled forward and placed his chin on the block. His hair fell past his eyes and hid his face. Cold touched on Soren's face and made him start. He looked up to see the smallest snowflakes start to fall. They settled in Zaki's hair. Soren was so close he could see them melt in an instant. The executioner drew back the ceremonial axe, sharpened and polished for the occasion. One sharp, short 'thock' sounded. It was done.

Crimson gushed forth upon the gathering snow.

THE
SHATTERED
CROWN

ONE

The dragons came with the darkness; insidious shadows that swallowed the earth with voids of light. Screams arose from the ground before they had given any other sign of their presence.

The humans were becoming more cautious, Cies noted. It mattered not. No being could stand before dragon-kind, least of all mortals. With a slow-burning satisfaction, he opened his fiery maw and dove from the air, followed by his gleeful kin.

Destruction came to Harring that night.

TWO

Soren slouched in his armchair before the fire with his feet stretched out to feel the faint warmth. The fire was too small to fill the entire space, and the cold of winter nipped at him. His high-ceilinged drawing room was rarely warm, but now, somehow, the insipid breeze found its way inside, and it chilled him to the core. Not even the midday winter sun brought warmth and respite; only a cold and flat light.

"More wood, please!" he called. A scurry sounded outside the door as his serving boy scuttled off to fetch another pannier of wood. Soren rose, stiff-limbed. He paused at the sharp rap on the door.

"Yes?"

"The Lord Steward of Pandora," his guard announced from without and pushed open the door.

"Lord Behan," Soren greeted him with a smile.

"Your Majesty." Behan's bow was not as low as it ought to have been, prevented by the stiffness of his arthritic joints.

Soren invited him to sit by the hearth instead, and Behan sunk into the chair with a grateful groan, whilst the boy returned and rebuilt the fire, and Soren hovered about the feeble warmth.

"What news?" Soren's face fell as Behan shook his head. "Another?"

"Yes. Harring."

Soren's gut wrenched as Behan said the word. *It surely cannot be Harring?* His eyes closed for a moment, as he said a silent prayer for his friend, Garth, and his daughter, Lindy, in that isolated and windswept place. No help would reach them there. *I pray they are safe.* He swallowed past the lump in his throat. "How many?"

"At least half have been killed, or fled and not returned. The other half managed to escape, and have since returned to their homes, though nothing remains of them. This news comes with latest word from Denholm."

Soren's mouth twisted in a grimace. He knew Lord Verio of County Denholm would have nothing positive to say. He waved at Behan to continue.

"Verio is threatening to shut the city gates. He has seen an unprecedented influx of refugees seeking shelter and safety behind his walls. In his own words, the city is 'overrun with them like rats'."

Soren growled an inhuman sound of rage. Verio was a despicably selfish man, but his words betrayed an even deeper contempt for his people.

"Yes, quite," Behan continued, with a shake of his head. "Hardly words of good taste. Soldiers are being killed alongside civilians, he reports. All his efforts are in vain, and he seeks now to consolidate his own safety. His weapons are of no use whatsoever against the dragon attacks. They attack from the sky with great spurting jets of flames, bulk that shatters buildings, and claws and teeth that can rend anything in their way. Even on rare occasions when close combat is possible, their hide is far too thick to pierce with any blade, and they are too dangerous to approach or survive. No defence stands before them. Verio is counting on his castle itself to provide enough fortification for him to outlast any attacks."

"And the people of Denholm county?"

Behan did not answer.

"Are left to fend for themselves," Soren answered his own question, his lip curling in disgust. "The man is a coward."

"He is, indeed, but, perhaps faced with such a foe, he cannot be blamed for wondering how he can survive if they attack his city."

Soren stood for a moment, trying to imagine experiencing a dragon attack. He recalled the fearsome bulk and presence of the dragons he had met, and could imagine only too well the fear they would strike into unfamiliar hearts. Yet, he could not understand why they attacked. The dragons he had met were fierce and terrifying, but bound to peace. *What had changed?* He repeated his thought to Behan, but the older man shook his head and sighed.

"I cannot fathom it myself, Sire. The witness accounts state all property and structures were wholly destroyed by fire and physical strength. All livestock are killed—most are consumed. People are killed and left. In any case, we must look to what we may do. The attacks move south and west through Denholm county—and they increase in frequency. We receive news of fresh attacks daily. There are, and we have, no defences to stand in their way. What can be done?"

"I know not," replied Soren, with a heavy heart. "Soon, they will breach the Grey Mountains." He knew dragons could fly over the passes with ease."And then..."

"Pandora."

"Yes. We could be next. It is perhaps only a matter of time before they attack us."

The consequences were implied. There would be no way to defeat such a foe.

The two men remained in silence, both gazes lost in the crackling flames of the fire that greedily wrapped itself around the fresh logs. Shivers crawled down Soren's freezing spine and every hair stood on end, even as his front roasted in the crescendoing heat.

Soren was foolish to think he had found peace for himself, and for Caledan, he realised. *Does peace ever come?* he wondered. He was at last rid of his usurping, murderous uncle, Zaki, and for now the ambitious and aggressive southern king, Harad, too. However, now he had a far greater problem—and no idea how to solve it. He pushed back his rising panic at the hopelessness and helplessness of the situation.

"I must make contact with the Eldarkind," said Soren at last. "If any should know of what is happening, it is they. Their race is as old as the dragons. Their magic could aid us."

"If I may suggest something of pertinence, Sire?"

Soren indicated for him to proceed.

"Your mother had a mirror," he said, watching Soren expectantly.

Soren raised his eyebrow, nonplussed.

"With this mirror, she could look upon lands far away, and

speak with the Eldarkind as if they sat as close as you and I now."

"How is this possible?"

"Their magic, of course. Scrying, they call it. The ability to see far. The mirror was a gift from Queen Artora to your mother upon her coronation. After her untimely death, I hid its purpose. To Zaki, it was nothing more than a mirror, and I felt no need to furnish him with the truth. He was unworthy, and underestimated the value of the Eldarkind."

Soren's lips pursed at the mention of his uncle, whose face flashed before his eyes.

Always the same face. The one of surprise and pain in the moments before he died; and then the lolling limpness of his head and the unseeing glaze on dead eyes that would only trouble Soren in his nightmares. It was still raw. Soren swallowed. "There is no time to lose. I must speak with Artora at once. Take me to the mirror."

THREE

Tarrell, the new king of the Eldarkind, stood with his hands clasped behind his back, admiring the splendour of the winter mountain vista before him. It was barren, a blank canvas of snow and bare meadows, but beautiful nonetheless. Everything was enriched now that the full flow of magic had returned to Ednor.

It rushed through his bones and his body hummed with the energy of it; rejuvenated and revitalised. He revelled in that, and the relief that accompanied it. It was only now the full power of the energy stream had returned that he could appreciate how much of it had been stifled—choked, and siphoned away—though he understood not where.

"My lord," his aide called, and burst in without waiting for invitation.

Tarrell turned and frowned, about to admonish him, but his usually unruffled aide's agitation gave him pause.

"The dragons are here."

"I beg your pardon, Alikar?"

"They are here," Alikar repeated, shaking his head in bewilderment.

"Who? Myrkith-visir?"

"No, Sire. The dragon who leads them calls himself Farran. He claims urgent counsel with you."

"So be it." The dragons were far too large to enter the building. "I will meet with him in the courtyard."

The rumbling reverberated through the hallways as Tarrell strode outside. *What on earth is the meaning of this?* He had been unable to scry with Myrkith-visir for days. The mirror had turned as black as night and he feared the worst, but did not understand it.

"Lord Tarrell." The dragon named Farran had a rough, gravelly voice.

"Farran, it is my pleasure." Tarrell executed a short, sharp bow before tilting his head back to show his fleshy under-jaw to the dragon.

Farran dipped his head almost to the ground before rearing to reveal his own chin. The dragon greeting revealed a vulnerable point as a sign of trust to both enemy and friend.

As Farran lowered his head to eye level with Tarrell, for he towered over the Eldarkind several times his height, Tarrell stole a chance to examine Farran's company. Bloody. Muddy. Exhausted. *What has passed?* Tarrell wondered.

"Draw fresh water for these guests. Bring fresh meat also." Eldarkind scattered to carry out his bidding. "What has passed?" he repeated his question to the dragon.

"Bahr of the Fire."

Tarrell stilled. He met Farran's giant eye. "You have had dealings with him." It was not a question. Bahr of the Fire, a fire elemental of the oldest and greatest nature, had lain in the darkness, bound by ice for a millennia. His affinity to fire, and his role in shaping the existence of the dragon race had occurred as a concern to Tarrell. *What if Bahr has sought their allegiance?* Before he could ponder any more, Farran replied.

"We have, and he did not visit us with amity in mind. Myrkith-visir is dead. Our clan is divided and at war."

Tarrell's jaw dropped open. "Myrkith-visir has passed? How did this happen? Who leads your clan now?"

"Bahr came, and with him, he brought fire, death, and a traitor by the name of Cies. His magic had twisted and grown Cies to unnatural proportions. Myrkith-visir denied him claiming us as his own servants, but Bahr and Cies had many supporters in the clan. There was a battle. Myrkith-visir sacrificed himself to end Bahr, but Cies lives on, and he has claimed the clan for himself."

"Bahr is dead?" Tarrell comprehended what it meant. Now,

he understood why their magic had diminished, and how it had returned. Tarrell exhaled with a deep sigh of ambivalence. The Eldarkind had lost their queen, Artora, the most fair and just, but Bahr of the Fire was dead, and thus she was avenged. No longer would Bahr skulk in the shadows, silently poisoning their very life force.

"You do not submit to Cies's rule?" Tarrell added.

Farran growled, and his anger was echoed by those around him. "No! We do not accept the rule of a coward who was banished from our clan. He is not fit to call himself our kin, let alone lead us."

A much smaller black dragon pushed forward from the crowd. "I name myself Myrkdaga, son of Myrkith-visir. My sire died the most noble of deaths. We do not submit to traitors. I follow Farran-visir, my sire's nest-mate. He will return honour to our clan and deal revenge on Cies of the silver scales."

Tarrell bowed to the black dragon. "I offer my condolences at the loss of your father."

Myrkdaga turned without reply and walked away with smoke rising from his nostrils and a low growl in his throat.

"This does not give you leave to come here Farran-visir," Tarrell turned his full attention back to Farran, now affording him the title of head of his clan. "You have strayed from your ancestral lands. Do you realise the implications?"

His clenched fist tremored a little, as the anger built inside him. "The Eldarkind have spent a thousand year abiding by the terms of our pact; now you have strayed from its conditions. You have broken the pact!" he accused.

Farran snorted, and Tarrell stumbled back, coughing as smoke puffed into his face. "The pact was broken already. It has been crumbling a long while—you know this to be true, you feel the magic, too—and it is His doing. Bahr has been weakening us for centuries as He devised His escape."

Tarrell was not convinced, though he privately admitted it did make some sense. Bahr's death slotted all the pieces of the puzzle together. He was silent for a moment, in contemplation. "Can we make contact with Brithilca-visir? He will no doubt have wisdom that may aid us in this. He will not be subject to any corruption by Bahr or Cies."

Farran rumbled his agreement.

Farran joined Tarrell later, away from prying eyes, in his private courtyard. The cloudy sky dimmed with the impending sunset, and the chill of the mountain air deepened. Tarrell came wrapped in furs, and even Farran warmed himself; the glow of fire in his throat revealed that much.

In the centre of the stone-flagged space, a still, shallow pool lay motionless. Tarrell paced towards it as Farran began the summoning. A low crooning emanated from his throat, rising and falling in pitch, and ebbing and flowing in intensity. The ethereal sound, charged with unspoken, ancient magic, made every hair on Tarrell's body stand on end, and shivers crawled down his spine.

The surface of the water vibrated, rippling from the centre to the edges, as though a pebble had been cast into it. And then, the water broke its bounds and soared upwards, twisting, turning, and writhing. Flowing rivers crisscrossed one-another as a form constructed itself: impossibly huge, made of far more water than that which had been in the pool.

Tarrell followed it with awe. He had never seen a dragon summoning before, and it was enchanting. In seconds that felt like hours, the form of a dragon stood before them. Made entirely of water that flowed through itself, creating ripples of reflected light that dazzled the courtyard, it stood towering over him—as large as Farran—and its feet were rooted in the water.

"Farran-visir. Tarrell-visir," the form greeted them with a deep, rumbling voice that sounded as though it spoke from a great distance away.

Tarrell, overcome for a moment by the wonder of what he had witnessed, and the privilege of meeting the father of dragons, dropped to one knee in the lowest bow he had ever offered another. "Oh, Brithilca-visir, this is a great honour."

"Brithilca-visir," murmured Farran.

"I know why you have summoned me," said Brithilca. His great snout swung between them as he regarded each in turn with a watery eye. "The clan is fractured, as it ought not to be, and there is no peaceful resolution. Cies already seeks you."

"He seeks revenge for his exile," growled Farran. "But the revenge will be ours. For Myrkith-visir and our fallen."

Brithilca did not reply. "There are far greater events set in motion that if left unchecked, will have devastating consequences for all. Bahr of the Fire is vanquished, yet His kin awaken."

"More? More like Him?" Tarrell said, aghast. Farran's growl rose in intensity.

"You know the old tales," said Brithilca. "You know who created the world and all upon it. Their slumber is ending. You must not let them rise."

"The records," said Tarrell. He knew where to begin looking. The oldest archives of the Eldarkind held records of the elementals, and where they would sleep. "Many have been lost," he recalled with dismay. Fire, decay, and water damage had destroyed many of the oldest records over their time.

"Begin with what knowledge you have," said Brithilca. "Seek them, and do it now, for my vision has long been clouded where they are concerned. I cannot see them as I once did, and I fear the worst."

"At once," said Tarrell, shaken. Bahr had damaged much: the Eldarkind's magic, their lifespan, and more besides. He dreaded to think of the consequences of more like him rising from their wards. The elementals had been bound with good reason: they had created the world and all upon it, and would also be its destroyer, if given the chance.

"And what of my kin and I?" asked Farran.

Brithilca looked towards him and took his time to reply. "You must work with the Eldarkind. If you wish for our race to be united once more, you know what you must do."

Farran bowed low.

A disembodied keening arose, and Brithilca unravelled before them. Water crisscrossed once more as it deconstructed and tumbled in splishes and splashes back into the pond, which rippled, and was soon still.

Tarrell and Farran stood in silence in the dark, digesting their meeting.

"We have much to do," said Tarrell at last.

Farran grunted. "Yes. But for now, we require needs more basic. Kotyir can no longer be called our home. I ask you on behalf of mine kin and I, if we may seek refuge with you here, in Ednor."

"You and yours are most welcome, friend," Tarrell agreed without hesitation, but his mind drifted back to Cies. "Yet, I do not wish to become involved with your clan wars. Brithilca's words are clear. A much greater threat looms—heavens help us. We must stop the rise of the elementals or we are all doomed. I will not have you bring more danger to our doorstep."

"The danger is here whether you will it or not," growled Farran. "Cies is a ruthless dragon through and through. Whether you stand against him, or not at all, mark my words, he will destroy you without a second thought."

"And you would have him come here?" said Tarrell. "You would have him destroy my people, all for sheltering you?"

"Of course not! Yet, wherever we are, should he defeat us, you will be next on his mind. He will not hesitate to eliminate you, so you do not threaten him."

"It is still none of my concern. Our purpose is to act for the greater good. If you feel the need to engage in petty strife, do so. But mine and I will not intervene. Choose your home in Ednor as you will. You are welcome for as long as you wish. I bid you goodnight." With that, Tarrell turned and strode away. He entered the building through the glass double doors where his aide awaited him.

"How long are they to reside with us, and where are they to stay?" Alikar asked.

Tarrell sighed. "I do not know. But we shall have to ensure they are well fed. Did you count them?"

"Upwards of six dozen. The winter stores will not see us through if they are to join us. What do they eat?"

"Raw meat, I believe. I shall have to enquire."

"We do not have the livestock, that is certain."

"I know, but I cannot turn them away. They are our allies. We must find alternate means of keeping ourselves this winter." He scowled to himself. Something else to worry about.

"As long as they stay far enough away from our habitations, hopefully all will be well. We have had some trouble already."

Tarrell stopped abruptly and fixed Alikar with an eagle-eyed stare. "Explain."

"A dragon may have knocked down a wall with its tail and ah—" Alikar gulped, "—stole, roasted, and consumed a goat."

"Confound it!" Tarrell exclaimed. "See our kin compensated, and have sharp words with everyone. We are to avoid confrontation. I shall see this reaches Farran's ears. He needs to control his kin. They are our guests, but they may not take what they wish and abuse our hospitality."

FOUR

"Where is he?" Eve said. Her eyes searched each brown-robed monk frantically—and fruitlessly—as they returned to the monastery. "Did you find him?"

Each day she had watched and waited for their return, sitting as long as her health permitted her in the freezing cold, swaddled in blankets. It proved difficult to endure after her own illness, for she had returned from the North with a raging fever that had left her delirious and incapacitated for weeks.

Exhausted and drained, she still dragged herself outside to keep watch, determined not to languish. At the very least, even if she was incapable of venturing back into the wilderness, she could do that. Until, that was, Abbot Hador discovered her as he always did, and, with gentle chiding, ushered her back inside to warmth and recovery.

Now, she could not move fast enough. Her chilled limbs were slow and stiff as she jogged with an awkward gait, still shrouded in blankets. The monks before her were weary themselves, and clambered from their horses with grunts and groans as the last members of the company plodded through the gate.

Riding on the very last horse was the familiar figure she sought, and her heart leapt in her chest as she perceived him. He was not awake, his horse guided by another, and stirred only slightly when his brothers pulled him from the saddle.

Eve rushed forward as he fell limply into their grasp. Luke's eyes flickered open, unseeing as she called his name, and with a moan, he slid forward into her arms, unconscious again. She crumpled under his cold weight, as monks rushed to aid them both. His skin was ice to the touch, and he was a leaden bulk. His hair was tangled and matted in her hand.

591

"Will he recover?" she asked, aghast.

The monks had no answer.

Inside the brightly lit, warm and dry infirmary—a log cabin with two beds and all the medicinal supplies that would fit—Luke's outerwear was peeled away. Mismatched gloves, a coat with tattered fur lining, and leather boots that had taken much wear and tear were stripped and piled in the corner.

Eve stifled a sob as she saw his bruised skin, but that was not the worst. Dark fingers. Dark toes. "What is it?" she whispered, aghast. The healer did not answer, and instead examined Luke from head to toe in great detail, peering, prodding, and turning Luke this way and that upon the bed.

"It is not as bad as I first feared," he said eventually.

Eve held her breath for what might come next.

"He has suffered chilblains and frostbite on his hands and feet. Alas, the frostbite will not recover, but unless it turns gangrenous, I have no need to amputate."

"Amputate?"

"It means to cut off a limb by operation."

No... Eve blanched. *I should have rescued him. Somehow.*

"The chilblains will recover with my ministrations. They ought to be kept warm and dry at all times," he added for Eve's understanding.

She nodded, feeling relieved, and his eyes flicked back to Luke. "When will he wake?" she says.

"I cannot answer. I do not know what has befallen him."

I do, Eve thought, but she said nothing. *This is my fault.* The memory of his prone form, frozen in place upon the gigantic icy throne in the dark cavern, haunted her nightmares still. *I should not have let him sacrifice himself for me.*

"You may wait with him until he wakes, if you wish. I am finished for now."

"Thank you." She did not look up as the healer left.

"Eve."

The familiar voice jolted her from slumber. Eve opened her eyes slowly. She was still in the infirmary, slumped against Luke's bed with her head resting upon it.

"Eve?"

She gasped and bolted upright, suddenly awake.

Luke's warm brown eyes regarded her. He smiled—a tired smile, but one nonetheless—and reached out a bandaged hand to her.

A grin widened upon her face, and she reached to hug him, reveling in how warm and alive he felt. "Luke!"

"Am I dreaming?" he said thickly, with a swallow.

Eve rushed to give him the cup of water from the side table. "No. I'm so glad you're here. I'm so glad you're awake. I'm so glad!"

"What happened to you? I did not think I would see you again. You made it back?"

Eve's smile faltered. She had returned—alone. "Nolwen. Nelda. They..."

"I know."

Tears welled in her eyes, as they had done many times before. She shook her head. "Bahr," she said past the lump in her throat. "He killed them all."

"I know," Luke said softly. He stroked her hair. There was little else to say. What else could be said? They had journeyed north, full of hope, with the well wishes of the Eldarkind and the support from Hador's men. It was intended to be a simple task to establish Bahr of the fire slumbered on. They could not have expected that with so much ease, he could have risen from his binding and broke the wards upon him—or that they would have paid the ultimate price.

"We are lucky to be alive," Luke acknowledged.

"How did you escape? It seems a miracle to see you again, and so soon. It should have been impossible. The only way the bond would break is with the death of Bahr, and we know I could not accomplish that."

"I don't know." Luke frowned. "I woke and I could move. I was no longer bound to the chair—I have no understanding of why. I left as quickly as I could. I nearly died trying to escape the mountain. I could not find the way out. Just as I gave up, I felt the breeze upon my skin, I found the entrance, and then I left without looking back. Hours passed, and then days. I have no recollection of the time. I saw a fire in the distance. I could not reach it. I was so close! The next thing I remember was being surrounded by my brethren. It was so good to see their faces. I thought I would die that day."

Tears spilled from Eve's eyes. "I'm so sorry I didn't—couldn't—return for you."

"You returned, though? Here? Alone? That is a feat enough in itself."

"Yes. I've spent these last weeks ill with fever. I wanted to leave with the search party to find you, but Hador wouldn't hear it."

"I'm glad of that," said Luke. He smiled and she mirrored it. Her face ached from it; she was so glad to see him.

"What now?" she said. "What happens now? With Bahr? With us?"

"I care not about Bahr, only that we are out of that accursed place and far away from Him. As for us? I don't know."

"I'll have to return to Arlyn. I cannot stay here much longer by Hador's generosity, and my father will have need of me. No doubt if he has returned home from the war, he will worry where I am. I am almost well enough to travel. Will you return with me?" she invited.

Luke's brows furrowed, and he dropped his gaze. "I don't know. I gave my word as my bond. I'm a brother here, now. I do not know if it be something I can walk away from."

"But you would if you could? You would return to Arlyn with me? Your mother, if you haven't already sent word, misses you greatly."

Luke's eyes flicked to hers. "I wouldn't be parted again," he said quietly. "Not after what we've endured." He reached towards her with his bandaged mitts, and held her close again.

Eve leaned into his chest and closed her eyes. Questions crowded her mind, but she had no answers save for two: that she wanted to return home, and wanted Luke by her side, whatever the consequences.

FIVE

Cies let out a gigantic belch and surveyed the scene about him with lazy contentment. His stomach bulged after the feast. Charred wool and bloodied, blackened, and cracked bones surrounded him—the last remains of the herd of sheep. Behind him, the barn blazed merrily, crackling, spitting, and bathing his hide with a growing heat. What humans were there were dead or fled. Cies did not care which. His kin gorged themselves around him, whilst the smaller dragons bickered and fought over scraps of meat.

Cies' prey was left for him with no contention. Whether out of fear, respect, or a healthy mix of both, he enjoyed the trappings of leadership. No longer did he have to prove himself to earn a full stomach. No longer did he have to answer to another. The faintest snarl escaped his throat unbidden. He would not have to follow a worm like Myrkith again. As long as he could lead—and do so without challenge—he would be satisfied to do as he pleased, and that suited him perfectly.

As he shifted to grab another carcass, now eating for greed, he hissed as painful spasms ripped and tore through his every muscle from head to tail. It took all his strength to remain still, but he could not move. To show weakness would be suicidal to his leadership, and he would not sacrifice that after all his hard work. The spasms subsided, and he regarded his clan from the corner of his eyes. They still gorged themselves. It appeared no one had noticed. The tiniest breath of relief escaped him.

It was true Bahr's magic had brought great benefits: he had brute strength and uncharacteristic bulk. Yet, since Bahr's death, it had also weakened him with debilitating spasms, and unevenly accelerated his growth into twisted forms that were sometimes awkward to manage. No more did the magic fuel him and grow his bulk and strength, for Bahr was gone. Cies could feel the magic slowly sapping away from him, no matter how much he desperately tried to cling onto it.

Cies shifted his stiffening body. A spike of anger made him growl, as another wave of pain rippled down his spine. He regarded the sheep before him. He was too annoyed to eat now, and flung the beast away. It sailed to the other end of the dark field, where it was claimed by several younger dragons on the fringes of the group, whose voices and snarls rose in a cacophony of challenges as they fought over it.

Divoky crowed into the night, a fierce and joyful roar that carried through the dark sky, no doubt striking fear into the hearts of those who heard it on the ground far below them. Cies let his deputy celebrate, but his own mood was marred by the pain that still ached in his bones.

"This is far greater a life than scraping our existence on Kotyir," said Divoky with a smile showing his gleaming, white teeth. "We are true to our form now, and we have reclaimed our position in the world. No longer hiding, but making the world tremble in fear before us!" He laughed, and his grin widened with grim satisfaction.

"It is only the beginning," Cies snarled. "We cannot be truly strong until Farran and his worms are defeated. As long as their rebellion holds, we are not at ease to enjoy this life." Cies could not stand the idea he would be defied, and that Farran and the rest of his followers would get away with it. Every wing-beat west drove them closer to Farran and his dragons, and Cies planned to end them one day soon. At any cost.

"They are cowards," spat Divoky.

"Cowards, indeed. Worms, and traitors, and filth," snarled Cies, his anger rising. "I will follow them to the ends of this world if I must, to make an end to them. I will not suffer their existence!"

"Where are they?" asked Divoky.

"They will be at Ednor, as Farran stated."

"You do not trust that?"

"He is not stupid enough to attempt to bluff us. I know it to be true. He seeks shelter with the Eldarkind." Cies's lip curled in disgust. *Dragons, seeking the protection of a weak race such as they.* They would also receive their comeuppance from Cies. He had no use for them. The Eldarkind had had the dragons at their beck and call for millennia, and that ended here and now with him. He would quash any notion of servitude, and any threat their magic posed.

"We fly west to Pandora now, yes?" Cies could hear the excitement in Divoky's voice. He knew the younger dragon wanted a taste of bigger and better spoils, but that would not be granted, yet.

Cies pondered a moment. He had considered it, yet, now his mind returned to Farran. He could see the other dragon in his mind's eye, smug and safe with the Eldarkind in their rat's nest Ednor. Fury rose again.

"No," he growled. Fire roiled in his belly and spilled up his throat. "Crushing our opponents is of greater importance. We fly to Ednor at once. Farran will rue the day he crossed me, as will all those who follow him. Their likes will rue pandering to the whims of the Eldarkind with their pathetic agreements and pacts. The Eldarkind will understand we are their masters, not they ours. Pandora will be ours for the reaping when we are finished."

Those dragons who soared alongside him heard his words. Gleeful rumbles rippled out through the clan as his words were relayed to all. Cies let his inner fire burst forth with an almighty roar, taken up by his clan until the sky burned bright with their flames.

SIX

Eve slipped into the infirmary, which was toasty warm compared to the frigid fog outside. Luke was awake, sitting in his bed reading a thick book.

"Eve!" He greeted her with a smile, placing the book open on his lap so he could clasp her hands in his. A smile stretched across her face as she beheld him. Shadows still sat dark under his eyes, but their unmistakable warm twinkle had returned. Her Luke was coming back.

"You can read this?" she said, wrinkling her nose. The Luke she knew had hated school as a child, and could barely read or scribe.

"Yes. Brother Ormund was kind enough to teach me. I'm glad he did; this is so interesting. It's a history of the monastery. Did you know the first abbot was named Dunnottar? And the first site of the monastery was at the crossroads to the south? The construction of this site commenced a hundred years later, under direction of Abbot Arbroath."

"Very interesting," Eve said, but her smile faded. This was a very different life to lead, and one that would not see them on the same path.

"How long are you to stay?" asked Luke.

"I…" She did not want to think about leaving, but knew she must. "I'll leave as soon as I feel well enough," she answered noncommittally. "I cannot stay, you know this. I have my duties to my father and to Arlyn, not least of all, but I'm a woman. I'm grateful for Hador's generosity in allowing me to remain for so long already. However, I need to be strong enough to make the journey unaccompanied."

"You cannot travel alone," Luke said. "It's not safe."

Eve held her hands up and shrugged. "I have no-one with me. The abbot has no men to spare. There is no-one who can accompany me." They sat for a moment in silence, the unsaid heavy between them. "Are you to remain here?"

Luke sighed, and ruffled a bandage hand through his tousled hair. "I'm not sure I am able to leave. If I can, will you wait for me to accompany you home?"

Eve nodded. That was what she had hoped.

"I will ask the abbot what may be done—if I can be released from my oath." Luke said, staring into nothingness, deep in thought.

"I'd like that," Eve replied quietly. *Would Hador release a brother bound by oath?* She had no idea, but a growing realisation that the course of her future might depend on it. She did not want to be separated again after they had endured so much. They shared a hesitant smile, and she placed her hands upon his. He grasped them in his warm hold—feeling reassuringly alive again—and yawned, extricating a hand to drag it across his face. The twinkle in his eyes had diminished, and Eve could see how weary he was. She excused herself, and stood to take leave, but he did not let go and tugged her back to her chair.

"Please, stay."

She acquiesced and perched on the chair. They sat in companionable silence, but her mind and heart raced, and unseen to Luke, her foot tapped upon the floor. She still carried terrible guilt about leaving him in the very bowels of Juska Mountain and not rescuing him herself. A growing part of her felt as though, after being told by Tarrell that Bahr could not be beaten and Luke was doomed, she had utterly failed him by believing it—as if the worst thing she could have done was to give up on him in her own heart.

She looked up to see Luke asleep. His head lolled on the pillow and his dark eyelashes resting on his cheeks. Eve extricated herself from his grasp as quickly and quietly as she could, and left without waking him.

"You left?" he said first, looking quizzical, when she visited again.

Eve flushed, dithering at the door. "You were so peaceful, I didn't want to disturb you." *And I felt sick to the pit of my stomach that I let you down.*

"I spoke to Hador."

Eve moved towards him, a thousand questions burning on her tongue.

"I asked him to release me of my bond, so I may return to Arlyn and try to rebuild my life—the correct way. Mother needs me, and it was foolish and selfish of me to abandon my life and forsake her. And... I want to be close to you too. After everything that has happened, I don't want to be apart."

"What did he say?" she whispered, twisting her hands together.

"He agreed I may leave. I'm released from my oath and bond to this place."

Relief flooded through her, and she embraced him, her awkwardness forgotten.

"Hador said I—we—will always be welcome here, for which I am grateful."

Eve did not reply, save to squeeze him tighter. Her skin tingled as he kissed her forehead gently.

There was a clatter from without and they sprang apart; the door opened to reveal Brother Ormund with another volume of history. Eve cooled her burning cheeks with the back of her freezing hands, her gaze averted, whilst Luke greeted his comrade with a secretive smile on his face only she could fathom.

SEVEN

The mirror was an innocuous object, covered with a dusty sheet. It stood in the corner of an abandoned chamber that was stuffed with accoutrements of all shapes, sizes and purposes. The servants struggled to free it of the maze of clutter, grunting and groaning under the strain, and coughing from the dust clouds that puffed with every step. Under Behan's watchful eyes, it was moved to Soren's quarters, where it was placed in a small drawing room away from prying eyes.

There, Soren unveiled the mirror, sweeping away the sheet in a cloud of dust to reveal the six-foot tall sheet of glass. A frame inlaid with mother of pearl surrounded it, and other than some small marks, it was spotlessly clean, despite the state of its shroud. Behan was ready with the incantation, noted in written form for him to use. Soren took the scrap of parchment, frowning as he beheld the slanted script and unfamiliar word.

"Leitha," he said. The word was unfamiliar and his tongue stumbled; he hoped he had said it correctly, for he had no understanding of how the magic worked.

A moment of nothing passed, and then the surface of the mirror plunged into blackness. Soren gasped and stumbled backwards, but as the mirror's surface swirled with things unseen, he could not help but edge forward once more, his jaw open in wonder as he beheld shapes coalescing inside the glass. By the time the room within solidified, Soren was almost touching the glass with his nose, and his outstretched fingers trembled millimeters from the mirror's surface.

It was a wondrous sight to behold. Soren stepped back to examine the mirror, which stood there, silent and unassuming. He looked behind the mirror, facing a corner of the room where two stone walls met—and the back of the mirror; plain, unassuming wood. With furrowed brows that rose into incredulity, accompanied by a delighted laugh, he looked into the mirror once more, examining every detail of the room before him.

Light, airy, and high-ceilinged, polished floors led to tall windows, through which he could see mountains. Mountains which were hundreds of miles away from him, appeared only hundreds of metres away instead. He shook his head. *Amazing.* He grinned at Behan, who smiled back, despite not seeming even half as impressed, but Soren suspected it was because this was nothing new to him.

"Hello?" Soren called into the mirror. "Hello?" he called a little louder.

Rustles, and then footsteps sounded before him from inside the mirror. A tall figure swept into view. Soren closed his mouth, which had been hanging open in awe.

"Your Majesty," said the figure, a male Eldarkind, offering a deep, sweeping bow. "It is a pleasure to meet you at last."

As he spoke, Soren regarded him curiously. He was far taller than Soren, it appeared, and long, pale hair flowed in a straight river down the back of his muted green robe, which fell from its high collar all the way to the floor. His brow was crowned in a delicate and interweaving silver and gold circlet. "My name is Tarrell. I am the king of the Eldarkind."

King? Soren thought, confused. *Where is Queen Artora?* After a moment's pause, his manners took over. "Your Majesty, it is a pleasure, also."

Tarrell smiled a thin-lipped smile that hid many feelings Soren could not discern. "I see your confusion. It is with a heavy heart I must tell you Queen Artora passed some weeks ago, of a sickness that could not be cured."

"I am sorry to hear. My deepest condolences for your loss," said Soren, though the words were an empty courtesy; he had known little more about the queen than her name.

"I thank you," replied Tarrell. "It has been a difficult time, but as ever, we move forward. How may I be of assistance to you?"

Soren took a moment to recover his thoughts. The wonder of the mirror, and speaking with an ethereal person both there and not there was distracting. "Dragons," he began. "The dragons are attacking along the east coast. The toll is terrible and growing and we have no means to defend ourselves. Last I met them, they were not hostile. I cannot fathom what has changed."

Tarrell's face closed, and his mouth set in a thin, grim line, but he did not seem surprised, which, in itself, surprised Soren. Tarrell explained to Soren, who listened aghast, of the recent rift in the dragon clan, and Cies's quest for destruction and revenge.

Soren took several moments to comprehend Tarrell's words, and his thoughts lingered on Myrkith-visir. The giant, black dragon had seemed invincible to Soren. *And now he is gone.* "This is grave news. By your words, they cannot be stopped by us, then. We need your assistance. Surely, your magic can help us?"

"There are greater events at play," Tarrell warned. "As I have said to Farran, I am reluctant to intervene my people in a matter which is not of the utmost importance."

"What about our pact?" said Soren, growing frustrated.

"The pact is broken," Tarrell replied flatly. "As it has been for some time now." He told Soren of all that had passed with Bahr of the fire, and of the awakening of the elementals as a result of the pact's failure. "It has been a long time in the breaking, and the consequences are dire for all of us. Cies is just the start. If he can be defeated, that brings some security, but worse will follow. We ally ourselves still with Farran and his clan, as we ally ourselves with you. That remains unchanged. But our priority is seeking to rebuild the pact."

"Why?" Soren questioned. "If Cies is the more pressing issue, then we ought to unite against him."

"Farran will have to fight that battle himself. Petty clan wars are no concern of ours, though we gladly offer any ally shelter. Our concern is for the greater go—"

"My people are being slaughtered!" Soren snapped. His cheeks were red balls of fury. "You would stand and do nothing whilst Caledan is destroyed? How is that aiding your allies?"

604

"You do not understand our mutual predicament!" Tarrell snapped back; the first sign he had lost composure. "The elementals have slumbered, bound, for a millennia. If they are allowed to rise, the world over will burn and be destroyed. Cies may seem a destructive force beyond measure to you, but I assure you, one rampaging dragon and his ragtag band of followers bear no measure of significance against the threat of the elementals. Mark my words, they are rising. They will come, and they will destroy us all if we do nothing."

Soren was caught off guard by Tarrell's fervent words. Something worse than Cies? He could hardly imagine it, but Tarrell seemed serious enough, and that alone was cause for concern. Soren swallowed. "How can we rebuild the pact?" He knew nothing of it, save it existed as some agreement that bound together the three races of human, Eldarkind, and dragon, in a lasting peace.

"We are not presently sure," Tarrell admitted. "It has been a millennia since the original pact was bound. We are combing through our oldest archives, and seeking the counsel of the great dragon Brithilca, but he is being as cryptic as ever."

Soren nearly laughed. The Eldarkind were cryptic enough to him, so Brithilca must be in an entirely different league altogether.

"I suggest you do the same," added Tarrell. "Mayhap we will find something of use between us."

Soren's amusement faded and he did not answer. There was even more serious work to be done, yet he had no idea where to start, and he was no closer to resolving the dragon attacks.

EIGHT

The walk to the crossroads was long and painful, but at least the exercise kept the chill at bay, for the day was clear and bright, and the winter sun did nothing to warm them. The monastery had no horses to spare, and so this part of the journey was to be on foot, though they hoped to hire horses at the crossroads; neither were capable of walking to Arlyn.

Both Eve and Luke were weakened after their infirmities— Eve still had not the strength to restore them with the help of her magic—and the weight of their packs dragged them down. Luke had insisted on taking both packs, but Eve refused, knowing he was barely capable of lifting his own. It was difficult to decide which of them was in a worse state.

It was the first day without a snowstorm that week, and despite Hador's protests that they were not fit to travel, Eve insisted on leaving. Some part of her felt a growing sense of urgency, as if they had tarried too long. Already, she could not recall how many weeks—months, even—it had been since she had left Arlyn. Five, she counted, and perhaps another. For Luke, it had been even longer still.

As they trudged on in silence, her thoughts turned homeward to Arylyn, her father, to Luke's mother and to what awaited them there. Hador had already informed her the fighting in the south had ended, and all had returned home. King Soren had defeated the uprising. That meant her father would have returned to Arlyn some moons ago. She no longer feared his wrath, though, she realised. After all she had endured, the anger of a mortal man counted for little next to the maleficent intent of limitlessly powerful elemental magic.

Days later, they trotted through the familiar gates of Arlyn with relief that they had managed to procure horses to ease the journey, and for the sight of home. It felt surreal to return to a place they knew so well, but that felt so strange after months of nothing but wilderness and trees. Here, the din of people and businesses was overwhelming, and stone buildings towered above them, cutting out the weakening late-afternoon light.

"It's been a long while," noted Luke.

"And much has passed," Eve added.

They parted outside Luke's house. He dismounted and handed her the reins to his mount. Before he turned away, they shared a smile and a long look, filled with everything between them. She did not want to ride away, but home beckoned for both of them. At the corner, she paused and twisted in the saddle to see Nora clinging to her son—Luke hugged her just as hard—and sobbing into his cloak. A small smile crossed her lips. *That's been a long time coming and well overdue*, she thought gladly.

Minutes later, and she clattered into the courtyard, which bustled with familiar faces. They hailed her with surprise and warm welcome, banishing the awkward feelings of displacement and surrealism. The smell of home blasted into her face as she opened the front door: log fires, pine fresheners, and something roasting in the kitchens. For a moment, she stood on the threshold with eyes closed and a grin on her face, listening to the old sounds and immersing her senses in things she had not even realised she missed before she shut the cold out behind her.

The maids greeted her excitedly and ushered her into the kitchens for food, saying how dreadfully in need of feeding up she was. The familiar henpecking warmed her heart and she chuckled to herself. She waved them off, saying she needed to see her father first.

"He's in the drawing room, Lady Eve," they told her.

That's unusual, she thought. He could usually be found in his study at this time, but then, she had lost track of the days. Perhaps, he was resting instead of working. She flitted up the stairs and corridors. It mattered not that she had been gone so many months, she still knew the place as well as the back of her hand. It was good to feel the familiar stone flags beneath her feet, and the smooth, whorled wood paneling underneath her fingers.

"Enter," her father called after she knocked on the drawing room door.

She entered without delay to find him seated by the fire reading with a blanket thrown over his legs. She had not seen her father at rest for many years, which was even stranger, and when he turned round, she stopped dead in her tracks. He was grey and drawn. His face lacked its usual healthy edge and his eyes were dull. Even his hair looked thin. He stood slowly and his arms shook as he pushed himself out of the chair. Tears pricked her eyes as she rushed to embrace him.

"I've missed you, Father." Eve fought back a rush of tears and emotion that her father did not.

"I've missed you, too, my little dove," Karn's voice cracked as he clasped her close for a long embrace. "I've been worried sick. I did not know where you were."

"What month is it?" Eve asked, biting her lip. *He looks as though he's actually been worried sick.* It was disconcerting to see the only stable pillar of her life so infirm and worn.

"Let's see, we are a few weeks into the second month of the year."

I've been away five months, Eve realised with a shock. *Five months...* "You're not mad with me?"

Karn's eyes flashed to hers and he gave a tired smile. "I am ill," he said, "and war once more opens my eyes to the real issues of the world. It matters not, my little dove, only that you are home safe. I trust you went with good reason."

She nodded, her eyes cast to the floor. "I did." She did not say where she had been—and he did not ask. She could see he was too exhausted, so she took his arm, guided him back to the warmth and comfort of his chair before the hearth, and tucked the blanket around his legs again.

With a roll of her aching neck, she at last unclasped her cloak and sat at her father's feet, snuggled into the sheepskin rug and leaned against his legs whilst the fire comfortably roasted her back.

"What ails you?" she asked.

He placed a hand on her head for a moment, and took a while to reply. "The tolls of war were hard," he said at last. "I cannot sleep on account of the horrors I have seen and I cannot rid myself of this damned chill. It permeates me to the bone." His legs quivered behind her. "I worried for you also, of course. We have had no news for months, save a message from Ednor apologising for the delay in your travels and promising your return soon, but with no explanation for your absence."

Eve opened her mouth to speak—to explain what had happened, as best she could try—but her father continued, and so she subsided.

"I need your help, Eve. I have a greater need of you now than ever I have before. I know I have prepared you well, and although I always feared and knew this day would come as much as I hoped it never would, I know it is time I ask for your help whilst I battle this forsaken infirmity. I know I can trust you to lead Arlyn in my absence. I would rest easier knowing Arrow county were cared for by her daughter. Will you aid me in this?"

Eve's shoulders slumped. A year ago, she would have been excited by the prospect: independence, control, and finally, a chance to prove herself. It was not so simple now, not so idealistic. *I don't want to lead any more. I don't want to be the son he never had. I want to be me. Can I do this?* she wondered. Her father's poor state concerned her and dampened her relief and contentment at returning home. *There is little choice. He is not fit to lead.* She accepted his offer with a sombre heart.

Karn heaved a shallow sigh of relief and sunk back into his chair with a small moan. "That gladdens me. Seek Hoarth, Captain of the Guard, about the defence and running of the town to begin with. He will tell you all you still need to know about how to manage Arlyn day to day. Water. Trade. Supplies." His voice trailed off.

"Father?" Eve twisted to look up at him. His eyes fluttered closed.

"So tired," she heard him murmur. "A little rest."

She stared at him for a moment, sadness welling in her heart, and then, as silent as a mouse, she left.

It was a few days before she could chance a meeting with Luke again. Eve's head reeled from days of meetings with this important person and that to discuss everything from landholdings and winter fodder for the animals to the town's defence plan, and she was relieved to sneak away to the isolation of the wall to stand guard with him for a while.

Luke's position within the town guard had been restored despite his absence, though he was on light duties whilst he recovered, and stationed at the far end of the wall as far away from trouble as there could be. His fingers remained bandaged under his mitts.

"My lady," he said gruffly as she approached.

She laughed. "My lady? Really?"

His face was tucked deep inside the fur lined hat. He glanced furtively around them. "I didn't know if anyone would be listening."

"They're not." She laughed and tucked her arm into his. "Walk with me." Obediently, he strolled alongside her to the most secluded end of the wall, where it met the soaring crags of the March Mountain foothills. They settled upon the battlements companionably, shielded from the wind by the crenellations, which was a relief. Her cheeks and nose were rosy with the sting of it, and she huddled closer into her fur-lined collar.

"How's your mother?" Eve asked.

Luke's eyes crinkled as he smiled. "She's doing well. In frail health, you understand, but you know what she's like: as fiery and independent as ever. She's glad I'm back, and I am, too. I don't know if she could manage without me looking after her."

"It must be hard at the cottage—you said the roof was leaking?"

Luke scowled. "I can't fix that blasted hole, no matter how

hard I try. The water always finds a way back in."

"Well, I have a suggestion. You and Nora should move to the keep. Your mother will be well cared for—warm and fed—through the winter, and looked after whilst you work. You won't have to worry about her."

"And me?" Luke turned to look at her, his eyes shaded under long, brown lashes, and his expression was inscrutable.

"You can stay with her. I'll make sure you have adjoining quarters, and you can dine with the staff. It'll be much nicer for you both. We have plumbing for hot water, which I'm sure will be much more pleasant for your mother."

"And we would be closer," Luke added.

"I suppose so." She shot him a sidelong glance and a half-smile.

He grinned back and tucked her under his arm. Suddenly, she felt warmer than should have been possible on such a cold day.

Her contentment faded minutes later when he enquired after her father. She talked of his illness, though Luke had heard most of the gossip on the wind through his fellow guards.

"Has he... Has he mentioned your future prospects?" he asked with some trepidation. "Marriage?" he added when she looked at him with a blank face.

She scowled and her jaw set firm. "No," she replied, with a steely glint in her eye. "He has not. And it matters not. Dane is dead, and I consider my betrothal ended. Father is too ill to think of it, thank the heavens, but I will tell him when he's well enough I have decided my own fate. I won't marry unless I choose my own suitor." The fire melted from her. "I won't be forced to marry someone I do not choose." Her voice was subdued. "I'm sorry. I wasn't strong enough to choose you, and I was so silly for not realising I wanted to until it was too late." Tears pricked her eyes and she struggled to fight them back.

Luke pulled her closer and stroked her arm in reassurance.

"I'm sorry for not coming back for you. I feel like I failed you." The tears fell now and she could not stop them.

"Oh, Eve." Luke wiped her tears away with his mitt, and his

lips warmed her frozen forehead with his kiss. "I know you would have returned were it possible. Please, don't berate yourself. Look, here we both are now. Home, safe, and where we belong: together. Now, we have a chance to start over, if you want to take it?"

"You mean for us?"

"Yes."

"To court?"

"Yes." His determined expression made her smile.

"I'd like that."

His grin spoke volumes as he lifted her chin with his mitt. His firm, warm kiss made her heart leap and was full of the promise of a better future.

Luke and Nora relocated to the keep within days, much to Nora's excitement. Luke watched his mother with quiet contentment as she sat next to an open fire, warm and dry for the first time in months. Life there suited her, though she would not accept charity and had taken to offering her services and experience as a seamstress.

Luke was content; he could leave her and go about his business without fear for her health here, and it brought him closer to Eve, which he could not deny lifted his heart more than he cared to admit. Each time they passed in the corridor and shared a touch of fingers, or just a glance and a smile, the frisson excited him, but it was not enough.

"When will you tell your father about our courting?" he asked when they met again, this time in a dusty storeroom in the cellars. It was not the first time he had asked; she had already brushed the question off once. His lips pursed as he recalled the sting of feeling like he wasn't good enough. *Will it always be this way?*

Eve leaned up to kiss him again, and he could not resist as her lips were the sweetest thing, but, after a few seconds, he pulled back and asked again. She bit her lip. "I dare not in his current state. He is so frail."

"But what of us?" Luke asked indignantly. "Is this all we are?" He gestured around them. "Dust, cobwebs, and shadows? Skulking and chance meetings in the darkness? Snatched moments here and there? Neither moving forward nor backwards? I know I cannot raise a house for you, yet, but I ought to make my intentions clear to your father, at least, and before that, you need to."

"I... I thought this would be best for now," Eve stammered. "Is it not good enough for now that we live under one roof? We can easily meet, with both of our parents confined to their chambers. We've never spent so much time together. Don't you enjoy that?"

"Of course," Luke replied gruffly. "But we hide it from them and everyone else! It's like you're ashamed of me—of us." His eyes bored into Eve, and she squirmed in his gaze.

"No! I never would be! I just don't know how to tell my father just yet. His condition worsens if anything. He does not recover. I worry about upsetting him further—"

"Why, because I'm not some grand lord?" Luke's tone was scathing.

"Yes!" Eve raised her voice, exasperated. "I've made my choice and I stand by it—I stand by you—but there's a time and a place to tell him. You have seen his current state. It is not now, and it is not yet."

"Is it ever going to be the right time for us to come out of the shadows?" Luke scoffed in disgust, and his lip curled in a grimace. He stood, quiescent for a long moment, and his anger softened, but the wall of disappointment that replaced it was even worse to see. It was clear he searched for an answer, but she had none to give.

"I..." Eve faltered, unsure how to voice her thoughts. *It's not about you! No... It's not you? You are enough? No—argh!*

He shook his head, turned, and walked away without another word.

"Luke!" she called after him, but he was gone. She swallowed. Guilt stabbed at her again. *We finally had a chance to be together—even in secret—and I spoiled it.* The disappointment, and hurt, in his eyes still bored into her as if he stood there.

NINE

"This is the fifth sheep this week," said the Eldarkind through gritted teeth. "What's more, the rest are in such terror that they have fled the pastures and several are still missing. We cannot continue like this."

"Peace, Ilskun," said Tarrell. His expression was purposefully impassive. "The dragons are carnivores and are wont to catch and eat their kills." He held up his hand to stop Ilskun's interruption. "I am aware this is unsustainable. I will speak to Farran-visir and ask that he and his clan hunt further afield, where they shall not encounter our own livestock."

Ilskun scowled, not placated. "It may be so, but tell them also to keep their kills further from Ednor. It is unsavoury for everyone to witness such barbarism."

Tarrell acknowledged Ilskun's requests before dismissing him. He waited until the door had shut before he let out a great sigh of frustration and retreated to the window to stare upon the meadows and contemplate.

By all accounts, the dragons were unwelcome guests; this was not the first complaint. Already, he had heard how the bulk and size of the dragons had damaged much in Ednor: pavements and roads were crushed and broken, stonework knocked off buildings as they passed, and fences and even walls had been swept aside like piles of leaves by their tails. The complaints of missing livestock exceeded these grumbles in number, and even Tarrell himself was concerned about how long they could coexist with the dragons in Ednor, though he dared not admit it to anyone else.

Conflict at home was the last thing he needed when such momentous things were at stake outside the shelter of Ednor. *Patience*, he thought to himself, as he had many times before. *Patience*.

He would have to show the patience his people understandably could not after the impositions on their lifestyles. Greater things were at stake than a broken wall or a missing goat. They would see that soon enough.

Tarrell's day improved with the return of one of his scouts. Sendari entered his office, executed a hasty bow, and gulped the cold glass of mint water whilst Tarrell waited for his report, his fingers tapping upon his knee in impatience. *Finally, good news at last. I hope.*

"Lord Tarrell, I thank you," Sendari said. He sunk into the chair opposite Tarrell with a grateful groan.

"I welcome you back. What news?"

Sendari swept a sweaty mop of brown hair away from his eyes with a grimy hand. He had travelled hard, Tarrell noted. "It is becoming harder to move through Caledan of late," Sendari began. "Even in the regions around Pandora where we have ever been welcome. The people are scared. The suspicion and fear created by the dragon attacks is making them ever more distrustful of anyone different, or foreign." He tugged at his hair. "I had to travel in disguise so as not to attract too much attention."

Tarrell shook his head in dismay. "This is ill news, indeed. If we are unable to travel freely, this may hinder our plans. Tell me where you have been. Did you fulfill your duties?"

"I did, Sire. I have travelled south and east across Caledan, across the isthmus, and roamed far to the north of Roher and Ladrin. I travelled the endless sands to where Arandulus of the Waters lies entombed."

"And is all well?" Tarrell leaned forward in his chair. His hands gripped the armrests.

Sendari faltered and he shot Tarrell a troubled glance. "All is well, as expected, but there is the slightest taint upon the air I cannot identify."

Tarrell stiffened and fixed Sendari in his steely gaze. "Explain." His voice was quiet, but his tone brooked no argument.

"The faintest shadow on the energy stream," he said. His nose wrinkled as he frowned. "It was like the flow of magic itself had some darkness within it as I have never seen to such an extent before. And yet, all was well. Nothing stirred. Nothing struggled against its bond. Arandulus sleeps soundly, as best I could determine."

"It begins," murmured Tarrell. "Or rather, it continues. Arandulus awakens as Bahr awoke."

"It cannot be so," Sendari said, aghast.

"That shadow is unmistakable. If you felt a taint upon the magic stream, it is happening. The slow unbinding and attrition of the magic that holds them is coming to pass. Is it not the same at the site where Oronimbus of the Air lays bound?"

Sendari had already returned from a previous mission west of the March Mountains and outside Caledan's domain to visit a spot deep in the wilderness. In a steep-sided valley, where the white water flowed fast, Oronimbus rested at the junction of two rivers. There, the water ran fastest and most turbulent.

Tarrell remembered his skin crawling with unsettlement as Sendari recounted how, despite the turbulent meeting of the waterways, the place in the deepest water were Oronimbus slumbered was as still as a millpond, as if the creature within could lessen the impact of the water of its own volition.

"It was the same with Oronimbus," Sendari confirmed. He hesitated. "It ought not to have been still in the very storm of the waters and yet, the water binding of Oronimbus is stronger, or He is weaker. If anything, Arandulus was worse. The taint of Her magic was much stronger. The energy stream was darker, and I could see the energy river's unnatural flow around Her, where with Oronimbus, there are little visible disturbances. I lay a new bond with Arandulus, and it seemed to have a little effect."

That was no consolation. Not all the elementals had been accounted for, and Tarrell knew if Arandulus struggled against her bonds, others did, too. "It is only a matter of time. I thank you, Sendari. You bring valuable news. Rest awhile before your next scouting, and leave as soon as you may. I fear we are running out of time."

Sendari bowed and left. As the door snapped shut, Tarrell cradled his head in his hands. His fingers massaged his temples as he tried to alleviate some of his stress. It was worse than he feared. The elementals already struggled against their bonds, and successfully.

First, clashes between his kin and the dragons. Then, the threat from humans. Now, their worst enemies of all arose. All three races: man, dragon, and Eldarkind would have to come together to see the pact be remade to bind the elementals in time to save them. That peace would not come to pass until Cies was defeated, Tarrell realised. Cies caused the rift of distrust between human, Eldarkind, and dragon, and Cies was the cause of their own strife with Farran and his dragons, who would not have to coexist alongside them if Cies was removed.

Cies was the key. *He must be defeated, and all who follow him if we are to have a chance of success to remake the pact and bind once more those who ought to lie sleeping forevermore. We must defeat Cies before the elementals awaken, but by then, it could be too late.*

Tarrell sent summons at once for Farran to join him, and for Soren to scry with them later that evening.

"Well met, Farran-visir," Tarrell said as the great dragon set down in the clearing with a resounding thump.

Farran replied in kind as he folded his giant wings away.

"What's this I hear of an incident this morning?" Tarrell asked, his tone carefully measured.

Farran rumbled. "My apologies. It would appear my kin is at fault."

Tarrell huffed and paced before the dragon. "We cannot have this happening! Each day, we keep treading on each other's toes instead of living in peace and harmony. My people feel threatened and they come to me, fearful and angry. Can you not control your kin?"

Farran's growl turned into a snarl that made even Tarrell take

617

a step back.

"I mean no offense," said Tarrell, but he offered no apology for what he had said and pressed on instead. "It's difficult not to be frustrated with the situation when our home is being destroyed and our carefully tended livestock frightened to death. We have ample space in Ednor outside the bounds of our dwellings. I am loathe to ask you to relocate further away—after all, we are allies—but it seems we cannot live in such close confines together."

"I agree. We have a mutual problem." Farran did not acknowledge the dragon's part in that, Tarrell noted. "Perhaps, our kin—dragon and Eldarkind—need to understand our joint predicament. Perhaps then, they will all see the need to cooperate and cease this pettiness."

Tarrell's eyes narrowed at the insinuation his own people were at fault, but he swallowed his pride, because Farran's idea was sound. "This could work," he conceded. "The enemy is not here. It... Cies... is out there, and he is coming. We must work with each other, not against each other. We have left this too long."

"And so," Tarrell summarised, having explained his scout's findings and his own conclusions. "We must rebuild the pact in the limited time we have remaining. I do not believe this is possible whilst Cies remains as a threat dividing all three of our races. In light of this, I believe we need to discuss our strategy going forward. It may be in our best interests to unite on this matter. Our three races are as in need of each other as ever, both in relation to Cies and to the elemental threat."

"We need your help now; we have needed it for weeks!" replied Soren through the mirror, scowling. Tarrell could see he was trying to bite his tongue. "We cannot defeat Cies alone, or at all, without your assistance. We do not have the knowledge or the strength. How can you concern yourself with the threats of the future above what endangers us all now?"

"Do not concern yourself with that just yet," Farran rumbled.

"Where are the attacks?"

"In the east and the south."

"Do they travel in a particular direction now?"

"Yes. West and north, on a direct course with Pandora. Please, I cannot protect my people from them," Soren implored.

Farran did not respond immediately, but his rumble intensified. "They are coming for us. I am sure of it."

"Your kin can fly across the country in mere days. Why are they not already upon us?"

"Perhaps, they do not yet dare. Perhaps, they are unsure of our location. Or, perhaps, Cies enjoys his terrorising so much he does not make haste."

"Regardless," replied Soren. "Whether they come for you or not, at this moment in time, my own people cannot sleep sound at night knowing they are safe. Every man, woman, and child is at risk wherever Cies goes. What can I do? How can I defend my people? I cannot do nothing, Farran-visir. How can my people look to me, trust me, follow me, if I do nothing?"

Tarrell and Farran shared a look. "Humans were never meant to be able to defeat a creature such as us," Farran replied eventually. "Our armour is impregnable to all your weapons, fire strengthens us instead of damaging us, and we are creatures of both night and day. We are wise and cunning enough to elude and to hunt you. Bahr of the Fire made us well. Our one weakness is water, in any of its forms: steam, water or ice. In great quantities, it will harm us and if we are submerged in water, we perish." Farran paused. Memories of Myrkith-visir and other clan members plunging into the cold seas to their instant death flashed across his vision.

Soren took advantage of his lull. "How is this possible? From the reports, we cannot get close enough to have any chance. Your kin kill us from a distance with fire, or attack with such speed from the dark skies that we can neither see you coming, nor defend against you. Even if we could catapult huge volumes of water at a distance with perfect precision, we would be hard pressed to triumph. As I see it now, we are hopelessly outmatched.

"I have ordered the evacuation of many outlying villages to

the larger towns and cities to keep them from harm's way. Whether they heed my warnings is their own choice, but, even if they do, they are not safe. Do you know how that feels, to not be able to help the people who depend upon you? I could as easily be sending them to their deaths, depending on where Cies chooses to destroy next. If you value our alliance as you say you do, you must help us," Soren implored.

"There is nothing we can do without openly engaging with Cies," Tarrell said, "and we are not ready to do so yet." He averted his gaze.

That enraged Soren further. "Whilst you wait, my people die. Make yourselves ready soon."

With that, the mirror plunged to black and returned to reflect Tarrell's own troubled face. He did not need to look at Farran to know the dragon felt as he did: their two races were too much at odds to unify yet.

TEN

Far to the north of Roher, on the border with Ladrin, the desert breeze blew warm and stifling under the baking sun as Tulia toiled in the fields alongside the other women of the village. It was a hard life she led now, far from the glamour of being the future king's concubine, but she was glad for it. It was a much simpler existence. In the village, no one asked questions. No one cared where she had come from, what she had done, and why she was there. As long as she worked alongside them to sow what they would reap, they welcomed her to share what little they had.

She wiped her brow with a dirty hand and stood for a moment to shrug the sling into place. On her back, bound by the fabric, her son babbled.

"Hush, Haroon," she said absentmindedly, bending over to toil again. He babbled back at her, and she knew that behind her back, his bright blue eyes, the spitting image of his father Zaki's, would be watching the world around him with quiet intelligence. One day, he would grow strong, and then… what? She did not know. Named for her own father, she had no doubt he would grow into a fine man.

"You'll get used to it soon," said old, wrinkled Sarana with a wink and a toothless grin. "I bore twins one year. Now they were heavy."

Tulia smiled fondly at the old lady. Sarana had taken her in when she'd been at death's door with starvation. "You can carry Haroon if you wish."

Sarana laughed and wagged a hand at her. "No, no, I think not, Tulia. My turn is done; now it is yours."

With a smile, Tulia bent over again to dig furrows in the earth with her sharpened stick. Soon it would be time to sow a new year's crop here in the hook of the river where the earth was full and rich. *The ground is soggy today, unusually so, though we haven't had rains for a while,* she thought absentmindedly. She dug shallow trenches, well above the waterline, but today the water rose in the bottom of them, bubbling up as if it were trying to break free of the earth. In minutes, her feet were surrounded with water—unnaturally icy in such a warm climate. Tulia paused, and looked about her. The other women were already muttering in confusion. And then the water started leaping into the sky.

"What demon's work is this?" Sarana shrieked, making warding signs with her hands.

Tulia looked to the sky and gripped her stick tighter at what she saw, as if somehow, it could protect her from nature itself.

What had been a hazy, sunny sky minutes before, was now piled high with black clouds. Shivers crawled down Tulia's spine as she stood, still and alert, scanning her surroundings. *This is not natural.*

The women were already gathering, clutching hands in fear. Some chanted prayers whilst others spat upon the ground and kicked up the dust to keep back whatever demon was at work. They watched, as the earth continued raining upwards, under the piling storm.

The water drew to one single point, where it began to form a great ball and then into a being with arms and legs, as tall as the sky. Its legs reached down to the earth and its head was crowned by the storm. The air rushed with wind and an unnatural roaring and keening that set Tulia's nerves on edge. The ground under their feet shuttered as it raised a giant leg and stepped towards them—again and again. The women scattered, screaming.

"The Gods have cursed us!" wailed Sarana. "Come child!"

Tulia followed, dropping her stick as the others had abandoned all theirs. What good was a stick against a god—or a demon? She had never seen Sarana run so fast, but the fear of gods had taken her.

Tulia's own heart beat in a frenzy as she ran, barely keeping her own fear at bay. She clutched Haroon to her chest just as the storm broke over their heads. Water lashed upon them so hard and fast, Tulia could see naught but a wall of water. The ground was slick beneath her feet and she laboured, struggling for balance.

She looked back, and wished she had not. Impossibly, the river had broken its banks and was rising into the air as if by this god's will. More water than could possibly be in the river crashed down and raced across the fields towards them all, and the village some distance away on its spindly stilts.

Tulia let out a fearful whimper and pressed herself even harder. Behind her, the surge of water churned up crops and furrows and was an advancing dark wall of debris.

"Run!" Tulia shrieked as loudly as she could to anyone who could hear her, ripping her voice apart with the force. She knew the village would not withstand this; the stilts were meant for gently rising waters, not an assault. But her voice was lost in the maelstrom and she could neither see nor hear any others. There was only her and Haroon. For his sake, if nothing else, she knew she had to escape.

The area was littered with rocky outcrops and she altered course, sprinting towards the nearest one as the roar of water grew behind her. Tulia threw herself onto the rocks and clambered as high as she could, reaching with her bare toes and grimy fingers for every crack and crevice that could bear her higher, away from the water. She wedged herself in a fissure twice her height off the ground and paused, shaking as exhaustion rolled over her. She looked out just as the water hit.

Not a moment too soon had she arrived. Already, the village was swept away, a jumble and tumble of broken wood, and the water battered the bottom of her own sanctuary with a force that rattled her. She braced with all limbs against the rough rocks through the worst of the impact, watching helplessly as her new life was swept away.

The watery god—or demon—advanced still, every step an earthquake. Tulia shrunk into the shadows, clutching her son tighter as it approached. It was so tall now that she could not see its head. Closer and closer. It stepped over the rock and, for one yawning moment, Tulia could see great legs of swirling water with vortexes of debris smashing inside. Freezing cold drops showered upon her. And then it was gone.

Tulia did not emerge for a day, until the water had subsided, and all that remained was muddy debris baking in the sun. She descended from the rocks and returned to the village, dazed and scared. The previous day seemed a surreal nightmare; a figment of her imagination. The sun was once more hot and baking upon her skin. The breeze warm and comforting. The birds wheeling in the sky. Yet reality left clues; a ruined field, debris piled high, and a missing village.

It was nowhere to be found. Where it had been was a flat plain, with a few snapped foundations.

Tulia combed the area for the rest of the day, but she found no one.

The next morning, only two other survivors could be found: the village dog and a boy half her age, who was wide-eyed and would not speak.

Tulia had to admit defeat. She murmured a silent prayer, knowing she would not see kind, old Sarana again, nor any of her new family. No tears came; she had learned long ago how to wall away her emotions from even herself.

"Time to find a new home." It was not the first time Tulia had had to start over. She knew it probably would not be the last, either. She beckoned the boy, chose a direction, and began walking.

"What is this nonsense?" snapped Harad as he rose from his throne. The figure prostrated on the ground before him shrunk further into the floor, as if trying to press himself through it.

"I beg your pardon, wondrous and mighty majesty," stuttered the figure. "But I swear on my life, every word is true! The demon destroyed everything in a great flood. There are only four of us that survived, and—"

"Silence!" roared Harad. He gestured at a guard, who kicked the prostrated supplicant for him. The man suppressed a cry of pain.

"You dare to spread news that the gods are displeased with Roher and seek to punish us? I will not hear another word of this treason. Punish this man accordingly for his lies." With a sharp slash of Harad's hands, soldiers jumped forward to grab the man. He protested, shrieking, as they dragged him from the throne-room.

"Let that be a lesson to anyone who seeks to spout such filthy, treasonous poison," said Harad. Eyes dropped to the ground as his gaze stabbed at each of them. Climbing back onto his throne, he scoffed and beckoned the next supplicant forward with a sharp twitch of his finger.

It was the first, but not the last time that week, that Harad heard tell of a great demon or god of water drawing forth floods that destroyed lands and killed entire villages. By the middle of the week, he was apoplectic that he could not suppress such nonsense. By its end, he was concerned it was true, though he would never admit it.

So many rumours coming from such a widespread area could not be all a lie, surely? His troubled thoughts recalled his devastating losses in Caledan. He had blamed them on Zaki. *Incompetent rat, curse his soul.* Yet if the gods punished Roher, perhaps they instead held Harad responsible? It was an uncomfortable thought.

We are too weak to resist an invasion or wage war now that our army is devastated and our weapons, too. Perhaps the gods punish me for overreaching. Perhaps they punish me for weakness. He growled at the thought. Never before had he felt so vulnerable. It was not a feeling he enjoyed. Life was much more comfortable with a stockpile of weapons and a fully garrisoned army waiting to do his every bidding.

He paced his quarters like a caged animal, waging war inside his own head. He could not speak of this to anyone. To admit an insecurity was to invite defeat. Least of all could he speak to his family; even Janus, his son and advisor, was a snake he would sooner kill than trust. *He wants my throne almost as much as I do.*

"I shall have to increase operations," he said to himself. He had already ordered the conscription of all men above the age of sixteen. Now, he would have them from fourteen. Plenty more young, strong bodies to bolster his ranks and keep his throne secure.

After the third nobleman had reported an attack by the next week amidst other tales pouring in from the north, however, Harad was forced to dismiss his ideas it was a fabrication of treasonous minds. He summoned Janus at once. He may not have trusted his son, but he knew he could rely on him for this.

"Find me the truth of the matter, Janus."

ELEVEN

Eve perused the letter with interest. As she read, her fingers rubbed over the now broken royal seal and the grain of the parchment. With each line, her cousin, Soren asked, and at times even begged, for her help with the Eldarkind and the dragons, explaining that they had joined forces in Ednor and were for now withholding assistance from Caledan, leaving it at the mercy of rogue dragon attacks. He explained everything; the struggling relationships between the three races, the attacks across Caledan, which left a gnawing worry in the pit of her stomach, and his own need for eyes and ears in Ednor.

"I need you, Cousin," Soren wrote, "to aid me as never before. Be my eyes and ears in Ednor. You are their kin; they will not look to you as an outsider as they would anyone else I could send in your stead. I need you to advocate for me, strengthen my position, and ensure my voice and Caledan's pleas are heard and answered. We are in grave danger and desperate need of their help if I am to have any success in defeating the rogue dragons and saving our realm. I tell you in confidence and to impress upon you the urgency of the situation. If left unchecked, Caledan as we know it could well be destroyed."

Eve let the wad of parchment fall into her lap. It took many minutes to digest its contents, and she re-read it thrice. Her hand tremored as she fought back frustration at what Soren asked of her.

I have only just returned home, she thought bitterly, *and settled back into the fold.* She thought of her father, frail and in need of her care, Luke, and their blossoming friendship as they both settled back into their own lives, and her own promises to herself to never again do anything she did not want. That did not stand when it came to the orders of her king. She swallowed. *I have no choice, yet again.* Unbidden, her fists clenched around the letter. She crumpled it and with all her might, threw it at the wall.

Confound it!

Her father took the news better than she thought. He understood the cost of duty above all else, so, perhaps, it was not surprising.

"I shall be fine," he said, smiling his now customary wan, tired half-smile, half-grimace. "I have run Arrow county for more summers than you have seen, my little dove."

Eve was not at all convinced, but she had no choice. "Take care of yourself," she told him sternly, feeling more nursemaid than daughter. "I will return as soon as I am able."

Karn grasped her hands in his own. His skin was dry and cool to the touch, almost insubstantial. She clasped his hands harder, as if to imprint the memory of them into her skin. "Be safe, Eve."

"I will, Father."

Before she left, her last visit was to Luke, with some trepidation. *Of all the times to leave,* she mentally berated Soren. *Would that it be whilst we fought.* Luke was less than pleased at her sudden mission, but she could not discern whether it was because of the nature of the task, or the fact they were no longer in harmony.

"Will you come with me?" she asked on impulse, though her voice wavered a little with uncertainty. "I leave at once."

Luke shook his head. "Mother needs me."

Eve swallowed and nodded. She had expected nothing less, given how frosty things were after their last meeting, though she had hoped for more. "I... I thought as much. Here." She pulled a small wrapped parcel from her pocket and handed it to him. "A scrying mirror. I enchanted it so that at my bidding, sight and sound shall pass through it, so we do not have to truly be parted."

Luke issued a gruff, "Thank you."

"Look to it at sunset each day?" Her statement turned into a question.

Luke nodded.

There was an awkward pause, a long, yawning silence between them.

"Well, I must leave," said Eve. She stepped forward to give him a tight embrace, which after a moment of surprise, he returned, and then she stepped back, turned around, and walked away without looking back.

Eve left as quickly as she could. She saddled Alia, checked her saddle bags had been packed with everything she had requested, and rode out into the valley, hoping the faster she rode to Ednor, the sooner she could return home to mend what was broken.

Eve arrived in Ednor just as the sun set, casting all in fiery red light as it dipped behind the mountains. Each day on her journey, she had scried Luke and spoken to him, though briefly. Things were still cold between them, as much as she hated it. Tonight, she had forewarned him they would not speak, knowing she would be still on the road for the final push to make Ednor before dark.

As she rode, Alia's hooves were a rhythmic drumming upon the grassy meadows of the mountain valley. Her tumultuous thoughts over her troubles with Luke and her worries with her father calmed as she soaked in the familiar sights and sounds.

The valley was as it had been on her first visit: lush, green, and full of life; far different to the barren and eerie valley she had last visited. Yet, on the breeze drifted birdsong and the strangest roaring she could not identify. Her heart leapt into her mouth with a burst of fear-soaked adrenaline as she sighted dragons flitting high above distant peaks.

Quickening Alia's pace, Eve rode faster until she reached the cover of the woodlands and familiar Ednor—once more bustling, and thrumming with life, vitality, and beauty. Magic hummed through her veins and she was almost dizzy with the strength of it. Her skin tingled and the very air seemed to vibrate with energy. For a moment, she simply closed her eyes to be lost in the full flow of the energy stream and reveled in the power of magic returned as she had never felt it before. It was good to be back.

Eve had already scried ahead and Tarrell awaited her at the gates of Ednor's simple palace. He helped her from Alia himself and sent the horse away with a groomsman. Tarrell offered her a sweeping bow and greeting in Eldarkind, and she took the chance to examine him. Tall, refined, and with a hint of steel, she determined from his stance, eyes, and the set of his jaw. He dressed in sweeping robes, far more ceremonial than his predecessor, Artora, and Eve gauged he would not be so informal as she. Eve returned the greeting and bowed herself, noting Tarrell's surprise in his raised eyebrow. She suppressed a smile. *Not all ladies curtsy.*

They walked leisurely into the complex with Tarrell engaging in small talk, much to her growing frustration.

"Perhaps, we have more pressing matters to discuss," she said as politely as she could, though her tone was cutting.

He smiled gravely and bowed his head in acquiescence. "I sense you are angry with me?"

Eve paused, unsure and taken aback by his remark.

"Perhaps, you still hold anger that we did not come to your aid regarding your friend."

"Yes," Eve said, realising that frustration still burned within her. "I offered to sacrifice everything for Artora—for you—and you repaid me with nothing. For all you knew, I could have died out there, and you would not have come to rescue me. So, yes, I am angry. I asked you for the help I so freely gave, and not only did you abandon me, you doomed him."

She fell silent; her own outburst had shocked even her. *I haven't said that to anyone, not even myself, before.* The resentment bubbling within her was surprising, and not a feeling she enjoyed, but it was true.

"I understand your frustration, Lady Eve, but there is much more you ought to know, which your cousin, the King, may have hinted at, that led to our decision not to intervene. Would that I could have helped."

Tarrell led her to the same drawing room Artora used. It was strange to be in this place again. Eve had twin memories: the bright and vibrant queen that glowed with her own light, and the dying queen, who had been pale, haggard, and as frail as a leaf. The spirits of Nolwen, Nelda, and Artora were with her in that moment. She could almost hear Artora's rich, warm voice, see Nolwen's lazy smile, and feel Nelda's warm hug. Eve swallowed past the lump in her throat. There was still raw grief attached to their memories, and a fierce ache of longing. She missed the first extended family she had known from her mother's side more than she could describe. *So many years unspent. So many memories we will never make.*

"Please," Tarrell waved his arm to invite her in, as she teetered in the doorway. "Come. Sit."

Obediently, Eve sunk onto a chair in front of the large windows, overlooking the familiar meadows, now bare of flowers and cold after a hard winter, and composed herself. "You know why I am here, I believe?" she asked Tarrell.

"King Soren informed me of your purpose here, yes. You are welcome to stay for as long as you please."

"I thank you, Lord Tarrell." She paused as drinks were brought to them, and took hers eagerly. The hot cup warmed her stiff hands. "What did you mean earlier, when you said there was 'much I ought to know'?"

Eve listened in silence as Tarrell explained from the beginning; he echoed the fragments Artora had told her. The elementals did not disappear, as was the commonly told tale, but they were, in fact, bound by the pact of men, Eldarkind, and dragons, which Artora had last hinted at. He explained, to the growing chill rising through her, of the breaking of the pact, of Bahr's rise and his demise at the hands of the dragons—Eve at last understood how Luke came to be free—of the return of magic, and of the threats that now loomed.

As he spoke of Bahr, vivid memories overwhelmed Eve and suddenly she was there again, in the freezing caves, darker than night, with Him; Bahr of the Fire. She felt the cold and fear as she had then. Her tongue tingled with the taste of tainted air and magic— and that cursed place. The mere memory made her nauseous. The feeling of the tingling, tainted magic faded as she shook herself and the warm, soothing magic of Ednor caressed her senses again, enveloping her in warmth and wholesomeness; a reassuring touch against the dark things of the world.

Eve realised Tarrell was watching her in silence. "More like him?" she said, unable to keep the dread and fear from her voice.

"More like him," Tarrell replied sombrely. "They sleep for now, but some stir already and it will only be a matter of time before they rise and we are faced with the greatest challenge since our races first united."

Eve did not respond, trying to process what he had said. *I hope they do not call upon me to try and bind such a thing again. Bahr was nearly my undoing.*

"This is why we could not help you rescue your friend," Tarrell explained. "The wellspring of magic was tainted beyond measure. Now, it runs pure again, but even so, the elementals' magic and their binding is too strong for the likes of us to journey to the ends of the world, binding them to sleep for eternity once more. It cannot be done. We must instead remake the pact between humans, Eldarkind, and dragons."

"What of the dragons?" Eve asked, trying to understand exactly what was happening. Soren had spoken about dragon attacks, not elementals.

"Ah, you pre-empt me," said Tarrell. "The threat of the elementals is certainly our greatest threat, but it is not our most pressing. Remaking the pact is our priority, yet we cannot do that when Eldarkind, man, and dragon are not united. When the pact failed, the dragon clan split into two factions: those who wanted to uphold the peace between our races, and those who did not. The latter, led by a dragon named Cies, seek to end both the dragons who reside here under our protection and friendship, and us also, for the simple reason that they bear no love for us. After we are vanquished, we believe they will take over the realm of Caledan as their own, and woe betide any human who defies them."

Eve had only briefly met dragons at her time in Pandora, long ago, and had little understanding of the huge and highly intelligent creatures; just a healthy respect and fear.

"Therefore, our new priority is to address the issue of the rogue dragons, who are currently, as your cousin has told you, spreading fire, fear, and destruction across Caledan. Soren will find this most agreeable, I presume, as he has already discovered none can stand in their way. He will be free of them soon. We have already determined they seek to challenge us without delay."

"Is Arlyn safe?" Eve asked. Her first thoughts were of her father, Luke, and her people's safety.

Tarrell did not answer, and when she pressed him, would not.

"I cannot guarantee anything, Lady Eve. Humans cannot stand before them."

A tingle of fear shot through Eve's stomach at his words. "Can the Eldarkind?"

"It is possible, but to do so, we must work in cooperation with the dragons here, which is proving difficult, given the vast differences between our races. We hope and presume they speed to Ednor, and do not divert, so we may engage Cies. We have the best chance of all three races here in Ednor to engage him successfully."

"What can I do to protect my people?" Eve pressed him.

Tarrell drummed his fingers on the armrest of his chair as he considered her question. Eve shuffled with impatience as the silence stretched. "Protective wards may help," he replied eventually. "I fear there is little you can do to defeat them in the case of an attack, but you may be able to protect your people from harm by drawing on the power of nature to sustain enchantments. That is more than can be said for most of Caledan."

Then all is not lost. Eve knew she could cast such enchantments if she needed to. "They are coming here beyond any doubt, though?"

"Yes."

"Then, if they fly west, there is a risk to my homeland"

"It is us they seek, not you."

Eve didn't feel reassured. She could see the dragons high on the peaks, soaring and looping through the clouds. It was not hard to imagine them striking fear into hearts wherever they travelled, especially under cover of night. According to Soren, certain death and destruction was the fate of all that came into their path, and Eve could not help but think of Arlyn. The town had fortifications, but it would be no match for dragons.

In her mind's eye, she saw hordes of the great, nameless beasts falling from the sky and her town roasting in flames, and shuddered. If Arlyn were to fall into the sight of the dragons, that would be its fate, regardless of any ward she could cast. Her muscles twitched, and only her duty to Soren kept her sitting with Tarrell. Every muscle urged her to return home as quickly as possible, to do whatever could be done to keep her people safe—just in case.

Not for the first time, she wished she could follow her own desires instead of duty.

Tarrell saw her consternation, for he leant forwards, and caught her gaze. "Nothing may happen at all," he said. "All may be well."

Eve was not reassured.

As she unpacked her few possessions into a small bedchamber that looked over the valley, she could not help but worry about what to do. The obvious solution was to lay a protective ward. She paced back and forth. *Before that, I'll need to let everyone know. What will they think? Will they take me seriously? Will they trust me if I need to use magic to protect them?*

Magic was a maligned thing in Arrow county, to the extremity that Eldarkind were not welcome there after a thousand years of fairy tales had twisted them into villainous and malevolent characters. Even Lord Karn had had to keep his wife's lineage and his daughter's half-blood status a close secret, for fear of repercussions.

Not to mention the dragons: creatures from myth and legend, never seen in those parts in living, written or spoken memory. *How can I return home talking of the Eldarkind as our allies, 'good' dragons and 'bad' dragons? They'll call me a madwoman, especially if I talk about more wars and battles to come after so many have only recently returned from fighting*

Zaki… and many have not. It will already take years to recover from such losses and rebuild lives.

She sighed. This would require some thinking. It had been a long day, and there was much to consider. Now, she knew the full picture of events from Tarrell.

That evening, she scried Luke and was glad to see his familiar face after a day of unsettling revelations.

"Are you well?" he asked. "You seem… I'm not sure."

Eve shook her head, and briefly recounted what Tarrell had told her.

Luke did not respond, except with a huff of surprise at her news. His hand worried at his beard as he contemplated what she had said.

"I need your help, Luke," Eve asked, when he did not reply.

"Are you that scared?"

"Bahr—or more like him—are rising, the dragons are coming, and we have no way to defeat either of them. Of course, I'm scared!" The goosebumps on her arms had little to do with the night chill. "They're destroying everything in their path, and you saw what Bahr could do, which was far worse. Arlyn is in danger!" She knew her message was garbled, and pushed on to try and impress her seriousness upon him. "I don't feel safe. They are coming. Will you come for me, so I can ride safely home? The dark of night feels all the more terrifying now that I know what it hides."

"I cannot come," Luke replied after a pause.

"Why?"

"I need to stay here to care for Mother, and I have my job to do. You do not understand that I cannot drop everything for you."

"Nora will be fine; we have servants who can care for her. I need you." Her voice was almost plaintive. She hated feeling so vulnerable, but it was true; she trusted him as no-one else, and felt safe with him as with no-one else. More than anything, he was the one person she had always been able to count on. *He's never rejected me before; maybe I deserve it after how we left things.* For a split second, she could see now how he had felt when she had refused to talk to her father about their relationship.

"Do you?" His voice was flat, and his eyes dark in the mirror. "What for? What are we?" He threw up his arms. "What is this? I should drop everything for you. Again? My mother needs me, and I won't desert her again on your account. She has nothing and no-one else! Look where it got me last time: abandoned, nearly dead at the end of the world and no good to anyone."

Eve recoiled at the resentment in his voice. "This isn't a whim, Luke. It's serious, as it was last time. You followed me willingly; I didn't even know! How is that my fault? You chose to sacrifice yourself, but you blame me for the consequences? I tried to save you and I could not. They all *died*. What else could I do? Return and freeze to death with you, or try and find help? You know I didn't want to leave you. How many times must I apologise—atone—for it?"

Her own frustration took over as the guilt she had suffered those past months at what had happened emerged. "I managed to make it back to civilisation. I sent you help. I still feel guilty I couldn't return myself, and I've tortured myself over that. I had every intention of returning. I would never abandon you! I was so ill and delirious after what I endured to send you help, the abbot would not hear of it. What else could I do? I need you, now. I need someone I can trust with my life. Of course, I would ask you first and foremost."

"When will you learn that not everything revolves around you—what you feel and what you want? I'm not your serving boy to do your bidding," growled Luke. "I'm not a dog to follow you around. It feels that way, as if I'm at your beck and call! Not today. You have the Eldarkind and their magic. Ask them." He vanished.

Eve ended the scrying and her hands shook with anger as she packed the mirror into its case.

"Damn it all, why doesn't he understand how important this is!" she snapped to the empty room. "What else can I do? I apologised for leaving him, I apologised for being unable to return, and still he holds his own choices against me." She stomped around the room, muttering darkly until her anger had run its course, and then she threw herself into a chair and sighed.

There is so much unresolved between us, and I don't know how to fix it. I know he hurts. His accusation that she abandoned him when he had chosen to sacrifice himself and encouraged her to leave, confused her. *How do I make him understand it's not like that?* Her eyes closed, but she could not escape her own thoughts.

Our feelings must place second; there is so much more at stake. Should I leave? she pondered. *Should I return home? Perhaps, I overreacted. Maybe it will never come to pass. Arlyn could be perfectly safe.* She tried to ignore the worrying niggle and looked out onto the still, calm valley. It was peaceful and wholesome. Nothing to fear here. It was easy to be scared in the night, for it was full of terror and overpowering fear if allowed into a susceptible mind.

That night, she kept the candles burning, but even so, she had an unsettled night's sleep. In the morning, she awoke and, despite feeling exhausted and bleary-eyed, felt better in the light of day. It was cold and clear outside with blue skies as far as the eye could see. *Maybe I should stay here, for now, as Soren has asked.* She prayed and hoped all was well for her home, and that her return, and her fears and worries, were unwarranted.

TWELVE

The letter bore the seal of House Orrell. Soren rested it atop the pile of opened letters, before scanning the next from House Balaur, his cousins and family to the south. He had already received letters from Arendall, Varan, and Denholm. Not many houses remained unaffected, for few counties had not yet been marred by the horrors of the dragon attacks.

Another day, another attack. The pattern did not cease. The attacks travelled west and north, and thankfully had missed Pandora, but it was still little relief. Evacuated villages had been all but destroyed, and their residents crowded into towns and cities. They were full to bursting, running short of food and water, and rates of crime and sickness escalated, yet there was no way in sight to stop the attacks, and no way for Soren to offer his people any chance of safety.

Soren dropped his latest letter onto the pile just as Barclay of House Walbridge rapped on the door and invited himself in. Soren grinned and welcomed him warmly, grateful for the respite from his duties.

Barclay was his own age, and an unexpected friend and ally, despite the differences of their parents. His father, Lord Willam Walbridge, had never been a staunch supporter of Soren's mother, Queen Naisa, and Soren had struggled to keep Willam's allegiance during the testing times of his short reign so far. A friendship with Willam's son proved both useful and enjoyable, and Soren was frequently reminded of Edmund's advice, though it seemed an age ago since he had given it.

"Be careful in whom you place your trust, Soren," Edmund had said. *"The sons of your enemies could be your friends, yet the sons of your friends could well be your enemies. Judge each person on their own merit, but be careful in*

whom you place your trust."

Usually, Barclay was a confident, relaxed, and carefree young man who loved to joke and fool about, but today, he was uncharacteristically subdued. Soren stilled, as trepidation uncoiled in his belly.

"There's been another attack," said Barclay. He refused to meet Soren's eye.

"Where?" The knot of tension within Soren that rarely disappeared clenched again.

Barclay shook his head, much to Soren's confusion. "No, not a dragon attack. This one is different." He paused, and briefly met Soren's glance before looking away again, staring at the sheaf of parchments on the desk as if his gaze could burn a hole through them. "An Eldarkind messenger was attacked."

Soren's heart sunk. *No...*

"He lives, but barely."

"Who would do such a thing?" Soren's dread turned to shock and then to anger.

"The perpetrators are not yet apprehended, "Barclay admitted.

"You must determine at once who dares attack our allies."

Barclay looked up again, and this time, his gaze did not fall. "Are they our allies?" His brow furrowed. "They are strange beings, and seem to have walked straight out of myth and legend. In my home county, they are less than benevolent."

"Such tales are twisted lies, I assure you," Soren was quick to correct him, and tried to hide his shock at Barclay's ill-informed view. "I assure you, they are the most noble of races, ever our allies, and work for the force of good. We seek to ally with them more than ever before in the face of these new attacks, alongside those dragons who also side with our cause: one of peace and harmony."

Barclay was incredulous, and he regarded Soren as if he were a stranger, or had lost his wits. "You want us to ally with dragons? Have you lost your mind?"

"I am your king," Soren reminded him frostily. "You are my good friend and so I forgive you that, but do not presume I am ignorant. I know secrets which are never spoken of. I know of things beyond your ken, and I bear these burdens so Caledan might live in peace." Soren leaned against the desk, feeling overwhelmingly tired all of a sudden. Kingship; it was such a weight to carry. Edmund was gone; his closest friend and confident, and one of the few others who knew most of the kingdom's secrets. Now, only Behan, the Lord Steward of Pandora, would share such knowledge. It would always be that way, Soren's secrets to bear until his heir was of age to know them; a long and lonely existence with the burden of those secrets.

"I apologise, Soren," said Barclay. "I mean no offense. You know I would not. I simply cannot understand how we would ally with a creature so barbaric. Look at what these dragons do." He gestured to the pile of letters, for he knew their contents. "I have read some of your letters. I have heard the tales. I have seen the pleas for help. How can we befriend, and trust, such monsters?"

"Because they are not all thus," said Soren, as a gnawing desperation rose inside him. Barclay would not be the only one who held this view, or felt strongly enough to express it. There would be more; many more. *How can I convince them all?* Soren fought back the feeling of overwhelm.

"I fear I must call a council meeting on this before it spreads further. I can no longer act alone in this, and we must ally with the Eldarkind and dragons. It is not only critical to our survival we do so, but it sends a message. I will not tolerate attacks on our allies. An alliance is the only way we may be sure of defeating those which conspire to destroy our nation." He omitted to mention the threat of the elementals. "Send the summons."

"Yes, Sire." Barclay bowed and left, leaving much for Soren to contemplate. His head felt heavy and overburdened as it had already been without this fresh problem.

Soren surveyed the solemn, impassive faces of the council sitting before him around the round table as the council meeting began. Lord Steward Behan, seated to Soren's right, hefted himself out of his chair with a groan and an audible creaking of his bones, to call a member of each county to stand forth in attendance. It was the only ceremonial flourish before the matters at hand were discussed.

Each member stood in turn. To Soren's left hand sat Barclay and his father Willam of House Walbridge. Lady Elsard of House Orrell was more stern-faced and thin-lipped than usual. Rafe of House Bryar, son of Asquith the traitor and just as untrustworthy, dabbed the sweat from his tufty moustache with a silken handkerchief as he bobbed his head in greeting. Godwin of House Bryar, the other loyal spur of the house, cast sidelong glances of disgust at his young, distant relative.

Lord Heligan, chief amongst the law readers was a welcome ally, as was his cousin Lord Finihan of Duncombe, and Doren of House Kinsley, brother to another dead traitor, Loren. Filling the second to last seat next to Behan was Theodore, older cousin to Dane, nephew of Edmund, and new Lord of Arendall House. Soren still could not adjust to how uncannily alike in appearance he was to Edmund and Dane. Last of all to arrive, red-faced and muttering apologies, was Soren's cousin, Ilyas of House Balaur. He attended on behalf of his father, who minded over Balaur territories to the south. It was his privilege to give the first account of the day.

By his account, it appeared Lowenmouth, the heart of his county, was in grave danger of being attacked, but the dragons had veered north, and nothing had been seen or heard since. They were still on high alert.

Lord Verio was, unsurprisingly, not present, having refused to leave the safety of his stronghold in Denholm county. He had been hit hard by the attacks, but Soren reckoned his absence was due more to cowardice. He said nothing, for Tristan, Verio's son, attended in his stead; instead, Soren graciously welcomed him with as much politeness as he could muster. Tristan was the shadow of his father, puffed with the same intolerable air of self-importance.

As Soren looked about the table once more, he realised Lord Bron of Rainsford was absent and had sent no-one in his place, though Behan, of the same house would stand in for him. No one from Arrow county sat, either. Karn was sick and Eve was on his own private business. Still, Soren regarded those before him feeling pleased. Not only was it the largest council gathered in a while, most of those attending were loyal to him, which was reassuring, given what he had yet to accomplish.

"I welcome you all," Soren began, his hands spread in invitation. "You are aware in part why you are here: to discuss how we can put an end to these dragon attacks."

Furious murmurs erupted as those about the table expressed their fear and anger at the devastating attacks. The clamour grew as they berated any lack of solution. Many of them had been personally touched, and Soren was taken aback by their vehemence. *This could be more difficult than I anticipated*, he thought, but there was little choice; onwards, or defeat.

Soren held up his hands to quiet them, but it did not work. "Your attention, please!" he shouted. Eventually, they subsided enough to listen, though now all seemed riled and in disagreeable moods, much to Soren's dismay.

"I have a solution." That captured their attention. Now, every eye was fixed upon him, every mouth was shut, and they leaned forward almost as one. "We cannot defeat these dragons. That is a fact. We cannot get close enough, we do not have the weapons to harm them, and we have not the strength to best them. You know this to be true." He looked into the eyes of every man and woman there, and saw the truth of his words reflected in their eyes. *Good. We are agreed on that, at least. Perhaps there is some hope yet.*

"There is one solution. We must ally ourselves with those who can. You remember, the dragons were my allies when I cast down Zaki. They have been our allies for a thousand years, as have been the Eldarkind, in a pact invoked by my forebear and the first King of Caledan, King Beren the Unvanquished, First of his Name."

They still watched him. Soren felt the pressure of their attention boring into him, like a rabbit transfixed in the eye of an eagle. "Not all the dragons are those perpetrating the attacks. That is only the minority. The majority of the clan still wish for peace and

642

the old alliance to hold." He exaggerated the numbers to give them hope the situation was more favourable; a gamble he hoped which would pay off.

"The dragons and the Eldarkind have the skills and the strength needed to defeat these rebel dragons who lay waste to our land and break the peace between our races." *It's now or never.* "We must invoke the old alliance, and ally ourselves with the Eldarkind and the dragons." He braced himself for their response, but was overwhelmed by their forceful denunciation of his plan. Barclay remained quiet, though his expression spoke volumes; he had already had chance and forewarning to say his piece.

Reeling from the overwhelming attacks now coming from all sides, he took a moment to regroup before he stood tall again, now with a thunderous expression upon his face that gave some pause for thought even before he spoke.

"Cease this madness!" he said. "Listen to reason. Of old, dragons, men, and Eldarkind fought and they were to tear each other's races to pieces. All would be destroyed, and there would be no winners. So, instead, they forged a lasting peace to ensure all three races could live in prosperity."

Soren glared around the room, challenging anyone to interrupt him. "That peace has now been broken by a mere handful of dragons, who rebel against this notion of good sense, which has endured a thousand years." He knew the numbers were far worse. The clan had split in half, and possibly more had defected to Cies. He could not be sure, but it was irrelevant; he could not afford to add more fuel to the fire. *Better to let them think we have the greatest chance; that this will be easy.*

"We must join with our allies to defeat them. We cannot do it alone; our many recent losses show this. We need the magic of the Eldarkind, and the strength of the dragons; and they are willing to give that in order to restore peace for themselves, also. We must act in good faith now, before it is too late," Soren stressed.

He was at once shouted down as a deafening uproar ensued.

"Dragons cannot be trusted!" snarled Tristan.

"Where have these feckless Eldarkind been through our

wars?" Lady Orrell said haughtily.

"Cowards!" Rafe said, with spittle flying from his mouth. The irony was not lost on Soren.

"Hiding goodness knows where!" Willam pounded the table. He hated cowards.

Soren was shocked by the hate, anger, and fear he saw upon their faces. He was surrounded by wide eyes, flaring nostrils, and thunderous brows. Hands were slashed, clawed hands were shaken, and fingers were wagged as each strove to shout their opinion.

"They are not monsters!" Soren replied, trying to make himself heard. "Dragons are wise creatures as old as the world—as are the Eldarkind! We need their wisdom and their strength. We need them!"

It was no use. He stared at them all as if they were strangers, wondering why they were so alienated from him when he was trying to do the right thing. *Why can they not see?* In that moment, he missed Edmund more than ever; a voice of calm and support throughout everything, a steadfast friend. Even Ilyas, his cousin and loyal supporter, was muttering darkly and shaking his head, with his brows furrowed in anger. Soren understood his people had felt the devastation firsthand, but he had hoped Ilyas would be more receptive to a solution; even a drastic one.

Will anyone trust me on this? Soren wondered. After all it had cost to secure their hard won loyalty regaining the country from Zaki and repelling attacks from Roher, it seemed as though all that support had vanished in an instant.

THIRTEEN

Janus left at once with a band of his most trusted riders to see the truth of the matter for himself. He chose the closest reports to investigate, but even so, they were three days ride from Arrans.

He could see the devastation from miles away as they crested the last hill before the valleys rolled away into the northern deserts. Beyond the river which marked the edge of Roher, there was nothing but waves of sand. But before it, cutting deep into the valley, was a trail of devastation no man could create.

Janus rode hard, pushing his riders the last of the way until they galloped through uprooted woods, through crop fields that were now heaps of dried mud, and past the remains of villages that were nothing more than piles of firewood. As they rode through the mess, his men were silent, observing the destruction about them.

There were no people, nor habitation left to question about what had happened. Janus kept riding with his men in tow in the direction the trail of debris left. They rode for another day before they espied the storm ahead, and then Janus could see only too clearly the truth of the matter for himself. He paused upon the edge of the forest, watching the dark clouds whorl and grow miles ahead of them, and the figure as tall as the sky that walked over the lands, preceded by a dark wave that glinted in the storm-refracted light.

His men muttered prayers to The Mother to protect them and The Warrior to give them strength. Janus said nothing, watching the spectacle before him and not knowing what to make of it. He knew his men were devout and fearful of the gods' wrath. He knew only their loyalty to him would keep them from speaking treasons or worse. And he knew what they would think: that the gods were angry with them, that Roher was out of favour, and perhaps, after the army's recent losses in Caledan, that their wrath was aimed at his father.

Janus needed to see no more. It did not matter if he coveted the throne for himself; there would be no throne to covet if they did not fix this mess and placate the gods, for this would cause an uprising that would endanger them all.

Harad was greatly troubled by his reports, but he knew Janus would not lie in this, for it affected his own future. The safety of Harad's crown was Janus's guarantee of kingship. Janus would selfishly guard that.

"The gods are displeased, then," Harad said, scowling. "But with what?"

Janus shrugged. "It matters not. We must be seen to appease them for the people's sake, and their continuing faith. It cannot be stopped by force, that is clear." He had already described to his father at great length what he had seen.

"I agree. We shall host games and feasting in the gods' honours. They must commence tomorrow. We have no time to waste! Make the arrangements. These must be our grandest. We must show our strength to the people, and the gods."

Harad's advisors swiftly assembled to take note of his ideas.

"It shall be three days, yes, three days, of games and feasting. I want every male hard-labour slave in the city over the age of eighteen bought and sent to the arena. Their masters shall be compensated. Three coppers a single, and a silver per half-dozen." Harad paused to glare at his treasurer who had begun to fuss over the cost.

"The price of the gods' happiness is immeasurable. Let it never be said I saw fit to scrimp and scrape. Mind, I am not foolish. Levy a tax to pay for it. 'The Gods' Tax' it can be called. People cannot say no to their gods." *Where was I? Ah, yes.*

"Three days of games. I want fighting, I want wild animals, I want crowd-pleasing, blood-thirsty entertainment. I want feasts that revel coronation celebrations." Harad paused again whilst his chief of ceremony held a whispered conversation and sent his underling scurrying.

"Yes, quite. The arrangements need beginning immediately."

"Sire?" Janus said. "What is to be done with those slaves who are not killed in the games?"

Harad met his son's eyes. They were as ruthless as his own, but he knew he would shock Janus with his revelation. "On the third day of the games, at the closing ceremony, they shall all be sacrificed to the gods." He was right. Janus's eyes widened almost imperceptibly, but he was smart enough not to say anything, and instead nodded and saluted his father.

"Sire, are... are you sure this is wise?" said his chief of ceremony.

"It is drastic, yes." Harad spread his hands wide and shrugged slightly. "Yet, what is more important? The happiness of our gods? Or... no. Of course, only their contentment is of value to us. We are all but slaves to them. Sacrifice was practiced until some short decades ago. Why as a boy, I remember it from my grandfather's rule. It served us well then, and will serve us well now to return to the favour of the gods. Our slaves should be honoured to lay down their lives to serve our gods in the next life." His tone was soft and honeyed, persuasive, but it sharpened.

"These are my orders and I expect to see them carried out with meticulous precision. Anyone who does not fulfill their duties will join the sacrifices on the third day."

Janus and Harad watched them with identical cold eyes as they bowed, and scraped, and left in a hurry.

"Are you sure that was well done, Father?" Janus questioned in his usual arrogant manner.

"You ought to remember I am your King before I am your father," replied Harad coldly. "I am doing what I feel is best to secure our future on the throne. You would do well to appreciate it."

Janus inclined his head. "My apologies, Father." Harad could tell the words were hollow. Janus was a cold, callous, and ambitious man just like himself. At times, it was something to be proud of, at others, something to be frustrated by. *Ever as I train him to be a strong*

647

king, he looks for a chink in my armour. Harad loved Janus as little as Janus loved him. Crown Princes in Roher did not survive on their father's warmth; they were far more motivated by their deaths.

The games were held, and the capital city Arrans held festivities that were well attended by all in the city and those who were able to travel in time for the hastily put together events. Nothing could be faulted. Harad's councilors were skilled at hosting many such events. It was but a trifle to them to do it at such short notice. Harad was pleased. Everywhere, he saw revelry and pleasure, and not a trace of fear of the gods' wrath upon them.

Yet, his closing gesture shocked them all. Only the heavy army presence and forced enjoyment by his supporters staved off dissent as thousands of slaves were herded into the arena in chains, offered to the gods, and sacrificed. The sand, especially transported from the nearby coast for the purpose, was not enough to soak up all their blood.

Their bodies burned long into the night on giant pyres that covered the city in a heavy, sickly smog. Up in flames they went, along with other offerings to the gods; fine fabrics, crafted goods, jewellery, food, and wines.

Harad was satisfied; he had made his point. His people feared him more than they feared the gods, and in that, they were wise. For now, at least, both they and he were assured the gods were placated, so he could return to ruling Roher in peace. No greater or grander an event could have been thrown, no more lavish, or expensive, and certainly, no more generous to the gods in lives and chattel. As the cleaning operation began and Arrans returned to business, Harad was confident he had solved their problem. No more would this god trouble Roher. He had shown the gods his strength and knew they would be appeased.

FOURTEEN

Myrkdaga lazily uncoiled in the cave as the mid-afternoon breeze swept in and tickled his nostrils. The air was different, here in Ednor. Sweeter. No salt from the sea, for one. It was filled with the scent of life and nature, instead of the barren desolation of Kotyir. One by one, he stretched every limb, right down to the tip of his claws, before unfurling his wings, shaking them, and refolding them neatly by his side.

A pang of hunger snaked through his stomachs, and he considered whether to move. There were no hard choices here; food was guaranteed, not hard won. Myrkdaga had to admit, it was enjoyable to feast on fat, well-fed beasts rather than the best Kotyir had to offer: wiry, tough mountain goats. As the pang reappeared, more insistent this time, Myrkdaga stirred, contemplating a hunt for a juicy deer to stretch his wings and fill his belly.

"Oy!" A voice cut through his thoughts. Myrkdaga was already enjoying a fresh, warm kill in his mind's eye. "Who's there?"

Myrkdaga moved faster, his scales hissing as they slid over each other. He poked his head out of the cave, and almost collided head first with a young, red-faced Eldarkind, who squeaked and scrambled backwards as he was confronted by the huge dragon head.

Myrkdaga rumbled, slow and menacing, let coils of smoke tumble from his nostrils, and stared at the young Eldarkind with narrowed eyes. He rather enjoyed scaring people, and had mastered the art of freezing creatures in their tracks with just one gaze. They made for easier meals.

To his surprise, the now pale-faced Eldarkind recovered from his shock and stepped forward, jabbing a finger at Myrkdaga. "You! What are you doing in my cave? Get out!"

Myrkdaga could not decide whether to be surprised or

impressed, but he had no intention of complying. He rumbled louder and opened his jaws so the sound swelled around them. "How dare you speak to me thus. I am Myrkdaga, son of Myrkith-visir!"

"You don't scare me." The Eldarkind had to shout above Myrkdaga's rumbles. "You're only a small dragon!"

Myrkdaga spluttered with disbelief. *This pathetic worm has the nerve to call me tiny?* He had never been called small by something as tiny as this being.

In Myrkdaga's moment of distraction, the Eldarkind surveyed the landscape. "Hey, you've destroyed all my things!" He stepped closer to Myrkdaga, now with a snarl of his own. "This is my cave, and you—" he jabbed at Myrkdaga again, though not quite touching him, "—have no right to come here and break everything. I built all of this by hand! It's taken me years! I didn't create all this so some jumped up dragonet could smash it to pieces. It's not yours to touch, or move, or break. Get out of my cave, now!" He picked up a fractured piece of wood and threw it at Myrkdaga. It bounced off Myrkdaga's shin. There was a moment of silence.

"Make me!" Myrkdaga growled. He opened his maw and roared his loudest in the Eldarkind's face, forcing him to clap his hands across his ears and scream a spell of protection, but, to Myrkdaga's extreme annoyance, he did not retreat.

With a huff of annoyance, Myrkdaga retreated back into the cave, curled up, and went to sleep. Breakfast would have to wait. He had a point to make.

The unmistakable thud of another dragon arriving widened Myrkdaga's smile, until he heard Farran's voice outside.

"What is the meaning of this?" Farran snarled. "I could hear your commotion across the valley!"

As Myrkdaga poked his head out of the cave, the Eldarkind cowered before Farran, visibly shaking. Myrkdaga's smugness increased.

"Farran-visir, thank you for your concern, but there is nothing to trouble you with. I was sleeping quite peacefully when I was disturbed and accosted by this insolent rat. I taught him not to wake a sleeping dragon." Myrkdaga made to withdraw back inside the cave, but froze at Farran's command.

"Is this true?" Farran's gaze incapacitated the Eldarkind.

"N-no, sir!" he eventually said, more of a forceful squeak than anything else.

"Then tell me your version of events." Farran shot a sidelong glare at Myrkdaga.

"My name is Lorellei, sir. This is my cave! I found this dragon sleeping in my cave, having destroyed all my possessions—" Lorellei gestured around him, and it was plain to see that seemed to be the case. "—and when I challenged him, he roared in my face and would not leave. I had to cast a spell to save my ears from bursting!" he added indignantly. He stood a little straighter, his fright forgotten in his anger. "I will not be bullied by a dragon!" He quailed however, as Farran rumbled, turning his gaze from Lorellei to Myrkdaga.

"Is this true? Did you destroy items from within this place?"

"I did," said Myrkdaga sullenly. "I don't know why that should be a problem. I'm a dragon! My sleeping comforts are far more important than some pieces of carved wood."

"Enough!" snapped Farran. "This is precisely the kind of behaviour we seek to avoid. Myrkdaga, I am disappointed in you. The Eldarkind are our friends and allies, and they offer us sanctuary; you know from what. Find another place to stay, and be sure to help Lorellei restore his dwelling."

Myrkdaga began to protest, but Farran cut him off with a sharp glare and warning growl.

As soon as Farran departed, buffeting them so hard with gusts of wind that Lorellei fell over, Myrkdaga opened his jaw and hissed at the Eldarkind, before taking to wing himself.

"Wait! You're supposed to help me!" Lorellei shouted after him.

"Help yourself!" Myrkdaga snarled.

FIFTEEN

The breeze blew from the north and west, and upon it, Cies could smell dragons. Familiar dragons, ones he had not smelt in quite some time. And there was something else, too. A smell he did not recognise, but one that wove strongly with the smell of Farran's kin, and one he could identify because of that: Eldarkind. Cies opened his mouth in a hiss of delight and strained his wings to fly faster, so he could meet the cowards who had led him on this merry chase all the way to the northern reaches of the world.

The sun already slipped from its zenith, hanging low in the sky to the south. Dusk was his favourite time to attack, but he would not wait that long today. He was too eager for the taste of fire and blood and death. An almighty roar tore from his throat, and, one by one, his dragons took up his war cry. As one, they flew behind him, hugging low to the ground and racing across the grassy meadows so they could not be seen as silhouettes against the darkening sky.

Before anyone could spy them, react, or signal the alarm, Cies was upon Ednor. With the greatest grim glee, he spurted far-reaching jets of flames from his maw, mirrored by his kin. In seconds, Ednor was burning to the sound of his fires crackling, his prey screaming, and his kin roaring. This was the part Cies loved the most, picking them off one by one. He struck one Eldarkind with a swipe of his tail, sending them into a tree with a sickening crunch from which they did not rise. Another he caught with a snap of his razor sharp teeth, shaking the lifeless form for good measure and tossing it aside. A third was fried to a blackened crisp in a second of his white hot fire.

He could not enjoy himself for long, however, because the roar of his enemies heralded their arrival. In an instant, the sky was a mess of claws, teeth, fire, and wings. Dragons tore at each other

652

with tooth and claw, sending Eldarkind fleeing for cover. Blasts of air from powerful wing-beats battered the air, and anything else that stood in their way. With the arrival of Farran and his kin, some of the Eldarkind rallied. Cies could once more feel the stinging, tingling hits of their spells upon his hide in a most peculiar way. It was a small annoyance he could withstand, and nothing more, so he dismissed their presence again until he saw the Eldarkind wielding blades that glowed with blue fire.

The magic burned his nostrils from a distance, and he wheeled up and out of their reach to assess this new threat. The blades looked insubstantial, shorter and thinner than a dragon claw, and yet this magic, he knew, was harmful. Sure enough, he could see it slicing through dragon-hide even easier than his own teeth or claws could whenever dragons were foolish enough to stray within their reach. He growled and examined the blue flames, unable to discern them. This was something to be wary of.

The shriek of a dragon distracted him from his thoughts, and as he surveyed the wider battlefield once more, he could see the tide had turned. Those who entered the reach of the blue flames fell, not to rise again, and the damage to his attack was done; the Eldarkind and Farran's dragons surged forward in a renewed attack.

Cies was pushed back with his kin, some of whom were injured; wings rent, missing claws, and teeth wounds puncturing their hides. He attacked all the more ferociously as the fires swelled around them.

Myrkdaga joined the fray with fury and vengeance burning through his heart. He blasted an inferno of white-hot flames towards his enemies, and joined in fighting with tooth and claw, using his bulk to smash smaller dragons out of the way, but he was not foolish. He knew he was not a large dragon by any means, and others larger than he would not hesitate to kill him with ease, so he stayed out of the way on the fringes of the fight, targeting the smallest and puniest of Cies's followers. It would be many years before he could challenge the likes of Cies's bulk and strength.

A familiar cry caught his attention, and he looked down to see Lorellei amongst the flames, cornered by a dragon of Myrkdaga's size. The Eldarkind glowed with light and stabbed towards the dragon like lightening, but the dragon caught him, battering him with a claw. Lorellei crumpled, and the dragon closed in.

Myrkdaga dropped from the sky like a stone to intervene. He crashed onto the other dragon, snapping his jaws around his neck, but Myrkdaga's enemy was larger than he, and Myrkdaga lost his grip. Now he was too close and too low to retreat, so he was forced to engage in close combat. Mid-air, they writhed, a flashing dance of sharp edges, attacking and retreating in a deadly dance serenaded with hisses, snarls, and roars. Pain lanced through Myrkdaga with every injury suffered, but he continued relentlessly, out of the air and onto the ground.

As Myrkdaga landed, a tree root caught him and in an instant, he was on his back. The larger dragon pinned him by his neck, constricting his breathing. He struggled futilely, as stars danced across his vision, and thrashed. Myrkdaga landed glancing blows, and some well placed scores, but it was no use, the other dragon had his weight pinned down and it was only a matter of time before Myrkdaga ran out of breath and energy.

All of a sudden, a white light so bright Myrkdaga had to close his eyes emanated from behind the dragon on top of him, silhouetting his form. The dragon released him and retreated, squealing in pain. As the bright light blinded him, Myrkdaga took his chance regardless. He sprang to all fours, and as his vision cleared, attacked with all his remaining strength.

Lorellei was beside him looking worse for wear, but fighting off the dragon with a flame-ensorcelled blade. With every strike, the metal shrieked, and skittered off the dragon's hide in a blaze of sparks, but every hit left lingering trails of blue flames that seemed to cause the dragon growing pain. With a look and a nod to each other, Lorellei and Myrkdaga wordlessly drove into a two pronged attack, dividing and circling their enemy instinctively, to attack from two sides and conquer him.

As they converged at full speed, the dragon launched himself into the night, out of their reach and their sight, to the sound of their cheers. As they met eyes, the heat of battle faded, and they stood in silence for a moment.

"Thank you," they muttered simultaneously with their eyes averted, but Myrkdaga could not hold back a grin, and neither, it seemed, could Lorellei. *Perhaps the Eldarkind aren't so feeble, after all*, Myrkdaga pondered, and perhaps they were more alike than he cared to admit. A grudging, small respect, had formed. Very small. And very grudging. But there nonetheless.

Lorellei jumped and punched the air with a whoop, unable to contain his excitement. "I've never fought a dragon before!" His eyes glittered with heady excitement.

"Clear your mind," Myrkdaga warned. Already his excitement had faded, and his eyes scanned their surroundings—out on the fringes of the battle—because he knew the fight was not over. *One enemy vanquished does not mean a battle won.*

With that, they dove back into the fray still erupting around them.

SIXTEEN

Eve had fallen asleep reading a book on earth magic in the reading room, but she awoke to a nightmare. The world had descended into a hell described straight from the book of God. Fires burned everywhere Eve could see as she stumbled out of her room, disorientated after being woken by the din in the middle of the night.

Dark smoke stung her eyes and she scrabbled to hold the door frame. It was the only way she could determine which way was up in the confusion. Choking smoke blocked the hall, and there was no sense of an exit. Black and billowing clouds made the darkness complete around her, and, unfamiliar with that part of the building, panic rose within her as the sound of crackling fires and the clashing outside deafened her.

Pushing back the panic for a moment, she checked herself over. No pain, or injuries. Her sword, which she had taken with her after a brief sparring practice, was still in its scabbard at her hip, but she had nothing else with her. No light. No water. Nothing to cover her mouth with. As if reminding her, she retched and coughed once more, but the smoke was so thick she could not rid herself of it. A fear far greater than that which she had felt even confronting Bahr of the Fire took hold of her and she shook with terror as she stumbled along with both hands pressed to the wall.

Her eyes were closed, useless as they were in the dark, and she took the tiniest breaths filtered by the cuff of her sleeve, though it didn't seem to help. The coughing overcame her and, in a fit of dizziness, she sank to the floor to discover both visibility and breathing improved.

For a few seconds, she lay there, taking shallow breaths of the sour air, before crawling with slightly renewed vigour towards the bottom of a door. With a hard shove of her shoulders, it opened, and the breath of a breeze tickled her cheek. Her heart leapt in her chest, until she saw the way before her more clearly as the smoke shifted. Ahead, the light grew, but it was not the cold light of a starlit sky, it was the bright, hungry glow of fire.

She cried out in fear and exhaustion, but the only way was forwards, for now she recognised the great entrance hall, and the smoke rose to reveal the way out. Through danger. Fire encircled the space, clinging to the walls, the wooden floors, and the fabric hangings. The air, now partly cleared of smoke, burnt her lungs with its fire-fuelled heat. It seared her eyes and skin, and her lips felt like they would crack and peel with the intensity of it. Eve realised her mistake, and looked back, but now the way she had come was cut off by the fire as it devoured all in its path. A squeak escaped her lips as she looked around and realised she was surrounded by a wall of flames.

Her heart pounded in her chest and she felt both ice cold and a feverish heat as she trembled from head to toe, and looked one way and another, like a rabbit frozen in a fox's glare.

A gap in the flames opened, and without a thought, she sprinted. Flames lashed at her, searing her skin. Sparks skittered. Flames danced across her. As she burst through the other side, she was on fire; a living flame. Locks of trailing hair were ablaze, every hair on her arms was singed off, and she screamed as the pain of the heat bit into her skin.

Hands grabbed her, patting her roughly down and cold water doused her. The shock of it made her gasp big breaths that didn't seem to take in any air. Eve sunk, shivering, to her knees, in shock and unable to discern the muffled voices around her before she fainted.

SEVENTEEN

Tarrell pushed forward with his kin as the dragons before them fell back from the ferocity of their attack and the strength of their magic. Together with Farran, they rallied to form an orderly and hard attack at the flagging dragons before them. They were still reeling from the ferocity and suddenness of the attack, but Tarrell pushed that deep under a layer of honed concentration and mental clarity. The result of years of meditation and control over his own mind urged him to push forward. He was determined to unify everyone in that one moment.

"We are struggling in the cold," shouted Farran mentally to Tarrell, soaring high above the battlefield. From the heights, he could see vast swathes of Ednor aflame, and below him, both air and land was a twisted mess of battling Eldarkind and dragon, kissed here and there with the blue fire of Eldar magic. "Though we have had some time to acclimatise, which will aid us in the long term—" He broke off to smash a dragon from the sky and bathe its falling body with flames. "We tire now, and we fight dragons fresh from the warm climes of the south."

"For us, it is the opposite!" Tarrell replied, darting in to slash at the tip of a dragon tail that slithered too close. He was rewarded with a howl as the end sliced clean off. "We are well used to the cold, but these fires; we cannot withstand their flames or their strength. Worse of all, our weapons are useless unless the dragons land, for they can attack well out of our reach."

"I fear the upper hand will slip away if we do not seize it now. We begin to hold them back. We cannot falter. We must push now!" Tarrell had the fleeting mental image of Farran saying it through gritted teeth, if that were possible for dragons.

"On your word, friend," Tarrell shouted. Farran soared high

above him, dealing crushing defeats to any dragons who fell into his path.

Farran's roar above him signalled his acknowledgment, and suddenly the air was thick with more wing beats as dragons strove to be at the very front of the drive to push Cies and his followers away from Ednor, and low enough to be vulnerable to the Eldarkind's blades.

Tarrell drove his kin forward with a rallying cry, and the fire on every sword blazed brighter and stronger as the magic feeding them was reinforced.

As one, they drove forward on foot and on wing. The dragons saved their fires: to preserve themselves against the cold, and because they would not be of aid against dragonkin. The Eldarkind chanted a discordant and disjointed song that bound precision and sharpness anew into their blade.

In a moment, they met the enemy, and drove back Cies and his kin with such fierceness they were caught off guard, complacent still in their surprise attack. Farran's dragons attacked those in the sky, diving upon them to knock them from the air, rent wings and inflict great gashes that rained purple blood on those below. On the ground, Eldarkind attacked, weaving and dodging between their enemies, striking and withdrawing beyond the flames, flailing claws, and teeth, to leave trails of blue fire lancing pain through Cies and his kin, and sword cuts nicking scales.

The organised attack made short work of Cies; and before they knew it, the night was silent. Dragons melted away into nothingness, until even their wing beats could not be heard over the raging inferno that continued to grow, feeding on Ednor.

Tarrell did not let down his guard, and Farran returned to patrolling the lofty heights. For a time, there was silence. Tarrell stood, his sword raised and every hair on his body risen and shivering. Every inch of his skin was alert and tingling. His breath stopped, but his heart pounded on in his ears like the thud of a dragon in flight. Thud. Thud. Thud. Nothing. Nothing in the darkness came for them. The drumming of his heart pattered with the drumming of landing dragons upon the hard ground as Farran signalled the descent.

Once more, the flames crackling leapt into focus, and the chatter of Eldarkind and dragons became a cacophony. Still, Tarrell stood, seeking anything in the valley, but, before him, the valley was dark. The brightness of the flames behind him obscured his vision; it was a void of the blackest night. They were out there, he knew. Somewhere.

"They have fled," said Farran, breaking the spell upon him.

Tarrell breathed a sigh of relief, but he did not dare ask.

"Far away. They will return."

"For now, we are safe, though?"

"For now."

Tarrell felt too numb to be angry. He was in shock now that the action of the night had faded. He turned to survey the devastation. A good portion of all he could see was burnt or smouldering.

His kin moved about, quiescent themselves at the devastation before them. There were many injured to tend to. They wandered pale-faced and bleeding, clutching injuries and helped along by their kin. And then there were the dead, who lay splayed and broken; scattered like autumn leaves upon the forest floor.

Tears glistened on his face as he walked amongst them, mirrored by his kin, as what had passed now sunk in.

There would be much work to do to make Ednor good and whole again, Tarrell knew.

The scale of the devastation was only clear the following morning in the cold light of a new dawn. Blackened and charred structures still smoked. Much had been flattened; collapsed through fire, or the bulk of dragons, whose bodies lay across entire buildings, having reduced them to rubble. Their death toll had been low, but the Eldarkind's was much higher.

The more Tarrell saw on his slow walk through the once lively and beautiful streets as Farran plodded next to him, the more his anger grew; a cold, inexorable rage that seethed in the pit of his stomach. He could barely wait to be out of earshot of his kin before he turned to Farran and unleashed the fury.

"Look at what you have brought to my people and our home!" he accused. "Death and destruction! Such suffering we did not deserve for our compassion to you and yours!"

"Cies would have sought you eventually, and without us to aid you, you would have been entirely at their mercy," Farran growled. "There is something far greater in motion. You ought to know that and act upon it!"

"Yes, we must remake the pact, and we cannot afford for this." Tarrell gestured at the devastation around them. "This will take years to make good, and what of my kin until then? Shall we freeze and starve in the meantime? What of those who ought not to have died? Their death is on your conscience!"

Farran rumbled menacingly. "I refute that, yet I understand your grief. We must remake the pact and the only way it will be achieved is by defeating Cies. Only then can the three races be in harmony. Only then can the pact be restored."

Grief broke through Tarrell's anger and he faltered in his rage. For a time, he sunk onto a blackened stone and simply thought, only realising Farran still stood beside him when his reverie broke some time later.

The anger was useless, he knew. And the grief. They would not be dismissed easily, and nor should they, but they would not help in what now lay ahead of the Eldarkind and the dragons. Tarrell knew the truth in Farran's words, as reluctant as he was to admit it. "You may be correct," he conceded. "If there is strife between the three races, the pact will not bind. Cies and his followers need to follow the ways of peace... or be defeated. The former is unlikely and therefore," Tarrell sighed, "the latter is our only choice if that is the case. Even if you are right, how can it be done? It is clear we are sitting targets."

"We must play to our strengths," Farran hinted. When Tarrell looked at him, nonplussed, Farran sat on his haunches and elaborated. "We struggle in the cold, and you struggle in the heat.

How can we combat that?"

Latching on to the problem at hand, Tarrell set aside his anger. "Protective spells from the cold and heat respectively."

"Yes, for our sakes, but I meant in the form of attack. How can we use this information to weaken our enemy? What of your blue fire blades? They did much damage with their cold fire. How did that happen?"

Tarrell shook his head. "I know not much about them. In my lifetime, I have not seen a blade behave thusly, though I am very gladdened they did, for without their imbued magic, we would have had a harder fight."

Tarrell drew the blade that still sat at his hip, examining its unremarkable, and now silver, surface. Experimentally, he moved it slowly closer to Farran, who watched with one giant eye. As the blade drew closer to the dragon, it glowed with a blue light, mirroring the previous night.

"Stay still," Tarrell said, as he scrambled to his feet and moved back. With all his might, he ran towards Farran and swept the sword in a mighty arc towards him. At the last moment, he deflected the blade into the ground, just as it erupted into blue flames. As the energy of his attack faded, so did the flames until they sputtered out and once more left a blade that was extraordinarily cold.

Farran huffed a ring of smoke from his nostrils. "Interesting."

"I do not know this magic," said Tarrell, frowning. "But it is mighty useful. Our master smiths of old were great blade-smiths and spell-casters if they could make our blades so strong and powerful that they can endure thousands of years and still be thus. I must speak with our master smith and see if he can explain it. We need this protection if we are to succeed."

The master blade-smith caressed Tarrell's blade like a treasured artifact, and examined it in silence for many minutes whilst Tarrell waited. He was not usually impatient, but now he had to force his foot to cease tapping upon the cobbled floor of the smith.

"It is a beautiful blade," Jarnsmi said with an approving nod. "An old blade, too."

This Tarrell knew, for its lineage was recorded from his grandfather's hands at the time the pact was made a thousand years before, and even earlier than that.

"All the old blades are made thusly," replied Jarnsmi in answer to Tarrell's question. "The heirlooms of Ednor tell a tale of our history. All the oldest blades were made with such magics to repel our old enemies the dragons. Unused as weapons against claw and scale for a thousand years, such skills have slept, but now they awaken as our old enemy seeks to challenge us once more."

"Does the magic have a limit?" Tarrell asked, wondering if the magic might have been used up in the battle. To his surprise, Jarnsmi laughed.

"No, for it will draw the energy of the world to sustain it, such was the skill of my forefathers. Then, should that fail, it will call upon the wielder, and, last of all, the blade itself, so above all, the blade and the spell endures."

"What of our newer blades?"

Jarnsmi shook his head. "The art has not been practised in a thousand years, given there was no need. It is a complex and lengthy process I only know snatches of theory from, but it is not used in our modern weapons."

"Can it be?"

Jarnsmi pursed his lips and pondered. "No," he said eventually. "It would take weeks now to forge a blade using this technique; a slow and lengthy process during which I would need to research the old ways and practise them. I am sure the outcome would be less than perfect."

Tarrell tried to stave off disappointment. "Not all carry blades as old as the times of the wars. Not all will have the protection afforded, or the ability to defend themselves. Can the protection be added to weapons already wrought?"

"No." This time, Jarnsmi was quick in his reply. "The spells do not take to cold metal already wrought. As with all spells, they must be imbued when the blade is in the making and the spells must be cast at precise points in the forging to bind with the metal for all time."

Tarrell deflated. He had hoped there was some solution. "What of those who do not have old swords to protect themselves?"

"The ice-fire itself can be made," suggested Jarnsmi. "It can be coated upon the blades, or whatever surface you chose. It will be nowhere near as long lasting, though."

"Still, that could help us." Tarrell latched onto the idea, and his excitement grew. "As we carry fire in jars to travel with on occasion, we could also make and store this, no?"

"Theoretically," Jarnsmi acknowledged. "If it be stable enough."

"We must test it. Will you retrieve the old records and put to practice this theory with any of our kin you deem could help?"

"I will."

Tarrell swept out to call a meet of dragons and Eldarkind to share his news, confident he had found a way to successfully defend them against Cies.

"Will we not be sitting ducks, as we were this time?" Sendari asked, as a host of all able-bodied Eldarkind and dragons met that evening.

Tarrell shook his head as the spark of an idea formed. "I have an idea which can avoid this, though it requires the cooperation of our dragon friends. The Eldarkind and dragonkin could fight together, as one, in the sky, where dragonkin are most powerful and where we can lend our abilities in close quarters."

"How is this possible?" asked Farran.

"We, ah, we could ride upon you."

Angry roars erupted around them as dragons stood, flexing their wings, kneading the ground with their claws, and shouting down his idea.

"We are not like these mules you ride," Farran said, glowering. "We are not beasts to be ridden."

Tarrell bowed his head to Farran and held up his hands, which had little effect to quiet the insulted dragons before him. "I cry your forgiveness," he shouted above the din. "I meant no offense." He paused as the discontent subsided. "With greatest respect, unless we can do this, how can we get close enough to Cies and his kin to aid you? We either sit on the ground, waiting to be picked off by flame, or attacked from above; or we join you in the skies to both protect you and fight with you: tooth and claw, magic and blade. Will you not allow us to engage in a fair fight?"

He looked around. The Eldarkind had already shrunk away in doubt, still unsure of their 'allies', whilst the dragons recoiled with open disgust at being asked to be beasts of burden.

Unexpectedly, the young black dragon, Myrkith's son, Tarrell remembered, stepped forward.

"I will fight alongside you," Myrkdaga said. Smoke dripped from his nostril as his growl deepened. "I would see Cies, coward of the silver scales, destroyed and my sire avenged at any cost."

Lorellei pushed forward through the ranks of Eldarkind. "We fought well together. I would be honoured if you would consent to bear me into a new battle." He bowed to Myrkdaga.

"You understand I am not your beast to be commanded," said Myrkdaga stiffly.

"I do."

"No liberties will you take with me. You will treat me with utmost respect at all times."

"I shall."

"Then I will bear you, as I bore King Soren."

Lorellei grinned, and there was a fierce challenge in his eyes as he moved to stand next to his new dragon partner.

Tarrell's eyes widened at Myrkdaga's words. There was a story here he did not know. After a moment, he recovered his composure. "Myrkdaga, I am honoured and gladdened by your commitment. Together, we can succeed. Lorellei, for your willingness to stand first, I will bestow upon you the greatest sword of your house to fight with. Are there any more amongst you who would follow this fine example?"

When all was said and done, only a few dragons came forward to consent to Tarrell's idea, and Tarrell struggled to recruit enough Eldarkind to match them. *It will have to do*, he thought as he surveyed the paltry gang before him. Nevertheless, with Farran's insistence to his kin that it was necessary, he partnered Eldarkind with dragon, so one could fight from the ground and one from the air, always in constant contact with each other and able to help where needed. Those with spelled blades he gave the most important task of ensuring those Eldarkind on the ground were protected, and he hinted at his solution that would allow more of them to temporarily give their blades the same power.

"Now, we wait," Tarrell finished. "Set a watch," he instructed.

"Fly patrols," Farran added to his own kin.

The group made to disperse, until a voice piped up. "When will the attack come?"

"With the dark," Farran replied grimly. "Cies will want the element of surprise, and the cloak of darkness. We must use all of our senses to detect him, and the night to our own advantage. He will not want us to regroup. He will be swift to seek retribution."

EIGHTEEN

Bang! Bang! Bang! The smash of hammer upon nail drifted through the window into Soren's study, jarring his already pounding head. He peered out over the square in front of the castle. Out of sight, he knew a messenger pinned up the first of a stack of decrees bound for all corners of western Caledan.

"It should not have come to this," he said with a scowl as he paced around his study.

Behan stood by the door with his hands clasped, examining the rug beneath his feet with greater interest than normal. He made a noncommittal noise as a reply.

"The Eldarkind are our allies," Soren stressed, glaring at Behan, who would not meet his eye. "Surely, you do not think otherwise?"

Behan met his eyes for the briefest moment, shook his head, and looked to the floor again.

Soren halted, his consternation rising, and looked at Behan. "Never have you been silent on a matter, Lord Steward. Speak to me now, Behan."

At his name, Behan shuffled uncomfortably. "They are not natural creatures, Sire." He detailed what his many intelligencers reported back. "People are scared. After the dragon attacks, they fear anything they do not know. Who are these fleeting fey folk, with pale hair as bright as starlight, smooth faces, and lilting voices? Where do they travel from and to, and how do they travel so unseen and unheard? In the west, you know of the old tales of the fey folk. Are they to come to steal our babes, make us take leave of our senses, rob us? Which tales they know determines their fear."

"You should be able to sift rumours from truth, though, Lord Steward."

Behan twisted his hands together." It is difficult to know what to believe in times such as these," he admitted.

"I expect better of you than this," said Soren, a hint of sharpness about his tone. He narrowed his eyes. "For a thousand years, the Eldarkind—and the dragons—have guarded our borders, our people, and kept the peace of Caledan, whether or not it was known. They are our allies, now and forever."

Behan surprised him by meeting his gaze with a surprising fire in his eyes. "You cannot think this of the dragons, surely?" He bobbed his head apologetically as Soren glared at him for speaking out of turn, but his eyes still fixed upon Soren with a passion he was taken aback by.

"Not all dragons are our enemy," Soren said, wary of Behan's strange mood. "There are a few bad eggs in every race. That I need to issue a decree stating it is against our laws to attack a member of the Eldar race—who have never done anything to harm us—is unthinkable."

"That you have to issue a decree at all shows the magnitude of the problem," replied Behan quietly.

Soren tremored with frustration at his words, and before he could say anything he would regret, he left. It would take a lot more than words to change Behan's mind.

"Good morning, Sire." Barclay strolled in with a nonchalant grin on his face and bowed as low as he could without tripping over; wobbling as he almost lost his balance.

Soren did not smile.

"Come, what ails you, Soren? It's far too nice a day to be glum." Indeed it was; a fine and warm winter's day, and the snows had almost melted, but Soren could not shake the chill in his heart.

"There have been more attacks on the Eldarkind, and Behan thinks I'm a madman for issuing the decree to protect them." He trusted Barclay intimately with most details these days, and was glad for the close friendship they had developed.

Barclay nodded, but his grin faded.

Soren huffed, and threw his hands up. "What? Say it! Everyone clearly knows something I don't. Damn it, be honest with me."

Barclay sighed and regarded Soren solemnly, with all trace of merriment gone from his eyes and his voice. "I say this as a friend, you understand?" A trace of anxiety flitted across his face, causing Soren to frown as he beheld it.

"There is a... growing discontent, shall we say—that you will not have seen for yourself—and a distrust of your actions. People see you fraternising with what they perceive as the enemy. There are whispers you are losing your mind and are not sane or fit enough to rule."

Soren froze, not even breathing. "Swear you do not lie to me."

"I swear it."

"Who says such things?"

"Who doesn't? What is a rumour but a wildfire of words? Come, you know how court works."

"And what say you?" Soren held his breath as Barclay deliberated his answer.

Barclay faltered and his mouth twisted. "I count you as the dearest of friends, Soren, this you know. I think you not mad, but I cannot help think what do you is madness. Dragons? Dragons! They attack us, and yet you want to befriend them?"

Soren held his tongue for the moment. "And what of the Eldarkind?"

"You know my feelings. They're a strange people, and I cannot fathom them."

"Barclay, will you trust me on this, if I ask you to?"

Barclay paused.

"I know how difficult it may be; how counterintuitive. I say what I said before: I know things not privy to most. I act with reason, and in Caledan's best interests, always. Now, more than ever, it is crucial to find a way forward. Believe me, I have tried to find another solution. The only way is to ally with the Eldarkind and the dragons. At least, those who remain on the side of good. Those who attack

669

us are not one and the same. The alliance would be primarily to seek their defeat in the short term. As my subject, my advisor, and my friend, will you trust me in this?"

Soren could see the indecision in Barclay's eyes and the instinct to say no. It danced on the tip of Barclay's tongue, as his lips parted to give his answer, and then paused.

"Yes," said Barclay at last. His tone was not convincing, and the set of his jaw betrayed his concern, but Soren would take that for now. Once given, he knew Barclay's word was good. He hoped he could still trust that.

Soren found himself wandering aimlessly through the castle, lost deep in thought, until he arrived at the archives where all the castle's records were kept under lock and key. He let himself into the dark room and stood for a moment. A deep sigh escaped. *I must find a way to rebuild the pact.*

"There must be some written record of how it was achieved," he mused aloud. He looked around. It was the first time he had ever visited, and he was surprised by the size of the room before him. What he had expected to be a broom cupboard, going by the diminutive size of the door, was, in fact, a tall, airy space in one of the castle voids.

It was filled with crooked shelves right to the ceiling, which was lost in the gloom, and ran to his left and right in between the castle's interior walls. It was a gloomy place, dark and forgotten, with a thick silence that was hard to break. It was dark, too. The only light came from lanterns that had not been cleaned in many years, and they burned dim and faint. Soren paced slowly, running his hand along the spines of a row of books, reading their titles as he passed. Every shelf was filled with heavy old tomes and countless stacked and bundled sheaves of papers.

"May I assist you, Your Majesty?"

Soren jumped out of his skin at the noise and spun around, grasping the shelf for support. Before him stood the wizened old record keeper standing four feet tall, an ankle-long beard tucked into his belt, and a robe that drowned him.

"Y… yes," said Soren, with a cough, to cover his surprise.

Inspiration struck. *He should know this place well!* "Show me where the oldest records are kept."

The old man hobbled to an antechamber with Soren close in tow. A door so small Soren had to bend over almost double led into a pitch black space. Light blossomed over the cupboard as Soren passed a lantern in. It was cold, Soren noticed, distinctly chilly, and it smelt old, of things that had lain for an age, gathering dust and mould.

"Is there anything in particular you wish to see, Sire?" wheezed the record-keeper into his handkerchief.

"Do you have any records on the pact?" Soren kept his tone intentionally light.

The record keeper's nose scrunched and his bushy eyebrows wriggled. "Which one, Sire?"

"Ah, I'm not sure," said Soren, feigning ignorance, and suppressing his disappointment. Of all the agreements made, if the old man didn't recognise mention of 'the' pact, he did not know anything, Soren surmised. "That will be all. You may return to your duties. Thank you for your assistance."

The old man bowed and backed away with a curious glint in his eye, leaving Soren alone in the tiny room.

He searched through every document in there with painstaking slowness; some of the documents were so old they cracked as he opened them, threatening to fall apart. He searched until the day was late and dust caked him from head to toe, but it was fruitless. He could find nothing that mentioned the Eldarkind, dragonkin, or pact of any kind. As he shut the last tome with a huff of frustration, he admitted defeat for the day.

NINETEEN

"Oh thank goodness!" Luke cried from the wall as Eve plodded towards Arlyn gates on her weary mount. She was just as exhausted, having not even slept in the saddle as she rode home without delay after the horrors she had witnessed at Ednor. She heard his voice, but did not have the energy to lift her head, and only when he appeared beside her to grab the reins and help her slide from the horse, did she see the consternation upon his face at her poor state.

"I was so worried!" he fretted. "What happened? Are you okay?"

She didn't answer. Her throat was parched dry and she could not find the words. Instead, she reached for him and buried herself into his chest, breathing in the scent of leather and horses, which made the most welcome change from the stench of fire and death that had clung to her for days. As she shook with exhaustion, she finally allowed the tiredness to overtake her.

"I need a healer," she croaked, and clutched at him as her legs buckled. He steadied her in strong arms.

With help, he escorted her back to the keep, shouting for assistance as they arrived in the courtyard. Maids arrived and an outcry arose at the poor state of their mistress. A healer appeared, and Eve was put to bed. Luke hovered about awkwardly, not allowed into the room, but not wanting to leave. As the door opened and closed with each new visitor, Eve saw him peering in, but she didn't have the energy to smile.

They undressed her from the clothes she had worn since the attack, and her body was as sooty, blackened, and burnt as her garments. Her skin was festered with blisters, pale and infected, and she could not hold back the screams as they peeled the scraps of fabric away, for they had fused with her skin, which was red, white, and oozing.

Worst of all were her arms. The healers tried to clean her as best they could, but the soot in her wounds caused even more pain as they tried to rid her of it, to the point where she nearly fainted due to the white-hot pain every touch overloaded her senses with.

Luke's face peered through the gap once more as a maid scurried out to fetch honey, lavender oil, and cloths. She was soon back. The soaked cloths were a cold relief against the hot fury of her skin and the lavender's scent masked all traces of fire and pus. Hands held up her limbs, body, and even her face as they wrapped her in the cloths, and she knew this would be her fate for weeks without magic, but she had not the strength to perform the magic needed to heal her burns, so extensive as they were and as tired as she felt.

Eve did not have to see the rest of her body to know it would be marred with a multitude of scars, magical healing or not, but that was a thought for another day. For now, she had to do battle with the burns that already began to angrily sting again as the cooling effects of her bandages wore away.

Last of all, they brought in sheep-shearers. Her hair was all but gone; they roughly chopped it at the shoulders and burnt chunks littered the floor. Her eyebrows were gone, too, they told her; but they were blonde to start with, she reasoned in her quiescent state. It was a little loss compared to all else.

Like a child, she tipped her chin back to accept the draught: a sleeping potion infused with pain-easing remedies. Within minutes, she sank into blissful slumber; a haven away from the pain.

Eve awoke to Luke sat at her bedside, with his gaze boring into her. He started as she opened her eyes and sat up from his slouch. "Eve! Welcome back."

"Water."

He hurried to hold the cup to her lips and tip it so she could drink the cool, refreshing water. She savoured every drop flowing down her parched throat and lay unmoving as he returned the cup to the side-stand, testing out her senses. The pain had dulled, but returned with a vengeance as she attempted a twitch. Waves of exhaustion still rolled over her.

She had not expected her return to be so. She had dreaded seeing Luke again for one, still unsure what to say, but he seemed to have forgotten their quarrel for now.

"What happened?" asked Luke. "When you didn't scry, I was so worried."

In a dull monotone, Eve explained haltingly, and in as few words as she could, of the dragon attack on Ednor, and how death, fire, and fear like she had never known came upon them in the night. "I barely escaped with my life. I've never been so scared before. I don't know which is worse: the dragons or the fire."

"I'm so glad you're here. You're safe now. I'm sorry I didn't take you seriously."

Eve nodded. They fell into silence. What more could be said? Their previous quarrel seemed trivial in light of what had happened, but it still nagged at her. "When you said I abandoned you," she said slowly. "Did you mean that?"

"I–" Luke looked away. "It's hard at times to know," he mumbled. "I asked you to leave, but I didn't want you to. Would you have come back for me?"

Her instinct was to laugh off his question because to her it was ridiculous, but she could sense he was serious. "Of course." *There's more to this.* "Why would you think anything else?"

Silence lengthened between them.

"I suppose I spent so much time chasing after you, that I never stopped to wonder if you would do the same for me."

Realisation dawned on Eve. "And you were hurt that I didn't return for you—personally."

Luke's silence was her answer.

"And that made you doubt everything between us."

"Sometimes... Sometimes, I do doubt this will work." He gestured between them. "Look at us."

"It doesn't matter. After all we have been through." She shook her head. "I can think of no one I would rather be with. Your rank doesn't matter; neither does mine. To me, you're Luke. Just Luke. *My* Luke; and I would have returned for you the moment I could."

"Thank you," he muttered, and his hand shook slightly as he placed it atop her bandaged fingers. The pressure made her burnt skin scream with pain, but she did not flinch, instead, savoring the feeling of peace between them once more.

"I'm so relieved you're safe," he said. Eve could see the frustration within him; at himself for not heeding her warning.

"You couldn't have known," she said. A thought struck her, and she bolted upright, shuddering as pain ripped through her. "The dragons could be coming here! I must warn everyone! We must prepare!"

Luke tried to stop her from moving, but her entire body was covered in burns and bandages, and he was loathe to touch her. "You cannot get up—you must rest."

"There's no time, Luke. If Ednor falls… even if it doesn't, we might be their next target. Their attacks are already rife across east Caledan. The west could be next." She ignored his protests and forced her legs to swing over the side of the bed, dangling until her toes brushed the floor. For a moment, she paused, gasping, and shook her head until the feeling of passing out faded.

"Help me," she commanded.

Luke rushed to her side and gingerly supported her as she staggered to the door. "Where are you going?"

"To the forest," she said through gritted teeth. Stars danced before her eyes and her skin crawled with irritation and pain. Eve ignored Luke's protests and pushed forwards so he had no choice but to help her. Strange looks followed them as they moved excruciatingly slowly through the keep and out into the gardens, for she wore only her nightgown which billowed in the breeze.

Every movement hurt: the ache of the long ride and the increasing agony of the burns. As Luke opened the door, Eve sighed in relief as the cold air froze her skin. She held onto Luke doggedly and started up the hill, through the herb gardens and into the forest. They moved at a snail's pace and out of sight of all Arlyn past the tree line until they came upon a clearing. Eve let go and sunk to the floor with a moan. Luke cried out and moved to raise her to her feet, but she stopped him with a sharp slash of her hand.

"Stand back," she warned.

The sodden ground welcomed her. Water soaked through her garments and in seconds, her cloak was drenched. It was cold and foggy, too. Now, the cold was not a comfort, but a leech. Eve shivered with cold and nervous anticipation.

She buried her hands into the freezing, wet mosses that carpeted the forest floor, entwining her fingers in the soft fronds and took a deep, steadying breath before she began to call the magic forth. Carefully selecting the energy of the large beings of the land in her mind—trees, fungi, and that which would not be weakened by her needs—she called out in the old tongue.

"Ia kvedja a ethera ro feld att mina ethera endurnyja, mina sarr laekna, ja min heild endr efla. Nema adeins a ethera etrele ja jurta spenna, ja inge skada einhevrr lifanti hlutur fram mina coinsiasa."

I call forth the energy of the land to replenish my energy, heal my wounds, and make me whole again. Take only that energy which can be spared of the trees and the plants and bring no harm to any living being on my conscience.

Magic crawled up her arms from the ground, visible if she half closed her eyes, coiling and trailing over her skin. It was an angry tingle at first contact that subsided into a soothing caress as the magic took hold. A sigh of relief escaped her lips as the agony subsided and her energy grew as the spell replenished it.

It could have been minutes or hours, she had no concept of time, only feeling, as the magic staved off the cold biting into her from her sodden clothes, and banished the stinging burns. The pain faded, and her aches dissolved. Eve felt her well of energy grow again until she no longer felt dulled by exhaustion, and relished in the feeling of sharp clarity and focus.

As the magic faded, she waited, until the last drops had gone, and then she stood. Taking a deep breath and filling her lungs with the pure air of the forest, which now felt refreshing instead of bitingly cold, she remained standing, and still, with her eyes closed, mentally checking every part of her body. All was well. Her hands flew to her hair. It had not grown back, but little had she expected that.

Eve opened her eyes and gingerly pulled back some of her bandages. Her arms were indeed healed. It seemed as though they had been healing for a month, not days. She swallowed. The pus filled, oozing, inflamed skin was gone, but now rivers of rippled scars covered her. White scars, slightly reddened, crisscrossed her arms, and she knew most of her body would be the same. She tugged the rest of the bandage away. Even her hands were scarred. She stared at their ugliness in a moment of fascination and disgust, before a wave of despondence swept over her at her state. There would be no fixing this, not even with magic. Forever now, she would be marred.

Luke appeared beside her. "That's amazing. You are healed!" A smile broke his face. "You are well?" he frowned at her sadness.

She nodded slowly. "I am well," she murmured, "but I will never be as I was. I cannot rid myself of the scarring." Feeling self-conscious, she pulled the bandages over her skin again and rubbed her arms as her cheeks reddened.

Luke clasped her hand, giving it a squeeze. "It doesn't matter." He caught her gaze and stared at her. "It doesn't matter," he repeated. "Only that you're well." He smiled, and her lips twitched in reply, but it was all she could manage.

They returned to the keep where the maids and healer were in awe of her strength and sudden recovery.

"By the grace of Eldarkind magic, I am healed," she told them. It set muttered gossip aflame throughout the keep, but she did not care. *Let them talk*, she thought. *One day soon, they will discover who I am, and it will matter not that one of their own has magic, for it shall save them all.* If her plans came to fruition.

She insisted above their protests that she was well enough to continue in her duties, and sent them scurrying to fetch the captain of the guard and his deputy.

Whilst she awaited for their arrival, she had a brief respite, and took advantage of her solitude to scry Soren.

Her appearance shocked her. It was the first time she had seen herself in a mirror since before leaving for Ednor. She touched the places where her eyebrows had been, fingered the harsh edge of her hair, and traced the flame-like scars up her neck.

Soren was equally appalled at her state, and more so when she revealed she had been in a much worse condition and would still be without magic to heal her. She showed him briefly the scars upon her arms to illustrate her point. Pity filled his eyes. She knew why, but did not dwell on it. It did not matter, now.

"Cousin. I am so very sorry for sending you into harm," Soren's voice was fervent, and Eve thought she could see a tear in his eye. "I feel responsible for this."

She shook her head. "It is what it is, Cousin. You were not to know. I scry with you now because I am returned home to Arlyn. I—" Her voice broke. She cleared her throat. "I have never been so scared in my life. The danger is clear. I need to prepare our defences. I do not know if Arlyn could be next. The Eldarkind and the dragons barely fought Cies off, and I know we stand no chance. What I saw... What I experienced... I cannot... I cannot say. It is so horrific." She swallowed. "I cannot let my people suffer the same. We must be ready to flee, for we cannot defend against these creatures. I apologise for failing in my duty." She bowed her head to him.

It was Soren's turn to brush aside her apology. He shook his head, and his mouth set firm. "You have not failed. Stronger men would have quailed where you stood firm. Your commitment to your people is noble and admirable. Your duty is to honour and protect your countryfolk. I understand that. They are lucky to be led by you now."

They briefly spoke of the Eldarkind, and Eve detailed the destruction of Ednor in the raging fires and the casualties of the attacks.

"I left with little notice," she added. "As a result, I have little understanding of Tarrell or Farran's plans, but I know they would be pushed to succeed against further attacks."

Soren sat back in his chair. "Even the Eldarkind and the dragons fail in this?"

She nodded. "It is no easy task, that is certain."

Soren exhaled a long puff of disbelief, and pondered awhile. "This is ill news, indeed. I have not been able to scry with the Eldarkind for several days now. I imagine this will be the cause."

"Yes. Much of Ednor was destroyed, and the main buildings suffered the worst. They are much preoccupied with ensuring the injured and dead are cared for, and the living have somewhere to stay."

There was little to say after that, and they exchanged some empty pleasantries. Eve shared her father was still ill and unable to fulfill his duties. Soren shared how his sister was flourishing in court life, sheltered from matters of state. Eve was glad, for Irumae had already suffered much beyond her years.

"I hope to see you both in the flesh soon," she said with a smile.

"May it be so," Soren hoped.

Soren wished her well, and she him, though they both knew it was very much against the odds with what lay ahead.

Awaiting her in the drawing room once she had finished was Hoarth, captain of the guard, and his deputy, Nyle. Her father was not present; still too ill to attend. It felt strange to meet people there, Eve noted as she sat in her father's chair. This was where her father held his meetings, which she had never been allowed to attend and was instead sent to play, school, or be scolded for trying to eavesdrop. Now, she sat in his chair, conducting his business. His presence was heavy in the room, despite his absence, as if he leaned over her shoulder.

Luke entered behind her and closed the door with a soft snap, but he did not sit with them. He was there as her guard, not her confident.

Eve invited them to sit, gesturing with a bandaged hand. Their lingering glances told of their interest in her condition, as they openly stared at her shorn hair and bandages.

"My lady," they said in unison, bowed, and took their seats.

"Forgive me the intrusion, my lady," said Hoarth. "I do not mean to pry, but I expected you to remain abed for quite some time. You seem remarkably well given the extent of the injuries you suffered, as they were described to me."

"I am much better than I was, thanks to the grace of Eldarkind magic," Eve said.

Hoarth stiffened and his eyes narrowed.

"Captain, please suspend your prejudice. Nyle knows of the Eldarkind; he accompanied me once to Ednor." Eve glanced at Nyle. His own eyes were hard. He had less than fond memories of that trip, and she hoped he still did not bear her ill-will for what had happened. "He can vouch they are a fair and noble race and their magic is a force of good. They bear no resemblance to the wives tales." She stared pointedly at him.

"It is so," Nyle said begrudgingly.

Eve nodded, satisfied. "By the grace of their powers, I am healed. Their blood flows in my veins," she dared to admit, "and I am blessed with magic. I have healed myself from the gravest of my injuries, so I may help Arlyn prepare for what may come." Ignoring their shock, she peeled back her bandage to reveal a scarred arm and hand. "This injury happened not a week ago. See how I have healed it? I will always bear these scars, but magic means I lived through them, and return whole to lead my people once more."

They did not reply—in shock from that admission, she presumed—so she continued, knowing she now had to show her strength for them to trust and follow her.

"I thank you for joining me today. Let us return to the business at hand. We have no time to delay." She detailed what had happened in Ednor again; her duties there, and what had befallen the Eldarkind and the dragons who allied with them and now resided there. "I witnessed this first hand. I survived. Barely," she emphasised. "The Eldarkind and the dragons were barely a match for those that attacked. We will not be able to stand in their way. You have heard the reports from across Caledan. It is all true. They could well come here next, or soon, and we must prepare."

Hoarth shuffled in his chair. "Surely, this is unnecessary. They would not trouble us so far west."

Anger rose in Eve. She ripped off all her bandages and stood to show him scarred flesh on every limb. "This covers my entire body," she said to him with bared teeth and red cheeks. "I am fortunate to have magic to be able to heal myself, but even so, I endured this for days with no ministration as I rode night and day, to return in time to warn my people. Would you like this or worse to be the fate of your wife? Your children? Parents? Friends?" she snarled.

"I do not have time to waste with disagreements. The dragons have come to the west. The Eldarkind and their dragons may yet drive them off, and then where will they go? They will not disappear. They could well come here. They will not wait on courtesy to attack. As they did at Ednor, they will come with the night and we will all be dead before we know it. I do not want to suffer what I have witnessed again, and I will protect my people from it whether you like it or not."

Hoarth subsided, taken aback by her vehemence, and Nyle sat as imperturbable as ever. Eve dared not look towards Luke, who had moved to stand behind her.

Eve grasped one of her father's blankets lying across the back of the chair and draped it across her naked legs. "Set a guard up night and day." She softened her tone, but kept the edge so they would be in no misunderstanding that she meant what she said.

"I want our walls constantly guarded. I want alarms sounded the moment any man, woman, or child hears so much as a whisper of anything. I care not if it is a false alarm. I would much rather the entire town be roused and return to bed cold and grumpy than for the alternative, for fear of inconvenience could mean we miss our chance and all end up roasted in our beds."

Hoarth nodded. Worry lined his face.

Good, she thought. *Perhaps he begins to take me seriously.* "We also need to have an evacuation plan in place. Where can our people gather if Arlyn is attacked? We must find somewhere everyone can reach quickly, without being detected, that will be safe beyond measure. Where can they go?"

Hoarth sat up, now his input was required. He stroked his beard and chewed his lip as he contemplated. "The forest?"

"Hmm," replied Eve noncommittally and shook her head. "Even if it is wet, I'm not sure it can withstand dragon fire, or hide our people."

"The lake?" suggested Nyle.

"Too open," Eve dismissed the idea, as frustration grew. She did not want to alienate them with her refusal to entertain their suggestions, but the ideas they proposed would not prove fruitful solutions. "The dragons may not suffer water, but their flames can travel many hundreds of yards. We cannot outrun or outreach them."

Behind her, Luke shuffled and coughed. "Erm." They turned to look at him, and he coloured slightly at their attention.

"Yes?"

"I don't mean to interrupt. What about the mines?"

Yes! Eve thought. "The old iron workings! I had not thought of that. Brilliant idea." A brief smile flashed across her face, and Luke smiled in response as she turned back to Hoarth and Nyle. "This could be the solution we need, no? They are close, they are safe, and our people may stay there without fear of detection. The dragons attack mostly from the air, and do not land very often. Are the caves safe?"

Hoarth shrugged and grimaced. "I cannot be sure. Folk don't go in them for good reason, but they could be shored up with ease to be sure."

"Make it so," Eve decided. "Send every man you have to reinforce the walls and ceilings where you can. Nyle, I want you to brief the town cryer. He must inform everyone of the danger and what to do when and if the time comes."

"My lady," they replied in unison, stood, bowed, and left.

Eve sat back in her chair and closed her eyes in relief. That had been both harder and easier than she had expected. *I hope they have some understanding of what we face… and are committed to following my orders.*

"Thank you for that," she said to Luke, and reached out to squeeze his hand in thanks. As she saw the scars on the back of her hand once more, she faltered, and pulled her hand out of his grasp, self-consciously covering it with the blanket. "You look tired," she said. "Rest. Eat. I'll be fine. Go."

Luke nodded and turned away, but before he reached the door, he returned to stand before her. Gingerly and gently, he freed her hand from the blanket and placed a soft kiss upon the scars before he left.

She swallowed and placed her palm across the back of the hand he had kissed. The skin felt so strange and wrinkled. It would take a long time to accept her new body, but perhaps it were not so dreadful and hideous as she feared.

Shortly after he left, she followed suit, and headed in the opposite direction, out of the keep and towards the woods once more with an idea forming from her earlier spells and the works in Ednor she had read about the powers of earth magic. Could she draw upon the power of the earth again to protect her people with a ward of colossal proportion? There would only be one way to find out. *I might not be able to fight dragons, but I can protect my people,* she thought determinedly.

TWENTY

It was clear that the gods had not been appeased. The devastation continued apace across northern Roher, and the streams of refugees flooding into the capital clogged the streets. Already, Harad had ordered the roads to be purged, with any beggars cast out into the merciless desert and stragglers flogged publicly in the squares, but it did not seem to dissuade them from arriving in ever increasing numbers, as if their king could protect them.

They would think it his duty, Harad knew, yet what more could he do? He had thrown games, made sacrifices, ordered Roher to complete days of fasting and prayer, and the capital of Arrans to be purified throughout. Nay, this could not be a god, for no god would think him weak, Harad reasoned. *This must be a demon.* That did not make his predicament any easier; demon or god, it mattered not. He could vanquish neither.

Harad doubled the conscription rates, lowered the conscription age to twelve, and doubled the city guard to ensure his control of the army, and thus the country, was secure. To keep his citizens busy and free of dissent, he doubled the days of fasting and praying, whilst spreading news that Roher could not be forgiven by the gods until its citizens had atoned for their wrongdoings. *Let the fervent punish themselves to please their gods. I pray this demon leaves us alone.* Harad's bluff would not stand to be called.

TWENTY ONE

Farran was correct. With the night came the dragons. This time, no cacophony heralded their arrival. This time, it was a silent descent of deadly assassins from the sky. Frantic horns rang out as the first fell from the stars, and the warning keening of Farran's watching dragons snaked through Ednor, signalling them to spring into action.

Myrkdaga met Lorellei's eyes with grim glee, and Lorellei gave him a shaky smile before clambering up Myrkdaga's leg to sit upon his back. He fumbled with the makeshift straps that would lash his legs in place and keep him safe during Myrkdaga's aerial manoeuvres, and grasped the loop around one of Myrkdaga's back spikes in front of him. Last of all, he checked his sword was accessible by both hands. Being ambidextrous would come in useful that night, he was sure.

Myrkdaga shuffled and stretched under Lorellei, testing out this new and unfamiliar weight upon his back; it would take some adjusting to ensure his flying remained stable. Though Lorellei was not heavy to him, the slightest adjustment in weight was the difference between a well-executed loop and tumbling out of the sky. Myrkdaga was ready for the challenge.

"Ready to fly, friend?" said Myrkdaga, his grin wide and toothy.

"Ready!"

Myrkdaga launched into the air. His wings snapped out and beat powerfully to speed them upwards. Lorellei whooped. Myrkdaga wobbled under his weight just a little, and shifted his wing position and tail to his new balancing position, trying small manoeuvres to test his balance.

"This is amazing!" said Lorellei into his mind. They had

agreed to communicate this way throughout the battle, so the wind and din could not snatch their words away.

"Welcome to my life," said Myrkdaga with a joyful roar. As they soared away from Ednor, Myrkdaga rose in thermals, for his strategy as a smaller dragon was to stay on the fringes of the battle and pick off those dragons he could outmatch.

"This breeze is low, which is good for stable flight," he told Lorellei. "And yet I do not welcome it, for it stinks of dragons." He growled.

Lorellei did not answer. All dragons smelled fairly odious to him, not just Cies.

At last, they levelled out, soaring high above Ednor valley. Lorellei struggled to look down; it was dizzying.

"Now, we are in our ideal position," explained Myrkdaga. "Above the enemy. Best to be here, as it's far harder to be attacked from below without warning, and far better to attack from high, approaching behind your enemy, so they cannot see you until it is too late."

"Won't they see us if they look up?"

"No. Look. Ednor burns." Myrkdaga pointed his head towards Ednor, which had once again erupted in flames as dragons swarmed over it. "The night sky means little light coming from above. For us, our enemies will be silhouetted below against the fire whilst they shall be so blinded by its light we shall appear from the darkness as wraiths." Already, his keen night vision was enhanced by the light of the flames; shapes darted thither and yon, indicating both his kin and enemy. His nostrils flared, tasting their scents upon the air.

"Wait for my direction," warned Myrkdaga. "Attack only those I attack, for I can tell friend from foe, even in this confusion. Are you ready? I'm about to dive." His wings fluttered as he caught himself from diving, thinking it best to warn his Eldarkind counterpart first.

Above him, Lorellei gripped him tighter between his thighs, and wound his hand into the loop. "Ready."

"Hold on tight!" Myrkdaga shut his wings and dropped from

the sky like a stone, gradually opening them to corkscrew out of the sky, faster and faster.

"Aaaaaargh!" Lorellei had to close his eyes against the sickening blur that threatened to claim the contents of his stomach

"Now!" Myrkdaga cried.

Disorientated, Lorellei struggled to draw his sword, which glowed blue, and brandished it before him, careful not to touch Myrkdaga. As he regained his composure, he had but a moment to perceive the dragon below as they approached it at breakneck pace. Lorellei focused all his attention on their foe, and his blade erupted into blue ice-fire as Myrkdaga sunk teeth and raked claws into the dragon before them. Lorellei leaned forward and slashed, catching the wing membrane. The dragon shrieked, and sped away. Myrkdaga snapped out his wings and it felt to Lorellei like they had slapped into a wall in mid air. Myrkdaga laboured, flapping his wings to gain height again.

Lorellei vomited over the side of Myrkdaga's shoulder, and the remains of his evening meal rained on those below. He sighed with relief. At the very least, that felt better.

They repeated the tactic on another smaller dragon, and this time Lorellei kept his concentration better. He clung on for dear life and kept his eyes open with sheer determination, though they stung from the wind rushing past them. As they approached this time, his sword was already ready and aiming, and together they delivered blows that left bloodied furrows from Myrkdaga's claws and trails of blue fire from Lorellei's sword across their opponent.

"That was well done," Myrkdaga grunted.

Lorellei whooped on his back, exhilarated by their success. His eyes, slowly improving in the darkness, though nowhere as sharp as Myrkdaga's, scanned the skies for their next engagement.

All of a sudden, a great weight crashed upon them, crumpling Myrkdaga's wings, and crushing Lorellei against Myrkdaga's hard, sharp-edged scales.

Myrkdaga roared in frustration as a larger dragon plummeted towards the ground with Myrkdaga firmly in his grasp, and Myrkdaga knew what it was about to do. He struggled, but could not escape.

Lorellei moved upon his back, wriggling free of the straps lashing him in place.

"What are you doing?" shouted Myrkdaga.

Lorellei did not answer, save with an incoherent battle cry. He freed his sword arm and began to hack with all his might at the dragon who held them, leaving rents in the dragon hide; it swirled with blue flames that crawled into the wounds. A giant twitch of the dragon dislodged Lorellei and he fell with a high-pitched scream into the abyss. Myrkdaga roared, an ear splitting, determined roar, and pushed with all his might away from the dragon, making sure to dig his claws into the wounds Lorellei had left.

Free of his enemy, Myrkdaga fell into a dive, the fastest he had ever performed, seeking the blue blade falling beneath him. At the last second, as the ground hurtled to meet them both, he caught Lorellei and snapped his wings out to break their fall into a gliding descent that tumbled them into the tree tops. As impact approached, Myrkdaga cradled Lorellei in his claws, tipped onto his back, and broke the force of the crash landing with his own body.

After a second of allowing himself to be stunned, Myrkdaga shook his head with a growl, clearing away the stars that danced before his vision. Delicately, he opened his claws to reveal the crumpled form of Lorellei, shaking like a leaf. He set the Eldarkind on the ground, where he did not rise, but instead sat, a gibbering wreck.

Myrkdaga surveyed their surroundings whilst he waited for his companion to regain his senses. They had fallen far from the battle, it seemed. He could hardly smell fire or dragons here, and he could not see any sign of flames through the trees. They were on the outskirts of Ednor, he surmised. He looked back down at Lorellei, who was managing to clamber to his feet with the support of a tree trunk, though still shaking.

"I thought I was dead," Lorellei stuttered. "Thank you."

"Anytime," Myrkdaga said gruffly. "Thanks for your help, too. Without your quick thinking and bravery—or foolishness—we would both be dead now."

Lorellei nodded. His face was as pale as the moon.

"The battle is not over. Are you ready? We still have more to do."

Lorellei straightened and coughed. He took a deep breath, and met Myrkdaga's eyes. The fear was still there, and exhaustion was beginning to show, but there was determination, too. "I'm ready."

The cost could be counted when dawn came anew. More broken, blackened buildings. More bodies. More injured to tend to.

Farran and Tarrell walked amongst the smouldering ruins in silence. Both were exhausted after a long and sleepless night. They had watched into the darkness, but Cies had not returned after their sustained and organised defence.

"He is gone for now, at least," murmured Farran. "He could not stand before us."

"We were nearly spent also."

"Cies does not know that. We presented a strong and unified front to him. He will know there are easier victims to terrorize, not least because he will be severely weakened, both in body and in leadership. He has much work to do before he can challenge us again."

"Where is he now?"

"I do not know," Farran rumbled.

"What would you do, if you were he?"

Farran paused. "I would regain my strength, and I would ensure no division in my clan. This defeat will weaken him. Dragons do not follow loss and defeat; only strength and success in battle. He will need to prove himself again to his followers."

"Surely, this means they will attack again?" Tarrell stopped, aghast. *We cannot sustain this.*

Farran stopped also, and met his eye. "He will not attack here." The implication was clear.

Tarrell shut his eyes momentarily and swallowed. In his mind's eye, he relived the past two battles, and knew no others stood a chance of resisting Cies as they had. "It will be a massacre," he said through gritted teeth.

"It is inevitable."

Tarrell shook his head. He refused to believe it, yet he knew it to be true. They had managed to save themselves, but nothing could be done for those in Cies's path.

"We must gather our kin. We cannot continue as we are."

"We are too isolated here," Tarrell addressed his kin and Farran's, who watched him with shadowed eyes and hunched shoulders.

"As you know, our sole purpose is to rebuild the pact, to ensure our true enemies lay sleeping, and the peace of our realm and others is saved. We can only accomplish this by defeating Cies to unite our land and three races in peace once more. However, we cannot do this alone." He paused, to meet the eyes of those before him. Their gazes bored into him. He could feel the weight of their losses as his own.

"After the events of the past days, Cies will not return here. We are safe for now. Yet, he will choose easier prey. Humans who cannot evade or repel him. We cannot remain here and allow innocents to suffer when we have the power to vanquish him. It is our duty, under the terms of our pact, broken as it may be, and I intend to uphold it."

Dragons rumbled their assent, and Eldarkind nodded, but many looked doubting. He could understand why. Their victories had cost them much.

"Will you follow Farran and I away from Ednor, to help in whatever way we may?"

TWENTY TWO

The messenger was clearly an Eldarkind in disguise. His hair was dark brown, but sleek and shiny, and his face was covered in uncharacteristic stubble. Unlike the Eldarkind messengers who came before him, he wore the clothes of a human messenger, and carried the royal seal that would grant him unbarred access to the king's own confidence. Yet, the slender set of his jaw was unmistakable. Soren ushered him in, casting a glance at the empty corridor outside. His guards, facing forwards and staring into nothing, closed the door behind him.

The messenger sagged with relief as the door snapped shut. Soren poured him a hot drink from the kettle by the fire, so he could warm against the winter chill that permeated inside the castle as relentlessly as always. A plate of steaming food arrived minutes later, and Soren fidgeted, waiting for him to finish eating. The last mouthful was barely in the Eldarkind's mouth before Soren asked, "What news?"

The Eldarkind swallowed the last morsel and rose to his feet to execute a sharp bow, despite his obvious exhaustion. "Sire. Allow me to introduce myself. I am Sendari and I travel at the behest of Lord Tarrell." He explained of the attacks on Ednor. The news was bleak. Death tolls, destruction, and many injured; Sendari spared no details, and by the end of his recount, Soren gripped the arms of his chair with white knuckles.

"This explains why I am unable to scry with Lord Tarrell?" he questioned.

Sendari confirmed his suspicion. "Much has been destroyed. There is not a mirror or pool left from which to scry in Ednor. That is why Lord Tarrell sent me. I travelled without stopping to reach you as soon as possible."

Soren frowned. "This is ill news indeed. I am sorry for your losses. I have had no word of further attacks. Does this mean Cies is vanquished and will trouble Caledan no more?"

His heart sunk as Sendari replied. "It is unlikely, Sire. Lords Tarrell and Farran believe he will choose an easier target to allow him to consolidate his power after a humiliating defeat at our hands, and that means an attack on your people. He may well have already attacked. I rode here without delay, but your human messengers are not so fast. News will be slow to come, or it may not come at all."

"We are vulnerable, then." Soren sighed. "We do not know where he will strike, or when. And yet it matters not; we cannot defeat him."

"We are only vulnerable in isolation," Sendari cautioned. "We must work together in this, my Lord urges you. I come at Lords Tarrell and Farran's behest because they wish to negotiate a relocation of both races to Pandora. We are isolated and vulnerable, too, but they believe by working together, we can succeed."

A relocation, Soren pondered.

"Our people are not yet convinced it is the best option," Sendari admitted, biting his lip. "The dragons are all for it, being— pardon me for saying—a bold and more confrontational race. My people are more cautious. We have never before abandoned our sanctuary in Ednor, and many are loathe to do so now. Lords Tarrell and Farran request your opinion on this matter with great urgency."

"I am in two minds myself," Soren replied. "I believe our best chance lies in unification, and a relocation to a stronghold like Pandora makes great sense. Together, we could defend a position of strength. We have the fortifications, resources, and position.

"However, there is too much discord at present sowed to act on this." He explained about the growing intolerance and even hatred towards both dragon and Eldar races, but his words were brief. Sendari had his own knowledge of this, first hand. "Peace is barely holding. I fear a coup or worse, and any proposals of an alliance have so far been shouted down most strongly. Take this news back to Tarrell and ensure him I support him fully and will do all I can to ensure we three races can work together. On my part, it requires great tact to orchestrate. I will do my best. Ensure he can scry with me soon—I would speak with him and Farran. I am gravely concerned."

Soren summoned Behan to share the news the moment Sendari departed for Ednor. However, the steward was not as responsive as Soren had hoped.

"You cannot be glad for the attacks upon Ednor, surely?" Soren asked, dreading the answer. "You cannot celebrate the weakening of Eldarkind."

Behan did not respond to deny it.

"You do not count them as friends?"

"No!" said Behan, and scowled most uncharacteristically. "Where have they been throughout the years of your mother's and grandfather's reign? Hiding in the mountains whilst our people fought and died when the Roherii invaded."

"They are a peaceful folk, and not bound to die for us, and why should they? Surely, the fact they are willing to abandon their homeland and stand with us, when they themselves are attacked, proves they are our allies?" Soren knew he was getting angry, for he could feel his cheeks reddening and could not keep the scowl from his own face, but he fixed Behan in his gaze and tried to remain calm. Losing his temper would not help.

Doubt crept into Behan's face, and he tapped his fingers together. "I cannot say, Sire."

"These are our allies," Soren pressed. "Remember, they have come to our aid in times of gravest danger before, unasked and unpaid. They have laid down their lives with us, because we are their ally. And now, they are prepared—and preparing—to do so again, despite their homes being devastated, and despite many wanting to stay 'hiding in the mountains', as you say. Everything they hold dear is gone, perhaps, and still, they have the courage to stand hand in hand with us in this. How can they be evil? Have you ever known them to be thus? Is this gesture an evil one?"

"No," said Behan, reluctantly.

"I should think not," said Soren determinedly. "So, why do you distrust them now? Of all people, I trust you highest." Soren softened his tone. It was not lost on him the absurdity of a man of his age chastising an elder, whether he was king or not. "You are wise beyond your many years, and well-versed in our history—our shared histories."

"It is hard to know who is friend and who is foe in these troubled times," Behan admitted.

"They are not our enemy," said Soren simply, with a shrug. He could not shrug off his concern, however. He knew he owed a great debt to Behan for his support in earlier troubles: for regaining his throne from his usurping Uncle Zaki, and for supporting him doggedly when storm clouds of treason were brewing in his attempts to stave off an uprising and hunt down Zaki. Without Behan's support, he would have failed in all tasks. Without Behan's support, he would no doubt be dead now, captured and executed by Zaki.

Soren could not shake the apprehension that grew at potentially distancing his most staunch supporter, and someone he trusted so deeply, but Behan's opinions were growing dangerously intolerant. If it were true of his greatest supporter, what did it say of others? If Behan did not support him, who else would be like-minded?

As they feasted in the hall that night, Soren felt in a bubble on the top table, set aside from the usual revelry and casting a suspicious eye over all who attended. Their smiles were friendly and their eyes shone with merriment, but to him, all seemed cold and calculating, and Soren could feel a palpable tension. *Am I imagining things?*

Barclay slid into the chair beside him. Lost in thought, Soren started at the interruption, but smiled with relief at who had joined him. "Well met, Barclay."

Barclay replied with his usual lopsided grin, and slouched in the chair, reaching forward to grab a chicken thigh, which he picked at idly. "It's not hard to see you have something on your mind, Soren. What ails you?"

In hushed tones, careful to not be overheard by anyone, Soren recounted his meetings with Sendari and Behan, and his fears that his support was dwindling in this crucial time.

"Will anyone try and rise against me?" he asked Barclay.

Barclay tossed his bone aside and cleaned his fingers meticulously on a napkin before tossing it in a crumpled heap on the table. "Well, you know you can count on me, on House Walbridge, I mean. Father is still lord, of course, but he's getting on a bit now, and not what he once was. I command a good deal of respect from our men, and I am set to succeed him."

"Thank you," Soren said, throwing a grateful smile to his friend. *Who would have thought I could count on House Walbridge first and foremost*, he mused. "I am fairly sure I can count on the rest of House Balaur to support me. Uncle Andor and Cousin Ilyas have ever been good to me. The other houses are bound to me by loyalty or ward, but I feel it counts for so little in these testing times. I feel these bring out the best and worst in men."

"I can toast to that," said Barclay wryly. "Don't forget the womenfolk, though. They're not as sweet as they appear. It's a good thing House Orrell is so small. Lady Elsard certainly fancies herself for queen, though gladly no one else thinks it. She'd be a mean and shrew-like ruler." He pulled a comical face of disgust, but wrinkled his nose at Soren's grim response. "Oh, come, I meant a jest. She would not dare. She's ambitious, not stupid."

"Mmm," replied Soren. "Perhaps, I should up my guard, or get my food tasted." He sighed.

"You could be worrying too much."

Soren forced out a chuckle. "I might be, but I've been around this court too long to be naive to what happens. I have always relied on Behan to deal with any plots, and yet his demeanor worries me. Speaking of which, I have not heard such whispers in a while, which is suspicious in itself. Is he hiding things from me?" Soren knew the question was rhetorical, and Barclay could not answer, but he wished he could discern the truth. *Is it omission or neglect on Behan's part? Either way, I am vulnerable.* Soren did not fancy eating anything now, and looked at his plate grimly.

Beside him, Barclay stood, and clapped him on the shoulder. "Worry not, Sire. I'll keep my eyes and ears open, and my nose to the ground. I wouldn't concern yourself. You're king, and it's as simple as that. If they don't like it, they have to lump it. That's the perk!"

Soren forced out a smile as Barclay turned away, but it fell as soon as his friend left. He swallowed. The pressure was palpable. *I have to act, but how? I cannot let this insecurity rule me, for that alone will be my downfall. Yet, how can I plow ahead with a course of action so vehemently opposed by so many others? What's worse: insanity or incompetence?* He hoped they did not talk about him like this, but Soren knew it was a futile wish.

TWENTY THREE

Sustenance, and a lot of it, was needed to recoup after the defeats at Ednor. Another day and another village was burnt to the ground and all its livestock eaten; bones and all.

Cies looked upon his clan with suspicion. He knew they would be questioning him behind his back—it was only a matter of time before he discovered it—and he would not suffer dissent. Their eyes fixed upon him slyly, watching and waiting for him to prove himself, and the biggest looking for their opening to challenge him.

One dared challenge him for the biggest cow, rushing forward with wings outstretched, and teeth bared in a hiss. Cies defended his prey, roaring deafeningly loud and pinning his opponent down by the neck. He grasped the dragon in his powerful jaws and shook it like prey, tightening his vice-like grip until the dragon could struggle no more for its breathlessness. Cies ached with the effort, but he would not show it.

He released the other dragon after a pronounced pause, and met the eyes of all those who looked up from their feasts to regard the spectacle. His bold stare sent the message he wanted. *Challenge me and I will crush you.* Cies tossed aside his challenger like a twig and it backed away hissing, with hate in its eyes.

Cies turned back to his meal, knowing he would not be challenged again—at least, that night—and glad for it. The cold hastened the weakening of Bahr's magic, it seemed, for he felt somewhat worse for wear.

They had flown down from the mountains to milder climes, where the forests sheltered their plump prey and would guard them from the worst of the howling winds. There would be no sleep, merely a few hours of laying still and resting with open eyes and alert minds to rest their muscles before moving on, but it was a stop they needed nonetheless. It was still too cold, even out of the cold heights. Cies knew the south was warmer, and he did not want to fly back to Kotyir; despite those isles being an oasis of warmth and sustenance, they were in the midst of cold bleakness. Besides, to fly back to their homeland would be defeat to him, and he could not tolerate that.

His plan was to move south; closer to the warmth that would enliven and sustain them, not this cold that stripped them of their strength and sapped them of their energy. He told his followers just that, in no uncertain terms, proposing they move south and replenish themselves in warmer climes.

"You would flee like a coward?" said a dragon big enough for Cies not to challenge him at that.

Cies snarled instead. "How dare you insult me. No, I have a better plan, one that will aid us as it weakens our enemy." He paused, waiting for the other dragon to subside. It drew its head back into the shadows and he continued. "We ought to wait for Farran to weaken himself—and all those worms who follow him—in the cold north, whilst we grow strong in the warm south. The lands there will be rich and plentiful." His voice was silky and smooth as it painted a picture none of them could resist.

"They'll be full of prey for the taking—fat, juicy and plentiful—and humans for conquering, and we can return in the high spring, waxing whilst our enemies wane. They will cower before us; them, and their little Eldar friends who think their clever magic tricks can defeat or intimidate us." He scoffed.

"We have already shown Caledan we are unbeatable. No human may stand before us. Now, let us conquer new lands without anything to get in our way. Let us show every human we meet our ferocity and strength. No longer are we bound to such weak races as humans and Eldarkind. No longer do we have to suffer this humiliation." Cies' grin stretched wide over white, serrated teeth. "Who will fly south with me?"

Roars drowned him out. Smugly, he sat on his haunches and watched his followers work themselves into a blood-lust-like frenzy.

They flew through the night, so energised were they, following the March Mountains south, until new lights were spotted on the horizon. They twinkled in the distance. An invite. Cies was full; his stomach strained from how much he had eaten. Now, though, he had a message to send to the humans and to his clan. He was unbeatable. No one could stand before him.

TWENTY FOUR

The bells and horns rang out deep in the night, rousing Eve from her slumber with a curse, as, bleary-eyed, she realised what they could herald. A frisson of fear jolted her awake in an instant. *Please, be a false alarm.*

The fire burnt low in the grate, giving her just enough light to see by. She threw on a jumble of clothes, donned some light armour and snatched up her sword, which was now always close to hand. As she ran downstairs, the rest of the house was alive with noise, already rousing, and when she reached the courtyard, her father was waiting. Men carried him out on a makeshift palanquin, but he was struggling to sit up and insisting he was well enough to walk or ride. Her cheeks blushed with embarrassment for him.

"Let him down," she ordered. The men complied without delay and soon her father stood, held up by two of his guards. He was as haggard and drawn as ever. "Come, Eve, we must leave."

"I cannot," she said to him. "In your stead, I am the Lady of Arlyn, and I must see everyone safe." She drew close to him. "I am protected, do not worry," she breathed into his ear. She prayed the wards would hold, and that they would do as she asked. They encircled not only her, but every living thing within Arlyn's walls, drawing upon the power of nature to sustain them.

"Be safe, my little dove."

She pecked him on the cheek, and nodded to his escort. "Quickly, now. Take Lord Karn to safety. Ensure no-one you encounter is left behind. Go."

She turned away, surveying who else was in the courtyard. Luke aided his mother across the hard ground. Eve strode across to them, and greeted Luke with a sharp nod. "You know what you must do?"

"I do." Luke was equally grim. It was Luke's task to escort the people of Arlyn to the caves and protect them from harm.

"Keep them safe."

"I will."

They shared a long look with much unspoken, but it was time to part; Eve had a different task. She swallowed and turned away.

There was no time to watch as her father was led away, or as Luke shepherded people down the quickest path. Eve mounted Alia without delay and rode for the town with the few guards who had insisted on her need for protection.

Arlyn was already well alight as she rode from the courtyard; the high walls protected the castle from the winds, but they also hid the town from view. She could hear no screams, because the roar of the inferno, and something much worse, drowned out all else.

Eve fought back the rising panic that clawed through her with memories of that terrible night of Ednor. *It's real. They're here.*

She could not help but pause under the shadow of the gates in awe and terror before her. Dragons, illuminated by sickly orange light from below, dove upon the town, wreathing it in jets of flames that instantly ignited whatever they touched. After a moment of hesitation, Eve forced down her panic, and rode for the walls where Hoarth awaited.

Hoarth indeed stood atop the walls, sweating in the heat as waves of scalding air rolled off the growing inferno.

"Nock! Release! Nock! Release!" his command rolled down the line of archers upon the walls. They loosed quick successions of arrows, peppering the dragons, but their volleys soared away into the dark, and skittered harmlessly off dragon scales. Eve took only a moment to appraise the situation. *Hopeless.* "Captain, order a retreat."

"I protest, my lady! We cannot abandon the town."

"What would you have me do?" she snapped. "Our arrows are clearly of no use. We cannot fight them with swords—we cannot fight them at all. Sound the retreat. The town is lost, and our people must be our priority. We can rebuild a town, but we cannot bring back the dead."

Hoarth failed to hide his scowl, but saluted her and signalled for a retreat.

"How many are dead?" Eve asked, as archers just about managed to form an orderly scramble off the wall.

"None of mine yet," replied Hoarth, as he and Eve filed from the wall last of all. "Report!"

"One."

"Two."

"Three."

His archers replied by number, until Hoarth was satisfied they were all present. "By some miracle, we are alive yet, though some bear injuries," he said with gritted teeth.

Eve hid a small smile. *Perhaps, my wards work after all.* "That is lucky beyond measure," she said. "Fall back to the caves, now. Conduct a sweep of the town and bring any stragglers with you."

Hoarth snapped a salute and bellowed at his men to form up. In seconds, they had disappeared into the chaos.

Now, with no one to distract her, the panic rose again as Eve realised how far the fires had spread, how tall they towered and how close they were. She fought to keep her breathing steady and push aside the rising panic that inexorably crawled through her.

She closed her eyes for a moment, but that made it worse. All too suddenly, she was aware of the heat pressing in from all sides. Beside her, Alia whinnied and pranced, with the whites of her eyes rolling and her mouth frothing. She tugged at her halter with increasing strength.

"Woah, girl, woah." Eve rushed to sooth her. "Not long, girl. Nearly safe, girl," she said, as much to Alia as to herself. She mounted Alia and untied her, gesturing to the guards who waited still in the saddle for her. "Come, we'll do one last sweep through the main streets." *The side streets would be overtaken by fire by now*, she knew. She shuddered at the thought of burning debris raining down on them.

Squeezing her heels into Alia, her horse bolted forward, needing no encouragement, and only Eve's confident and steady hands kept her under control as they raced through the town. Thatched roofs burned merrily as far as the eye could see, and slate roofs cracked under the heat, already caving in. Shutters were blown out and doors were gaping maws into fiery bellied homes. The air was scalding hot and choking with ash, smoke, and debris, and floating specks created pockmarks of black on their garments. Eve could not help but notice when they alighted on her hair and skin. They caused no damage or pain.

The ward is working, she realised with relief. Smoke blocked any hint of the night sky. They could see nothing, but the roars of dragons wheeling above them, and the ear-splitting spontaneous combustion of their fiery jets igniting the town were deafening. They were not safe yet.

They rode on through the empty streets, meeting more stragglers the closer they got to the old mines. Eve and her men chivvied them on urgently, sacrificing their horses for those more in need. Alia was soon burdened with an old woman and two children whilst Eve ran on foot beside her. Eve's men followed suit.

Shingle beaches met them on the far side of the town, where it gave way to the still and calm waters of the lake. Standing in contrast to the chaos behind them, The lake was glass still and as peaceful as any other night. The night sky was clear and bright here; the moonlight cool in contrast to the dirty orange at their backs. This was the most exposed part. Eve looked back towards the town, hoping the wall of smoke would shield them for long enough.

They straggled in silence; a long, gangly line, around the shore of the lake, until they reached the small pricks of black in the cliff face that signalled the old mine workings. Into the dark, dank cave they went, ushered by Eve and her guards, down into the black bowels of the earth. It was lit further in where the light could not be seen from outside, and it was far more welcoming, with friendly, though fearful, faces waiting.

Men lined the passage, offering reassurances and direction to those who entered. Many were hysterically sobbing or in silent shock. Eve followed and was last of all to reach the large cave that the mines snaked off. It was warm, dry, and well lit; and safe, thanks to her instruction. Newly cut wood lined it, shoring and doubly shoring areas to make certain they were safe.

Her people were not quiet, but neither did they talk. Instead, a fearful murmur echoed and whispers chased around the cavernous space; a thousand voices of worry for every one. Some had already begun the process of salving and bandaging burns and cuts with whatever they had to hand.

As Eve moved through them, they greeted her with deference and many clasped her hands, muttering fervent thanks. She smiled back at them with smiles as hollow and scared as their own, whilst laying a gentle hand on a shoulder, head or hand as she passed. *Now they understand the danger of which I spoke*, she thought, though she wished it had not come to pass. She had never wanted to be proven right less.

Her father greeted her with relief. Set aside from most, he had relative privacy. She greeted him, but moved on, searching the grubby faces until with relief, she spied Luke. Relief blossomed in her chest and she rushed over to clasp hands with him for the briefest moment. Even in her fear, his mother gave her the smallest of smiles before her brows scrunched and her mouth twisted once more in concern.

"Thank goodness you're both well," said Eve.

"And you," said Luke. She could hear the fervour in his voice, and longed to sit and rest, but it was not over yet.

"I must go back. I must see if there is anyone else," she said, careful to not be overheard.

"You cannot go back out there," Luke hissed. "It would be madness!"

"I have no choice. I could not live with myself if any were harmed."

"I'm coming with you, then." Luke scrambled to his feet.

"You should not leave your mother."

"Go with her," said Nora sternly.

Eve smiled, grateful, and squeezed Nora's hand in thanks before they left the strange homeliness of the cave and dove back into the cold, dark, and choking night. From their vantage point across the lake, it was clear to see that Arlyn was devastated, or it would be, by the time the fires had burnt out. The tower of fire and smoke reached as far as they could see into the sky, and the entire town was alight, it seemed.

There could still be people trapped. She had no way of knowing, but her conscience would not let her rest. *What if the ward fails?* Those inside the caves had had miraculous escapes, whether they realised it or not yet, but she could not be sure how long the protection would last.

As they prepared to mount to return to the town, darkness swept over them, blotting out all light. A dragon as big as the sky soared over them, wheeling back towards the town. With a screech, it burst a jet of flame into the air.

Eve shrank back into the shadows of the cave.

"It's not safe," said Luke grimly, moving back into the shadows too and sheltering her with his body; his instincts taking over. "We cannot go. They will see us."

He was right, Eve hated to admit. If any lived out there, Eve would have to trust to her wards that they would find safety.

It felt like an age until the cold, grey light of day arrived, and with it, silent apprehension of what lay outside. A sleepless, never ending night filled with the sound of crackling, spitting and roaring of fire, and the hiss of the rains that eventually came was a nightmarish lullaby.

Eve was first to venture back to Arlyn. Fires burned plentifully, though the worst was over. Stone houses were piles of rubble on the ground, and wooden buildings nothing more than charred ruins. The dragons at least, were gone.

Eve sent for all those who were fit and able to come from the caves. Immediately, lines were set up to pass water along to dampen the fires, in whatever vessels could be salvaged. It was a lengthy, tiring process. Fires burnt out before they could be put out, but it needed to be done.

Whilst they busied themselves with that, Luke was in charge of accounting for all the townsfolk. Of all its residents, only five were unaccounted for, presumed dead. Eve said a silent prayer, grateful for her ward, which undoubtedly saved a huge number of lives. Her ward only protected against the dragon attack however, and it did not include other ailments; so, there were many injuries to tend to, from falls to cuts and scrapes. They were better injuries than the alternatives she had witnessed at Ednor.

The keep was mostly intact as its walls were so strong and thick the fire could not penetrate them. Yet, many of the outbuildings were destroyed: servants' quarters, kitchens, and stables. Eve ordered the injured to be treated in the castle, for it was the only solid space left in the town. Healing supplies were eked out as far as they could go; what had been left in the town was destroyed. People took only what they could carry, or nothing at all, so many were without food, water, clothing, and shelter.

It was a dire situation to be in, in the middle of winter. Those who had space in undamaged buildings gladly shared it, including Eve, who gave over her room to a family with four young girls. They were naive of the dangers of the previous night, and thrilled to be spending the night in a castle despite the smoke damage to all the furniture.

As the sun began to set, Eve set off to the woods for some moments of quiet recollection, away from the hubbub, where she could begin to solve the problem of how to keep her people warm, dry, and fed without any shelter or food. But as she came upon the clearing where she had laid her spell, it was much changed. Every tree was dead, bare, and barren. Every blade of grass was shrivelled to nothing. Every plant. Every flower. Every moss. Every fungi. Every living thing within a radius as far as she could see was decimated.

This was the price of my ward, Eve realised with sadness, placing her hand upon the lifeless bark of a tree. *So much energy was needed.* She had not realised just what it would cost to protect her people from the dragons' attack.

Eve sunk to the floor, wrapping her hands in the desiccated mosses. There was no life here now, only freezing water that pooled around her hands and knees.

"I'm sorry." She knew the dead things could not hear her, but she was. "I'll make this right, somehow."

TWENTY FIVE

Soren read Eve's letter. It shook in his trembling hand. She wrote of the attack in Arlyn, sparing few details, and other small villages in Arrow county. Her news told of the utter devastation and many dead in the county, though the people of Arlyn had been spared thanks to her wards. She requested a lengthy list of aid: food, healing provisions, cloth, and all manner of practical things that had been lost. He did not spare much time to re-read her requests as he knew in the chill of winter, they would need such things and soon.

"Make a copy of this list and send as much as we can spare, immediately," he instructed.

He pondered a moment on his cousin's plight. It was hard to think of Pandora lying in ruins and hopelessly without provisions or shelter, and yet, that was what she faced in Arlyn. He had hoped it would not come to this, not after what she had endured in Ednor, but it seemed the fates had a different plan for her. He would send all he could, he knew, but it would be only a fraction of what was needed.

His frustration grew as he read more news of the day, for most of the other reports mirrored Arlyn's: attacks and devastation heading south along the March Mountains, and struggling villages and townships elsewhere that had previously been destroyed requesting similar help. He could take no more.

"Summon the council at once!" he shouted to the messenger who waited outside, and strode from his chambers.

As his lords arrived in various states of hurriedness and some looking decidedly rumpled, Soren paced, filled with anger and in silence as they sat. Not one word was spoken and the tension was palpable. They sensed him, and he sensed them.

"Well met, Lords, Ladies," Soren greeted them, his voice

clipped. "We have urgent business today." Today, he would not waste breath on pleasantries. He explained without preamble the devastating dragon attack on Arlyn and Arrow county.

A murmur arose at his words, and a shocked babble grew as those before him wondered at it amongst themselves.

"We must act now," said Soren, glaring at them all. This was not optional any longer, and he would not suffer their objections and dithering. "We must ally with the dragons and Eldarkind against this."

The expected disagreement arose, and he cut them off.

"Silence," he said, in a dangerously brittle tone, and slammed Eve's letter on the table. Those closest to him jumped. He read a few choice excerpts. "Would you like this to be your kin? Your homes? A village might be expendable to you, but not to me. A hundred villages might be expendable to you, but not to me. A town? A city? Pandora? Arlyn was defensible, and it lies in ruins. Pandora is defensible. It too will suffer the same fate unless we act. What stops us from becoming the next target? Blind luck. Would you like to be burnt alive in your beds?"

Lady Elsard flinched at that, and all eyes flicked away from his searching glare, unwilling to meet it.

"They. Will. Come. It may be tomorrow. It may be a year, but they will come for your homes and they will come for Pandora. Would you look to Caledan's utter destruction because you were too proud to work with those who have ever been our greatest allies?

"I ask you to support me. Have I ever led you wrong? I may be young, but I have been sorely tested, and each time, I have led Caledan to victory and peace. I have shown my character to you. I have shown my worth. I will do whatever it takes to save Caledan, whether you support it or not. I do this for all of us. The choice is yours: stand with me, or burn."

Barclay rose with a scrape of his chair. His face was closed and solemn. "I will stand with you."

A shadow of fury crossed his father Willam's face at Barclay's insubordination, but he stood, too. "If my son stands, then I stand first," he said. "My lands and my people are at stake, but I will not give my command to the Eldarkind!"

"Hear, hear!" came the sudden outcry, and his indignation was mirrored by all around the table.

"Command is given to no man, or Eldarkind," Soren said, though he thought them foolish for not wanting to accept the advice and knowledge of those far wiser than them. *This will be something to overcome, but not today.*

"Each shall have order of their own command, as has always been the case. I will manage the Eldarkind and the dragons. I will ensure they act in our best interests." It was a promise he wasn't sure he could keep, but the mood changed in the room perceptively and suddenly, those who a moment ago had shook their heads were instead nodding.

Lady Elsard stood next, slowly, and pointedly. She looked around the room regally, as if she expected them all to hang off her every word. "I will support this, if there is the means to kill the dragons by our own hand. I will not stand huddled in the shadows with the womenfolk and children awaiting the grace of the Eldarkind to save us. I want power in my own hands and in the hands of my men to deal death to these abominations."

Her sentiments were echoed by others.

Soren held up his hand to stem the flow of conversation. "So, am I to infer that as long as no Eldarkind interfere with your command, and as long as we have means to fight on our own terms the dragons who harry us, you will all stand for this?"

"Aye," came the many-bodied response.

Soren rushed back to his quarters at once, having sent away the council to summon their forces to Pandora. He had one last thing to do before the ball would be set rolling, unable to be undone: invite the Eldarkind and the dragons to Pandora. The scrying mirror now worked, and Soren called forth the magic.

Tarrell was swift to appear, and they exchanged terse greetings.

"The worst has come to pass," said Soren grimly.

Tarrell's shoulders slumped. "I have been unable to scry these last days. Where?"

"Arlyn. Much of Arrow county. Now, the attacks continue, moving south." He recounted the details once more.

Tarrell did not respond for some time and stood, shaking his head. "I knew the risks, but I did not expect this. Cies has gone over and above to exact his revenge. I feel responsible. If we had not driven them off, if we had killed them, instead, this would have been prevented."

"Do not blame yourself," Soren said. "Casualties in Arlyn were limited, thanks to Eve's wards. It could have been far worse. There was no way to prevent it."

Tarrell nodded, but his face was lined with grief and guilt. He stirred at last, from his reverie. "Your accounts match mine, at least. I scried Cies but a few minutes before you happened to call for me. He appears to be moving south, and swiftly. They follow the coast, but do not fly over the sea. I have spoken to Farran, and he is adamant it confirms his theory they fly south to warmer climes where they can grow stronger. The cold of our northern climate weakens them. Farran thinks we are rid of him for now, but that he will return."

"Then we must act, before he does."

"Agreed."

"You are prepared to relocate to Pandora?"

"At once. We can arrive within but two days."

"Then come without delay, please. We will host the dragons in the castle grounds and receive the Eldarkind at the castle." Soren did not mention that was because he did not trust his lords to welcome their new allies.

"I thank you for your generosity, Soren. We will see you on the morning after tomorrow." Tarrell drew back, about to end their connection.

"Wait!" Soren held his hand up. "Make a grand entrance," he said. "My people have grown to fear the dragons greatly, and even your people to some extent. They will be suspicious. They will expect savagery. Make the grandest entrance you can, so we may persuade them otherwise."

Tarrell regarded him for a moment, his expression inscrutable.

"I'm ashamed to ask what will be obvious to you, but there is no room for error." Soren's cheeks began to burn. It felt ridiculous to ask a guest to behave, as though they would not; especially, those as noble as the Eldarkind or the dragons, and yet Soren could not afford for this to go wrong.

Tarrell smiled sadly. "I hope the tensions between our three races will soon be behind us. Certainly, the dragonkin and my own kin are much closer after our shared battles. I am sure we can unify all three races once more, when we are together in Pandora."

Soren hoped he was right.

Within a day, news spread through Pandora about their incoming allies and the forthcoming celebrations to welcome them. Soren hoped they would be treated with respect, not feared or harmed. He was nervous, though. The mood was still volatile, or so it seemed to him, but he kept second guessing himself until he was not sure of anything.

As the Eldarkind began to arrive upon dragon-back, making just a grand an entrance as he had hoped, Pandora's citizens flocked to the streets to welcome them. At first, screams of fear rang out, for the approaching dragons were huge and fearsome. But as they alighted outside the city, and the Eldarkind dismounted and formed ranks for their civilised parade to the castle, the mood turned to celebration, much to Soren's relief, as the citizens realised the dragons and the Eldarkind were no threat. In the light of day, their grand entrance into the city left no uncertainty; these were intelligent and benevolent races, not the terrifying savages that destroyed towns and villages.

The noblemen and women of the court greeted their new guests extremely civilly, much to Soren's relief, and they dined and feasted that night in the great hall, with great braziers burning and the vast doors thrown open to the dragons. The dragon crowded in the courtyard to dine on fresh meat, out of sight of their human guests.

It went as well as Soren could have hoped, and he formally welcomed the Eldarkind and the dragons to Pandora. In turn, Tarrell and Farran went to great lengths to state their peaceful and friendly intentions; Tarrell much more wordily than Farran, as was his nature. Soren breathed a huge sigh of relief as the day was done.

TWENTY SIX

Soren, Tarrell, and Farran met the following day in the great hall; the only place in the castle that Farran could fit through the doors. He basked happily before the huge open fire, rumbling with contentment as they reflected with relief at the success of their arrival.

"Perhaps, there is little to fear now that we are here," said Tarrell.

"I am glad you are here regardless," replied Soren. "We are in need of hope as much as help. If my people see you as our allies—and I hope they already do—it will give them great hope to know that we fight fire with fire."

Farran grinned, revealing great, jagged teeth. "Fight we shall. I look forward to the day I next meet that cowardly worm, Cies. It shall be his last."

Soren was not convinced by the dragon's bravado and confidence. He looked to Tarrell. "Can we do this? Is it possible?" he asked frankly. "I have trawled through our oldest records. Nowhere can I find mention of how dragons can be defeated. Rather, the opposite. The only way we could survive, judging by records from King Beren's reign, was to ally with the dragons."

"It is possible... with our help," said Tarrell. He explained their strategy from the previous battle with Cies, and, most crucially, how the old blue ice-fire magic had crippled their enemy. "It is a weapon most fearsome that it seems they cannot stand against. This, and working together, are our best hopes. We stand a good chance."

Farran rumbled his agreement.

"How do we procure some of this ice-fire magic, and what is it?" asked Soren.

"It is fire infused with ice magic, and it has the power to

quench a dragon's inner fire. In large quantities, I have no doubt it could kill. In the quantities we have, it physically hurts them. It allows our blades to pierce their hides with ease, which human weapons cannot do at all.

"This magic is a lost art in some ways; our oldest blades are created with such spells imbued. We no longer have the knowledge, or the time, to create such weapons before they shall next be needed. However, my smiths have already experimented successfully to create the essence of the ice-fire in isolation. It can be used to coat non-magical weapons and thus, gives them the capabilities of an ice-fire blade until the effects wear off."

"This means that we could use it?" Soren leapt at the chance to have a weapon that could make a difference in this fight. He felt helpless otherwise.

Tarrell hesitated. "It is a secret of the highest nature. Moreover, it is not given freely away, for it has the power to harm other living things, also. We cannot give it into hands that may misuse it." He fiddled with his furs, tugging them closer and folding his arms.

"But we need it," Soren replied. His brows furrowed. "Without it, we are as near as useless. We won't be able to fight Cies. We'll be nothing more than sitting ducks! I won't have my people fight to die, but neither can I command them to retreat. They will not allow you to fight this battle for us. Sharing this weapon could give us a fair chance. Without it, we have no hope of success. Will you not afford us the chance to defend our homes and our people?"

"I appreciate your problem," Tarrell replied delicately. "However, humans have not exactly demonstrated that they can be trusted to the level we would require to share a weapon of this nature."

Soren's frustration spiked as Tarrell continued.

"We are... intuitive of human nature. We can see how distrustful and fearful your kin are of us—of both our races," he said with a glance towards Farran. "Even now, when they know we are no threat to them. Humans, armed with a weapon that could kill dragons? This could backfire on those who are their allies."

"I beg you, Lord Tarrell. We need this. Without it, we will be utterly useless in the fight to come; nothing more than spectators waiting for our own doom. Please, allow me to show you we can be trusted. I will see to it personally that it is given the highest security and secrecy. On my shoulders be it, if any mishaps occur." Soren stood tall and straight, bearing Tarrell's scrutiny and Farran's, whose great orb of an eye watched him unblinking.

Eventually, Farran huffed, and Tarrell sighed. "We will hold you to that. It is greatly dangerous in the wrong hands."

Soren's spirits lifted with hope. "When may I have some to test?" His fingers twitched with enthusiasm. "I want to try it on swords and arrows, see what can be done with it." His imagination teemed with ideas.

Tarrell held a hand to stymy him. "I have not decided yet. I will consider it."

Soren was forced to swallow his pride and accept Tarrell's decision. *Patience*, he cautioned himself. *It is not a no.*

Their conversation turned back to Cies and where he might be. No further reports had arrived from Caledan that hinted to his whereabouts, but his trail of destruction implied his destination.

"So, you believe he moves south from Caledan, then?" Soren mused once Tarrell and Farran had explained their theory. "Will he attack Roher?"

"He may yet travel that far south, but our best guess is he will return to us to seek out the personal grudge he had on Farran and the clan who remain here in Caledan."

"Wherever he roams, he will be back," growled Farran.

Soren stilled. "I heard reports from the steward yesterday that trade lines are disrupted from north Roher of late. Goods once plentiful are now scarce—and their prices high—and some of the usual traders have not arrived at all this season. We are unable to find certain wares at all. Could Cies and his dragons have something to do with this?"

Tarrell and Farran shared a meaningful look.

"It could be," said Tarrell.

Soren narrowed his eyes. *What is he not telling me?*

"I think needs must. I must scry Cies, and… Arandulus."

"Aye," agreed Farran ominously.

Who? wondered Soren. He discovered soon enough as they retrieved Soren's scrying mirror at Tarrell's behest. A nonplussed servant carried it to the top of the tower where Farran could land to join them, for he could not fit inside the castle.

"*Leitha Cies*," Tarrell said. The mirror swirled black and cloudy until the image cleared, revealing Cies flying over hills of sand and arid desert plains. His scales were dazzled by the sun and in all directions, all that could be seen was an ocean of dunes and barren hills undulating to the horizon.

"He is north of Roher." Tarrell frowned and squinted, leaning into the mirror to try and see any details he could. "Alas, I cannot fathom where. From the direction of the sun, he flies east."

"He flees," Farran scoffed. "Come. He is not worth our time. Search for Her."

"Who is it you seek?" Soren asked, his curiosity thoroughly piqued.

"Arandulus of the Water," Tarrell replied sombrely. "I spoke to you of the elementals rising from their bindings? Bahr was but one. The bonds holding Arandulus in slumber are weakening, and I know She struggles to rise from Her prison. Arandulus sleeps north of Roher, where the sea of sand stretches as far as the eye can see. It is remote, so no human would ever stumble upon Her. And yet, if She has arisen, She could easily cause enough chaos to disrupt the Roherii trade routes."

"Does Cies seek Her?" Farran lifted his head and growled.

Tarrell allowed himself a bark of laughter. "He will not know She sleeps there; or that he passes Her so close. If he did, he would flee as far as he could. She has no love for dragonkin. Arandulus would destroy Cies in a heartbeat, whether he sought to ally with Her or not. He bears the gifts of fire—of Bahr—and that is enough to earn her enmity."

Farran rumbled, darkly amused. "That would save us much trouble."

"*Lessa.*" Tarrell turned back to the mirror. He took a deep breath. *"Leitha… Arandulus ro foss."*

Once more, the mirror plunged into darkness and Tarrell waited with bated breath as it cleared. Soren leaned forward and Farran snaked his head closer.

A great storm. Flashes of lightening upon a darkened landscape that ought to have been bright sunshine, and the glint of light on water where there should have been none. Soren's skin prickled. The mirror sharpened, and he gasped as he saw the watery figure as tall as the heavens stalking through the dunes, followed by a flood of epic proportions.

"No…" whispered Tarrell.

"It is too late. She has risen," growled Farran.

"I don't understand," said Soren.

Tarrell tore his gaze away from the mirror where the figure blazed a trail of watery destruction to Soren. "It is worse than we warned. I told you of the threat from the elementals, but now that they are awakening, it lends even greater urgency to us all. We must defeat Cies to be able to rebuild the pact. And we must mend the pact before we can bind the elementals anew."

Tarrell came to Soren that night as pensive as he had been that afternoon upon discovering Arandulus was free of Her bonds. Soren received him, surprised he had come. Wordlessly, Tarrell handed Soren a small black pouch made of a woven material he had never seen.

Soren opened it and pulled out the small, clear, stoppered bottle inside. It was filled with a blue substance like no other. Neither solid, not liquid, nor gas, it emitted its own blue-white light that undulated around the bottle of its own volition like a living flame, though starved of air it must have been in the container. Soren looked at Tarrell, the question clear in his eyes. The gravity of what he held was not lost upon him.

He was solemn as Soren had not seen him before. "With this gift goes my trust," said Tarrell quietly. "This is but a small sample of our ice-fire. I have my kin preparing more night and day so we shall be ready when the time comes. In the meantime, I entrust this to you for your use only, for any testing you may wish to carry out. Look inside the bag."

Soren did as he was instructed and pulled out two gloves, made of an identical material to the pouch.

"The pouch and gloves are the same material. They are woven of both cloth and spells of protection, so the bottle shall not break, even if you dropped it from the highest tower of this castle. The gloves are a necessary precaution. Wear them when you handle it, or you will come to great harm. Skin is no match for the ice-fire. It will harm dragons and men alike, it is so powerful."

Soren made to put the gloves back in the bag, though he was still captivated by the beauty of the ice-fire. Tarrell caught his wrist before he could move. "Do not let anyone touch this, promise me."

Soren nodded, and held it more gingerly, still worried about breaking it. "I promise I will keep it safe. The Lord Steward will know of somewhere it can be kept, where it shall not be taken or tampered with." He placed the bottle in the back and tightened the drawstring handle, holding it carefully. From the outside, the bag was nondescript; something that the eye would easily pass over. That would serve discretion well, Soren hoped.

TWENTY SEVEN

Soren inspected the dragon's wound cautiously. She radiated warmth in strange contrast to the chill held by the last winds of winter that crept inside his furred cloak. He pulled it closer as he bent forward to peer at the clean rend through her scarlet scales—which oozed violet blood—and the sparks of blue ice-fire that lingered on her still.

She growled, a constant low rumble of discontent, occasionally whimpering with the pain and snarling when the Eldarkind working to heal her prodded too hard, or for too long.

"Tell me what happened, Iolanta," Soren asked.

Iolanta opened one of her ruby red eyes just a crack. "The human threw the essence of ice-fire at me without provocation." She snarled. "I should have roasted him where he stood."

"But you did not," said the Eldarkind, not looking up from her work. "For I was on hand to stop it. An eye for an eye never ends well."

"You are not the one being poisoned by your very bane," Iolanta snarled.

"Peace," her healer whispered, and placed a hand softly on Iolanta.

Iolanta huffed unhappily and smoke puffed from her nostrils.

Soren suppressed a cough. "What happened next?" he prompted.

"I immobilised the pair of them," said the Eldarkind, as if it was as simple as that. "We were in the gardens. I was admiring the view over the great lake from the treetops when I saw the human behaving most furtively. I climbed down to follow him. I recognised the pouch of ice-fire at once, for I have been helping to create it. Before I could ask what he was doing with it, Iolanta appeared and the human attacked. I alerted Lord Tarrell and Farran-visir at once—and yourself by our trusted messenger." She met Soren's eyes almost apologetically.

Soren suppressed a scowl. It did not need to be said that a human messenger would not have acted with discretion on this matter. "Where is the perpetrator now?"

"In the dungeons," said Behan as he arrived with ruddy cheeks. He leaned heavily on his walking staff heaving great breaths as he recovered.

Soren turned immediately. "Do we have his identify? And how on earth he came to possess ice-fire? I charged you to protect it!" he gestured sharply at Behan. "I vouched personally for our good conduct."

Behan shuffled and his eyes did not lift from the ground.

"What is it?" Soren pressed him.

"My nephew," Behan admitted in a voice barely louder than a murmur. "I asked him to carry the ice-fire to Heligan directly, where he has a place for safekeeping anything which needs protecting. My arthritis pains me greatly today and I cannot walk so far or fast. I thought it would be safer to send it with him, for he could carry it to safety far faster than I." Behan bowed his head in shame.

Soren stood in stunned silence for a long moment. "Bedenor did this?"

Behan jerkily nodded. "I do not know why he acted thusly. I told him of its great importance and the urgency of its safekeeping. I have always placed my faith in him."

"You realise the difficult position this puts me in?" Soren said softly. "The dragons may well want an eye for an eye, and I cannot refuse them."

Behan's eyes closed, his brows furrowed, and he bit his lip.

Bedenor prowled around the narrow confines of his cell. The dark, windowless space shrouded him in shadows barely lit by the slow-burning oil lamps hanging outside. "I did it because I do not want to associate with monsters and heathens," he snarled.

Soren could tell he bore a deep-seated anger that had nothing
to do with Iolanta; she had been in the wrong place at the wrong
time. He sighed. "They are not monsters and heathens," he said,
though he knew words would not convince Bedenor, such was his
fervent belief. "They are our allies, and as befits their status, harm to
them is treated as harm to any man, woman, or child under our laws.
You realise this must carry the same weight as if you had attacked a
fellow human?"

Bedenor stopped his pacing to stand squarely in front of
Soren on the other side of the barred gate. His set jaw jutted out
mutinously and his arms were folded under corded shoulders. "I
do."

"And you accept the consequences?"

Bedenor did not answer. *How can he accept the consequences of a
decision he does not agree with?* Soren suppressed another sigh and gritted
his teeth. "So be it. You may await my judgment."

He left without another word and did not look back, in case
his own anger surfaced. Bedenor had sealed his own fate, whether
or not he accepted it. His actions made Soren's own position even
more precarious.

It was Soren himself who had sworn to accept the
consequences of any misdemeanour. What would be his fate? *This
could jeopardize my forces being able to use ice-fire, at the very least.* He did not
like to dwell on what the more severe punishments could be.
Regardless, he had a difficult decision before him: to bring Bedenor
to justice for maiming what most others would see as nothing more
than a beast, or to risk alienating his Eldarkind and dragon allies by
letting Bedenor go, and condoning his actions by association. Either
way, it would cause strife.

"No matter what I do, I will not please everyone, especially
during times of strife such as these," he admitted aloud to himself.
It felt more real to say it, and it made his heart sink even more. *What
else can I do?* He was realising more and more that with every new
conflict in his rule, he would make new friends. And new enemies.
It does not matter what I do, whether I think it right or wrong, they will only

judge me on their own views.

He recalled his rule so far. Scenes of critical decisions flashed past him, as well as the lives changed, for better and for worse. He felt no guilt though; no regrets. *I tried to do my best. I tried to be fair in everything. I tried to be selfless. Have I been?* It was difficult to judge. Caledan's needs and his own blurred into one at points.

Soren hoped he had made the right choices. Even his own morals were clouding. Once upon a time, he would never have thought violence was the answer, and yet here he was, planning yet another battle; the only viable option he could see to create a lasting peace. *And that violence will alienate—is alienating—more people, though I do it for their own benefit. It is my right and duty to safeguard Caledan, even though it may cost me dearly. Stay the course,* he told himself. *As long as I believe I'm doing the right thing, I can do little else.*

He sighed. To ruminate would achieve nothing, and he was no closer to deciding Bedenor's fate. On this, he had no intuition, and no answer. The more he deliberated, the more he realised there was only one choice.

It was fair, he thought, to tell Bedenor of his decision. Behan was present also, dithering behind him and wringing his hands.

Bedenor stood in silence to hear his fate. His eyes still held a fiery spirit of rebellion, and he met Soren's troubled gaze with a hard stare that showed no weakness.

"As you maimed one of theirs, I shall let the dragons decide your fate. Your life is forfeit to their judgment. It would be the same with any other ally, so it shall be with they, though they are not human."

Behan emitted a squeak. Bedenor did not flinch or respond.

Soren turned to Behan. "I will see every man, woman, Eldarkind, and Dragon in Pandora in Castle Square for the passing of judgement."

Behan paled. Soren did not blink. He knew Behan would think Bedenor to be made an example of. In truth, he did not know what Farran's judgement would be. Bedenor could well be held to account. Farran would not, or could not, tell Soren. Soren hoped his hunch was right, that maybe, just maybe, the dragons would show clemency for the greater good. There would be a fine line to walk between the alliance holding or failing, and he could not see which path would hold either. Anxiety swirled in his stomach.

Soren's fingers drummed upon his folded arms as he waited impatiently with the rest of Pandora's inhabitants in Castle Square. A faceless crowd surrounded them. He stood upon the raised dais in the middle of the square where a heroically posed monument to King Beren stood, with Behan, Heligan, Farran, Tarrell, and Bedenor. The first days of spring were balmy and the sun streamed upon them, but Soren's skin prickled with a chill he could not shake.

Lord Heligan led the proceeding. As Chief Law Reader, it was his duty. He explained what had passed to those assembled, many of whom did not know what had occurred for Soren had insisted it be kept as secret as possible for fear of inciting more hate-crimes.

"Bedenor has already admitted his guilt in this and shall be punished accordingly as if he had harmed a fellow human." Last of all, he delivered Soren's judgment over the rumbling crowd whose tongues wagged at the news. "As with any other case, we defer judgment to Farran-visir, as it is his kin who has been harmed." Heligan bowed to Soren, and then to Farran, and stepped aside to stand shoulder to shoulder with Behan, who was visibly trembling.

Farran moved forwards on all fours in silence. His eyes transfixed Bedenor, who stood in shackles. A hush fell over the watching crowd, who bunched together and moved away from the approaching dragon. His bulk was huge to behold, and a wide berth surrounded him.

Tarrell stood next to Soren and shifted his balance. Soren thought he heard a whisper, but when he flicked his eyes to the Eldarkind, his mouth was firmly shut and he regarded the scene before them with an inscrutable expression.

"It is my duty to pass judgment, and pass judgment I shall," rumbled Farran. His voice carried across the square, where not a person made a sound. He opened his jaws, and all could see that fire burnt within. A wave of heat rolled over those closest, and scattered screams broke out.

Bedenor let his first sign of fear show, as his chains clinked together. Soren could see how tightly he grasped his hands together to stop the shaking. His lips were clamped so firmly shut they were nothing more than a thin line and a sheen of sweat glossed his skin. Behan was his mirror, though he did nothing to stop his quaking.

Soren moved, about to step forward without even thinking—to do what, he did not know—but a slender and strong hand held him back in an iron grip.

"Wait," Tarrell commanded in a low voice, not relinquishing his grasp on Soren until he sunk back. He stopped moving, but every muscle tensed. Behan had no such compulsion. He leapt forward on unstable legs, his stick clacking on the stones. Guards leapt forwards to catch him as he overbalanced and pulled him out of the way, so he could not intervene, though they looked as sickened as he.

Farran's jaw inched open, wider and wider in a slow, inexorable movement until all those gathered could see fire spewing forth from the white-hot forge in his throat. Flames licked his towering teeth and the commotion of the crowd grew louder as they pushed backwards to escape him. Anger overtook fear, and Farran roared to silence them. In a moment, he spurted a jet of flame high into the air that ignited their screams once more. Without further ado, he blasted a white hot jet of flame at Bedenor.

Behan collapsed in the arms of the guards restraining him. Sickly fascinated, they could not tear their eyes away to look at him.

Tarrell watched on, stony faced. Heligan closed his eyes. Soren looked. He had no choice. It was his duty. The light burned his eyes, as did the horror of what he saw, but he forced himself to stare regardless. His breath was ragged as the heat roiled over them. Now he felt no chills on his skin, only deep in the pit of his stomach at what he witnessed.

After but a moment, though it seemed like an eternity, Farran clamped his jaws shut with a clack that echoed around the square, shutting off the inferno. Silence fell over all. As the heat and the smoke cleared, cries of amazement rang out. Bedenor remained standing, shaking like a leaf from head to toe—and unharmed before them. He was blackened and dirty, but Soren could see he was clearly unharmed.

"How?" he murmured in wonderment.

"I… I… Alive. I'm alive," Bedenor stuttered. His face was snow-white under the soot. "I don't understand."

Farran turned to the crowd and as he swung his head and giant neck above them, causing them to flinch and fall silent at once. "I have given you my retribution," he growled. "Let no man stand before us. We are allies. Our bond means no harm ought to pass between us. I have shown you our power against those who have earned its full brunt."

Tarrell stepped forward. His pale hair shone in the sun as he raised his chin. "And I have protected him against it. We are your allies," he mirrored Farran.

"On this one occasion, I shall show clemency," Farran warned. He moved, and the crowd scrambled to back out of his way and clear a path. He snaked his way through them all, back to the castle. The floor shook with every step and his tail skittered and hissed across the flagstones.

Tarrell followed with Soren and Heligan. Behind them, guards carried the still form of Behan and Bedenor, now unshackled, accompanied his uncle. Tears of relief trailed pale lines through the soot on his face.

Soren's heart sang with his own relief, and a weight felt lifted from his shoulders. For a moment, he allowed himself to feel the awe of what had just happened. For a moment, he thought his plans had failed. That Farran would exact the revenge which, in all honesty, he had earned, on Bedenor. Soren could not have blamed him for that. Retribution was owed, though it would have made relations even more strained between the three races.

Soren was glad Farran had acted as he did; it was the best possible outcome. Surely, now that the dragons had shown mercy and clemency and the Eldarkind their unswerving loyalty towards the alliance, there would be no reason for any to doubt them.

The midday sun burned the back of his neck as they retreated.

There was not much time remaining to them before Cies would return.

This is but one part of the puzzle. Soon, it will be time.

Twenty Eight

Spring arrived quickly after that. Where there were the last frosts of winter, suddenly a warm spell arrived to dispel them. Balmy air and baking sunshine coaxed birds and blossoms forth until the air was rich with the sound of birdsong and the sweet smell of nectar. Buds swelled on trees which exploded with greenery, and a new season of vitality took Pandora.

Soren's eyes were blinded to it that day, as he was deep in discussion with Tarrell and Farran in the castle grounds. Still, he was glad he no longer had need of his winter cloak. There had been no trouble in the week since Bedenor's atonement, but a greater threat loomed, and with each warm day it grew: Cies. They all knew he would return after the weather had turned. It was just a case of when.

Training commenced with all three races working together, and progressed well. Soren's men drilled in great regiments upon the plains outside Pandora, and local fighters were flooding in as each house sent their reserves, with more promised from those further afield.

The drills were more for working as a team rather than practicing close quarter combat. Soren knew there would be little of that. He had poured most of his focus into training the archers and longbowmen, who were honing their skills from dawn until dusk on makeshift ranges. Soon, their arrows would be tipped with ice-fire, and his men would stand a chance of success.

Tarrell had been careful to produce limited amounts since Bedenor's misdemeanor, and it was stored under lock, key, and the watchful guard of Eldarkind eyes and magic. It would not be released until the very last minute. Soren hoped they would have time to distribute it. He had tried to persuade Tarrell to release it sooner, but he was unrelenting. Soren could not blame him. He knew Tarrell bore his own guilt about the mishap for having supplied the ice-fire to humans in the first place. Soren had swallowed his pride on that matter and given Tarrell his pick of the vaults to store it in.

After spending the morning touring the training ground, they secreted themselves away in a remote part of the castle grounds beside a pond to scry Cies for themselves.

"*Leitha Cies*," Tarrell intoned. The muddy water rippled in response, and, in a few moments, the reflection of the sky had disappeared and they looked upon Cies basking in arid surroundings and bright sun. Light bounced from his silver scales as they shimmered and glowed in the heat haze.

"He could well be in the deserts north of Roher and Ladrin, or perhaps further afield. It is difficult to tell," Tarrell mused.

"He will be stronger already," said Farran. "He looks peaceful, yet he will be plotting his revenge this very second. A dragon defeated will never stop seeking it. It will torment him." He sounded pleased at the prospect.

"When?" Tarrell stared at Cies's still form.

Farran rumbled and did not answer immediately. "He could remain until the height of summer, for all we know. That would see him at the zenith of his strength, but equally ours, too. If I were he, I would wait until midsummer."

Tarrell ground his teeth. "We do not have so long. Arandulus already walks again."

"Perhaps, when we are ready, we can make Cies come to us."

Soren cocked his head and looked at Farran quizzically. Tarrell seemed just as perplexed.

"With the Eldarkind's help, we could speak with Cies through one of your scryings. He is short-tempered and rash. It would be too easy to goad him into returning at our bidding and when we are ready, before the warmth of the south and the desert sun restores his health too much. They will be here within a few short days if they make haste, which, if we bait him well, I foresee him doing. He is impetuous and quick to seek vengeance."

Soren and Tarrell shared a glance. Soren could not discern Tarrell's thoughts, but his own were clear. Either way, they would have to face Cies. Which was worse: a confident dragon or an enraged one? Soren could not be sure.

"You think that best?" Tarrell asked.

"I do. Perhaps, dragons alone, we would be evenly matched. Perhaps, even outmatched for they have had the favour of the deserts; that could lend them an edge. However, with Eldarkind, humans and ice-fire, I am certain they cannot stand before us. Each day we delay, they grow stronger far faster than we may. It is spring, but it is not warm enough here for us to thrive. My bones still ache with cold."

"I will acquiesce to your expertise," Tarrell said, bowing his head towards Farran.

"Are we agreed?"

"Make it so," said Soren grimly.

Farran rumbled. His grin widened and his eyes narrowed to slits. "Make it so," he echoed with glee.

"When shall we set the date of this… summoning?" Soren asked, as his eyes were drawn to Farran's impressive teeth. *Thank goodness he is on our side.*

"No more than half a moon away. It will be the fourth month of the year and the southern sun will be waxing to full strength."

They parted with Soren both heartened and nervous. They had the number of men, Eldarkind, and dragons. They had the weapons: the dragons themselves, for one, Eldarkind spelled blades, and the ice-fire for his own men. Theoretically, Soren reasoned, it should be simple. But dragons were an entity unknown to him.

Cies would be stronger from his time in the south, and he was imbued with elemental magic. What did that mean? It would not be easy, he was certain of that. He had seen dragons on the warpath, and just three dragons: Myrkdaga, Feldith, and Feldloga had made short work of Pandora's fortifications when Soren had returned from exile. Soren had felt the power of Farran's fire, too. He could not imagine it tenfold, or a hundred-fold, but he did not need to. Pandora was at risk of that alone.

Thoughts began to coalesce. Eve had warded the people of Arlyn. Perhaps, the Eldarkind could do the same for Pandora itself and its people? His thoughts returned to Eve and her healing abilities. It seemed like an age since she had laboured in the healing houses of Pandora, and Soren suspected they would be needed, also. He had not summoned any men from Arlyn, busy as they were with rebuilding the town, but he had need of Eve. Another pair of magical hands would not go amiss, and neither would her healing skills.

He returned to his drawing room and the Eldarkind mirror to scry her at once. She looked tired as she answered his calls. Dark shadows hung under her dull eyes.

"How goes repairs?" Soren asked.

"Well, thank you, Cousin," Eve replied. "I am most grateful for the men you have sent, and the crafts folk. Everyone now has temporary shelters, and with summer on its way, we're busy with the reconstruction. The weather has been kind to us so far, for which we are lucky. We are surviving."

"I'm glad to hear it. I did not ask for men from Arlyn county, knowing how much you needed them—"

"I'm grateful for that, too, Soren," Eve cut in, giving him a wan smile.

Soren nodded. "But I do have need of you."

Eve raised her eyebrow, but did not speak, so he continued.

"I need your help in the battle to come. Your healing skills, your magic. You know what we face. I need every pair of hands I can find, and yours most of all."

Eve faltered and could not speak for a moment. "I am flattered you ask," she replied carefully, "but Arlyn is without a leader if I leave. You know my father's ailments do not permit him to take on his usual duties. I am needed here."

"All will be well," a man's voice said. Soren could see a man in guard's attire step forward.

"Luke…"

"I promise you, E… Lady Eve," Luke replied, his eyes flicking to the mirror. "Your father seems a little recovered; you need not worry for him. Captain Hoarth is doing an excellent job of overseeing the restructuring of the town with the masons and carpenters, and I can accompany you, as usual, to keep you safe."

Eve flashed him a small smile, and Soren could sense something between them, but he did not enquire. There was no time to waste on niceties, and his cousin's indiscretions were her own matter.

Her face clouded. "What if it is like Ednor, like Arlyn, all over again?" She shuddered, and Soren could see the horror in her eyes as if she was reliving it again.

"It will not be like that," Soren leaped on the opportunity to reassure her. "We are prepared. The battle is of our choosing in place and time. We will triumph. There will be no retreat. There will be no defeat. Pandora and its people will remain safe and whole. There will be no devastation. I promise you will be safe."

"If you are so prepared, what need have you of I?"

"Great need. There will be casualties. We cannot avoid that. Human, Eldarkind, even dragon. My healers cannot cope with it. We need someone like you, with your capabilities. I do not ask it lightly of you. Will you come?"

Eve looked towards Luke, clearly torn.

He nodded. "It's your duty, Eve. To king and country."

"What of Arlyn?"

"Arlyn will be fine. Hoarth is a good man. Your father is recovering," Luke repeated. "We have our most skilled men, and, thanks to our king—" he dipped his head to Soren, "—master craftsmen from Pandora to help us."

Eve did not reply, and looked away from them both. Soren could see she waged a battle inside her own mind then. At last, she looked up, her face troubled and unsure, but, as he watched, it set in determination.

"I cannot do it, Cousin. Forgive me. We have our own ill and injured here to tend to. How else can they be healed except with my magic? We have lost all else, and can forage little from the land at present. I cannot leave them knowing this. My people look to me for hope and leadership. If I leave, what does that say to them?" Her eyes flicked to Luke. "And of myself." Her voice grew quiet. "Ednor... Arlyn... I cannot endure that again." She cleared her throat. "All I have done, I have tried to do for duty to others. I cannot abandon what is the most important duty to myself. Not now. Forgive me." She raised her chin in defiance.

Soren searched her face, but found no doubt there. He sighed. "With greatest respect, Cousin, I shall not order you to come. If you truly feel this is the best course, I will honor your judgment. We have the Eldarkind and the dragons. We shall manage without you. Continue your work in Arlyn."

Eve held up her shoulders as they threatened to sag with relief.

Soren hoped she was right and that one pair of hands would not make the difference.

The first day of the fourth month dawned with the clouds as seething and brooding as Soren. He stood in silence with Tarrell and Farran upon the battlements of Pandora, watching over the plains where his archers and fighters practised under scudding clouds and wheeling dragons.

It was time.

They prepared in the dark vaults, away from all prying eyes, where the ice-fire was kept. A perfectly circular pool of water as still as a millpond and as dark as night lay in the centre of the vaulted cellar. Soren had never seen this part of the castle before and wondered at its purpose, but it would serve them now, regardless of its origin. Farran, thanks to the underground cavern that supplied Pandora and the wide tunnels under the castle, managed to squeeze far enough in so he too could join them. His neck stretched through the door and his head both rested on the floor and butted the ceiling.

Soren and Tarrell stood equal measures apart around the pool, with Farran in between them. Farran opened his mighty jaws and a crooning sound filled the cellar, echoing from every wall and pillar in the dark place and vibrating Soren to his core. Tarrell stayed silent, mouthing words with no sound whilst his eyes fixed on the pond.

This was no ordinary scrying, Soren could tell. Farran's voice rose in pitch and intensity, now speaking guttural words in a language Soren did not understand, and Tarrell's words grew louder, too. The hairs on Soren's skin prickled. Cies appeared upon the water, and, as Soren watched, Tarrell and Farran fell silent. Cies slowly turned his head to stare Farran in the eyes.

Farran spoke then; more harsh, guttural words in his tongue that grated on Soren's ears. Cies snarled and replied in kind. They continued to speak, back and forth, and their conflict rose in intensity until Cies cut Farran off with a roar. His open jaw filled the pond and Soren saw fire brewing within. Cies unleashed a jet of white-hot flames towards them. Soren stumbled backwards and Tarrell leaped forwards, shouting to end the connection. Fire spurted from the surface of the pool just as Tarrell closed the scrying. Crackling flames and hissing, vaporized water deafened Soren. The fire was blinding. The darkness and silence that followed blanketed them.

"It is done," said Farran grimly. "He will come."

Come Cies did. The watch was doubled night and day, with all Pandora on standby. On the second day, the sun did not set. A horizon of flames lit up the sky. The wall of flames marched towards them as Cies burned all in his path. Soren watched from the battlements with Farran and Tarrell. It was an intimidating scene, as Cies intended.

Waiting was the worst, and Soren knew they could lose no time in preparing.

"Sound the bells," he ordered.

TWENTY NINE

The wall of fire arrived at Pandora before the next day was out, bringing with it winged demons that soared through the flames and smoky skies, raining hell upon its inhabitants.

Pandora's women and children and the old and the infirm, huddled out of sight, deep beneath the citadel in the vaults of Pandora castle. It was to be their impregnable refuge. The healers were there, too, at Tarrell's advice. Soren thought the healing houses, deep in the city walls, would be safe, but an attack from above rendered all vulnerable, Tarrell warned. This would be a new kind of warfare, Soren realised.

As they awaited the approaching inferno, Pandora's walls bristled with soldiers. Their armour was aglow with the reflection of fire. Archers and longbow men stood stony-faced, staring out between the crenulations with fingers tapping upon their bow handles or rifling through their arrows; anything to keep the nerves at bay.

Soren awaited on top of Pandora cathedral's tower, ringed by his finest longbow men. It was the best vantage point in the city, and he wagered, the best chance of reaching the dragons. The castle lay under a light guard for now; to be their defence should they have to fall back. The dragons waited there, itching for the battle to start.

Song rose from the city as Eldarkind stood around Pandora with their arms up-stretched to the sky, singing in the Eldartongue of protection and warding, and weaving a great spell of protection for mother earth to keep them. Soren could not make out the words, but they filled him with a sense of reassurance not even the approach of Cies could break. At least, until the songs ceased. Then, the creeping dread took hold once more.

It seemed both an age and an instant before Cies arrived. But all too soon, Cies was upon them. There were no exchanges, no parlays and no delays. He descended upon them in a halo of fire, and flames and hell descended from the heavens with him.

The moment they were within range, Soren gave the command to attack. Horns blew across the city to pass on his order. The first volley of arrows sailed into the sky, tipped with glowing blue fire. Arrows swam through the sky like glinting fish. Many sailed to nowhere, but some found their target and the roaring of the oncoming storm of dragons changed as they hit. The arrows left blue-white skittering trails that lingered over the dragon's scales.

"Again!" he shouted. "Release at will!" He winded the horn himself to give the order.

Cies and his dragons held back nothing in their attack, bathing the city with trails of fire that set swathes of Pandora ablaze.

The first Eldarkind ward failed with the first attack, much to Soren, Tarrell, and Farran's dismay, but it was no surprise. Tarrell had already warned there was insufficient magic to hold it. If nothing else, it was a faint hope. Soren hoped they could succeed, but even he was not sure how they could stand before such an attack. None of his men could survive dragon fire, he knew that much.

At last, dragons and Eldarkind engaged. Farran, followed by his clan, took off from the castle garden in stealth mode, rising fast and high with the Eldarkind mounted upon them, ready and waiting with ice-fire blades. They were shielded from view by the waves of smoke that rose from Pandora, but it would not be long before they were spotted.

With Lorellei astride, Myrkdaga soared behind Farran.

"Are you ready?" Lorellei said into his mind with a grin. Myrkdaga could hear the edge of fear hidden behind Lorellei's bravado.

"I have been anticipating this day for many moons," said Myrkdaga with grim glee. "Retribution at last." A gust of wind buffeted them and Lorellei did not answer for a moment, too busy tightening his grasp upon Myrkdaga.

"You… you will seek to challenge Cies yourself?"

Myrkdaga growled. "No. I cannot stand before Cies. He is too powerful for me to defeat. I am no fool. But he will be cast down by one of my kin, I know it, and then my father's justice will be served. Myrkith-visir will be avenged, and the coward and traitor, Cies of the silver scales, will be no more. As he deserves."

"You do not come for the alliance, do you?"

Myrkdaga scoffed. "No. I care not for the petty wishes of humans and Eldarkind to play nicely. I have no enmity towards either of your races, but you ought to be stronger. You ought to be able to fight off dragons. Perhaps, Eldarkind, with your ice fire swords and your magic can, but these humans… I have never seen such numerous and incapable creatures. Their homes burn and all they can do is send pointy sticks into the sky? It baffles me that we must ally with them, but for now, I care not. I come for Cies and Cies alone."

Farran turned on his wing to descend, and Myrkdaga gritted his teeth. "Hold on. Here we go." He tucked in a wing and pivoted on the spot, to plummet from the sky as fast as a falling star. On his back, Lorellei hunched close to his scales, closing his eyes to slits against the wind slicing past them.

In moments, the sky darkened as they entered the plumes of smoke. The only hint of dragons around them was a dull flash within the murk. Lorellei kept his blue sword at the ready, awaiting Myrkdaga's direction, for his dragon counterpart could sense his foes with greater accuracy.

"Left!" was the only warning Lorellei received before a dragon loomed in the smoke. Lorellei slashed his sword in wild desperation, just managing to nick the hide. Lorellei jolted as Myrkdaga used the dragon's own bulk to push away from it. He swallowed and gripped his sword tighter. *Calm.* He took a deep breath, trying to focus his energy. That was all he had time for before they were in the fray once more.

Again and again, they darted in and danced away, attacking with stealth and speed and melting back into the smoke to protect them. Myrkdaga rent with claws and teeth, and Lorellei sliced and stabbed with his sword. Their opponents roared with pain and surprise, but by the time they realised where the attack had come from, Myrkdaga was gone, onto his next target.

Their attacks proved a useful distraction. Before long, Cies and his dragons were nearly all engaged in battles in the sky, and had ceased their assault on Pandora, leaving the archers and longbow men there free once more to come out from cover and pepper them with arrows.

Myrkdaga hissed as he dodged one. "These humans cannot tell us apart!"

The distraction was needed, for the city was already well on its way to destruction. The casualties came thick and fast once the last Eldarkind wards had failed and Cies and his dragons picked off men and Eldarkind on the battlements and savaged dragons in the sky.

Another wave of fire bathed the city. The smoke stung Soren's eyes and clogged the back of this throat. Still, his men fought on, firing arrow after arrow. They glistened with sweat as the inferno roasted them as the hot air rose from the city far below. *How much longer can we continue this?* Soren wondered. Their efforts did not seem to be doing much at all.

"Pandora is mostly aflame," Tarrell relayed to him mentally. He rode Farran far above Soren. "The wards are not holding. The last is about to fail. Cies has destroyed the surrounding lands; there is no longer anything to draw forth energy from, for it feeds the fire instead. We cannot offer you any more protection. Your men will be slaughtered. Pull them back!"

"I will not fall back yet," Soren said, determined not to give up, but the reports relayed from the dragons, Eldarkind, and his own men, were not favourable. *Damn it!* Soren cursed to himself. His eyes searched the smoke above them. Dragons writhed in the sky, paying little heed to the humans below them. *Are we so inconsequential?*

The docks were aflame, the city outside the walls blazed, and the fires were spreading inside the walls, too. He could see them approaching the cathedral and creeping through the streets, leaping from building to building. No one would survive those infernos if they were trapped, Soren knew, for the docks were mainly wooden buildings. The castle seemed intact, for the fighting had not reached quite so far into the city yet. *It is only a matter of time,* Soren caught himself thinking, before he had time to stifle the thought. He gritted his teeth. *I cannot think like this.*

"Can you drive them lower?" Soren asked. "We need them closer. We cannot do much damage from afar."

"We will try," replied Farran. He dove through the clouds until he could see Soren glinting in armour on top of the cathedral, and crashed into a younger dragon, knocking it clean out of the sky. Its fractured body plummeted, crushing buildings as it crashed into the ground. The airborne fight descended until both halves of the dragon clan were well within range.

"Take care!" Soren warned his men. "It will not do us well to harm our own allies." He grabbed a longbow himself and stepped forward into the line of men. "Loose at will!"

His muscles screamed as he drew the strong bow, and the string sliced into his hands with its resistance. After a moment, he lined his target with his single open eye and loosed. The arrow soared into the air and through the dragon's wing membrane in a burst of blue fire. His men cheered at that and hastened to follow his example, peppering the dragons who flew within range with arrows. Their attack did not go unnoticed for long. Dragons turned their attention to the annoying, small beings on top of the tower and hurtled towards them.

"Fall back!" Soren screamed at the top of his voice, and they scrambled to shelter inside the tower. The heavy wooden door slammed closed just at the last second. A lick of fire snatched at them through the gap as flames battered the tower where they had stood only moments before. The roar of the fire and the rumble of crumbling masonry deafened them all.

The tower shook from the assault. It sounded as if the dragons were battering it or tearing it brick from brick. Soren dashed down the stairs to where a slit window penetrated the wall. Sure enough, chunks of falling masonry pummelled the ground below them. Above him, the door crackled and buckled as the ironwork melted under the heat and the thick, hardened wood eventually gave up and burst into flames, too.

We cannot go out there now, Soren thought. *Our attack is over. For the moment.* "Fall back," he ordered, and stood aside as men filed past him down the stone stairs. Heels thumped upon the stone and bow-ends tapped, but not a word was spoken. He looked into the face of each man as he passed. They all wore the same look of grim fear and uncertainty.

"Fall back to the castle gate," Soren ordered, raising his voice so all could hear. "We have the best vantage point there over the city and fortifications." He made sure to sound more confident than he felt. "Get there any way you can. Split up if needs be. Be safe. I will meet you there. We must be quick, before the ways are closed by fire."

"Yes, Sire," echoed up the tower as they acknowledged him. Last of all, he followed, with one look back to the door, or the hole where it had stood. It seemed the dragons had turned their attention elsewhere.

Soren paused. Gingerly, he stepped back upstairs towards the top of the tower. Remnants of iron nails glowed molten on the blackened and burnt stone floor. Nothing was left of the door but ashes. As he peered out, smoke obscured his view, but he could see dark outlines of vast dragons wheeling through the air. Hot air gusted through the door towards him, and the heat of the fire in the stone burned his feet as he stood. He retreated quickly.

By the time Soren had descended from the tower, he was alone. It was deathly silent in the huge space, save for the dull booming of destruction outside. With quick eyes and nimble feet, he jogged through the huge space, searching for anyone who might have been there. It was deserted, to his relief. A giant crash sent him sprawling to the floor in self-defence. As he looked up from behind a stone pew, he saw several of the giant, stained glass windows had been smashed. Now, he could hear the crackle of the flames, the cracking of stone, and the screams of the dying.

I have to leave now, Soren realised. *This was a fool's mission.* He mentally kicked himself, but pushed the thought aside. There was no time for chastising. His life depended on being able to reach the castle safely.

The huge cathedral door was half open. One leaf trembled on its hinges. As he stepped from the cool dark of the cathedral and outside into the murky light of the smoky day, several dragons plummeted from the sky to land in the square before him.

Soren took a step forward to greet them when one opened its jaws and sent a jet of flames spilling around the square, lighting up anything that it touched. With a gasp and a suppressed cry, Soren jumped backwards into the shadows once more, his heart leaping from his chest. *I cannot get out!* He hoped his men had made it to safety. There were no other exits he knew of from the cathedral.

"Tarrell! Farran!" he shouted in his mind, hoping they would hear. "I'm trapped in the cathedral!"

"We're coming." Tarrell's reply was grim.

Soren peered around the edge of the door. The dragons had not noticed him, but they blocked his way. The shadows deepened as another dragon, larger than them all, landed. *Silver. Cies!* Soren forced down the rising panic that threatened to bubble over. Cies was huge—even larger than Farran—and corded with muscles which bulged under tightly knit glistening scales that formed an impenetrable armour.

"Cies is here!" he shouted to Farran, who growled in response.

Soren fingered his sword, which had been coated with ice-fire. He was sure that might annoy Cies, but he had no doubt about the abilities of his blade. *What use is a needle against a giant? Can it even pierce his hide?*

He swallowed and his other hand tightened on the bow. The

quiver still hung on his back. He felt. Three arrows, all tipped with ice-fire. *They're better than nothing.* He stood inside the door, mostly hidden from view, and lined up a dragon through the open crack. In quick succession, he nocked, drew, and loosed the three arrows, threw the bow to the floor, and put all his weight against the door to close it.

The hinges were oiled and smooth and it closed without a sound, but he could not hear over the squeal of outrage from the dragon he presumed he had hit. He did not pause to look, and thrust harder. The hinges might have been smooth, but the door was not meant to be moved by one man. For all his efforts, it shut frustratingly slowly, leaving a yawning gap that did not seem to shrink between the two leaves.

As the door clanked shut, Soren peered through the keyhole to see a blur of silver approaching. A great bulk smashed against the door, catapulting him backwards. Soren sailed through the air and smashed into the unyielding stone floor. He gasped for air and blinked, but all he could see was black and stars for a moment. As his head cleared and his lungs relaxed, his senses came rushing back. Everything hurt. His shoulder particularly, where it had leaned against the door, and his back and legs where he had crashed into the floor. The sound of the impact had been deafening, and as his vision cleared, he froze.

The gutteral roar silenced even Soren's pounding heart, which rattled against his ribs; each beat a kick in the chest. He trembled from head to foot, faced by the gaping maw of the giant, silver dragon before him. Cies's head towered above him, and his hot fetid breath made Soren gag. His head snaked through the doors, but his shoulders would not fit through. Cies gnashed his teeth in frustration, stretching as far as he could reach. About Soren lay shards of stone, torn from Pandora's cathedral by Cies's jaws, which darted towards him, coming just short. Claws screeched furrows into the stone-flagged floor. The muscles in Cies's neck corded and bulged as he strained.

Soren lay on his back, just a few feet out of reach, but already, under Cies's battering, the stone was grinding and shrieking, as if it might give way at any moment. Slowly but surely, Soren was certain Cies would succeed. Soren looked to his blade. It seemed so short and frail compared to even one of Cies's enormous teeth. Its reach was too short, and even if it could cut Cies or harm him with the ice-fire, Soren would be incinerated by fire, or caught in those unrelenting jaws before he could do anything about it.

The stones quivered and chunks began to crack off the door frame. Cies squeezed closer. Soren scuttled backwards, scrambling with his hands to drag himself away. Cies pushed forwards as far as he could, wriggling his shoulders; he roared in frustration and snapped his teeth as Soren moved further away.

It was all the encouragement Soren needed. Ignoring his complaining body—pain seared through him with every movement—Soren took his chance, scrambled to his feet, and ran. He jogged awkwardly, lopsided, as his body tried to compensate for its injuries.

A mighty crash sounded behind him. Soren chanced a glance backwards. His heart leaped into his mouth. Through the door, or what was left of it, the silver dragon leapt forward, through the collapsing wall as stones that would crush a man fell around Cies like pebbles. Each pace of Cies was worth ten of Soren's, and each step shook the very foundations beneath them.

With a cry, Soren doubled his efforts, forcing his screaming body into a sprint. There was no way Farran and Tarrell would be able to save him now. He gritted his teeth against the pain. Safety. The tiny door behind the altar that might offer shelter was too far away. He would never make it. *Why is this cathedral so damn big,* he fleetingly thought, desperately searching for an alternative. No pillar or pew would shelter him.

With his last strength, not daring to look behind him again, Soren dashed up the wide stairs of the dais and threw himself towards the dragon throne. A pitiful shelter, Soren knew, but if he could just make it behind Brithilca's frozen wings, made of the strange, impenetrable material that no one could fathom, perhaps he stood his best chance.

The ringing in his ears crescendoed with the pounding in his head and the rattling of his body, which felt like it would shake itself apart from the weight of the behemoth pounding behind him. As he dove, ducking under the protective shield of the wings, a shiver rippled through him and a wave of golden light rippled across his skin.

In the instant that he stopped, the throne of the dragon kings, guarded by what some said were the petrified remains of Brithilca himself, moved. Soren's breath caught as Brithilca's wings snapped shut about him. Silence and darkness was immediate. All Soren could feel was the floor shaking beneath him.

THIRTY

Soren froze, unsure what had happened. Every muscle was tensed. Every sense tingled on high alert. The floor jolted him repeatedly. *Cies must be trying to find a way through Brithilca's protective shell*, Soren reasoned, because they were growing more intense and frequent. His mind detached from his emotions, and, for a moment, the world dropped away. *I'm going to die*, he thought quite calmly. Not even Brithilca's statue could survive a dragon attack for long, magic or not, Soren was sure.

"I can endure for as long as you need me to." The deep, calm voice of Brithilca spoke into Soren's mind.

Soren gasped and looked about, but it was pitch black; not even a chink of light entered. He placed his hands upon the wings that surrounded him. They were warm to the touch, as if alive. "Brithilca?" *It cannot be.*

"It is I. Do not give up. Do not despair."

"How can I survive? If… If you release me, there is no way I can withstand Cies." Soren did not want to think about what awaited him on the other side.

"Soren, the pact must be rebuilt between man, Eldarkind, and dragon at any cost. The elementals must not be allowed to rise, for they will destroy us all. Cies is but a small test."

"I cannot defeat him, though! What can a human do against a dragon?"

"You are not alone. Help comes. Worry not. I will release you not a moment too soon, or too late, but you have a part to play in this. You can make a difference." Brithilca growled, cutting off Soren's protest.

"We have no time! Listen. I must share with you how to remake the pact!" Soren could hear the urgency in Brithilca's voice.

"The knowledge has been lost to me for centuries. The elementals clouded my vision with their magic as they sought to undo the pact. I must impart it to you, now, lest it be lost once more!"

All of a sudden, Soren was in another place and time, in a body and mind not his own. Thoughts raced through his head—someone else's thoughts, someone else's knowledge.

"Beren," Brithilca's voice said into his mind.

The sky was dark and the air was clogged and choked by the night's fires. Lurking in the heart of the murk was a figure of darkness.

"Bahr," Brithilca growled.

Bahr faded in and out of sight, wreathed in flames and black, roiling smoke—a great curtain of black that darkened all as far as the eye could see. This close, Bahr was a truly terrifying sight. Three times the height of a man he stood. His skin, if it could be called such, was so dark that his face had no features beside eyes that burned like fiery pits and a white hot maw that looked like the bowels of the earth. Standing tall and immobile, he loomed forebodingly, his black form visible by the void of light it created.

Men, Eldarkind, and dragons waited in silence, ready in their positions. All night, the dragons had worked upon the lofty heights of the glacier, under the shroud of the smoke, the dark, and the Eldarkind's concealing magic, blasting away at the glacier until a great lake of water and slush had formed. It pooled behind the cliff of the glacier wall, which held it back from the valley like a dam. Beren, Falykas, king of the Eldarkind, and Brithilca, chief amongst dragons, waited for him, too, ahead of their forces and first in the line of danger.

Soren stared at Falykas. He was so like Tarrell. And Brithilca. He had never seen anything as impressive as the glittering blue dragon. He was not so muscular as Cies, whose form was twisted out of proportion. No, Brithilca was everything a dragon should be: sleek, powerful, and beautifully deadly.

Cracks rent the air as Bahr moved towards them. Not a word did he utter, but he did not need to. They had seen his mind and knew his intentions. He would not waste his words before he crushed them, they were sure.

It was time.

"Prepare!" Beren ordered his men. Soren felt the body he inhabited move. He was only a spectator. *Behind him, swords hissed as they were drawn, bows creaked as they were pulled, and axe hafts thumped upon the*

ground. His soldiers were grouped with bands of Eldarkind; they would be casting spells, protected by the iron of his men.

At a seemingly unspoken instruction, the dragons took to the wing as one, to soar high above those left on the ground.

All too soon, Bahr was upon them. As before, they were engulfed in thick smoke that clogged their lungs and veiled their sight. Beren stood ready with his men to defend their Eldarkind counterparts, who had already raised their hands to the sky to begin chanting. All pointed towards the glacier to combine their magic as one.

Roars and shrieks sounded from overhead as dragons attacked Bahr with fire and physical might. They, and Bahr's loud responses, masked the cracks and groans of the collapsing glacier as it cracked, but did not break.

Beren's men stood in protective circles around the Eldarkind as Bahr drew closer. Some drew close enough to strike him; not all were fortunate enough to live. Their iron blades melted as they penetrated him, yet Bahr's screams indicated they had caused some pain.

His giant, black hands raked from the heights to indiscriminately grab anyone within his reach. Each man he grasped died a painful death. He tossed them into the heights to fall to their death, incinerated them in an instant, or slowly burnt them to death and fused them with their melting armour as he held on his burning grasp and squeezed the life from them.

The Eldarkind renewed their spells, chanting louder, faster, and with more vigour than before until the cracks in the glacier became a rumbling that engulfed them all. Now would be the difficult part: stopping the water from drowning them all. Their voices rose in intensity as the storm mirrored them. It battered them all with gusts that were hard to stand up in, and the dust raised from the ground sliced unprotected flesh and dashed itself into open eyes.

"Forward!" bellowed Beren. They surged as one mass, surrounding Bahr as the glacier gave way. Huge blocks of ice tumbled down from the heights to smash into a million shards upon the ground, which annihilated anything that got in their way. The groan and roar of countless gallons of displaced water followed as the Eldarkind frantically gesticulated at it, now crying their incantations with hoarse voices. The water tumbled down upon them all, bouncing off the valley bottom and twirling up into the sky in great spouts that formed rivers in the air, which soared towards Bahr.

He snarled in anger, deafening them all, and battered those surrounding him with fiery globules and his massive limbs, sending swathes of men and Eldarkind falling. It broke some of the magic, and swathes of water fell from the sky, battering those below like a waterfall. Bahr screeched as he was caught by it, and a great hissing went up as fires were extinguished around them.

Then, Bahr attacked anew, raining fire and death upon them all. Beren looked up. Giant water snakes wrapped around Bahr. He vaporised them with fireballs wherever they drew too near him, all the while, raining devastation on those below. Dragons harried him from above. Bahr batted them from the sky as if they were flies, and wreaked his own painful magic upon them. Beren's mouth fell open in despair.

"We must act now! We must bind him!" Falykas shouted, fighting his way through to Beren across slippery ground covered in mud, blood, and bodies. Brithilca darted out of the sky to join them. "Are you prepared to do whatever is necessary?"

Beren hesitated, but only for a moment. "Yes."

"Take my hand!"

Beren rushed to comply. Falykas grabbed his hand in a vice-like grip and placed his other palm on Brithilca's flank.

"We cannot kill him, so we must bind him," Falykas explained quickly. "My people do not have the strength to do this alone. I must ask of you possibly the greatest sacrifice. Brithilca, I need your strength and Beren, I need the wards of your iron. We must bind ourselves together—combine our strengths—to have what is needed to succeed. I do not know if we shall live to see the end of this."

Beren swallowed. There was no other way. Every moment he hesitated, another of his men died, and the threat to his home grew with Bahr's strength and lust for vengeance. He squeezed Falykas's hand tighter in response. Brithilca curled himself around them, his head level with theirs, to protect them from the worst of the battering gusts.

Falykas bared his teeth, took a deep breath, and shouted into the sky in the tongue of his own people that Beren did not understand. His words were snatched away into the maelstrom. "Storr andas, ia kaskea uan att aslura, inge flytte, inge tenkir, inge endra, ja inge eiende. Brun anda Bahr, ia sinuar uan nedan isen ja foss. Ia sinuar uan yta detthe, mina ethera, a ethera ro mina Eldarkin, a jarn ro ungrkin, ja a styrkr ro dragonkin, asti a lok ro timi!"

Soren heard the unfamiliar words as Brithilca translated them into the speech of man in his mind, "Great spirits, I command you to sleep, unmoving, unthinking, unchanging, and unyielding. Fire Spirit Bahr, I bind you under ice and water. I bind you with this, my energy, the energy of my kin, the iron of man, and the strength of dragonkin until the end of time!"

Beren felt Falykas's magic rip through him and he braced himself against Brithilca's hot scales, which hummed under his fingers with Brithilca's strength. His body felt both on fire and doused in cold water as ice-fire rippled through every nerve to the tips of his fingers and toes. He could barely see past the hump of Brithilca's body. Outside that protective shield, his own men fell to the ground as the same energy rushed through their veins.

As one, every piece of armour on his body shivered and melted into liquid that fell up into the sky. Rivers of metal twisted and turned, glinting in the darkness with their own light as they joined with the liquid iron of his men's armour and weapons. They tumbled together towards the heart of the darkness, not touched by the cutting winds or dissuaded from their path. The giant darkness at the centre of the storm that was Bahr was soon swathed in the constricting threads of metal and the water that remained, like a shining cocoon in the sky.

Dragons hurled themselves out of the way, struggling to land in the gale-force winds. Eldarkind stood tall with their arms stretched to the heavens, their lips locked in a silent chant that mirrored Falykas's words.

Bahr's dark form struggled against the bond, and the rings of metal and water expanded as he fought. Falykas dropped Beren's hand and grasped his knife. He swept the blade across his palm and grabbed Beren's hand to open a long gash in his palm, too. Swirling around to Brithilca, whose eye regarded him for a moment, before his head dipped in acquiescence, Falykas plunged the short blade into Brithilca's soft, fleshy underjaw.

Boiling hot, giant droplets of purple blood rained down upon Beren and Falykas, who lifted up his hand to catch the violet liquid on his own crimson palm, before locking his hand with Beren. Their three bloods mingled as he shouted the incantation one last time.

Brithilca howled a shriek that added a new layer of deafening noise to the storm and began, scale by scale, to disintegrate before them. He glowed as bright as molten metal as he disappeared in a shower of sparks. Tears streamed down Falykas's eyes and he raised them to the heavens to follow the sparks as they sought the eye of the storm.

Beren closed his eyes to the storm as it intensified around them, and prayed to the skies they would succeed. Without the shelter of Brithilca, debris and wind battered them, forcing Beren away from Falykas. In the muddy air, he could see nothing and no one around him. Beren fell to one knee and hunkered on the floor, swaying with each blow until his senses abandoned him and he sunk into darkness.

The visions faded and suddenly, Soren was back in his own body. Pain stabbed through him once more. Soren's head span as he tried to process what he had just witnessed, seemingly with his own eyes and body.

"Magic, and strength, and iron," growled Brithilca, interrupting his confusion. "Magic, and strength and iron," he repeated, enunciating every syllable. "These three things you need to remake the pact."

Soren nodded. "What of Cies?" He stumbled as the floor shook once more, and braced himself on Brithilca's wings.

"In that, I cannot help you. This fight is yours to face. It is nearly time. Are you ready? I can give you one parting gift."

"No! Wait!" Soren cried, but it was too late. A chink of light appeared, and another and another as Brithilca's wings cracked open. Soren rushed to draw his sword, which glowed a fiery, flickering blue, and held it before him, blinking as his eyes adjusted to the dull light, which was blinding after the darkness.

"Now!" Brithilca's voice cried, and the statue moved with as much speed as a living dragon. Above his head, Brithilca's jaws opened and a jet of blue fire spurted out towards Cies, who towered above Soren with glittering eyes that were full of rage.

The flames struck Cies square in the chest and he yelped a piercing shriek that drove into Soren's head. Soren paused for just a moment, but he knew this was it. *I'm not going to live through this*, he thought, but there was no time to be scared. *I might as well do my worst.*

Behind Soren, Brithilca fell still and the fire stopped, but as Soren rushed forwards, the blue flames did not dissipate. Instead, they clung to Cies, just like ice-fire. Soren reached Cies's clawed feet, and with a battle cry as fierce as he could muster, hacked at what he could reach of Cies' legs. Cies stumbled backwards, distracted by the flames and this new annoyance when behind him, a roar announced new company. Through Cies's dancing legs, Soren saw Myrkdaga land just inside the cathedral doors with an Eldarkind on his back and relief blossomed.

Myrkdaga dashed forwards on all fours and attacked Cies with tooth and claw, whilst the Eldarkind on his back cried in their strange tongue and leapt from Myrkdaga's back onto Cies with his flaming blue blade. He danced over Cies's writhing form with uncanny balance and agility, peppering him with flaming blue cuts as Myrkdaga bit and clawed the giant silver dragon.

Cies turned away to face these new foes, hobbling on cut paws and Soren took his opportunity to slice off the tip of Cies' tail, too. Cies roared again and half-turned back to face him with fire brewing in his throat.

Panic and adrenaline washed over Soren, and then he remembered the small bottle of ice-fire he had brought, just in case his blade needed re-coating. He dropped his sword, fumbled for the stopped bottle, and ran towards Cies. The heat was unbearable and the jaws were more terrifying as they closed in on him, but Soren knew he could not falter. He removed the stopper from the bottle and tossed it into Cies's open jaws.

It sailed into his giant maw, dwarfed in an instant even as blue fire tumbled from the open neck of the clear bottle. The bottle danced through the air, creating a shimmering trail of flames into Cies' mouth, bounced off his spiked tongue, and into his throat.

In an instant, the white-hot fire brewing in Cies' throat turned the deepest blue, and he sputtered and choked. Soren dove aside as Cies spurted a jet of flames, but they were blue and cold. Cies thrashed as the fire consumed him from the inside, sending Lorellei tumbling from his back.

Cies swiped at Myrkdaga, but the young dragon held on with hate glowing in his eyes as he shredded Cies's wings, until, at last, he was knocked clear and sent tumbling through several stone columns and into the cathedral walls, which shook from the impact. Soren scrambled to his feet to run, but Cies' claw caught Soren, rending his armour from chest to midriff, and then his tail battered Soren too, sending him sailing through the air. Soren smashed into a pillar and sunk to its bottom in a crumpled heap.

Time slowed. He watched in slow-motion as Cies thrashed. More pillars collapsed and the roof caved in, raining slates. Buttresses fell. The vaulted ceiling tumbled in pieces, no longer beautiful and strong, but as missiles. Cies roared as they struck him. They fell as deadly rain, thudding into the ground and fracturing into infinitesimal pieces.

Myrkdaga rushed to Soren's side, carrying Lorellei in his jaws, and gingerly deposited the unconscious Eldarkind beside the fallen king. The young dragon sheltered them all against the pillar, screeching in pain as he was hit time and again with falling masonry. Glass shattered, leaving no window intact. Cies' scales glowed blue, and the blue ice-fire peeked between them, bursting to emerge. Emerge it did, and through the smallest gap in Myrkdaga's wings, Soren saw the silver dragon consumed entirely by the blue flames. With one final shriek, Cies fell to the ground and did not rise.

Soren blinked slowly. The pain was overwhelming. White hot and fierce. He could feel hot blood leaking down his front to pool in his lap. With every beat of his slowing heart, it pulsed out. Myrkdaga had sunk to his haunches under the brutal barrage, and his weight and warmth smothered Soren. Soren tried to move, but no part of his body worked. He couldn't breathe it hurt so much, and his chest would no longer obey him.

The pact, he tried to say. *I must remake the pact. I know how. I cannot fail.* No words emerged, only the faintest moan. The tightness of his chest was painful now. Soren's lips cracked open in an attempt to suck air in, anything. He wanted to take a breath so desperately, but it would not come. *I… have… failed…*

He would die. He would never rebuild the pact. He had failed. There was no energy or effort left to be sad, or angry; or feel anything. Soren's eyes slipped shut and he faded into darkness.

THIRTY ONE

Myrkdaga dragged the still forms of Soren and Lorellei through the collapsed cathedral wall just as Tarrell and Farran landed. Farran's wings battered the square in warm winds filled with ash and smoke that made Myrkdaga cough.

Farran galloped towards him with Tarrell close behind. "Where is he?" Farran growled.

"Dead," said Myrkdaga. "Cies is dead."

"What of Soren?" Tarrell asked urgently as he surveyed the devastation before them with wide eyes.

"Here," Myrkdaga said.

Tarrell rushed to his side.

Farran passed them without a word, and leapt onto the piles of rubble, digging through them to discover for himself.

Tarrell placed a hand on Soren's forehead and felt for a pulse before doing the same with Lorellei. "We have no time to speak of what has passed. Can you fly? We must try to save them."

Myrkdaga nodded. "I can fly." *Barely. But I will not desert them.* He looked down at the pair. Lorellei looked in peaceful slumber, but Soren was a bloody, rent mess.

"Take Soren to the castle, now. I will have healers waiting." Tarrell shook his head. His eyes lingered over the wounds, which still oozed blood. "I do not know if we can save him. We must try. I will take care of Lorellei." He placed his hands on Soren and sent a blaze of magic surging into the fallen king. "Mayhap that will help."

Myrkdaga gathered Soren in his clawed feet as gently as he could and took off with a giant leap into the air. His wings screamed with pain as he laboured, flapping them harder and harder to gain speed and altitude.

Pandora burned beneath him in a raging inferno. Ashes

floated up on the heat, tickling Myrkdaga's nostrils as he breathed them in. He paid little heed to it, glancing down only to look at Soren. He was sickly in the murky orange glow, and the blood was dark and thick upon him. He felt cold in Myrkdaga's claws, and he moved not at all. *I cannot even sense breath from him, nor heartbeat.* Myrkdaga's eyes lingered over him. There was precious little hope to be found here. He was not sure what even Eldarkind healers could accomplish.

His thoughts turned to the pact. Cies was vanquished. All he had sought was accomplished. But of course, Farran sought the greater good, as did Tarrell, as did Soren. Where would that be now without Soren? Myrkdaga had seen Bahr and he did not wish for others like him. He growled, gritted his teeth against the pain, and pushed harder to reach the healers at the castle. *Almost there.*

"Farran!" Tarrell cried, hovering about Lorellei for the dragon still dug with the needs of a madman. "We have work yet to do!" He bent over once more to murmur words of healing into Lorellei's ear. He was relieved to see a small flushed tinge on Lorellei's cheeks and the faint rise and fall of his chest.

Tarrell's words were drowned by an almighty roar as Farran uncovered Cies's body beneath the rubble. "Cies is dead!" he shouted into the minds of everyone who could hear; friend and foe alike. "The traitor and worm is vanquished, never to rise again. Come and see for yourselves." He spat the challenge out and began to tug Cies's giant body from the ruins so it could be seen.

Cies had not died a good death. The edge of every scale was burnt to a white, fine ash, and they were faded and pitted with damage from the ice-fire magic. Cies' eyes were closed, but through the slit of his eyelids, Farran could see dull, lifeless pupils. He grinned with satisfaction and tugged harder until Cies' crumpled form lay in a heap upon the ruins. He roared again and spurted a giant jet of fire into the sky.

"All you who followed Cies of the silver scales; the traitor, the coward, and the outcast. Come see what has happened to your mighty leader!" Farran crowed into the night. His eyes glittered with glee. Dragons of his own clan alighted around him, and they roared with him of their prowess, shouting into the darkening skies of sunset.

Farran might have acted for the greater good, but he was no soft dragon. A clan head had to be ruthless. "Hunt them down," he said to his clan. "All who defected. Kill any who will not join us. There can be no peace for us until they are all gone." Dragons took to the sky in a whirlwind, and he followed them into the air with grim resolve. It was no enjoyable thing to kill kin, but for the future safety of the clan, and the future of the pact, there was no other choice.

Tarrell exclaimed with frustration as Farran left. "Dragons," he said through gritted teeth.

Lorellei murmured an intelligible sound and Tarrell bent closer to here.

"St..u…. Stubb..orn…" Lorellei opened his eyes slowly, groaning. "My… head…"

Tarrell sighed with relief. "I am glad you are alive, Lorellei. Well done." He placed his hands upon Lorellei's shoulders and channeled some of his own energy into the younger Eldarkind to revitalise him.

Moments later, Myrkdaga landed with a crash and a thud. "Well met, friend," he said with a toothy grin at Lorellei.

Lorellei slowly sat, and used Myrkdaga's bulk to pull himself to his feet where he swayed unsteadily. "Well met, indeed." Lorellei grimaced. "What happened? We're not dead."

"We defeated Cies," Myrkdaga replied smugly, a puff of smoke bursting from his nose.

Lorellei had no answer for that. Speechless, he surveyed the wreckage around them and his eyes fixated on Cies' body. "I did not think it possible."

"We are not done yet. There will no doubt be dragons who will not acknowledge defeat. Will you fly with me once more?"

"I would be honoured, friend." Lorellei winced as he clapped Myrkdaga on the leg. *What is necessary, is not always easy,* Lorellei reminded himself and clambered onto Myrkdaga once more with a pounding head, aching body, and a drawn sword.

It was swiftly done after Cies' defeat. Many smaller dragons meekly surrendered in the face of Farran's clan, the Eldarkind, the humans, and the ice-fire magic. There were few to defeat in combat, and fewer still who ran, for cowardice was not a common trait amongst dragonkin.

Those who had surrendered were not welcomed back into the clan, but viewed with suspicion. They were to remain, for now, outside Pandora under the watchful eyes of dragons loyal to the clan, where they would cause no trouble.

Then, it was all hands needed to put out the fires still raging in places of the city. By all accounts, Pandora was ruined, but before it could be rebuilt, it had to be quenched. In this, the dragons could not help due to their vulnerability to water, but the Eldarkind's magic made up for that as they drew water from the ground to extinguish the flames whilst Pandora's people made human chains to pass buckets from the lake into the city.

THIRTY TWO

Soren's eyes opened just a crack to warm, inviting light, but it blinded him, and his eyes slipped shut once more. That was strange. He had not expected to awaken again. His head pounded. He tried to swallow, overwhelmed by the dryness of his mouth, but his muscles would not obey him.

Everything was almost silent; the only sounds the rustle of something nearby.

"Nngh," Soren managed to say. That hurt, too. Everything hurt. His front more than anything; it was on fire with pain. His breaths were laboured and shallow, for each hurt even more.

"Don't move," a firm, reassuring voice said.

Tarrell, his lethargic mind suggested. Soft hands—more than one pair—were cool and soothing on his skin.

"You took quite a beating," Tarrell said, somewhere above him. "Welcome back to the land of the living, Soren. We were not sure you would make it for quite some time."

Beside Soren, Tarrell and his team of Eldarkind healers continued to labour, soaking dressings and applying them to Soren's bloodied body to gently clean it.

It had been a long healing over several days, and Tarrell's own eyes threatened to droop shut, but he was determined not to fail. Without Soren, the rebuilding of the pact and the saving of all they held dear would be lost. Tarrell would give everything he could before he let Soren slip away, because the alternative did not bear thinking about.

They had needed all their skills and concentration to save him, for Soren's wounds ran deep and he was on the verge of death as they tended to him. It had taken hours of joint spell casting to knit Soren's broken flesh back together, mend broken bones, and replace his blood loss.

Tarrell looked over the king's broken body. There would be a reckoning yet. Soren would have much to come to terms with. Even the Eldarkind could not work miracles.

"Water," Soren whispered hoarsely. A cool trickle of liquid ran down his throat as someone carefully tipped it through his cracked lips. "Thank… you." He slipped back into unconsciousness, hounded by shadows of fragmented dreams.

It was easier the next time. Everything still hurt, but this time, Soren managed to open his eyes. Gaunt and exhausted, Tarrell continued waiting on him. He slumbered sitting up with his head tipped to one side, but jerked awake as Soren twitched his limbs under the coverlet. *My chamber*, Soren realised. "What happened?" His voice was hoarse. Soren tried to prop himself on his pillows, but, once more, his body would not obey, and Tarrell placed a hand gently on his shoulder to stop him.

"Do not move. Not yet."

Soren lay back obediently. Full of questions, he opened his mouth, but unsure where to start.

"You may now add 'dragon slayer' to your list of titles," said Tarrell with a wry smile. "Cies is gone—vanquished forever—thanks to you and your quick thinking. Myrkdaga says you were quite heroic, in a reckless sort of way." Tarrell explained what had happened after Soren passed out.

"I thought I would never wake again," said Soren quietly. There had been no time to reconcile with his death, but he had been so certain that was the end.

Tarrell regarded him with an inscrutable face, remaining silent for a while before he replied, "You very nearly did not wake, Soren. I… we… have done our best. You are alive, and that is what matters."

"What do you mean?" said Soren. He frowned.

"We cannot make all whole again. You were too deeply

injured. Time will tell how this will affect you, but for now, you have some scarring."

Soren struggled to sit up. Tarrell made to stop him, but he shook his head. "I want to see."

At Tarrell's word, his Eldarkind attendants dragged forward a tall mirror, and Soren slipped his feet over the side of the bed to sit up. His legs, he noticed, were covered in bruises: purple blooms of all shapes and sizes that spread across his skin. *Armour isn't dragon-proof, then.* Soren dragged his gaze away from his legs, which seemed otherwise intact, to look in the mirror. He swallowed.

He was naked under the covers, and it meant not a detail escaped him when he tugged them back; though, it would have been hard to miss. A giant, red scar, freshly healed, swirled from his shoulder to his hip, across his chest and stomach. It was hideous. The skin was angry and vibrant, not yet healed, with scabbing and pale areas on the edge of infection.

"You broke a leg when Cies threw you aside," Tarrell said quietly, watching Soren for his reaction. "Several ribs. Fingers. One of your arms. An ankle. These were easy enough to heal, for the most part, though, you may notice stiffness and aching for a while. This, though… Cies's claw rent your armour with ease, like shearing though fabric. You lost so much blood you were almost beyond saving. That alone will leave you weakened for a short time. This wound was not something we could heal whole again. With some further ministrations, we will ensure it gives you no pain and will not be susceptible to infection, but you may not be able to fight and move as you did, for the flesh of a scar does not knit together properly again."

Soren could not take his eyes from the wound. He had rarely considered himself handsome, but now his athletic body would be forever marred by this.

"Come, you must rest some more. We still have work to do before you are ready to try walking."

Soren slid back into bed obediently, but he could not erase the unsightly image of his battered body from his mind.

Better alive and scarred, than dead? he asked himself.

759

In a few days, Soren was able to walk with minimal pain and the wound on his chest gave him little trouble, save where the scar tissue tugged at him strangely as he moved. That would take some getting used to.

As soon as he was able, he met with both Tarrell and Farran to discuss what had happened. There was much news to be shared of the battle and what had happened since, but they had won, and that was all that mattered to Soren.

"I am grateful for your help, Lord Tarrell. Without you…" Soren gestured to himself and drew a finger across his neck.

Tarrell smiled and bowed his head. "I am relieved that we could save you."

"Farran-visir, well met," Soren executed a short bow to the dragon, grimacing as his body warned him not to bend too low.

"Well met, Soren-visir," Farran rumbled, affording him the dragon's term of respect.

Once they had discussed news of the battle, for Soren did not recall anything after his battle with Cies and there was much he had missed, it was time for Soren to tell his own strange tale of how Brithilca had saved him from certain death at Cies' claws and shown him of the making of the original pact.

Soren explained it as best he could, painfully aware that he might sound insane, but Tarrell and Farran listened intently to his every word without a sound. They did not speak until he had finished.

"I wish we could have seen this for ourselves," said Tarrell longingly. They scried Brithilca at once, but the spectral dragon had only disappointment for them.

"I have no doubt what you say is true, Soren," Brithilca said gravely. "However, once more, my mind is clouded and I cannot see that which you speak of. I am sorry."

"What did Lord Falykas say? Can you remember the exact words?" Tarrell leaned forwards.

"I…" Soren was about to deny him further, but he found that

he remembered it with crystal clarity. "I need a quill and parchment at once, before I forget it!" he said.

Tarrell rushed off to fetch one and returned momentarily, with a freshly inked quill held at the ready.

Soren repeated Brithilca's translation of the binding pact. "Great spirits, I command you to sleep, unmoving, unthinking, unchanging, and unyielding. Fire Spirit Bahr, I bind you under ice and water. I bind you with this, my energy, the energy of my kin, the iron of man, and the strength of dragonkin, until the end of time."

Tarrell scribbled the last words and blew on the parchment to try the ink. "What else? That cannot be all, for we attempted similar wordings to rebind Bahr of the Fire, Arandulus of the Water, and others; and all have failed. Tell us every detail of what passed. There must be an answer in what you saw."

Soren closed his eyes and brought forward the memory that was not a memory, reliving every detail, and trying to recall anything that might be material.

"The dragons," Soren said slowly, his eyes still clamped firmly shut as visions flashed through his mind. "They had melted a glacier. The Eldarkind were using the water to trap Bahr. It held Bahr at bay, but not for long. And then... Falykas spoke the incantation. Beren's armour melted from him, and flew into the sky to join the water encircling Bahr. It seemed to slow him. Iron, it would have been at that time. There are few remnants left now. It was not enough."

Tarrell and Farran listened with bated breath.

"Falykas cut his own palm," Soren continued, "and Beren's, and mingled their blood. He cut Brithilca too—dragons have purple blood!" Soren exclaimed. "Falykas caught the blood in his palm, and then shouted the incantation again. I think it was the same one—the words were lost to the wind. This time, it felt different. I could feel the magic ripping through me—Beren—through all of us. Brithilca vanished; he glowed like white hot fire, and disintegrated to nothing. Beren lost consciousness." Soren opened his eyes. "That was all I saw."

"I can continue," said Brithilca. "I remember now... some small details, as if through a haze. Beren and Falykas lived on. Bahr was imprisoned in ice, and my spirit inadvertently became his guardian. I have soaked up the magic and power of the bound elementals, as I have that of my kin for a millennia now. We must do this with Arandulus before it is too late. Soren, as your gift to the pact, we need iron. Tarrell, of you and yours, your magic. And Farran, of thine and mine, our strength."

"So, that is how it is done," mused Tarrell. "The pact is in the blood, iron, strength, and the binding itself."

"And in the elemental's greatest weakness," added Brithilca. "For Bahr, it was water, in any form. For Arandulus, it will be different."

"Earth," said Tarrell.

"There is no time to be wasted if Arandulus walks the earth once more," said Farran sombrely.

"Will you go at once to bind Her?" Soren asked.

"Yes," Tarrell replied, and met his glance. "And you must come with us. We need your blood, and your iron."

"I will need some time. We do not use iron to make our armour or our blades anymore. I shall have to raid the forges and the stables and such places to gather some. Do you have need of more of my men?"

Tarrell and Farran shared a glance Soren did not need explaining. "No."

Soren dipped his head in acquiescence. "I understand. Will you permit me to put my affairs in order before I leave? I have much to do." *And a plan of my own.*

He left anyway, once he had extricated himself from their polite goodbyes. He had not asked permission to leave, it was merely a formality, a politeness. Soren summoned the council at once.

Barclay was first to arrive. "Well met, Soren! By jove, I thought we'd lost you." He strode forward and clasped forearms with Soren, his face beaming with a relieved smile. Soren noticed he looked worse for wear himself and bore bruising to his face.

Barclay raised an eyebrow. "Oh, this?" he said airily. "A mere bump, compared to your injuries."

Soren grinned, though his smile faded as other council

members began to file in. Soon, they all sat, awaiting his command. Not one of them walked without an injury of some kind. That pleased him in a strange way. It meant they had all fulfilled their duties. Even Rafe, son of Asquith the coward. Perhaps, he had injured himself trying to flee. The thought materialised before he could stop it. Soren's lips twitched in a smile, and he pursed them shut instead.

First, he collected their reports from the battle. All were similar. Fire. Destruction. Heavy losses to the archers' ranks. And little they could do. Their thoughts already turned to the devastation outside. Few areas of Pandora had escaped unscathed, and many had been totally destroyed. But they all agreed, grudgingly in most cases, that without the dragons and the Eldarkind, they would have been completely defeated.

"Quite," nodded Soren. "I hope now, that you can see the value of why I pushed so hard for an alliance?" He looked around the room, but got little more than reluctant nods. "Our oldest allies shall remain our strongest. We have but one more task to complete together, and I must leave you for this." That grabbed their attention. All eyes were now fixed on him and not a word was spoken.

"Roher. What are the latest reports, Barclay? I asked you to keep records of traders. Behan? News from our ambassador?"

"Strange indeed," said Behan, speaking first as his rank was most senior. "Our eyes and ears in Arrans tells of chaos in Harad's court. By all accounts, and these have been verified by crown prince Janus, a god or demon walks the earth, spreading destruction and death on Roher. None may stand in its way. Harad is increasing his army as quickly as he can with boys younger and younger, and he puts on the most lavish and barbaric shows of power to appease these Roherii gods. By all accounts, it sounds bizarre. I cannot fathom the truth of it myself."

"Your report corroborates this?" Soren turned his attention to Barclay.

Barclay nodded. "The traders tell much the same story and we suffer losses to wares from Ladrin and east Roher, most notably of all. All the sea and western land routes are open, but it seems the north roads out of Roher are closed, for some reason. There is a story of a great being of water as tall as the sky who washes away all before it."

Soren nodded gravely. Arandulus. He had seen Her for himself, and would have described Her exactly the same. *A great being of water as tall as the sky*, he mused. "Strange, indeed, it seems, I know, but I know it to be the truth. What has risen is no god or demon, but an elemental of water who has lain bound for a millennia. The old stories of King Beren are true. He did make a pact with dragons and Eldarkind, and into that pact they made a binding to subdue the elementals to everlasting slumber, to save all three of our races. The pact is broken, and the elementals are rising. They bear no love for us. For our safety, we must turn to this new enemy at once, and defeat it."

Groans arose from the council, and questions. Soren held up a hand to stymie them.

"I know of a way to stop this being, and form a lasting, binding, meaningful peace with Roher."

The council fell silent at once and all leaned forward expectantly.

"The Roherii are powerless against Arandulus; for that is what the being of water is called. She is a powerful water elemental. They can do nothing to stop Her, however great their armies grow, because humans are of little consequence to Her, as they are to other elementals. We have something the Roherii do not. An alliance with dragons and Eldarkind; the very beings who can stop the elementals." Soren did not mention the pact. *Let them believe that we need our allies more than they need us… it is probably true.*

"It is my plan to offer Roher terms of peace, on the condition we banish Arandulus for good. We seek to do this anyway, but I do not see why we cannot also help our own cause. I am under no illusions. Our truce with Roher is weak, at best. I am certain when they grow strong enough, unless we have an agreement they will adhere to, we will be at their mercy again. We have a city, nay, a country to rebuild. We do not need that, too."

"So, why not leave this being to destroy them?" said Willam of Walbridge, Barclay's father. "Why sacrifice our men, or our... allies... to save the Roherii, for a peace treaty we doubt they will uphold anyway?"

"Because Arandulus bears no love for any of us. She will happily destroy the Roherii, and we would most likely be next. Not to mention, the other elementals who also awaken from their long slumber bear us all enmity," Soren explained patiently, though he could not be cross with them, for it was a lot to understand. "Regardless of Roher, I am duty bound to assist the dragons and Eldarkind in binding Arandulus once more; and her kin. Yet, we can do it in such a way to exact a lasting promise from Roher. If they believe us to be capable of defeating gods, will they be so quick to attack us in future? I think not."

"If we do not do this, these... elementals... will seek conflict with us?" Theodore of House Arendall said with a wrinkled brow.

Soren nodded, regarding them all solemnly. "It will be worse by far than the battle we have just endured. Caledan, all its people, and any trace of our existence will be wiped from the face of the earth with ease when they rise. It is not 'if', it is 'when'. The sooner we act, the easier it will be to contain this."

"What do the Eldarkind and the dragons need from us?" Theodore was still confused.

"Myself, primarily. I must be there when the binding is made, and strangely, iron, and plenty of it. Do you know of the old fairy tales of iron warding against fey beings?" He looked around the table with a furrowed brow and watched them nod in confusion. "Well, it appears this is much the truth. Iron will be our gift to the binding. I need as much as we can find, immediately. Send your men to raid the forges, stables, anywhere we might find some. By the word of the Eldarkind and the dragons, we cannot succeed without it."

As they departed, Soren could not help but feel a small pride at what he had accomplished. Somehow, despite all the odds, he had secured his role as king. They would follow him for now. Perhaps, for a long time, even into the strangest of situations. At last, he felt like a man, not a boy. If he could only manage to defeat Arandulus, and in the process bind Roher to peace, he would earn their loyalty for life, he was sure. *If only.* Soren suspected it would not be as easy as he hoped.

THIRTY THREE

Soren handpicked a dozen of his most trusted men to accompany him, and Barclay as his right hand man. They were to travel to Roher immediately with all the dragons and those Eldarkind who were not needed urgently in the healing houses for the gravely injured. His men were none too pleased, however, when they discovered they would be travelling on dragon-back, but there was little other choice. Soren was glad. It was a much smoother ride than on horseback, which he appreciated more than he could say, for his body screamed at him still.

Travel to Roher took three weeks at best; a long and arduous route by sea, and a dangerous and deadly one by land. Yet on dragon back, they would arrive within days. Soren could see the growing worry in Tarrell; his tight lips, troubled eyes, and constantly moving fingers told a tale his voice would not. There was no other option; time was running out, and Soren told his men as such.

"I have chosen you because, though you number few, you are the greatest men I could have by my side in what will be the most crucial battle of our lives. You have already been briefed on the nature of our visit. I know it is difficult to comprehend what we face. Even I struggle. Yet, I would not choose any others to go into battle with." His lips twitched in a smile as they saluted him: their fists brought up to their chests in the old way that was so rarely used now.

They rode three apiece on the largest and strongest of the dragons, who could bear their weight with ease. The entire dragon clan had mobilised and flew with them, even those who had defected to Cies. Farran wanted to keep them close, and this would be their chance to prove themselves, or die trying, in his mind.

It was dawn when they departed, and dusk settled as they descended to find a place to camp that night. The dragons did not need sleep, but their human and Eldarkind counterparts flagged. A day spent on dragon-back in the frigid, gusty air of the heights was too much to bear through the night. Already, they had flown south from Caledan and across to the mainland above Roher, where the deserts swathed the land.

A dark blot on the pale sands was their home for the night; a small oasis for them to drink at. As they landed, the heat of the sand from that day's sun baked them until they stood under the shelter of a few scraggly trees. It was a world away from the lush greenery of their homes. As they filled their water flasks, the huge disc of the sun slipped, bloody red, beyond the horizon, leaving them in the dark and quiet of the desert night.

The next day, they alighted just north of Arrans, Roher's capital city, and Soren set his plan in motion. The dragons and Eldarkind would not accompany him. Instead, they remained far from the capital; away from the roads and anyone who might spy them. This was the part of his idea that Soren had the least faith in. *Trust the plan*, he said to himself.

Soren and his dozen men dressed in their finest clothes, buckled on their armour, and unfurled the Caledonian banners which they had brought with them for this very purpose. Soren cast a critical eye over his band as they assembled. Not the finest envoy he could imagine, but certainly a more impressive sight to appear from the desert than their dusty travelling attire.

The late afternoon sun scorched them, and Soren could feel perspiration dripping down his torso as the heat roasted him. They approached the walls of Arrans, where the road ran through an impressive gatehouse. The red stone towered above them, ending in triangular crenellations that were uncomfortably reminiscent of dragon teeth. As they stepped into the shade of the guardhouse, Soren felt unnervingly like he was walking into a real dragon's mouth. Here he was, one of only thirteen men, about to set foot inside an unfriendly capital. Here he was, with no fall back plan and no means of escape. Here he was, placing himself knowingly at the mercy of a powerful king who would not hesitate to crush him if he so chose. *Trust to the plan*, he repeated.

Guards watched them approach with obvious confusion. No horses. Shining armour. Banners. *We must look like a mirage to them.* Soren's lips twitched. The portcullis was raised and the way clear. *Only traders must pass through here for Roher did not expect an army*, Soren thought, but as he made to walk through, the guards scrambled to stop him.

He chose an appropriate look of disdain and stepped back as one made to bar his way, coming so close as to contact him.

"I request an immediate audience with King Harad," said Soren in a tone that brooked no argument and sought no permission.

Barclay stepped forward with a warning glance at Soren. "Have His Majesty informed at once that King Soren of Caledan, of the Throne of the Dragon Kings, Dragon's Bane, Eldar-friend, Dragon-friend, First of his Name, seeks counsel at once."

The guard looked them up and down, and his eyes lingered on the banners. He called sharply and another scurried out of the gatehouse. "Caledonians." He gestured at Soren.

"I translate," said the newcomer in a thick accent. Barclay repeated his request, and the man bowed. "At once." He spoke quickly and urgently to his comrade, who saluted and jogged through the gate to mount one of the horses tethered in a shelter inside. Within moments, he had galloped into the city in a cloud of dust.

"Please, here." The remaining guard waved them forward, into the cool shade of the gate. "He is getting, ah…" he fumbled for the right word and shook his head. "Horse. Many horse, for you."

The thunder of hooves roused them some minutes later as the man returned with thirteen mounts for them, all fitted with strange saddles and bridles, and walked them past a mounting block so Soren and his men could mount. Soren stepped onto the mounting block with as much grace as he could muster. Even in the shade, the heat was overwhelming.

They rode through the city at speed, but even so, it was a rush of sensory overload. Arrans was sprawling; far more vast than

Pandora, for it spanned a valley that sunk between several hills and spread as far as the eye could see. They rode on wide, paved roads, but if he glanced left or ride, Soren could see shaded alleyways of bare dirt snaking between buildings that grew more ramshackle the further back they ran from the main street, which was kept immaculate.

Ahead, on the tallest point of the city, he could see a sprawling palace that had nothing in common with Pandora, either. His own castle felt poxy compared to it. The streets became wider, cleaner, quieter, and more affluent the further they travelled into the city. Ramshackle slums were replaced with towering stone build buildings with impressive facades and high walled gardens.

Here, the roads had gutters for waste water and a raised pavement each side of the road. Roherii men and women walked along it, dressed in clothes the likes of which Soren had not seen before: draped robes and dresses of the finest floating silks and in the most vibrant dyed colours.

The grandest of them did not walk at all, but were carried in chairs and palanquins by uniformed servants. All Soren could see through the translucent curtains shielding them from onlookers and the sun was the shadow of a face and the flash of jewellery, and then they were gone in a cloud of perfumed air as their bearers loped past.

There was no time to admire the grand walls and gates of the palace, nor stop to stare at the manicured gardens—lush and green, bursting with flowers, and scattered ornamental fowl and exotic beasts scattered about—for they were rushed inside the palace immediately.

Soren dismounted and followed his guide inside, shadowed by his men, who did not move to take their armour off despite the heat, and kept their fingers close to their swords and their eyes roving for signs of a threat.

They strode over polished marble floors, through frescoed high-ceilinged halls, and past priceless works of art. It was lavishness like Soren had never seen before; purely for pleasure, over Pandora castle's need for function first. Indefensible, he thought, as he spied floor to ceiling windows open to the elements. His guide paused outside a grand door. Soren could not discern the wood, but it was covered with elaborate carvings and embellished with wrought metal designs. As Soren watched his guide slip inside, he noticed that even the door handles were elaborately designed. *Gold?* he wondered. The giant doors opened suddenly before him, silent on their hinges, and his guide gestured them into the huge space of the grand hall beyond.

Soren stood tall and proud and marched inside, knowing his men would be in identical form, with his banners held proudly as they were announced.

"His Supreme Majesty King Harad, Third of his Name, King of Roher, Ladrin and all the Lands of the West, welcomes King Soren of Caledan, of the Throne of the Dragon Kings, Dragon's Bane, Eldar-friend, Dragon-friend, and First of his Name," a booming voice introduced him.

Harad sat before them, statuesque, on a grand throne that sat on a stepped dais high above their heads. It was imposing, luxurious, and a display of wealth and power. The throne was studded with gems and precious metal designs, and Harad sat with a heavy crown atop his head, draped in golden and purple fabrics, and displaying a gaudy amount of jewellery. He looked like a sculpture.

It was far from Soren's last meeting with Harad—his first—outside the gates of Pandora all that time ago. Then, he had worn crafted armour that enhanced his physique into a fearsome warrior. Now, Soren could see that, although fearsome and impressive, his hair had greyed somewhat more, and he had descended ever so slightly more into the corpulence of middle age.

Harad met his gaze as Soren strode across the smooth, polished floor that reflected his gleaming armour, and offered him a slight bow, as an equal. "Your Majesty," said Soren, straight faced and impassive. Harad, he noted, looked more than a little surprised to see him—as was to be expected—but he recovered with grace, as Soren expected.

"Your Majesty," Harad greeted him, but did not rise from his chair. His eyes, which had widened ever so slightly at Soren's entrance, now closed again as Harad resumed his customary shrewd and impassive expression.

Soren noticed his glance furtively checking the room. They were surrounded by guards, he knew; some visible and some hidden in the shadows behind the vast columns which held up the lofty ceiling. *Harad will be calculating whether to hear me out or not bother.* They were vastly outnumbered, and in the heart of his enemy's territory. *Trust the plan,* he steadied himself again.

"I thank you for receiving me at such short notice, Your Majesty," began Soren. "I ask that you send your men away, for I bear urgent news for your ears only."

Harad scoffed, but Soren's grave expression did not waver. "I know of your current predicament," he said quietly, focusing his attention on Harad, who sat forward in his throne, straining to listen. Soren stepped forward until he was at the foot of the dais. Guards leaned forward, too, but Harad dismissed them with a flick of his finger and they sank back into their positions. "I know of the being of water, as tall as the sky."

Harad blanched.

"I warn you now. You will not want any other to hear what I must tell you." Soren drew himself up tall and firm, exuding a confidence he did not feel, and did not let his determined expression flicker.

Harad regarded him inscrutably, not giving any hint as to his thoughts. His eyes glittered under a shadowed brow his crown cast over his face. At last, he shifted on his throne and stood. At a slash of his hand, guards melted away. "Pray, continue." He stepped slowly from the dais.

Soren suppressed a grim smile as King Harad descended to his level. *I have his attention piqued, at least.*

"It—She—is called Arandulus. She is an elemental. I suppose a god of sorts. She terrorises Roher, yes?" He looked to Harad, but he gave no response. *Of course, he does not want to admit weakness, even in private.* "And you cannot stop her." No response, not even a twitch. Harad watched him guardedly now, like a predator. "I can defeat her."

Harad froze and fixed Soren in an eagle eyed stare.

"I *alone* can defeat her," Soren repeated. "I can restore peace to Roher... and stability to your rule. It is undermining, no? Not being able to help your own people."

Harad scowled, at last showing a chink in his seemingly impregnable armour. "No man can defeat this demon," Harad sneered, but he was flustered by Soren's unrelenting calm demeanour. "What is this madness?"

"I promise you," said Soren, letting a smile slip. "I can deliver you from this being."

"How can it be done?"

Soren paused, and his tongue darted out to wet his lips. "I cannot reveal it. Naturally, it is no ordinary method I use. But I promise you, it can be done, and by I alone. You will have to trust to that." Soren could see Harad's inner struggle. *He is not one to relinquish control, power... or to trust.*

"It cannot be done," Harad said at last with a sneer.

"I promise it. On my honour as a king," said Soren solemnly. "Naturally, in exchange for this great deed, I would require something in return."

Now Harad regarded him with curiosity. *At last, we speak the same language: business.*

"Will you accept my offer? If you think it impossible, what do you have to lose?"

"What do you desire in return?" Harad's tone was guarded.

Soren suppressed a laugh. *Ever the businessman. He does not want to lose in this; as if the stakes could be higher for him!* "I will defeat Arandulus, the 'demon' who terrorises you, in exchange for a meaningful, lasting peace treaty between our two nations."

Harad was speechless.

"What say you? Is that a worthy price to pay for the salvation of your nation? By the accounts I hear, Arandulus ravages Roher and there is nothing you can do to stop her. It is only so long before your people lose faith in you." As it had happened with himself and the dragon attacks. *That was a dark time.*

A flicker of anger crossed Harad's face. "I can—"

"Not deal with this alone," Soren interrupted him. "Humour me, if you think it so impossible. You have nothing to lose and everything to gain. If I succeed, peace is restored to your country and your rule will be secure once more. I will receive just recompense. If I fail, well, you do not have to fulfill your end of our agreement, and you are no worse off than before." Soren watched Harad carefully. He was clearly calculating his own conclusions, for his eyes focused unseeing into the distance. *He will be wondering whether it makes him any less of a man to accept help… and realising that Caledan will be ripe for the taking should I fail. The stakes are high for me, too. Trust to the plan…*

"I will agree to this," Harad said stiffly.

Soren smiled, a thin lipped smile of gladness, but not relief. This was just one step in a plan in which many things would have to come to fruition for success to be ensured. "I am most pleased to hear it, Your Majesty. I would suggest time is of the essence. I have less than two days at best before I must leave to complete my end of our bargain. I wish for our peace treaty to be negotiated and signed by then."

Harad was not used to taking orders, or instruction, it was clear. A muscle in his cheek twitched and he clapped. A servant appeared in a flurry of movement from seemingly nowhere. Harad fired a rapid babble of Roherii at him, and the servant bowed, scraping the floor with his robes, and rushed away. "It shall be done," Harad said grudgingly.

The negotiations took two days to complete, and Soren itched to leave. Tarrell and Farran's own sense of urgency filled him.

They were made all the more difficult by the fact Soren did it alone, without the usual customary delegation that would assist him. Only Barclay accompanied him to negotiations, and the Caledonian ambassador to Roher, who Soren had never met before—a distant cousin to the Orrell family—who was glad to speak with someone else from his homeland.

He was a quiet man. Soren guessed anyone would have to be a private person to succeed in Roher. The Roherii court was a tense place, each watching Harad for his actions. Harad was quick to punish his enemies, and angering him never ended well. *It must be a hard job here. Mind, the ambassador gets paid handsomely for his 'troubles',* Soren knew.

Luckily for Soren, between the three of them, they had managed to pour over the draft agreements, which were riddled with intentional omissions, misleading, and unfavourable terms. Even in such need, Harad would not offer a fair deal, it seemed. Soren had not expected anything less from the shrewd king. *Everything is business with him. The more he can gain, the better.*

"We are fast running out of time," Tarrell warned him again as Soren scried him using a small mirror he had secreted into the palace upon his person.

"I progress as fast as I can," Soren answered, dragging a hand across his face. He was tired. It had been a long day of negotiating. Peace treaties, as it happened, were intricate, fiddly, and time-consuming to decide.

"We appreciate that, Soren," Tarrell sighed. "But for our two races, Arandulus is the more pressing issue."

"We sign the treaty tomorrow morning—at last. I will leave immediately."

Tarrell was as satisfied as he could be, and it would have to do. *It is too late now to change the plan.*

As they ended the scrying, Tarrell turned to Farran with a sigh. They scried Brithilca next. The blue dragon flitted across the glass, filling its surface with his bulk.

"We have Eldarkind magic," Tarrell mused, "and a suitable binding to use. We have your strength and fire, too," he nodded at Farran, "though I suspect your fire will not sit you at an advantage in this fight?"

Farran rumbled in agreement. "No, indeed."

"You have my strength for the binding also," said Brithilca. "Remember, she cannot harm me in my current form, and I have an idea of my own. There is a way that I can use Arandulus's own magic and power to make myself a physical form with your help. Farran, you know how to summon me into water; think of it on a grander scale. I will be immune to her water based attacks, and can channel your strength and magic if you remain in close proximity."

"Will it succeed?" asked Tarrell.

Brithilca was silent. "I cannot be certain," he said eventually. "Yet, we are of limited options. The clan is susceptible to her magic and her water, so I must try. If we are not careful, she could end the entire clan on a whim."

Soren signed his name with a hideously impractical quill, made of a feather so large he could barely control its bobbing top as he wrote. But it was done, and the ink dried on a treaty more meaningful than any which had been signed in the past hundred years. It was not time to celebrate yet. *There is much to accomplish first.*

"A copy will be sent at once to Caledan?" he looked to Harad with a raised eyebrow. Harad nodded curtly. "I thank you. I retain the second copy, and you the third." He took the roll of parchment from Harad's aide.

"I will require proof," said Harad suddenly, regarding Soren through half-lidded eyes.

Soren froze. *Proof. There will be nothing left to show.*

"I shall send my firstborn, Janus, with you. He shall report to me on his return, what has passed. The treaty will take effect with the destruction of the demon you call Arandulus."

Soren thought quickly. "He will journey on horse?"

"Naturally." Harad's eyes narrowed again. "My men tell me you arrived from the desert with none of your own. Do you require mounts?"

"Ah, no, I have my own mounts outside the city." Soren avoided the question skillfully.

Within the hour, they were on their way. Soren and his dozen men, and Janus, who was a copy of his father, only some decades younger. He had the same ruthless feel, and Soren was under no illusions that there would be no camaraderie between them. *This is business to Harad. He will trust no one.*

Harad accompanied them, too, much to Soren's chagrin. He was clearly curious about the 'mounts' that Soren would not describe. *Perhaps, he thinks I have bred special horses or beasts.* Soren suppressed a chuckle. There would be nothing for it but to reveal his allies; a secret weapon of his own, he supposed.

Soren was glad that Janus had brought his own mount. It was still a sore point with the dragons that they bore their allies like beasts, and he had no intention of asking them to bear the son of a man he bore such enmity to. Perhaps, this could work out well. Tarrell and Farran will not wait for Janus. *Perhaps, by the time he catches up with us, our task will be complete.* Soren could only hope.

They crested the hill behind which the dragons and Eldarkind camped, and Soren heard Harad and Janus curse under their breath. They halted, wide-eyed and open-mouthed on the brow of the hill, regarding the sprawling camp of dragons and—to the Roherii—humans. Soren slyly examined them. A mix of fear, wonder and desire was written upon Harad's face.

Harad rode forward to Soren. "Such wondrous beasts are these. What are they?"

"Dragons," said Soren, and left it at that. He would not furnish Harad with more than was necessary.

"Where come you by these?"

Soren did not answer.

"What price do you demand for me to buy one, or perhaps more, from you?"

"They are not for sale," Soren said swiftly, annoyed by the lust in Harad's eyed. He looked at Harad scornfully. "They are our allies, not beasts of burden. They act only under their free will. I could not compel them to follow you if I tried." *At least, we are their allies,* Soren thought gladly. *I would fear to be their enemy.*

"Free will, you say," mused Harad. The lustful look had not disappeared him his eyes and Soren disliked the thoughtfulness with which he said it.

"Well met, Farran, Tarrell," he said as they approached. "I bring with me King Harad of Roher, and his son, Prince Janus." It was as much a warning as an introduction that meant 'do not speak freely'.

"It is a pleasure to make your acquaintance," murmured Tarrell with a bow as Soren introduced him.

Farran regarded them with inscrutable eyes, and did not offer the same bow he had offered to Soren upon meeting him. *His instinct is right*, thought Soren, as he watched Farran's wariness around Harad and his son.

"We must be away at once, yes?" Soren prompted.

"At once," Tarrell said. "We already make ready to leave."

"We shall fly far and fast," Soren said to Janus with no apology. "I thank you for telling us where Arandulus currently roams. Follow us as quickly as you can."

"I am not to ride these beasts like you?"

Farran began to growl.

"Come, I can pay if it a question of price. What say you?" Janus stepped forward hungrily.

"We are no beast of burden," growled Farran, and stabbed his head towards the Roherii prince.

Janus stumbled backwards and his face paled when Farran's teeth were bared in his face.

"I would not do your bidding if you asked it, and it certainly cannot be bought." Farran's lip curled in disgust; a surprisingly human reaction.

Harad stood back from the exchange, Soren noted, but his eyes still held a gleam of insatiable desire and curiosity.

THIRTY FOUR

The dragons, with the Eldarkind, and Soren and his men flew north-west swiftly, leaving Janus to trail them on his mount. He scrambled to keep up at first, but as they drew further and further ahead, gave up punishing his horse, which was well suited to riding in the desert, and settled for a steady pace instead.

It was a unanimous decision not to wait for him. There was no need for him to know of the pact and their magic, and much to do after Soren's delay in Arrans. It weighed heavily on all their minds of the need to catch Arandulus by surprise to hold the advantage, for the dragons were incredibly vulnerable to water and not even Eldarkind magic would be able to protect them from her wrath.

Flying as high as they did, they needed little direction from Janus, they discovered, for Arandulus was large enough to be visible ahead of them or, at least, Her storm was. Dark clouds piled high into the sky, and underneath them was an inky blackness they could not discern.

Arandulus moved quickly, for She was already almost at the isthmus of land which separated Roher and the mainland from Caledan.

"She will be seeking Bahr," Farran said grimly. "She will know he has perished, and Kotyir will draw Her, for it contains the last remnants of his magic."

They approached and dove into the roiling clouds sinking below them where they could spy Arandulus in the gloom. She marched inexorably north with her back to them, and the dragons stormed her at once, bathing her in swathes of fire. She turned and shrieked an inhuman sound of rage that grated on their ears.

"Spawn of Bahr!" she hissed, and turned her attention to

them. Soren's dragon—followed by those who carried his men—dove to the ground to land against the rising winds. They carried something else important, too: iron, and much of it.

"Encircle Her," Soren shouted to each man and dragon pair. "Do not break the circle at any time. It will be our failure if you do. Do not touch the water. Stay out of her reach and beneath her notice and watch your heads," he added, ducking to avoid a flying twig. "Am I clear?"

They all nodded, and quickly set to dividing the iron between them equally. Then, Soren was on his own with his dragon and his iron. For a moment, he stopped and looked up; and wished he had not. Arandulus towered above them, as tall as he could see. Her waters were white and dark, thrashing and tumbling over and amongst themselves.

Soren could see other things, too: trees, stones, and worse debris whipping round inside her form. Where her feet tethered to the ground, water rushed and surged, and Soren leaped onto his dragon so they could fly just out of reach of the water that snatched anything it could into its grasp, even as she plucked dragons from the sky and quenched their life in her wet fists.

Far above him on Farran's back, Tarrell began the incantation, which was taken up by the mouths of his kin, and the dragons crooned, calling Brithilca forth. Farran stumbled and stopped as Arandulus reached a giant watery arm to grab him.

Farran dove out of her way, but was not quick enough, and she grasped his tail. He screeched in pain and flapped wildly, but he could not escape her. A shape blasted out of Arandulus's side, a giant spray of water, as if she was flesh sliced by a sword.

She looked down, and, momentarily distracted, released Farran, who dashed away into the darkness to regroup at a distance. The water solidified into the huge shape of a dragon bigger than even Farran: Brithilca, though he was made of water, not flesh and scales. He roared, though it sounded strangely muted, as if he did so underwater, and attacked Arandulus mercilessly.

Tarrell resumed his spells as Brithilca harried Arandulus. With every second that passed, Arandulus grew more enraged and her assault grew more fierce. Dragons fell from the sky, their life quenched by her waters, to smash into the ground far below in a giant plume of sand.

Soren watched with horror, struggling to stand in the battering winds. It seemed like the tide of battle was turning, and they would not succeed as easily as he had hoped. There was little he could do but wait with his pile of iron, all the while suppressing the growing doubt within him.

Even though her assault was deadly and devastating, it seemed to fuel the dragons, and they rallied into performing even more daring manoeuvres to maintain their fiery attack. Brithilca's watery form flew around her, darting towards Arandulus and creating giant, scathing cuts through her that dashed water out into the air as if she bled it. Her form diminished as her water was vaporized by the relentless dragon fire and contained by the Eldarkind magic that constricted her. Bands of glowing light and swathes of fire that moved under the control of the spell encircled her form.

Soren could not help but watch slack-jawed with the rest of his men. He started as the iron beside him clinked and looked down. It moved of its own accord, rattling together as horse shoes clinked with anvils and nails, and then it seemed they melted, into shining liquid drops. Just like in his visions of Beren. They shivered and leapt into the sky, and as he looked across the plain, he saw glinting droplets flying towards Arandulus from all directions. They hit the bands of fire with splashes that cascaded sparks and joined into bands of glowing, molten metal that encircled Arandulus.

"No!" she snarled, and her eyes blazed blue like lightening on a summer's day. "No!" She struggled but could not snap the bonds. "Twice wronged, you shall pay dearly for this!" she raged at them, trying to stagger in any direction, but she could barely move.

Farran dropped from the sky with a thud behind Soren that made him jump, fearing he was about to be flattened by debris.

"Here!" Tarrell called, and he pulled out a knife.

Soren immediately understood and sprinted towards him in the growing gale as air battered and buffeted him. He hunkered behind Farran's bulk as Tarrell jumped from Farran's back, slashed both of their palms, and joined hands to mingle the blood. Soren bit back a cry.

Tarrell turned without delay to Farran, who tilted his head to offer the fleshy underside of his jaw. The knife nicked his hide swiftly, and Tarrell caught the giant purple drop of blood that fell, just as Falykas had in Soren's vision. The three bloods mingled on Tarrell's hand, and he closed his fist around the liquid and called the incantation again as Farran leapt into the sky to continue the battle.

"*Foss anda Arandulus, ia kaskea uan att aslura, inge flytte, inge tenkir, inge endra, inge eiende i a feld. Ia sinuar uan yta detthe, mina ethera, a ethera ro mina Eldarkin, a jarn ro ungrkin, ja a styrkr ro dragonkin, asti a lok ro timi!*"

Water spirit, I command you to sleep, unmoving, unthinking, unchanging, unyielding in the earth. I bind you with this, my energy, the energy of my kin, the iron of man, and the strength of dragonkin, until the end of time!

Tarrell's words were snatched away into the wind and they could do little but watch as Arandulus shrunk inside the growing bands of fire and metal. There were chinks in her cocoon, and she sought to escape. Great, arching jets of water spurted from them, but each time, Brithilca snapped at them with his own watery jaws and they disintegrated or Arandulus snatched them back inside her prison.

The forms in the sky collapsed in upon themselves and Arandulus emitted a keening shriek that split Soren's head. He closed his eyes as if it could shield against the sound, but even when he clutched his hands to his ears, he could not stop it piercing into his skull.

All of a sudden, the sound ceased and Soren opened his eyes again. What remained was a ball of twisting fire, molten metal, and pure light in the sky, shrinking into itself again and again. Arandulus still struggled to escape, but the loops of water spurting out grew less and less, and the watery form of Brithilca did not need to act before the force of the magic binding Arandulus pulled her essence back itself.

Soon, nothing was left but a ball the height of a man. Dragons converged on it from all directions, whipping their wings in a strange pattern. Sand rose from the desert into the maelstrom to form a vortex that shrouded Arandulus, and Soren could see it drove into the ground, boring a hole so deep he could not see the bottom. Through the flying sand, which was so sharp Soren had to half close his eyes to shield them, he watched as the orb descended into the hole.

The dragons changed to a new formation and a new pattern of beating wings, and the tornado of sand fell to the earth, now funnelled back to the hole from whence it came until the sand was settled again and nothing could be seen of Arandulus. Just a hump in the ground remained where she had displaced the sand.

Brithilca rumbled, soared over them, and disintegrated into a flood of water that plummeted from the sky as his spirit left its physical form.

Dragons roared with pride and joy, soaring into the sky and performing arcs and somersaults whilst others landed. Eldarkind slipped off their mounts and congregated by Arandulus' resting place. Tarrell, Farran, and Soren rushed to join them.

Already, the storm clouds were disintegrating and cracks of sunshine became swathes of pale, hazy desert sky. Mud baked. Puddles sunk into the sand. And soon, there was no clue as to what had happened.

As the Eldarkind and dragons congratulated each other, Soren looked up. On the horizon was the figure of a horse and a man. He galloped towards them and Soren jogged to meet him.

Soren was pleased to see that Janus was slack-jawed and speechless.

"You saw?"

Janus swallowed and nodded. His face was full of fear as much as it was questions, judging by the look of his twisted brows.

"Tell your father of this. I consider our treaty binding as of this moment." With great satisfaction, Soren turned and walked away. Only when he was out of sight of Janus and amongst the dragons and the Eldarkind did he let his shoulders slump with a huge sigh of relief. *Trust to the plan. We did it.*

THIRTY FIVE

It was a slower return to Pandora, but only just, for the dragons were battle weary, but there was still one urgent matter to attend to: the re-binding of all other elementals before they awoke. Soren considered that the pact was remade after facing Arandulus, but Brithilca had one last plan in mind that would not only seal the alliance between men, Eldarkind, and dragons, but rid them of the threat of the elementals forevermore.

There was no time to waste. As they arrived in Pandora, they flocked to the ruins of the cathedral where Brithilca's indestructible statue still stood amongst the collapsed walls and the devastated structure. Only the tower remained almost intact whilst much of the rest of the building was razed. Cies' damage of the columns holding the roof had done their job. It had collapsed almost entirely, pulling the walls down with it.

Stonemasons were already busy carting rubble away from the site and trying to organise the ruins, but it would be a process that would take decades to complete. As the dragons landed, the masons stopped work and stood back, watching curiously before they scrambled to sink into low bows when they recognised Soren. They made to down tools and leave, for the dragons overwhelmed their workspace, but Soren shook his head. "Stay. Witness this."

Soren stepped through the rubble carefully, flanked by Tarrell and Farran. Dragons ringed them, sitting on their haunches with their wings folded neatly away and with Eldarkind intermingled. As one, the dragons began to croon. The sound never failed to send shivers down Soren's spine, for magic flowed in their voices. The sound drew others, and before long, a growing crowd of Soren's people accumulated around them, standing and watching in silence.

Soren halted before the dais on which Brithilca's somehow

miraculously undamaged statue sat, waiting. A crack rent the air, and a second, and a third, and Brithilca's statue, inhabited by the spirit of the great dragon himself, slowly came to life as the dragons' song died. Brithlca stood and spread his wings, flexing them and unfurling them so they cast a great shadow.

Soren dropped to his knees, as did Tarrell, and Farran raised his chin to the stone dragon.

"Brithilca-visir," they murmured as one.

"Farran-visir. Tarrell-visir. Soren-visir. My kin and my allies," Brithlica rumbled. His great head swung from side to side as he swept his gaze over the still growing crowd. "Once, in the days of old, there was a man-king, an Eldar-king, and a dragon-king. King Beren, King Falykas, and myself. We warred. The land and its peoples were scarred. Yet, a greater threat than each of us endangered us all. Gods, you humans called them. Elementals, they are known to Eldarkind and dragonkin.

"We saw no option but to unite against this common enemy. In doing so, we succeeded. Our enemy, the elementals who sought to destroy us all, were vanquished, but not forever. In the thousand years since, they have lain in slumber. An alliance between men, Eldarkind, and dragons was forged, and for a millennia it endured, but it was broken by the corrupted magics of the elementals as they sought to escape their bindings. Our great bond unraveled. Apart, we were as weak as we had been when war divided us. Apart, the pact failed.

"Today, we bind the pact anew, and stronger than before; with openness so that we may all live freely together in harmony and prosperity, safe in the knowledge that those who seek to rise and destroy us shall all remain bound to lie in slumber for aeons more, until our three races end." Brithilca looked to Soren, Tarrell, and Farran. "Are you ready?"

Tarrell brought his knife to bear again, and cut into his palm once more. He had healed it before in seconds, as he had done with Soren's and Farran's cuts when they had faced Arandulus, but they had all three known it would not be the last time they gave their blood to the pact. He nicked Farran's throat again, and sliced into

Soren's palm. Once more, he mingled their bloods and held out his palm to Brithilca, who sniffed it.

Tarrell took a deep breath and looked Brithilca in the eyes. "Thank you, Brithilca-visir," he said softly.

Brithilca rumbled. "I have endured over a millennia now, trapped in an existence of darkness and an absence of sense and life. For a thousand years, I have been unable to feel the sun on my face, the wind beneath my wings, and the fire in my belly. I am strong, but I am tired. I gave my life once for the pact. I will do it again willingly, to see it endure for the life of our three races, and have my peace, too."

Farran responded in a tongue Soren could not understand— the dragon's own language, he supposed—and Brithilca replied in kind.

Last of all, Brithilca turned to Soren. "The dragon throne will be no more, and neither will the crown. You understand that the value of neither of these things lies in the item, but in you. Beren would have approved of the choices you have made."

Soren swallowed and blinked away the tears. All those years sitting before this immobile throne dreaming of adventures with dragons, and now, he had had an infinite amount more to do with Brithilca than he had ever thought possible—more than anyone else. It was still not enough, and still too dear to part with. *So much I will never know.*

His respect for the great spirit was even greater than that he held for the dragons and the Eldarkind, and he had not known Brithilca had suffered so over the years. It added to the ache in his heart for the sacrifices Brithilca had made, and the sacrifice he was about to. For, as Brithilca had informed them, he had the residual strength and magic to ensure that the pact could be rebound for as long as their three races endured, and, most importantly, the bonds upon all the elementals would be re-wrought at once. But in lending his strength, he would end his existence; trading his life, for all of theirs.

Tarrell approached Brithilca, who bent his head so that Tarrell could place his palm and the three bloods on Brithilca's muzzle.

Tears streamed down his face as he spoke. "*Storr andas, ia kaskea uan att aslura, inge flytte, inge tenkir, inge endra, ja inge eiende. Ia sinuar uan yta detthe, mina ethera, a ethera ro mina Eldarkin, a jarn ro ungrkin, ja a styrkr ro dragonkin—*" Tarrell's voice cracked, "*—asti a lok ro timi! Vid innsigala okur sattmala yta dreyri ja fjolkynngi, att lengi sem okur thrir tegundir pola; ungrkin, dragonkin, ja Eldarkin.*"

Great spirits, I command you to sleep, unmoving, unthinking, unchanging, and unyielding. I bind you with this, my energy, the energy of my kin, the iron of man, and the strength of dragonkin until the end of time! We seal our pact with blood and magic, to endure as long as our races; mankind, dragonkin, and Eldarkind.

As he spoke, the dragons crept into song once more. Their crooning now sung of loss and ends, and reverberated through everyone there. The Eldarkind wove their own melody into it, rising high to the dragons' low tune, speaking of binding and forging, of sleeping and mending. As Soren watched, all of them glowed with an inner light, and magic tingled upon his own skin. Sparks danced through the air, and when Soren squinted, he was sure he could see a river of light flowing around them all.

Soren stepped forward to place his own hand atop Tarrell's, and Farran joined them. Soren's mouth opened, and he sung, too, though he did not know the words or understand them. His mouth was not his own; magic found the song for him, and soon sound swelled around them as it spoke through the watching men, women, and children in a tongue they did not know.

The light grew brighter and brighter around them, forcing Soren to shield his eyes. Before them, the stone figure of Brithilca grew warm, and then hot to the touch, and began to disintegrate into sparks, just as he had done a millennia ago, as Soren had seen through Beren's eyes. This time, however, Soren knew there would be no spectral remnant of the great dragon. His heart ached with sadness and gratitude for Brithilca's sacrifice, and, at last, he let tears spill down his face unashamedly.

In but a few moments, Tarrell's and Soren's bleeding hands raised into mid-air, as last of all, Brithilca's head disappeared and one last trace of his voice echoed around them. "Thank you..."

Their song crescendoed and faded. First, the humans faltered, and then the Eldarkind, and last of all the dragons until all that remained was silence. The air was thick with magic and sparks floated upon the breeze. The tingle of it lingered upon Soren's skin, and he could see trails of light glistening over Tarrell and weaving across Farran's scales.

They shared a look heavy with sorrow. It was done. The pact was remade, and the threat to the three races extinguished for as long as they would endure, with all elementals rebound to sleep. They had wrought a peace that would last many millennia more, but there was no joy in that moment, as there ought to have been. Not even relief, for the cost had been great. Almost too great to bear.

Soren looked to the damaged throne sitting upon the dais. It looked bare and small and vulnerable without the figure of Brithilca guarding it.

THIRTY SIX

Even a few weeks had made a difference as stone buildings sprang up and many wooden constructions were already finished, thanks to the townsfolk of Arlyn all pitching in to help under the direction of Soren's master builders.

Eve walked the streets, which were still black with fire damage in places, and piled high with rubble. Before the dragon attack, this would have looked like devastation, but already she could see how far the town had come in a short time. There was much more to do in Arlyn and throughout Arrow county—and much more to be healed, but that would come in time.

Eve was glad, most of all, to be able to help build and restore things rather than destroy them. She had had her taste of war. Death and suffering was not for her to inflict, and she never would; she was quite certain of that. One good thing had come of this. Through all the suffering her people had seen, she had also shown them her magical skills and that the powers of the Eldarkind were a force for good.

She had openly used her powers to heal those in need. Never would she be ashamed of her identity again. Now, she could be proud of her heritage and her skills, and be certain of her place in the world at last. And her people, through knowing and trusting her, trusted in that also.

A few of the Eldarkind had arrived several days before on their way home from Pandora to rebuild their own lives. They had stopped to help her, too. Tarrell was amongst them. It seemed he felt personal guilt for the attack on Arlyn, though he could not have foreseen or prevented it. Together, they healed the people's injuries and left to start their own lives once more.

After that, instead of hushed tales of child-stealing terrors in the night, the people whispered of the Eldarkind, with their hair of starlight and their healing hands, and Eve's by extension.

Eve's father left the running of the county wholly to her, and that was a responsibility she made her own. His health had neither improved, nor deteriorated. He endured. Eve was sad, but it only made her more determined to succeed in her own way.

"How goes it?" asked her father when she visited that afternoon. He was in the drawing room again—his new favourite haunt—with another book and a fire, even though it was spring and warming fast.

"Well," she replied, and recounted the week's progress.

"I am most glad, my little dove. I am proud of you." He smiled and Eve grinned herself, pleased with the praise. His face filled with warmth when he smiled, and Eve loved that. His cheeks were pinker today. *He looks much better today. Today is a good day.* A frisson crossed her stomach and she stood taller. *Today is the day.*

"Father, I have something to tell you."

Karn's brow furrowed and his lips twitched in a small smile, amused at her seriousness. "Yes?"

"I wish to marry. I have found a husband. I will not be dissuaded."

Her father laughed reflexively. "I beg your pardon?" He looked at her askance. "You are serious?"

"Yes."

He quieted. "What have you done?"

"Nothing!" Eve protested and blushed. "Worry not, Father. I've cast no shame upon our family. I mean, that you wished me to find a husband, and I do not want to marry anyone I do not choose for myself. I have found a prospective husband of my choice."

"Who?"

"Luke. Lucan, I mean," she stumbled, affording him his proper name.

"The guard?" Her father was incredulous.

"Yes."

"And you want my blessing?"

Eve stood straighter. "Yes."

Her father sighed. "Did you know I defied my father's own will to marry your mother?"

Eve frowned. "What?"

"I did." Karn chuckled. "He did not speak to me for a year, but I was so in love, I did it anyway." He shook his head. "If you truly feel so strongly, I cannot force you otherwise. Above all else, I desire your happiness and security. I want you to have a husband who will care for you the rest of your days. If you place your faith in this choice, then I shall respect your wishes. You... You are no longer a little girl, Eve."

She knew he referred to her managing Arrow county on his behalf. *No, I am not,* she thought. That innocence was lost forever. Her father's improvement was slow, if at all. Eve knew she would have to lead the county for much longer in her father's stead. She excused herself and ran to find Luke, who was toiling on one of the myriad of building projects.

For a moment, she stood to watch him as he heaved and hauled rubble with a crew of strong, young men. His muscles corded under the strain and he was too lost in his concentration to notice her. She could not help but smile.

"Luke," she called softly after a few moments. At once, he stopped and looked up, grinning as he saw her. He straightened and wiped a grimy hand across his sweat-stained brow. Eve beckoned him over, and he excused himself and jogged towards her.

"Is everything well?" he asked.

She nodded and smiled, unable to keep the grin from her face. "I spoke to my father. About... us."

Luke's smile faded and his expression clouded. "And?" he asked cautiously.

"He gives us his blessing."

Luke raised his eyebrows and she nodded to confirm it. He broke into an even wider grin. "Then it means?"

"Yes."

"You will be my wife?"

"Yes."

Luke paced forward and grabbed her in a tight embrace. She

held onto him, not caring that the dust and grime smeared her clothes—nor who saw them embrace.

"Not yet, though," she added.

He released her, looking puzzled, but she gestured around them. "We have work to do first."

Luke smiled ruefully. "That we do."

As they sat upon the walls later that day, looking down over Arlyn as the sun set behind the mountains, Luke tucked her under his arm. "For all that has happened over the past couple of years, I cannot help but be glad." He squeezed her closer.

She patted him on the chest. "I am, too." Her eyes fixated on her scars once more, and she was glad Luke did not seem to see or mind them. She was still not used to them herself. And then, her eyes lingered on his own blackened fingertips. The frostbite had not healed as the monks had rightly said, but neither had it gotten worse.

Those were just the visible signs of all they had endured, and marks they would carry for life. Yet, the physical remnants seemed inconsequential to what else they had endured, and what they had become as people: strong and independent, and the choosers of their own destinies.

"What a journey," Eve said. *Somehow, the path wandered and I still find myself exactly where I would want.*

"It's been a long one."

"Mm. There's much more to come yet."

"I'm sure."

"But for now, some peace, I hope," Eve added.

Luke chuckled. "I hope so, too. I promise, by the end of the year, I'll have a house raised for us. I'll ask your father for your hand, as I ought to. We'll do this properly, as we should have done the first time around."

"I'd like that very much." Eve leaned closer and Luke planted a kiss upon her forehead and clasped one of her scarred hands in his own maimed grasp.

THIRTY SEVEN

The halls of Pandora castle were the noisiest they had ever been. They should have been at their quietest, for the dragons left for Kotyir swiftly and the Eldarkind for Ednor, but Soren had opened the castle to the citizens of Pandora. So much of the city was destroyed and they had nowhere else to go. He would not see them out on the streets. It was against convention and wholly unplanned, but Soren had to admit, it was the most welcoming the castle had felt in a long time.

It was meant to be lived in—used, Soren thought with satisfaction. Families occupied every spare room, and some slept in the corridors. Some of the lords thought it an atrocious judgment, but Soren did not give a mind to their concerns. He would not have his people starve outside and endure cold nights and the spring rains without shelter. Soren had seen the slums of Roher; they were frail, shoddy, and squalid. His people would be treated differently. And so the castle filled each night with the chatter of a thousand voices, and emptied each day as they all left—Soren included—to lend a hand rebuilding the city.

It would take a long time, and several generations to rebuild parts, like the cathedral, but Soren left those in ruins. Housing came first, at whatever price the crown could afford to give the people who had lost everything.

It was the first time since he had been a naive prince that he worked without fear or worry, for it was the first time he had not needed to watch over his shoulders for the threat of assassination, the worry of treason, or the pressure of war looming.

Somehow, against all the odds, he had done it. He had regained his throne from Zaki, the usurper. He had avenged his mother and brought her murderer to justice. He had even removed the threat of Roher. Not even his mother had managed to curb Harad's ambition.

Most importantly of all, he had secured a new, lasting bond between the three races of men, Eldarkind, and dragons that would see peace and a secure future for Caledan long after he had gone. Now, they could live openly together, and their alliance could be celebrated. Dragons would be the champions of the realm, and the Eldarkind's magic would become the tales of legend, not twisted fairytales.

The danger of Cies was gone forever, and the much greater threat of the elementals, also. Though, that was something most of Soren's people would never know of. They did not need to know the real terrors that haunted nightmares.

Soren toiled that day alongside his subjects, feeling proud of all he had accomplished. A new age would dawn, an age of lasting peace, he hoped, now that he had proven himself. It had not been easy, and it had cost a lot to achieve.

With each brick he lifted, another face swam across his memory. His father. His mother. Edmund. Dane. There were countless others, too. Many had died that he had never seen or known. He wished it could be different. It did not seem worth it in a way, that they would not be here to see it, but he was glad their deaths had not been in vain. *My parents and Edmund would be proud of me, now. If only they could see.*

He had gained, too: new friendships and alliances that never would have seemed possible.

He was no longer a naive prince, that was certain. Now, Soren was a strong king, secure in his realm. *Perfectly placed to lead it for many peaceful years.* War would come again one day; that much was inevitable. He had learned at great cost that peace only seemed to come from violence. Perhaps he could change that, and perhaps he could not. But for now, there was peace, and Soren, King Soren, First of His Name, Dragon's Bane, Eldar-friend, Dragon Friend, Bane of Elementals, Vanquisher of Roher, and Bringer of Peace had earned his rest.

THE END.

THANKS FOR READING
PLEASE LEAVE A REVIEW

Thanks for reading *The Shattered Crown*. This is the end of the Books of Caledan series, but I will return to Caledan for more stories in the future! I hope you've enjoyed the adventure with Soren, Eve, and everyone else.

If you did, please leave a review on Amazon and Goodreads. These help me find new readers to transport to the magical land of Caledan!

Join Team Meg at fiction.megcowley.com to download free stories from each of my series, hear my latest fiction news, get advance previews of new books, find out new releases first, discover great book recommendations, reading deals, access bonus content and more.

Keep reading for a sneak peek of my new series, Morgana Chronicles – Arthurian legend as you've never read it before!

APPENDIX: THE LANGUAGE OF THE ELDARKIND

THE ELDAR TONGUE
A guide to translating and pronouncing the tongue of the Eldarkind.

Again – endr – *end-ur*

All – navan – *na-vahn*

And – ja – *jah (hard j as in jar)*

Any – einhevrr – *eye-n-hef-ur*

As long as – lengi sem – *len-gee sem*

Bind (v) – sinuar – *sin-ooh-ARR*

Blaze – Loga – *log-uh*

Blood – dreyri – *DRAY-ree*

Bring – koma – *koh-ma*

Catch – fang – *fang*

Call up/forth – kvedja – *k-ved-JA (hard j as in jar)*

Changing – endra – *end-RAH*

Conscience – coinsiasa – *coin-see-ass-uh*

Creatures – kaperur – *-kap-air-uhr*

Dark – Myrk – *murk*

Darkdawn/Dark-of-the-dawn – Myrkdaga – *murk-dag-uh*

Dark flame – Myrkith – *murk-ith*

Dawn – Daga – *dag-uh*

Dawnfire – Dagabrun – *dag-uh-brun*

Do harm to – skada – *SKA-dah*

Earth – Feld – *fel-dt*

Earthblaze – Feldloga – *fel-dt-log-uh*

Earthflame – Feldith – *fel-dt-ith*

Elder (sign of respect) – ellri – *ell-ree*

Elemental – anda – *an-duh*

Else – annao – *ah-now*

End – lok – *lock*
Endure – pola – *pol-uh*
Energy – ethera – *et-air-ah*
Everywhere – kallikkiala – *kah-lih-kih-ah-luh*
Father – Isa – *ee-sah*
Fire – Brun – *brun*
Flame – Ith – *ith*
Free/Release (v) – Lessa – *less-uh*
From – frama – *fram-ah*
Great – storr – *store, with 'r' lengthened*
Green – Gren – *gren*
Greenscales – Grenskarle – *gren-scar-l*
Heal – laekna – *lake-nuh*
I – ia – *ee-ah*
Ice – isen – *ih-sen*
In – i – *ih*
Iron – jarn – *jar-n*
Leader – Visir – *viz-ear*
Light – Leioss – *lay-oss*
Living – lifanti – *lih-fan-tee*
Magic – fjolkynngi – *f-yolk-kin-gee*
Make – efla – *eff-lah*
Making – elfad – *elf-add*
Mankind – ungrkin ('young kin') – *unger-kin*
May – kan – *can*
Me – min – *minn*
Mother – Ema – *eh-mah*
My – mina – *mee-nah*
Night – Natta – *nat-ah*
Not/un -inge – *in-geh*
Nothing – ingeth – *in-geth*
Of – Ro – *row (as in to row a boat)*
Old one – anda – *an-dah*
On – fram – *fram*

Only (just) – adeins – *add-aynes*

Our – okur – *o-cur, with 'u' lengthened*

Pact – sattmala – *sat-mah-lah*

Plant/s – jurt/a – *jurt/jurt-ah*

Races (species) – tegundir – *teg-un-deer*

Release/Free – Lessa – *less-ah*

Replenish/renew – endurnyja – *eh-durn-ya*

Rise – Risa – *ree-sah*

Scale/s – Skarl/Skarle – *s-karl/s-karl-uh*

Seal – innsigala – *in-sig-ah-la*

See – Leta – *let-ah*

See far (to scry)- Leitha – *ley-tha*

Shield – rond – *rond*

Sleep (v) – slura – *s-lure-ah*

So that – sa att – *sah at*

Spare (verb) – spenna – *spen-ah*

Spirit/elemental/old one – anda/s – *an-da/an-da-s*

Stay – sitya – *sit-yah*

Strength – styrkr – *steer-keer*

Sword – sverd – *s-v-aired (with a clipped 'd')*

Take – nema – *neh-mah*

The – a – *ah*

Thing – hlutur – *h-luh-ture*

Thinking – tenkir – *ten-keer*

This – detthe – *det-teh*

Time – timi – *tih-mih*

Three – thrir – *th-rear*

To – att – *at*

Touch – taka – *tah-kah*

Tree/s – etre/le – *et-reh/et-reh-leh*

Un/not – inge – *in-guh*

Under – nedan – *neh-dan*

Until – asti – *ass-tee*

Water – foss – *foss*

We – vid – *vid*
Whole – heild – *h-ile-d*
With – yta – *ee-tah*
Wound/s – sar/r – *s-are*
Yielding – eiende – *ay-ee-en-day*
You – uan – *oo-an*
Your – uana – *oo-an-ah*
Young – ungr – *unger (as in 'hunger')*

ELDAR TONGUE PHRASES
A guide to translating and pronouncing the phrases of the Eldarkind found in The First Crown, The Tainted Crown, The Brooding Crown, and The Shattered Crown.

Make a shield of the air so that nothing else may touch the blade. – *Efla rond ro a lofti sa att ingeth annao kan sverd taka.*

~

Rise from the ground with the energy of the sapling. – *Risa frama a feld yta a ethera ro a etre.*

~

Fire spirit, I command you to sleep, unmoving, unthinking, unchanging, unyielding in the ice. – *Brun anda Bahr, ia kaskea uan att aslura, inge flytte, inge tenkir, inge endra, inge eiende i a isen.*

~

I bind you with this, my energy and the energy of all living creatures everywhere until the end of time. – *Ia sinuar uan yta detthe, mina ethera ja a ethera ro navan lifanti kaperur kallikkiala asti a lok ro timi.*

~

I bind you with this, my energy, the energy of my kin, the iron of man, and the strength of dragonkin, until the end of time! – *Ia sinuar uan yta detthe, mina ethera, a ethera ro mina Eldarkin, a jarn ro ungrkin, ja a styrkr ro dragonkin, asti a lok ro timi!*

~

I call forth the energy of the land to replenish my energy, heal my wounds, and make me whole again. Take only that energy which can be spared of the trees and the plants and bring no harm to any living being on my conscience. – *Ia kvedja a ethera ro feld att mina ethera endurnyja, mina sarr laekna, ja min heild endr efla. Nema adeins a ethera etrele ja jurta spenna, ja inge skada einhevrr lifanti hlutur fram mina coinsiasa.*

~

Water spirit, I command you to sleep, unmoving, unthinking, unchanging, unyielding in the earth. I bind you with this, my energy, the energy of my kin, the iron of man, and the strength of dragonkin, until the end of time. – *Foss anda Arandulus, ia kaskea uan att aslura, inge flytte, inge tenkir, inge endra, inge eiende i a feld. Ia sinuar uan yta detthe, mina ethera, a ethera ro mina Eldarkin, a jarn ro ungrkin, ja a styrkr ro dragonkin, asti a lok ro timi!*

~

We seal our pact with blood and magic, to endure as long as our races; mankind, dragonkin, and Eldarkind. – *Vid innsigala okur sattmala yta dreyri ja fjolkynngi, att lengi sem okur thrir tegundir pola; ungrkin, dragonkin, ja Eldarkin.*

LIMITED TIME OFFER
DOWNLOAD A FREE BOOK AT
fiction.megcowley.com

It's easy to kill a man. It's hard to kill a dragon. Is it impossible to kill a god?

Bahr, the god of Fire and War, is terrorising the land, annihilating men, Eldarkind and dragons alike. Nothing can stand before him and Beren, chief amongst men, faces everything he loves being lost to Bahr's fickle fires.

After witnessing Bahr's devastating power, Beren despairs, until the mysterious king of the Eldarkind offers him one glimmer of hope – but it comes at great cost. To have any chance of success, Beren must have faith in the enigmatic Eldarkind, set aside his lifelong differences with the dragons, and place his trust in the enemy who has destroyed his home and family. Unless he does so, they are all doomed.

As Bahr's vengeful eye turns to their hostile alliance, their differences threaten to divide man, Eldarkind, and dragon. Can Beren forge the strongest allies from his bitterest enemies before Bahr destroys them all?

Discover how the epic fantasy tale begins in this prequel, *The First Crown: A Caledan Novelette*, set 1,000 years before the *Books of Caledan* trilogy. If you liked *The Lord of the Rings*, *The Inheritance Cycle*, or the *Books of Pellinor*, then you'll love the *Books of Caledan* series.

Chapter One

I raced across the field as the freezing air of early autumn piled up the storm clouds above me, further darkening the early evening. My outstretched hands pushed aside rough golden stalks of wheat that rustled fitfully in the breeze, and the first blobs of rain burst on my exposed skin.

In a stride, the heavens had opened, pounding me with ice-cold water. As I floundered over the dry-stone wall, the muddy ground clutched at my boots and my sodden clothes constricted my movement. Behind the wall, under the shelter of the ancient oak tree, I paused for a respite.

Ahead lay Uncle Anreth's cottage – Aunt Elaine had already closed the shutters – but light spilt from the doorway, illuminating the unfamiliar horses tethered outside. Curiosity pulled me from shelter towards the open door. Excitement fluttered in my belly. Was Fa home at last?

"Morgana! I've been calling for you," said Aunt Elaine, but her voice lacked its usual, sharp annoyance. "Come in, child. We have visitors."

I was too interested in the visitors to retort at being called a child and slipped past her to stand shivering by the fire.

They were all there – crammed into the single room – Aunt Elaine, Uncle Anreth, Cousin Thomas and my own younger brother and sister, Garlais and Alaina. It was already too crowded to house yet two more visitors, who stood with their heads bowed in the low-ceilinged room. My heart sunk. It wasn't Fa.

"Pray continue, sirs," said Anreth, with a troubled glance at me.

The tallest stood a little straighter until his head bumped the ceiling. "Now that all the children of Gorlois are present, we bear a message for his kin. We are sent directly by His Majesty, King Uther, to convey his greatest sadness and love to you for the loss of your father and kinsman Gorlois upon the battlefield. He was slain protecting his king and died a valiant death. His sacrifice was so noble, and his friendship and counsel to the king so valued, that King Uther has decreed Sir Gorlois to be knighted even in death, and this title passed on to his son and heirs."

My knees didn't feel strong enough to hold me up, and I sunk to the floor.

"Fa was... slain?" Alaina said. Her button nose wrinkled in confusion. Garlais stood in silence with no expression upon his face.

"Yes, little one, your papa is dead," said Elaine softly. She drew the young girl close, but Alaina squirmed in her grasp with no hint of sadness about her. She didn't know what death was.

"It can't be true," I said. "Fa promised to return. He promised!"

The soldier's expression softened. "I'm afraid I speak the truth. We leave you this royal decree."

"I cannot read," muttered Anreth. His ears burned red as he bowed his head.

"It matters not. It bears the royal seal. King Uther leaves land for Sir..?" He looked between Thomas and Garlais as if unsure who he should speak to.

"Garlais," Elaine said, pointing to her nephew.

"For Sir Garlais as his own, and gold as a poor recompense for the loss of his father." He handed over the royal decree – a roll of parchment sealed with white wax – and a woven bag with clinking contents to Anreth. "We also bear his sword."

He offered the wrapped blade to Garlais, who took it hesitantly and looked it up and down. Garlais' brow wrinkled in confusion. The giant two-handed blade was nearly as tall as him.

"What of his girls?" said Elaine.

The soldier looked between Alaina and I. "I have a second letter for Lady Morgana. You are invited to reside in Camelot henceforth as King Uther's ward. You will present yourself at his return to Camelot from conquest at the next new moon."

No mention of Alaina. I ignored what he had said. "What of my sister?" I asked, laying a protective hand on her shoulder.

The man shrugged. "She must find a husband or kin to care for her."

Elaine clutched Alaina close. "I would not see my brother's children suffer any more than they already have done," she said. Tears rolled down her cheeks.

I neither heard nor saw the soldiers take their leave. My senses shut the world out, with a blanket of nothing. I jolted as Elaine gathered me into a tight embrace, now openly sobbing.

"He promised to come back," I mumbled. "I don't understand."

"My poor loves, now you are orphans," Elaine wailed, drowning out my words. "You shall not be alone. We will care for you as we have done these last years."

"Elaine," hissed Anreth. "We have not the space or the food! Winter comes upon us."

"Quiet yourself, Anreth! We shall manage as we always have done. I will not turn my brother's children into the night!"

Anreth retreated to his pallet, grumbling.

I felt constricted. Elaine's grasp strangled the breath from me and my wet clothes bound my skin. I struggled free from Elaine's arms and dashed out into the dark. It did not matter which direction I ran through the rain. I would find her way home like I always did – as sure-footed as the goat.

When I could run no more, I sank onto a sodden, moss-covered stone. Although the rocky overhang overhead kept off the worst of the rain, the rising wind tossed sheets of water across me. I huddled into the muddy cliff. My limbs shook uncontrollably, but I could not tell whether it was from nerves, cold, or both. I clutched my tunic closer, wishing I had a cloak or anything to keep warm and dry.

As if he could read my thoughts, Emrys jumped into my lap. My numb fingers clutched at his fur and I held him close, my face buried in his purring midriff.

"Emrys! How did you find me? How are you dry?" The surprise of the ginger cat's arrival pushed all thoughts of my father away for a second.

Emrys nuzzled his head against my face. "I'll always find you, mistress. And I'm a cat! I don't like getting wet. So, I don't."

"Oh, Emrys..."

They sat in companionable silence. Emrys was always patient – he didn't trouble himself to rush anything. I loved that. He knew just how to make me feel better. Just like father did. Had done. Tears leaked from my closed eyes, into Emrys' fur.

"It can't be true," I mumbled.

"I'm sorry, mistress." I did not have to explain. Emrys knew what I spoke of. He usually did. I had long given up questioning how.

I had always been able to talk to cats, but I had learned the hard way at an early age not to speak of it. The other children had thought I was a sorceress, and even my family did not tolerate it. On reflection, it was no wonder I liked cats more than I did people. Cats were easy to please, but people were fickle and judgemental. Emrys was different, though. Whilst most cats told me of hunting and stalking, Emrys was like a person in a cat's body and the closest thing I had to a friend.

I recalled how we had met. On the day of Alaina's birth – and our mother's death – a mewling kitten had appeared on the doorstep and refused to leave. Father had eventually relented and let me feed it. That night, the young Emrys had curled up and slept next to me. Father had not had the heart to throw it out after my pleas.

"I never thought I could miss him more than I already did," I said. The ache in my chest testified to that. It had been a long summer without him – duty bound to campaign with his king. I had never met a king, but I disliked this one.

Father's last gift was one of the giant hugs that dwarfed me. I could still feel his beard tickling my cheek and smell the wood smoke and soap of his clothes if I tried. Never again. I swallowed past the lump in my throat.

When I could bear the shivering no more, and when even Emrys began protesting that my crying was making his fur wetter than the rain, I stumbled home on numb feet.

The fever lasted for days.

When I awoke, clear-headed for the first time since that night, my limbs were sore and my throat dry. The cottage was empty – the fall harvest would be well underway in the fields with even little Alaina helping – but for Emrys who curled up at my feet.

"Water," I croaked through cracked lips.

"None here," replied Emrys, not moving a muscle.

I struggled to my feet and stumbled outside. The day was dull, but the light bright enough to hurt my eyes. I hobbled to the cowshed where the comforting, cool gloom enveloped me once more. The cow lowed in greeting and nudged at my hands for food. I absentmindedly patted it and dragged the milking stool and bucket forward. A few squirts later, my practised hands had expressed several mouthfuls of warm, creamy milk. I gulped it eagerly. Emrys mewed at my feet, but I drank every drop before setting the pail down to collect some more.

"I wanted some of that!" Emrys flicked his tail in irritation.

"I needed it more. You can have some of the next lot." I scratched at the base of his tail until Emrys subsided into purrs and then continued my milking. The rhythmic squirt of liquid into the bucket lulled me. After the illness, I did not have the energy to be upset in any case. A dull emptiness sat inside me.

"What am I going to do, Emrys? Why have I been summoned to Camelot – and not Alaina or Garlais?"

"Well, Garlais inherited your father's land and his home, in addition to the king's gifts." Emrys curled up next to my feet, outside the splash zone.

"That belongs to Garlais. What of Alaina and I?"

"I cannot say. I don't think your brother would abandon either of you. You've been a mother to him these last few years and Alaina is the family darling. I am sure Elaine will care for them both, and Garlais will see Alaina provided for in years to come."

"I'm ordered to leave so soon. It's not fair! I don't want to go; what will Garlais and Alaina do without me? I'm a mother to them; we've never been parted. We'll have no income until Garlais is old enough to earn. We've got no animals, no crops, and no stores for winter. Our home might not be fit to live in anymore. As it is, we don't even earn enough to pay our keep to Elaine and Anreth for what food of theirs that we eat."

"Your father left them enough coin to see Garlais and Alaina through, and you will be provided for in Camelot. Worry not, mistress."

His words did not ease my concern.

The sound of singing distracted me. It swelled in volume as the family returned with the harvest and songs of bounty. Noticing my distraction, Emrys uncurled and stuck his head in the bucket of milk to steal his fill. I scrambled to my feet, feeling revived after my drink, and went outside to help.

Chapter Two

"The king invites us personally to welcome him back to Camelot!" Elaine squealed, her cheeks red and her eyes sparkling as she looked at the scroll again, though she could not read. "*Personally*!"

"We don't have to go, though." I scowled.

"Oh hush, Maggie! Of course, we do. A king's invite is not a request. You have been invited to live in Camelot castle with the king and his family; what a great honour! I imagine he will find you a highborn husband, and you shall want for nothing ever again.

Besides, we shall set foot in Camelot itself! Oh, how exciting. I shall wash our finest clothes in the morning, and we'll bath too. I'll spare nothing. Alaina, you can pick lavender and rosemary from the herb garden to scent them with. If we are invited to a private audience, we cannot disappoint!"

"I don't want to go," I growled.

Elaine slapped the back of my hand with her wooden spoon. I snatched it away and glowered at her. My hand stung fiercely.

"What's gotten into you, girl? You've always wanted to visit the town; now you get to live there as a personal guest of the royal family. What could be greater?"

"That stupid king is the reason my father's dead! I don't want to meet him, I don't want to live in his stupid castle; I don't want to do anything he says!" Hot, angry tears pricked my eyes. I stormed out before Elaine could chide me again or my tears could fall.

I climbed the oak tree and nestled in the branches. My anger ebbed with the rustling of the leaves. Maybe it would be nice to visit the town – Elaine was right, I had always wanted to. The town was where the knights jousted, learned to fight and there were lots of interesting things to see. I loved the village fields and the open space, but it was lonely and it was boring. Living in Camelot, though? That would be something else entirely.

"The distraction would be nice for Alaina and Garlais at least," I said to myself with a sigh. Alaina had started to understand Fa would not be coming home, and Garlais had retreated into himself. I had to do it for them.

"Who's there?" a sharp voice said.

I froze.

"You'd better not be spying on me! Come out!"

Through the lattice of leaves, I could make out the unmistakable bright, auburn hair of Falla. I stopped breathing.

"I'll come and get you myself." Falla's voice was dangerously spiteful.

I uncurled slowly and climbed down the tree until I stood with my back to it, facing her. Though Falla was a year older, she was the same height as me, but somehow made me feel an inch high.

"Dirty witch! What were you doing – prying?" Falla's lip curled at the sight of me, and she shoved a fist at me to ward off magic.

I clenched my jaw. "None of your business. Wasn't spying on you anyway. Better things to do." My own first wasn't to ward off magic, as I thought about punching her.

To my surprise, Falla laughed. "Were you making a tree house? A new home? Have your family turned you out? It's about time!"

I glared but did not answer, although insults filled my mouth. I shouted them in my mind instead. Falla always used my own words against me, and somehow made my tongue tie itself in knots. I hated how flustered she made me.

"I'm not surprised. You don't belong here anyway. You're the black sheep of the family with your ugly looks. I'd be surprised if you weren't a changeling."

I could feel my face burning. Still, I held my tongue. My clenched fists shook by my side as I stood my ground, glaring at Falla with open hatred. As usual, she had struck a nerve. I was well aware my strange appearance cast me aside from my sandy-haired, brown-eyed family. My own hair was jet black, even darker than father's, and my bright blue eyes were a gift from the river goddess that matched no one else. I had the physical traits of a sorceress, though I was no more a sorceress than anyone else. The gods and goddesses had been cruel to curse me so, surely?

Falla's eyes sparkled with spite. "It's so sad that your parents had to die to escape you, but they're better off no—"

With a screech of frustration, I launched myself at her. A squealing Falla fell backwards to the floor with me on top of her.

"Shut your mouth, you cow!" I slapped her around the face as hard as I could and tugged on her long hair. Before she could recover, I leapt to my feet and dashed away.

Fury fuelled me into the woods to my favourite dell, where

the peace of the forest enveloped me. I did not see the basket lying on the path until it was too late. I crashed into the ground with a mighty smash, whilst the basket flew over my head, spilling its contents all about.

Dazed and winded, I lay gasping in the mud that was now plastered across my face, hair and clothes.

"Confound it, you clod of a girl!" Bony hands with an iron grip and unyielding strength hauled me to my feet. I was surprised to find it was the tiniest, most wizened old woman I had ever laid eyes on. What stopped my breath was the old lady's eyes – eyes of water – glaring at me with unconcealed fury.

"Do you know how long it took me to collect those mushrooms? Now I shall have to begin again!"

"I- I'm sorry," I stammered. My anger dissipated, replaced by shock and curiosity, and more than a little fear. It was the first time I had seen anyone with eyes that matched my own, though the woman's wispy, white hair was as different to mine as it could be. Blue eyes though? And mushrooms? This old lady was a sorceress, I was certain. And everyone knew that you ought not to anger a witch. Behind my back, my hand clenched into a fist to ward off witchcraft and evil. I hastened to help her pick up as many undamaged mushrooms as we could find, all the while sneaking sidelong glances at my furious and muttering companion.

"Be more careful!" snapped the woman in parting. She glared at me, transfixing me, before turning away and leaving with surprising speed.

I watched her disappear into the trees until even the sound of her passage – the cracking of twigs and the rustling of foliage – had ceased. Only then did my fist uncurl.

"I don't like her." Emrys seemed to appear from nowhere. I scratched him behind the ears in greeting.

"Well I didn't exactly help myself there, did I?"

"It's not that. She didn't smell right."

"Emrys! You can't say that!"

"Not in that way. I mean something about her smelled…

different."

"Well, I haven't seen her before. She'll be from a different village. Maybe they make different soaps or use different herbs." I did not speak my fears aloud, scared that she would hear me, and fly back here to curse me in a rage.

"Hmm," Emrys replied noncommittally. "Come home, anyway. Elaine wants everyone to bathe before you leave for Camelot." Emrys looked me up and down. "You'll definitely need to wash your hair this side of winter now. What a mess!"

"I don't want to go, Emrys." The change of topic distracted me from the growing fear; now the surprise of running into a sorceress has passed, the apprehension grew. I hurried away nonetheless.

Emrys did not reply.

"Why me?"

"I'm sure you'll have to go to discover that," Emrys replied.

"Fa isn't coming home." I swallowed past the lump in my throat. "Garlais and Alaina are all I have left, and I'm all they have left. How can I leave them now? How can I start over, in another new place, filled with strangers? Knights, and ladies, and royals… I don't know how that world works. I know farming and hunting, not… well. Whatever they do at court. Not that."

"It scares you?"

"Of course. This might not be my home, but it's as close as. Elaine and Anreth have cared for us for a long time, now. I belong in Camelot even less than I belong here." Falla's words still stung in the back of my mind.

"You'll find a new home there, I'm sure. It might not be forever. Think of it as an adventure, away from the fields and the animals."

"Mmm," I replied noncommittally.

Anreth shook his head as I returned to the cottage, caked in dirt. "What on earth have you been doing, girl? Wash in the stream, now. You're not traipsing that mud in here."

"But we're to bath tomorrow – the stream will be freezing," I protested, but I knew it was futile. Anreth's will was iron.

As I shivered that evening, damp, next to the fire, Anreth muttered on about the poor harvest seeing them through winter, whilst Elaine chided him.

"Oh, hush complaining."

"Well, we have three extra mouths to feed over winter, now Gorlois isn't to return."

"Two. Morgana will live in Camelot; the king will feed her."

"Two then. The harvest was poor enough without us stretching it to feed two more mouths."

"Gorlois left coin for the children. I'm sure Garlais wouldn't mind us using a little bit to make sure we had enough food for the winter – would you, Garlais?"

"No, Aunt Elaine," Garlais replied dutifully. He sat on his straw pallet fiddling with the hilt of his father's sword as his fingers traced its details, and did not look up as she addressed him.

"See, Anreth. We'll be just fine. Stop fussing."

Anreth subsided into intelligible grumbles.

I turned my face to the flames. Anreth was right. It would be harder for them to survive the winter if I remained; one more mouth to feed. I had lived through bad harvests before; mother had gone without so we could eat. It would be wrong of me to put so strain on them, I knew. Father's inheritance wouldn't much help; it was for Garlais and his future, not food for us all.

Not for the first time, my thoughts turned to the king my father had died for. Why would anyone die for someone else? I supposed it had something to do with orders and duty. I'd never do it. A part of me was curious to see the king, to try to understand why father had laid down his life for this man.

"I'll go to Camelot," I said as the fire died in the hearth, and aunt and uncle dozed on their chairs.

"Of course you will, dear," mumbled Elaine sleepily.

"Too right you will," muttered Anreth.

Soon, they were asleep where they sat, and I laid out on the pelts before the fire, with Emrys tucked under my chin.

"I'm going to find this king and give him a piece of my mind," I whispered fiercely to Emrys.

"You're going to confront a king?" Emrys asked. "You do realise that's not the done thing, right?"

"My father died for him. I have a right to know why."

"Hmm," was the only reply I received for a long moment. "Well, don't hold yourself to that. A lot may happen before you find yourself face to face with the King of Albion."

I breathed in the aroma of the dying fire, the pelts, and the herbs drying in the rafters as my eyes drifted shut. It would perhaps be a long time before I smelled the scents of this home-from-home again.

"Confront a king..." I could hear Emrys chuckling to himself.

Buy your copy of Magic Awakened to discover the legend today!

About The Author

Meg is a *USA Today* Bestselling Author and illustrator living in Yorkshire, England with her husband, son and two cats Jet and Pixie. She loves everything magic and dragons.

Meg thanks her parents for her vivid imagination, as they fed her early reading and drawing addiction. She spent years in the school library and in bed with a torch, unable to stop devouring books. At home, Meg had a 'making table', where her mum and dad contained the arty mess she created with various drawing and craft projects. The first story Meg remembers writing as a child was about a clever fox (it was terrible, and will never see the light of day). At school, if Meg wasn't reading a book under the desk, she was getting told off for drawing in all her classwork books.

Now, she spends most of her days writing or illustrating in her studio, whilst serenaded by snoring cats.

Visit www.megcowley.com to find out more, and connect on social media, or check out her books on Amazon at author.to/megcowley.

Join Team Meg at fiction.megcowley.com to hear all her latest fiction news.

Made in the USA
Columbia, SC
06 December 2018